W9-CBI-889

FALL OF ANGELS

L.E. Modesitt, Jr.

TOR®
fantasy

A TOM DOHERTY ASSOCIATES BOOK
NEW YORK

This is a work of fiction. All the characters and events portrayed in this book are either products of the author's imagination or are used fictitiously.

FALL OF ANGELS

Copyright © 1996 by L. E. Modesitt, Jr.

Cover art by Darrell K. Sweet
Maps by Ellisa Mitchell

Edited by David G. Hartwell

A Tor Book
Published by Tom Doherty Associates, LLC
175 Fifth Avenue
New York, NY 10010

www.tor.com

Tor® is a registered trademark of Tom Doherty Associates, LLC.

ISBN-13: 978-0-812-53895-3
ISBN-10: 0-812-53895-1
Library of Congress Catalog Card Number: 95-53221

First Edition: June 1996
First Mass Market Edition: July 1997

Printed in the United States of America

0   9   8   7

L. E. Modesitt, Jr.'s Recluce

"This is a writer who cares about his characters and his world. This is disciplined fantasy, not fluff. L. E. Modesitt, Jr., is uncompromising when it comes to the effects of magic, both on the natural world and on the human heart. There are no cheap solutions to the problems of Recluce. Because of that, it is a world worth returning to."

—Megan Lindholm, coauthor of *Gypsy*

Fall of Angels

"Modesitt's character development is solid, and the novel makes intriguing use of technology in a fantasy setting. . . . Fans of the series should enjoy this sixth entry, particularly for its explication of the myths and legends of latter-day Recluce."

—*Publishers Weekly*

"*Fall of Angels* is an excellent lost-colony story in the tradition of Marion Zimmer Bradley's Darkover series or Julian May's Exile saga. Modesitt follows the very real concerns for food, latrines, shelter, medicine, and the struggle for power within the group, while tracing the lives of gifted men and women in the process of becoming legends."

—*Locus*

"Mr. Modesitt delivers a gripping tale with complex and imaginative characters to hold readers in total thrall."

—*Romantic Times*

TOR BOOKS BY L. E. MODESITT, JR.

THE COREAN CHRONICLES

Legacies	*Darknesses*
Scepters	*Alector's Choice*
Cadmian's Choice	*Soarer's Choice*

THE SPELLSONG CYCLE

The Soprano Sorceress	*The Shadow Sorceress*
The Spellsong War	*Darksong Rising*
Shadowsinger	

THE SAGA OF RECLUCE

The Magic of Recluce	*The Order War*
The Magic Engineer	*Fall of Angels*
The Death of Chaos	*The White Order*
The Chaos Balance	*Magi'i of Cyador*
Colors of Chaos	*Wellspring of Chaos*
Scion of Cyador	*Ordermaster*
The Towers of the Sunset	*Natural Ordermage*

THE ECOLITAN MATTER

Empire & Ecolitan
(comprising *The Ecolitan Operation* and *The Ecologic Secession*)
Ecolitan Prime
(comprising *The Ecologic Envoy* and *The Ecolitan Enigma*)

THE FOREVER HERO

(comprising *Dawn for a Distant Earth*, *The Silent Warrior*,
and *In Endless Twilight*)

THE GHOST BOOKS

Of Tangible Ghosts	*The Ghost of the Revelator*
Ghost of the White Nights	

TIMEGODS' WORLD

(comprising *The Timegod* and *Timediver's Dawn*)

The Parafaith War	*Gravity Dreams*
Adiamante	*Archform: Beauty*
The Octagonal Raven	*The Ethos Effect*
The Green Progression	*Flash*
The Hammer of Darkness	*The Eternity Artifact*
*The Elysium Commission**	

*forthcoming

For David Hartwell
Who was willing to look at something different
from the beginning

INITIAL CHARACTERS

Crew of the United Faith Forces' frigate WINTERLANCE

RYBA	Captain, also a Sybran nomad
NYLAN	Chief Engineer, half Sybran
SARYN	Second Pilot, half Sybran
AYRLYN	Communications Officer, non-Sybran
GERLICH	Weapons Officer, Sybran, nonnomad
MERTIN	Logistics Officer, Sybran, nonnomad

Marines attached to the WINTERLANCE

FIERRAL	Commanding Officer
BERLIS	
CESSYA	
DENALLE	
DESINADA	
ELLYSIA	
FRELITA	
HULDRAN	
ISTRIL	
JASEEN	Also a combat medtech
KADRAN	
KYSEEN	
LLYSELLE	
MRAN	
RIENADRE	
SELITRA	
SHERIZ	
SIRET	
STENTANA	
WEBLYA	
WEINDRE	

NORTHERN

CANDAR

Gulf of Candar

Gulf of Murr

RECLUCE

EASTERN OCEAN

The WORLD

EMitchell 1995

I.

THE FALL

I

"THERE WERE ANGELS in Heaven in those days, and there were demons, and the demons were the creators and the creation of chaos . . .

"In that distant battle between the fires of the demons and the ice lances of the angels, the very skies twisted in upon themselves, and the angels, who came from cold Heaven, were cast down and strewn across the stars.

"Those angels, the first and last from far Heaven, when they found the world, knew not where they were, nor could they see even the stars from whence they had come. And they descended unto the Roof of the World.

"There they built the Citadel of the Winds, the tower called Black, with those chained lightnings yet they had retained, carving unto themselves a high refuge and a reminder of their past.

"So as they had come, so earlier had come those from the lands and heritage of the demons, and those were men who believed not that women should wear blades nor speak their minds and thoughts.

"In the time of that first summer came armsmen, inspired by the demons, and there were battles across the Roof of the World, and blood . . .

"Thus continued the conflict between order and chaos, between those who would force order and those who would not, and between those who followed the blade and those who followed the spirit.

"Of the great ones were the angel Ryba, Nylan of the forge of order and the fires of Heaven, Saryn of the dark blades of death, and Ayrlyn of the songs. . . ."

Book of Ayrlyn
Section I
[Restricted Text]

II

"WHAT ARE YOU going to do when you get back to Heaven? Visit your family?" asked Saryn in a low voice, barely audible above the hiss of the ventilators. As second pilot, she had control of the *Winterlance* while the captain dozed in the command couch. Saryn's eyes were glazed, her mind half on the neuronet.

"I'll probably think about that when the time comes. Might be a long time," pointed out Nylan. "Headquarters has extended all flight officers' tours another two years." The engineer's thoughts flicked across the power net, only a section of the full neuronet, as he answered.

"Why don't they just say that we're stuck until we drive the demons out?"

"Top angels—excuse me, Cherubim and Seraphim— express their commands more temperately." Nylan cleared his throat. "Where are we headed?"

Saryn expressed a mental shrug through the net. "I've got the coordinates, but the captain didn't say why. We're positioning for an underspace jump, and awaiting further orders."

ALLNET CALL! ALLNET CALL!

As the neuronet alert jabbed through his thoughts, Nylan stiffened and glanced around the bridge of the United Faith Forces' frigate *Winterlance.*

Ryba—the captain—hit the net so quickly, her thoughts cold and clear across the neuronet, that Nylan wondered if she had ever been asleep.

At times like these, the engineer wondered if he ever really had known the captain. He knew that she drove herself, that she spent hours in high-gee exercise, that she knew and practiced not only unarmed martial combat, but even the antique twin sword exercises of Heaven's Sybran horse nomads—and that the blades on her stateroom wall were razor sharp and had sharpened points as well. Then, she had been raised in the nomad heritage where women fought and commanded—and she did command.

Nylan stifled a yawn and eased fully into the net, catching the last of the on-line feed.

". . . line two to be led and coordinated by *UFFS Winterlance* . . . line three to be led by *UFFS Stormsweep.* Action will commence at 1343 standard . . ."

"Shit . . ." The contemptuous word that floated unattached through the net came from Saryn, who had just released the conn to Ryba, although Saryn had stayed linked to catch the incoming message.

"Right enough," affirmed the captain, her tone not quite sardonic. "Twelve towers, and only fifty of us, and half are destroyers with barely adequate D-draws."

Saryn stood, wiggling her fingers. Then she tried to massage her neck with her left hand before settling back into her couch and trying to rest while Ryba reoriented the *Winterlance* prior to setup for the underspace jump prior to the attack.

With a deep breath, Nylan stretched. The engineer could check the files for the whole message, but the captain had it, and he knew enough—more than enough. The demons had a picket line of towers across the transit corridor, with webs into the underspace that would effectively cut the United Faith Alliance in two.

The damned towers that drew power from who knew where and how were almost invulnerable—almost. Except when enough de-energization was concentrated on the nexus points in their energy links, and then the entire line went up into pure energy. Most of the time, though, it was the angel ships that went up in energy.

The towers had to be hard to build, because there were only about fifty known to exist. That still meant enough to quarter the UFA and to disrupt trade and communications totally.

"Engines . . . interrogative fusactor status." The captain's inquiry burned into Nylan's thoughts.

The engineer suppressed his annoyance. Ryba could have dropped into the power subnet easily enough; it wasn't as though the *Winterlance* were anywhere close to jump or combat yet. He slipped deeper into the system and ran through the checks, then pulsed the summary to her.

"Thank you, engines. Power net looks good."

Nylan straightened in the couch and watched as the captain studied the displays—the ones spread across the front of the cockpit, and those in her mind. Her thoughts flicked through the *Winterlance*'s neuronet, making course adjustments, tweaking the power flow from the twin fusactors, and studying, again and again, the icy images of the demon ships of the Rationalists.

"Lots of power there, Ryba," observed the wiry white-blond engineer from his third seat. His unvocalized words flowed through the neuronet to her.

"I wish you two would speak aloud. All those empathetic overtones mess up the net." Ayrlyn, the comm officer, took a deep breath, although her words were also unspoken, flowing through the net with ice-burning overedges.

Empathetic overtones? Just because they occasionally slept together? Nylan glanced sideways to the fourth seat where the brunette sat, her thoughts restricted to the comm-net, as she monitored everything from standing wave to demon frequencies.

"Net's faster." Ryba's no-nonsense words snapped across the net with their own burning edges.

Nylan winced and decided to check the power subnet again.

"Ten till jump. Time adjustment will be negative five for sync."

The engineer moistened his lips. Backtime twists out of jumps seemed to give the angel ships an advantage, but the power requirements on the fusactors meant they had to be rebuilt almost every third sortie, and eight units was the max backtime possible for an angel cruiser. The destroyers could go ten, but their underspace mass drag was less. So were their shields.

A negative five meant the force would contain at least one heavy cruiser, with three to five de-energizer draws. That also meant trouble.

"Trouble . . ." As if to confirm Nylan's concerns, Ayrlyn added the single word verbally.

"Weapons . . . interrogative D-status."

"De-energizers are ready, Captain." Both Gerlich's voice and "net voice" came across as a smooth deep baritone, smooth as the man himself, unusually so for a full Sybran. Of the ship's officers, half were full-blood Sybran—Ryba, Gerlich, and Mertin—big, broad-shouldered, and, despite their size, most at home in the chill of the high latitudes of cold Sybra. Ayrlyn was mostly Svennish, and Saryn and Nylan were about half and half.

"Interrogative mass distribution."

"Within parameters, Captain." Mertin squeaked, despite his size, both in person and on the net, perhaps because he was barely out of the Institute.

The time clicked by silently as the *Winterlance* hurled toward her underspace jump point, as the dozens of other angel ships converged on that same jump point.

"Stand by for jump."

"Engines, standing by."

"Comm, standing by . . ."

The acknowledgments flicked across the net, sequentially yet instantaneously.

"Jump . . . NOW!"

The *Winterlance* dropped underspace, with a rush of golden glory, as though on spread wings, that instant of pain/ecstasy enduring forever, yet gone before it had begun . . .

. . . then realspace slammed tight around the cruiser.

The rep screen flared bright with the images of nearly fifty angel ships, arrow-wedged toward the glittering line of light held together by the mirror tower ships of the demons.

Nylan could sense the dark image of a trapped angel transport, an insect struggling futilely in the web of energy, struggling with full drives, with shields, yet unraveling into dust and energy in the instants after the angel force dropped toward the demon mirror line—that impossible energy web that stretched across seemingly empty space to snare any angel ship within light-years, in real or in underspace.

"Full shields. Everything you can get me, Nylan."

"Yes, ser."

"Begin overlap . . . now!"

"Full shields in place, Captain." Nylan dropped himself down through the net practically to the individual flux level, to smooth the energy flows, and to develop maximum power for both screens and propulsion fields.

At the same time, he had to fight the feedback created by the overlapped shields of the cruisers flanking the *Winterlance*. On the right was the *Polarflow*, on the left the *Deepchill*.

The *Polarflow*'s engineer was either rough or new, or both, and the power fluctuations from the ship created unnecessary energy eddies across the entire shared shield, eddies that fed back into the *Winterlance*'s powernet.

"Smooth your fields, three!" snapped Ryba over the command net. Three was the *Polarflow*, and Nylan nodded.

The worst of the energy fluctuations smoothed, but Nylan shook his head. The other engineer just didn't have the touch, and nothing except experience would give it to him or her.

The problem was that the demons wouldn't give that much time, either, before the mirror towers lashed the fluctuations into energy storms whose feedback would rip the *Polarflow* apart.

The representational screen showed the first line of angel ships, the destroyers, sweeping "down" toward the picket line of light.

"One, close up."

Ryba's commands seemed distant as Nylan, his senses deep in the power subnet, merged the fusactor flows into an eddy-free flow.

"Line two . . . begin D-sweep at my mark. Five, four, three, two . . . MARK!"

The darkness of the ordered shields of the second line deepened as the cruisers accelerated toward the tower ship pickets, a darkness all the more profound for its depth, a depth that radiated the smoothed harmony of merged energies.

A blinding line of light flared through the screens, through Nylan's mind, shivering him to the tips of the nerves in fingertips and toes, and leaving his eyes watering.

When his mind cleared, long before his eyes, he could sense through the net that that blinding line of light from the tower ships had shattered the first line of attacking angel forces, nearly a dozen fast destroyers.

Still, without so much as a flicker in the overlapping screens, the *Winterlance,* and the second line, dropped its darkness toward the mirror-lights of the demons, and Ryba squared the ship on its tower-shattering course.

"De-energizers."

"Charging," came Gerlich's affirmation across the net.

The screens of the Rationalists' tower ships flared and merged, creating a shimmering wall that seemed to reflect all electronic signals and visual images back through the *Winterlance*'s neuronet.

Ryba winced as the signals knifed through her skull; Nylan dropped off the top level of the net. So did Ayrlyn.

"Activate D-one." The captain's thoughts were cold, even

though Nylan knew she trembled in the command couch, even as the combined signals of the angels' fleets and the demons' towers flared back through her mind and her body.

"D-one is activated."

"Activate D-two."

"D-two is activated."

Nylan moistened his dry lips, finally opening his eyes, then easing back onto the neuronet's top level, where his senses slipped across the screens and inputs that the captain juggled as line two began the sweep through the probing disruption lines cast by the demons.

With twelve towers and only fifty angel ships, he didn't expect too much from the de-energizer beams of line two, except that the demons' towers would have to draw on their own power, rather than use laser or solar energy to hold the reflective focusing against the angels' fleet. It often took four lines to even get the reflective shields of the demons to dim.

Nylan watched the representational screen—no visual scans would show the intertwinings of energies and positions that marked the angel-demon conflicts. The energy draw beams converged on the selected nexus point, the two from the *Winterlance,* two from the *Deepchill,* and one, of course, from the struggling *Polarflow.*

"Three! Get that D-beam in position."

There was no response from the *Polarflow,* but somehow the demons' towers shifted in space, and the D-beams flared into nothingness.

The captain flattened the propulsion fields and slewed the ship sideways at a right angle to the course line, then even before the frigate was reoriented, pulsed the de-energizers twice more on the nexus linch point between the shields of two towers.

Another pale amber de-energizer beam struck the same linch point, then another, and then a fourth.

"Power, Nylan. Power!"

The engineer dropped into the neuronet, and a hundred flashes of energy ripped at him, enough that his whole body burned, as he boosted the fusactors to nearly twenty percent over rated maximum and channeled everything but the power to the ship's screens into the de-energizers.

Two disrupter fields bracketed the *Winterlance,* and Nylan dropped his senses into the lowest power sublevels, smoothing fields and trying to anticipate the feedback effects.

Somewhere, on the neuronet levels above him, he could sense the implosion as the *Polarflow* was sucked into overspace chaos.

Ryba dropped the frigate's ambient gravity to near-null while lifting the *Winterlance* almost on her tail.

The demon disrupter brackets faded.

Sweat poured from Nylan's forehead and down across his closed eyes as he eased the flux lines into smooth lines of power from each fusactor and merged them. He let the right fusactor rise to one hundred ten percent rated output and the left to one hundred nine percent until just before the hint of electronic chaos began to appear. Then he dropped both to just shy of max.

Even so, the system telltales began to flash amber, like pinpoints of pain through Nylan's body, and he took the ventilation system off-line to compensate, knowing the two dozen marines would start cursing even as the cold air stopped flowing from the ventilator jets.

The flight crew members were used to the loss of ventilators in combat, and were usually too preoccupied to worry, but the backup combat troops weren't. They hated serving as backups, but ever since the *Icewind* had captured a demon tower, the angel high command had insisted on two squads of marines on each cruiser. Of course, reflected Nylan, no other cruiser had even come close to a tower ship, and the angel scientists had yet to figure out how the damned tower worked, except that it somehow both created chaos perturbations and used them to distort realspace.

Two sets of disrupter beams probed around the *Winterlance.*

Ryba dropped the external energy levels to nil, then pulsed screens.

Nylan scrambled through the mid-level powernet, cooling feedback, and unsnarling the energy loop from the second fusactor, always more sensitive to field effects.

A third beam switched to the *Winterlance* as the *Deepchill* went to chaos.

The captain dropped the nose and most of the screens, jamming all the powerflows into acceleration, and demanded, "Power!"

Nylan rammed the fusactors into emergency overload, nearly one hundred twenty percent of rating on each, letting his nerves burn as he damped the swirls.

The third line of angels began to attack the towers, but the disrupter beams all seemed to remain searching for the *Winterlance,* bracketing the cruiser on all sides.

Nylan swallowed. With no gravity in the *Winterlance,* the ship warming rapidly, the ventilation off, and the captain playing spaceobatics to avoid the Rats' focused ion disassociators, his guts were twisted into knots, his eyes pools of pain, and all he had to operate with were the net and his senses.

"Shields!" Ryba dropped the acceleration to nil.

The fourth line of angel ships, including the heavy cruisers, swept in from below, and dozens of de-energizers licked at the towers, but the disrupters still slashed at the *Winterlance.*

Nylan reshifted the power flows into overshields, calculated, and recalculated. The *Winterlance*'s screens were strong enough for perhaps two simultaneous demon beams—once, twice at the outside.

One disrupter slid across the screens, and Nylan moaned as the power burned into his brain, even as he shifted the screen focus to blunt the dull, aching, and chaotic combined power drain and overload.

A sound like splintering glass, shattering static, and pure chaos screeched through the comm bands as the mirror ships' nexus point collapsed and fundamental chaos backsurged from the disintegrating Rat picket line.

Angel ships scattered, some underjumping blind, others swallowed by the chaos vortex unleashed by the nexus point's collapse.

Ryba dropped the shields and pulled full acceleration.

The fundamental chaos—a white vortex swirling in no directions and all directions—glittering with the focused and reflected energies of the Rationalists' tower ships—slammed through the *Winterlance,* twisting and tumbling the frigate through a dark funnel—into a red-tinged whiteness framed with black order.

The same blackness flooded over the overloaded engineer.

III

NYLAN SHOOK HIS head. He hadn't expected that he'd be able to shake his head—or that he'd even be alive. Then he tried to access the neuronet, but nothing happened. He concentrated on the power system, and got the mental image of the board. The mental readouts matched the visual console before him, but he had no feeling of being on the net, just the mental picture.

Both status images revealed that the fusactors were dead—almost as if they did not exist.

He frowned.

"Darkness! Look at you . . ." murmured Ayrlyn.

"What?" asked Nylan.

"Your hair is silver—not old silver, just silver."

"Enough on hair color! Where are we?" Gerlich's words growled from the speaker.

"We're trying to find out!" snapped Ryba. "It takes longer manually."

Nylan stared at the captain—whose dark brown hair had clearly turned black—a dark jet-black. Jump transits didn't change hair color—that he knew. He turned toward Ayrlyn, whose brown hair had become a fiery red, not orange-red or mahogany-red, but like living flame.

Were they all dead? Was this some form of afterlife?

"So . . . where are we?" asked Saryn, her hair still brown, perhaps slightly darker, a shade more . . . alive.

As he waited for the captain to answer, Nylan glanced at the board before him, where half the displays were either dead or showing meaningless parameters, and then back at the captain. Finally, he shrugged and waited.

"Nowhere I've ever seen," Ryba finally answered. "The nav systems don't match anything, but we're practically on top of a planet, and I'll have the orbit stabilized in a bit."

The engineer frowned. The odds on underjumping, especially blind and unintentionally, and ending up near a planet, any kind of planet, were infinitesimal.

"Nylan, is there any way to get more power?"

"The fusactors are dead, Captain. I'll try again." Nylan concentrated on the fusactors, ignoring the dead net, trying to call up and replicate the feeling of smooth power flows.

For a moment, perhaps several units, some form of power flowed, but Nylan felt as if it were flowing from him, not the fusactors, and the blackness began to rise around him.

He let go of the image. "That's it, Captain." He didn't know why, but he couldn't do more.

"Might have been enough." Ryba's words were grunted.

The engineer returned to study the readouts before him, regretting the slowness of the manual inputs. Since the captain said nothing, Nylan began to use the long-range sensors to gather data on the planet, cataloguing each piece of data as it hit the system. A warm water planet with no electronic emissions; clear day-night rotational pattern; no moons of any size; no light concentrations on the dark side; roughly Heaven-Sybra-standard gravity, assuming that the mass balance was somewhere near norm.

He trained one sensor on the sun and swallowed.

"Stable orbit . . . I think," announced Ryba, wiping her forehead with the back of her black shipsuit sleeve. She turned in the couch and frowned. "You were right, Ayrlyn. About the hair color."

Nylan nodded to himself. Was the spectrum, the visible

spectrum, different? How could it be? The ship's lights were still the same. Or were they all different?

"Where are we?" asked Saryn. "Does anyone know?"

"A demon-fired long way from anywhere—that's certain." Ryba wiped her forehead again, looked back at the screens once more, and then at Nylan. "You were doing something with the sensors, Nylan. What do they show?"

"I'd have to say that we're not in our universe."

"Not in our universe? How could we not be in our universe?"

"Would you prefer dead? The afterlife of the demons? Those are your choices. Personally, Captain, I prefer the alternative universe."

"And what might lead you to this conclusion, Ser Nylan?" Ryba's voice was chill, the polite voice of disagreement that Nylan hated.

"A number of little things, beginning with the odds of blind underjumping and emerging near a planet. In our universe, that kind of jump would have turned us into dust and energy. The fusactors are both dead, and they shouldn't be. The indicators show that the firin cells are discharging at half their normal rate, despite twice the emergency load."

"At least there's a planet down there."

"That's another problem. It's a water planet, and it's in what would be a habitable zone—assuming that such a thing existed with a yellow-white star this hot. But it's on the fringe for most of us."

"You're half-Svennish, aren't you?" snapped Gerlich over the speaker. "Trust a Svenn to pick a hot planet."

"He didn't pick it," pointed out Ryba. "How hot is it?"

"*If* the sensors are accurate . . . the sea-level surface is like Jobi, but warmer. Too hot to be comfortable for us, but fine for demons. There are a couple of high-altitude plateaus that would be perfect—especially in the smaller continent, but setting a lander down there would be murder."

"Trying to live in a place hotter than Jobi would kill most of us—except you and Ayrlyn," responded Gerlich's voice.

Saryn swallowed in the background, but Nylan said nothing.

"It wouldn't be a revel for us." Ayrlyn's brown eyes seemed to flash blue.

Ryba nodded curtly, but not quite so coldly. "Anything else?"

"I *think* there's some form of life down there, and there shouldn't be, not without some form of moon, or unless we're looking at a planoformed world. But there aren't any electronic emissions."

"Maybe it's a lapsed colony world."

"Could be. Whose? How long has it been isolated?"

"Stop it, please . . ." said Ayrlyn. "If the fusactors are down, can we fix them? If not, what do we do?"

"We die or colonize." Ryba looked coldly back to Nylan. "Atmosphere?"

"Rough analysis indicates low CO, oxygen about twenty-two percent, mostly nitrogen. There's nothing obviously wrong, but I can't rule out toxic or chronic trace elements in the soil or atmosphere."

"Inhabited?"

"The traces I've picked up say so." The engineer shrugged again. "Could be anything, but it's carbon-based, and, if I had to guess, probably some form of humanoid. There are some regular patches that could be fields and some lines that could be roads . . ."

"Better than savages, but not much."

"You could be jumping to conclusions," pointed out Ayrlyn.

"I have to go with the odds." The captain glanced back at the readouts. "And we're continuing to lose power."

"This whole world is against the odds."

Ryba turned and called up the visual display of the smaller continent on her console. "Nylan, Saryn, Ayrlyn . . . come here."

"Captain? Gerlich here. What's the drill? The marine force leader wants to know. So does Mertin."

"We're in stable orbit, but we'll have to abandon the ship.

We're surveying landing sites. You can commence figuring loads for the landers. Something along the line of configuration C."

"Self-sustaining?" came the weapons officer's voice.

"That's affirmative. Local culture looks primitive, but organized. Roads and fields, and that probably means things like blades, archers, and cavalry or the local equivalent if they have horses or what passes for them. Mass density is standard, and that means metal-working."

"Understood. All four landers appear operational . . ."

"Fusactors aren't going to work here, Gerlich," added Nylan. "You'll have to modify the configuration for that."

"Fusactors work everywhere."

"Not here, wherever here is."

The captain looked at Nylan. "You sound absolutely certain."

"You can have Gerlich test the survival fusactor, but it won't work."

"Weapons . . . the engineer is probably right, but test the fusactor and let me know."

"Will do, Captain. How much time do we have?"

"Take enough time to do it right, Gerlich. We're operating on stored power. We can't take the tier two firin cells, but try to make room for the fully charged cells left in tier three."

"What tools?"

"All the hand tools, and"—Ryba looked at Nylan—"two sets of laser cutters."

Nylan nodded.

"No energy weapons?" asked Gerlich.

"The heavy-weapons head for one laser. Hand weapons might be useful for a time, but we probably won't have any way to recharge them. All the slug-throwers the marines have. And take all your clothing—especially sweaters or warm things—even if you have to wear it or stuff it into cracks in the landers. And blankets. I can guarantee we won't be coming back for anything."

"We'll get working on it, Captain."

Ryba turned to the bridge crew and gestured to the screen. "Where do we go down? Here's the planet."

The four clustered around the single wide screen.

"Four major continents. The one that looks like a fish—roughly—has an island off it." Ryba glanced at Nylan. "Would we be better off on the island?"

The engineer shook his head. "It's hot; it's so dry that the sensors don't show any moisture, and there are no signs of habitation. It's also pretty rocky."

"What about the big southern continent?"

"Isn't it hot?" asked Saryn. "It's not that far south of the equator."

"Very hot," admitted Nylan.

"You don't seem very positive, Ser Nylan," commented Ryba. "Each unit we sit and talk costs us power, and all you do is say no."

Nylan shrugged. "I'd vote for the second-largest continent. It's got some high mountain plateaus in that western range. It's spring or early summer now, and we can land. There's greenery there, but no signs of habitation—probably too cold for the locals, and it might be helpful not to tramp on anyone's boots."

"It's hundreds and hundreds of kays from any access to oceans or major rivers," pointed out Ayrlyn.

"We're not exactly into seafaring," Nylan said dryly.

"Fine," said the captain. "We land on this mountain plateau. We get a defensible position—maybe. We get snow and ice over our head in the winter, a short growing season, and probably not much access to building materials."

"We also have more time to establish ourselves before the local authorities, or what passes for such, show up," answered Nylan.

"It's insane to try and put a lander into a mountain pasture. It could be just a high-altitude swamp," protested Saryn.

"The odds are against that, and there are two areas where we could land. Each is twice as long as a lander's set-down distance."

"Twice as long in the middle of mountains that could rip a lander into little shreds."

Nylan shrugged. "How long will anyone last if we set down on those hot and flat plains?"

"We don't even know if they have local authorities, or if the locals are intelligent, or if they even look remotely like us," protested Saryn. "This is insane."

"I think you just validated the engineer's suggestion," said Ryba. "There's too much we don't know, and we don't have the energy to shuttle things off the ship. Besides . . ." She left the sentence unfinished, but Nylan knew the unspoken words. Except for removable power supplies, weapons, and tools, the *Winterlance* would shortly be unusable in any case.

"Trying to hit mountain landing areas? That's crazy."

"You're right," Nylan agreed. "Except that trying to land anywhere else would be even riskier. The landing is high risk, but it makes survival lower risk. Take your choice."

"We're opting for long-term survival," announced the captain. "I'm not interested in merely prolonging existence enough to die of heat exhaustion on a nice flat plain where landing is easy. I'll begin computing the entry paths," the captain announced. "Nylan, would you do a survey of your equipment to see if there's anything else that could be useful planetside?"

The engineer nodded as the captain assigned the responsibilities for cannibalizing the *Winterlance*.

IV

"HAVE YOU DETERMINED the cause of the great perturbation between order and chaos—the one that shook the world last evening?" asks the white-haired man dressed in the more traditional flowing white robes.

The younger, but balding, man straightens and looks up from the circular glass in the middle of the white oak table. "Ser?"

"I asked, Hissl, about the great perturbation. Jissek still lies in a stupor, and my glass shows that waves flooded the Great North Bay."

"Waves always flood the Great North Bay, honored Terek." Hissl inclines his head to the older magician, and the summer light that reflects off the roof of the keep of Lornth and through the window glistens on his bald pate. "I do believe that order fought chaos in the skies, and that times will be changing."

"A safe prediction," snorts Terek. "The times always change. Tell me something useful."

The man in the white tunic and trousers stands and bows to the older white-clad man. "There are strangers approaching from the skies."

"There are always strangers approaching. How do you know they are from the skies?"

"The glass shows a man and a woman. The man has hair colored silver like the stars, and the woman has flaming red hair, like a fire. They are seated in a tent of iron."

"An old man and a redheaded weakling?"

"The man is young, and the woman is a warrior, and they bring other women warriors."

"How many?" Terek walks to the unglazed window of the lower magicians' tower, where the shutters tremble against the leather thongs that hold them open. His eyes look out upon the barely green hilly fields above the river.

"A score."

"I should tremble at a score of women warriors? This is the message of such a great disturbance?"

Hissl bows again. "You have asked what I have seen, and you mock what I tell you."

"Bah! I will wait until Jissek wakes."

"As you wish. I have warned you of the danger."

Terek shakes his head and turns toward the plank door that

squeaks on its rough hinges with each gust of the spring wind. He does not shut it as he leaves.

Hissl waits until he can no longer hear the sound of boots on the tower stairs. Then he smiles, recalling the lances of winter that the strangers bear, and the breadth of the women's shoulders.

V

NYLAN WENT THROUGH the manual controls a third time, as well as through the checklist once more. Then he studied the rough maps and the readouts again. He had one of the two landing beacons, and his was the one that the other three landers would hone in on—assuming he managed to set down where he planned, assuming that he could find the correct high plateau in the middle of the right high mountain range without getting spitted on the surrounding needle-knife peaks.

The second beacon would go down with Ryba—in case he ran into trouble.

"Black two, this is black one. Comm check." Nylan watched his breath steam as he waited for a reply.

"One, this is two. Clear and solid."

"Good. You're cleared to break orbit."

The engineer took a deep breath. "I'm not quite through the checks. About four units, I'd guess."

"Let us know."

"Will do."

In the couches behind him were the eight marines assigned to his lander. The craft wasn't really a lander, but a space cargo/personnel shuttle that could be and had been hastily modified into a lifting body with stub wings for a single atmospheric entry in emergency situations. Only one of the four landers carried by the *Winterlance* was actually designed for normal atmospheric transits, and it had far less capacity. That was the one Ryba was bringing down with the high-priority cargo items.

Although Nylan had more experience in atmospheric flight than Saryn or even Ryba, he wasn't keen about being the lead pilot through an atmosphere he'd never seen, belonging to a planet he suspected shouldn't exist. Because he was even less keen about dying of starvation or lack of oxygen in orbit, he continued with the checklist. Still, the business of trying to hit mountain plateaus bothered him, even if it were the only hope for most of the crew. "Harnesses strapped and tight?"

"We're tight, ser," responded Fierral from the couch beside him, the blue-eyed squad leader, who once had been a brunette, but who now had become a fiery redhead as a result of the *Winterlance*'s strange underjump. "It wouldn't be a good idea to be floating around here anyway, would it now?"

"No," admitted the engineer. He took another deep breath before flicking through the remainder of the checklist.

He scanned the screens, then thumbed the comm stud. "Black one, this is two. Breaking orbit this time."

"We'll be tracking you."

"Thanks." Nylan pulsed the jets, amused as always that it took energy to leave orbit, then watched the three limited screens as the lander slowly rose, then dropped, although neither sensation was more than a hint with the gentle movements. He knew those movements would be far less gentle at the end of the flight.

The first brush with the solidity of the upper atmosphere was a dragging skid, and enough of a warming in the lander that Nylan's breath no longer steamed.

The second brush was longer, harder, like a bareback ride across a fall-frozen stubbled field just before the snows of a Sybran winter began. And the lander warmed more.

Nylan studied the screens, not liking either the temperature readouts or the closures.

"Make sure those harnesses are tight! This is going to be rough."

"Yes, ser."

With the third and last atmospheric contact, the lander bucked, stiffly, and then again, even more roughly, as the thin whisper of the upper atmosphere slowly built into a screaming shriek.

Whhheeeeeee . . .

The lander was coming in fast . . . too fast.

Nylan flared the nose, bleeding off speed, but increasing the heat buildup. Then he dropped it fractionally.

Whheeeeeeeee . . .

The lander bounced, as though it had skidded on something solid in the upper atmosphere, then dropped as if through a vacuum. Nylan's guts pushed up through his throat, and he could taste bile and smell his own sweated-out fear.

"Friggin' pilot . . . not made of durall steel . . ."

"Does . . . best he can . . . wants . . . to live, too . . ."

"Don't apologize for an engineer, Desinada . . ."

Nylan tried to match geographic landmarks with the screens, but the lander vibrated too much for him to really see.

The sweat beaded up on his forehead, the result of nonexistent ventilation, nerves, and the heat bleeding through the barely adequate ablative heat shields, and burned into the corners of his eyes, as his hands and mind worked to keep the lander level.

The buffeting began to subside, enough that he could see ocean far below and what looked like the tail of the fish continent ahead.

He checked the distance readouts and the altitude. He'd lost too much height. After studying the fuel reserves, little enough, he thumbed on the jets and flattened his descent angle.

At the lower speed, though, the effect of the high winds became more pronounced, and the edges of the stub wings began to flex, almost to chatter. With little enough power, the engineer could do nothing except hold the lander level, and wish . . . He tried to imagine smoothing the airflow around the lifting body, easing the turbulence, soothing the laminar flow, and it almost seemed as though he were outside the ship, in a neuronet, a different neuronet, almost like smoothing the *Winterlance*'s fusactor power flows.

The chattering diminished, and Nylan slowly exhaled.

Another hundred kays passed underneath, and he thumbed off the jets, hoping to be able to save some of the meager fuel for landing adjustments.

Far beneath him, the screens showed what seemed to be a rocky desert, a boulder-strewn expanse baked in the sun. Ahead rose the ice-knife peaks that circled the high plateau that was his planned destination.

He thumbed the jets once more, again imagining smoothing the airflow around the lander. Surprisingly, the lander climbed slightly, and Nylan permitted himself a slight grin.

The DRI pointed to the right, and the engineer eased the lander rightward, wincing as the lifting body lost altitude in the maneuver.

All too soon, the high alpine meadows appeared in the screens as green dots—small green dots, but the southernmost one grew rapidly into a long dash of green set amid gray rock.

The lander arrived above the target meadow, except the meadow showed gray lumps along the edges, and a sheer drop-off at the east end that plunged more than a kay down to an evergreen forest.

From what Nylan could tell, the wind was coming out of the east, and he dropped the lander into a circling descent that would bring the lifting body onto a final approach into the wind. He hoped the approach wouldn't be too final, but the drop-off allowed the possibility of remaining airborne for a bit if the long grassy strip were totally unusable.

As he eased around the descending circular approach, the lander began to buffet. Nylan kept easing the nose up, trying to kill the lifting body's airspeed to just above stalling before he hit the edge of the tilted high meadow that seemed so awfully short as he brought the lander over the ground that seemed to have more rocks than grass or bushes.

He eased the nose up more, letting the trailing edge of the belly scrape the ground, fighting the craft's tendency to fish-tail, almost willing the lifting body to remain stable.

The lander shivered and shuddered, and a grinding scream ripped through Nylan's ears as he eased the craft full onto its belly. The impact of full ground contact threw Nylan against the harness straps, and the straps dug deeply into flesh and muscle. The engineer kept compensating as the lander skidded toward the drop-off, slowing, slowing, but still shuddering eastward, and tossing Nylan from side to side in his harness.

With a final shudder, the lander's nose dug into some-thing, and the craft rocked to a halt.

For a long moment, the engineer just sat in the couch.

"We're down." Nylan slowly unfastened the safety har-ness, trying to ignore the spots of tenderness across his body that would probably remind him for days about the rough-ness of his landing.

"Did you have to be so rough?" asked Fierral.

"Any emergency landing that you can walk away from is a good one. We're walking away from this one."

"You may be walking, ser, but the rest of us may have to crawl." The squad leader shook her head, and the short flame-red hair glinted.

"Are you sure he's done?" asked another marine.

"We're done." Nylan touched the stud that cracked the hatch. There wasn't any point in waiting. Either the ship's spectrographic analyzers had been right or they hadn't, and there was no way to get back to orbit, and not enough sup-plies in the ship to do more than starve to death—especially since no one knew where they were and since there were no signs of technology advanced enough to effect a rescue.

The air was chill, almost cold, colder even than northern Sybra in summer, but still refreshing. A scent of evergreen accompanied the chill.

With a deep breath, Nylan stepped to the hatch on the

right side of the lander and used the crank to open it the rest of the way. "It smells all right."

"I can't believe you just opened it. Just like that," said Fierral.

"We didn't have any choice. We're not going anywhere. We can breath it, or we can't." Because the lander had come to rest with the right side higher than the left, Nylan had to lower himself to the ground.

". . . can't believe him . . . kill us all or not . . ."

". . . least he doesn't dither around . . ."

"Neither does the captain . . . probably why they get along . . ."

Leaving the voices behind, the engineer slowly surveyed what was going to be their new home, like it or not.

The landing area was a long strip of alpine meadow, perhaps five kays long and a little more than two wide, bordered on three sides by rocky slopes that quickly rose into the knife-edged peaks that had shown so clearly on the screens. To the north was a ridge, lower than the surrounding rocky areas, almost a pass, through which he had brought the lander. The entire meadow area sloped slightly downhill from the northwest to the southeast, one of the reasons the landing had seemed to take longer than necessary, Nylan suspected. To the southwest, beyond the rocky slopes, rose a needle peak, impossibly tall, yet seemingly sheathed in ice.

"Freyja . . . blade of the gods," he said quietly.

"It is, isn't it?" said Fierral from behind his shoulder. "How did you get us down?"

"It wasn't too bad."

Fierral glanced back to the west, along the trail gouged out by the lander. "That's not exactly a prepared runway."

"No." Nylan laughed. "Would you give me a hand? We need to set up the beacon for the others."

"They can land here?"

"The beacon makes it a lot easier. You can lock in a direction and rate of descent."

"I would get the hard landing."

"We're here."

"Wherever that is." Fierral wiped her sweating forehead and glanced around the high plateau. "At least it's not *too* hot."

Behind them, the other marines dropped from the lander.

Nylan looked at the track he had made. From what he could tell, most of the rocks were small, nothing that would create too many problems. Rising from the grass between the rocks were small purple flowers, shaped like stars, that rose on thin, almost invisible, stems.

Nylan forced his thoughts from the fragile flowers and turned toward the lander itself. From what he could see, the ablative coating on the belly had been largely removed by the shrubbery and rocks.

"We've got some work to do—quickly. We need to set up the beacon and see if we can move the lander a bit." He headed toward the lander and the emergency beacon it contained. Fierral followed.

One of the marines walked the several hundred steps eastward from the lander, pausing just short of the sheer dropoff.

". . . frigging long way down . . ."

Nylan nodded. They had come a long ways down. He just hoped that they didn't have to fall any farther.

VI

HISSL STUDIES THE images in the glass. Four rounded metal tents squat amid the late spring grasses that carpet the Roof of the World. On the high ground in the northwest corner of the grassy area, the silver-haired man hammers stakes in place in a pattern which Hissl cannot determine through the mists of the glass.

Thrap! At the sound, Hissl squints and the image in the screeing glass fades into swirling white mists that in turn vanish, leaving what appears as a circular flat mirror in the center of the small white oak table. He turns. "Yes?"

"Hissl, Jissek has recovered, and we are here."

"Do come in." The man in white erases the frown and stands, waiting, as the two other men in white step into the room.

Terek closes the door and smiles.

Hissl returns the smile and bows. "I am honored."

"What do you make of the people of the iron tents?" asks the rotund Jissek. "From where did they come, do you think?"

"From beyond the skies—that is certain."

"Why do you say that?" asks Terek.

Both Jissek and Hissl look at the older wizard. Terek looks at Hissl as if waiting for an answer.

Hissl takes a deep breath before he speaks, ignoring the frown his sigh evokes from Terek. "There are many signs. It would appear that the tents flew down to the Roof of the World—"

"Flew? Iron cannot fly."

"They flew," confirmed Jissek.

"The people who were in the tents look mostly like us, but they are not. I have never seen silver hair on young people or hair that is red like a fire. And they sweat, as if the Roof of the World is warm, as though it might be hot like in the Stone Hills or the high plains of Analeria in midsummer."

"That seems little enough. What else?"

"They are mostly women. Out of a score, only three are men. Their leader is a woman. At least, she is shaped like a woman. And all the women bear what look like weapons, though I cannot be sure."

"The angels, you think?" asks Jissek.

Hissl shrugs.

"Angels? Bah . . . tales to frighten children with. That's all."

"Every wizard who can scree will see these women, and such tales will get passed, especially to those few who follow the black."

Terek pulls at his smooth chin. "Such tales . . . that would not be good. Perhaps someone should travel west."

Hissl and Jissek exchange glances. Finally, Hissl, the youngest wizard, the only balding one, clears his throat. "Would it be . . . proper for us to undertake such a mission—given the concerns raised by Lord Nessil of Lornth?"

"That might work to our advantage," points out Terek. "Lord Nessil would not wish the example of armed women to be made known, especially to the Jerans. Their women ride with the men, and he has had some trouble . . ."

The other two wizards nod.

"He would appreciate our concern, *and* he would be most intrigued with women of silver or fiery red hair."

"These . . . angels . . . might not take to being taken," says Hissl.

"Have they shown weapons? Thunderbolts, or firebolts such as we can bring?"

"No," admits the balding wizard. "Not that we have seen used."

"Then fourscore armsmen should be more than enough."

"As you wish." Hissl inclines his head.

"I will recommend, of course, that you accompany His Lordship." Terek smiles. "Since you have discovered the strangers, you should share in the rewards. And one wizard should be more than enough. We would not wish to imply a lack of confidence in the abilities of His Lordship."

"No . . . no, indeed," murmurs Jissek, wiping his forehead.

"You are most kind, High Wizard." Hissl offers a head bow. "Most kind."

VII

THE LANDER SHELLS formed a square on the rocky upper slope of the alpine area, adjacent to one of the two small streams that wound through the grass and shrubs, and below the staked-out pattern that Nylan had made. One of the shells contained several body-sized dents, and plastic foam filled a long gouge on the left side. On the uphill side of the shells were several plastic-covered stacks—the disassembled sections of the landers' exterior removable parts.

The wind whispered in from the north, barely above freezing.

Nylan and Ryba lay together in the forward part of lander one, sharing the command couch, under the light thermal blanket that was more than warm enough for them.

Only the faintest light crept in through the short corridor from the hatch, but Nylan had no difficulty seeing. With the silver hair had apparently come some form of enhanced night vision that took in the objects around him in the dimmest of light. He looked at Ryba, short hair tousled, face calm in sleep—not quite relaxed, but he had never seen her completely relaxed.

Beyond the couch were their clothes . . . and the twin blades Ryba had brought down from the *Winterlance* and begun to wear. Nylan did not shake his head. She was doubtless correct in assuming that the blades would have to serve as a defense before long and in accustoming herself to their use. What weapon could he use? A blade probably, since Ryba could teach him, although the idea of an edged weapon bothered him. But where would they get blades?

Though he knew the basics of metallurgy, he'd never tried anything so primitive as smithing, and he had no idea if there were any metallic deposits nearby. Charcoal he could make, if he ever had the time, and he could devise some sort of bellows, but they would be useless without iron or copper. The landers held enough steel alloys, but a primitive smithy would be hard-pressed to reach temperatures high enough to melt or cast them.

He took a long, slow breath.

Ryba's eyes flickered, and then, as always, she was awake. "What are you thinking about?"

"Weapons, smithing, how to use the materials in the landers . . ." He shrugged, suddenly conscious of her nakedness next to him.

"That's not all you're thinking about," whispered Ryba.

Nylan could feel himself blushing.

"And after last night? Shame on you."

Nylan nibbled on her neck.

"Not now . . . I can hear someone in the back."

"They certainly heard last night," he hissed back.

"It's different in the morning. Besides, we've got a lot to do. The growing season is so short. We'll have to get those grow-paks figured out and started. They're really designed as deep-space hydroponic units, but there are instructions for conversion, and there's one planet or soil-based unit." The captain swung her feet onto the chill composite flooring of what had been the cockpit area.

Nylan swung his feet to the other side, aware of the warmth of her back against his and of the faint scent of evergreens and the whispering of the wind outside.

Ryba pulled on her shipsuit, as did Nylan. He followed her into the dawn, and toward the stream to wash up. Neither spoke.

As the day lightened, long before the sun had edged above the tree-fringed eastern horizon that lay beyond the drop-off, Nylan had whittled a small limb into shavings, then used one of the matches to light the cook fire. He looked down at the match, then shook his head. "Strikers, maybe."

"Strikers?" Ayrlyn broke off a handful of dried end branches from the dead tree limb that several marines had dragged nearly a kay the day before.

"Steel and flint . . . maybe I could cut some pieces from the lander and bend them into an arc, attach the stone. Haven't seen any flint, though."

"You are planning for the long haul, aren't you?" Ayrlyn fed more of the tinder into the small flickering flames, flames duller than her flaming hair.

"Not so long. Three boxes of matches might last a local year if we used only one a day. We don't exactly have a chemical-processing industry here." Nylan picked up a plastic bucket, checking the scrapes on the gray material, then began to walk toward the stream.

"Does he sleep?" Saryn limped toward the fire that Ayrlyn fed, leaning heavily on the rough staff that allowed her to avoid putting too much weight on the hardened foam cast around her broken right leg.

"Neither he nor the captain seem to need much." Ayrlyn yawned.

"Where's the captain?"

"In number two with Mertin, sorting through the growpaks," answered the engineer, returning with a full bucket of water. "She wants to get started on laying out fields and planting."

"We've been down less than an eight-day, and she wants us to be field hands?" asked Saryn.

"What about Gerlich? Where's he gone?" inquired Ayrlyn.

"He's got the one bow and the arrows—out hunting. He claims there's something like a wild boar out there." Nylan gave a short laugh.

Saryn shook her head.

The captain and the junior officer emerged from the shell of lander two and walked toward the fire. Mertin ducked to avoid the line of smoke that seemed almost to seek his face.

From lander four emerged Fierral. The red-haired marine commander and the two ships' officers converged on the fire, stopping well back.

"Why the fire?" asked Fierral. "We've still got firin cells."

"Cooking. We're saving the cells for things we can't duplicate locally," answered Ryba.

"Such as?"

Two more marines eased up toward the fire.

"Powering the combat laser, if we need to." Ryba adjusted the makeshift hairband to keep the short and thick black hair totally away from her face.

Nylan emptied half the water into the kettle and swung it out over the fire on the makeshift crane. He frowned as he set aside the bucket.

"You don't approve, Ser Engineer?"

"I hope we can avoid that. The combat laser gobbles power. The more power we can use for constructive purposes the better."

"I take it you have some ideas?"

Nylan stood. "I've been studying the geology. There's something that looks like black marble, except it's not. It's tougher, but it's not as hard as granite, and I hope it cuts more easily—with a laser."

"Houses?" asked Saryn.

The silver-haired man shook his head. "A tower, something like that. It makes more sense. That's what I staked out—good solid footings there."

"How long 'fore we start building something, ser?" asked one of the younger marines standing behind Ayrlyn.

"That's not the first priority," snapped Ryba. "The lander shells are fine for now. What we need to get in the ground is food. We also need to survey the forest and the meadow here to see what's likely to be edible, while we still have the analyzer and some power."

Nylan nodded.

"And . . . we'll still need timber of some sort to roof, floor, and brace the engineer's tower."

"We might not need planks except for flooring and bracing," Nylan volunteered. "There's a dark gray slate that splits into sheets pretty easily."

"Good . . . I think."

"What's in the emergency grow-paks?" Saryn leaned back on the flat stone, stretching out the leg with the cast.

"Maize, although I don't know about whether the stream will supply enough water . . . potatoes that ought to do well in a cold climate, some high-protein beans."

"Get the potatoes in first," suggested Nylan.

"Potatoes?" asked Mertin, stepping up beside Ryba.

"They grow just about anywhere, and we could exist on them with only a few supplements. The ground seems all right." The engineer poured the rest of the water from the bucket into the pot. "They keep better than some of the other plants, although you could dry and grind the maize into a flour, I think."

"Seems?" asked Saryn.

Nylan shrugged. "It might take generations to determine if all the trace elements are there, but I'd bet they are."

Ryba looked at him.

"If it's not perfectly planoformed, it's a natural duplicate of a hot humanoid world. It feels right."

"Are we going to rely on feel?"

"We'd better figure out something to rely on besides high technology that won't be around much longer."

"Feel . . ." Ryba frowned. "Let's finish eating and get to work on those fields. The growing season can't be very long here. Once we get everything we can planted, then we'll worry about game and timber and longer-range priorities."

Fierral nodded, stiffly, like the marine force leader she remained.

Saryn straightened on the rock where she sat and winced.

Nylan glanced uphill across the starflower-strewn grass and bushes—and rocks—to the staked outline of the foundations of what he hoped would be a tower . . . if they could get to it. If the locals didn't show up in force first . . . If . . . He clamped his lips together, ignoring the sidelong look from Ryba.

VIII

THE EARLY-MORNING sun glared out of the blue-green sky and bathed the sloping meadow, and the figures who toiled there, glinting off the few exposed metal sections of the lander shells and off the small spring that fed the stream.

Ryba stood above it all, on the top of the rocky ledges above the dampness of the meadows in the wind that blew steadily from the northwest. With her stood Fierral and two marines. All four looked to the northeast, down the rocky ridge line.

"There . . . you can see them, at the base of the ridge there. It's almost as good as a road." Fierral pointed. "They're pretty clearly headed here. And there are a lot of them."

"I'd expected a little more time before anyone found us. I wonder how they knew." Ryba frowned, then shrugged. "I suppose that's not the issue now."

"What do you want us to do?" asked the blue-eyed force leader.

"Act innocent. Keep the sentries in place and use the mirrors to signal me when they get close. Position the rifles there in the rocks where you can sweep them if you have to. Try not to use them until you really have to. I'd rather save the ammunition. Make sure the rest of the marines have their sidearms with them. We only have the pair of rifles?"

"Just the two," Fierral affirmed.

"Give one to each of your best snipers—besides you— and put one where you are and the other on the far end of that downhill clump of rocks."

"Not a bad cross fire." The force leader nodded.

"Then set up the rest of the marines where they can take cover quickly if they have to. They might have archers or something."

"I didn't see anything like that through the glasses," Fierral said slowly. "You don't think they're peaceful?"

"With more than fifty horses in a primitive culture? That's the equivalent of a half-dozen mirror towers." Ryba snorted. "No . . . they're not peaceful, but we'll pretend they are, and I'm betting they'll be trying for the same impression, too."

Fierral raised her eyebrows, just as flaming red as her hair, but said nothing and waited for Ryba to explain.

"It's simple. The way the approach runs here, you have to come up the ridge, and that's exposed. Nylan was right. It's a good spot for a tower—or a castle. The rocks behind there are too sharp to bring horses through, and too steep. So"—Ryba shrugged again—"without modern weapons, it would be hard to take. But first we have to survive to build it. Anyway, they'll pretend to come in peace, unless we attack first, just to get close, and they think we'll be drawn in."

"Men," laughed Fierral.

"They may be transparent, squad leader, but they're still dangerous." Ryba turned. "The engineer will be doing the prep work for his tower, and I'll keep a handful busy with the ditching. We might as well do something while we're waiting. It will be a while. They'll walk the horses up here so that they're fresh for the battle they're pretending they don't want. Try not to kill the horses. We'll need them."

"Besides you, who can ride?" asked Fierral.

"You'll all have to learn, sooner or later. This way, we won't have to buy mounts."

The other two marines looked from the hard face of their squad leader to the harder face of the captain.

IX

"LORD NESSIL, THE ang—the strangers are just over the rise, not more than twenty rods beyond the tips of the gray rocks." The armsman in brown leathers keeps his voice low and looks up to the hatchet-faced man in the heavy purple cloak. Blotches of moisture have soaked through the armsman's leather trousers, and green smears attest to his crawling through underbrush and grass.

Lord Nessil brushes back a long lock of silver and black hair, then smiles. "Are they as attractive as the screeing glass shows?"

"Pardoning Your Grace, but I wasn't looking at them that way." The armsman's eyes flicker to his right as another trooper leads his horse back to him. "They don't seem bothered by the chill. They wear light garments, like they were in Lydiar in midsummer, but I wasn't looking beyond the clothes, more for blades, and only the black-haired wench bears one. A pair she has."

"A pair of what?" asks Nessil.

Lettar looks down at the grass.

"For that, Lettar, you shall have one to enjoy." Nessil laughs softly. "Women warriors, and only one has a blade. I shall enjoy this." He turns toward the wizard in white. "What do your arts show, Wizard?"

"There are less than a score that I can scree there, eighteen in all, and but three men. They bear some strange devices that radiate some small measure of order, and others that bear some measure of chaos. They have set up a spindly windmill that will be ripped apart in the first good wind." Hissl inclines his head.

"What would you have us do, Wizard?"

"I would like your men to preserve their devices. We might learn something from them. I cannot advise Your Grace on tactics, My Lord. You are the warrior. I can but say that they are likely to be more formidable than they appear. I cannot tell you why."

Nessil laughs again, still softly, but more harshly. "You caution me that they could be formidable, but not why. Thus, if I succeed in capturing them all, I will be pleased." His face darkens. "If I fail, you may claim you warned me. Wizard's double words! Ride beside me, Ser Wizard."

"Pardoning Your Grace, but what shall we do? Ride down on them?" asks Lettar.

"No. We will be civilized. We will ride up and demand their surrender for trespass. That way, we might get them all. We do outnumber them more than three to one." Nessil looks at Hissl. "And we get the wizard close enough to use his firebolts if need be."

"What about the men?"

"If they resist, kill them. If not, we can always use them somewhere. Try to save as many of the women as you can. I've never had a silver-haired wench—or one with fire-red hair." Nessil offers a boyish grin and looks along the line of threescore mounted troopers. "Shall we make our appearance? Bring out the banners. After all, we do come in peace, one way or another."

Hissl's eyes glaze slightly, as if he is no longer quite within his body.

Then the horsemen ride toward the low rise, over which looms the ice-needle peak that dominates the Roof of the World. The banners flap in the brisk wind that blows out of the north and spins the windmill beyond the crest of the hill.

The starflowers left in the meadow on the far side of the ridge—those that have not been destroyed by the cultivation or wilted as their season has passed—bend in the wind.

X

ABOVE THE PLOT where Gerlich and several marines half toiled at ditch-digging, partly sheltered by a line of boulders, Nylan studied the laser, and the array of firin cells in the portable rack. He mumbled and made another adjustment to the powerhead on the laser.

"Why don't you just try it, ser?" asked the stocky blond marine behind him.

"Because, Huldran, we can only replace a fraction of the power."

"What about the emergency generator?" Huldran nodded her head toward the man-sized but flimsy-looking windmill set near the crest of the hill. Beneath it was a small array of solar cells. Both the cells and the generator fed through a convertor into a single firin cell.

Nylan laughed. "The laser uses more energy in a few units than the generator supplies in a day." After another readjustment to the powerhead, he straightened and wiped his sweating forehead. "It gets hot here in the day."

"Yes, ser." Huldran wiped away the sweat from her fair-skinned forehead.

"I heard that, Ser Engineer," said Gerlich from the plot. "It's frigging hot here. It would have been hard to try to live any lower. I'll bet those lowlands are like the demons' hell." The shirtsleeved Gerlich blotted his brow and handed the makeshift spade to one of the marines. "Your turn."

"Yes, ser." The dark-haired marine took the shovel and continued digging the ditch that would divert stream water through the plot. Her eyes continued to scan the rise to the north as she slowly dug.

Three other marines grubbed at the ground with makeshift implements resembling hoes to clear away the mixture of what appeared to be grass and a high-altitude clover bearing occasional reddish blooms. Their eyes occasionally darted toward the top of the ridge or toward one of the rock formations. The shortest marine wiped her forehead, her hand unconsciously touching the slug-thrower at her belt.

"How long do we have to play at being innocent would-be peasants, anyway?" asked Gerlich.

"Until our visitors arrive," responded Ryba from the end of the small plot. "In any case, you've proved you can toil with the best, Gerlich." She motioned to the former weapons officer. "You can even bring in game with a bow—even dangerous game." Her eyes flicked to the rack where another marine had stretched out the hide of what appeared to be a cougar and studied a small manual. "No one knows what to do with the hide. What do you know about making bows and arrows?"

"Not much. I use them. Others make them."

"We're all going to have to do some making here."

Gerlich smiled lazily and shrugged.

Ryba's hand flicked, and, as if by magic, the tip of one of the steel blades appeared at the brown-haired man's throat. Her eyes met his, as they stood there, the captain almost equal in height to the husky weapons officer, and in breadth of shoulders.

Gerlich swallowed.

"In case you've forgotten, I'm not only captain, but I'm

tougher than you are—and so are most of the marines, in case you get any ideas." Ryba's blade vanished back into the scabbard. "Now . . . do you want to try to figure out how to make something useful?"

"You've made it clear I have little choice."

"None of us do, not if we're going to survive. I intend to make sure that we all do."

A light flashed across Ryba's face, and she squinted, then turned toward the sentry up in the rocks. After a moment, she called, "Ready! Stand by for visitors."

"Ready, Captain," responded Fierral, squaring her broad shoulders.

To the north of the plot, but to the right of the rockier ground where Nylan's crude stakes marked the tower that might never be built, Saryn sat in the shade of a boulder and used one of the three survival knives to pare down a fir limb into the shaft of what would be another shovel. At Ryba's command, she eased her own slug-thrower out of the holster and onto the flat rock. She stopped peeling and carving, but still held the knife loosely.

Beyond her, still partly sheltered by a line of boulders, Nylan made yet another adjustment to the powerhead on the laser. He straightened, then frowned as he both heard Ryba's command, and somehow felt the presence of horsemen beyond the ridge.

Was it just his imagination?

Ryba walked uphill toward the rocks until she was less than a dozen paces from where Saryn and Nylan worked. "Company's about to arrive."

"Wonderful . . ." mumbled Nylan. "We're barely planet-side an eight-day, and someone has decided to start a fight. Humans are such peaceful creatures."

"We're angels," hissed the dark-haired Saryn.

"Same same," muttered the engineer back.

"High Command would have your head for that," pointed out the second pilot.

"We'll never see High Command again."

Saryn shivered.

"Keep your slug-throwers ready," added Ryba. "Aim for the body."

The ground vibrated slightly as the horsemen crossed the top of the ridge. In the van were two young men bearing purple banners, followed by a man in a purple cloak thrown back to reveal an iron breastplate and a large hand-and-a-half sword worn in a shoulder harness.

Ryba reached for the slug-thrower at her hip.

"That won't do much," observed Nylan. "They'll just think it's magic of some sort. I suspect that they only recognize blades and arrows as weapons."

"I don't care what they call it. We have to stop them."

"Will it hurt to talk?" Nylan asked. "They look too like us not to be human."

"I suppose not, but if they're really human, they're here to fight." Ryba's eyes flicked toward the ridge where the head marine stood. The snipers remained hidden. "Fierral has her troops ready to gun down the whole mass of them if I give the order."

"All of them?"

"If necessary." Ryba's face was hard. "People don't like facing the unknown. If they're hostile, I'd rather have them all disappear. We could plead ignorance in the future. It's hard to plead ignorance when there are witnesses."

The three studied the riders as the horsemen rode down toward the angel encampment. Beside the purple-clad leader rode a man cloaked totally in white, and Nylan could even feel a sense of whiteness, tinged with red, emanating from the man, who was the only one not carrying visible weapons. That lack of weapons bothered the engineer.

"Watch out for the one in white," he said quietly as his hand drifted to the standard-issue sidearm that he had never used against the demons of light or their mirror towers.

"I'll keep that in mind." Ryba kept her broad shoulders square as she stepped forward and somewhat away from the rocks.

The horsemen drew up in a rough line, a sort of half-circle centered on the small plot being ditched. The marines in the plot had lowered their hoes, and their hands rested by the butts of their sidearms.

The man in the purple cloak reined up well short of Ryba, inclined his head, and declaimed something.

"Not good," whispered Nylan. "They know she's in charge."

Ryba inclined her head slightly, then, without turning her head, asked, "What did he say?"

"The general idea is that we don't belong here."

"I could tell that myself," snapped Ryba, her eyes still fixed on the man in purple.

The leader of the locals added a few more words, the last ending in what seemed a partial snarl.

Ryba looked back at him, then responded in an even tone. "I suggest you do the same to yourself."

Purple cloak drew the big hand-and-a-half sword, holding it at the ready.

"Now what do you suggest?" asked Ryba.

"Put one of those Sybran blades through him and run like hell from the guy in white," suggested Nylan.

"I'm afraid we can't recognize your authority." Ryba's voice was almost musical.

Another sentence followed from the local's leader, and he gestured toward the heavens overhead.

Nylan pursed his lips. Did the locals know they had come from space?

"Returning to where we came from is clearly impossible," Ryba responded.

The sword jabbed skyward again.

"No."

The purple-cloaked man barked a command. The sword swept toward Ryba as he spurred his horse forward, as did the other horsemen.

"Fire at will!" yelled Ryba.

Even before the local's heavy blade was within a body length of Ryba, the purple-clad rider was sagging from the big horse, a length of Sybran steel protruding from his chest.

The other horsemen continued to charge whoever happened to be close, blades out and looking for targets, maintaining a rough double-line formation. Only the man in white held back, his eyes scanning the meadow area.

Crack, crack, crack, crack . . . Even the first staccato impacts of the marine slug-throwers that echoed across the high meadow hurled nearly a dozen armsmen from their mounts. One of the purple banners fluttered to the ground.

The others ignored the sounds and rode toward the handful of marines in the open.

Crack! Crack! Crack! More slug-throwers discharged, and more horsemen tumbled, their frozen faces wearing expressions of disbelief.

Nylan aimed at the man in white. *Crack!*

Nothing happened, but the engineer had the feeling that somehow the ceramic composite shell had fragmented before it reached the target.

Crack!

With a long and dramatic-sounding set of phrases, the man in the white tunic and trousers raised his right hand and gestured.

Ryba dove behind the nearest boulder, and Nylan ducked. The two of them jammed together.

Whhssttt! The firebolt seemed to bounce off the rock, flared over the half-hoed field, and smashed across the side of the nearest lander. White ashes cascaded onto the meadow. Where the firebolt had struck was a gouge in the dark tiles that showed metal beneath.

"Frig . . ." muttered Ryba. "Personal laser! Can't believe it."

Whhhssstt!

Another firebolt flared above them, gouging a line of fire through the meadow clover.

Whhhssstt!

Crack! Ryba's shot also failed to reach the man in white.

"That's no laser." Nylan peered over the edge of the boulder, then frowned. The man in white was gone, although Nylan thought he could feel someone riding up the hill.

More feelings that seemed to be correct, and that bothered the engineer.

"Where did he go?" snapped Ryba.

"Forget him!"

Crack! Crack! Crack!

Nylan lifted the slug-thrower as two horsemen, low in the saddle, swept around the end of the rocks and headed toward them.

Both the captain and the engineer fired again.

Crack! Crack! Crack! When the hammer came down on the empty chamber, Nylan scrambled to the other side of the rock, emerging a moment later. His mouth dropped open as he saw Ryba on one of the horses, chasing down, and slicing open one of the hapless armsmen, and then another.

"Get the damned horses!" yelled Ryba before she rode uphill after a fleeing mount.

Nylan looked at the nearby horse, then flung himself behind the boulder as another horseman galloped toward him.

Crack! Crack! Crack!

The slugs whistled over Nylan's head, and one of Saryn's shots dropped the horseman.

"You'd better reload!" suggested Saryn.

"Thanks!" Nylan, crouching behind the boulder, fumbled the second and last clip into the slug-thrower. He hoped the marines had more firepower. He also hoped they were better shots than he'd proved to be.

When he scrambled up, there were no horsemen nearby, just the mount of the man Saryn had dropped. Nylan, ignoring his apprehensions about grabbing onto anything ten times his size, grasped the reins of the nearby mount, which promptly reared. "Now . . . now . . ." He tried to be reassuring, but the horse reared again, nearly dragging him off his feet before it settled down.

Whhheeeee . . . eeeee . . . eeee . . .

"I don't like it any better than you do, fellow, lady, whatever you are." Horses? What was he doing hanging on to horses on an impossible planet? He tried not to shiver and concentrated on calming the horse.

Slowly, somehow, he managed, even as he looked across the meadow. He swallowed. From what he could see, there were large numbers of bodies strewn almost at random. Three of them, beyond the plot, wore shipsuits.

Absently, Nylan patted the neck of the horse.

Wheee . . . eeee . . .

He glared at the beast that towered over him, and, surprisingly, the animal seemed to whimper. Patting the animal's neck, he added, "Just take it easy."

His eyes flicked across the meadow, then toward the top of the hill where Ryba had reined up.

"They're gone, frig it!"

Nylan led the horse toward the lander shells and the half-grubbed and ditched plot, not quite sure what to do with the animal. At the least, he needed to find someplace to tether it. Several marines were working over two angel bodies as he led the horse toward the nearest lander, where, absently, he tied the reins around an internal door loop. No one was going to be closing the door anytime soon.

Then he hurried through the fallen horsemen. One moaned as Nylan passed. He looked down at the hole in the man's abdomen, and his guts twisted at the blood. The man moaned again. Nylan knelt. There wasn't much he could do.

The soldier muttered something, blood oozing from the corner of his mouth. Had he fractured ribs in his fall from the horse? The man's hand clutched Nylan's, and he muttered, "Nerysa . . . Nerysa . . ."

His hand loosened, as did his jaw.

Nylan closed the dead man's eyes and slowly stood. Then he walked toward the group between the end lander and the plot where three gathered around a prone figure in a shipsuit.

"It's no use." One of the marines sat back and wiped her forehead.

The unmoving figure was that of the junior officer—Mertin. Above sightless eyes and streams of dried and drying blood, his forehead looked slightly lopsided.

The marine stood. "Those blades are more like iron crowbars. Not much edge. Damned sword caved in his temple. He just stood there and shot, never ducked. He got about four of them."

Nylan looked toward the other grouping. "Who's that?"

"Kyseen, I think. Mangled leg. Three of them hit her at once. She got two. The third got her with his horse. She still got him."

Nylan shook his head. The entire fight still seemed both horribly real and terribly unreal.

From what he could tell, several other marines were also down.

From the hillside above, Ryba rode downhill, leading three more riderless mounts. More to the west, another marine and Gerlich were on horseback, trying to corner several more of the riderless horses. Nylan counted nearly a score of mounts being held, tethered, or chased.

Nylan glanced back toward Kyseen.

"Dumb bastard!"

Since she sounded as though she had a chance for recovery, and since he was certainly no medtech, he walked back toward the uphill side of the lander shells where Ryba was directing the construction of something where the horses could be tethered.

"Nylan!" ordered Ryba. "Get a couple of marines and check the bodies. Those that aren't too badly wounded we'll try to save for information. Gather all the weapons, anything valuable, and have your detail bury the rest deep enough that scavengers, or whatever they have here, won't get them. Keep any cloaks or jackets or armor or boots—if they're in good condition."

Nylan nodded. While he didn't like the idea, he understood the need.

"Don't bury any of the dead horses yet." Ryba made a sour face. "Maybe we can butcher some and stretch out the concentrates."

Nylan frowned. Horse meat? Maybe it would be better than concentrates, but he had his doubts. To stop thinking about that, he asked, "Who got away besides the fellow in white?"

"Maybe a half dozen. One or two were wounded, I think." Ryba turned her mount toward the end of the meadow where Gerlich lurched in the saddle as his mount nearly carried him into an overhanging pine branch. "Use your legs, Gerlich, and your head!"

Nylan pointed to the three nearest marines. "You, you, and you—we're the scavenger-and-burial detail." He saw Huldran. "You too, Huldran. We'll start up by the rocks and sweep down. Carry the bodies to the lower end of the meadow, near the drop-off." He gestured.

"That's a long ways," pointed out a tall woman, who, like him, had come out of the mysterious underjump with silver hair.

Nylan tried to remember her name. Was it Llysette?

"Llysette, it's downhill—"

"It's Llyselle, ser."

"Sorry. In any case, Llyselle, it is downhill and away from the water, and it's going to be hard to bury them deep enough to get rid of the smell. There are rocks there, for a cairn, if necessary."

"Yes, ser." The four gave him resigned looks.

"Why don't we just drop them over the cliff?" asked Huldran.

"That would probably just cause more trouble with the locals, and we don't need that."

"How would they know?"

Nylan shrugged. "I don't know, but they've got something—call it technology, call it magic. They knew Ryba was our leader, and they knew we came from space or the local equivalent."

"Great . . ." mumbled one of the other marines.

"Stow it, Berlis," said Huldran tiredly. "The engineer's usually been right, and these days that counts for a lot. Let's get on with it."

"Take any weapons, knives, any gadgets or coins. Jewelry,

too," added Nylan. "The more we find, the more we might be able to figure out about these people."

The sun had dropped behind the mountain peaks by the time Ryba, Gerlich, and their work crew had completed a makeshift corral for the captured mounts and by the time a large cairn and five individual graves had been completed and filled in the southwestern corner of the open area, just beyond the end of the meadow and less than two dozen steps from the beginning of the drop-off.

Saryn was by the cook-fire area, making an attempt to butcher a dead horse. Nylan shook his head, but kept walking toward the stream. He needed to get the blood and grime off himself, if he could.

Not much more than an eight-day and already five were dead—Mertin and four marines. Then, again, reflected the engineer, without the combat-trained marines and Ryba, things would have been worse, much worse.

Nylan bent down and washed the rock dust and dirt from his hands in the narrow stream. Then he walked back toward the lander where they had stockpiled the plunder, such as it was, from the corpses. They had gathered nearly three dozen of the heavy iron blades that scarcely seemed sharp enough to hack wood. After thinking about Ryba's Sybran blade and how she had sheared right through the local plate and chain mail, Nylan shook his head.

He neared the lander, and Ayrlyn, who stood by the single remaining local. The man half sat, half lay almost against the side of the end lander on a thin tarp. The pale green eyes surveyed Nylan, and the man spoke.

Nylan almost caught the words.

"He's asking if you're the only true man here," said Ayrlyn from his elbow. "He wants to give you his sword. Or he would if he still had it."

"Honor concept, I suppose."

"Only men have honor here? Are we in trouble!" snorted the former comm officer. Her brown eyes flashed that impossible shade of blue.

"If I take his sword, I'm responsible for him, I suppose."

"Something like that, I'd guess."

"Does that mean he gives his word not to escape, or is it meaningless nonsense?" Nylan's voice was hoarse, tired.

"Who would know?"

Nylan stared at the local. "I'll take his moral sword, or whatever. Tell him that if he breaks his word, he'll wish no one in his family had ever been born." Nylan was tired. Tired and angry, and he just wished that things hadn't degenerated into slaughter so quickly.

Even before the flame-haired comm officer started to speak, the man paled, and words tumbled from his lips.

Ayrlyn looked sideways at the engineer. "For a moment, I thought you almost glowed." She shook her head, and fires seemed to shimmer in her hair. "Whatever you did, he claims you're his liege. His name is Narliat." She lowered her voice. "You did *something* that scared the living darkness out of him. He called you master or mage, something like that."

Nylan rubbed his forehead. "This place makes me feel strange. It's almost like being on the net, except it's not." He almost could understand the man's words, and the language was somehow familiar, but not quite. He kept rubbing his forehead.

Ayrlyn looked at him. "It is strange. I've had a couple of flashes like that, except it's more as though I could feel the trees or the grass." She glanced around nervously. "I'm not crazy. I'm not."

"We're probably just tired." Nylan looked at the prisoner. "Now what?"

"Tell him to stay here, and he will."

Nylan did, and Ayrlyn repeated the words. Narliat bowed his head.

The two angels walked toward the cook fire where Ryba waited. Nylan glanced to the rocky outcropping where a pair of sentries were outlined against the twilit sky.

The captain turned her head. "How many in the cairn?"

"Forty-three."

"Forty-three? That many?" burst out Kyseen from the litter by the fire.

"That few," said Ryba. "There were almost sixty, I think. Probably another three or four were wounded. They'll probably die, if the locals' medical care matches their weapons. That means almost a dozen escaped."

"Killing two thirds of an attacking force sounds pretty good," pointed out Saryn.

"I'm more worried about the one in white," mused Nylan. "It wasn't a laser, but he had a lot of power."

"It doesn't make sense. Whatever weapon he used burned right through the lander's ablative tiles like they weren't there—until it got to the thin steel undershell. That's not a laser. The ablative tiles would have stopped even a small weapons laser." Saryn winced as she shifted her position on the stone.

"Call it magic," suggested Nylan.

"Magic?" Ryba's eyebrows lifted.

"There's something here like a neuronet—"

"You think this is all imagination? That we're really trapped in the *Winterlance*'s net?"

"Oh, frig . . ." muttered Gerlich.

"No. There are too many independent variables for a net to handle, especially the interactions and apparent actions between individual personalities. Also, there's a feel about the net," explained Nylan. "It's not here."

"Thus speaks the engineer." Gerlich's tone was openly sarcastic.

Nylan ignored it.

"What do you think of the local swords?" Nylan asked Ryba. "You're the only one with any experience, I think."

"Not quite," said Gerlich. "I did club fencing for a while."

"So did I," added another voice. "Sers . . ."

Nylan looked at the wiry silver-haired marine.

"I'm Istril," the marine explained apologetically.

"That's a help," said Ryba slowly. "You're all going to have to use blades, I think, before the year is out, anyway. Maybe sooner. Unless we can manufacture bows and learn archery."

"Why . . ." started a voice farther back in the twilight. "Oh . . . sorry."

"Exactly. Fierral took inventory. That little firefight cost us nearly three hundred rounds. That's actually pretty good. One in nine shells counted. Except we only have about six hundred rounds left. That's maybe two battles like we just went through." Ryba bowed to the marine force leader. "Without the marines, we'd all be dead or slaves."

Ryba turned to Nylan. "I fear you were correct, Ser Engineer, about the need for a defensive emplacement, a tower."

Nylan nodded. "You never answered the question about blades."

"Most of their blades are hatchet-edged crowbars. That hand-and-a-half blade the leader carried is a fair piece of work, and so was one other thing like a sabre. Why did you ask?" Ryba smiled tightly. "You don't ask questions, ser, unless you know the answer."

"I saw what your blade did to the local leader," Nylan replied honestly. "I just wondered what the comparisons were."

"If we could find blades like mine, it would give us an advantage—not so much as slug-throwers—but I don't see those for a long, long time to come."

Neither did Nylan.

"But," continued the captain, "I don't know how we could find or forge blades like mine."

Nylan frowned, then pursed his lips. Was there any way? He shook his head.

"What about the language?" Ryba turned to Ayrlyn.

"That doesn't make sense, either. It sounded like an off-shoot of Anglorat," said the comm officer.

Nylan nodded, mostly to himself. He should have recognized it, but he hadn't expected the demon tongue to show up here.

"What was that idiot saying? Where were you, anyway?" asked Ryba.

"Where you put me . . . on the other side." Ayrlyn gave a

slight shiver. "I didn't get it all, and some of the words didn't make any sense, but the general idea was that we had to surrender because we were trespassing on his lands—"

"His lands?"

"His lands."

"Darkness help us," said Ryba. "We would knock off the local ruler. That can't be good."

"It might be very good," mused Nylan. "Anyone else might decide to wait a while before taking us on."

"Either that, or they'll all be up here on some sort of holy war against their version of the demons. That's what we probably look like to them."

Nylan laughed.

"What's so funny?"

"We got here because we were fighting the demons, and as soon as we land, we're fighting more demons."

"You think this place was a Rationalist colony?" Ryba's eyebrows knit together.

"How could it be? It's not even in our universe," snapped Gerlich.

"Maybe they got here like we did," suggested Saryn.

"We don't even know how we got here, not for sure," pointed out Nylan. "Or where *here* even is."

"You obviously have some ideas, O Bright One," snapped Gerlich. "So how do you *think* we got here?"

"We were at the focus of a lot of energy, more than enough to blow the boards and the *Winterlance* right out of existence. We're still around, even if it's someplace strange—"

"Are you sure we're just not dead, or imagining things?" asked Ayrlyn.

"The physical sensations seem rather intense for being merely spiritual and mental . . . and I explained the limitations of a net . . ."

"So you did."

Nylan turned to look fully at the taller man. "So . . . listen. I'll listen to your knowledge. If we don't listen and save every bit of knowledge we have to share, we'll be dead—or our descendants will suffer more than they have to—or both."

"That assumes we'll live that long," snapped Gerlich.

Ryba's blade flickered again, and the cold steel touched Gerlich's neck. "I'm getting very tired of having to use force to keep you in line, but it seems like that's all you respect."

"Without that blade . . ."

Ryba handed the blade to Istril, the small marine. "Hold this."

Gerlich looked puzzled.

"Some people never learn." Ryba's foot lashed out across the bigger man's thigh.

"Missed, bitch." Gerlich charged.

Ryba danced aside, and her hands blurred. Gerlich slammed facefirst into dirt and clover, then scrambled up and took a position, feet wide, hands in guard position.

Ryba feinted with her shoulder, once, twice.

Gerlich did not move.

The captain seemed to duck, then with a sweep kick knocked Gerlich off his feet, although the brown-haired man scrambled and slashed at her arm. Ryba took the arm, and Gerlich went flying into the meadow.

He rose slowly, holding his arm.

"It's only dislocated," snapped Ryba. "I could have broken your worthless neck. So could most of the marines."

"Why didn't you?"

"Because you have some stud value. But I could break both your arms and keep that."

Nylan shivered at the chill in Ryba's voice. He looked up at the unfamiliar stars. They looked very cold, and very distant.

Gerlich slumped and slowly walked forward toward the fire.

"Jaseen, can you snap that back in place?" asked Ryba.

"Yes, ser."

"Do it."

Gerlich sat down on a boulder, while Ryba reclaimed her blade and sheathed it. Nylan glanced across the faces of the twenty-two women—all but the two standing in the rocks as sentries—and then at Gerlich. Things were going to be different . . . very different.

He repressed a shudder.

XI

NYLAN LAY ON his side of the couch in the darkness listening to Ryba's soft and even breathing. A faint cold breeze wafted forward from the open lander door, bringing with it the scent of fire smoke and evergreens.

The engineer closed his eyes, then opened them. Less than six hundred rounds of ammunition—that was what stood between them and being captured or killed by the locals. The battle laser might be good for another skirmish, but it wouldn't be much good once the fighting reached the hand-to-hand stage, and that meant a cold decision to wipe out the locals before they even charged the angels.

And after that? The locals wouldn't go away. It might be a few seasons or years before they attacked again, but given human nature, they would. Then what would the angels have left for defense? Ryba had agreed to build a tower, and that meant he had to design one that was simple and relatively quick to construct, big enough for growth, and proof against a cold, cold winter that probably lasted more than half the local year. Ensuring that the tower could hold off any lengthy attack also meant figuring out a water supply that couldn't be blocked . . .

He sighed.

"You're still awake?" asked Ryba.

"I thought you were asleep," said Nylan.

"No. I was thinking."

"So was I. What were you thinking about?"

"You name it, and I was thinking about it," she answered

slowly. "Weapons, the locals, weather, crops, housing, your tower, the next generation, how to feed horses through the winter, how to get to the winter . . ."

Nylan nodded, then added, as he realized that, while he could see her, she didn't seem to have the same night vision he did, "I was thinking about the tower."

"I told you that you could use the lasers to cut stone to build the tower. Just make it big enough for three times the numbers we have."

"Four," suggested the engineer.

"If you can do it. There's not that much power in the firin cells." Ryba reached out and squeezed his hand. "It isn't going to be easy."

"No. And the building season won't be much longer than the growing season. Some of the evergreens look solid enough, and straight enough to provide the timbering we need. But we'll have to cut green timber, and that's going to be hard with one axe and one portable grip saw."

"You just can't stack stones on top of each other, though, can you?"

"Not unless we want to use huge blocks, and we don't have enough people to move things. We'll need mortar of some sort, but there has to be clay somewhere around here, and, unless I'm mistaken, there are old lava flows across the way."

"What does lava have to do with mortar?"

"I haven't found any limestone nearby. So I'm hoping that I can either pulverize some of the lava or that there's some compressed ash that I can use with the clay. It's going to take a little experimenting."

"What about glass?"

"Shutters, probably, for the first winter, except for what I can make out of the armaglass screens, but they're small. There's one small handsaw besides the grip saw. If the emergency generator holds up for a while . . . if I can figure out how to make mortar . . . if . . ." Nylan took a deep breath. "Too many ifs . . ."

"Yes." She squeezed his hand again, and he squeezed back.

They lay silently for a time longer.

"Those swords we got from the locals aren't much better than iron crowbars," Ryba finally said into the darkness.

"That bothers you, doesn't it?"

"You can't forge replacement shells for the slug-throwers, can you? Or make powder?"

"I could make black powder, if I could find the ingredients, but it would destroy the guns within a season, I think. There's too much residue. That's even if I could cast shells out of the copper I don't know even exists."

"Better blades ought to be possible . . ." mused the captain. "Somehow . . ."

The silence dropped over the couch again, then lengthened into sleep as the scent of the fire was replaced with the colder late-night air, the stronger smell of the evergreens, and the hint of the oncoming rain.

XII

AFTER WIPING HIS forehead, Nylan handed the crude shovel to Huldran. "Keep clearing this rock off, all the way downhill to the stakes there. Make sure the dirt goes way outside the stakes, or you'll have to move it again."

"Yes, ser," answered the stocky blond.

Nylan took his makeshift twine-and-weight level and measured the slope of the clear rock shelf. The rock ledge uncovered by the digging sloped enough that the tower foundations would have to be stepped and leveled. With the brush of pine branches, he gently swept the dust and dirt off the rock around one crack that extended the length of the cleared area, bending down and using his hand to gauge the width.

On a flat expanse of rock to the west of the tower foundation area, two marines took turns using crude stone sledges on the chunks of reddish rocks. Beside them Saryn took a small hammer and pulverized the small pieces into dust, and then swept them into one of the few plastic buckets.

Khhhcheww!!! Chhhew!!!

"Frigging dust!" snapped the former second pilot, shifting her weight and the cast on her injured leg.

Khhchew!!!

Despite the sneezing, Saryn kept pulverizing the reddish rocks.

Over the hammering came another set of vibrations. The engineer raised his eyes to see Ryba riding up, her eyes surveying the area.

"Are you still digging holes?"

Nylan glanced at the captain sharply, then exhaled as he caught the glint in her eye. "Yes. We're still digging holes." He gestured, then swallowed, and continued the explanation he felt stupid making. "If I get the foundation and the lower level right, the rest will be easy. If not . . ."

"I'm glad you take it seriously." She wiped her forehead. "We're going to need it, and a stable or barn as well."

"I don't know how long the laser will last . . ."

"It lasts as long as it lasts. Then we try something else." Ryba's voice was matter-of-fact.

"Any signs of the locals?"

"Istril thought she saw someone in purple on the far ridge, but whoever it was didn't stay around. There's a road down along the bottom of the ridge, more like a trail. I'd say it's one of the high passes across the mountains, probably more direct, but colder." Ryba turned in the saddle, studying the fields and the surrounding slopes, then looked back at Nylan. "Gerlich says there aren't any signs of local hunters in the higher woods. Not much in the way of larger game, either. That cat seems to be the top of the predatory chain. There are some goats, probably escaped domesticated animals or their offshoot, some horned sheep, and a lot of smaller animals, all off the mammal evolutionary tree. The

goats and horned sheep run at the first sign of anyone nearing. There are traces of what might be deer, but no one's seen
any."

"Goat and mutton are the animal-protein sources, then?"

"And the deer. Horse meat, possibly, and there have to be
cattle, somewhere."

"Why?"

"Where did the leather come from for those saddles and
reins? Or those vests?"

Nylan felt stupid. "Of course."

Ryba glanced toward the marines pounding rocks, and
toward Saryn, who wore a floppy hat she had scrounged
from the plundered goods. Ryba blotted her forehead, then
steadied the horse, which sidled away from Huldran. "Sand-
stone? Why are they crushing that?"

"Volcanic ash. It's almost too hard, but if we crush it and
mix it with some other stuff, and some of the clay at the base
of the ridge, it sets pretty well, maybe too well, sort of like
a stone epoxy. We won't be able to mix much at once, and
that's going to be a problem."

"It hardens too quickly?"

Nylan nodded. "All or nothing. It either sets quickly, or
it's slop."

"When will you start actually building?"

"Not until I get the footings set. Another couple of days
probably. The first line of stones—that will really be like a
sill—has to be perfect. We'll do a double wall up to the
third-floor level, fill it with stone chips and clay for insula-
tion—"

"Whatever you think." Ryba nodded and turned the horse
down toward the section of the meadow that resembled a
field of sorts.

As she left, Nylan pondered. Did he really need to cut all
the stones? How big, or small, should they be? What pattern would optimize the energy usage and prolong the laser's
useful life?

He took a deep breath, then laughed. He was taking too
many deep breaths.

"No! I'm no friggin' field hand! You take your turn in the fields, too! Your ship's scrap, and you're no better than the rest of us now."

Nylan looked downhill and to the eastern part of the field from where the voice carried up across the meadow.

One of the stocky marines, one of the few not only bigger but broader in the shoulders than Ryba—Nylan thought her name was Mran, but he'd never been good with names and hadn't been concentrating that much—held the crude hoe like a staff, daring the captain to force her to return to work.

Nylan missed Ryba's response, but she vaulted out of the saddle and handed the reins to Siret, one of the three marines with silver hair like Nylan, and one of the more quiet marines, though Nylan thought the deep green eyes saw more than most realized.

"Big trouble, ser," observed Huldran. "Mran's tough, and she's a hothead."

The four other marines in the field drew back, slightly, but watched as Ryba carefully slipped off the crossbelts that held her blades and the belt and holstered slug-thrower, then laid them across the roan's saddle.

Mran smirked—Nylan could sense the expression as he and Huldran hurried downhill toward the field.

Then Ryba said something.

"You and who the frig else?" demanded Mran.

"Just me."

Except for his and Huldran's steps, and the faint rustling of the wind through the evergreens beyond the meadow, a hush held the meadow. Even the few remaining starflowers seemed held in stasis. Nylan wanted to shake his head, knowing what would happen. Mran didn't understand what Ryba really was.

"You afraid or something, *Captain?*"

"No . . . I'm giving you one last chance to get back to work. If you don't, some part of your body won't ever work right again." The words were like ice. "I didn't think even you were stupid enough to take on someone raised as a nomad and wired as a ship's captain."

"You don't scare me, *Captain*."

"That's your problem, Mran, not mine. Get back to work."

"Make me."

"All right. You were warned." With the last word, Ryba *blurred,* as her hardwired reflexes kicked in.

Mran tried to slash with the hoe, but dropped it as Ryba's foot snapped her wrist. The marine used her good hand and reached for the pistol, but the captain followed through with stiffened hands and an elbow. A second *crack* followed the first, and Mran looked stupidly at the second damaged wrist—but only for a moment before she crumpled into a heap.

Ryba slowed to normspeed and smiled. "Anyone else think I shouldn't be in charge of things?"

"No, ser," came the ragged chorus.

Her face hardened. "Surviving in this place isn't going to be easy, and I don't want to have to keep doing this sort of thing." She glanced toward Nylan. "I might add that the engineer, the second, and the comm officer could have done the same thing, except that they don't have the advanced martial arts training, and they would have had to kill Mran. Disabling is harder." She smiled again and looked down at Mran.

The marine's eyes unglazed, and hatred blazed from them.

"Next time, I'll break your neck first. The only reason you're alive is the same reason Gerlich is alive. There are too few of us for genetic purposes, but you cause one single bit of trouble, and I'll drop you over that cliff without another thought. Do you understand?"

"Frig you!"

Ryba took a deep breath. Then her foot lashed out. *Crack!*

Mran's head snapped back, and the lifeless body slumped onto the field.

Ryba looked at the marines. "I never want to do this again—ever. But I will if I have to. We won't survive if everyone thinks she can second-guess me. I'll listen to ideas, and I have, and I've taken them. But there's no room for this sort of thing."

As Ryba belted on the crossbelts, Huldran turned to Nylan. "Hard woman."

He nodded. "I'm afraid she's right. According to our local source, old Narliat, we're regarded as the evil-doers from the skies, and force of arms and surviving up here in the cold are all that are likely to save us. More democratic systems don't work well with large egos, and marines and ship's officers all have large egos." Nylan snorted.

"Frigging lousy situation." Huldran's green eyes glared momentarily.

"Let's try to make it better." Nylan shrugged, and turned to walk back toward the incomplete tower. He didn't know what else Ryba could have done, not without creating even more problems in the days ahead, but he didn't want to talk to her at the moment. Even if some people, like Gerlich and Mran, or Lord Nessil, the dead local leader, seemed to respect only force, Nylan might have to accept it, but he didn't have to like it.

He looked back to where Ryba mounted. He suspected Ryba was shaking, inside—high speed took a lot out of a body—but the captain seemed as solid as the stone Nylan labored over as she turned the roan toward the next field.

XIII

"WHAT WILL YOU do with the cowardly wizard, dear?" asks the heavyset and gray-haired woman who sits on the padded bench in the alcove.

The black-bearded young man pulls down his purple vest and walks toward the empty carved chair with the purple cushion, then turns back to face her. "Much as I distrust Hissl, Mother dear, I wouldn't call him cowardly. According to the handful of troopers who returned, he was attacked, and he used his firebolts. After Father and nearly twoscore troopers were killed, he retreated. If he hadn't brought them back, we still wouldn't know what happened for sure. Then I would have had to rely on Terek's screeing, and I don't like that, either. He's even more devious than Hissl."

"All wizards are devious. That was what your father said, Sillek," the lady Ellindyja responds.

"He was right, but they have their uses."

"What will you do with Hissl?"

"Nothing."

"Nothing? After he led your father to his death? Nothing?" Ellindyja's voice rises slightly, its edge even more pronounced.

"What good will killing him do? We've just lost three squads of troopers, and it looks like we now have an enemy behind us, right on top of the Roof of the World, possibly able to close off the trade road to Gallos. Lord Ildyrom and his bitch consort are building a border fort less than a half day's march from Clynya, and the Suthyan traders are talking about imposing more trade duties. Sooner or later, we'll have to fight to take Rulyarth from them or always be at their mercy." Sillek pauses. "With all that, you want me to kill a wizard and get their white guild upset at me? Create another enemy when we already have too many?"

"You are the Lord holder of Lornth now, Sillek. You must do what you think best . . . just as your father did."

"What good would executing Hissl accomplish?"

His mother shrugs her too expansive shoulders. "The way you explain it, none. I only know that difficulties always occur when white wizards are involved."

"I will keep that in mind." Sillek turns and walks to the iron-banded oak door, which he opens. "Take the wizards and the others to the small hall."

"Yes, ser."

Sillek holds the door to his mother's chamber and waits as she rises. They walk down the narrow hall to the small receiving chamber where he steps up and stands before the carved chair that rests on a block of solid stone roughly two spans thick. The lady Ellindyja seats herself on a padded stool behind his chair and to Sillek's right.

Seven men file into the room. The five troopers glance nervously from one to the other and then toward the two wizards in white. None look at Lord Sillek, nor at his mother, the lady Ellindyja. Hissl's eyes meet Sillek's, while Terek bows slightly to the lady before turning his eyes to Sillek.

"Who has been in the forces of Lornth the longest?" Sillek's eyes traverse the troopers.

"Guessin' I have, ser. I'm Jegel." Jegel has salt-and-pepper hair and a short scraggly beard of similar colors. His scabbard is empty, as are the scabbards of all five troopers. The left sleeve of his shirt has been cut away and his upper arm is bound in clean rags.

"Of the three score who rode out with Lord Nessil, you are all who survived?"

"Beggin' your pardon, ser, but we aren't. Maybe a dozen rode down the trade road to Gallos. Welbet led 'em. He said that you'd never let anyone live who came back with your father left dead."

"That's the way it should be . . ."

Sillek ignores the whispered comment from his mother, but the troopers shift their weight.

"Why did you come back?" he finally asks.

"My consort just had our son, and I was hopin' . . ." Jegel shrugs.

"Did you ride away from my father in battle?"

"No, ser." Jegel's brown eyes meet those of Sillek. "I charged with him." His eyes drop to his injured arm. "Got burned with one of those thunder-throwers, but I followed him until there weren't no one to follow. Then I turned Dusty back."

"Dusty?"

"My mount. I ran into the wizard at the bottom of the big ridge—him and most of the rest. Most went with Welbet. The rest of us came back with the wizard."

"What did you think of the strangers?"

Jegel shivers. "Didn't like their thunder-throwers. One woman—she was the one with the blades—she threw a blade, and it went right through Lord Nessil's armor, like a hot knife through soft cheese. Then she took his horse, and slaughtered three, four of the troopers with both the blade and the thunder-thrower, almost as quick as she looked at 'em."

"Were they all women?"

"Mostly, ser. Except the one I got. He had a thunder-thrower, but it did him no good against my blade."

Sillek's eyes turn to the second trooper.

"I be Kurpat, Lord Sillek. I couldn't be adding much."

"Did you leave my father?"

"No, ser."

Sillek continues the questioning without finding out much more until he comes to Hissl.

"And, Ser Wizard, what can you add?"

"About the fighting, Lord Sillek, I can add little, except the thunder-throwers throw tiny firebolts, much like a wizard's fire, but not so powerful."

"If they were not so powerful, why are so many troopers dead?"

Hissl bows his head. "Because all of the strangers had the thunder-throwers, and because the thunder-throwers are faster than a wizard. If your father had twoscore wizards as powerful as Master Wizard Terek, there would be no strangers."

"Pray tell me where I would find twoscore wizards like that?"

"You would not, ser, not in all Candar."

"Then stop making such statements," snaps Sillek. "Don't tell me that twoscore wizards will stop the strangers when no one could muster so many wizards. Besides, you'd all be as like to fight among each other as fight the strangers."

"Pray answer a widow's question, Ser Hissl," requests Ellindyja from the stool on the dais. "How was it that you counseled my consort to attack the strangers?"

Hissl bows deeply. "I am not a warrior, Lady. So I could not counsel the lord Nessil in such fashion. I did counsel him that the strangers might be more formidable than they appeared."

"But you did not urge him to desist?"

Hissl bows again. "I am neither the chief mage of Lornth"—his head inclines toward Terek—"nor the commander of his troops. I have expressed concerns from the beginning, but the chief wizard advised me that, since I could not prove that the strangers presented a danger, we should defer to the wishes of Lord Nessil, as do all good liegemen."

"You, Chief Wizard," Ellindyja continues, "did you counsel Lord Nessil to attack the strangers?"

"No, my lady. I did inform him of their presence, and I told him that they were appeared likely to stay."

"And that some were exotic women, I am sure."

Hissl's lips twitch.

Sweat beads on Terek's forehead before he answers. "I did inform him that several, men and women, had strange silver or red hair. I also told him that they had arrived from the heavens in iron tents and that he should proceed with care."

"You, Ser Hissl, did you bid him proceed with caution?"

"Yes."

"Then why did he attack them?"

"My lady," responds the balding wizard, "we rode up in peace, but the leader of the strangers refused to acknowledge Lord Nessil, even when he drew his mighty blade."

"I see. I thank you, Ser Wizard." Ellindyja's voice is chill.

Hissl offers a head bow to her.

"Go . . . all of you." Sillek's face remains blank as the five troopers and the wizards walk quietly toward the door.

XIV

NYLAN ADJUSTED THE single pair of battered goggles and then lifted the powerhead of the laser in his gauntleted hands. The wind blew through his hair, and the puffy clouds scudded quickly across the sky, casting quick-moving shadows across the narrow canyon where the engineer stood. The chilly summer wind carried not only the scent of evergreens, but of flowers, although Nylan could not identify the fragrance. The starflowers had all wilted or dried up, but lower yellow sunflowerlike blooms appeared in places, and long stalks that bore single blood-red blooms jutted from crevices in the rocks at the western edge of the meadow—and from between the rocks in the cairns.

Fifty steps down the dry gorge stood a horse harnessed to a makeshift sledge. Two marines—Berlis and Weindre—waited by the horse for the cut stones that Nylan hoped he could deliver. He also hoped the laser lasted long enough for him to cut a lot of stones.

He touched the power stud, and the laser flared. Nylan could almost feel the power, like a red-tinged white cloud, that swirled from the firin cells into the laser. He released the stud.

"What's the matter, ser?" asked Huldran.

"Nothing major," he lied, thinking that it was certainly major when the ship's engineer imagined he could see actual energy patterns. His head throbbed slightly with his words, and he massaged his temples. The effect was almost like coming out of reflex step-up.

The wind whistled through the branches of the stunted pines farther back and higher in the narrow gorge. He moistened his lips.

"Are you all right, ser?" The stocky blond Huldran bent forward.

"I will be." *I will be if I can get my thoughts together,* he added to himself. As he looked around the gorge, he wondered whether, if he cut the stones correctly, he could also hollow out spaces so that the area in front of his quarrying could eventually be walled up or bricked up for stables or storage or quarters.

Then he shook his head. He was getting too far ahead of himself. The power swirl—why was it familiar?

"Something . . . but nothing bothers him . . . got nerves like ice . . ."

He tried to push away the whispers from Weindre and concentrate on the power flow. Flow—that was it! It was like a neuronet flow. He touched the stud again, briefly, and concentrated, ignoring the sweaty feeling of his hands and fingers within the gauntlets.

The laser flared just for a microinstant, but that was enough.

Nylan squared his shoulders and studied the rock, then aimed the head along the chalked line. The white-red line of invisible fire touched the line. Nothing happened, except that the rock felt warmer, hotter, redder.

"Frig," Nylan muttered under his breath, as he cut off the power again. He'd been certain that the laser would cut through the rock. Lasers cut *everything,* from cloth to metal. Why wouldn't they cut rock?

Because, his engineering training pointed out, they burned through other substances, and the rock could absorb more heat than cloth or sheet metal, and it didn't accept the heat evenly, either.

"Problems, ser?" Huldran blotted the sweat oozing across her forehead.

"Some basic engineering I need to work out."

He needed to work out more than basic engineering.

After taking another deep breath, he triggered the laser once more and reached out with his thoughts, as though he were still on the neuronet, ignoring the impossibility of the setting, and smoothed the power flow. This time, the rock began to smoke along the focal line of the laser, and a slight line slowly etched itself along the chalk stripe.

Nylan depowered the laser, and checked the power meter—half a percent gone for nothing, nothing but a scratch on black rock.

"Ser?" Huldran stepped forward to look at the black stone.

"We're getting there," he lied, pushing the goggles back and wiping his damp forehead. "It's slow. Everything's slow."

"If you say so, ser."

Could he narrow the focus, somehow use the netlike effect to redirect the heat into a narrower line? If he couldn't, the laser wasn't going to be much good for stone-cutting.

Replacing the goggles, he checked to see that the head was set in the narrowest focus, then triggered the power. As the fields built, he juggled the smoothing of the power flow and his efforts to channel power into the thinnest line of energy possible. For an instant, all he got was more stone-etching, then, abruptly, the lightknife sliced through the black rock.

Nylan's eyes flicked to the power meter—the flow was half what it should be. He stopped his—were they imaginary?—efforts to smooth the flow and felt the red-white swirl and watched the meter needle rise and the slicing stop. Hurriedly, he went back to his not-so-imaginary efforts to reduce the laser power flow fluxes, letting himself drop into the strange pseudonet feeling that eased the energy flows to the laser and reinforced the energy concentrations. Even though he had no scientific explanation for the phenomenon, his efforts reduced the energy draw of the cutter by nearly fifty percent, while cutting stone in a way he wasn't certain was possible, and he wasn't about to turn his back on anything that effective, whether he could explain it or not.

As the tip of the laser reached the end of the chalked line, Nylan eased it back along the second line, then along the third, before releasing the stud. He wiped his forehead with the back of his forearm, then knelt, adjusted the powerhead, and positioned the laser for the undercut.

Still concentrating, he powered the laser, smoothed the flow, and drew it along the line. Then he released the stud, and, using the gauntlets he had pressed into service to protect his hands from rock droplets, he tried to wiggle the stone. The whole line wobbled.

He nodded and began the cross-cuts.

When he finished those, the line of clouds had passed, and the sun was again beating down on him. The first individual building stone came away from the black rock easily, and Nylan smiled and lifted the goggles.

"Take 'em away, Huldran."

The stocky blond marine motioned to Berlis and Wein-dre. "You two—come and help."

Nylan plopped down on a low stone and wiped his fore-head, feeling even more drained than when he had ridden the *Winterlance*'s net, more drained than from overuse of reflex boost. His eyes flicked downhill. Through the narrow open-ing in the gorge he could see most of the field to the east of the tower site. Thin sprigs of green sprouted from the hand-furrowed rows. To the north, where he could not see, there were longer green leaves from the field where the potatoes and other root crops had been planted in hillocks.

"These are heavy," grunted Weindre, staggering down to the sledge with a single block.

"That's the idea," said Huldran. "We can't waste power on small blocks. Besides, bigger blocks are harder to smash with primitive technology. So stop complaining and get on with carrying."

When the three had cleared out the half-dozen blocks, Nylan stood and chalked more lines, longer ones, and went back to work.

By the time he had finished the next line, his knees were wobbling. He sank onto the stone after he depowered the laser and pushed the goggles onto his forehead.

"Darkness—the engineer's white like a demon tower." Huldran looked at Nylan. "Don't move." She turned to Berlis and Weindre. "You can still load those blocks on the sledge. Berlis, you can lead the horse down the gorge and out to the tower site." The stocky blond marine looked at Nylan. "I'll be right back. Just sit there."

Nylan couldn't have taken a step if he'd wanted to, not without falling on his face, not the way the gorge threatened to turn upside down around him.

He sat blankly until Huldran returned and thrust a cup in front of his face. He drank, and the swirling within his head slowly subsided enough for him to take a small mouthful of the concentrate-fortified sawdust called energy bread. He chewed slowly.

Ayrlyn walked up the gorge carrying a medkit, stepping

around Berlis and the slowly descending horse and sledge.

"What happened to you? You look like you stayed on boost too long."

Nylan finished the mouthful of bread. "I think I overdid it."

"What do you mean?"

"A variation on the law of conservation of energy and matter, or something like that." Nylan wiped his forehead with the back of his forearm.

Ayrlyn looked at Huldran, who looked at Weindre. Weindre shrugged.

"This place allows me to operate on something like the neuronet, and I can smooth the power flows to the laser and focus the laser into a tighter beam. That lets me cut with about half the power. It's not free, though."

The flame-haired former comm officer nodded. "Heavy labor? Like boost?"

Nylan nodded.

Huldran's blond eyebrows knitted in puzzlement.

"On the ship's net," Nylan tried to explain, "the fusactors supply the power to sustain the net. It's a small draw compared to the total power expended by the system, but it's real. This . . . place . . . is different. I can replicate the effect of the net—but I have to supply some form of power, energy—and it's just like working."

"That local in white . . . ?" began Ayrlyn, her eyes widening.

"Probably something like that, but I don't know." Nylan finished off the chunk of energy bread, and took another gulp of the nutrient replacement. "It's frustrating. I find a way to save power, and it's limited by my strength."

"It's a lot faster than using a sledge and chisel to quarry the rock," pointed out Ayrlyn.

"It's slow."

"Can anyone else do it?"

"I don't know." Nylan shrugged. "I'd guess it's like being an engineer or a pilot or a comm officer. If you have some basic talents, you can learn it, but . . ."

"Can you use the laser again, and let me try to watch or follow?" Ayrlyn looked around. "You two try also."

Nylan stood and stretched. "I'll cut a few." He used the chalk and roughed out the lines he needed, then picked up the powerhead. "Ready?"

"Go ahead."

He dropped the goggles in place, touched the stud, and began to smooth the fluxes, trying to be as gentle as possible, and realizing that the gentle efforts were nearly as effective and not quite so draining.

After the first cut, he stopped. "Well?"

"I couldn't see or feel anything," said Weindre.

"No," added Huldran.

"There's a sort of *darkness* around you," said Ayrlyn, "and that darkness seems to focus the whiteness—it has a hint of an ugly red—of the laser."

Nylan nodded. "That feels right. Do you want to try it?"

"No!" Ayrlyn's mouth dropped open after her involuntary denial. "I . . . I don't quite know why I said that."

"Something in you feels rather strongly. Do you have any idea why?"

"The white of the laser. It feels wrong . . . really wrong . . . disordered . . . ugly." Ayrlyn shuddered.

"I couldn't see anything like that," said Huldran, "but I watched the power meter, and you're using a little less than half what's normal, except for the first few instances. It seems to be cutting better than I ever saw."

"What is this place, anyway?" asked Weindre.

"Who knows? A different universe, maybe, where the laws of nature, physics, are different. Not a lot different, or we wouldn't be surviving, but different." Nylan picked up the laser again. "And if we don't get enough stone for the tower, we won't be surviving." He disliked his own tone, perhaps because it reminded him of Ryba's attitude. What was happening to him? He was seeing patterns and neuronets that couldn't be and getting ever more critical of Ryba. And yet he worried about sounding like her.

"You'll have to take it slowly," insisted Ayrlyn.

"Unless you can find someone else who can do it," pointed out Huldran.

"Why don't I see if I can rotate some of the marines up here, just to see if anyone can do it—or even sense what you're doing?" asked Ayrlyn.

"Fine. But there's only so much power here."

"I'll send them," said Ayrlyn firmly. "Take your time."

"Yes, mother fowl."

"Cluck, cluck . . ."

Nylan grinned and readjusted the goggles. "Ready?"

"Yes, ser."

He lifted the powerhead again.

XV

"How DID PEOPLE come here?" asked Ayrlyn, moving back from the heat of the cook fire.

"The old ones?" Narliat edged toward the heat and half turned to face the redhead. "The old ones came a long time ago."

In the growing late twilight of early summer, Nylan sat behind the two, concentrating on Narliat's speech and trying to catch the meanings of the slurred and modified Rationalist words.

". . . like you strangers, they came from the skies . . . not in tents of iron, but upon the backs of iron birds . . ." Narliat gestured with the healing hand, and the missing thumb and forefinger did not seem to hamper him as much as the still-splinted broken leg.

"Were there people already here?" asked the comm officer.

"There were the druids, the people of the Great Forest, and many others . . . especially those in other lands beyond Candar—"

"Candar?" asked Nylan.

"Ah, the wizard, he does speak." Narliat turned to the engineer. "Candar—that is all the lands that are surrounded by the oceans here, the lands of Gallos and Lornth, and Jerans, and Naclos, and Lydiar in the east."

"Candar is the name of the continent," said Ayrlyn.

"It is Candar, not continent," explained Narliat. "Candar is where the old ones landed . . . the old tales claim that the mighty iron birds took all of the plains of Analeria to land. That is how big they were, and their wings shadowed whole towns . . ."

"Analeria is the high plains region east of these mountains," added Ayrlyn, brushing flame hair from her eyes, still acting as a comm officer.

". . . and the old ones were glad, for they had fled from the awesome ice lances of the angels of Heaven. The wizards, the white ones, they say that you are fallen from the angels of Heaven. Is that true?"

"We've certainly fallen," quipped Nylan, slowly, in what he recalled from his service indoctrination in Rationalist dialect, "but—"

"So they were right!" Narliat's eyes widened. "You are angels. Do you freeze everyone to death who opposes you? Are you going to freeze me?"

"No," said Ayrlyn and Nylan, nearly simultaneously.

"What does our friend have to say?" Ryba, both blades on her hips, looked down at the three.

"He was telling us about the old legends. Sit down. If you can follow tangled Old Rat, you might find it interesting," suggested Ayrlyn.

Ryba eased herself onto a cut-off tree-trunk section that served as a seat. The remainder of the tree had been laboriously cut into a handful of planks with the single collapsible grip saw.

"She is the cherubim—or a seraphim. Truly, she was terrible," stammered the local armsman.

"Terrible?" murmured Ryba. "How delightful."

Nylan frowned, but only cleared his throat.

"You were telling us about the old ones," prompted Ayrlyn, "how they came to the high plains of Analeria on the backs of the great birds . . ."

"Those birds, they had feathers whiter than snow, and the tips of those feathers were like mirrors, and they even turned back the sun . . . and the old ones brought with them the knowledge of metals, and of the cold iron that turns back the fires of chaos . . ." Narliat paused and looked up at Ryba.

Nylan followed the local's glance, trying to picture the captain as Narliat saw her—an angular face, with a regular but sharp nose and high cheekbones, pale clear skin that tanned only slightly, dominating and penetrating green eyes, broad-shouldered and muscular without being overly stocky, and short hair that had become so dark that it seemed to swallow light. In fact, she looked like an avenging angel.

"The fires of chaos?" asked Ayrlyn. "What can you tell us about the fires of chaos?"

"No wizard am I," declared Narliat, and his eyes went to Nylan, then back to Ayrlyn. "Those who are wizards control the fires of chaos."

"Like the man in white?" suggested Nylan.

"Hissl? Yes, he is . . . he was one of Lord Nessil's three wizards."

"He still is," added Nylan. "He escaped. Hissl did, I mean. What about this Nessil?"

"Lord Nessil—your seraphim killed him with the iron lightning she flung through him." Narliat coughed. "He was the lord of Lornth, and Lornth claims the Roof of the World."

"Not anymore," said Ryba.

Nylan's eyes looked down toward the cook fire where various small rodents had been spitted and were being turned. The horse meat from the animals killed in the attack had been tastier than the rodents, but not much. A lot of the meat had been wasted, because they'd had no way to preserve it. Ryba hadn't been pleased with that, Nylan reflected, not at all. Then, some days, she didn't seem pleased about much. That hadn't changed much, though, not from when she'd had a sound ship under her.

On the far side of the fire, Gerlich leaned close to a lithe marine—Selitra. The former weapons officer, who had taken to wearing Lord Nessil's hand-and-a-half blade, said something, and they both laughed, but Selitra glanced sideways at Ryba, who remained concentrating on Narliat.

Charred and fire-roasted rodents, mixed with the vanishing ship concentrates, were scarcely Nylan's idea of a good meal. Ayrlyn had found some roots that resembled—or were—wild onions, but without cook pots, their culinary value was minimal.

". . . the lords of Lornth came out of the Westhorns here, many, many years ago, almost as long ago as when the old ones came in from the skies on their mighty birds with feathers like mirrors . . ."

"Are there any traders that cross these mountains?" interrupted Nylan.

"Traders?" asked Fierral from behind Nylan.

"We've got some local coin now, and some jewelry, and a bunch of blades. We could buy a few things—like sledges or wedges, cook pots. Most traders don't care about politics." Nylan cleared his throat. "Maybe other things."

"But . . . to trade with the angels . . . who would dare?" declaimed Narliat.

Nylan suspected that, had it not been for the stories, there might already have been traders, or some travelers, on the high road that crossed the mountains and ran below the ridge that led up to the high meadow.

"Anyone who wants coins," suggested Ryba.

Narliat looked blank, and Ayrlyn translated.

The armsman grinned. "Skiodra."

"Is he a trader?"

"That is what he calls himself, but he is a thief, and his guards carry blades that are often in need of sharpening."

"Sharpening?" Fierral's red hair glinted as she shook her head.

"They get nicked when they fight," said Ryba dryly.

"How do we find this Skiodra?"

"He will find you if you fly the trade banner."

"We don't have a pole or a trade banner," pointed out Ayrlyn.

"Poles we can make," said Nylan, turning toward Narliat. "What does a trade banner look like?"

"A trade banner." The armsman shrugged. "It is a white banner with a dark square in the middle."

"We can put something like that together."

"With what?" asked Ayrlyn. "I didn't notice such things as needles or thread in the survival paks."

"There are some needles in the medical kits—for sutures," said Ryba.

Nylan frowned, wondering why Ryba was so familiar with the medical kits. That hadn't been her training at all. Then again, as captain, she'd looked at everything. He'd been mostly involved in solving the shelter problem.

"We'll also have to make a show of force when this Skiodra shows up."

Ayrlyn translated for Narliat.

"Skiodra is very polite if you are strong." The armsman shrugged. "If not, you become slaves, and he sells you to the traders from Hamor. That happened to a cousin of Memsenn's. She lived on a farm outside of Dellash. One day Skiodra passed by, and when her consort came home, she was gone. He chased Skiodra's men, and they killed him."

"Not a pleasant fellow." Fierral's fingers went to her sidearm.

"I don't think any of Candar is what we'd term peaceful," said Ryba. "The only way to ensure peace is through strength."

"That was what Lord Nessil said. But . . . now that he is dead, it may be that the Jeranyi will march, or the Suthyans." Narliat edged closer to the fire, then looked at the angels around him. "Truly, you are people of the winter. Is Heaven cold?"

"Colder than Candar, even than here," replied Ayrlyn, "except maybe in winter."

Across the fire, Gerlich and Selitra stood and eased away into the shadows, hand in hand.

Ryba and Nylan exchanged looks.

Ayrlyn snorted. "Poor woman. Thinks she's special."

"I've warned them," added Fierral, "but it does get lonely."

"I would make you less lonely . . ." volunteered Narliat.

Fierral shot a look at Narliat, who immediately glanced at the darkness beyond the fire.

"He's learning Temple fast," laughed Ayrlyn. "Even if it's not that different from Anglorat."

"Too fast," said Fierral.

"Supper's ready," called Saryn. "Such as it is."

At the call of supper, even Gerlich and Selitra reappeared, no longer quite hand in hand.

Nylan followed the others, getting his helping of mush and chunk of blackened rodent, as well as a few berries and a chunk of wild onion. The roughly circular wooden platter was the result of a collaboration between some of the marines and Narliat.

He sat farther from the fire, on a boulder overlooking the landers, using his fingers and a crudely carved spoon he had made. The slightly charred rodent was tastier than the mush, but he ate both, and washed them down with water from the plastic cup he had claimed and kept.

Beside him, Ryba ate, equally silent.

After he finished, Nylan stood. "I'm going to rinse this off, and rack it, and wash up. Then I'm going to collapse."

"Wait for me." Ryba finished her last mouthful of mush. "I won't be too long. I have to check with Fierral to make sure the sentries are set."

"All right." Nylan walked over to the side branch of the stream, diverted for the purpose of washing, and rinsed off the wooden platter, then used the scattering of fine sand to wash his hands. After that he rinsed them and splashed off his face.

"Next," said a voice.

He looked up to see Ayrlyn standing there. "Sorry." He stood and moved away from the stream.

She smiled. "You don't have to be."

"You're doing well with Narliat."

"He figures he'd better do well. He doesn't have any-where else to go. Besides, he likes the ratio of men to women."

"Has anyone . . . ?"

"Right now, Ryba would have their heads, but that won't last. She probably knows that, too. She thinks of every-thing." Ayrlyn paused. "Just be careful, Nylan. She uses everyone."

He nodded, hoping the darkness would cover his lack of enthusiasm.

Ayrlyn bent to rinse her platter, and Nylan walked to the lander, passing a pair of marines on the way. One was Hul-dran, the stocky blond who helped with stone-cutting; the other a solid brunette whose name he had not learned.

"Evening, ser."

"Good evening, Huldran. Are you on sentry duty?"

"Not tonight. Not tonight."

Once in the forward area of the lander, Nylan pulled off his boots. Then he sat in the darkness for a time barefooted, before he pulled off the shipsuit that, despite careful wash-ing, was getting both frayed and stained.

When Ryba still did not appear, he finally stretched out, folding the cover back to just above his waist. His shoulders and his forearms ached, and his feet hurt. He also worried about Ryba—their relationship. A lot of the time she was distant, commanding, just like he imagined an antique nomad-liege of Sybra. Of course, that was her heritage, and Candar seemed to reinforce those traits.

In the distance, he could hear laughter, but could not rec-ognize the voices.

As his eyes began to close, he heard footsteps on the hard floor of the lander, and he propped himself up on his elbow.

"I told you I wouldn't be long." Slowly, Ryba slipped out of her boots, and then out of the shipsuit, and eased under the thin cover. Her lips were cool, but found his, and her skin was like satin against him.

Later—much, much later—they eased apart, although Ryba's hand held his for a moment.

"Don't go away." Ryba rolled away from Nylan. "I'll be back in a moment."

"Where would I go?"

She ruffled his hair slightly and pulled on her shipsuit over her naked body, thrusting her bare feet into her shipboots—boots that were beginning to wear, as were everyone's.

Nylan wondered absently if traders had boots, or if footwear would become yet another problem. He leaned back on the couch, letting the cool air from the door waft over him. Sometimes . . . on the one hand, Ryba was a good leader, captain, whatever, and she was receptive, sometimes aggressive in sex . . . and yet . . . he sometimes felt more like an object than a person.

His eyes closed. It had been a long day, as were they all, and he was barely aware when Ryba returned, slipping off her suit and lying beside him under the thin blanket that was almost too hot.

XVI

THE SUN HAD barely cleared the trees on the eastern side of the sheer drop-off at the base of the meadow when Nylan laid the endurasteel brace and the crowbarlike local blade beside one of Ryba's Sybran blades. Beneath the blades was a crude quench trough, half-filled with water and the hydraulic oil for which there was really no other use—not for centuries, probably.

Then the engineer walked around the working space outside the base of the unfinished tower construction. Should he consider a dry moat as well? He shook his head. Half the year or more a moat would be a bug-filled mess, and the other half the high snows would render it useless.

"Stop spacing out. Get on with it," he muttered, turning to the firin cells. The power bank was down to twenty percent, and the system wouldn't work at levels below twelve. His eyes went to the windmill, which turned in the lighter morning breeze. The cell being charged was over eighty percent. Another day might find it at ninety percent if the wind picked up, if . . .

Nylan laughed ruefully. Far less than a day of continuous heavy laser usage would discharge one bank of cells, and it would take nearly half a local season to recharge the individual cells in just one of the four banks they had brought down from the *Winterlance*. The more he tightened the beam and the shorter the energy pulse, though, the less the effective power drain, and that meant some things were less power-intensive. Darkness knew he'd better find less power-intensive ways to use the laser.

With a little more than half the stone for the tower cut, he'd exhausted two banks and most of the third. The emergency charger had recharged three cells, but each bank held ten. Still . . . he had gotten more proficient with managing the laser's power flows, and each row of stones took a shade less power. Also, the cut edges and leftover chunks could be used, perhaps for the less exposed inside walls.

Terwhit . . . terwhit. The call of one of the birds—a green and brown scavenger—drifted across the high meadow from beyond the field, along with the smoke from the small cook fire.

The engineer studied the curves of the Sybran blade again, with his eyes, senses, and fingers, frowning as his senses touched a slight imperfection in the hilt. Then he grinned. Who was he deceiving? He was no bladesmith, just a dumb engineer trying to figure out how to counterfeit a workable sword while no one was around to second-guess him if his idea didn't work—using questionable techniques in an even more questionable environment.

Terwhit. With a rustle of feathers, the small greenish-brown bird flitted from a twisted pine in the higher rocks behind the partly built tower toward the firs in the lower southwest corner of the high meadow.

Nylan ran his fingers over the Sybran blade again, then

picked up the endurasteel brace he had unbolted from one
of the landers. Again, he forced himself to feel the metal. It
also had several imperfections hidden from sight—Heaven-
based quality control or not.

Finally, he powered up the firin cell bank, pulled on the
goggles and the gauntlets, and picked up the heavy brace.
After readjusting the laser, he pulsed the beam, slowly cutting along what felt like the grain of the metal. He pursed
his lips, considering the apparent idiocy of what he did—
guiding a laser with a sense of feel he could not even define
to create an antique blade out of a brace from a high-tech
spaceship lander.

The heavy tinted goggles protected his eyes, although he
realized that he wasn't using his vision, but that sense of feel,
a sense that somehow seemed to break everything into de-
grees of something. What that something was and how he
would categorize it were more questions he couldn't answer.

He didn't try, instead releasing the power stud and letting
his senses check the cut and the metal—which felt rough,
almost disordered.

With another deep breath, he flicked on the laser and
spread the beam for a wider heat flow, using his senses and
the power from the laser to shape and order the edge of the
blade, trying to replicate something like the feel of the
Sybran blade.

After the second pass, he unpowered the laser and pushed
back the goggles, wiping his forehead. Then he bent and
picked up the plastic cup, swallowed the last of the water in
it, and set the empty cup back on the ground beside the cell
bank where the power cable wouldn't hit it.

One of the marines—Istril—sat atop one of the rocky
ledges and watched as he readjusted the goggles and studied the model blade again.

Once more, he picked up the metal that had been a brace
and triggered the laser, shifting his grip, and trying to ensure that his gauntlets were well away from the ordered line
of powered chaos emanating from the powerhead.

After his first rough effort at shaping the blade, he turned to the curved hand guards and tang. As he shaped the metal, he tried to smooth it, just as he once had smoothed power fluxes through the *Winterlance*'s neuronet. When the rough shape was completed, he unpowered the laser and checked the cells—a drop of less than one percent so far. Not too bad for a first try.

He pushed back the goggles and blotted the area around his eyes, then studied the blank blade. Even with one rough cut, the shape looked better than the local metal crowbars.

He could feel Istril's eyes on him, but he did not look toward the rocks. The smoke from the cook fire was more pronounced, as was the hum of people talking. He did not look toward the landers, either. Instead, he inhaled, then exhaled deeply and replaced the goggles and lifted the laser.

Trying not to feel like an idiot, he triggered the laser and continued to use his mental netlike sense and the power of the laser to work the metal, almost to smooth the grains into an ordered pattern while trying to create the equivalent of a razor edge on both sides of the blade.

By the time he finished with the laser, not that long it seemed, sweat poured down his forehead, out and around the goggles, and his knees trembled. Done with the laser, he set the powerhead down and waited as the metal cooled toward the color of straw.

The oil-and-water mixture in the crude trough felt right, but whether it was . . . time would tell. Using the modified space gauntlets, he swirled the mixture in the trough and eased the blade into it, letting his new sense guide the tempering—or retempering. Then he laid the blade on the sheltered sunny side of the black boulder where it would complete cooling more slowly.

He set aside the goggles and checked the power meters— a drop of one percent, maybe a little more. He nodded. He could make something that looked like a blade, but was it any good?

As he saw Ryba's broad-shouldered figure striding grimly

toward him, he offered himself a smile. He'd get one opinion all right—and soon.

"Why did you take my blade? It had to be you. No one else would—"

Nylan held up a hand to stop her. "I'm guilty. I didn't hurt it. I needed a model, and I didn't want to feel like a fool."

"Model for what?"

His eyes turned toward the flat rock where his effort rested.

"Darkness! How did you do that?"

"Art, laser, dumb luck—all of the above. Don't touch it; it's still hot enough to burn your skin, and I don't know if it will work. It looks right; it feels right, but I'm no swordsman. It could shatter the minute it's used. I don't think so, but it could."

Ryba stepped up to the blade and looked down at the slight curves of the deep black metal. "It's beautiful."

"Technology helps," Nylan admitted. "But I don't know if it will even work. It could break apart at the first blow."

"I don't think it will." Ryba looked at him. "It looks like it will last forever."

"It doesn't matter what it *looks* like. It's how it feels and lasts."

She studied the blade again. "I need to teach you more about using blades. It would be a shame for someone who can create this not to be able to use it well."

"You don't even know if it's right."

Ryba's dark green eyes met his. "About some things, I can tell."

Nylan shrugged.

"How many of these can you make?"

"Over time, enough for everyone, and probably a few more. I'd guess a little less than a two-percent charge on the bank for each. But I don't want to do that many until we've got enough stone for the tower."

"We need both."

"It will take more than half a season with the portable generator to fully charge a whole bank of cells. We've gone through nearly three banks, and that only leaves one that's completely full. We'll probably have the first recharged before we finish the tower. I haven't done the math, but I could probably forge ten blades on a depleted bank if I recharged two cells. But I need a base load of twenty percent for stone-cutting."

"You've got piles of cut stone here," pointed out Ryba.

"It's not enough." He shrugged. "Right now, the mortar's the problem, but I think I've got that set."

"That's a terrible pun."

"Didn't mean it that way."

The former captain looked at the smooth and sheer black stone wall that rose nearly twice her height, then at the square door frame whose base stood nearly her height above the visible base of the tower. "You're building a demon-damned monument."

"Why are you letting me? Could it be that I'm right?"

Ryba laughed. "The others look at this, and they all see that it can be done, and that we're here to stay. Nothing I say is as effective as your killing yourself. They all see how you drive yourself. But is everything that you've planned really necessary?"

Nylan pointed to Freyja—the ice-needle peak that towered above the unfinished tower, above the other mountains. "You can tell from the ice on those peaks that the winter is as cold, if not colder, than northern Sybra. Also, a tower isn't enough. We need stables, and next year, we'll need more storehouses, and workrooms for all the crafts we'll need to develop, and we'll have to defend them all. I'll end up cannibalizing the landers for metal and everything else, because that's easier than trying to develop iron-working from scratch or than trading for it. Once we run through the plunder, what can we use to buy goods? Or food? I certainly haven't seen traders galloping to find us. Also, there's going to be a gap between when we lose all high technology and when we can master lower technology."

Ryba looked at the blade. "What gap?"

"It would take me days to forge a blade like that with coal

or charcoal and hammers. Maybe longer, and that's if I knew what to do. That's if I had an anvil, if I could find iron ore, if . . ." He snorted. "How long will the emergency generator and the charging system last? Maybe a local year . . . and it might quit in the next eight-day."

"Then you'd better do at least a few blades, and others, as you can fit them in. We're going to need them. I hope not soon, but we will."

Nylan wiped his forehead. "I'll try to balance things. Has anyone heard anything about this so-called bandit trader? Can't we get something from him? Big cook pots, even cutlery?"

"I'm working on a list. What do you think we really need?"

"Some heavy cloth, wool maybe, and something like scissors, to cut it, thread and needles. We're not equipped for winter. There were—what?—two cold-weather suits in the paks? Any dried or stored food we can buy. What about something like chickens . . . for eggs? The concentrates might last until mid-winter. Salt. Some of that stuff Gerlich kills could be dried and salted. Oh . . . I need to figure out how . . . never mind . . ."

"What?"

"I'll use the laser to glaze it. That will make cleaning it easy."

"What?" repeated Ryba.

"The water reservoir, cistern, whatever you want to call it. I'd like it to be on the second level in the center, but I don't know if I can work that. I still haven't quite figured out piping or a reservoir near the head of the spring. We'll run hidden piping, like a siphon, so we can have some continuous water flow in winter or if we get besieged . . ."

"You are a pessimist."

"A realist."

"Probably," she admitted. "What if the laser goes?"

"There are two spare powerheads and a spare cable. I can use the weapons head, if I have to, but the power loss is enormous, and that might not work at all. If it goes now, we do it the hard way, and not nearly so well, and people die. If it lasts into winter, then I should have the basics done."

"Dreamer."

Nylan grinned ruefully.

"Go get something to eat." Ryba motioned to Istril, who had edged down the rocks, and who hurried up in response to Ryba's preemptory gesture. "Istril . . . would you watch this equipment while the engineer eats? Don't touch it, and don't let anyone else, either." Ryba pointed to the blade that Nylan had used as a guide. "Use that if you have to."

"Yes, ser." Istril's eyes flickered to the black blade on the stone. "You made . . . that . . . ser?"

"I tried," conceded Nylan.

"It's beautiful . . . sometime . . . could you forge me one?"

"Istril should get one of the first ones."

Nylan sighed and nodded at the slight silver-haired marine. "It's cool now. Pick it up and see if it's half as good as it looks."

"You mean it?"

Ryba and Nylan nodded.

Istril touched the hilt—designed to be wrapped in leather—and slowly lifted the blade. She stepped back and lowered it, then smiled.

"Is it tough enough?" Nylan asked. "Bend it or something."

Ryba lifted her blade. "Just blade to blade."

Nylan watched as they fenced, the silvery metal of the Sybran blade glittering against the black of his.

After a time, they both lowered their weapons, and Ryba wiped her forehead. A moment later, so did Istril.

"I think it might be better than mine," said Ryba, "at least in blade work. It might not be balanced right for throwing."

"It's beautiful," said Istril.

Ryba looked at Nylan.

He nodded at Istril. "It's not perfect, but you may have it. The hilt needs to be wrapped."

"It's too good for me."

"Then you'll have to get better for it," said Ryba. "In return for the blade, you'll have to teach the engineer how to use one."

"Can I start now?"

"After I eat, and only for a little," said Nylan. "We've still got a tower to build."

XVII

"I WAS NOT exactly amused by your reference to the chief wizard the other day before Lord Sillek," begins Terek.

"You are the chief wizard," points out Hissl calmly, "and I only spoke the truth. To have done otherwise . . ." He shrugs.

"There is truth, and there is truth," says Terek slowly, shifting his bulk as he ambles toward the table with the screeing glass upon it.

Hissl remains silent.

"Let us see if you can find anything which may impinge upon these . . . fallen angels. For if something does not, sooner or later we will be called to help avenge Lord Nessil's death."

"The longer before we ride to the Roof of the World, the better."

"I would prefer never to ride there," replies Terek.

Hissl concentrates. The white mists part, and a half-built tower appears, a tower whose walls seem as smooth as glass and as dark as winter water unruffled by wind. A silver-haired man struggles to position a long slab of stone to form the top step in a wide stone staircase.

"Great wizardry . . ." mumbles Hissl, the sweat beading on his forehead from the effort to maintain the image.

"It would take a score of scores to take that tower even now with the weapons they have." Terek paces away from the table. "Those stones seem steeped in order."

"Could you not fire it?" Hissl relaxes, and the image fades.

"Now—but what if they roof it with split slate? It would be two or three eight-days before Lord Sillek could assemble a force and ride there. Can you see Lord Sillek building siege engines upon the Roof of the World?"

"He could," suggests Hissl. "Anything is possible for a great lord."

"You are so dense. What would Lord Ildyrom be doing once he discovered Lord Sillek and his engineers and most of his armsmen were upon the Roof of the World?"

"So Lord Sillek leaves them alone? Is that so bad? It's only good for summer pasture anyway, if that. What does he lose?"

"Honor . . . face. *We* told Lord Nessil about the strangers. If his son and heir cannot defeat them, what do you think he will do to us? And it will be us, not just me, Hissl."

Hissl pulls at his chin. "It could be a cold winter."

"In irons below the castle, your hands and arms would be burned apart—if you lasted that long." Terek glances at the glass. "See if you can find anything else."

"What?"

"Anything."

Hissl concentrates once more, and a band of riders now appear in the screeing glass, with one of the lead riders bearing a white banner with a dark square in its center.

"Traders . . ." mused Terek. "Almost armed like bandits."

"Skiodra, probably . . ." muttered Hissl, the sweat beading more heavily on his forehead with the effort of holding the second image.

"Can you open it a little more?"

Hissl concentrates, and more sweat pours off his forehead, even as the mists widen to reveal dark pines and rocks, and a needle peak in the background.

"It looks like the Westhorns, along the high road toward the Roof of the World." Terek smiles. "Skiodra is just the type to steal what he can and destroy the rest. He only trades when he has to." The chief wizard rubs his hands together.

"What if he trades them weapons?" Hissl releases the image and blots his forehead.

Terek frowns and stops rubbing his hands. "That's not the problem. They have weapons. They have more weapons than they have soldiers, if that's what those women in dark gray are. What if they trade weapons for goods? Even a poor sword is worth half a gold."

"You said Skiodra is not much better than a bandit."

"Let us hope he is an effective bandit—a very effective bandit."

Hissl nods, but his eyes drop to the glass.

XVIII

NYLAN STUDIED THE staircase again, considering the wisdom of such a massive central pedestal. He'd had five purposes in mind—to provide a central support for the square tower, to make flooring each level easy, to provide an interior storage space, to allow for firm stone steps, to provide for chimneys, and to provide an interior air tunnel for ventilation. All that was well and good, but its construction had slowed that of the tower wall, still only slightly above the second level.

He put his foot on the nearest brace, wiggled it gently. Because Nylan had no really accurate way of calculating loads, he was estimating and feeling the bracing, setting the stripped logs that formed the bracing for the floors only about three handspans apart.

"Cessya, this isn't solid on the outside."

"Weblya is bringing up some wedges now. Then we'll mortar it in place." Using the crude tripod crane, Cessya and another marine eased another timber toward the stone-lined slots.

"Frig! It's still too big. Needs more trimming."

As the big roan bearing Ryba neared the tower, Nylan

stepped away from the long flat section of stone that would anchor the next section of the staircase and started down the stone stairs.

Ryba had tied the roan's reins around one of the larger building stones when Nylan met her. She now carried one of the Sybran blades and the second blade Nylan had forged in the other Sybran scabbard—as well as the holstered slug-thrower.

Nothing like a walking armory, he reflected. "Where have you been?"

"I've been checking out the approaches from the west. We're better protected than I thought. You can't get here except by coming up the ridge. I stopped to see how you were coming before I go check out the road. There still haven't been any signs of travelers—just scouts from Lornth."

"How do you know?"

"They wear purple. Subtleness isn't exactly ingrained in the local culture." Ryba started up the steps. "Let's see how things are going."

"Not bad, actually."

When they reached the spot where Nylan had been working, he glanced down toward the fields and the meadows that surrounded them, now dotted with the small sunflowers. A silver-haired marine weeding in the field suddenly dropped her hoe and dashed across the ditch, where she vomited.

"Ryba? Did you see that?"

"What?"

"Look down there. She looks sick." The engineer pointed.

"That's Siret. She's sick, but it's not an illness. I suspect her contraceptives have worn off—if she's been taking them at all."

"I haven't seen Gerlich with her." Nylan didn't think the thoughtful silver-haired marine was the type to go for Gerlich.

"Who's been looking?" Ryba shrugged.

"You did make a point about stud value with him."

"That's true." Ryba half laughed. "You'd think you were building this tower to stand forever."

"I figure that it will be a generation before anyone can expand on what we build. If they're prosperous, fine. If not, this buys them time."

"Assuming we can finish it."

"We could roof what we have now and get better shelter than the landers."

"You're talking four levels?"

"Six. We've almost cut enough stone for five on the outside walls, and I could do the inside walls with mortar and uncut stones if necessary."

"What about heat?"

"I'm thinking about a crude furnace. But that's the reason for a tower with an underground foundation, except we'll cover part of the lower level with stone and soil on the outside. Heat rises, and that's going to be important in the kind of winter we have here."

Ryba shook her head. "You'd better hope the laser holds out. Or that you learn to forge with local materials." She paused. "Is there any way you could shape those local blades into something better? That wouldn't take as much power as cutting and forming them from the lander braces, would it?"

"I don't know. Do you want me to try?"

"Let me think about it. How many of those killer blades have you done?"

"Three so far."

Ryba glanced toward the ridges where Nylan had quarried the black stone. "We're going to need more. Demondamn, we'll need more of everything."

"I know."

"What about the stable?"

"We can't do everything. I've been cutting the stone so the space could be used for storage, or for stables. The overhead would be low."

"Outside of spacecraft, Nylan, they're called ceilings." Ryba laughed.

"I might get used to it someday." He cleared his throat,

then shrugged his shoulders, trying to loosen them. "Back to work."

The sound of hooves echoed from the west, and Ryba glanced toward the top of the ridge and the approaching rider. "Kadran's in a hurry. We've got close to enough mounts, but not nearly enough people who know how to ride."

"Most of us were raised to ride ships, not horses."

"Look where it got you."

Nylan grinned ruefully. Sometimes, he really wondered about Ryba. She was planning to build a culture, a kingdom, as a matter of fact, without even a look back. She'd killed one marine and threatened to cripple Gerlich. At the same time, Nylan didn't see that much of an alternative, not when everyone seemed to respond only to force.

He moistened his lips. For all Ryba's apparent indifference to the past, the engineer still couldn't help wondering about his family, his sister Karista, and his mother. They'd all be told he was dead, and he wished they knew he was alive. He shrugged to himself. Assuming they were in another universe, was it better for them to think of him as dead? No, but there wasn't a thing he could do about it.

Ryba had already left the tower to wait for Kadran. Like all the marines, Kadran was full Sybran—big and tough.

Nylan looked up the uncompleted staircase, then turned and followed Ryba. He'd like to know what was happening, and Huldran would ask.

"There's a bunch with a trading flag riding up toward our banner," announced Kadran as she rode up. "They've got a lot of weapons showing."

"That's probably wise in this culture," said the captain. "We'd better respond in kind."

"Ser?" asked Kadran.

"You find Fierral, and have her get all of you ready for another attack. It shouldn't come to that, but our local friend says some of these traders will take everything you have if you're not tough.

"Tell Istril to come with me, and get Gerlich and have him

wear that big crowbar he's so fond of. And have Ayrlyn and Narliat come." Ryba turned to Nylan. "You, too. That will make three and three."

"I wouldn't know how to swing one of those things. I've had maybe three lessons, and Istril died laughing the first time," protested Nylan.

"Strap on a pistol and the blade. The locals don't see the slug-throwers as weapons. We need to get moving. Meet me over by those rocks as quickly as you can. I need to gather up the coin and jewelry we've got, and some of those crowbars that pass for blades." Ryba untied the reins and vaulted into the saddle of the roan.

As Ryba and Kadran rode off, Nylan shouted up into the unfinished structure. "Huldran! Cessya! Weblya! We've got company. Drop what you're doing, and form up with Fierral."

"Where, ser?"

"Up by those rocks, I think. On the double!"

Huldran laughed. "That's Svennish. 'Double-quick' is marine."

"Double-quick, then."

Nylan began to half walk, half run toward the lander that held his sidearm and the blade he had formed and did not still know how to use.

By the time he had reclaimed his gear and splashed water on his face and hands to get rid of the worst of the dirt and grime, and hurried up to the meeting point, Fierral and two others watched from the top of the western ledge, the weapons laser ready.

Nylan hoped they didn't have to use it. He fingered the pocket torch he had gotten from the lander, wondering if such a simple item would be useful, but he wanted something that would suggest power that didn't involve hurting or killing anyone else.

The remaining sixteen marines—all wearing sidearms—were deployed in two groups, each group with a clear field of fire. Kyseen, her face white, and her leg still in a heavy splint, sat on a boulder at one end of the rocks with the easternmost group.

The traders, dressed in half-open quilted jackets and cloaks, had halted downhill from the trading banner.

Ryba glanced around the group, all in thin uniforms or shipsuits, some still sweating from their haste. "Before we start . . . the one thing we don't trade is any of our weapons— or the new blades Nylan has forged."

"Those blades . . . they are worth golds . . . many golds," suggested Narliat.

"They'll cost us far more than that if the locals get their hands on them. We can trade any of the captured blades, but that's it."

"How much are those armsmen's blades worth?" Nylan asked Narliat.

"Whatever Skiodra will pay."

Nylan gave the smaller man a sharp look.

Narliat stepped back a pace, then stammered. "That is true, but the worst of them would have cost Lord Nessil nearly a gold."

"Good. That should help."

"Let's go. We'll leave our pile of trading goods here." Ryba fingered the leather pouch at her waist that contained almost all their local coins.

The six walked slowly down to the banner.

"Where do we stop?" Ayrlyn hissed to Narliat. Her eyes flashed blue.

"A dozen paces this side."

As the six angels stopped, eight of the traders stepped forward, leaving perhaps a dozen men with the horses and the four carts.

The traders stopped on the far side of the banner. For a moment, the only sound was that of the wind, and the faintest *clink* of harness chains from the traders' cart horses below.

After another moment, the biggest trader, wearing a huge blade like the one Gerlich bore, and a breastplate, stepped forward another two paces. "I am Skiodra," he declaimed in Old Anglorat with an unknown accent so thick that Nylan could barely follow the simple declaration. "You wish to trade?" Skiodra inclined his head to Gerlich, the biggest man in the angel group.

Before Gerlich could speak, Nylan stepped forward and smiled politely at the bandit-trader. "Yes." Then he gestured to Ryba. "This is Ryba . . ." He groped for the Old Anglo-rat word, and added, "Our marshal . . . leader."

Skiodra squinted slightly. One of the traders behind Skiodra, with a bushy blond beard, grinned broadly.

"And you do not let anyone else do the speaking, O Mage?"

Mage? Nylan certainly hadn't thought of himself as a mage, especially with a blade in an ill-fitting scabbard strapped around his waist.

"Pardon . . ." Narliat cleared his throat and looked at Ayrlyn and then Nylan.

Nylan nodded.

Skiodra's eyes flicked to the splint on Narliat's leg and to the ruined hand. The blond man behind him continued to grin.

"Honored Skiodra," began the armsman from Lornth, "best you and your men tread lightly with your laughter. Lord Nessil did not, and he lies under a pile of rocks above the cliff. Even his wizard could not save him. The . . . marshal"—he struggled with the unfamiliar word—"hurled one of those angel blades through his breastplate. Never in my years as an armsman, never have I seen anything more terrible."

"You may not have seen much," suggested Skiodra, before looking past Narliat to Nylan and then Gerlich. "Can she not speak for herself?"

"I . . . speak . . ." answered Ryba in Anglorat, "but not your words well."

"How do we know you speak the truth?" asked Skiodra. "This . . . minion . . . speaks well, but fine words are not truth. Nor do they buy goods."

"Does that matter?" asked Nylan. "You are traders. We would trade. If you insist . . ." He shrugged and turned to Gerlich. "Take out that crowbar, slowly, and show it to him . . ."

A thin trader with a scar on his face and a mail vest show-ing through a tattered tunic scowled at the word "crowbar."

As Gerlich extended the hand-and-a-half blade, Skiodra's eyes widened.

"That . . . it is a great blade," he admitted.

"Put it away," commanded Ryba. "Just be ready." With-out letting her eyes leave Skiodra, she said in an even voice to Nylan, "Tell him that he's dead meat if he tries anything funny, but that we can probably make him some credits or whatever they call it."

"You understand that, Narliat?" asked Nylan.

"Yes, ser." Narliat cleared his throat. "Most skillful trader . . . you have seen Lord Nessil's great blade. Lord Nessil came here with threescore armsmen. A dozen or less es-caped with their lives . . ."

"Why do you speak for them?"

Narliat looked down at the splint and raised his ruined hand. "What else would you have me do? They are angels, and who with wits would cross them?"

"I see no angels."

Ryba stepped back and raised her hand.

Hhsssttt!

A single flare of light flashed, and the top of the pole and the trading banner that had flown from it vanished. A few ash fragments drifted down around the Candarian traders.

Nylan tried not to wince at the power used in that quick burst.

Narliat gulped, but cleared his throat. "I did say they were angels."

Skiodra managed to keep his face calm. "Why would an-gels trade?"

"We could not bring everything we need with us," an-swered Nylan haltingly. "Do you not buy food when you travel?"

"You only want food?"

"Or something that provides food, like chickens."

"The great Skiodra does not deal in chickens, like some common . . . peasant . . ."

"Let him offer what he has," suggested Ayrlyn. "Don't ask for anything."

Narliat glanced at Ryba, then Nylan. They nodded at Narliat.

"Noble Skiodra . . . since my masters know not what you might have to offer, it might be best for you to show what you have."

"You might best do the same."

Narliat looked to Nylan, who nodded again.

"We will bring some goods," answered Narliat.

Skiodra lifted his hand, and the four carts began to wind their way up from the road at the bottom of the ridge.

Ryba turned and gestured. Four armed marines moved toward the piles of supplies near the top of the ridge.

Nylan looked westward to the darkening clouds that promised the first real rain since they had landed.

The first cart held barrels.

"That—the orange one," explained Narliat, "that is dried fruit from Kyphros. The white ones are flour. The seal means it was milled in Certis . . ."

"How much do they generally run?" asked Ayrlyn.

Narliat glanced nervously from the redheaded comm officer to Skiodra, who cleared his throat.

Ryba put her hand on the hilt of the blade Nylan had laser-forged.

"Uh . . . I couldn't be saying, ser, not exactly, since it'd depend on when Skiodra bought them and where."

"Three silvers for the flour and a five for the fruit," said Skiodra.

Narliat's eyes widened.

Nylan snorted. "That's about triple what the trader paid for them."

"You wish to travel to Kyphros to get them for yourself?" asked Skiodra.

"Excuse me," said Nylan. "Four times what he paid. Maybe five."

The slightest nod from Narliat confirmed his revised guess.

"So, the noble trader paid—what?—half a silver for each barrel of flour, and he wants three. Six times . . . that's nice if you can get it." Nylan laughed.

"Ah . . . my friend . . . how would you pay for the feed for all those horses and men? It is not cheap to travel the West-horns—and the flour, it came from Certis, and those fields are on the other side of the Easthorns . . ."

The engineer repressed a sigh. A long afternoon lay ahead, and the air was getting moister with the coming of the storm. "A half silver a barrel for your expenses, for each two barrels, I could see," he added. "That would be more . . ."—he groped for the word—"fair."

"Fair? That would be ruin," declared Skiodra. "You mages, you think that because you can create something for nothing that every person can. Bah! Even two silvers a barrel would destroy me."

Narliat's eyes flicked back to Nylan.

"Such destroying . . . that would buy you fine furs. Even a handful of . . ." He looked at Narliat.

"Coppers?"

"Coppers. Even two coppers in gain a barrel would make you the richest trader."

"I said you were a mage. That may be, but your father had to be a usurer. You would have my men eat hay, and my horses weeds. Even to open trading, as a gesture of good faith, at a silver and a half a barrel, I would have to sell the cloak off my back."

In the end, they agreed on nine coppers a barrel for the ten barrels of flour.

"What do you have to offer?" asked Skiodra, as a boy, act-ing as a clerk, chalked the number on a long slate and showed it to Nylan. It looked like a nine, but Nylan still glanced toward Ayrlyn and Narliat, who nodded.

"Try the small sword," suggested the armsman.

Nylan presented it.

"A nice toy for a youth, but scarcely worth much," snorted Skiodra.

"Lord Nessil paid a gold for it," asserted Nylan.

"A gold, and he was a rich lord who was cheated, or sleeping with the smith's daughter . . ."

It was going to be a longer afternoon than he had thought. Nylan refrained from taking a deep breath. "Lords don't have to bargain, noble Skiodra. If they think they are being cheated, they kill the cheater. The blade is probably worth two golds, but a gold is what he paid, and it's scarcely touched."

"Your father and your grandfather both were usurers, Mage. How your poor mother survived . . . I might consider, out of sentiment, and because of your audacity, five coppers for that excuse of a weapon . . ."

The sun, had it been visible through the heavy clouds, would have been nearly touching the western peaks before Skiodra packed what remained back into his carts and departed—not quite smiling, but not frowning, and promising to be back before harvest.

"So what do we have?" Fierral's eyes went from the carts of Skiodra to the supplies, but the redheaded marine officer's hand stayed on her sidearm.

The piles, bales, and barrels represented a strange assortment of goods. Besides nearly thirty barrels of flour, corn meal, and dried fruit, and a waxed wheel of yellow cheese, there were bolts of woolen cloth, a pair of kitchen cleavers, two large kettles and three assorted caldrons, two crude shovels, an adz, two sets of iron hinges big enough for a barn door, but no screws or spikes.

Nylan looked away from the assorted goods and held out his hand, feeling the tiny droplets of rain. As he listened to the rumble of distant thunder, he frowned, feeling that the clouds almost held something like the *Winterlance*'s neuronet.

Ayrlyn looked from the clouds to Nylan. "I know."

Ryba frowned, then asked Narliat, "You think they'll be back?"

Narliat shrugged. "Maybe yes, maybe no. It matters not."

"It doesn't matter?" asked Ayrlyn, brown eyes questioning.

"Others will come, now."

Nylan hoped so. They needed more supplies, a lot more, if the winter were anything like he thought it was going to be. And they needed something like chickens. He thought chickens could last the winter if they were in a place above freezing out of the wind. Then he took a deep breath, realizing that was just a hope. What did he really know about anything like that?

"I hope so," said Ryba, echoing his thoughts.

A low rumbling of thunder punctuated her words.

"We need to get this stuff into the landers or under cover." Ryba turned. "Fierral? Have your people get this stored. The cloth needs some dry places—maybe lander three. Nylan, how much covered space is there in your tower?"

"Not a lot yet," the engineer admitted. "Only the bottom level of the center is covered yet, and that's where the lasers and firin cells go."

"Then it will all have to go in the landers for now. That will make things tight."

"I'll see about getting the next level floored and roofed," said Nylan. As he hurried back to ensure that the lasers were stored against the oncoming rain, he wondered if he would ever get caught up to the needs they faced.

He fingered the torch in his pocket, and gave a half-laugh. He'd never even thought about using the beam. That was the way so many things worked—when it came time to use them, he forgot or did something else.

Overhead, the thunder rolled, and the fine rain droplets began to get heavier, and the sky darker.

XIX

THE RAIN STILL fell the next morning, but the droplets were fine and sharp, carried by the winterlike wind out of the ice-covered heights to the west. Low clouds obscured Freyja and all the mountains, except for the ridges closest to the landers. Even the partly built tower seemed to touch the misty gray underside of the clouds.

Nylan paused in the door of the lander, looking down at the gooey mess below. After a moment, he stepped into the mist-filled air, and his boots squushed in the mud. Some of the clumps of grass—even the yellow flowers—bore a snowy slush, and he looked back at Ryba. "This is one of the better reasons to get the tower finished. We're not going to have dry and sunny weather all the time."

His eyes dropped to the mud underfoot, and he frowned. "We need clay."

"Clay? What does that have to do with rain and weather?" Ryba stepped into the gusting rain.

"I should have thought of it sooner. We'll need bricks, and maybe I can make some clay pipes for water and the furnace. The right kind, and I can make a big stove so people won't have to keep cooking over fires."

"You're still hung up on that furnace, aren't you?"

"The main hall will have a big hearth and fireplace in case it doesn't work." He shrugged. "We also need to get water from the springs to the tower, and that means pipes."

Ryba laughed. "You'd think you'd been born doing this sort of thing."

"Hardly. I hope I don't make too many mistakes. I'm overlooking a lot of things, except"—he snorted—"I don't know what they are because I've overlooked them."

They stopped before reaching the cook fires, and Ryba

studied the fields, wiping the water from the ongoing drizzle from her face. A long, boot-deep trench crossed one corner of the potato field, and one hill had been undercut by the running water. Two marines were reclaiming it, while a third was digging a diversion trench across the uphill side of the field.

"Denalle, would you finish that demon-damned diversion so we're not fighting water and the frigging mud?" demanded one of the two trying to keep the potato hill from collapsing into the narrow stream of cold water.

"Stow it, Rienadre. You want to fight through these plants, you do it. They got roots tougher than synthcord. I'll be happy to change places with you."

"Shiiittt . . ."

The two marines in the field stood up as the gooey mass of soil collapsed into the still-widening trench.

"We're going to help you, Denalle, before we lose more." Rienadre and the other marine trudged toward the edge of the field.

"This really isn't that good a locale for crops," Nylan said.

"I know, but until we can develop more trade and maybe find some animal that does well up here . . ."

"Sheep or winter deer or something. Even chickens or some sort of domesticated fowl."

"None of which we've seen," Ryba answered curtly. "Not chickens, and the goats scatter into the rocks if they so much as hear a hoof click."

They walked through the drizzle to the cook-fire area, where Nylan got a slab of bread that Kyseen had tried to bake in a makeshift oven and some purple food concentrate. He looked at the off-white center and nearly black crust of the bread, so flat that it looked more like a pancake. He supposed that was because Kyseen had no yeast or whatever made bread rise. After another look at the black-edged mass, he broke off a section and chewed. The bread was only half-cooked and soggy in the middle, but—if he avoided the carbonized outside—it tasted better than the purple concentrate.

Nylan frowned. Some of the partitions in the landers were thin metal. Perhaps he could unbolt them, and without too much power usage, turn them into baking sheets for the oven he hadn't built. After a laugh, he took another mouthful of the soggy bread. He was thinking about making items to fit in things he wasn't sure he could build, and that assumed that he found something like clay, that he could turn it into brick, and that the laser held out—just to begin with.

He finished the last bit of the heavy slab of bread and the slice of the pungent yellow cheese, rinsed his wooden plate, and set it back with the others, and went to find Ryba.

He found her talking with Fierral at the far side of the cook fires.

"Rain or no rain, we need some sentries. The locals are tough, and I don't want someone lofting arrows into us. Or whatever."

No bowman was going to risk ruining good strings in the rain, Nylan felt, but he said nothing.

"Yes, ser," Fierral answered, then looked toward Nylan, her red hair plastered against her skull by the dampness.

"I wanted to talk to Istril about where I might find some clay." Nylan brushed the water off his forehead to keep it from running into his eyes.

"You're not going to work on the tower?" asked Ryba.

"I'm not about to take out the lasers in this weather. The timbers will have to dry anyway before they're mortared and wedged in place."

"What about the clay you're using in the mortar?"

"That's not quite the same. Without the ash . . ." Nylan shook his head. "Besides, I'm hoping to find something that's easier to use and fire. Istril said that she'd seen some spots that might be clay, somewhere down below."

"Wouldn't the locals already be using it?"

"Large deposits, yes. I just want enough for bricks to build some inside walls, maybe a stove, and some water pipes."

Ryba shrugged and turned to Fierral. "Can you spare Istril?"

"That won't be a problem, Captain. Or should we start calling you marshal?"

Ryba grinned. "Whatever works."

Istril was still sleeping in the third lander, and, while Nylan washed up and went to find out something about the horse situation, she ate.

When Istril arrived, the slim marine vaulted into her saddle. Nylan climbed into his, banging himself with the blade he had forged and still barely knew how to swing without hitting himself.

Thankfully, Istril let her horse walk uphill toward the tip of the ridge that seemed almost into the mist that hung below the clouds. Nylan let his beast follow.

"I don't know as what I saw, ser, is what you want, and it's down a little ways. It wasn't like dirt, and it was almost slimy."

"All we can do is look. That sounds promising. Even if it is clay, it will take some experimenting to see if we can fire it."

"Fire it?"

"Turn it into things—pipes for water, bricks, maybe things like plates or pots. That means building a kiln or an oven of sorts." He grabbed the horse's mane as the beast lurched downhill.

They rode in silence until they reached the exposed section of the ridge, little more than a narrow way bordered on each side by rocks that dropped sharply away. Most of the rocks on the north side were still covered with ice left from the winter that held some of the night's snow above it.

Nylan looked down toward the forests that began well below the bottom of the ridge. They would have to circle back along the bottom of the ridge on the north. In the distance, kays below, he could see and sense a narrow stream emerging from the rock pile. He massaged his back. "How long will this take? Isn't there a shorter way?"

Istril led the way down the ridge line, keeping her mount close to the windswept hard rock near the center. "Be a while, ser, but you don't want to take the short way down there."

"What short way?" Nylan's words came out as he bounced in the unfamiliar saddle, reflecting that any saddle would have been unfamiliar.

The silver-haired marine laughed. "Over the cliff. Where we're headed is really just below the landers. A long way straight down."

"Oh." Nylan readjusted his weight in the saddle.

By the time they reached the bottom of the ridge and crossed the cold narrow stream, Nylan felt the tightness in his legs. The rain had dropped off more to a soft mist, and the clouds above appeared a lighter featureless gray.

"Sometimes we see those scouts in purple, but lately they've pulled back. Don't see any travelers, but Narliat says that we won't until it gets warmer, toward midsummer. People don't cross the Westhorns that much."

"That's what they call these mountains?" asked Nylan. "The Easthorns are the other big range, then."

"Guess so." Istril drew her blade and ran through a set of what looked like blade exercises as the horses paralleled the small stream. When she finished, she wiped the blade on a scrap of something tucked in her belt and sheathed it. "Good blade, ser."

"Thank you. I wish I could use one the way you and Ryba do."

"Practice. Never thought I'd have a real use for it." She laughed softly and leaned forward in the saddle. "There! Look up on the hill."

Nylan looked. A tawny catlike creature vanished behind a bushy pine.

"Those are the big cats. They don't like us much. I think there are something like bears, too, but I've only seen tracks."

Nylan glanced up at the nearly sheer rock wall that began on the far side of the stream. "Hard to believe we're up there." He looked back toward the thick trunks of the evergreens where the big cat had vanished. Would it have been better to bring everything down the ridge?

"It's less than a kay ahead, in and out, just above where the other little stream joins," explained Istril.

The two streams joined below a reddish-brown mound that held some bushes Nylan didn't recognize, and only clumps of grass. Just above where the two streams joined, a narrow log, a fallen fir limb, lay half in and half out of the water. A brownish green frog smaller than Nylan's fist squatted on the water-peeled limb, then plopped into the stream and vanished.

After dismounting and tying the horse to an evergreen branch, he jumped across the stream, nearly plunging back into it when his worn shipboots skidded on the slippery ground. He grabbed a bush and steadied himself, then bent down and scooped up some of the clay, almost as plastic as dough. The consistency seemed right, but how could he tell?

"Can we start a small fire here?"

"I can probably find some sticks." Istril brushed a lock of silver hair back over her ear and dismounted.

While the marine gathered brush and some small branches, Nylan experimented with the protoclay. It looked right, felt right, but would it fire right? He rolled out several small balls with his hands, then some flat sections, and one small crude potlike shape, then another.

His striker, when he had finally used Istril's knife to scrape some thin dry shavings, worked in getting the fire started. They added drier branches and waited until there was a small bed of coals, on which Nylan, after wetting his hands in the chill water, placed his test items.

Then he washed the reddish clay off his hands in the water that chilled all the way up his arms. While the clay balls and flat sections baked on the coals, coals that occasionally hissed in the few drops of water falling from the gray sky or nearby trees, Nylan slowly trudged up the narrow gorge, looking up to his right as he went. Up there, somewhere, was the plateau where the landers rested.

Istril trudged beside him, looking more to the sides as she did. "Doesn't look like many people have been here."

"Probably not. You saw how cold those traders looked—and we were sweating." Nylan stopped and looked up the cliff. If they had rope . . . perhaps they could get some rope the next time—if there were a next time . . . if the traders had rope. He studied the cliff. The vertical was still more than four hundred cubits, and probably treacherous at the top. Plus . . . the fired clay wouldn't be that strong and that meant any sustained banging against the rocks would probably crack it unless it were heavily padded—and that meant even more rope and equipment.

If he built the firing hearth up the branch of the creek, which would be dry most of the time— He pulled at his chin. Either the clay went up on horses, or the finished bricks and pipe did.

There was enough wood nearby. He hoped the two-person saw they had bought from Skiodra would help in cutting wood for the firing. Or would it be needed for planks and timbers? Could they use one of the smaller saws on the deadwood to get firewood? Why did he think things would be simple?

Finally, he turned and started back down to the coals.

"Be a long trip to bring things up," observed Istril.

"Very long. But there's a lot of wood here, and not nearly so much up there."

"That makes sense, ser."

Nylan hoped so.

He used a stick to ease one of the balls out of the coals. While the ball had cracked in two, the half coated with ash seemed hard enough. The other side was still damp in parts.

While he could feel that the clay was right, he decided to wait a while longer for the other pieces. He had the feeling that, so far as the clay and brick works were concerned, he—or someone—was going to be doing a lot of experimenting, and a lot of waiting.

XX

"I SEE YOU still intend to let those women flaunt their defiance at you from the Roof of the World." The lady Ellindyja holds the needlework loosely.

"When did you take up needlework?" asks Sillek.

"When I found myself no longer useful to the Lord of Lornth, I took up the diversions of my youth." Ellindyja eases the outer wooden hoop off, readjusts the cloth over the inner hoop, and replaces the outer hoop. Then she picks up the needle.

"We haven't replaced the armsmen we lost."

"Nor your father's ring. Nor his honor." Ellindyja's voice is acid-edged.

"The *present* Lord of Lornth would appreciate any suggestions you might have, my dear mother, which do not either bankrupt me or leave our lands open to Lord Ildyrom."

"I have been thinking, Sillek—about heritages and honor."

Lord Sillek purses his lips, then asks, "What of something besides an attack we cannot afford."

"Well . . . if one must resort to more indirect and more merchantlike means, Sillek, my son, surely there must be some . . . adventurers . . . out there who might want a reward of sorts, perhaps some small parcel of almost worthless land, and a title . . . even a pardon . . . if necessary." Ellindyja smiles brightly.

"Hmmmm . . ." Sillek paces to the tower window and back. His fingers touch his trimmed beard. "Not nearly so expensive as troops. It might even reduce the banditry—one way or another."

"I am more than happy to be of service, Sillek—as I was for your father. He was a most honorable man."

"I don't think we'll make the offer through a broadsheet, though."

"No . . . that would be too overtly merchantly. Tell your wizards and your senior armsmen, and make sure that the traders' guild knows. That is the way the better merchants operate."

"I do so appreciate your advice." Sillek paces back to the window, glancing out into the slashing rain that has poured off the Westhorns. "Your advice is always welcome." He only emphasizes the word "advice" ever so slightly.

"I am so glad you do."

Sillek does not turn from the window, not until he forces a smile back upon his lips.

XXI

NYLAN SPLASHED HIS face again, trying to wash away the stone dust, then took a long swallow of the cold stream water. The water carried away some of the acridness and dustiness that seeped endlessly into his nostrils and dried his throat. After another swallow, he walked back toward the tower. In the foot-packed clay area beyond the rough stacked stones and the space where Cessya and Huldran alternated splitting the slates for roofing tiles, Istril and Ryba were working at blade practice, using the wooden wands that were far safer for beginners.

Nylan shivered. His turn would be coming up. He set down his cup on the nearest pile of black stone and watched as Saryn and Ryba began to spar. Despite the partial splint that remained on Saryn's leg, their wands flickered, faster, and then even faster, until Nylan's own heart and lungs seemed to be racing. Even Istril and Siret had stopped, both silver-haired marines following the action. As Saryn limped backward and lowered her wand, the engineer finally caught his breath.

"Ah, yes," came a voice from the sunny side of a pile of cut stones meant for the sixth level of the tower.

Nylan leaned over to see Narliat drinking in the reflected heat from the stone. "Yes?"

"The she-angels, those two, and I see why Lord Nessil is dead."

"You liked Lord Nessil?" Nylan tried to keep his voice neutral.

"He was more honest than most, but he was terrible when he was angered, and he was angered a lot. That is not what I meant, Mage. I am a man, too, and I was an armsman." Narliat shrugged. "I would not lift a sword against your she-angels. They would kill me in three strokes, even the one who is crippled, and I have killed a few men. They were poor farmers, but they were strong, and I did not want to die." Narliat looked back to the practice space where Ryba had followed Saryn's lead and set aside her weapon. "I see the she-angels, and I see the whole world change."

Nylan could feel the sweat oozing from his forehead as he stood in the sun. He looked down at the local, wearing a jacket and huddled against the black stone, almost for warmth. "You're cold?"

"Not if I stay here." Narliat smiled. "You will make your tower warm, will you not?"

Nylan looked toward the stones, looking more like dark gray in the sunlight than the black they had seemed when Nylan had cut them from the mountain. "Not that warm—"

"A tower—on the Roof of the World. Only the angels would dare—"

"Nylan! Since you're not cutting or setting stone, let's get your practice done now." Ryba motioned.

Narliat grinned as the engineer trudged toward the practice area.

"Here you go." Ryba handed Nylan one of the hand-carved wands. "It's not balanced the way I'd like—"

"I know. We've been through this before." Nylan lifted the wand. The last few times he'd actually managed to keep Ryba from tapping him at will, but he had no illusions about his ability to hold off a master swordsman or armsman or whatever they were called.

"Set your feet."

Nylan shuffled into position.

"Not like an old man, Nylan."

Behind them Nylan could see Saryn motioning to one of the marines.

"Pay attention," snapped Ryba.

He took a deep breath and tried to focus on the wand, on Ryba's face, framed in jet-black hair, and upon her wand.

"That's better. Ready?" Her wand thrust toward him, and he parried, clumsily, barely deflecting it.

"You can do better than that." This time her wand was quicker, and Nylan tried to counter, but the edge of the wood thwacked his shoulder.

"Ooo . . ." He wanted to rub it, but had to dance aside as another slash whistled toward him, and another . . . and another.

Somehow, he managed to slip, block, deflect, and dance away from most of the captain's thrusts and slashes.

"All right." Ryba stepped back. "That's what you should be facing, but most of the locals aren't that good. Most don't use the points of their blades, but the edges, and that's different."

Nylan shook his head and blinked, then blotted the sweat from his eyes.

"They use heavier blades and try to beat you to a pulp." Ryba picked up the wider wooden weapon, the one with a wooden blade that looked more like a narrow plank than a practice weapon. "You need to work on deflecting a heavier blade. You can't meet it directly, not without losing your own blade or risking having it broken." She took the bigger wooden slab in two hands. "Ready?"

"Yes," said the engineer, even as he thought, *No.*

The first time his light wand met Ryba's heavy one, the

impact shivered all the way up his arm, and he staggered back, dancing aside to avoid another counterstroke before the third one slammed into his thigh.

"You'd be crippled for life if that had been a real blade, and if I hadn't pulled it at the end. Demon-damn, Nylan, this is serious, and these things can kill you—and they will."

"Fine for you to say . . ." he gasped. "You grew up with them."

"Get your blade up. Get it up."

He raised his wand, ignoring the pun, and waited, then half ducked, half slid the heavier wand.

"Better. Get it back up." Ryba sent another slash at his open side.

Nylan jumped and slid his wand over hers, then drove the heavier blade almost into the dirt.

"Good. Use their momentum against them. Those crowbars are heavy."

But it didn't seem that heavy for Ryba because she whipped it back up and around, and Nylan was backpedaling again, and again.

Still, in between all her hits, he did manage to drop the heavy wand into the dirt once more and actually strike Ryba on the shoulder, lightly.

Finally, she stepped back. "Not bad. You've got a feel for it. Right now, you could probably hold off the weaker locals. You just need more practice." Ryba smiled. "I can see that you'll be good—very good—with the blade." Her smile vanished, replaced momentarily with a look Nylan could only term somber. "It won't be easy." She looked toward the tower and shook her head.

Nylan lowered the wand, his entire body dripping sweat. Practicing against Ryba was worse than carting heavy stones up the seemingly endless tower steps, and probably a lot more futile. He handed the wand back to her. "Sometimes," he said, "it feels futile. I'll never be as good as you are."

She took the wand from him, lowering her voice. "You don't have to be. You're an engineer, and you're going to be a wizard or a mage or whatever they call them." Ryba paused. "Narliat already thinks you are." Then she added, "But you still need good basic defense skills, and that means more practice."

Nylan wiped his forehead with the back of his forearm. "Mage?"

"It has to do with the way you use the laser. You ought to be able to use this local net or whatever it is for more than that." Ryba offered a forced smile. "I know you can."

"Thanks. You're so encouraging."

"I know what I know." She shrugged. "Only sometimes . . . unfortunately." Then she looked toward the two marines standing back beyond the stacked slate, and pointed at the silver-haired one. "Llyselle, we don't have forever."

Nylan trudged back to the stream to wash his face again before he returned to the business of setting stone in the walls of the tower. Even the cold water didn't cool him much. The yellow sunflowers had begun to wilt, and were being replaced by small white flowers that hugged the ground between clumps of grass. Nylan felt like one of the wilted yellow flowers.

As he passed the practice area, he glanced at Narliat, sitting in the sun and fingering the splint on his leg. Nylan laughed to himself as he realized that the armsman was in no hurry to remove the splint, no hurry at all.

"She's tough," observed Huldran as Nylan lifted another stone and began to lug it up the stairs.

"Very," grunted the engineer.

"So are you."

"Not like she is."

"You're just as tough, ser . . . in a different way. She couldn't build the tower, and we'll need it, and you aren't a fighter. You're a defender."

"Suppose so . . ." Nylan continued up toward the top of the fifth level where he set the stone on the rough planking. Then he turned and headed back for another stone. Above him Cessya and Weblya wrestled another of the big timbers into the stone slots.

He was carrying up the fifth stone, and almost wishing

he were back practicing when Huldran asked, "Are you about ready for more mortar?"

"Start mixing it. One more stone, and we'll be ready."

"You've almost got the north side filled in between the supports."

"With luck, we'll get the west done, too." He continued up the stone stairs, almost tripping on the top step. By the time he returned with the next stone, Huldran was stirring the mortar components together.

"This tower will last forever," she said.

"Maybe."

"The captain says it will, longer than any of our descendants will live here, and that's a long time."

"She said that?"

"Yes, ser."

Nylan paused before lifting the stone into place, then said, "Can you bring that tub up when you're done?"

"Not a problem."

After reaching the fifth level and setting down the oblong stone, Nylan took a deep breath, then measured the six heavy stones, and rearranged them in the order he wanted. What had Ryba meant by saying that the tower would last forever?

While he waited for Huldran, he glanced out toward the southwest, taking in the ice-needle of Freyja, the peak that glittered in the midday light like a de-energizer beam sensed through the *Winterlance*'s net. He swallowed. That was past, and no reminiscing would bring back that time or universe.

This was indeed a different place, not that different on the surface, but more different than most of the angels realized. Still . . . Ryba's comments—both the ones he had heard and those reported by Huldran—bothered him. Was she getting delusions of grandeur, of some sort of omnipotence? How could she say she knew what was going to happen? Was she getting delusions because she had trouble accepting that she could no longer wield the *Winterlance* like a mighty blade to smite the demons?

"Here's the mortar, ser." Huldran eased the trough onto the planks.

With the trowel—another laser-cut adaptation—he began to smooth the next line of the reddish-gray mortar across the top of the stones already set.

Clang! Clang! The off-key sounds from the crude triangle gong resounded across the Roof of the World.

"Bandits!"

Nylan eased the fifth heavy stone into place on the mortar, trying to ignore the whinnying of horses and the shouted commands.

"Istril! Take the lower trail! Try to cut them off. Use the rifle."

"Fierral! Run the second group . . . with Gerlich . . ."

"Form up! Form up . . ."

By the time Nylan finally could let go of the stone and hasten up the steps to look over the top edges of the outer wall, he only saw the dust of departing marines, riding off behind Ryba and the redheaded force leader—and a dozen marines remaining with blades and sidearms stationed in the rocks on each side of the top of the rise.

From the far side of the rise was what was becoming a packed road down the ridge, Nylan could hear hooves. In time, he reflected, they should consider putting in marker cairns or something for winter travel. Or, considering the mud, a real paved road.

A horse—carrying double—trotted back over the rise and downhill. Blood streamed down the face of the marine riding in front.

"Medic! Medic!" shouted the other rider.

"That's Denalle!" said Weblya, balancing on the last of the big beams she and Cessya were setting in the slots, the beams that would form the floor for the sixth level of the tower and the roof of the fifth.

"She's bleeding and got an arrow through her arm," added Cessya.

Nylan watched for a moment before going back to the stones. The mortar would set before he got the last stone in place if he didn't hurry, and there wasn't anything he could do that Ayrlyn or one of the combat medics couldn't do better.

He laid out another line of mortar, then lifted another stone into place, trying to ignore the conversation between the two marines above.

". . . think he feels he can't waste an instant . . ."

"You look at that ice up there. You want to be in one of those thin-shelled landers when the snows are up over our heads?"

"But . . . Denalle's hurt . . ."

"What can the engineer do that the medics can't?"

"Glad I'm not an officer . . . or the captain."

"No . . . I wouldn't want to be in her boots. Or the engineer's."

A whispered remark came next, followed in turn by a laugh.

"You'd better not. You'd really be in trouble."

Nylan blushed, but laid another line of mortar. After he set the sixth stone, he carried the nearly empty tub of mortar down to the yard space where Huldran was using the sledge and a wedge Nylan had made to split slate.

Clunk!

"Damned stone . . . doesn't always split right," grunted the stocky marine.

"I know. Nothing works quite the way we want."

"You didn't use all of it?" asked Huldran.

"No . . . can you powder it or something?"

"Do that all the time. Just spread it out on the clean section of stone there—the one with the dents in it. When it dries, we turn it into powder and add it back in."

A cooler breeze whipped across the meadow and the tower work area, along with the shadow from a puffy and fast-moving cloud.

"Wind feels good," commented Huldran.

"It'll make it easier to finish the sides before the day's over."

"You think you can?" asked the stocky blond.

"There's enough stone cut, and I'm trying to let the generator recharge some more firin cells before I have to cut more. The captain wants me to forge more blades, and . . ." Nylan shrugged.

"You're trying to have enough power to finish the tower and do that?"

The engineer nodded before returning to carting stone. He had almost finished getting what he would need before several horses appeared at the top of the rise and headed down toward the landers. Over one horse was another body, one clad in olive-black.

Nylan shook his head. Did every bandit attack mean another death?

He watched as the mounted marines rode straight for the smoldering fire where Kyseen, hampered in combat by her broken leg, struggled with cooking.

Nylan still hadn't done much on that front, besides designing the kitchen layout and the stoves for the tower. He hoped that the bandits who had attacked Denalle and the others hadn't done too much damage to the brick-making operation, but he wasn't about to say that out loud.

The engineer recognized the slim, silver-haired figure of Istril, and he waved. "Istril!"

The marine turned her mount toward the tower, after saying something to the two others and letting them continue toward the landers.

Nylan and Huldran waited, then the engineer gestured. "Who?"

"Desinada." Istril reined up.

Nylan vaguely remembered the woman; she'd been among the group that he'd brought down on his lander. "Sorry."

"That sort of thing happens here. A lot, it seems."

"Anything good?" asked Huldran.

"One of them had a purse." As she turned the horse toward the landers, Istril lifted the leather pouch and shook it, letting Nylan and the three marines hear the clank and jingle of mixed coins. "Not that I wouldn't have Desinada back for a dozen of these and then some."

"Was anyone else hurt?" Nylan asked.

"No. Rienadre ducked behind your brick oven and winged one of the bastards. I got the other one. We think one got away, maybe more, but Berlis ran down the winged one. He gave her some lip, and she ran him through. She gets mean sometimes."

"Yeah . . ." muttered Weblya. "Like always."

"Thank you." Nylan inclined his head to Istril.

"No problem, ser." Istril turned her mount back toward the landers.

More hoofbeats announced the return of Ryba and the rest of the marines, along with two more mounts, each with a bandit's body slung across the saddle.

Nylan nodded and bent to lift another stone. "Back to work."

"Don't you stop for anything, ser?" asked Cessya.

"Winter won't." Nylan started up the stairs.

"One more timber," announced Cessya. "Just one more."

"Then we got to saw planks," pointed out Weblya.

"Oh, yeah . . . it's my turn on top. You get to be in the pit."

"Thanks."

The sun had dropped behind the western peaks before Nylan mortared in the last stone on the fifth level of the eastern wall. Despite his best resolves, he still had the gaps in the southern wall left to do. Another day before Cessya and Weblya could wedge and mortar the big timbers into place and start on placing the planks. He trudged down, carrying the empty mortar trough.

"We'll take that, ser," said Weblya.

"You're going to finish it even before it starts to chill, aren't you?" asked Cessya.

"The walls and roof. We might even be able to use some of the armaglass for windows in a few places, if the laser holds out." Nylan coughed, trying to clear the stone and mortar dust from his throat. "I wanted to get the stoves and furnace in, too."

"A furnace?" The two looked at each other.

"Pretty crude. Wood-fired, and wide heat ducts. A big air

return down the stair pedestal—that's already in place."

"You think big, don't you?"

"I suppose so, but you need space when there's snow outside over your head." Nylan smiled wryly. "The snow nomads didn't do all that winter hunting just for food. If they'd all stayed around the fires, they'd have killed each other." He frowned. "We probably need some timbers inside so that people can work on skis after it gets cold."

The two marines shook their heads as the engineer checked the laser, still stored in the space under the lower stairs, and then walked up the hill toward the portable generator with a single firin cell.

He checked the readout on the cell being recharged—over eighty-three percent—and disconnected it, replacing it with the discharged cell. Then he walked back down to the tower where the three marines had cleaned the trough and racked their tools.

"I'm going to wash up before dinner," he said.

"What is dinner?" asked Huldran.

"Gerlich brought in two wild goats, or sheep or something. So we're going to have a goat stew. Meat's too tough for anything else," answered Weblya.

Goat stew, reflected Nylan, probably meant goat meat, wild onions, and a few other unmentionable or unidentifiable plant-root supplements, all thickened with some of the corn flour. "Wonderful."

He plodded toward the streamlet that seemed to narrow each day. They hadn't really had much rain in almost two eight-days. That could mean problems for their attempt at crops.

After washing, he walked through the twilight toward the landers and the cook fires, his face cool from the water and the wind off the ice of the higher peaks.

The smell of smoke and bread and wild onions told him that, again, he was among the last to eat.

"Here, ser." Kyseen handed him one of the rough wooden platters heaped with dark stew, a slab of the flat, fried bread on the side. The edges were only dark, dark brown this time, not black.

"Thank you." Nylan took it and looked around for one of the sawed-off logs that served as crude stools.

"You can sit here, ser." Selitra slipped off a log seat. "I'm finished."

Nylan offered a grateful smile to the lithe marine and sat. "Thank you." His legs ached; his shoulders ached; his hands were cracked and dry. And he still hadn't finished the fifth level of the tower.

He tried the bread; it wasn't soggy, and it even tasted like bread, but heavy, very heavy. He dipped it into the brown mass that was stew and chewed. Either he was starving or the food was improving. Probably both.

"Do you mind if I join you?" asked Ryba. "I ate a little earlier."

Nylan nodded. "I was trying to finish the outer part of the fifth level. We didn't quite make it." He looked north to the dark shape of the tower.

Ryba's eyes followed his. "It's impressive."

Nylan snorted. "I just want it to be warm and strong."

"Just? I recall words about furnaces, stoves, and water."

"Those all go with being secure and warm." He dipped the corner of the bread into the stew and scooped more into his mouth.

"Those weren't common brigands," Ryba said quietly. "Their blades and bows were better than those of some of Lord Nessil's armsmen."

"Bounty hunters?" Nylan finally asked.

"I think so. The local lord has probably offered some sort of reward to get rid of us. We'll probably see more bandits or brigands, maybe even a large force by the end of the summer."

The engineer shook his head.

"Your tower looks better and better." Ryba's fingers kneaded the tight muscles in his shoulders.

Nylan swallowed. "I'm not sure I like being right in quite that way."

"It's better than being wrong."

He couldn't argue with that and looked toward the larger fire, where the marines had gathered around Ayrlyn.

"What about a song?" asked Llyselle.

"A song?" questioned the red-haired comm officer, her voice wry.

"About how you angels routed the bandits," suggested Narliat.

"I don't know about routed," muttered Denalle, her eyes dropping to the dressing on her right arm. Her left hand strayed toward the second dressing that covered her forehead, then dropped away. With a wince, she closed her eyes for a moment.

"I don't make up songs that quickly," answered Ayrlyn.

"But you are a minstrel, are you not?" asked Narliat.

"This is a verbal culture," pointed out Saryn.

"Too verbal," growled Gerlich, glaring at Narliat.

Nylan could feel himself tensing at Gerlich's response and forced himself to let his breath out slowly.

"And it has too many wizards," added the hunter. "And I don't understand why the wizards serve the nobles, the lords, whatever they are. Those wizards have real powers."

"The wizards, they cannot stand against cold iron," answered Narliat, "and there are not a great many wizards."

"Still don't see . . ."

"Oh, Gerlich . . ." murmured Ryba, barely loud enough for Nylan to hear. "Think, for darkness' sake."

Nylan thought also, about cold iron, wondering why cold iron would prove a problem for a wizard. He could handle it, and Narliat said he was a wizard.

"Cold iron?" he finally asked.

"Why yes, Mage. The white ones, they cannot handle cold iron. It's said that it burns them terribly." Narliat shrugged. "I have not seen this, but I have never seen a white wizard touch iron. Even their daggers are bronze."

Nylan frowned. Why would that be so? "Thank you."

"Now that we have that cleared up," Ryba said too brightly, "how about that song?"

Ayrlyn picked up the small four-stringed lutar she had brought down from the *Winterlance,* just as Ryba had brought the Sybran blades.

"How about this one?" Ayrlyn strummed the strings, adjusted one peg, then strummed again, and made another adjustment before clearing her throat.

A captain is a funny thing, a spacer with a net,
an angel gambling with her death, who never lost a bet.
The captain, she took us to those demon-towers,
then brought us back right through Heaven's showers . . .

Nylan winced, knowing that the second verse would be bawdy, and the third even bawdier, then glanced at Ryba, who was grinning.

"I've heard worse versions," she said. "Much worse."

Raucous laughter began to rise around the fire even before Ayrlyn finished the last verse.

". . . and she served him up well trussed, well done!"

The laughter died away.

"An old song? A Sybran song?" asked Denalle.

"I don't know many," admitted Ayrlyn, "but there is one." The redhead readjusted the lutar, then began.

When the snow drops on the stone,
When the wind song's all alone,
When the ice swords form in twain,
Sing of the hearths where we've lain.

When the green tips break the snow,
When the cold streams start to flow,
When the snow hares turn to black,
Sing out to call our love back.

When the plains grass whispers gold,
When the red blooms flower bold,
When the year's foals gallop long,
Hold to the fall and our song . . .

Nylan glanced around the fires, then to the unlit and dark tower looming against the white-streaked peaks, and back to the marines. More than a handful of faces bore eyes bright with unshed tears. Some marines blotted damp cheeks when Ayrlyn lowered the lutar.

Huldran slowly walked out into the darkness, and Selitra laid her head on Gerlich's shoulder, sobbing silently at the old Sybran horse nomads' ballad.

"How about something a bit more cheerful?" suggested Ryba.

"I'll try." Ayrlyn readjusted the lutar and began another song.

> *When I was single, I looked at the skies.*
> *Now I've a consort, I listen to lies,*
> *lies about horses that speak in the darks,*
> *lies about cats and theories of quarks . . .*

"Lies about cats and theories of quarks . . ." mused Nylan. "They're all lies here, I suppose, at least the quarks."

"You don't think quarks are real here?" asked Ryba. Her hand rested lightly on his forearm, warm in the cool of the mountain evening.

"Who knows what's real, or what reality even is?" he answered.

"Where we are is real."

And that was a definition as good as any, Nylan thought, his eyes taking in the almost luminous ice of Freyja, the needle peak that would dwarf even the most massive tower he would ever be able to raise.

XXII

"LORD SILLEK LET it be known that he would not be displeased at whoever reduced the squatters' holding on the Roof of the World to rubble and returned the seal ring of his father." Terek pulls at his chin as he walks to the tower window.

"He's not taking another army up there," answers Hissl, leaning back from the glass upon the small table.

"We discussed that earlier. In his position, would you? This approach will encourage every cutthroat in Lornth to attack those women."

"What good will that do?" Hissl stands and walks toward the second open window to let the breeze cool him. "Lord Nessil had score three armsmen. Not even Skiodra has that, and you saw how he backed down when he came face-to-face with those devil women. What could a handful of brigands do?"

"Lord Sillek has to do something. The . . . expedition to the Roof of the World was rather . . . embarrassing for Lord Nessil . . ." Terek turns back toward Hissl.

"For his family, you mean?" asks Hissl. "A corpse is beyond embarrassment."

"Young Lord Sillek wishes to avenge his father."

"And to solidify his position?"

"He's willing to grant lands and some minor title to whoever succeeds. Something like Lord of the Ironwoods, no doubt." Terek laughs. "There are bound to be some who feel that no women can be that dangerous." The chief wizard shrugs. "Besides, there are not that many of them, and for every one that is killed—that will make things easier for Lord Sillek."

"Let us see," muses Hissl ironically. "Lord Nessil lost

forty-three armsmen, and those angels lost three. Say there are two dozen left up on the Roof of the World . . . why, that means Lord Sillek, or someone, only needs to sacrifice around four hundred armsmen." Hissl's voice is soft and smooth. "And that would be in a battle on an open field. It might take ten times that once their tower is completed. Do you suppose we could persuade Lord Ildyrom, Lord Ekleth of Spidlaria, and—"

"Enough of your foolishness," snaps Terek. "The lord's stratagem against those angels cannot hurt him."

"Do you believe they are really angels?" asks Hissl.

"It might be in our interests to claim that they are—or at least that they are fallen angels."

"Some of them died. Angels don't die," points out Hissl.

"I believe that was one of the men."

"There were four graves for their own, and there are still two men walking around. That means three of the women died."

"You are rather tedious, Hissl," says Terek.

"I am attempting to be accurate."

"Then let us call them fallen angels. That makes them seem more vulnerable." Terek pauses, then adds, "And what other . . . *accuracies* . . . might you add? Helpful accuracies?"

"Those thunder-throwers . . . I do not think that they will be able to use them for too much longer."

"Would you stake your life on that?"

"Not at the moment. In a year . . . yes."

Terek waits. "Go on. Explain. Don't make me drag everything out of you."

"Only a handful of them are experienced with blades— the leader, one of the men, and one of the smaller women. But they are teaching the others. The thunder-throwers are more effective than blades. So . . ." Hissl shrugs. "Why are they spending time learning a less effective weapon? Also, they have begun to build a tower."

"On the Roof of the World? One winter and they'll be dead or ready to leave."

"I don't know about that." Hissl touches his left cheek

with his forefinger, and he frowns. "We were wearing jackets and cloaks. The wind was cold. It was still just beyond spring up there. They were in thin clothes, and they were sweating—all of them."

"We will see." Terek pulls at his chin again. "We will see."

"Yes. That is true." Hissl frowns ever so slightly, then smiles.

XXIII

THE GREEN THAT had sprouted from the hand-furrowed rows of two of the fields rose knee-high in places, waist-high in others, depending on the plants. The potatoes had been planted in evenly spaced hillocks, but the green-leaved plants nearly covered all the open ground of the third field, except along the diagonal line where the water from the storm eight-days earlier had created a trench, since filled in.

Behind the fields, the landers squatted, droplets of dew beading and then streaking the metal. Well beyond them were the large cairn and the seven others, including the latest one for Desinada. Already, dark blue flowers grew from between the cairn stones to mix with the red blood-flowers that were fading as the summer passed.

Nylan turned to the west, where, in the dawn, the fog seemed to rise off the squared structure of black stone that dominated the area above the field. The final upper sill of the wall stones stood more than ten times the height of a woman. Rising out of the middle of the tower was a square construction of mortared stones, and at the central point about half the rafters for the roof were connected. The remaining rafters were lined up in the stone working yard below the tower.

Nylan stood in the dawn and studied the south-facing

opening that would be the doorway. While the heavy pins had been set in the stone lintels, the door had yet to be built, as did the causeway to it.

His eyes flicked from the tower base up the black stones. No great work of art, but it would be big enough and strong enough to do what would be necessary, unless the locals decided to drag siege engines through the mountains, or spent seasons building them and supporting the builders with an army. Neither seemed likely. Then, he reflected, nothing about the planet was terribly likely.

At the sense, rather than the sound, of someone approaching, he turned toward the landers.

"You don't sleep much, do you?" Ryba stopped several paces short of him.

"Neither do you, apparently."

"Burdens of leadership, curse of foresight . . ." Ryba cleared her throat, then turned toward the tower.

His eyes followed hers. "Still a lot to do. Sometimes, more than sometimes, I wonder what else I've forgotten."

Her hand touched his shoulder. "It's beautiful . . . the tower, and I can see, you know, that it will last for generations. Maybe longer."

"You can see that?"

Ryba shrugged, almost sadly. "Some things I can see. Like the women who will climb the rocks searching for Westwind, for hope, for a different life. Like the men who will chase them, not understanding."

"Westwind?"

"I thought it was a good name. And that's what it will be called." Her laugh was almost harsh. "So we might as well start now."

Nylan turned to her. "You're seeing all this?"

"Nylan . . . you can bend metal and power, and Ayrlyn can touch souls with her songs, and her touch heals small injuries—and Saryn—she glitters when her hands touch the waters or a blade. Why shouldn't I, who rode the greatest neuronets of all, why shouldn't I have a power beyond the blades?"

"Foresight?" he whispered.

"At times . . . yes . . . It's only occasional . . . now . . . but I wonder . . ." She shook her head. "You think it's easy to kill one of your own, to be as hard as the stones in your tower? To see what might be, if only you're strong enough . . . ? To know that everyone will die if you're not . . ."

His hands touched hers, and found that her hands and fingers were cold, trembling, for all that he had to raise his eyes to meet hers.

XXIV

"THUS CONTINUED THE conflict between order and chaos, between those who would force order and those who would not, and between those who followed the blade and those who followed the spirit.

"On the Roof of the World, those first angels raised crops amid the eternal ice, and builded walls, and made bricks, and all manner of devisings of the most miraculous, from the black blades that never dulled to the water that flowed amidst the ice of winter and the tower that remained yet warm from a single fire.

"Of the great ones in those times were, first, Ryba of the twin blades, Nylan of the forge of order, Gerlich the hunter, Saryn the mighty, and Ayrlyn of the songs that forged the guards of Westwind . . .

"For as the skilled and terrible smith Nylan forged the terrible black blades of Westwind, and wrenched the very stones from the mountains for the tower called Black, so did Ryba guide the guards of Westwind, letting no man triumph upon the Roof of the World.

"For as each lord of the demons said, 'I will not suffer those angel women to survive,' and as each angel fell, Ryba created yet another from those who fled the demons, until there were none that could stand against Tower Black.

". . . and so it came to pass that Ryba was the last of the angels to rule the heavens and the angel who set forth the Legend for all to heed . . ."

Book of Ayrlyn
Section I
[Restricted Text]

XXV

SILLEK LOOKS DOWN the lines of horse, then back toward the west branch of the river, and the ford. Behind him, the fourscore armsmen shift in their saddles.

On the next rolling hill is another force of cavalry, under the white banner bearing a single fir tree—the banner of Jerans. Sillek studies the Jeranyi force, noting the varying sizes of the troopers opposing his. Men and women both bear arms, their mounts standing, waiting, in the knee-high grass.

"Barbaric," he mutters.

"The women?" asks Koric. The mustached and slightly stoop-shouldered captain spits out onto the grass. "Sometimes they're nastier than the men. Rather fight the Suthyans any day."

"Do you see Ildyrom over there?"

"He's the one in the green jacket. Verintkya's the big blond bitch next to him. She uses a mace sometimes, they say. Split your head with a smile, she would."

Sillek turns in the saddle. "Master Terek."

"Yes, Your Grace?" The chief wizard eases his mount closer to the Lord of Lornth.

"Will your firebolts reach the Jeranyi?"

"From here, ser? It's a long pull . . ." Terek's ungloved hand brushes his white hair. Behind him Hissl and Jissek watch Sillek intently.

"Yes or no?"

"Yes, ser." Terek holds up a hand. "But we can't send so many. It takes more energy to send bolts that far."

"Can you tell if Ildyrom has any archers there?"

Terek gestures to Hissl.

"There are a couple of troopers with the short curved bows, but no longbows, ser."

"So they can't quite reach us with arrows . . ." Sillek pauses, then turns to Terek. "Go ahead, Chief Wizard. Fry as many as you can."

Beside Sillek, Koric clears his throat. "Ser . . . begging your pardon."

Terek waits, as do Hissl and Jissek.

"Yes, Captain?" Sillek's voice is smooth—and cold.

"Using firebolts . . . I mean . . . what if they've got wizards?"

"Is that your real concern, Captain, or are you clinging to my father's outdated sense of nobility?"

"Ser . . ." Koric drew himself up in the saddle.

"Koric . . . I'm not interested in battlefield tales or boasts. I've got a bunch of bitch-women at my back with thunder-throwers. I've got Ildyrom and Verintkya trying to take over the good grasslands between the South Branch and the West Fork, and the Suthyans are raising the port tariffs in Rulyarth. Now, if I can get rid of Ildyrom without losing anyone . . . so much the better."

"Next time, they'll bring wizards," said Koric.

"There aren't many, if any, as good as ours." Sillek turns to Terek. "Is that not correct, Master Wizard Terek?"

"I believe so, ser."

"Good. Prove it."

Koric frowns as Terek concentrates, then points.

Whhhhssttt! With a whistling, screaming hiss, a firebolt arcs from Terek's fingers out over the valley between the two hills and falls across two Jeranyi troopers.

The twin screams shriek across the gently waving grasslands, and greasy smoke billows from the other hillside. A riderless horse rears into the midday sky, then lets forth a screaming whinny before bolting down the hillside in the general direction of Berlitos, the forest city of Jerans that lies more than four days of hard riding to the west.

The remaining Jeranyi horse hold, though the troopers on them seem to shift in their saddles before several arrows fly eastward. The shafts drop harmlessly in the tall grass well below the hilltop where the forces of Lornth wait.

"Another!" commands Sillek.

Terek frowns, but concentrates. A second firebolt arcs over the valley and toward Ildyrom.

The bolt splashes across the chest of a roan who rears, screaming, so suddenly that the rider is flung backward and falls into a crumpled heap. More greasy smoke rises as the fatally wounded horse falls and rolls, then quivers, in the damp grasses. A trooper dismounts, checks the still figure in the grass. Shortly, two Jeranyi troopers quickly put the body on a packhorse.

Then the fir-tree banner jerks, and then the Jeranyi turn and ride westward, disappearing behind the hilltop, leaving three piles of smoldering ash.

As Sillek watches, Terek takes a deep breath, and Hissl, observing the pallor on Terek's face, nods to himself.

"Now what, ser?" asks Koric.

"We follow them, discreetly."

"We could ride 'em down, maybe get rid of them."

Sillek holds in a deep breath, purses his lips, then finally responds. "How many armsmen did we lose?"

"Why, none, ser."

"How many did they lose?"

"Three."

Sillek nods. "And what happens if we do this every time they stop, until we chase them back to their earthen fort?"

"It won't get rid of their fort."

"No . . . but if we can kill five or ten troopers every time we meet and not lose anyone—how long before Lord Ildyrom is going to think about abandoning that fort? We can do the same to supply forces, you know?"

"He'll think of something, ser."

"He probably will, and we'll have to think of something better." Sillek motions, and the purple banners flutter in the light wind as the Lornian forces follow those of Jerans. "Preferably before he does."

XXVI

THE WHITE-YELLOW sun beat down across the Roof of the World, and Nylan wiped his forehead, glancing across the fields. The melting ice from the mountains to the south provided some water, but the two small streams that wound out of the rocks and meandered across the meadow area before they joined seemed to shrink daily. The meadow area around the fields now bore no flowers, only grass and low bushes, except for the stony patches where nothing grew.

Nylan's eyes followed the general path of the stream to the cut on the north end of the eastern plateau where the stream plunged over the edge, dropping in a thin line of silver to the creek bed on which, far below, lay the gorge that contained Nylan's fledgling brick-making operation. He hadn't tried the clay piping yet. The bricks were proving difficult enough. He took a deep breath. With the laser, he could work what seemed miracles, so long as the firin cells lasted, and yet trying to get the consistency and texture of a demon-damned low-tech brick . . .

With a shake of his head, Nylan turned, and as he walked back from the space in the rocks, feeling relieved, his eyes flicked over the tower. The outer walls were complete, and so were most of the inner walls. Cessya, Huldran, and Weblya had the roofing timbers in place, and the three of them were working on the cross-stringers, while he got the tiles ready.

At the southern base of the tower were the stacks of slate tiles that had slowly been split by Huldran, Cessya, and Weblya with the sledge from Skiodra and the wedges he had made with the laser—just waiting to be drilled so that the tower could be roofed.

He swallowed.

He'd never made provisions for waste disposal in the tower.

"Shit . . ." he mumbled. How could he have overlooked that? It didn't seem all that bad now, in the warmth of summer, but with ice and snow deeper than a man or woman, or deeper than that, some provisions definitely needed to be thought out—and he hadn't.

He walked toward the work yard and studied the tower again.

He could convert one of the fourth-level casements into a small facility, with an exterior drop shaft into a cistern-type enclosure with a drain for liquids. Maybe he could add another on the fifth level. But some sort of bathhouse or the like would have to be separate, and for safety's sake, have a separate water line—plus a covered and walled passage that could be blocked off in cases of attack, if necessary. Some part of the bathhouse probably ought to have laundry tubs, as well.

How . . . how could he have overlooked those needs, and what else had he overlooked? Then again, the difficulty of covering the piping and the heights had forced him to put the tower's cistern on the lower level.

Back in the yard, he rechecked the power levels on the block of firin cells—down to thirty percent—mentally calculating and deciding he might, *might,* make it through the day before replacing the block. He'd also planned to use the laser to craft another blade or two—Ryba was insisting that he needed to provide more weapons before the laser gave out. In between times, he'd already managed to forge nearly a dozen of the black blades that all the marines clamored for.

After scratching the flaking and itching sunburned skin on his forearm, he inspected the laser's powerhead with both eyes and his senses, still trying every trick he could think of to eke out the best use of the stored power that he was running through faster than the emergency generator would ever be able to recharge—assuming the laser even outlasted the generator.

Nylan finally eased the laser on and focused the beam, as much now with his mind as with the manual controls, to drill the necessary holes in the slate roofing tiles that Stentana would stack as he finished each.

The barrel of heavy spike nails that Ayrlyn had charmed out of a traveling trader two days toward the plains of Gallos was definitely going to be a help. Making nails was not something he even wanted to try with a laser, assuming he could even figure out how. The transaction, according to Narliat, had taken not only Ayrlyn's charm, but more than a gold in coin—and a gold was worth plenty in this culture—something like a season's work for a laborer—the looming presence of armed marines, and Narliat's guile. She'd also come up with another pair of heavy hammers and a huge chisel, plus, of course, some food. Nylan had appreciated it all, especially the cask of dried fruit from someplace called Kyphros.

He was drilling three holes in each slate, after having tested the idea by spiking several to sections of stringers that had proved flawed.

Once he got back into the rhythm of the work, Nylan moved through the big slates quickly, and that was a relief, because he felt everything he could do to stretch more life from the laser would make everyone's life easier.

In time, his arms began to ache, as they always did after using the laser, and his vision began to blur.

Clang! Clang! Clang! Someone banged the alarm triangle.

"Bandits!" yelled another voice, and before Nylan could

finish the hole he was drilling and cut the power flow and look away from the laser, Ryba and a handful of marines were galloping across the meadow and up the ridge.

"I thought we got the bandits earlier," said Cessya, wrestling a rough-cut stringer toward the makeshift earthen ramp that led to the tower door.

"This is probably another group," pointed out Nylan, his eyes on the additional marines taking up positions on the rocky heights that controlled the approach to the tower and the meadow and fields. He took a deep swallow from the cup and munched some of the stale flat bread, feeling guilty as he did, but knowing that he couldn't do what he did without the additional nourishment.

"Take a break, Stentana," he suggested. "It'll be a little bit before I can fire it up again."

"Power, ser?"

"Sort of." He smiled wryly, not wanting to explain that he was the underpowered part of the equipment. He walked up the ramp and into the shade of the second level of the tower, where he sat on the next-to-the-bottom step.

The triangle sounded again, and Nylan heaved himself up off the step and back out into the sunlight.

Three riders guided their mounts down toward the landers, following the trail past the tower yard. On the fourth mount, riderless, a body was slung across the saddle, a body in the black olive drab of a marine.

"Who?" asked Huldran as Istril led the horse past the tower yard.

Nylan looked at the laser and then toward Istril and the dead marine, but the body was facedown.

"Frelita."

Nylan didn't know the marine by name, since he hadn't learned them all, but he'd probably recognize her face—or recognize when she wasn't there at dinner. For a time, the tower crew watched the horses and their riders.

"We can't help them by looking," Nylan finally said.

"I'll be glad when the tower's finished," added Huldran.

Weblya laughed once. "Then we'll have to build a real

ramp, and some stables. There's a lot to do."

"How about a bathhouse with showers?" suggested Nylan. "And a place to do laundry?"

"Showers with ice-cold water? No, thank you," answered Stentana.

"He's working on a furnace," said Huldran. "Maybe he can give us a hot-water heater."

Nylan groaned.

Huldran grinned. "I can ask, ser."

"Let's worry about getting a solid roof on the tower first."

"Yes, ser." The blond squared her shoulders.

Nylan finished the last of the roof slates before the sun even touched the western peaks, with enough time—and power left—for him to shape two more of the black blades, although they couldn't be used, not easily, until some of the hides of the big cats killed by Gerlich were tanned—or until they got some kind of leather to wrap the hilts.

After that, Nylan stowed the laser cells back in the space under the tower stairs. Then he trudged to the upper stream and washed up as well as he could before making his way toward the cook fires.

Three repeated rings on the triangle called all but the sentries around the fires.

Ryba stood on one of the lengths of logs, and studied the group, waiting for silence. Her face was grim. "Frelita's dead. It didn't have to happen, but she really wasn't paying attention."

". . . poor woman . . ."

". . . should have watched closer . . ."

"You idiots!" snapped Ryba, her voice cold as a winter gale, cutting off the low murmurs. "Did you think that after one round of bandits, they'd all go away? We can't afford to lose one of you every time some idiot brigand shows up. Do you want to be the next one skewered by one of those arrows? There's no such thing as one band of brigands in a place like this. You kill one bunch, and more show up. And life is so frigging hard here that they don't care much if they die, so long as they have some fun along the way. Fun is food, wine, beer, and women—and they don't care how they get their women."

Saryn fingered the sharp edge of her blade, one of the better ones Nylan had done, and one of the matching pair that the former second pilot wore. ". . . I do . . ."

Her words were as clear as if she had been standing beside Nylan, and he frowned. How had he heard Saryn so clearly?

Ayrlyn, halfway between Nylan and Saryn, shook her head, then glanced at the engineer, raising her eyebrows. He shrugged back, trying not to cough as the smoke from the cook fire twisted toward him.

Perhaps it wouldn't be too long before Rienadre and Denalle had fired enough bricks to start building the big stove and the furnace in the lower level of the tower. Maybe completing the tower would help with some of the security. He pursed his lips. Who was he kidding? Crops had to be tended. Someone had to hunt. Others had to keep watch. The tower would be great against the winter, and at night—but not that much help in the warm days, except as a higher vantage point.

"Women are slaves here—outside of Westwind. And don't you forget it. There are few men off the Roof of the World who wouldn't want to kill you, humble you, rape you—or all three. We're the evil angels to a lot of these people. Now we can change that, and we're going to—but we can't do it if you get yourselves killed." A cast of sadness crossed the captain's face. "I'm sorry about Frelita. I wish it hadn't happened. And I'm still sorry about Desinada. But let's not let it happen again." She stepped down and walked through the marines toward Nylan.

He touched her forearm, and she looked at him, then nodded toward the tower. So they walked back up the gentle slope until the black stones loomed over them.

"It always takes death or force to get people's attention. And one death sometimes doesn't even do it," Ryba began. "I've got to act like some ancient dictator just to get people to follow common sense."

"Not all of us," suggested Nylan.

"Thank the darkness." Ryba sighed. "But they complain about sawing planks, cleaning saw blades, or making bricks. Don't they?"

"Sometimes."

"And what do you tell them?"

"I ask them if they want to spend the winter with a thin layer of metal between them and snow twice their height, eating frozen food and breaking their teeth—if they've got the strength to eat." Nylan paused. "Selling the tower's easy. They can see it. It's hard to sell alertness, or general pre-paredness, or anything people can't touch."

Ryba nodded. "Sometimes . . . sometimes, I get so tired."

Nylan put his arms around her.

She stiffened for a moment, then relaxed. "Have to re-member to take comfort when I can."

"That's all we can do."

After a time, they separated and walked slowly back to-ward the cook fires and a late supper. Overhead, the cold stars blinked out and shone down on the Roof of the World, each as cold as the ice that coated Freyja, as cold as the lat-est cairn in the southwestern corner of the Roof of the World, where there were getting to be too many cairns, too quickly.

XXVII

THE LOW GRAY clouds that had brought the long-overdue af-ternoon rain scud eastward and toward the mighty Westhorns as Sillek peers on his knees through both the twilight and the chest-high, damp grasses. Less than a thousand cubits away, across a slight depression, lie the earthen ramparts that sit on the last raised ground controlling the approach to the ford—and the road to Clynya.

Behind the ramparts are several tents, and more than a

handful of long rough-planked buildings with sodded roofs. The air smells of damp grass, soil, and woodsmoke.

"Can you set those buildings on fire, Master Mage?" he asks Terek.

"This grass is damp, ser."

"The buildings?" hisses Sillek.

"Yes, ser, but I'd have to get closer, much closer. They've cut away all the grass—"

"Burned it, I think," corrects Sillek. "You can see in the dark, can't you? Mages are supposed to be able to do that."

"In the dark? You want us to do this in the dark?"

"As I told Koric, I'm not a slave to an outmoded code of honor, Master Chief Wizard. That bastard Ildyrom disregarded honor and traditional boundaries when he seized the grasslands west of Clynya and built this fort to hold them. Honor says I should send my armsmen against a bunch of mongrel scum to have them killed? Frig honor. I intend to get the grasslands back without killing my men."

Terek shifts his weight from one knee to the other in the high damp grass, all too aware he does not wear the hip-length boots that Sillek does.

"When it gets dark, Koric and a handful of the best will escort you and the two other wizards down as far as you need to go. I want everything in that fort to burn—everything."

"But they'll flee."

"Of course." Sillek smiles. "I've thought of that, too. Now, let's get back and get ready." He glances to the darkening western horizon, then back to the thin lines of smoke coming up from the wooden huts behind the earthen walls.

Terek shivers, but follows the lord as the two creep back through the grasses, hoping that the sentries in the fort can see nothing but grass waving in the evening breeze.

". . . all this sneaking . . ." Terek mumbles to himself.

"Do you want to ride up front in a charge to take that fort, Master Wizard?" asks Sillek, still easing through the damp grasses in a crouch, grasses that bend and then spray Terek with the rain that has coated them.

Terek wipes his forehead. "No, ser."

"Then stop complaining. I'm a lot more interested in winning than in being a dead hero, and, from what I've seen, so are you."

When they reach the low hill that shelters the Lornian forces, Sillek straightens and massages his back.

Koric waits and listens as Lord Sillek explains.

". . . won't be too much longer before it's dark enough for you to start, Koric."

"Yes, ser."

Sillek touches his arm and lowers his voice. "Who else can I trust to ensure these . . . wizards . . . do as they're supposed to? I can't spare a score of horse or the archers."

"I understand, ser. I'll do my duty."

Both Sillek and Koric understand the words that Koric does not speak. *But I don't have to like it.*

"I know," Sillek says. "Just remember. It's the results that count." He studies the almost-dark sky and the stars that have appeared. "You'd better get started."

Koric nods.

Sillek wipes what moisture he can from his leathers, and boots, before mounting and beginning his instructions to the horse troopers.

As the skies continue to clear, and the white firepoints of the stars blink across the grasslands, Koric leads the three wizards through the grass. Watch fires glimmer at the four corners of the fort, spilling light into the darkness.

Another group from Lornth circles behind the wizards, heading for the ford in the West Fork. The dozen men bear longbows and filled quivers.

Farther from the Jeranyi redoubt, sheltered by the slope of the land and the chest-high grass, Lord Sillek and his horse wait, then he nods, and, almost silently, the troopers begin their roundabout ride to the south side of the road that leads from the ford to the fort.

The grass bends and whispers, showering Hissl with droplets. He wipes his face and follows, at a crouch, Koric and the chief wizard.

"Keep down," hisses Koric. "You mages get us discovered,

and you'll spend the next season in cold iron, if the Jeranyi don't catch us, and do it first."

Hissl takes a deep breath and wipes more water out of his eyes. Jissek just puffs along after Terek. Behind them follow a half squad of armed troopers, also creeping through the damp grass and darkness.

"Is this close enough?" asks Koric as he pauses and glances toward the watch fires that are little more than a hundred cubits away, their flames flickering in the light but steady wind out of the west that brings with it the smell of wood fires, probably from wood ferried downstream from the headwaters of the West Fork. Mixed with the wood smoke is the odor of cooking grease.

Hissl licks his lips, trying to ignore the growling in his guts.

"Close enough," admits Terek, "even for Jissek."

"You start when you're ready," orders Koric. "The others will watch for the fires."

"The center building is mostly wood," offers Hissl in a low voice.

"Thank you, Master Hissl," responds Terek.

"Stop it, you two," mumbles Jissek. "Let's get on with it."

"You also, Master Jissek," hisses Terek. "I'll do the first, then Hissl, and then you, Jissek. Take your time, and hit *something.*"

Whhsttt!

The first firebolt arcs out of the grass and drops into the fort— slamming into the side of a building where flames lick at the rough-dressed log wall.

Clang! Clang!

The Jeranyi warning bell echoes through the fort.

More fireballs arc out of the darkness and fall across the buildings within the earthen walls.

The bell clamors more, then falls silent as the sound of voices and muffled orders fill the once-still evening.

". . . mount up and fall in!"

"Archers! . . . Where are the frigging archers?"

"Fire! Water for the cook hall! Fire!"

Three additional fireballs, the first the largest, drop in succession into the fort.

"Aeeeeiiii!" A scream tells that at least one has struck more than wood.

The crackling of flames joins the chorus of orders and the whuffing and whinnying of hastily saddled mounts. The night air lightens with the growing flames from the buildings in the fort, with burning canvas, and the smell of smoke thickens as it drifts toward the wizards.

Another round of fireballs flares eastward. After his fourth firebolt, Jissek drops to his knees and holds his head. Terek snorts and flings another ball of fire toward the fort, and so does Hissl, who ignores the sweat beading on his forehead despite the cool night wind.

The flames continue to build, and the cool wind becomes warm, then hot, and the Jeranyi redoubt blazes with the light of a second sun.

Terek grunts as he lets go a last firebolt. "Can't do much more here."

"All right. Let's move back. Keep low until we're out of the light."

As all three wizards stumble after the surefooted Koric, the fort's gates open, and the Jeranyi horse ride quickly down the road toward the ford, in rough ranks, blades glittering in the light of dozens of fires.

The whirring of arrows, like soft-winged birds, is lost in the clatter and thump of hooves, in the low-voiced orders, and the crackling of the fire. The bodies slumping in saddles are not.

"Charge the river!" orders a strong tenor voice.

"The river!" adds a second, deeper voice.

The column straightens, and the Jeranyi forces gallop downhill, hooves thudding on the damp-packed clay of the road, before splashing through the water and heading into the darkness that leads to Jerans.

More soft-winged arrows fly out of the darkness into the backlighted horse troopers, and more bodies fall from saddles. Some few wounded riders are fortunate enough and strong enough to hang on and keep riding into the safety of the western darkness.

Shortly, the road is empty, except for more than two dozen bodies and two riderless horses.

Behind the empty road, the pillar of fire that had been a Jeranyi outpost slowly subsides, consuming as it does all that can burn, and filling Clynya, kays downwind, and the barracks there, with the odor of smoke and burned meat.

Later, much later, in the small upper room of the barracks, Sillek smiles. "That should give Ildyrom something to think about."

Koric nods slowly. "This time. What if he rebuilds?"

"This time, the wizards will watch. One of them will stay here with a detachment."

The three wizards exchange glances.

Koric nods slowly. "Might I?"

"If that would please you, Captain." Sillek turns to Terek. "I would appreciate it if Master Hissl might serve my captain Koric here."

"I am most certain that Master Hissl would be pleased," answers Terek.

"Indeed, I would be pleased, Your Grace," responds Hissl. His voice is low, only a shade more animated than if it were absolutely flat.

In the corner, Jissek wipes his forehead.

XXVIII

HIGH HAZY CLOUDS hovered above Freyja, moving slowly eastward, and behind them, to the west, lurked a hint of darkness.

Nylan cleared his throat and checked over his equipment, from the worn gauntlets and the scratched goggles never designed for such intensive use down to the crude trough of water and hydraulic fluid.

He ran his fingers over the blade he was using as a model once more before picking up another of the endurasteel braces from the landers. His senses, now more practiced, studied the metal, checking the imperfections hidden within.

With a deep breath, he pulled on the goggles and the gauntlets and touched the power-up studs on the firin cell bank. After picking up the heavy brace, he readjusted and pulsed the laser, slowly cutting along the grain of the metal. He'd finally gotten used to guiding a laser by feel, and he even didn't try to analyze what he was doing too deeply.

When he had completed the rough cut, he released the power stud and checked the cut and the metal—still rough, still partly disordered. Next came spreading the beam for a wider heat flow and to get the heat and power to guide the semifinished shape of the blade.

After his round of shaping, he concentrated on the hand guards and tang. As he cut and melted the metal, he eased the metal into shape and order, trying not to remember how he once had smoothed power fluxes through the *Winterlance*'s neuronet.

Almost as an afterthought, he tried to bind that . . . darkness . . . that accompanied the local net into the metal. He'd gotten better. Not only did the blade glow with a lambent darkness, but it felt more right for him. He'd keep this blade and pass the one he had been using along.

By the time he'd completed and tempered the blade, the power loss was only about a half percent from the cells— but he was exhausted as he slumped onto one of the extra wall stones and gulped down the water from the battered and scratched gray plastic cup. Perhaps the extra energy required by the darkness he had put in the metal?

He licked his dry lips and looked across the tower yard. Beyond the extra wall stones were the thicker slate chunks that would be used for flooring—at least in the lowest tower level and in the great hall.

The wind had picked up, its cooling welcome as it ruffled his unevenly cut short hair. Jaseen had tried, but the aesthetic effect left something to be desired. Not that he cared that much—or did he?

To avoid that speculation, Nylan glanced up beyond Freyja, noting that the sky was darkening, becoming almost black upon the mountains that formed the horizon.

"Frig . . . he's here early . . . and another miracle blade," mumbled Weindre to Huldran as the two entered the area outside the tower that was coming to be known as the yard.

"Don't complain. Your life just might rest on those blades. How many rounds are left in your little slug-thrower?" Huldran grinned at Nylan.

The engineer offered a quick smile in return, then glanced at the roof, where three sides were complete, with the black-gray slate tiles spiked in place. Only the east side remained unfinished, with three lines of tile in place along the bottom stringers.

They'd used mortar to seal the ridges, although Nylan knew something more plastic, like tar or pitch, would have been far better—but where could they find that?

"I know. I know," answered Weindre as she stopped in the yard. "But I feel so awkward with a piece of sharp metal in my hands."

"Better learn to get comfortable with it," suggested the stocky blond marine. "Otherwise you'll end up like Desinada or Frelita."

"You want us like the captain or the second, or Istril? They're scary." Weindre paused. "Even the engineer—pardon, ser—he's pretty good, and he doesn't practice that much."

A dull rumbling echoed off the western peaks, followed by another round of thunder. Three quarters of the sky was black, but the sun still shone in the east.

He forced himself up. "I'll need some help getting all this into the space in the center of the tower."

"Ser?"

Another roll of thunder pounded out of the mountains.

"This is going to be a demon-damned storm. Let's go! Now!"

"Yes, ser." Huldran grabbed Weindre by the arm, and the two marines unfolded the carry-arms for the firin cell racks.

Nylan began gathering tools and loose objects as the wind began to tear around him.

Overhead, the clouds gathered into a dark mass almost as black as deep space. The wind had risen to a whistling shriek by the time the three had stowed all the equipment, as well as the just-finished black blade, back in the tower, and Nylan had secured the heavy door.

"Now what?" shouted Huldran above the wind.

The lightning cracked across the sky, the white-yellow bolt reflecting off the ice of Freyja, the rumbling echoing back and forth between the high peaks after each bolt.

"Just stay here in the lower level of the tower," suggested Nylan. "We'll see how well we built."

Weindre looked at the two.

"I'd rather be here than in one of those flimsy landers," snapped Huldran.

Nylan sat on one of the steps, his eyes resting on the low lines of brick that represented the base of the stove. The furnace was waiting on the results of his efforts in firing clay piping.

Weindre glanced up the stairs, then followed Huldran over to a side wall. Unlike Nylan, neither sat—they just stood listening to the storm.

His eyes closed as he leaned back against the stones, Nylan let his senses follow the patterns of the storm. Even without straining, he could feel the interplay of chaos and order, like the power flows that occurred when the angels' de-energizers fought with the mirror towers of the demons. He doubted he'd sense that type of battle again, not with technology, anyway.

Like ice knives, the rain slashed down, heavy droplets dashing against the stone walls of the tower, then running in rivulets downward.

Clack! Clack!

Fist-sized hailstones banged off the stones of the tower walls.

A small trickle of water, blown through the unfinished main doorway, began to drop from one side of the stairwell above, down onto the packed clay of the tower's lowest level. Before long, the drops became a stream.

The wind continued to howl, and Nylan wished that he'd insisted that the big front door be finished and hung. He still hadn't done much more on the waste-disposal problem than rework the two casements.

The water had formed a large puddle, almost a small pond in the lowest part of the tower basement, that grew as Nylan watched.

Almost as suddenly as the storm had begun, the clacking of the hailstones died away, and the wind's whistling dropped off.

Nylan stood and eased his way up the steps and onto the water-soaked timbers and stone subflooring of the tower's entry level. From the doorless front portal, he looked out across the Roof of the World. The lower corners of the larger field were little more than knee-deep gullies, leading into a man-deep canyon that ran right off the edge of the plateau.

Even in the middle of the northernmost fields, some of the small potato nodules were half-exposed, hanging out over ditches. Only the stone cairns—one large and eight smaller ones—looked untouched. That figured.

Nylan shrugged and walked out into the drizzle, then looked back at the tower. The walls seemed solid, and the foundations untouched, although the open casements on the upper levels were dark with moisture. His eyes went higher. From what he could tell, only the lower line of slate tiles on the east side had been damaged, and about half, a good twenty, were either askew or missing.

Nylan hoped the laser lasted longer, because trying to hand bore or punch those slates would create a lot of broken tiles—and more than a little wasted effort for Weblya, Huldran, and Cessya.

"Shit!" Huldran's voice was bitter.

"That's only a handful of roof tiles," Nylan pointed out, turning back toward the landers and trying to ignore a sense of loss as he plodded through ankle-deep water and mud. He didn't know what he should—or could—do, but he needed to find out the rest of the damage.

"Yes, ser, but we didn't need any of this." Huldran walked at his elbow.

"Probably not. We should have expected it, though. I imagine fall, winter, and spring are all this violent, if not worse."

"Hate this place."

"You'd rather be down on the plains, melting into a pile of goo?"

"The whole friggin' planet, ser."

"None of us planned this. We do what we can." *And hope that it's enough and that we didn't do anything too stupid,* he added to himself. "We'll need to run wider diversion ditches around the field to stop this sort of thing."

Heaps of hail lay strewn everywhere across the meadow, and the drizzle that kept falling was tinged with ice flakes.

Ryba looked up from a prone figure where she and Jaseen, the combat medtech, struggled. "We need dressings, Nylan. Gerlich's out hunting, and he knew the storage plan by heart. Try lander three. Huldran, can you take charge of the diversion in the fields so that we don't lose any more crops?"

"Yes, ser." The blond marine was moving as she spoke.

"Will do." As Nylan turned to go for the medsupplies, he asked, "What happened?"

"One of those skinny little trees with the gray leaves—the storm ripped off a top branch. Kadran didn't even see it coming in the wind and rain. Went through her shoulder like a set of barbed arrows."

Nylan winced, but stepped up his pace.

He was halfway through the second bin in lander three when Ayrlyn joined him and started at the other end of the bins.

Nylan ran through an emergency medical kit. "There are a couple of modules missing here."

"Don't bother with that, Nylan." Ayrlyn frowned. "Great help here. This one says it's the emergency surgery section, and here's the section for emergency childbirth. Someone's been into it, but it's been resealed."

"Be a while before we need that." Nylan glanced through the lander door, but did not see the all-too-visibly-pregnant Ellysia. "How Gerlich . . ." He turned back and discarded the single remaining bone-splint kit.

"There are some stupid ones left. Every generation there always are. Not many, but she'd never considered birth control. Now, what about this—standard first aid—"

"That's it. We need to run that over to Jaseen."

"I'll do that. See if you can find any more. We might need them. Who knows what happened to those who were caught out in the open?" Ayrlyn grasped the sealed package and left while Nylan carefully worked through the dwindling medical supplies, before finding another sealed package of surgical dressings. He decided against taking them, but set the package in the now-empty first bin before leaving the lander.

In the short time he'd been in the lander, Ryba had managed to start the process of restoring order. Kyseen was rebuilding the cook fire, and straightening up that area, while Huldran had managed to divert the main flow of water from the bean field and had a crew working on the potatoes.

Ryba was checking over the mounts, and Istril headed off with two others to see about rounding up two mounts that had left the makeshift corral.

Everything, except the tower, it seemed, was makeshift, and he still didn't have the demon-damned thing finished— or even the plans worked out for the bathhouse and laundry addition and the jakes in the tower.

Slowly he walked back to the tower, where the lower level lay filled with puddles, one of them almost a half cubit deep. Drains. He had forgotten drains—another mistake to be rectified.

When he reached the tower yard, and the slowly vanishing puddles, he turned and looked up, studying the rain, now only falling steadily in a form somewhere between a fine mist and a heavy drizzle. The piles of white hailstones, like bleached bones, stood out on the green of the meadow.

Then he walked up into the tower and started up the stairs to check on the damage to the east roof.

As he climbed, he wondered about his brick-making and the crude oven, then shook his head. That had been low tech, and if the rains had carried it away, he would find a way to rebuild it.

XXIX

HISSL STARES INTO the glass, looking at the waving stalks of grass, and at the burned fort, with the few wisps of smoke still threading into the sky. Concentrating again, he waits for the image to re-form, and it does, showing an empty road that would lead to Berlitos, should he desire the glass to follow the track.

There are no signs of the Jeranyi. Hissl tugs at his chin. Ildyrom must have pulled back a long ways, perhaps as far as Berlitos.

The wizard frowns, and the white mists fill the glass, eventually showing a line of horse troopers trudging down a forest road behind the fir-tree banner. Since there are no forests near Clynya, that means Ildyrom has in fact stopped pressing his claim on the grasslands—for now.

The white wizard shakes his head. "You'll be stuck here for seasons—seasons, angel-damn!" His words are low, but they hiss with frustration.

He looks around the small room, then out the narrow window into the blue of the morning and over the low thatched roofs of Clynya toward the West Fork he cannot see from the second story of the barracks. As he does, the image fades from the glass.

"Terek . . . with you scheming in Lornth, how will I ever get out of here? If I'm successful, Ildyrom won't get the grasslands back, and I'll be stuck here. If I'm not . . ." He shakes his head and looks down at the blank glass.

In time, he studies the mirror once more, and the mists swirl, and in the midst of the swirling white appears the Roof of the World, and the black tower that stands, despite the storm, and the silver-haired figure in olive-black who trudges up the stone steps. The glass also shows the aura of darkness that surrounds the man in the glass.

"A mage, and he knows it not." After a time, Hissl gestures, and the image vanishes, leaving only a blank and flat mirror on the small table.

Finally, he smiles, tightly, thinking about bandits and the Roof of the World.

XXX

STANDING OUTSIDE THE lander, with the light wind that promised fall ruffling his hair, Nylan slowly finished the gruel that passed as morning porridge, along with cold bread, his thoughts on the tower once more.

Huldran and the others had been less than pleased when Nylan had insisted on putting a drain in the bottom of the tower, nor had Ryba been happy when he had used the laser to drill through some of the rock.

"A waste of power . . ."

Nylan disagreed—the lowest level of the tower needed to be dry. Dampness destroyed too many things. He swallowed the last bite of the lumpy gruel with a shudder and glanced toward the tower. At least the roof and doors were in place, and he could concentrate on making the place livable. Outside the front door, Cessya and Weblya had already begun to haul stones in to fill the space between the walls of the causeway.

The engineer walked over to the wash kettle and rinsed the wooden platter before racking it. He hoped that they could finish the tower kitchen before long—but he needed to work out the problems with making the water pipes. If the climate were warmer he could have just built a covered aqueduct, but that would freeze solid for half the year.

He walked back toward Ryba, his eyes rising back toward the dark stones of the tower that was somehow tall, squat, and massive all at the same time.

"What are you thinking?" asked Ryba. "You're not really even here."

"About water pipes, kitchens, laundry." He paused. "About building a bathhouse or whatever."

"I suppose you want to start a soap factory, too."

"Someone else can worry about that. I'm an engineer, not a chemist."

"Good." She laughed harshly. "The bandits are whittling away at our ammunition. We need more blades. Can you coax out another two dozen?"

"Another two dozen? Don't most of the marines have one?"

"They'll need two."

Nylan pursed his lips. "I can do some. I don't know how many. I thought the cells would be the problem, but there's a raggedness in the powerheads."

"And you had to drill a drain?"

"Yes . . . if you didn't want all the supplies to mold and mildew."

She shook her head. "You're stubborn."

"Not so stubborn as you are." Nylan wondered how long before everyone would think he was obsessed with building, if they didn't already. Why didn't they see that they had one chance—just one?

A single *clang* on the triangle echoed through the morning. Ryba and Nylan looked up to see Llyselle ride across the meadow. Llyselle bounced slightly in the saddle, but Nylan knew that he bounced even more when he rode. He didn't have Sybran nomad blood—or training. The tall, silver-haired marine reined up outside the cooking area, but before she could dismount, Ryba stood there, Nylan not far behind her.

"There's a herder down there, waving a white flag," Llyselle announced. "He's got some sheep or goats, and something in cages."

"Let's hope he wants to sell something." Ryba pointed at the nearest marine—Siret. "Go find Narliat, and Ayrlyn, and ask them to join us."

"Yes, ser." Siret glanced at Nylan with a strange look in her deep green eyes, then turned away, but Nylan could tell she was definitely thicker in the midsection, unlike Selitra. Yet Selitra had been sleeping with Gerlich, and she didn't seem pregnant. But Siret, the silent silver-haired guard?

Before long, Narliat limped up, using a cane, but without the makeshift leg cast he had worn for so long.

Ryba repeated Llyselle's explanation.

"Most herders would not come this high with you angels here. Once this was good summer pasture, but now . . ." The former armsman shrugged. "Times have been hard, and your coins are good. He would not have to drive animals all the way to Lornth or to Gallos. The cages—they might be chickens."

"What does the white banner mean?" asked Ryba.

"Ser Marshal, it means he wants to get your attention. Beyond that? I do not know."

"Hmmmm . . . we need all the supplies we can buy or grow, and they probably won't be enough." Ryba glanced up at the tower and then back to Ayrlyn and Narliat. "How do we approach this herder?"

"You walk down with a handful of people, I suppose," began Ayrlyn.

"Just one or two—not the marshal or the mage," added Narliat. "Powerful angels should not start negotiations with herders."

"We did with Skiodra," pointed out Ryba.

"That, it was different, because it was under a trade flag and Skiodra was himself there, and he is a powerful trader."

"If you say so." Ryba glanced around. "All right. Everyone! Get your weapons. Let's hope we won't need them. Meet by the triangle at the watch station on the right . . . by the road to the tower." She turned to Fierral. "Where's Gerlich?"

"Where he is every morning. Out hunting." The head marine's voice bore overtones of disgust.

"If he shows up . . . tell him, too."

Nylan hurried to the lander where he reclaimed his sidearm and the blade he had forged, which was too small for the overlarge scabbard. He tried not to fall over the damned thing every time he wore it. Ryba might never be without her weapons, but he couldn't work with a pistol at his side and a blade banging his leg.

Ryba had the big roan saddled when he reached the watch station.

The herder waited below at the foot of the ridge. Occasionally, the man looked up the slope, then back at the milling sheep, or shifted his weight as he leaned against the side of the cart.

Finally, after talking to Fierral and Istril, Ryba nodded.

Carrying the small circular shields they had reclaimed from the last brigands, with Narliat between them, Berlis and Rienadre walked down the ridge toward the herder, who had a white banner leaned against his cart. Beyond the herder were perhaps five ewes with their lambs.

Nylan and Ryba watched from the rocks at the top of the ridge as the three neared the herder. The herder and the three talked, with Narliat doing most of the speaking. Finally, Berlis turned uphill and gestured.

Neither Nylan nor Ryba could make out the words.

"Do you think it's all right?" asked the captain.

"I don't know, but nothing's going to happen if someone doesn't head down there. From what Berlis is trying to tell us, the trader won't trade unless a more important person appears."

"I don't like this," muttered Ryba.

"All right, ride down. That gives you more mobility—and have Istril and some of the others ready to charge like those old Sybran cavalry."

"Very funny."

"We need the sheep, and maybe those chickens, and you know it. So does the herder. He's gambling that you just won't steal them. You're gambling that it's not some kind of setup."

"Wish I could see . . . everything . . ."

Below them, Berlis gestured again.

"You can't?"

"It comes and goes, and some of it . . . makes no sense. Some is too clear." Ryba vaulted into the saddle. "Fierral! Istril! Stand by. Llyselle, you ride with me—on the right."

Nylan noted that the trees at the base of the ridge were on the right, but before he could speak the two started down the ridge, riding slowly. He kept watching, but nothing changed. The herder watched as the two riders neared, and so did Berlis and Rienadre.

Abruptly, Llyselle's horse reared, sending the silver-haired marine flying. Ryba bent low in the saddle, turned her roan toward the trees, and charged.

"Let's go!" Fierral and the others galloped down the ridge.

Feeling as if he were making a big mistake, Nylan followed on foot. He was halfway down the ridge, his worn boots skidding on the rocky ground before he realized he was alone.

Ahead, the mounted marines charged into the trees. Nylan heard the reports of the sidearms and saw the sun flash off Ryba's blade. He kept moving, but, by the time he neared the herder's cart, the action was over.

Llyselle was limping toward the cart, looking uphill past Nylan, and the engineer turned and saw Ayrlyn riding down, carrying two large plastic sacks with green crosses on them—medical supplies or dressings. Nylan wished he'd been smart enough to think of a horse or medical supplies, or something. Instead, he'd just run into the middle of what could have been trouble, too late to help and without any support.

He pursed his lips as Ayrlyn rode past. There was still trouble. Llyselle was holding her right arm, cradling it, as though it were broken or injured, and Narliat and the herder were still under the cart. Fierral and Istril had charged off downhill through the trees.

Nylan kept walking, his eyes checking on all sides. As he neared the cart and the beginning of the forest on his right, he saw several bodies near the trees, and one on the open ridge ground, with two marines beside her.

The downed marine was Stentana—an arrow through her eye. An arrow, for darkness' sake.

Nylan counted eight brigand bodies and, his eyes elsewhere, almost tripped over his scabbard. He caught himself and turned at the sound of hooves, reaching for the blade, but the riders were Istril and Fierral, and they led two more horses, each with a body slung across it.

Nylan turned toward the cart. There Ayrlyn was treating a wound caused where an arrow seemed to have ripped into Berlis's thigh. Llyselle stood beside Berlis, waiting.

"Strip the bodies and make a cairn down there, over by the rocks," commanded Ryba. "No sense in dragging them up the mountainside. Take all their clothes. We need rags as well as anything—but the clothes all need washing, and then some."

Since he didn't seem to have been much use, Nylan plodded toward the woods, and grabbed one of the bodies by the boots and dragged the corpse toward the rocks where Ryba had pointed, but toward an area where small boulders seemed more plentiful. Damned if he were going to make burial hard on himself, not for men killed as a result of their own failed ambush.

Nylan forced himself to strip the bandit, barely more than a youth despite the straggly beard and the scar across one cheek. The bandit's purse held only two silvers and a worn copper, but both silvers were shiny. The man wore a quiver, but had dropped his bow somewhere. He had no blade, just a knife that was badly nicked. As for clothing, he had worn a tattered and faded half cloak that had once been green of some shade, a ragged shirt, once brown, trousers, also once brown, but of a differing shade, and two mismatched boots, both with holes in the soles. No undergarments, and no jewelry.

After looking at the threadbare garments and cloak, Nylan agreed with Ryba's assessment of their use as rags. He also wondered how many vermin the clothes harbored. At the same time, in a way, he felt sorry for the dead man. Life couldn't have been that easy for him.

"Another attack?" Gerlich had ridden in from the trail to the west, the one that looped north from the ridge before descending and turning west, unlike the other two—one of which descended around the lower east side of the ridge and eventually led to Nylan's brickworks. Across his saddle lay three large and brown-furred rodentlike creatures, already gutted.

"This one was a little different," Nylan explained as Siret dragged another body across the ground and let it fall next to the one Nylan had stripped. "They used that herder there as bait."

"Dump the clothes there in that pile," ordered Fierral, still mounted, and pointed to the stack Nylan had made.

"What about the coins and other stuff?" asked Siret.

"You can keep a knife—if you don't have a belt knife," answered Ryba. "If you do, pass it to someone who doesn't. You can keep the local coppers, too. Share them if you think you can. Give any silvers or golds to the comm officer—Ayrlyn. We'll need those to buy food and supplies—from the next honest trader."

"They seem to have things well in hand," observed Gerlich.

The herder and Narliat had crawled out from beneath the cart. Berlis and Rienadre stalked toward them. So did Huldran and another seven marines. The herder looked up at the circle of marines. Then he slumped into a heap.

"He's just fainted," said Ayrlyn softly.

"Never saw angry women with blades," snorted Ryba. "What about the others?"

"I did nothing," pleaded Narliat. "Nothing, I swear it."

"Just stuff it," growled Berlis as Ayrlyn sprayed a disinfectant into the guard's wound. "Don't tell me how you didn't see it coming."

Llyselle leaned against the side of the cart, her face paler than her silver hair.

Brawwwwkkk . . . awwwkkkk . . . From the handful of cages behind the injured marine came the sound of chickens.

"Are there any other bandits around?" Ryba asked Fierral.

"Istril and I chased down the two who ran. Istril was complaining that she had to shoot them. She didn't want to waste the ammunition."

"We need to think about bows," snapped Gerlich as he eased his horse next to Ryba's. "We need some sort of long-range weapon."

"There are four or five here. Two got broken," announced Siret.

"We'd better start learning to use them," suggested Gerlich.

Nylan frowned. Gerlich was right. But could he build a better bow? One with a longer range? Out of some of the composites in the lander?

"Look out," whispered Istril. "The engineer's got that look again."

"What about these damned sheep?" asked Gerlich, gesturing around at the near dozen ewes and lambs.

"They're all ours," snapped Ryba. "We'll let the herder go."

"Don't forget the chickens," Nylan said. "Good source of protein."

"Pay him one copper. I only suggest," Narliat added hastily as Berlis glared at him while Ayrlyn continued wrapping a tape dressing around the wounded marine's thigh.

"Local custom?" asked Nylan.

"It is traditional for treachery. He cannot claim he was not paid."

"Fine. Nylan—you and Ayrlyn take care of it," said Ryba. "Just make sure he understands."

"He already understands," said Ayrlyn. "That's why he passed out."

Ryba pointed toward Denalle and Rienadre. "You two, and anyone else you can round up, figure out how to get these animals up over the ridge and into the grass on the west end. We can use the manure to fertilize the crops—or maybe compost it some way for next year. I'm no herder, but they'll provide meat at the least and maybe wool, if we can figure out what to do with it." She gestured up the ridge.

"Yes, ser." The two nodded and looked at the sheep, then slowly circled downhill of the milling animals.

The herder moaned, and Berlis levered her blade out, wincing, but the point was firm as it rested against the herder's neck. The man's eyes bulged.

"Go ahead. Explain it to him, Narliat," Ayrlyn suggested. She rummaged through the prepackaged medical gear.

"I have no copper."

Nylan fished out the purse he had taken from the dead bandit, extracted the single copper, and handed the worn coin to Narliat. "There."

Narliat looked at Nylan, turned to the herder, then to Berlis. Berlis retracted the sword. The herder swallowed, but did not move.

"Sit up," Nylan commanded in his poor Anglorat—good enough because the herder sat up slowly. "Go ahead," the engineer told Narliat.

"This is your payment. It is full payment for your treachery. There is no other payment, save death, should you reject this coin."

The herdsman gulped, looking toward Ryba. "Kind lady . . . they made me. They would have killed me. My ewes, they are half my flock . . . my children will suffer . . . Take the fowl . . . take them as my gift, but . . . the flock . . . ?"

Ryba's eyes were as hard as emerald. "Your treachery has killed a dozen men, not that they were worth much, and one of my marines, who was worth much. Another has lost the use of her arm, and a third took an arrow in the thigh. Don't talk of suffering."

Narliat looked at Nylan, and the engineer realized that the herder had not understood a word. "Our people have suffered from your treachery," Nylan explained in Old Anglorat. "You helped make that treachery. The marshal has been generous. Will you take payment or death?"

Narliat's slight nod confirmed that Nylan's words met the formula.

"And," Nylan added, though he could not have said why, "do not think to take the coin and reject the offer. Do not take the coin and curse us. For then you will live all your days as though you had died, and you will be tortured endlessly." He could feel something flash before—or from—his eyes.

The herder fell forward in another dead faint.

"Friggin' torps," said Berlis. "Man has no guts. Faints twice, and nothing touched him."

"The . . . mage . . . did," stuttered Narliat. "He—the herder—will never think a dangerous thought again."

"Impressive," said Ayrlyn.

The herder groaned and slowly picked himself up. "The coin . . . the copper . . . please . . . please . . ."

Narliat handed him the copper.

"Please . . . can I take my cart? Please let me depart."

"Go on," said Ryba.

The herder looked at Nylan.

"Go. Never forget."

"No, great one. No. No." The herder shivered as he slowly unstacked the four crates, each with a pair of chickens with reddish-brown feathers. Then he took the pony's reins and untied them from the stake in the ground. Leaving the white banner on the ground, he led the cart away, looking back over his shoulder every few paces.

"We need a cart," Nylan said, looking at the departing herder.

"A cart?" asked Ayrlyn.

"For firewood, bricks, you name it . . ."

"Fine," laughed Ayrlyn. "Saryn and I will work on it."

"You?"

"Why not? If you can build towers and forge swords, surely two of us can find a way to build a simple cart."

"Now that you've disposed of those logistics, how did you manage that last bit of terror, Nylan?" asked Ryba.

Ayrlyn frowned, but stepped back from the marshal as Ryba edged the roan closer to the engineer.

"What?"

"Terrifying that poor sot."

"He's not a sot, ser," said Berlis. "He's a worthless hunk of meat." Then she paused. "I have to admit that the engineer scared me for an instant, and I didn't even know what he was saying."

"I'm waiting, Nylan," said Ryba lightly.

The engineer finally shrugged. "A little applied psychology and a menacing tone in a foreign accent." His head throbbed slightly as he said the words, and he frowned.

"Psychology, my left toe," muttered Ayrlyn under her breath. "Wizardry, plain and simple."

Nylan flushed, but Ryba had eased her mount back slightly and missed the byplay. The engineer said more loudly, to catch Ryba's ear, "I still need to go down and check the brickworks. There's nothing I can do here right now, and I want to get the tower ready to live in."

Ryba opened her mouth, closed it, then said, "All right. I trust you'll use your senses to scout the way."

The slight emphasis on "senses" was not lost on the engineer, and he nodded. "I will, Marshal."

"Thank you, Honored Mage." She flushed at the title. "And Istril and Siret can ride with you." She laughed. "The silver angels."

Nylan frowned before he realized that the three of them all had the bright silver hair created by the underjump that had brought them to the Roof of the World.

"Siret can take Llyselle's mount," continued Ryba. "You can try one of the captured ones. They look spiritless enough even for you."

Nylan nodded. "That's fine."

". . . what was all that about?"

Nylan caught the question Siret whispered to Ayrlyn as he climbed into the saddle of the old bay.

"A little formality, that's all," Ayrlyn answered Siret in a dry tone.

After settling himself into the saddle, Nylan gingerly flicked the reins of the bay and followed Berlis and Istril toward the descending ridge road. As he bounced along, he wondered why he'd insisted on going to the brickworks. Was he worried that the brigands had found it and damaged it? Or because he had to do something after looking so stupid?

Belatedly recalling Ryba's admonition, he tried to sense beyond the trail that was still not a road, for all the travel between the clayworks and the tower. Slowly, he caught up with the marines.

"I'll go first," suggested Istril, "then the engineer."

Nylan started to object, then shut his mouth. If anything went wrong, with only three of them, it didn't really matter where he rode. Besides, given all the dead brigands, why would any who had survived stick around?

"Hate this frigging place," said Siret, now riding behind Nylan. "Everyone out to kill us, just because we're women."

"They seem to want to kill me and Gerlich as well," Nylan answered. "And Mertin might have had something to say about it. They don't seem to like any strangers."

"You're different, ser." Siret's voice held less anger. "The men here . . . they're not human."

"Even Narliat?"

"He's the same as the rest. He's just scared stiff of us, especially the captain, the second, and you, ser. Especially you, ser."

Why him? Ryba was far deadlier than Nylan. Why, Nylan

couldn't hit someone with a slug-thrower at nearly point-blank range.

The three rode down from the next rise in the rising and falling trail, and when Nylan glanced back, he saw only the sky, the plateau rocks, and the trees. Istril had opened more distance between them, and her head swung from side to side, her head cocked almost as though she were trying to listen for trouble or even sniff it out.

Nylan tried to follow her example, looking, sensing . . .

They continued down the winding trail, nearly silently, when a vague sense of unease drifted, as if on the wind, toward Nylan. He squinted, and looked toward the tall evergreens to the left, but the silence was absolute. That bothered him. All he could smell was the scent of pine, of fir.

But there was something . . . somewhere . . .

"Ser!" cried Siret.

Even before her words, Nylan had seen the flicker of motion to the left of the trail. As he yelled "Istril!" he turned in the saddle and drew and threw his blade toward the man who had stepped clear of the thick underbrush and leveled the bow at the slender marine who led the three angels.

In a fashion similar to working the ship's power net and the laser, Nylan smoothed the air flow around the spinning blade, extending its range, and somehow ensuring that the point struck first.

"Uhhh!" The brigand crumpled.

Nylan rode toward the forest, sending his senses into the trees, but felt no others nearby. Siret had ridden up beside him, her slug-thrower out in one hand. Istril had wheeled her horse, ducking low against her mount's back as she rode up.

Before the engineer and Siret reached the bandit, the figure convulsed, and a wave of whiteness flared across Nylan. He shivered and barely hung on to the saddle as the power of the death he had created washed over him.

"Ser? Are you all right?" Istril reined her mount up beside Nylan.

"He's fine," affirmed Siret.

"Fine . . . now," said Nylan after drawing a deep breath,

trying not to shake as he forced himself out of the reflex step-up that he hadn't even realized that he had triggered. He took another deep breath and glanced down at the dead brigand's young face—another man barely out of youth, looking for all the world almost like the one he had stripped farther up the mountain. Brothers? Or did a lot of dead bearded young men just look alike? He took another slow deep breath, wishing he had something to eat or drink.

Why all the bandits? Surely, the word was out that it was dangerous to take on the angels up in the mountains?

"You stopped him. He was going to shoot me, wasn't he?" asked Istril.

"Yes."

"Frigging right," added Siret, the deep green eyes cold.

"How did you know he was here?" asked Istril, adding belatedly, "Ser?"

"I just sort of felt that someone was here." Nylan dismounted and eased his blade from the bandit's chest, then wiped it clean before replacing it in the scabbard that the blade did not really fit. "And I couldn't reach him. Gerlich was right. We need longer-range weapons."

Istril studied him and pointed. "You have your sidearm."

Nylan swallowed. "I guess I really didn't think. So I threw the blade. I hoped it would distract him, anyway."

His head throbbed with the lie. He'd hoped to kill the bandit, plain and simple, and instinctively he'd known that he couldn't have with the slug-thrower. He'd always been a lousy shot. So he added, "I hoped it would kill him, but I wasn't sure I could do it. Not with a pistol." With his uttering of the truth, the sharp throbbing in his skull faded into a dull ache. The engineer rubbed his forehead. What was happening to him? Throwing blades on a low-tech planet, getting headaches from lies, forging blades with magic—or the equivalent, knowing that he could kill with a blade and not a sidearm. Was he dreaming? Was he dead?

He shook his head. The pain, the aches, the constant tension—they all seemed too real for death or dreams.

"Are you certain you're all right?" Istril's eyes continued

to survey the forest to their left, then the cliffs to the right.

"Yes. Mostly." Nylan bent and went through the brigand's purse. A few coppers, and three shiny silvers. A thin gold ring. A beat-up knife. He checked the clothing and boots. "Boots worn through and stuffed with some old leather." He stood and sniffed. "He had to have a mount somewhere."

The engineer cast out his senses again, searching not for more brigands, but the horse. "I'm not sure, but I think his mount is tethered back there."

"What about more bandits?" asked Istril.

"We thought we had them all," said Siret, "and this one popped up."

The engineer shook his head. "There aren't any. Not alive."

"Narliat says you're a wizard, too—a black one. Do you know what that means?" Istril glanced back toward the trail and then focused on Nylan.

"No." Nylan took the reins and began to lead his mount through the trees toward the horse tethered behind a massive pine just past a large boulder sunk in pine needles. "A black wizard? I've got enough trouble just being an engineer."

Istril ducked and rode after him. After a moment, so did Siret.

XXXI

"Now that you have reclaimed the grasslands, when will you reclaim the Roof of the World? And your father's honor?" The gray-haired Lady Ellindyja shifts her not-inconsiderable bulk on the upholstered bench in the alcove. Her fingers dart across the embroidery hoop, the needle shining like a miniature blade that she deftly wields.

Sillek stands behind the carved chair with the purple

cushion, resting his arms on the back. "The grasslands are reclaimed only so long as Koric and Hissl remain in Clynya. The moment they leave, Ildyrom's forces will return, in even greater numbers, no doubt. I send armsmen into the Westhorns, and I won't only lose the grasslands, but half the land between Clynya and Rohrn."

"If you cannot reclaim that honor, you must do something to solidify your position. You need an heir, Sillek." His mother's voice is flat. "You know you do."

"I also need score five more armsmen, control of Rulyarth, and Ildyrom in his grave."

"Not to mention regaining control of the Roof of the World." The needle continues to dart through the white fabric, trailing crimson-red thread.

"As I have told you, most honored mother, that might be a very bad idea, right now." Sillek straightens and purses his lips. "A very bad idea."

"A bad idea? To reclaim your patrimony? Given all that your father has done for you, Sillek, how could you possibly even think that, let alone say it so soon after his last sacrifice for you?" The glittering needle darts through the fabric like a cavalry blade chasing a fleeing footman.

Sillek waits until the pace of the needle slows. "I took your advice, dear Mother, and we are already reaping its benefit, and it has cost us little."

"Costs? You talk so much of costs." The needle shimmers, then plunges into the fabric. "Costs are for merchants, or for scoundrel traders."

"I am not being clear, I fear."

"Clear? I fear you are all too clear. You will give up your patrimony because your enemies are too much for you."

"I do not intend to forfeit my patrimony, Mother dear, and your assumption that I would do so speaks poorly for me, and not well for you. I would certainly never wish to relinquish that which my honored sire had gathered for my benefit or the benefit of our people." Sillek walks toward the alcove.

"Could you explain your logic to your poor benighted

mother, Sillek, Lord of the Realm? How can you retain your patrimony when you refuse to reclaim it? Are you a magician now?" The needle stitches another crimson loop in a droplet of blood that falls from a gray sword.

Sillek smiles. "From what Terek has told me, and from my other sources, so far the angels on the Roof of the World have destroyed at least three bands of brigands trying to claim my reward—that reward you suggested so wisely. And two of the lesser angels have been killed, and four or five wounded, while close to a score of brigands have been destroyed." His smile turns into a laugh. "I couldn't do nearly so well, and I certainly am in no position to lose another score three of trained armsmen."

Sillek glances out the window and toward the river. "Next spring . . . after winter up there—then we'll see."

"I do hope so, Sillek, dear. I do hope so." The sharp needle stitches in another loop of blood.

Sillek's lips tighten, but he does not speak.

XXXII

NYLAN OPENED HIS eyes slowly in the gray light that came through the open tower window. Although fall had scarcely arrived, the nights had begun to chill, enough so that the single blanket seemed thin, indeed. Blankets were not used in large numbers on spacecraft, and the few that had been brought down felt less than adequate for the winter ahead. That meant another set of items to be bought from the all-too-infrequent traders. Nylan blinked as he wondered how they could pay for all that they still needed.

Although the landers had been stripped of what would make the tower more habitable, that had provided little enough. The marines occupied the third level of the tower. Gerlich, Saryn, Ayrlyn, and Narliat occupied part of the fourth level. The fifth was used for miscellaneous storage, and Ryba and Nylan rattled around in a sixth level that had little in it except for the two lander couches lashed together and a few weapons and personal effects.

Only the shutters on the second and third levels were finished, the results of Saryn's and Ayrlyn's handicrafts, and there were no internal doors. Rags had been pieced together to curtain off the two jakes and provide some privacy. Nylan hoped that they could finish the bathhouse and additional jakes facilities before too long—not to mention the shutters.

As he moved slightly, Ryba's eyelids fluttered, and she moaned. He waited, but she did not open her eyes. So Nylan slowly shifted his weight more in order to look out through the casement. A trace of white rime frosted the outer edge of the window ledge, but the whiteness seemed to vanish as the first direct rays from the sun touched the dark stone. The hint of wood smoke drifted in the window, blown down from the chimney momentarily.

Over the crude rack in the corner hung their clothes, including the ship jackets that probably would not be heavy enough for the winter ahead.

Nylan's eyes shifted back to Ryba's face, to the curly jet-black hair cut so short and the pale clear skin, to the thin lips and the high cheekbones. Her eyelids fluttered again, and she groaned.

"Not yet . . . not yet," she murmured.

Nylan waited, almost holding his breath.

"No . . ."

He reached out and touched the cool bare shoulder. "It's all right. It's all right."

Ryba shook her head and moistened her lips, but her eyes did not open for a moment. Then she shifted her weight on the lander couch and looked directly at the engineer. "No it's not. I was dying, and I won't finish everything that needs to be done for Westwind, or for Dyliess."

"It was just a dream . . ." Nylan paused. "It was a dream, wasn't it?"

Ryba shook her head again, and squinted as she sat up.

Then she swung her feet off the couch, letting the blanket fall away from her naked figure, until it covered only her waist and upper thighs. Her back to Nylan, she faced the open window, looking out toward the northern peaks that showed a light dusting of snow from the night before. The faintest touch of yellow and brown tinged the bushes and meadow grasses.

"It wasn't a dream. It was real. My hair was gray, and I was lying here, except I was in a big wooden bed, and there was glass in the windows, and people in gray leathers were standing around me." Ryba shivered and then stood, padding to the clothes rack, where she pulled on her undergarments and then the brown leather trousers and an old shirt—both plunder.

"If your hair had become gray, that had to be a long time from now." He stood and stretched.

"Nylan . . . I wasn't finished, and it hurt that I didn't finish."

"Ryba," Nylan offered gently, "no one who really cares about anything is ever finished with life. And you care a lot." He forced a smile, then began to dress himself.

Ryba finished with the bone buttons of the trousers and then buttoned the shirt. "You're probably right, but it was real . . . too real."

"Another one of your senses of what will happen?"

She nodded. "They come at odd times, but some have already happened."

"Oh?" He hadn't heard that part.

"Little things, or not so little. I saw your tower almost from the beginning—and I know what the bathhouse will look like." She sat back on the joined lander couches that served as their bed and pulled on her boots.

"Who is Dyliess?"

"Our daughter. I'm pregnant, and she'll be born in the spring, just before the passes melt."

Nylan's mouth dropped open. "You . . . never . . ."

"She'll be a good daughter, and don't you forget that, Engineer." Ryba smiled. "I wanted the timing right. You can't do that much in the winter here, and next summer . . . we'll have a lot of problems when people realize we're here to stay. They think the winter will finish us, but it won't."

"Promise?" he asked.

"I can promise that, at least so long as you keep building." She stood in the open doorway at the top of the steps. "I want things to be right for Dyliess, and they will be."

"A daughter . . . you're sure?"

"You wanted a son?"

"I never thought—one way or another." He shook his head, still at a loss, still amazed.

"You'll have a son. I'll promise that, too." Her voice turned soft, almost sad.

"You don't . . ."

"I know what to promise, Nylan. I do." Her eyes met his, and they were deep and chill, filled with pain. "There's no time to be melancholy, Engineer."

The forced cheer in her voice contradicted her calm and pale face. As they looked at each other, Nylan could hear the hum of voices from below, and the smell of something cooking, although he wasn't sure he was in any hurry to find out what Kyseen had improvised for breakfast.

"We do our best, Nylan, in spite of what may be."

"May be or will be? Can these visions of yours be changed?" Nylan sat down on the couch-bed and reached for his shipboots, his eyes still on her.

Ryba shrugged. "Maybe I only see what can't be changed. Maybe it can be. I don't know, because this is something new."

"All of this is something new." Nylan pulled on his shipboots, getting so worn that he could feel stones through them.

"You need new boots. You ought to check the spares. We've only got about twenty pair left over."

"I suppose you're right." Nylan stood.

"I have to be. I'm the marshal. You have to, also. You're the mage. Now that we've settled that, let's see if breakfast is remotely palatable." She started down the steps, the hard heels of her boots echoing off the harder stone, and Nylan followed, trying not to shake his head. A daughter, for darkness' sake, and Ryba had named her, and seen her in a vision of her own death. At that, he did shake his head. The Roof of the World was strange, and getting stranger even as he learned more.

They walked toward the pair of tables stretched out from the hearth. In a room that could have handled a dozen or more tables that size with space to spare, the two almost looked lost. The benches had finally been finished, and for the moment everyone could sit at the same time.

Ryba marched toward the head of the table, but Nylan lagged, still looking around the great room, amazed that they had completed so much in barely a half year. Of course, the tower was really not much more than a shell, but still . . . He smiled for a moment.

Breakfast in the great hall had gotten regularized—a warm drink, usually a bitter grass and root tea; cold fried bread; some small slices of cheese; any meat left over from supper—if there had been meat served—and something hot, although it could be as odd as batter-dipped and fried greens or kisbah, a wild root that Narliat had insisted was edible. Edible kisbah might be, reflected Nylan, but something that tasted like onions dipped in hydraulic oil had little more to recommend it than basic nutrients. It made the heavy fried bread seem like the best of pastries by comparison. So far the few eggs dropped by the scrawny chickens had gone into the bread or something else fixed by Kyseen.

"Good morning, Nylan," said Ayrlyn.

"How did you sleep last night?" the engineer asked the redhead, who huddled inside a sweater and a thermal jacket and sat on the sunny south casement ledge that overlooked the meadow and fields.

"Not well. It's getting cold. When will the furnace be finished?"

"Not until after the shutters," he answered.

"The shutters won't help that much."

"Unless we cut a lot more wood and finish the shutters,

the furnace won't be much use," Nylan pointed out.

"Don't we have any armaglass at all?" Ayrlyn shivered inside the jacket.

"There's enough for six windows." He put his lips together and thought. "Maybe eight. Most of them ought to go in here. These are south windows."

"That's why I'm sitting here trying to warm up. I'm not a Sybran nomad," Ayrlyn pointed out, turning slightly on the stone so that the sun hit her back full on. "Saryn and I could make simple frames that would go on pivots if you could mortar the pivot bolts or whatever in place. Can you cut the armaglass?"

"If the laser lasts." Nylan laughed, then frowned as his stomach growled.

"You need to eat."

"I can hardly wait." The engineer glanced toward the table where Ryba was serving herself.

"It's not bad this morning—some fried meat that has some taste, but not too much, if you know what I mean, and there's a decent hot brew. Narliat showed Selitra a bush that actually makes something close to tea. Bitter, but it does wake you up."

"All right. Bring me a window design, and we'll see what we can do." He started toward the table.

"We need salt, demon-damn!" Gerlich's voice rose from the end of the table nearest the completed but empty hearth. "Without salt, drying meat's a tricky thing, and I don't want to smoke everything."

"I'll have Ayrlyn put it high on the trading list." Ryba's voice, quieter than Gerlich's, still carried the length of the room.

Gerlich strode by, wearing worn and tattered brown leathers rudely altered to fit his large frame and carrying a bow and quiver. "Good day, Nylan."

"Good day. How's the bow going?"

Gerlich stopped and shrugged. "It doesn't shoot far enough, or with enough power, but it's good for some of the smaller animals—the furry rodents." He grinned. "I'm tanning those pelts—Narliat told me some of the roots and an acorn they use—and by winter I might have enough for a warm coat." The grin faded. "There's not much meat on the fattest ones, and I don't know how good the hunting will be when the snow gets deep."

"I don't, either." Nylan paused. "Let me think about it."

"Do that, Engineer." Gerlich raised the bow, almost in a mocking salute, and began to walk toward the main door. "I'm going to try my luck at fashioning a larger bow."

"Good luck, Great Hunter." Nylan made his way to the table and sat down across from Ryba.

"It's not bad," she said. "The meat, I mean."

"What is it?"

"I didn't ask."

"One of those rodents, baked and then fried," said Kyseen, replacing the battered wooden platter with another half-filled with strips of fried meat. "The stove makes all the difference, and the bread even tastes like bread now. The eggs help, but those chickens don't lay them fast, and I'm letting 'em hatch a few, 'cause we'll need another cock, a rooster"—the cook flushed—"before long."

"If we had windows and that furnace," suggested Siret, with a shiver, "that would help, too."

Nylan glanced at her, and she looked away.

"You'll warm up a lot before long," added Berlis.

The silver-haired Siret flushed.

Nylan felt sorry for the pregnant marine and added, "I'm working on the furnace . . . as soon as we have more bricks." Gingerly, he used his fingers to take several strips of the fried rodent, and two slices of bread. There was no cheese, but there was a grass basket filled with green berries. He tried one, and his mouth puckered.

"Those green berries are real tart, ser," said Berlis, glancing at Siret.

Siret flushed, but said quietly, "It might have been better if that arrow had been centered between both thighs. It would have fit right there."

"Enough," said Ryba, but Siret was already walking past

the end of the table with no intention of returning. The marshal turned her eyes to Berlis. "Comments like that could get you killed."

"Yes, ser." Berlis's voice was dull, resigned.

Nylan ate more of the green berries and the fried rodent strips without comment. The bread was good, and he finished both slices down to the crumbs.

"What are you planning today?" Ryba asked.

"I'll try to squeeze in two more blades before I go back to the bathhouse. What about you?"

"Trying to put up a more permanent fence for the sheep. They got into the beans last night."

"I'd rather have mutton anyway," came a low voice from down the table.

"I would, too," admitted Ryba, "but we need both."

Those left at the table laughed, and Ryba took some more rodent strips. So did Nylan. Before he had finished eating, Ryba stood and touched his arm. "I'll see you later."

His mouth full, Nylan nodded.

After he gulped down the rest of his breakfast, he walked out the causeway and down to the "washing area" of the stream. In the shade of the low scrub by the water were a few small ice fragments, which reminded the engineer that the bathhouse would soon become a necessity, not a luxury. He took a deep breath, and then an even deeper one when he splashed the icy water across his face. The sand helped get the grease off his hands, but he wished they had soap, real soap.

"Along with everything else." Nylan snorted and mumbled to himself. He tried to ignore the basic question that the soap raised. How could he or Ryba turn Westwind into an economically functioning community?

Because the south yard had become the meeting place, training yard, and thoroughfare, Nylan carted the laser equipment out to the cleared space beside the bathhouse structure on the north side of the tower.

After he checked the power levels and connected the cables, Nylan looked from the laser powerhead to the endurasteel braces, then at the half-finished north wall of the bathhouse. Huldran was mixing mortar, while Cessya and Weblya were carrying building stones.

He lowered the goggles, pulled on the gauntlets, and flicked the power switches. Huldran had finished mixing the mortar and had begun to set the higher stones in the north wall by the time Nylan had finished the rough shaping of the blade.

He cut off the power, pushed back the goggles, and sat down on the low sills of the unfinished east wall of the bathhouse. Working with the laser was as exhausting as lugging stones. While his mind understood that, it still felt strange. Then again, the whole planet was strange.

After he felt less drained, he stood and walked around the bathhouse and uphill to the spring where he filled the plastic cup that would probably wear out even before he did. He sipped the water, too cold to drink in large swallows, until he had emptied the cup. Then he refilled it and walked back down and checked the firin cells.

"How many more blades will you do, ser?" asked Huldran.

"I don't know. There are enough braces for another dozen, but whether the laser will last that long is another question."

"Do we have enough stone?"

"Probably not. This afternoon, I'll cut some more. We may have to finish this with bricks. I asked Rienadre to create some molds for bigger ones, closer to the size of the stones."

"That's good, but I'd rather have stone."

"So would I, but we're lucky we've gotten this far."

"I'd not call it luck, ser." Huldran flashed a brief smile.

"Perhaps not," said Nylan, thinking of the nine individual cairns overlooking the cliff. He lowered the goggles and triggered the power, beginning the final shaping of the blade.

When he looked up after slipping the blade into the quench trough, Huldran had finished the north wall and was beginning on the east wall. He removed the blade and set it on the wall to finish cooling.

Clang! Clang!

"Bandits!"

A half-dozen horses clattered over the ridge and down toward the tower. The riders had their blades out as they headed for the tower. Behind them, Nylan could see two marines following on foot.

Crack! Crack! The two shots from one of the rifles—presumably from the lookout at the tower's northern window on the upper level—resulted in one horseman dropping a blade and clutching his arm. He swung his mount around and back uphill, but the others galloped toward the tower, directly at Nylan.

The engineer groped for the blade that wasn't at his side. Then, with a deep breath, he flicked the power switches on the firin cells back on, and dropped the goggles over his eyes.

"It ought to work . . ." he muttered.

As the power came up, he forced himself to concentrate, trying to extend the beam focal point through what he thought of as the local net, creating a needle-edged lightknife.

"Get the mage! There!"

The remaining five riders turned toward Nylan. The ground vibrated underfoot as they pounded downhill.

A field of reddish-white surrounded the focal tip of the weapon as Nylan, more with his senses than his hands, slewed the lightblade across the neck of the leading rider, then the second.

Nylan staggered, as his eyes blurred, with the white backlash of death, and his head throbbed. He just stood, stockstill, trying to gather himself together, to see somehow, through the knives of pain that were his eyes.

Another set of hooves clattered across the hard ground, these coming from the south side of the tower. As the second rider finally went down, Istril and Ryba rode past the tower, their blades out.

Ryba's throwing blade flew, and the third rider—his mouth open in surprise—collapsed across his mount's neck. The horse reared, throwing the body half-clear, and dragging the rider by the one foot that jammed in the left stirrup all the way to the edge of the upper field before the horse finally stopped.

Crack! Crack!

The fourth horse staggered and fell, but the rider vaulted free and ran toward Nylan, his blade raised, and his free hand reaching for the shorter knife at his belt.

The engineer swung the laser toward the attacker, readjusting the focal length with his senses, fighting against his own headache and the knives in his eyes. The white-red fire blazed, and the flame bored through the man. The corpse pitched forward, and the blade clattered on the stones less than a body length from Nylan's feet. Nylan went down to his knees, and stayed there, flicking off the energy flow to the powerhead as he swayed under the impact of another death, yet worrying that he had not cut the power earlier. They had so little left and so much to do.

The single remaining raider ducked under Istril's slash, started to counter, and looked at the stump of his forearm as Ryba's second blade flashed downward.

"Yield!" demanded the marshal, her eyes cold as the ice on Freyja.

The redheaded man, his hair a mahogany, rather than the fire-red of Ayrlyn or Fierral, clutched at his stump without speaking.

"Yield or die!" yelled Nylan in Old Anglorat, forcing himself to his feet, still clutching the wand that held the laser's powerhead.

"I . . . Relyn of Gethen Groves of Lornth . . . I yield." The young fellow was already turning white.

"Nylan, can you handle this? There's still a bunch below the ridge." Ryba had pulled her blade from her other victim, not leaving the saddle, then turned the roan toward the ridge, Istril beside her.

Relyn swallowed as he heard her voice and watched the two gallop uphill, joined by four others.

"You'd better get down." Nylan glanced around. Both Huldran and Cessya had left, either to find mounts or follow on foot with their weapons. "If you don't want to bleed to death."

As he struggled out of the saddle, Relyn looked closely at Nylan, seeing for the first time Nylan's goggles and gauntlets. Then he pitched forward.

Nylan set aside the powerhead and walked toward the mount and its downed rider, noting the well-worked leather and the tailored linens of the rider. The black mare skittered aside, but only slightly as Nylan dragged the young man toward the laser.

"Hate to do this . . ." he said.

A brief burst of power at the lowest level and widest spread cauterized the stump.

Nylan kept looking toward the ridge, but no one appeared. With his senses he could tell that Relyn was still alive and would probably live since the blackened stump wasn't bleeding anymore. The engineer wished he could have done something else, but what? He laughed harshly. Here he was, worrying about whether he could have done a better job saving a man who had been out to remove his head.

He left the laser depowered and walked to the wall where he picked up the blade he had just forged. Wearing the gauntlets, he could use it—if the need arose.

Should he chase after the others—or wait? He decided to wait, hoping he wouldn't have to use the laser again. He wasn't sure he could take any more killing. Since Relyn was still unconscious, he walked toward the black mare, starting with her to round up the three horses that had remained in the area, tying their reins to various stones on the solid part of the north wall of the bathhouse. Then he forced himself to check through what remained of the three bodies that he had blasted in one way or another with the laser.

Ignoring the smell of charred flesh, he methodically raided purses, removed jewelry, and stacked weapons on the partly built east wall. Then he went to work removing those garments that might still be usable. All three mounts had heavy blankets rolled behind the saddles.

"Oooohhh . . ." Relyn moaned, but did not move.

Nylan looked toward the ridge. Finally, he looped some cord around the unconscious man's arms and feet, and then climbed onto the mare, who backed around several times before finally carrying Nylan and his recently forged blade toward the ridge.

The wave of death that reached him as he crested the ridge almost knocked him from the saddle. All he could do was hang on for a moment before starting downhill toward the figures on horseback and the riderless mounts.

As he descended, he began to discern individual figures, and almost all those he saw were in olive-black.

A black-haired figure turned the big roan toward him. "Nylan! Are there any more by the tower?"

"Just the one I tied up. The others are dead. What happened here?"

"There must have been nearly thirty of them . . ." Ryba smiled a grim smile. "A handful got away. The others, except one or two, are dead."

"What about us?"

Ryba shook her head. "For this sort of thing—it's not too bad. We lost two, I think, and Weindre took one of those blades in her left shoulder. We're claiming the spoils of war right now."

"Did you notice that these weren't bandits?" he asked.

"What do you mean?"

"Good mounts, good saddles, good clothes, good weapons, and jewelry and a lot of coins," Nylan explained.

"We'll talk about it later. We need to gather up everything." Ryba rode back downhill.

Since she seemed to have everything under control, Nylan turned the black around and headed back up the ridge to the tower.

By the time he had reached the uncompleted bathhouse and tied up the black, Relyn's eyes were open.

"I gave my word, Mage," he snapped.

"I wasn't sure, and you weren't awake enough for me to ask you," returned Nylan in Old Anglorat as he unfastened the cords. He extended his senses to Relyn's stump. "That probably hurts, but you'll live."

"Better I didn't."

"I doubt that." Nylan massaged his forehead, trying to relieve the pain in his eyes and the throbbing in his skull.

"Have you never been exiled, unable to return? That is what will happen when my sire discovers I was bested by women, and fewer of them than my own solid armsmen."

"All of us are exiles, young fellow. As for the women, you might note that they're not exactly the kind of women you have here." Nylan felt very safe with that assertion.

"You don't jest," returned the man dourly. "They had small thunder-throwers—and their blades . . . had we blades such as those, things would have been different. Did those blades come from the heavens, also?"

Nylan looked down at the stony ground.

"You look confounded, Mage."

"My name is Nylan." The engineer didn't wish to answer, but even the thought of not answering was increasing his headache.

"Ser Nylan, surely you know where came such blades."

The engineer took a deep breath. "I . . . made them."

"Here? On the Roof of the World?"

Nylan nodded.

"Light! I must be cozened into attacking angels each worth twice any armsman, and supported by a mage the like of which our poor world has never seen." Relyn struggled into a sitting position on the wall. "You killed three of my men, did you not?"

"Yes."

"Might I look at that blade?"

Nylan looked down at the blade he had thrust through the tool belt. "This? It's not finished. The hilt needs to be wrapped." He eased the blade out, half surprised that he had not cut himself with it, though it was shorter than the crowbars carried by the locals. He showed it to Relyn, who brushed the metal with the fingers of his left hand.

"Would that I had a blade like that," said the younger man.

"They are for . . . the guards . . . of Westwind."

"Westwind?"

Nylan gestured to the tower. "That's what we have named it."

"Westwind." Relyn shivered. "Westwind. A cold wind."

"Very cold," Nylan agreed, thinking about Ryba's coolness after the battle. What was he supposed to have done? Sprung into the saddle and chased after them? He laughed, thinking of himself bouncing along on the black.

"You laugh? You laugh?"

"Not at you, Relyn. At me. I was thinking about how awkward it is for me to ride a horse."

"I do not understand. Do not all men ride? All mages?"

"Yes, but we don't always ride horses into battle." Nylan turned at the sound of hooves, watching as Huldran and Cessya rode up.

"You're already organized, ser, aren't you?" asked Huldran.

"Pretty much," Nylan admitted.

"Who's the pretty boy?" asked Cessya.

"I think he's the guilty one. He thinks his father will disown him for being defeated by a bunch of women."

"He's not bad-looking."

"They think you're not bad-looking, Relyn," Nylan said. "Even if you are the one who plotted this. Might I ask why?"

Relyn shrugged. "I am the younger son, and when I heard that Lord Sillek had offered lands and a title to whoever reclaimed the Roof of the World . . . I spent what I had. Now . . . I am ruined."

"If you had succeeded, we'd have been ruined," pointed out Nylan as he turned to Huldran. "Who did we lose?"

"Weblya and Sheriz. Weindre got slashed up, but Jaseen says she'll pull through. A bunch of bruises and cuts for everyone else, except the marshal." Huldran sighed. "It's going to get tougher. We're just about out of rounds. Best to use what we've got left for the rifles."

"I wouldn't know," Nylan said, "but that would be my suggestion."

"That's what the marshal told us." Huldran turned in the saddle. "We've got to make another big cairn. Siret's bringing down the cart for the bodies. Since you're all right, ser . . ."

"Go on." Nylan waved the two off. "Do what you have to."

"A curious tongue you speak, Mage. Some words I understand. You are not, properly speaking, an armsman, are you?"

"No. I'm an engineer . . . like a smith. I build things, like the tower, or this."

"Yet you slew three men, and you forge blades that . . ." Relyn groped in the air with his left hand. "And the women, they are mightier warriors than you?"

"For the most part, yes."

"Demons of light save us, save us all, for they will change the world and all that is in it."

Of that, Nylan had no doubts. And, from what he'd seen, it would probably be a better world—but would it be one that had a place for him? From Ryba's actions and gestures, daughter or no daughter, he wondered.

XXXIII

THE GRAY CLOUDS churn out of the north, and a cold rain falls across Lornth, heavier showers splattering in waves across the red tile roofs of the town. From behind the leaded-glass window, Sillek's eyes look south toward the river, though he sees neither roofs nor river.

"Sillek, did you hear me?"

He turns toward the alcove where his mother the lady Ellindyja adjusts the white fabric over one wooden hoop, then slips the second hoop in place to hold the linen taut.

Golden thread trails from the needle she holds in her right hand.

"My dear mother, I fear I was distracted."

"Distracted? The Lord of Lornth cannot afford distractions, mental or otherwise, and certainly not distractions of the nature of the . . . lady . . . Kirandya." Ellindyja knots the end of the thread with motions that seem too precise for the white and pudgy fingers.

"I suppose not." Sillek's words are harsh as he sits on the straight-backed wooden chair opposite the alcove bench. "You were saying?"

"Ser Gethen—you might recall him, Sillek. He has more than score ten in armsmen, and all the lands between the rivers north of Carpa, even a hillside vineyard. I think he has several daughters near your age as well, and the middle one is said to be quite a beauty."

"I don't believe you were talking about his daughters."

"Ah . . . no." The golden thread completes the edge of a coronet on the linen, and the needle pauses. "Ser Gethen had a son, Relyn or Ronwin or something. He heard of your offer of lands and a minor title for destroying those witches on the heights—"

"Your idea, as I recall," interjects Sillek, "and a good one."

"And the young fellow gathered his funds and some armsmen and attacked the witches. He had a score and ten men, well armed. A half dozen returned."

"I had heard something of his exploit, but only this morning. Pray, tell me—how did this news come to you?"

"The youth's mother—Erenthla—she and I were once close, and she sent a messenger. That's of no matter now, Sillek. You certainly should not expect me to be totally cloistered. What is of import is that Ser Gethen is less than pleased. Erenthla—she is Lady of Gethen Groves—conveyed that. Rather clearly." Ellindyja's needle flickers through the fabric, creating another lobe to the coronet taking shape on the linen. "She hinted at her liege's loss of honor and that it might be linked to your failure to uphold that noble heritage bequeathed to you."

"Since you are determined to pin this upon me, why should I be disturbed? The young fellow knew the risks. Any raiding has risks. And he was a hothead, from what I recall. The kind that thinks every fight brings honor." Sillek stands, then his brows knit. "He was killed?"

"Far worse—he was captured. Being captured by women —even angels—makes it most humiliating, especially for his sire. Erenthla was clearly distraught. I should not have to point this out to you. Of course, Ser Gethen was forced to disown him, but he was Gethen's second son of two, and second in the succession, and there are only sisters after him."

"Ah . . . the matter becomes clearer. I should court one of those sisters in the guise of placating Ser Gethen . . ." Sillek paces back to the window and stares into the heavy rain. His lips tighten and his fingers knot around each other.

"I did not suggest that. It is not a bad idea, but I was talking of honor, of the honor your failures have cost you, and now, Ser Gethen. The honor you have steadfastly refused to acknowledge or uphold. The honor that you subjugate to concerns more suited to a petty merchant. My son should not be a merchant, but a lord."

Sillek turns and slowly walks across the floor. He stops by the chair, and his eyes flash. "I am Lord of Lornth, and my father did not die for honor. He died looking for exotic women. Of that, I should not have to remind you, of all people. His honor, his duty, lay in preserving and protecting his people—and there he failed. He lost more than twoscore trained armsmen for nothing! I know what honor is. Honor is more than a reputation for seeking out danger mindlessly. It is more than attacking enemies blindly without regard to costs and deaths.

"You talk of honor, but the honor that you speak of so carelessly and endlessly will bring nothing but pain and needless death. There is no honor in destroying Lornth through mindless attacks on powerful enemies. There is no honor in squandering trained armsmen like poor tavern ale." His hand jabs toward Ellindyja as she starts to speak. "No!

I will hear no more protestations about empty honor, and should you *ever* throw that word at me again, you will be cloistered—in high and lonely honor in my tallest tower. There you can think of honor until your dying day. And may it comfort you, because no one else will. Do you understand, my dearest mother?"

Ellindyja pales. Her mouth opens.

Sillek shakes his head grimly.

Finally, she bows her head. "Yes, my son and liege."

For a time, silence fills the chamber.

"I still value your *advice,*" Sillek says evenly.

Ellindyja does not look up, as the unsteady needle slowly fills in the second lobe of the coronet she stitches.

"About Ser Gethen's daughter," he suggests.

"Courting Ser Gethen's daughter would not be a bad idea," Ellindyja says quietly, her eyes still on the embroidery. "No ruler is so rich that he cannot afford to look at both a lovely lady and lovely lands, and this . . . incident . . . left Ser Gethen with but one heir."

"Fornal is reputed to be outstanding in Arms."

"He may be," said Ellindyja, "but life is uncertain, as your father discovered. Although Ser Gethen is a warrior of caution and deliberation, I do know that he is less than pleased."

Sillek turns from the window. "You think I should go to Carpa and soothe his ruffled wings?"

"It could not harm you, and, since you are so preoccupied about the possible predations of Lord Ildyrom, rather than . . . other considerations, you would be close enough to return to Clynya, should that *remote* need arise." The pudgy fingers fly momentarily, and the golden thread continues to fill in the outline of the coronet.

"It is scarcely remote when a neighboring lord builds a fort on your lands." Sillek's face is stern, and chill radiates from him.

A jagged line of lightning illuminates the roofs of Lornth, and the crash of nearby thunder punctuates Sillek's observation.

"That is true. Perhaps you could make that point with Ser Gethen in person." The lady Ellindyja lowers her embroidery. She does not meet his eyes.

Sillek lifts his hands, and then lowers them. "We shall see."

"Sillek dear, I understand your concerns for the greater good of Lornth. I only provide those suggestions that I feel might be helpful for Lornth . . . and for preserving your patrimony."

Sillek's lips tighten again.

Ellindyja looks away. "Ser Gethen is upset, my son and liege. I cannot disguise that."

Sillek's eyes fix on her, but she says nothing.

"He is upset." He takes a deep breath and releases it slowly. "And it is true. You cannot change that. For your judgment in this matter, I am grateful, but . . . I do not appreciate even indirect references to honor and patrimony. Those are best reserved for cloistered towers."

"Yes, Sillek. You have made your point, and you are Lord of Lornth." Ellindyja bows her head again.

Sillek offers the faintest of head bows before turning back toward the door as another rain squall pelts across the roofs outside.

After the door closes, Ellindyja smiles sadly, and murmurs, "But you cannot escape honor."

The embroidery needle flashes, and the third golden lobe of the coronet forms.

XXXIV

WITH THE SHUTTERS in the great hall closed, the fire in the hearth left the room—the end closest to the fire—nearly comfortable for Ryba and the marines in just the light and tattered shipsuits they wore for heavy work. Although

Narliat had kept complaining about the chill, Nylan had re-
sisted using the new furnace, especially since the grates for
the ducts on each floor were not finished. Besides, it wasn't
that cold, not yet, and he worried about having enough firewood for the long winter.

Nylan wore his ship jacket, unfastened and open, as did
Ayrlyn and Saryn. Relyn and Narliat wore their heavy cloaks
wrapped around them, and sat on the right edge of the raised
hearth, their backs to the heaping coals and the logs of the
fire.

Two squat candles—among the few in Westwind and pro-
cured by Ayrlyn and Narliat—flickered on the table. The
candles and the fire managed to impart a wavering illumination to the great hall, although the corners were dark, as
was the end of the room nearest the stairs. Nylan could see
clearly without the light. That was not the case for most of
the others, as they squinted to see when they turned toward
the gloomier sections of the hall.

Ayrlyn had drawn one of the candles close to Relyn's
stump, because he had complained that the arm was chaos-
tinged.

"Chaos-tinged?" asked Saryn.

"Infected," explained the redhead, looking at the arm.

Nylan could feel as Ayrlyn extended her senses to examine the arm, much in the same way that he had manipulated
the fields around the laser.

"The arm's not infected," Ayrlyn said. "You'll live."

"What sort of life will I live, healer?" asked Relyn. "The
great warrior of Gethen Groves defeated by a handful of
women, and what kind of life awaits me?" He inclined his
head to Nylan. "And by an unknown mage." He snorted.
"Who would believe that less than a score of women, a single armed man, and one mage could kill nearly thirty well-
armed and -trained men?"

Nylan took another look at Relyn's stump. Crafting something like a hook or artificial hand might not be that difficult, and it might make the man more functional and less
self-pitying.

Gerlich smiled briefly at the mention of "a single armed man," then glanced toward Ryba. His smile vanished.

"Ser, they killed three score of Lord Nessil's men," suggested Narliat, raising his maimed right hand. "He even had a wizard with him. And we have not seen any of the great Lord Sillek's men, or Lord Sillek himself, come to follow his sire's example. Lord Sillek did succeed his father, did he not?"

"He did, armsman. That was why I was here."

"Would you care to explain?" asked Nylan, knowing the answer, but wanting the others, besides Ryba, to hear it from the local noble himself.

Ryba sat in the single chair at the end of the table—a rude chair, crude like all the other crafts, but Saryn had insisted that the marshal should sit at the end, and had made the chair herself. Ryba half turned in the chair to hear Relyn's words.

"Lord Sillek offered a reward of the Ironwoods and a title for whoever cleansed the Roof of the World."

"Cleansed?" asked Ryba coldly. "Are we vermin?"

While her accent in Old Anglorat left something to be desired, Relyn understood and swallowed. "Your pardon . . . but women like you are not seen elsewhere in Candar, nor across either the Eastern or the Western Ocean."

"There are women like us in Candar, and they will find their way to Westwind," Ryba said. "In time, all the lands west of the Westhorns will be ruled by women who follow the Legend—the guards of Westwind . . . I've mentioned the name before."

"The Legend?" asked Relyn.

Nylan glanced at Ayrlyn, who looked down.

"Ayrlyn? Now would be a good time to introduce your latest song."

"As you wish, Marshal." Ayrlyn walked to the far end of the hall where she removed the lutar case from the open shelves under the central stone stairs. She left the case and carried the instrument toward the hearth.

"What is this Legend?" asked Narliat.

"It is the story of the angels," Ryba said smoothly, "and

the fate of those who put their trust in the power of men alone."

Nylan winced at the certainty in her voice, the absolute surety of vision. Like her vision of a daughter, although that was certainly no vision. There were enough signs to Nylan, especially to his senses, but while he could not tell the sex of the child, Ryba had no doubts.

"All Candar will come to understand the vision and the power of the Legend," Ryba added. "Though there will be those who oppose it, even they will not deny its truth and its power."

Ayrlyn stood before the hearth, lutar in hand, adjusting the tuning pegs, and striking several strong chords before beginning.

> *From the skies of long-lost Heaven*
> *to the heights of Westwind keep,*
> *We will hold our blades in order,*
> *and never let our honor sleep.*

> *From the skies of light-iced towers*
> *to the demons' place on earth,*
> *We will hold fast lightnings' powers,*
> *and never count gold's worth.*

> *As the guards of Westwind keep*
> *our souls hold winter's sweep;*
> *We will hold our blades in order,*
> *and never let our honor sleep . . .*

As Ayrlyn set down the small lutar, Ryba smiled. The hall was hushed for an instant. Then Cessya began to clap.

"Don't clap. It's yours, and you need to sing it with her. Again, Ayrlyn."

The redheaded healer and singer bowed and strummed the lutar. Her silver voice repeated the words.

By the last chorus of "and never let our honor sleep" all the marines who had become, by virtue of the song and

Ryba's pronouncement, the guards of Westwind Keep had joined in.

Nylan tried not to frown. Had Ryba used the term "guard" before? Was she mixing what she thought she had said, her visions, and what she wished she had said?

Relyn looked at Narliat, and both men frowned.

"You frown, young Relyn. Do you doubt our ability at arms? Or mine?" asked the marshal.

"No, sher."

" 'Ser' will do, thank you. The term applies to honored warriors." Ryba turned away from the two at the corner of the hearth. "A good rendition, Ayrlyn. Very good."

Ayrlyn bowed and walked toward the shadows that shrouded the stairs.

Relyn glanced toward Ryba's pale and impassive face and whispered to Narliat. "She is truly more dangerous than Lord Sillek."

Far more dangerous, Nylan felt, for Ryba had a vision, and that vision just might change the entire planet—or more. Sillek and the others had no idea what they faced.

The engineer's sense of reason wanted to deny his feelings. Logic said that a mere twenty-plus marines and an engineer could not change history, but he could feel a cold wind every time he thought of the words Ayrlyn had composed, as though they echoed down the years ahead.

XXXV

IN THE NORTH tower yard, Nylan glanced from the armaglass panels up at the sky, where gray clouds twisted in and out and back upon each other as they churned their way southward, bringing moisture from the northern ocean.

Behind him Huldran and Cessya ground more lavastone for the mortar needed to finish the southern wall of the bathhouse and the archway in its center that would lead to the north tower door. As the powder rose into the air, the intermittent cold breeze blew some of the fine dust toward the engineer.

Kkkchewww!!! He rubbed his nose and looked at the two marines, working in their threadbare and tattered uniforms. Then he checked the connections on the power cables, and the power levels on the scrambled bank of firin cells he was using—twenty-four percent.

He lowered the goggles over his eyes.

Baaa . . . aaaa . . . The sound of the sheep drifted around the tower. Nylan hoped someone knew something about sheep, because he didn't. They gave wool, but how did one shear it? Or turn the fleece into thread or wool or whatever got woven into cloth? There was something about stripping the oil from the wool, too. Saryn or Gerlich probably could slaughter them and dress them, but how many did they want to kill—if any? And when?

What about the chickens? Kadran had them up in a narrow cut Nylan had made above the stables—a makeshift chicken coop. Would it be warm enough in the winter, or should they be in with the sheep or horses? Who would know? He couldn't attempt to resolve every problem, but he hoped someone else could figure out the sheep and the chickens.

He forced his thoughts back to the job at hand—cutting the armaglass to fit the window frames that Saryn and Ayrlyn had made.

Nylan studied the chalked lines on the scarred and once-transparent panels from the landers. If he cut carefully, and if his measurements were correct, he might have enough glass for eight windows—four for the great hall and the rest for the living quarters—one or two on each floor where people slept. In the coming winter, the tower would still be dark—they had no lamps and only the few candles.

His eyes flicked in the general direction of the second large cairn—and the eleven individual cairns. How could Ryba promise that Westwind would change history when two seasons had reduced their numbers by more than a third? Children? But how many?

"Stop it!" he told himself, lifting the powerhead.

Cessya and Huldran glanced up, and Nylan looked down at the armaglass, forcing himself to take a deep breath and concentrate on the cutting ahead.

He triggered the energy flow to the powerhead, and began his efforts to narrow the laser's focus even more. Unlike his efforts with stone or metal, the armaglass sliced quickly and easily, and Nylan soon looked on eight evenly sized pieces, each ready to fit into a frame.

After clicking off the power, he checked the cell-bank energy level—barely down at all. His eyes narrowed, and he looked at the armaglass sections, then pushed back the goggles and walked over to the frames. Each frame was complete, except for the top bar, so that the armaglass could be slipped into the grooves.

Still wearing the gauntlets, Nylan picked up a section and eased it into the frame. It stuck halfway down, but with some tugging and wiggling, he managed to push the glass all the way into the frame. Saryn and Ayrlyn could assemble and install the rest of the windows. Another problem resolved.

Then he looked back at the laser. Because he had used so little energy, he might even have some power to use for Gerlich's project, not that Gerlich had asked Nylan directly, beyond complaining about underpowered bows.

Nylan removed the fraying gauntlets and wiped his forehead with the back of his forearm. Cool breezes or not, using the laser left him hot and sweaty. After a swallow of water, he looked at the two smaller braces on the stone, along with the two long rods of composite beside them, then at the sketch that Saryn had drawn from memory.

Nylan studied the pair of braces once more, then pulled on the gauntlets and eased the goggles in place. The lenses were so scratched that he relied on his senses more than on his sight. All the equipment from the *Winterlance* was falling apart, overstrained and stressed from usage far heavier than ever planned for by Heaven's shipbuilders and the angels' suppliers.

Finally, he triggered the power to the laser. The composite sliced easily, and he quickly had the rough form he needed. Then he set that aside and began shaping the brace toward the ideal shape that Saryn had suggested.

The first long, slow pass with the laser left him with the metal too heavily bunched near the grip. After three passes, with the sweat streaming down his face and around his goggles, he had the shape he needed, leaving an open groove down what he thought of as the spine of the metal.

He cut the power flow and set the laser wand aside gently, removing the goggles and gauntlets and sitting on a building stone. There he wiped and blotted his face.

In the meadow to the east, the grass was browning more each day. The leaves of local deciduous trees, even those that seemed like oaks and had acorns, did not change color much. Half the leaves seemed to turn to a light gray and shrivel into almost thin strips clinging to the branches, while the other half dropped off. Why? He didn't know and might never.

"Ser?" asked Huldran as she carried a stone past him and toward the slowly rising southern wall. "What's that?"

"A bow . . . maybe."

"You'll get it right."

Nylan wasn't sure about that, but he put the goggles back on, and then pulled his hands into the gauntlets. After measuring the composite rod, he triggered the laser, trimmed the rod more, and then started to mold the metal around the rod.

EEEssssssTTT! The would-be bow exploded into burning sparkles, and Nylan threw it into a stone-walled corner. He backed away quickly and set down the wand as quickly as he could so that he could beat out the smoldering fabric on his upper arm. As he did, he thanked the high command for insisting on flame-retardant uniforms.

He took off the goggles and studied the ragged and now burned and holed right sleeve. A section of his biceps was faintly reddened, but he could feel just warmth, not the pain of a burn.

With that, he watched as his protobow collapsed into a puddled mass of metal and melted composite. What had happened? He knew iron-based alloys could burn, but the laser hadn't been that hot.

He glanced upward. Overhead, the gray clouds continued to twist back and forth on each other, but not even a sprinkle had fallen on the Roof of the World, let alone lightning.

On the other side of the tower, a procession of marines conveyed the last of everything remotely usable from the landers into the tower. Another group was systematically finishing the stripping of the lander shells and storing what could be used for future building or raw materials in the first lander, which had been dragged up next to the bathhouse wall. The second lander shell was at the foot of the narrow canyon where Nylan had quarried his stone, partly filled with cut and dried grasses for winter feed for the horses. Drying racks, made of evergreen limbs, ranged across the spaces below the ridge rocks.

Nylan glanced back at the cooling mess of metal. Beside him stood Huldran, just looking.

"Fireworks, yet?" asked Ryba from behind him. "How did you two manage that?"

"I haven't figured that out yet, but I was trying to form metal around a composite core—"

"The gray stuff—cormclit?"

Nylan nodded.

"It's pretty heat-resistant in a directional way—that's why it's used as a hull backing," pointed out the marshal.

"Oh, frig . . ." The engineer shook his head. Next time, he'd have to cut the composite so that the heat-reflective side was to the inside of the groove. It made a stupid kind of sense, although he couldn't have given the explanation a good physicist could have.

"I take it you figured it out?" asked Ryba. "You have that look that says you're so stupid not to have realized it from the beginning." She paused. "No one else would ever figure out your mistakes if you weren't so upset about them." She laughed briefly. "What were you trying this time?"

"Another weapon."

Huldran eased away from the two. "Need to set these stones, ser, Marshal, before the mortar locks up."

"Go ahead," said Nylan.

"We'll need every new weapon we can get," Ryba said.

"We're about out of slug-thrower shells?" asked Nylan.

"Maybe fifty, seventy-five rounds left in personal weapons, about the same for the two rifles. That's not enough." She shrugged. "What were you trying to make?"

"One of those endurasteel composite bows."

"We could use some, but where did you get the idea?"

"Gerlich was muttering the other morning about the lack of accuracy and range with the native bows."

"He always mutters—when he's around."

Thunder rumbled across the skies, echoing back from Freyja, and fat raindrops began to fall.

"Excuse me. I need to get the laser under cover." Nylan began to disassemble the equipment. First the powerhead and cable went back to the fifth-level storage space—into an area half built into the central stone pedestal—then the meters, and finally, the firin cells themselves. Ryba helped him carry the cell assembly. After that he set the cooled and melted puddle of metal and composite in a corner of the un-completed bathhouse. He might be able to use the mess in some fashion later . . . and he might not.

Then, through the scattered but big raindrops, he and Ryba walked up to the emergency generator, spinning in the fall wind. It too was failing, bearings squeaking, and power surging, but it still put power into the firin cell attached to the charger. Both charger and cell were protected by a frame-work of fir limbs covered with alternating layers of canni-balized lander tiles held in place with heavy stones.

"Still charging." Nylan carefully replaced the covering.

"You've made the power last longer than anyone thought possible," Ryba said.

Looking downhill at the tower, Nylan answered, "There's more to do, a lot more."

"There always will be, but Dyliess will appreciate it all. All of the guards will."

At the clop of hooves, both turned toward the narrow trail from the ridge, where Istril rode toward the front gate to the black tower.

"Trouble?" asked the engineer.

"I don't think so. She wasn't riding that fast."

They had almost reached the south side of the tower before the triangle gong rang. *Clang! Clang!*

"Those traders are back, Marshal," called Istril as she rode from the causeway toward Nylan and Ryba. "The first ones."

"Skiodra," Nylan recalled.

"He's the one. He's got nearly a score of men, and eight wagons."

"I told you we needed weapons," said Ryba dryly.

Nylan shrugged.

"Get a dozen marines," ordered Ryba, looking at Istril, "fully armed. Have the rifles stationed to sweep them if we need it."

"Gerlich is out hunting," pointed out Istril, "with half a squad."

"Get who you can." Ryba turned to Nylan. "You, too. You did so well last time that you can handle the trading."

Nylan shrugged, then headed to the washing area of the stream. He wished the bathhouse were completed. Then he laughed. The tower had gone more quickly than anyone could have anticipated, far more quickly, and he was still worrying, except it was about showers, and laundry tubs, and more jakes.

Ryba headed toward the stables. "I'll have a mount waiting for you."

"Thank you. I won't be too long."

After a quick wash and shave, with the attendant cuts, a return to the tower, and a change into his other shipsuit, he donned the slug-thrower he hoped he didn't have to use, and the black blade he had infused with black flux order. Then he walked down the stone steps, past the aroma of baking bread, and out the front gate of the tower.

As Ryba had promised, a mount was waiting, its reins held by Istril.

"They just left, ser, at a walk."

"Can we catch them by walking a bit faster?" asked Nylan. The not-quite-swaybacked gray whickered softly as he mounted.

"I think so." Istril grinned.

Nylan and the silver-haired marine with the warm smile joined the other eleven marines and Ryba halfway down the ridge toward the spot where the traders, dressed in the same quilted jackets and cloaks, waited by a single cart that flew a trading banner. Two were on foot before the cart, the remainder mounted behind the cart.

Skiodra, still the biggest man among the traders and wearing in his shoulder harness an even bigger broadsword than the long blade Gerlich usually bore in similar fashion, stepped forward. "I am Skiodra, and I have returned." His Old Anglorat did not seem so thick, but Nylan wondered if that were merely his growing familiarity with the local tongue.

"Greetings, trader," answered Ryba, still mounted. Her eyes did not leave his, and after a moment, the trader bowed.

"Greetings, Marshal of the angels. We bring more supplies. Have you blades to trade?"

"These are better," said Ryba. "We will bring them down shortly. What do you have to offer?"

"Are we sure they are angels?" interrupted the bushy-haired and full-bearded trader behind Skiodra.

Skiodra waited, enough so that Nylan understood the ploy.

"If you wish to join those under that cairn there," suggested the engineer quietly, pointing to the heaped rocks that covered the slain bandits, "you may certainly test the strength of your beliefs." He dismounted and handed the reins to Istril. Then he walked forward, slowly drawing his blade, the one he had kept because it was even darker than the others and seemed to hold darkness within its smooth luster, and extended it sideways and slowly. "You might also wish to touch this blade if you doubt." He smiled, knowing that he had bound some of the strange flux energy within the blade.

The blond reached for the blade, but his fingers never touched the black metal. Instead, he stepped back, his face pale.

Nylan extended the side of the blade toward Skiodra. "Perhaps . . ."

"No. My friend spoke too hastily."

As before, the first cart—the one with the banner this time—was filled with barrels.

"Shall we start with the wheat flour?" asked Skiodra. "I have the finest of flours from the fertile plains of Gallos, even better than the flour of Certis, and closer and fresher."

"And doubtless unnecessarily costly, for all that trouble, trader."

"It is good flour."

"I am sure it is," agreed Nylan, "but why should we pay for a few days' freshness when we will be storing it and not using it until seasons from now?"

"I had forgotten—until now—that, mage or not, you came from a long and distinguished line of usurers," responded Skiodra. "As I told you once, my friend, and I will accord you that courtesy, it is far from costless to travel the West-horns. This is good flour, the best flour, and that freshness means that you can store it longer, far, far longer . . . at a silver and three coppers a barrel, I am offering you what few could find."

Nylan tried not to sigh. Was every trading session going to be like the first? "And fewer still could afford," he responded as smoothly as he could. "Granting you the freshness, still five coppers would more than recompense your travel."

"Five coppers! Five? You would destroy me," declared Skiodra. "With your black blades, do you think that you can eat metal in the cold of winter? Or your soldiers, will they not grow thin on cold iron? A generous man am I, and for a silver and two I will prove that generosity."

Ryba's eyes appeared to look at neither Skiodra or Nylan, but remained on the blond trader.

"Such generosity would quickly bring you dinner on plates of gold and silver. At six coppers a barrel, you would be feeding your mounts sweetcakes." Nylan smiled broadly to signify his amusement.

"Sweetcakes? More likely maize husks begged from gleaning fields. A silver and one . . . not a copper less!" Skiodra looked toward the roiling clouds. "May the devils from the skies show you my good faith."

"Your faith, that I believe," answered Nylan. "It is your price that not even a spendthrift second son would swallow. Seven coppers."

"I said you were a mage. Oh, I said that, and blades like black lightning you may forge, but your father could not have been a mere usurer, but an usurer to usurers. You would have my horses grub stubble from peasants' fields. Even to give you a gift to start trading, at a silver a barrel, I would have to sell not only my daughter, but my son."

"At eight coppers a barrel, because I would reward your efforts to climb here, you would still have golden chains for your daughter."

"I could not sell a single barrel at nine coppers," protested Skiodra.

"How about eleven barrels for a gold?" Nylan's fingers slipped over the hilt of his blade as he sensed the growing chaos and tension in the big guard next to Skiodra and keyed in the reflex boost he had always worried about using, even on the *Winterlance*'s neuronet.

"Done, even though you will ruin me, Mage."

Ryba looked sideways, and the blade of the blond trader flickered—but not as fast as Nylan's, which flashed like a stroke of black lightning through shoulder and armor.

The blond trader's dead eyes were frozen open in surprise, and Ryba's blade rested against Skiodra's throat, as Nylan removed and cleaned his own blade, fighting against the throbbing and aching that battered his skull, both from the chaos of death and the agony of forced reflexes. Would every death hurt that much? Or would it get worse?

"This sort of thing isn't good for a trader," Nylan remarked conversationally. "People might get the wrong idea. We might think that you really wanted to rob us." He squinted, trying to fight off the pain.

"I did not know . . ." Skiodra looked toward the dozen armed men with bared blades who edged their mounts toward the mounted guards of Westwind.

"Let us just say that you did not," said Ryba. "You might tell your men to sheathe their blades. Could any of them have stopped the mage?"

"No." Skiodra looked toward his men. "The angels mean well, I think, and it might be best if you put your blades away."

About half did.

"Who wants a blade right through his chest?" asked Ryba with a smile.

A single man charged, and Ryba's left hand flickered. The dark-bearded man slumped across the horse's mane with the throwing blade through his chest, and his mount reared. The body slid into the dust.

The dozen mounted angels eased forward, each bearing an unsheathed and dark blade Nylan had forged.

Skiodra looked at the grim faces of the women, and the blades. The other five men sheathed their blades slowly, though their hands remained on their hilts.

"This really isn't very friendly, Skiodra," said Nylan. "Have you seen that your men all moved first, and they're all dead?"

Skiodra swallowed, eyes glancing at Ryba's blade, back at his neck.

"Doesn't that tell you something?" pursued Nylan. "Now . . . do you want to trade for your goods, or do you want us to slaughter you and take them?"

"How do I know—"

"Stuff it!" snapped Ryba. "We would prefer to trade, and you know it. You'd prefer to steal, and we know it."

A pasty cast crossed Skiodra's face.

"So we'll trade, and if you try anything nasty, we'll just kill you," concluded Ryba. "I thought you agreed to nine coppers a barrel for the flour."

"Yes, Marshal of angels."

As Ryba lowered her blade, Skiodra mopped his forehead. "What else do you have to offer?"

Skiodra forced a grin under his pale and sweating brow. "I might ask the same of you, Mage."

"How about two dozen of the finest blades produced west of the Westhorns, directly, more or less, from a place called Carpa. Of course," Nylan said lightly, "I expect that five of them would pay for everything in your carts with a few golds to spare."

"I slandered your father, Mage. You had to be whelped from a white witch and sired by the patron angel of usurers." Skiodra shrugged. "I cannot blame you for trying to get the best price, but your idea of fairness would have ruined Lestmerk, and he could get blood from stones and water from the sands of the Stone Hills."

"Now that we have that understood," laughed Nylan, doing his best to ignore his continuing headache, "what do you offer from the remaining carts?"

"I will show you, provided you bring down those blades."

"I'd say to bring ten," Nylan suggested to Ryba, "just so that the honorable Skiodra has a choice. And some of the breastplates, maybe."

Skiodra frowned, and Nylan translated roughly. "I suggested that the marshal bring a double handful to allow you a choice."

"Mage . . . you alone must be the patron of usurers."

Nylan shrugged. "Since you are the patron of ambitious traders, I'd say we could work out a fair trade."

Skiodra laughed, but the sweat beaded on his forehead, and Nylan wondered why. Did he seem that formidable?

Cessya turned her mount back up the ridge, presumably to bring down the cart and some of the blades captured from Relyn's forces.

In the end, Ryba and Nylan looked upon nearly thirty barrels of flours—maize, wheat, and barley; five bolts of gray woolen cloth; one bolt of a red and blue plaid; four barrels of dried fruit; two kegs of a cooking oil from something called oilpods; three axes; two saws; and enough other assorted goods to fill a wagon—plus one of Skiodra's carts, the oldest and most rickety. He'd even managed to get a barrel and a small keg of feed corn that might help the chickens through the winter.

The guards remained mounted until the trader's entourage was well along the road toward Lornth. Then, as half the women began to load the two carts, Nylan mounted and eased the gray up beside Ryba.

"This whole business is a little strange," he observed. "You notice that Skiodra didn't show up until after you made hash of young Relyn's forces. And this Lord Sillek—he's the son of the lord you killed in the first battle—he's offered land and a title for our destruction, enough that this young hothead—Relyn, I mean—was willing to take the chance."

"It's not all that strange," answered Ryba. "Skiodra wanted to see if we'd been hurt, and how badly. If we were weak, then he'd attack. Since he found us strong, he'll sell the information to someone. Lord Sillek, I suppose."

"Something like that," Nylan agreed. His eyes covered the goods that had cost eight blades and some breastplates. "We still have some coins."

"The flour and fruit will help, but it's going to be a long winter," Ryba said quietly, "even if we can get some more from those traders that Ayrlyn has been working with near . . . what is it? . . . Clarta, Carpa? The economics are the hard part—in war or peace, I suppose." As the last of Skiodra's riders disappeared beyond the ridge, she turned her mount uphill.

Nylan rode beside her, still bouncing in his saddle, wondering if he would ever learn to ride as smoothly as the others. "Do you think we can make this work economically? Westwind, I mean?"

"I already have," said Ryba slowly, "thanks to Skiodra and young Relyn."

"You don't sound happy. Is that another vision?"

"Not exactly. But the pieces I've already seen make more sense." Ryba shifted her weight in the saddle and turned to face Nylan. "Look how many bandits there are. Trading has to be dangerous. Westwind will patrol the roads across this section of the mountains—what are they called?"

"The Westhorns."

"And we'll charge for it. I think the sheep will make it."

"But that's trading lives for coin . . ." said Nylan. "More or less."

"Yes, it is. So is everything in a primitive culture. Have you a better answer? Can we grow enough up here to support even the few we have left? And if we could, could we keep it without fighting?"

"No," admitted Nylan.

"If they want to die by the sword, we'll live by having sharper and faster blades. Thanks to you, smith of the angels." Ryba did not look at Nylan as she rode past the sentry point where Berlis and Siret, and their rifles, had surveyed the trading.

Nylan could feel Siret's green eyes on him, and he nodded and smiled to the pregnant marine briefly.

"Smith of the angels?"

"For better or worse, that's your legacy, Nylan." Ryba kept riding, crossing the ridge crest and turning the roan toward the canyon that served as a corral until the stables could be completed.

"And yours? Or do I want to know?"

"Ryba, of the swift ships of Heaven. Ryba, one of the founders of Westwind and the Legend. Blessed and cursed throughout the history to come, I suspect. Don't ask more, Nylan."

"Why not?"

"Because I won't tell. Not even you. Not Dyliess, when her time comes. It hurts too much."

"You can tell me."

"No. If I tell, then you—nobody—will act the same, and we might not survive. I can't risk that, not with all the prices

everyone's already paid. And will. And will keep paying."
She kept riding.

Nylan looked toward the tower, and then at Ryba's dark
hair and the dark hilts of her blades. Ryba of the swift ships
of Heaven. Ryba, the founder of the guards of Westwind and
the Legend. He swallowed, but he urged the gray to keep
pace with the roan.

XXXVI

THE STOCKY MAN whose black hair is streaked with gray escorts Lord Sillek into the room at the north end of the courtyard, carefully closing the door behind him.

Two heavy wooden doors stand open to the veranda and
the shaded fountain that splashes loudly just beyond them.

Sillek glances around the room, his eyes taking in the inlaid cherry desk, the two bookcases filled with manuscripts
bound in hand-tooled leather, and the two cushioned captain's chairs that are drawn up opposite a small table. The
chairs face the fountain, and the north wind, further cooled
by the fountain, blows into the study.

"My sanctuary, if you will," says the gray-haired man.

"Quite well appointed, Ser Gethen," responds Sillek, "and
certainly private enough—although . . ." He gestures toward
the open doors and the fountain.

"It is more discreet than one would suspect." Gethen
laughs. "It took some doing before the sculptor understood
that I wanted a noisy fountain."

"Oh . . ." Sillek smiles, almost embarrassed.

"Please, Lord Sillek, do be seated." Gethen slips into the
chair on the left with an understated athletic grace.

"Thank you." Sillek sits almost as gracefully.

"My lady Erenthla has expressed a concern that you might
have come to the Groves as a result of her hasty note to the

lady Ellindyja. She wrote that missive while she was in some distress." Gethen clears his throat.

"I must admit that the receipt of the letter, certainly not its contents, did remind me that I had been remiss in paying my respects. My arrival represents a long-overdue visit to someone who has always been of great support and good advice to the house of Lornth." Sillek inclines his head ever so slightly.

Thrap. The knock is almost unheard over the gentle plashing of the fountain, but Gethen immediately rises, crosses the handwoven, patterned carpet, and opens the door.

"Thank you, my dear." The master of the Groves stands aside as a young blond woman carries a tray into the study. On the elaborately carved tray are two cups, a covered pot with a spout, and a flat dish divided into two compartments. The left contains carna nuts, the right small honeyed rolls.

Sillek stands, his eyes going from the confectioneries to the bearer, whose shoulder-length blond hair is kept off her face with a silver and black headband. Her eyes are deep green, her skin the palest of golds, her nose straight and even, and just strong enough not to balance the elfin chin and high cheekbones.

"This is my middle daughter, Zeldyan. Zeldyan, this is Lord Sillek."

Zeldyan sets the tray on the low table, then rises and offers a deep, kneeling bow to Sillek, a bow that drops the loose neckline of her low-cut tunic enough to reveal that her body is as well proportioned as her face. "Your Grace, I am at your service." Her voice bears the hint of husky bells.

"And I, at yours," Sillek responds, as he tries not to swallow too hard.

"We will see you at supper, Zeldyan." Gethen smiles indulgently.

She bows to them both, then steps back without turning, easing her way from the study and closing the door behind her. Gethen slides the bolt into place.

"A lovely young woman, and with great bearing and

grace," Sillek observes. "You must be proud of her." His fingers touch his beard briefly.

"My daughters are a great comfort," Gethen answers as he reseats himself, "a great comfort. And so is my only son, Fornal. You will meet him at supper as well."

"I never heard but good of all your offspring, ser." Sillek has caught the slight emphasis on the word "only," but still places his own marginal accent on the word "all."

"Your courtesy and concern speak well of you, Lord Sillek." Gethen leans forward and pours the hot cider into the cups. "Your father was not just Lord of Lornth, but a friend and a compatriot." He turns the tray and gestures to the cups, letting Sillek choose.

Sillek takes the cup closest to him and lifts it, chest-high, before answering. "A compatriot of my sire is certainly someone to heed, and to pay great respect to." Then he sips the cider and replaces the cup on the tray.

Gethen takes his cup. "The son of a lord and a friend is also a lord and a friend." He sips and sets the cup beside Sillek's.

Sillek glances toward the fountain, then back to Gethen. "You offered my sire your best judgment."

"And I would offer you the same."

"You have heard of the . . . difficulties I have faced recently, between certain events on the Roof of the World and Lord Ildyrom's . . . adventures near Clynya?"

"I have heard that certain newcomers are said to be evil angels, and that they have great weapons and a black mage with powers not seen since the time of the descent of the demons."

"We do not know nearly enough," Sillek admits, "but what I do know is that these so-called angels killed nearly threescore trained armsmen and lost but three of their number. They have also destroyed several bands of brigands who thought them easy prey. Unfortunately, they have also caused others pain, others who may have judged—"

"It often is not our judgment that matters, Lord Sillek, but the perceptions of others," interrupts Gethen. "When the perception of the people is that women are weak, those who fall to women are deemed even weaker and unfit to lead." The master of the Groves shrugs, sadly. "And those who lead, especially rulers, must follow those perceptions unless they wish to fight all those who now support them."

"That is a harsh judgment."

"Harsh, yes, but true, and that is why I, who loved all my children, have but one son, for I cannot endanger the others by flaunting dearly held beliefs." Gethen clears his throat.

Sillek waits without speaking.

"I understand you were successful in reclaiming the grasslands with a rather minimal loss of trained armsmen." Gethen laughs. "Rather ingenious, I think."

"I was fortunate," Sillek says, "but it ties up my chief armsman and one of my strongest wizards in Clynya."

"Hmmmm. I see your problem. If you attempt to secure the river, or Rulyarth . . . or send another expedition to the Roof of the World . . ."

Sillek nods.

"Perhaps you should take the battle to Ildyrom. It appears unlikely that the newcomers on the Roof of the World would move against anyone in the near future. Nor will the Suthyan traders."

"I had thought that, Ser Gethen. Still, Ildyrom can muster twice the armsmen I can. The other option would be to enlist support for a campaign to take Rulyarth, enough support to wage such an effort without removing forces from Clynya."

Gethen purses his lips, then tugs at his chin. "That might work, provided those who supported you were convinced that you would continue to work in their best interests. With the access to the Northern Ocean, and the trade revenues, Lornth could support a larger force of armsmen . . ."

"I had thought that, ser, but wished to consider your thoughts upon the matter."

"Hmmm . . . that does bear consideration." Gethen tugs at his chin again, then reaches for his cider and sips. "You would need to make a solid, a very solid, commitment."

"That is something that I would be willing to do, ser, especially for the good of Lornth."

"The good of Lornth, ha! You sound like your father. Beware, Sillek, of phrases like that. When a ruler talks of the good of his land, he means his own good."

"The two are not opposites, ser."

"True. And sometimes they are the same. Tell me, what do you think of Zeldyan?"

"At first blush, she is attractive and courtly. I would know her better."

"Should you wish for the good of Lornth, Sillek, I'd bet you will know her much better."

"That is quite undoubtedly true." Sillek forces a smile. "For you offer good advice."

"How good it is—you shall see, but I offer you all the experience that I have, purchased dearly through my mistakes." The gray-haired man rises. "I believe the time for supper nears, and Fornal and Zeldyan would like to share in your company."

"And I in theirs, and yours, and your lady's." Sillek stands and follows Gethen into the twilight of the courtyard.

XXXVII

THE WEST WIND, as usual, was chill, chill enough that most of those working on the Roof of the World had covered their arms, although only Narliat, stacking grasses on the drying rack, actually wore a jacket in the sunny afternoon of early fall.

In the colder shadow of the tower on the north side, as Huldran, Cessya, and Selitra worked to complete the stonework on the east and south sides of the bathhouse, Nylan tried to complete the bow he had failed three times with squinting through the goggles, coaxing power out of the cells and through the powerhead. The line of light and power flared almost green, and Nylan channeled the reduced power around the curved form he held in the crude tongs, smoothing the metal around the composite core, trying to shunt the energy evenly around the composite without burning the iron-based alloy.

With a last limited power bath, Nylan flicked off the laser and slipped the protobow into the quench—but only for a moment—before laying it out on the dented chunk of stone too flawed to use for building.

In the end, the shape differed clearly, if subtly, from the sketch that Saryn had provided so many days earlier. Still, a wide smile crossed his face. The bow had been harder, much harder, than the blades.

After a drink from the fired-clay mug, he picked up the second crude bow frame, already roughed out, and began inserting the composite core.

But just before noon, he had created three bows and dropped the energy levels to where he needed to replace two of the ten cells before continuing.

He also needed a rest, and something to eat.

After disassembling the laser and storing the wand and powerhead, the engineer walked around the tower toward the causeway and the main south gate to the tower.

The south tower yard, below the causeway, was getting more use, now that the tower was occupied, and the landers had been moved again and set up more for storage, either to the west of the tower or at the mouth of the canyon used for corraling the horses and for stone. A low rough-stone wall was rising around the yard, built by the simple expedient of asking the marines to carry small stones and put them along the lines Nylan had scratched out. There were enough stones around the tower, and the knee-height wall made a clear demarcation between meadow and the tower yard.

On the uphill side of the yard, near the causeway into the tower, Ayrlyn and Saryn were working to improve their cart, based on their ideas and what they had seen in practice in the cart obtained from Skiodra. On the downhill side, beside the remaining roof slates and building stones for the bathhouse, Gerlich and Jaseen sparred with the heavy wooden blades.

Nylan's eyes moved south where, on the trail-road down from the ridge, a thin, red-haired figure walked between the two marines, and Fierral followed.

Since Ryba wasn't around, Nylan waited until the four reached the base of the causeway. The marines stopped, and Fierral stepped forward, her eyes surveying the area before settling on Nylan.

The local, so thin she seemed to be little more than a child, barely reached Fierral's shoulder, although her tangled hair fell nearly to the middle of her back. Her pale blue eyes darted from the marines to Nylan. She shrank away and back toward the marines.

"Ser," Fierral began, "this local just showed up and bowed and bowed. Selitra and Rienadre don't understand the local Anglorat, and I don't do that much better, but I think she's asking for refuge or something. Do you know where the marshal is?"

"No one here will harm you," Nylan offered in his slow Anglorat, looking at the painfully thin figure.

The girl-woman looked down at the packed dirt leading to the causeway, and eased back until she was pressed against Rienadre's olive-blacks.

"She's clearly not fond of men. Better get the marshal," Nylan suggested. He turned toward the nearest of his tower workers, who had stopped on the far side of the causeway by the main tower door. "Cessya? I think Ryba's checking the space for stables up in the stone-cutting canyon. Will you get her?"

"Yes, ser. Wouldn't mind a break from lugging stone."

"Well . . . you could bring down a few of the larger fragments . . ."

"Ser?"

Nylan grinned.

"Master Engineer . . . someday . . . someday . . ."

"Promises, promises . . ."

Cessya flushed as she turned.

"You're a dangerous man, Engineer," said Fierral.

"Me?" Nylan laughed.

When the force leader, or armsmaster, just shook her head, Nylan's eyes crossed the south tower yard to where Ayrlyn was bent over the axle of the creaky cart. Saryn stood on the other side.

"Ayrlyn?"

The redheaded healer lifted her head. "Yes, Nylan? What great engineering expertise can you offer to stop the creakiness of the wheels?"

"Roller bearings, except I can't make them. Grease, otherwise, preferably from Kyseen's leavings or from animal fat."

"Grease?" Ayrlyn made a face. "I need engineering, and all you have to offer is grease? That was what you said yesterday."

"That's what they used for centuries. It's smelly and messy, but I understand it works." Nylan shrugged and grinned. "Can you give us a hand?"

"With what?"

The engineer motioned toward the local girl-woman. "We have a local problem. I need you and Narliat."

"That worthless loafer?" Ayrlyn took a deep breath, then wiped her greasy hands on a clump of grass. "He's pretending to stack grasses to dry. It's the easiest job he can find."

"I'll get him," Saryn volunteered. "You talk to the local kid, Ayrlyn. I still hate Anglorat." The former second pilot, limping yet, turned and headed for the grass-drying racks.

Ayrlyn wiped her hands on the grass again, then crossed the yard, where she stopped and looked at the small redhead. After a time, the girl-woman looked back.

"Who are you?" asked Ayrlyn.

"Hryessa." The name was so faint that all of the angels had to strain to catch it.

"Where are you from?"

"Lornth. The way was hard."

Nylan nodded at the long scratches, and the scabs, on the scrawny legs below the gray dresslike garment, and the purple and green bruises on the left side of the face. A white line in front of her left ear bore witness to a previous injury.

"Why did you come?"

"Because . . . because . . . I heard that you were angel-women, and that you had defeated Lord Nessil. Even the mages of Lord Sillek fear you." Hryessa pursed her lips as though she feared having said too much.

"Some of that is true," answered Nylan. "We have defeated Lord Nessil, and some of the bandits."

The small redhead stiffened and swallowed, but her eyes finally met Nylan's, although she shivered as she spoke. "They say that you are a black mage who devours souls and puts them into the stones of your tower."

"Oh . . . frig . . ." The expletive whispered from Rienadre's lips.

"I do not devour souls. All of us have built the tower," Nylan explained.

"You are too modest," interjected Narliat. "The mage made the tower possible, and he used a knife of fire—"

Hryessa shrank back until her back pressed against Rienadre's legs.

Nylan wanted to smash Narliat for making things harder, but Rienadre spoke before Nylan had figured out what to say.

"Easy, easy, kid," said the marine. "The engineer's good people." Rienadre patted the girl-woman's shoulder, and the small redhead straightened, more in response to the tone than the words she could not have understood.

"He is a good mage," explained Ayrlyn in Old Anglorat. "His works have saved many, and his tower will protect us all against the winter. It is only made of stones and timber and metal—nothing more."

Nylan tried not to wince at being called a mage. He was an engineer, and a poor excuse for one in a low-tech culture. That was all he was. Except . . . as he thought that, his head throbbed. Was he more than an engineer?

"You wanted to see us?" asked Ayrlyn.

"I had . . . hoped, great lady . . ." Her eyes fell to the clay underfoot. "I had hoped to find a place."

"It will be a cold and long winter," Ayrlyn offered.

"I do not care . . . you are women." Her eyes glistened, but the tears remained unshed, and Hryessa stiffened, gathering herself together in pride.

"You do not have to beg, or humble yourself," Nylan said softly. "The lady Ayrlyn only wished you to know that winter on the Roof of the World will not be easy."

"Is he really a man?" asked Hryessa, directing his words at Ayrlyn.

Nylan tried not to frown.

"Yes," answered Ayrlyn with a smile. "He is very much a man, but he is an angel, as are we all."

The sound of hoofbeats interrupted the process, as Ryba guided the big roan to a halt by the causeway, letting Cessya slide off first, then dismounted and handed the marine the reins. The marine led the roan to the hitching rail.

Ryba walked toward the group, halting beside Nylan and looking at the small redhead. "You are Hryessa," she said slowly, "and you have come for refuge. You are welcome." With that, the marshal smiled. "All such as you are welcome."

Nylan froze for a moment. How had Ryba known the woman's name?

Hryessa bent her head, then knelt. "Thank you, Angel of Heaven."

Ayrlyn's and Nylan's eyes met, and Nylan realized that they shared the same feeling—one of awe, a sense of experiencing something that transcended either of them.

After a moment, Ayrlyn spoke. "These others—they are also angels."

"But she is *the* angel," said Hryessa in a calm voice. "I have seen." She bowed again to Ryba.

Ryba inclined her head to Ayrlyn. "Would you take care of her? Get her washed and clean and clothed? And you and

Fierral need to work on sleeping arrangements and blade training."

"We'll take care of it." Ayrlyn nodded. After a moment, so did Fierral.

Hryessa frowned, her eyes darting from Ryba to Ayrlyn.

"They're going to make sure you get bathed, clothed, and fed," Nylan explained in Old Anglorat. "Then, you will learn our ways, and they will teach you the way of the blade."

"Teach me a blade, like an armsman?"

"Better, Hryessa, better," said Fierral in accented Anglorat.

Again, Ayrlyn and Nylan exchanged glances, and Nylan felt that they shared almost a sense of foreboding.

Ryba nodded and turned back toward the long hitching rail on the west side of the causeway, where her roan was tied.

"Let's go, Hryessa," suggested Ayrlyn, leading the young woman toward the tower.

Nylan headed for the stream to wash, wishing, again, that he had gotten around to finishing the bathhouse.

After washing, he turned back toward the tower and walked across the short causeway and into the great room. All eight narrow windows to the great room were open to admit the cool breeze. In four, the armaglass windows were pivoted and the shutters folded back. In the other four, without the armaglass, the shutters were just folded open.

In time, Nylan hoped, they would be able to afford glass for the remainder of the tower windows, but glass was a lower priority than food or weapons, especially now that Ryba had declared that the destiny of the guards of Westwind would be the double blades.

No wonder she had pressed him for the forty blades he had made so far!

He stepped toward the mostly filled tables. The grass baskets were filled with loaves of fresh-baked bread. Ayrlyn had finally brought back a yeast starter or whatever it was, and Kyseen had only exploded dough all over the kitchen a handful of times before learning how to mix flour, yeast, and water in making loaves suited to the big, wood-burning ovens that everyone had thought were too big when Nylan and Huldran had started laying bricks and mortaring in the metal cooking surfaces and oven grate slots.

Nylan sniffed the air, trying to determine the composition of the steam rising from the two big pots—one on each table. Some sort of stew, with local roots and greens tossed in.

Jaseen turned toward Nylan as he passed the end of the second table, and he noted the scratches on the medtech's forearms.

"What happened?" he asked.

"Frigging pine trees. The second and Kyseen discovered the cones have nuts, and you can roast them or bake them or whatever. Only problem is that if you wait for the cones to fall, the nuts are gone. Selitra and me, we've been climbing pines. I slipped, and some of those needles are like knives."

"I'm sorry."

"So am I. Frigging nuts. Bet they don't even taste good." She took a savage bite from the chunk of bread she held, and Nylan walked toward the hearth end of the first table.

Ryba, as usual, sat at the head of the table, and Nylan slipped onto the end of the bench to her left, the space that was always left for him.

As he sat, he noticed Ayrlyn leading Hryessa toward the second table. The local woman now wore leather trousers, boots, and a shirt somewhat large for her thin frame. Her face had been washed, and her hair had been cut short, marine-style.

As Hryessa looked down the table, her eyes widened, and she swallowed. Ayrlyn said something, easing Hryessa onto the bench and breaking off a large chunk of bread for her.

"There's our first recruit," noted Ryba.

"She's not that big," said Gerlich from the other side of the table.

"Given time, she'll be as good or better than any except

Istril or a few others." Ryba's words were matter-of-fact. "We'll see more before long."

Beside Saryn, Relyn frowned, struggling with a spoon in his left hand. "You will teach her the blade?"

"Of course. Why not?"

Relyn opened his mouth, then looked at Nylan. "Mage? What do you see when women have blades?"

"More men and women will get killed—at first." Nylan stood and spooned stew onto his trencher. "After that, most of those who die will be arrogant men."

"You sound displeased at that," Saryn offered.

"I'm displeased any time force is the only answer, and these days I'm displeased a lot," said the engineer as he re-seated himself, forcing his tone to be wry.

The silver-haired Siret smiled shyly and passed Nylan a basket of bread.

"Thank you." Nylan handed the basket back after breaking off a chunk of the heavy bread.

"You're welcome, ser."

"Would you pass me some, dear Siret?" asked Berlis.

"I certainly would, dear Berlis. About the time you bed a demon—except you already have. So enjoy it." The deep green eyes flashed.

"Talk about bedding . . ."

"If you want to bed a blade," suggested Siret, "just say another word."

"Guards!" snapped Ryba.

Both women closed their mouths.

"Thank you." Ryba turned to Nylan. "You were working on something different this morning."

"Yes. I finally got the bow thing worked out, I think." Nylan turned to Gerlich. "You might want to try it later this afternoon."

"Try what?" Gerlich lifted his eyebrows.

"A metal-composite bow."

"I'll try it, but I finally made one out of a local fir-type tree that works pretty well."

Nylan took a spoonful of stew. The meat and sauce tasted

more of salt and some spice than meat, but he was hungry and shoveled in several mouthfuls, followed with a bite of bread. The bread was better-tasting than the stew.

Perhaps because of the outburst between Berlis and Siret, the midday meal was relatively quiet, although Gerlich had a long and low conversation with Narliat.

After eating, Nylan went back to the north yard and the next group of metal-composite bows.

First, he laid out three more strips of composite, and trimmed them, before rough-shaping the braces into the bow outlines. After that, he turned off the power and rested for a moment, letting the chill breeze off the western heights cool him and dry his sweat-soaked hair.

Behind him, the clink of trowels and mortar and stone continued as the outside walls of the bathhouse rose. The walls separating jakes, showers, and laundry could be installed after the roofing.

His break done, Nylan adjusted the goggles over his eyes once more and eased power through the laser. He could sense the raggedness of the powerhead, and he sweated even more heavily as he strained not only to meld the metal around the composite core, but to keep the energy flow from the powerhead constant.

As he turned the curved shape in the tongs, his breath became more and more uneven, but he managed to smooth the last curves before shutting down the power and pushing the goggles back.

The quick quench was followed by his slumping onto a stone to rest.

Four bows. How many more could he coax from the laser? Should he stop and use the life of the powerhead to do the delicate stonework? He took a deep breath. He still had the other powerhead.

With a quick rest and a mugful of cold water, he went back to work on the next bow. The powerhead wavered more; Nylan strained more; and he took even more time gasping and recuperating. Five bows rested on the stones.

The third bow of the afternoon creased his arms with

lines of fire long before he finished, and left a knifelike pounding inside his skull. As he started on the final smoothing and melding, coaxing power out of the cells and through the powerhead, the line of light and power stuttered more and more in green bursts. Sweat poured from his forehead and around his goggles and even inside them.

His eyes burning, Nylan completed the last smoothing and flicked off the power to the wand, then set it aside and stepped toward the quench tub. He slipped on the clay, but caught himself as he dipped the bow into the quench for its momentary bath before laying it on the stone.

He sat on the stone for a long time, sipping water, eyes closed.

"Are you all right, ser?" Cessya finally asked.

"I will be." *I hope,* he added mentally, *considering I've created six bows that might not even work, nearly destroyed the laser in the process, and feel like the local mounts have tromped me into the stone.*

"Are you sure?"

The engineer opened his eyes and nodded.

"What are these?" asked Cessya.

"A new kind of bow—if they work."

"Do you need some help?"

"Well . . . if you could take the firin bank back to storage," Nylan admitted.

"Selitra! Give me a hand here. We need to store the energy cells," called Cessya.

Nylan slowly disassembled the power cables and the wand and powerhead while they carried the cells back into the tower. Then he followed with the laser components and stored them on the shelves above the power cells.

When he returned, the three were back at their stonework. Nylan extracted the woven bowstring from his pocket and tried to string the first bow. It took him three tries, probably because his arms were still aching.

Then he had to go back into the tower and find some arrows. Instead, he found Gerlich off the main hall.

"Are you ready to test the bow?" asked the engineer. "We'll need arrows and a target."

"Sure. Why not? I've got an area where I've been practicing at the south end of the meadow, near those scattered firs. We'll see what your toy will do, compared to the wooden one I worked out." Gerlich grinned, but the grin made Nylan uneasy.

The two walked back to the north tower yard, Gerlich with his own bow and quiver. The western wind felt good as it ruffled through Nylan's hair, and the engineer realized he was still hot. He handed the composite bow to Gerlich.

"Hmmm . . . a little heavy, and probably too short."

Nylan looked at the curves. "Too short?"

"Well, Relyn says that a proper bow should be chin high, about three and a half cubits local."

Nylan shrugged. His bows were not quite chest high, but, easier, he suspected, to carry on horseback.

"Let's see about the draw." Gerlich took the bow and mock-nocked an arrow. "Stiffer than it looks, but probably not strong enough for the average armsman." He grinned again. "Then, there's accuracy. Let's go and see."

Nylan followed the long-legged former weapons officer across the meadow to the half-dozen scattered firs. Circular targets on ropes dangled from the limbs.

"Those just twist and flap unless you hit them square and hard," said Gerlich. "Good training."

The engineer watched as Gerlich took a long arrow from the quiver, nocked it, and released the shaft.

The shaft *clunked* against one of the targets, spinning it, but the shaft did not hold and angled to the ground. Gerlich released two more shafts. The same thing happened twice more.

He handed the bow back to Nylan. "What you've got is accurate; it's easy to carry; and it's probably all right for hunting. I'd like something with more power, and I think most of the locals would also. It's good, but not in the class of your blades."

Gerlich lifted and strung the big bow, then sent a shaft

whistling toward the target. *Thunk!* The target swung in the light breeze, but the shaft held in place. "See the difference?"

Nylan nodded politely. One difference he had noted was that Gerlich had not drawn the composite bow to its full capability.

"I'll stick to my own bow and my toothpick, if you don't mind. Smaller weapons are fine for marines." Gerlich paused. "Is that all, Engineer?"

"That's all."

"I need to see about some game to fill the pots." Gerlich walked toward the trees, reclaiming the arrows and checking them, and resetting the targets. Then he raised an arm and walked briskly toward the canyon corral.

Nylan followed more slowly, wondering about both the bow and Gerlich. Why had Gerlich not drawn the bow fully? Was he worried that the metal might splinter? Nylan would never have given him a bow that he thought would fail.

"Is that your new bow?" Istril rode up to Nylan as he neared the causeway. "Could I try it?"

Nylan shrugged and handed it to her. "Gerlich wasn't impressed. He said it wasn't strong enough."

Istril laughed. "Brute strength isn't everything." She tried the draw. "It seems as heavy as his." She looked at Nylan. "We've got a target range up near the corral canyon. Do you want to see how it works?"

Nylan glanced to the west, where the sun hung just above the peaks. He wasn't going to get much more done before supper anyway. "All right."

"Climb up behind me," invited the marine. "Benja can carry double for a short ways, and it's faster."

"You're sure?"

"I'm sure."

Nylan clambered up awkwardly behind the slim marine.

"You're going to have to put an arm around me, ser, or you'll get bounced off after four steps."

Nylan flushed, but complied, and Istril flicked the reins. Nylan still bounced, but Istril seemed welded to her saddle, able even to open and close the crude gate without dismounting. When they reached the corral area, Nylan slid down gratefully into the shadows. "Thank you. I think I do better in the saddle than behind it."

"Most people do, ser." Istril slid down and unsaddled Benja. "You won't mind if I rub her down?"

"Of course not." As she worked on her mount, Nylan walked up the canyon to where he had cut the stone. The brickwork for the stables was almost finished, and rough fir timbers were stacked beside the walls. He ducked through what would be the door and studied the interior.

The rafters wouldn't be that far above his head, but the horses would have shelter at least. He walked outside.

Braaawwwk . . . awwwkkkk . . . awwkk.

From the smaller and more crudely bricked space where Nylan had tried to quarry more stones, before finding the rock fractured, came the sound—and the definite odor—of chickens.

Nylan turned and headed downhill.

Istril had just patted Benja on the flank, and the mare whuffed, then walked to the water trough.

"The targets are up there, on that side." Istril strode briskly uphill, and Nylan followed, marveling that the slender guard had so much energy so late in the day.

She paused. "There they are."

Three man-shaped figures—sculpted from what seemed to be twisted fir limbs—stood before a backdrop of gray that flowed from the canyon wall.

"The gray stuff behind them is sand and dirt. No sense in blunting arrowheads." Istril nocked a shaft with a fluid motion and released it.

Whunk! The shaft vibrated in the target, right where an armsman's heart would have been.

"Nice!" she exclaimed.

"Gerlich said it wasn't strong enough."

"Friggin' idiot. Beggin' your pardon, ser, but he is." Istril nocked and released a second shaft, which appeared beside the first. "Sweet weapon, ser, and there's plenty of pull here.

I'll show you. Might cost me a shaft, but we might as well find out."

The marine walked toward the target on the far right. When she reached it, she bent down and pulled a battered breastplate from behind the target, fastening it in place. Then she walked back to Nylan.

"We'll see how it does against the local armor."

"Can you spare a shaft?"

"I'd rather lose a shaft than my neck." Istril laughed, a warm sound. "It's better to find out now instead of in a fight." She set her feet, nocked a third shaft, and let it fly.

A dull *clunk* followed the impact, but the shaft slammed through the metal and held. At the sound, Benja barely looked up from where she chewed off a few clumps of mostly brown grass.

"I don't know what the big idiot's talking about." Istril shook her head. "This is smaller than his monster. It's easier to carry. It aims better, and it goes through armor. What else do you need?"

"The reputation for carrying the biggest bow and blade?" suggested Nylan.

Istril laughed again. Then her face cleared. "This is a killer weapon, ser. Any of the marines—I guess we're guards, now—any of us would carry this over anything else I've seen or used. Do you have any more?"

"Five others, but I don't have strings for them."

"Five? That's a good start."

"I don't know how long the laser will last," Nylan explained, "and I didn't want to make any more unless they were good."

"Good? With this and your blades, the locals won't stand a chance."

"Please don't humor me, Istril," Nylan asked.

"I'm not humoring you, ser. I wouldn't do that. We're talking our necks and lives."

"I didn't mean—"

"I know." Istril extended the bow.

"You can keep it. I wouldn't have the faintest idea of how to use it."

The faint sound of the triangle gong announced the evening meal.

"Thank you, ser. We'd better be headed down."

They walked in silence down to the tower, ducking through the fence poles and following the path to the causeway.

"Bread smells good," said Istril as Nylan swung open the heavy front door to the tower.

"Kyseen does that well."

"I think Kadran's been helping since her shoulder was torn up."

"That might explain it." Nylan gave a half laugh.

Istril set the bow by the stairs, and they walked to the tables.

"Testing the engineer's bow?" asked Gerlich politely.

Ryba's eyes flicked to Nylan. "You forged a bow?"

"Finally," the engineer admitted. "It's been difficult."

"I hope you didn't spend too much power on it," Gerlich added from his seat in the middle of the first table. Selitra sat beside him.

"You have to spend power to create anything," pointed out Nylan. "We need good longer-range weapons."

"Your blades are more effective," countered Gerlich.

"I don't think so," said Istril firmly. "I tested the bow, and it's perfect for a mounted guard."

"For a guard, perhaps, but I can put more power into the great bow," answered Gerlich.

"I'm sure *you* can," responded Istril politely. "But the engineer's bow works much better for a mounted guard, and I'm more than glad to use it. So will the others, I'm sure, since it's much easier to carry on horseback, and far more accurate than that monster you carry."

"It doesn't have the pull." Gerlich's voice carried an edge.

Ryba's eyes flicked between the silver-haired guard and the dark-haired man.

"It has enough power to go through a breastplate at combat range and that should be enough for anyone," snapped Istril.

"I thought we were talking true long-range weapons . . ."

"Enough," said Ryba quietly. "The engineer's weapons will be sung of long after we are all gone from Westwind. So will your great bow, Gerlich. There's room for both in history. It's been a long day, and we don't need an argument at dinner. In fact, we don't need arguments at all. We need to work together to get through the coming winter."

Nylan slipped into his seat quietly, glancing at the scattering of ashes in the cold hearth. "No fire?"

"It's not that cold yet, and it takes work to saw and split logs, even the dry deadwood," said Ayrlyn from across the table. Beside her, on the side closest to Ryba, sat Hryessa. Relyn sat on the other side.

"You're wearing a jacket."

"I'm not a Sybran," conceded the redheaded healer. "You're half Sybran, at least."

Nylan grinned and shook his head. "The wrong half, probably."

Dinner consisted of long strips of meat, clearly beaten into tenderness, and spiced with the hot dried peppers that Kyseen had found somewhere, then covered with an even hotter red-brown sauce. With it were lumpy noodles, some almost as thick as small dumplings, and some form of sliced root.

Nylan forced himself to take several circular root slices, but he ladled the sauce over everything except the bread. The bread seemed to get better.

The only beverage was water. They had a choice of bitter tea in the morning and water at night. The engineer wondered how long it would be before they might have something else.

Hryessa looked blankly at the barely smoothed wood of the tabletop while conversation continued. As Nylan started to eat, the local woman helped herself to another hefty portion of meat and dumpling noodles. She ate slowly, as though she were full, but could not believe that she would eat the next day.

Nylan refrained from shaking his head and took a second bite. By the time he had swallowed the mouthful of meat and dumplings, the sweat had beaded up on his forehead.

He drained his mug and refilled it, then blotted his forehead.

"The bread works better than the water," said Ryba dryly.

Across the end of the table, Ayrlyn nodded.

He took a mouthful and chewed. They were right. The burning faded, and he took another mouthful. After more bread and some water, he asked, "Is this the latest way for Kyseen to stop complaints about the food? How can you complain if it's too hot to taste?"

"I think it's good," offered Gerlich.

"He never had any taste to begin with," suggested Ayrlyn in a whisper.

"He still doesn't," muttered Nylan, adding more loudly, "You always liked things hot and direct."

A wave of laughter rolled down the table. Hryessa ignored the humor; Relyn frowned slightly, still struggling to eat with his left hand; and Nylan reminded himself that he had wanted to craft something for Relyn's stump.

"Better than cold and indirect," countered Gerlich.

Only a few chuckles greeted his remark, then small talk resumed around the two tables, especially at the end away from the hearth where Huldran and Cessya sat.

Nylan overheard a few of the phrases.

". . . bathing when there's ice on the walls . . ."

". . . better than stinking . . ."

". . . cares? No one but the engineer, and you know how dangerous that'd be . . ."

Nylan glanced toward the corner of the first table where Narliat sat beside Denalle, who was attempting to practice her Anglorat on the armsman. Narliat's face was bland, although Nylan sensed the man was fighting boredom.

Nylan concentrated on finishing his meal, although he required two more large chunks of bread to get him through the last of the spiced meat.

"No sweets?" asked Istril, her voice rising above the murmurs around the tables.

"What kind of sweets?" replied Gerlich.

"Not your kind, Weapons. You're as direct as that crowbar you carry. That's hard on a woman." Istril stood and walked toward the steps to reclaim the composite bow.

Relyn, sitting beside Ayrlyn, watched the slender marine. He pursed his lips, opened his mouth, then closed it. "How . . . ? No maΔn would accept that in Lornth."

"This isn't Lornth, Relyn," said Ayrlyn. "This is Westwind, and the women make the rules. Gerlich crossed the marshal once; she took him apart. She used her bare hands and feet to kill a marine who crossed her."

The young noble glanced at Nylan. "What about you, Mage?"

"Gerlich is better at the martial valors than I am, I suspect."

"You're better with a blade," said Ryba, "for all of his words about his great sword."

Gerlich's eyes hardened, but he turned and smiled to Selitra, then rose and bowed to Ryba. "It has been a long day, Ryba, and we will be hunting early tomorrow."

Ryba returned the gesture with one even more curt. "May you sleep well."

Gerlich smiled, and Nylan tried not to frown. He liked the man less and less as the seasons passed.

"You are a strange one, Mage," said Relyn slowly. "You are better with a blade than most, yet you dislike using it. You can wield the fire of order, and yet you defer to others."

"Too much killing leaves me unable to function very well."

"But you are good at it."

"Unfortunately," Nylan said. "Unfortunately."

Later, in the darkness, Nylan and Ryba walked up from the great hall, slowly, the four sets of steps that led to their space on the sixth level.

"Some nights, I get so tired," said Nylan. "It's easier to chop wood and do heavy labor than to use the laser these days. It's beginning to fail."

"Can you do any more of the bows?"

"I did six. I might be able to do some more, but I haven't cut all the stone troughs for the bathhouse and showers. I did get the heater sections done."

"A heater?" asked Ryba.

"It's not really a water heater, but I figured that I could put a storage tank with one side on the back of the chimney for the heating stove, because not many people will bathe in ice water in a room without heat. It probably won't get the water really hot, but it might make it bearable, and the back stone wall is strong enough to hold a small tank."

"You're amazing."

He shrugged in the gloom of the third-level landing, almost embarrassed. "I just try to make things work."

"You won't always be able to, Nylan."

"Probably not, but I have to try."

"I know." She reached out and squeezed his hand, briefly, then started up the steps again.

When they reached the top level, Nylan paused. Framed in the right-hand window, the unglazed one, was Freyja, the ice-needle peak faintly luminescent under the clear stars and the black-purple sky. Nylan studied the ice, marveling at the knife-sharpness of the mountain.

Ryba kicked off her boots and eased out of the shipsuit. Nylan turned and swallowed. Lately, Ryba had been distant, oh-so-distant. He just looked.

"You don't just have to look," she said in a low voice. "Today is all that is certain."

He took a step forward, and so did Ryba, and her fingers were deft on the closures of his tattered shipsuit.

"You need leathers," she whispered before her lips touched his. "Leathers fit for the greatest engineer."

"I'm not—"

"Hush . . . we need what is certain."

Nylan agreed with that as his arms went around her satin-skinned form, still slender, with only the slightest rounding in her waist, the slightest hint of greater fullness in her breasts.

Later, much later, as they lay on the joined couches that they still shared, Nylan held her hand and looked at Freyja, wondering if the peak had a fiery center like Ryba.

"I'll be back," Ryba whispered as she sat up and pulled her shipsuit over her naked form. She padded down the stairs barefoot, after picking up an object Nylan could not make out, night vision or not, from beneath the couch.

As the cold breeze sifted through the open windows—both the single window with the armaglass and the one with shutters alone were open—the engineer pulled the thin blanket up to his chest, and waited . . . and waited.

His eyes had closed when he heard bare feet, and he turned and asked sleepily, "What took so long?"

"I ran into Istril, and she wanted something," Ryba said. "I'm never off-duty anymore, it seems. I was able to help her, but it took a bit longer than I'd thought. She thinks a lot of you."

"She's a good person," Nylan said, stifling a yawn and reaching out to touch Ryba's silken skin, skin so smooth that no one would have believed that it belonged to an avenging angel, to *the* angel.

"Yes. All of the marines are good. That's one reason why I do what I do." Ryba let Nylan move to her, but the engineer felt the reserve there, the holding back that seemed so often present, even at the most intimate times.

And he held back a sigh, only agreeing with her words. "They all are good, and I do the best I can."

"I know." Those two words were softer, much softer, and sadder. "I know." But she said nothing more as they lay there in the cool night that foreshadowed a far, far colder winter—as they lay there and Ryba shuddered once, twice, and was silent.

Hryessa's words ran through Nylan's mind, again and again. "But she is *the* angel."

Darkness, what had they begun? Where would it end?

XXXVIII

SILLEK GESTURES TO the chair closest to the broadleaf fern that screens the pair of wooden armchairs from the remainder of the courtyard and from Zeldyan's family and retainers.

"You are most kind, Lord Sillek," murmurs Zeldyan as she sits, leaning forward, the husky bell-like tones of her voice just loud enough to be heard over the splashing of the fountain.

"No," says Sillek. "I am not kind. I am fortunate. You are intelligent and beautiful, and . . ." He shrugs, not wishing to voice what he thinks. Despite the apparently secluded setting of the chairs and low table between them, he understands that all he says could be returned to Gethen.

"Your words are kind."

"I try to make my actions kind," he answers as he seats himself and turns in the chair to face her directly.

"Necessity does not always permit kindness." The blond looks at Sillek directly for the first time. "Necessity may be kind to you."

"You speak honestly, lady, as though I were a duty. There is someone else who has courted you?"

Zeldyan laughs. "Many have paid court, but none, I think, to me. Rather they have courted my father through me."

"I would like to say that I am sorry."

"You are more honest than most, and more comely." Her hand touches the silver and black hairband briefly, and a sad smile plays across her lips. "Have you not courted others?"

"I am afraid you have the advantage on me, lady, for I have neither courted, nor been courted—until now."

"Why might that be?" She leans forward ever so slightly.

"Because"—he shrugs—"I did not wish to be forced into

a union of necessity." He laughs once, not trying to hide the slightly bitter undertone.

"You are too honest to be a lord, ser. For that, I fear you will pay dearly." Zeldyan's tone is sprightly.

"Perhaps you could help me."

"To be dishonest?" She raises her eyebrows.

"Only if dishonesty is to learn to love honestly."

"You drive a hard bargain, Ser Sillek." Her eyes drop toward the polished brown stone tiles of the courtyard.

Sillek reaches out and takes her right hand in his left. "Hard it may be, Zeldyan, but honest, and I hope you will understand that is what I would give you." Another short and bitter laugh follows, then several moments of silence. "I would not deceive you with flowery words, though you are beautiful and know that you are. But comeliness and beauty vanish quickly enough in our hard world, especially when courted for the wrong reasons."

"You are far too honest, Sillek. Far too honest. Honesty is dangerous to a ruler."

"It is, but to be less than honest is often more dangerous." Sillek frowns, then pauses. "Is it so evil to try to be honest with the lady I wish to join?"

"You might ask her if that is her wish."

The Lord of Lornth takes a deep breath. "I did not ask, not because I do not care, but because I had thought it was not your wish. I have appeared in your life from nowhere, and there must be many who have known and loved both your visage and your soul." He laughs softly. "I had not meant to be poetic, here, but my tongue betrayed me."

Zeldyan's eyes moisten for an instant, but only for an instant, before she turns her head toward the broadleaf fern.

Sillek waits, the lack of words punctuated by the splashing of the fountain. His eyes flick toward the end of the courtyard where he knows Gethen and Fornal make small talk about crops and hunting while they wait, and where, in another room, the lady Erenthla also waits.

When Zeldyan faces Sillek again, her face is calm. "What would say your lady mother?"

"Nothing." Sillek wets his lips. "Her thoughts are yet another thing. A fine match, she would think. She would say to me that the Lord of Gethen Groves has lands, and his support will strengthen Lornth and your patrimony, Sillek."

"You court strangely, My Lord."

"So I do. Say also that I court honestly." He offers her a head bow. "Would you be my consort, lady?"

"Yes. And I will say more, Lord. Your honesty is welcome. May it always be so." Zeldyan bows her head in return, then smiles ironically. "Would you wish my company when you deliver my consent to my father?"

Sillek stands. "I would not press, but I had thought we both might speak with your father, and then with your mother."

"She would like that."

Sillek extends his hand, and Zeldyan takes it, though she scarcely needs it to aid her from the chair. Their hands remain together as they walk past the fountain and back toward the far end of the courtyard.

XXXIX

NYLAN USED THE tongs to swing the rough bow frame into the focal point of the laser, struggling to keep the power flows smooth and still shape the metal around the composite core.

On the stones he used for cooling after the quench lay a circular cuplike device with a blunt—very blunt—hook and two bows—most of a morning's work. He hoped the metal cup and hook would serve as an adequate artificial hand for Relyn; he was tired of the veiled references to one-armed men.

His eyes went back to the two bows. All told, the engineer had made twelve over the eight-day before, each a struggle sandwiched between limited stone-cutting and building the heating stove for the bathhouse, and welding the two laundry tubs. Ellysia, relegated to laundry as a collateral duty because her obvious and early pregnancy had limited her riding, had immediately commandeered both. According to what Nylan had overheard, though, she refused to launder anything of Gerlich's.

Nylan permitted himself a smile at that, before he forced his concentration back to controlling the laser, and smoothing the metal around the cormclit composite core of what would be another bow.

As the tip of greenish light flowed toward the end of the bow, the energy flows from the powerhead fluctuated more and more wildly, and Nylan staggered where he stood, trying to hold the last focal point.

Pphssttt! Even before the faint sizzling faded into silence, Nylan could tell from the collapse of the flux fields around the laser focal points that the powerhead had failed. The engineer slumped. The other cutting powerhead was in little better shape. The weapons head, although scarcely used, would squander power, depleting the cells in a fraction of a morning—without accomplishing much, except destroying whatever it was focused on.

The last powerhead *might* last long enough to finish another handful of the composite bows.

He frowned. First, he needed to cut the shower knife plates. Then, if the second powerhead lasted that long, he could go back to the bows. At least, the black tower was finished. That is, the basics were—roof, floors, the hearth, chimneys, the stove and the furnace itself, and the water system from the tower wall to the lower-level cistern.

Everyone had needed something. Ryba had wanted weapons; everyone had needed shelter; the horses had needed stables; the tower had needed some windows . . . the list had seemed endless.

He disconnected the powerhead from the wand, glancing toward the uncompleted bathhouse behind him. Huldran,

Cessya, and the others were raising the roof timbers on the stables.

The single *clang* of the triangle announced the noon meal, and Nylan took the artificial hand and the broken power-head. He dropped off the powerhead in the tower, then found Relyn by the causeway. The mahogany-haired man sat on the stones watching Fierral and Jaseen spar, his eyes narrow.

"Greetings, Mage."

"Greetings. I brought you something." Nylan extended the device.

"What . . . might that be?"

"What I promised the other evening when I measured your arm." The engineer extended the artificial hand and mounting cup, measured to fit over the healing stump.

"It might be better than nothing, ser." Relyn took it in his good left hand.

Nylan felt himself growing angry, and the darkness rising within him, but he bit back the personal anger and chose his words carefully before he spoke. "It is no evil to lose, either a battle or a hand, to someone who is better. It is a great evil to refuse to struggle against your losses. I offer you a tool to help in that struggle. Are you too proud to use that tool? Does an armsman refuse a blade when his is broken?"

Rather than say more, Nylan turned and left. He was one of the first at table for the midday meal, rather than the last, but he refused even to look in Relyn's direction.

After he ate, Nylan excused himself and trudged back to the north side of the tower, where he set up the laser with the remaining powerhead.

On the other side of the tower, in the fields, the field crew—Selitra, Siret, Ellysia, and Berlis, who still complained about her thigh wound—were gathering the beans, and digging up some of the bluish high-altitude potatoes. The potatoes that didn't seem ready could wait, but with the threat of light frosts growing heavier, the last of the above-ground produce had to come in.

Between the carcasses dragged in by Gerlich and salted or dried, and the wild roots, and crops, and the barrels of assorted flours gotten in trading, Westwind might get through the winter—on tight rations. The food concentrates were almost gone, far faster than Ryba or Nylan had anticipated.

Clang! Clang! The triangle sounded twice.

Nylan looked up from reconnecting the second powerhead as Istril led four other riders uphill toward the ridge. Another set of would-be crop raiders, no doubt. There wasn't the swirl of the white chaos-feel on the local net that happened when large numbers of armsmen showed up. Why his senses worked that way, he didn't know, only that they did.

Since they didn't seem to need him, he turned his attention back to the work at hand. With the goggles in place, he studied the sheets of metal taken from lander three and the lines chalked on them.

Finally, he triggered the laser and began to cut the knife plates, quickly and without much smoothing. All eight went quickly, and he took a deep breath when the long-handled plates were completed. The rest of the "valves" could be worked out with local materials, if necessary.

He moved the leftover metal and laid out the three rough bow forms and the three composite cores he had already cut.

Maybe . . . maybe . . . the laser would last through all three.

At the sound of hooves, Nylan looked up. Istril led a mount, over which was a body. So did two of the marines who followed. Seven mounts, and three bows in all, and no obvious casualties for the marines. Nylan took a deep breath, then noticed that Istril had turned toward him.

She reined up well short of the laser.

Nylan checked the power and pushed back the goggles. "No casualties?"

"No." She smiled broadly. "The bows work well. Very well." Then the smile became a grin. "Gerlich doesn't know what the frig he's talking about. He couldn't have sent an arrow as far as your bows, even with that monster of his. It's technique."

Nylan nodded. "With most things, it's technique."

"The bows may save a lot more lives than the blades, ser. Ours, anyway, and that's what we're worried about." She paused, then flicked the reins. "We need to take care of these."

Nylan offered her a vague salute, watched as she turned her mount, then lowered the goggles.

The energy flows tumbled through the powerhead like green rapids, and Nylan felt he was using all his energy just to smooth them, and it took even more to begin to shape the rough metal bow frame around the composite.

Once more, his face was a river of sweat as he struggled with the laser and the shaping. And once more, he was drained, arms lined with internal fire and legs shaking, by the time he finished the bow and quenched it.

The powerhead was failing, yet, after what Istril had told him, the bows might be the most important thing he could make before the laser system collapsed. So he rested on the cracked stone he used as a seat, trying to catch his breath and regain his strength before beginning the next bow.

"So . . . the mage is working hard." Relyn ambled into the north tower yard. He carried Nylan's creation in his left hand.

"The mage always works hard." Nylan wiped his damp forehead.

"You sweat like a pig. Yet I see no weapons, no hammers, no hot coals."

"This is harder than that."

"What? You work the fires of the angels' hell?"

Nylan stood and walked toward the firin cell bank and the laser wand. "Watch. Then you can decide."

Relyn's lips tightened, but he said nothing as Nylan lowered the goggles. The engineer inserted the composite strip in the groove of the bow frame, then picked up both with the tongs and the laser wand with his right hand.

Again, the greenish light flickered, and Nylan wrestled with the fluctuating power levels as he molded metal around composite. Sweat streamed into and around his goggles. His arms and eyes burned, and his legs felt rubbery even before he quenched the bow and set it aside.

He pushed back the goggles and blotted his face dry, but

his eyes still burned from strain and the salt of his sweat. His tattered uniform was soaked. For a few moments, he just sat there, doubting whether the powerhead would last through another bow.

"Worse than the fires of the angels' hell," Relyn finally offered.

The words startled Nylan since, with all the concentration required, he had forgotten that the young noble had been watching.

"It's hard, but I wouldn't know about the angels' hell. I've only seen the white mirror towers of the demons."

"You look like men and women, but you are not." Relyn shook his head. "You bend the order force around chaos and form metal like a smith, and the fire you use is hotter than a smith's. Yet all the other angels say none but you can wield that green flame."

"I won't be able to do that much longer. The flamemaker is failing," Nylan conceded.

"That is why you work so hard?"

The engineer nodded.

Finally, Relyn bowed his head. "I have not been gracious, or noble. This . . . it is a work of art, and you were generous to create it for me, especially when you have so little of the flame left. And you put some of your soul in it. That I can see. I will use it, as I can, but I would not wear it after my last words when we ate—or yours."

Nylan understood that the statement was as close to an apology as he was ever likely to get, and that the words had cost the younger man a great deal.

"It is yours to use." Nylan paused. "I only ask that you use it for good, not evil."

Relyn lifted his eyes. "You have not . . ."

"No. I would not compel," Nylan said, mentally adding, *Even if I knew how, which I don't.* "The choice is yours. I don't believe in forcing choices. People resent that, and their resentment colors their actions and their decisions."

Relyn studied the smooth metal. "Now . . . I must think."

"About what?"

The younger man gave Nylan a crooked smile. "About what I have seen and what I must do."

"I wouldn't stay here," Nylan said bluntly.

"But you do."

"That's true, but I'm an angel. You aren't." As he spoke, Nylan found himself thinking that he was only half angel, assuming pure Sybran equated to pure angel.

"Even angels have choices, Mage." Relyn lifted his remaining hand, then turned and walked uphill toward the ridge.

"What was that about?" Nylan asked himself, walking back to the bucket by the wall. He drank and splashed his face before returning to the last bow.

He shouldn't have worried about the last bow. The entire powerhead fused solid when he triggered the power. He looked at the day's work—five bows. Seventeen bows in all. Not enough, but better than none.

He began disassembling the laser, and he had returned all the components, useless or not, to the tower, all except the bank of firin cells and the five bows, when Ryba rode down from the ridge and reined up.

"Both the cutting heads for the laser are shot," Nylan explained. "They're totally fused."

"What were you doing?"

"It doesn't matter. The total cumulative flow was the issue. The heads are only made to last so long. I got five more bows done."

"That's almost enough. Can you modify the weapons head?" asked Ryba, almost idly, leaning forward on the roan, her fingers touching the staff of the composite bow Nylan had given her—one of his better efforts.

"Not really. It's designed for maximum power disbursement in minimum time—that's a weapon configuration." The engineer unfolded the carrying handle on the right side of the firin cell frame.

"What about your . . . abilities?"

"I can channel the flows, shape them, but I can't hold back that kind of power flow. With the industrial heads, they're designed to be choked down, except it's not choked. They draw power at any level . . ." Nylan shrugged. Explaining how things felt with a new ability he couldn't adequately describe even to himself was difficult. He unfolded the other carrying handle.

"How much power do we have left?"

"Fifty percent on one bank of cells. The emergency generator might last long enough to get that bank to full power. Then again, it could quit any time. The bearings are nearly shot."

"That could power the weapons laser, couldn't it?" Ryba smiled again, almost cruelly.

"For a while. The cells might hold for a year."

Ryba straightened in the saddle. "You've done well, Nylan. The great smith and engineer. You built a tower, a bathhouse, stables, figured out how to heat them—and still left the weapons laser. I'll see you at dinner."

As she rode off, with the way she spoke, he almost wished he hadn't accomplished so much.

XL

"SER GETHEN of the Groves!" announces the young armsman-in-training, "accompanied by Lady Erenthla, and Zeldyan, of the Groves of Gethen."

The single horn plays a flourish, and Sillek, concealing a wince because the horn player is off-key, hopes that Gethen is not terribly musical.

Through the opening doors of the great hall step the three, walking up the green carpet toward the dais where Sillek and his mother stand. The lady Ellindyja remains slightly back and to his right, but close enough that Sillek can read her face.

In the hall are nearly threescore landowners and others of

prominence in Lornth, there to witness the formal betrothal.

Zeldyan, eyes downcast, walks behind her father and side by side with her mother.

"She'll do for a consort," opines the lady Ellindyja. "Good lands, good blood, good manners, and good looks. And Ser Gethen will back you on the campaign to take Rulyarth?"

"That was a deciding factor in announcing the betrothal," Sillek lies. "But I would have no more speech on that. The fewer who know, the better."

"I will keep silent, but I rather doubt that her father's support was the deciding point," suggests Lady Ellindyja. "She took your fancy, and you'll tell me that her father will support you to soothe me."

"I felt him out before I ever saw Zeldyan."

"If he knew you cared, he would have driven a harder bargain."

"He only has one son," Sillek says quietly, his lips barely moving and his face impassive as Gethen and Zeldyan approach.

The lady Ellindyja shrugs. "All ventures are a gamble. Had young Relyn taken back the Roof of the World, Ser Gethen would have doubled his lands and influence. Now he must support you more. Sometimes luck is as important as skill."

"Your advice was the deciding factor, Mother dear," whispers Sillek just before he steps down off the dais platform to greet Gethen.

Gethen inclines his head.

Sillek offers a half bow. "Welcome to Lornth, Ser Gethen." He turns to Erenthla. "And to you, lady." His last bow, and his deepest, goes to Gethen's daughter. "And to you, Zeldyan. I am honored."

Although Zeldyan's face displays a polite smile, a tinge of a flush colors her cheeks as she curtseys in response.

"Not so honored as we are," responds Gethen formally, and loudly enough so that those even in the back of the hall can hear.

"You do offer me honor in entrusting your daughter into

our family and care, and I assure you that she will in turn be honored and cherished," responds Sillek, turning his eyes from the father to the daughter.

Both Gethen and Ellindyja frown momentarily at the words "and cherished," while the white-haired Erenthla smiles briefly.

Zeldyan momentarily raises her eyes to Sillek, and they sparkle, before she drops them so quickly that not even Ellindyja sees.

"As a pledge of my trust," Sillek continues, "I offer you the seal ring of a counselor of Lornth."

A dark-haired youth, an armsman-to-be, steps forward with a small green pillow on which rests the golden ring.

"It is a token of my faith." Sillek's eyes are clear and direct as he faces Gethen, so direct that the older man pauses momentarily.

"You do me, and my daughter, great honor, Lord Sillek."

"Only your due, ser. And hers."

This time, at the untraditional reference to Zeldyan, Gethen does not frown, although the lady Ellindyja swallows.

A second young armsman approaches, with another pillow on which are two matching silver rings, each with a square emerald set in the center of a miniature seal of Lornth.

Sillek takes the smaller ring. "With this ring, I ask for your hand, lady, and with it, I pledge both my hand and my honor."

She extends her left hand, and Sillek slides the ring in place, adding quietly, "And my devotion."

Then it is Zeldyan's turn, and her voice is cool and firm, without bells, without brassiness, without softness. She lifts the larger ring, and Sillek extends his hand. "With this ring, I give you my hand, and accept your hand and your honor." As she slips the ring in place, her fingers tighten around his hand briefly, and she adds, "And give you the respect you deserve."

Gethen's eyes widen but fractionally, and then they cross with the lady Ellindyja's.

Sillek's and Zeldyan's hands remain locked for several instants, before Sillek finally says, loudly enough for all in the hall to hear, "Two hands promised in honor."

"Two hands promised in honor!" the onlookers chorus.

Sillek steps onto the dais and draws Zeldyan up beside him. After a moment, he gestures, and Gethen and Erenthla join them. All smile except the lady Ellindyja.

XLI

THE DULL RUMBLE of thunder echoed across the Roof of the World, and a line of rain slashed at Tower Black. Water dribbled through the closed shutters of the great room, but not through the armaglass windows. The coals left from the morning fire imparted a residual warmth . . . and some smokiness, because Nylan had added the hearth after the walls had been started.

Nylan sipped the cup of leaf tea slowly, lingering past breakfast. With his head still aching two days after the laser had failed, he wondered if the bows had killed the powerheads earlier than necessary. He massaged his neck again and looked around the empty room. The guards had left the table and were working, either in the lower level of the tower, or in the stables, out of the cold rain that had fallen for two days straight.

The inside tower drains were working, at least, and water seemed to be filling the outfall, from what he could see out the front door. Nylan smiled, but the smile faded as he thought of the uncompleted bathhouse and unfinished outside conduits to the cistern. He should check those drains before long.

He wished he'd been able to roof and finish the bathhouse before the rain. The heating stove in the bathhouse was only half-built. With the laser gone, he'd have to mortar the plates for the water heater in place, but he couldn't do any more brick and stonework until the rain stopped, and the clouds outside were so dark they were almost black.

Nylan took another sip of the hot tea that tasted almost undrinkable, but seemed to help relax rigid muscles and relieve the worst of the headache, and massaged the back of his neck with his left hand once again.

The main tower door opened and then closed. A single figure stomped wet boots, then headed toward the tables.

"You look like manure." Ayrlyn slid onto the bench across the table from the engineer. Her short red hair was wet and plastered to her skull, and rivulets of water ran down her cheeks.

"Manure feels better. You look wet."

"The joys of trying to locate logs and timber before the weather turns really nasty. We need more deadwood for the furnace and kitchen stove. It cuts easier." Ayrlyn wiped the water off her face, but another rivulet coursed down her left cheek right afterward. "There's a lot of internal work this place needs. That means green wood, and it's a mess to cut."

Nylan's eyes rose to the blank stone walls, the unfinished shelves, and the lack of interior walls. "You could say that."

Ayrlyn studied Nylan. "You look like a worn-out engineer."

"You look like a soaked and worn-out artisan and singer." Nylan paused. "I never did tell you how effective that Westwind guard song was."

"It's a terrible song," protested Ayrlyn.

"That's why it's effective. Every anthem ever written is terrible, either melodically or because it's lyrically tear-jerking."

"You've made a study?"

"No . . . but the Sybran anthem . . . you know, 'the winters of time . . . the banners of ice . . .' Or how about the Svennish hymn to the mother? Or 'The Swift Ships of Heaven'? Have you really listened to the words?"

"Enough." Ayrlyn laughed. "Enough."

"All right . . . but what about the Akalyrr 'Song to the Father'?"

"Enough! I said enough."

Nylan sipped his tea, trying not to grimace.

"That good?"

"It helps. That's all I can say about it." He set the mug down again. "Have you learned anything new from our friend Relyn?"

Ayrlyn glanced toward the end of the great room. "He's learning how to use that hand, but he still feels crippled—and angry. He's confused, too, because he owes allegiance to this Lord Sillek, yet he feels he was tricked. He also doesn't think much of Narliat . . . or of Gerlich, for that matter."

"He has good taste," Nylan said. "Has he told you anything new that we didn't know about this planet?"

"It's hard to say." Ayrlyn frowned. "He pretty much agrees with Narliat's story about the landing of the demons, and so does Hryessa. She's taken to Saryn, by the way. She sees Ryba as a goddess, and she can't relate to a goddess. Saryn's merely a mighty warrior. Hryessa also tells the demon story a little differently—the demons are the patrons of men and of the wizards, and white is the color of destruction here."

"Why wouldn't it be?" asked Nylan. "The demons of light are white."

"In a lot of cultures, especially low-tech ones, white means purity. It was in ancient Svenn, and in Etalyarr. Here, darkness is pure, and there's not much emphasis on cleanliness. All wizards are men, obviously."

"Wonderful." Nylan glanced toward the door and the stairs, but the great room remained empty save for them.

"Black wizards are rare. That's why Hryessa will look at you."

"Because I'm rare?"

"Because they all think you're a black wizard." Ayrlyn smiled.

"How would they know? I don't even know why what I do works."

"For Relyn, Hryessa, and Narliat, it's simple. White wizards throw firebolts without using tools or weapons. White wizards destroy people and things. Black wizards build things, like towers, tools, and weapons. Or heal. You build. So you're a black wizard." Ayrlyn shrugged. "You also have silver hair, and none of the white wizards do. They aren't sure about black wizards, since there aren't many."

"If I have to be one or the other, I guess it's better to be black." Nylan took another sip of the tea, trying not to make a face, then set the earthenware mug—a recent addition from Rienadre and the brick kiln—down and massaged his neck. "Your healing makes you a black wizard, too."

"I don't know that I'm any wizard . . ."

"You're a healer."

"A minor black wizard, then. Very minor."

Ayrlyn offered a quick smile, then continued. "Relyn seems to think that this Lord Sillek has his hands full. His western neighbor, a charming fellow named Ildyrom, has been trying to take over some grasslands. Young Sillek also is being choked by his northern neighbor. Relyn doesn't understand the government there, but it sounds like a form of council run by big traders. They hold the river near the Northern Ocean and all the ports."

"So he's got trouble on all sides?"

"According to Relyn. Narliat says it's not that bad, and all Hryessa knows is that food has gotten scarcer. Oh, Relyn also says that no one likes fighting the westerners—Jeranyi, I think they're called—because the women fight alongside the men."

"Rather chauvinistic culture."

"I'd say that's the rule, mostly. It's a warm planet."

"What does warmth have to do with male chauvinism?"

"It doesn't necessarily, except that women handle extreme cold better than men. Look at Heaven, where women have more than half the government. Some anthropologists theorize that cold tolerance is the whole basis of the Sybran culture." Ayrlyn spread her hands.

"Do these Jeranyi come from a cold culture? I didn't recall any mountains there."

"No. Maybe there's some other reason."

"Anything else?"

"He's given me a lot about local customs, trade, that sort of thing, but it's background. Helpful, but background. The other thing is that this Lord Sillek doesn't have an heir, or any surviving siblings. That bothered Relyn."

"Probably civil war if Sillek dies," mused Nylan. "Two out of three says this Sillek's definitely got his hands full." He looked down at the rapidly cooling tea and wondered if he could force himself to drink any more.

"That's my reading, but we're only going on what we've seen, and that isn't much, plus the in-depth reports of three locals, and the offhand remarks of traders." Ayrlyn blotted a thin line of water from her neck below her right ear. "Rain looks like it's never going to stop."

"It's probably snowing on the mountaintops." Nylan looked toward the windows, then swung his feet over the bench. "Time to check the drains."

"Drains?"

"The little details, like keeping the tower from being washed away. The things that get forgotten in the sagas of heroes and heroic deeds."

"Still bitter about that?"

"A little." He snorted. "But it's time to go get wet."

"I'm going to dry off some before I go back out there."

"I haven't been out, and I should have been." The engineer stood and carried the mug down to the north door of the tower, where he washed it in the one bucket, rinsed it in the other, and racked it in the peeled-limb framework leaned against the stone wall. The second slot in the upper left was his.

Then he closed his jacket and eased open the north door, which not only squeaked, but scraped against the floor stones. A blast of rain slewed across him, but he hurried out and closed the door behind him.

The water resistance of his ship jacket wouldn't last long, but he wanted to check the drains in the uncompleted bathhouse. The last thing he wanted was the rain undercutting the walls or their foundation.

A roll of thunder followed another line of what seemed

solid water that hit Nylan just as he ducked through the half-covered archway and into the unroofed bathhouse.

"Oh . . . frig!"

The water was already ankle-deep. Nylan plodded forward toward the first drain where he could sense some drainage. He pushed back his sleeves and thrust his hands into the water, ignoring the chill, feeling around, and finally finding a chunk of brick. He pulled that out of the mud, only to have something sharp scrape the back of his left hand. He heaved the fragment over the wall and bent down again, fishing through the muddy water and coming up with a long shard of slate. He threw that outside the walls and looked at his hand.

The rain washed away the blood from the thin cut as fast as it welled out, but the cut was only skin-deep. The water started to swirl down the drain, then stopped. The engineer sighed and went fishing again, this time coming up with a round stone just the right size to plug the drain.

He watched the water swirl and start to drain, and again stop.

After repeating the process nearly a dozen times, the drain seemed to be flowing freely, and he slogged through the instep-deep water to the other end of the bathhouse and the second drain—also plugged.

After four tries, he got the second drain running freely, but the first drain had become plugged again—with several more stone fragments.

All in all, Nylan slogged back and forth between the two drains nearly half a dozen times before the area inside the walls was drained, although several depressions remained as ankle-deep puddles.

Then he circled the tower, checking the rock-lined drainage way on the lower east side of the tower. While the drainage way was a narrow rushing stream that seemed to divert the deluge from the tower foundations, beyond the stones the water had already dug a trench knee-deep through the lowest point of the makeshift road to the ridge.

Nylan shook his head. They would need a stone culvert,

or something, to keep the road from being washed out with every heavy rainstorm. He took a deep breath and headed back to the north door of the tower, his shipboots squishing with every step.

Water-resistant or not, Nylan's jacket was soaked, as was everything else. But the drains were working, and the water from all around the tower was flowing freely into the outfall he had designed. Beyond the outfall . . . He just winced.

His head ached again; his neck and shoulder muscles were tight, and his eyes burned, and he trudged back to the north side of the tower. He turned the heavy lever, and the latch plate lifted. A strong push and the door swung open, barely wide enough for him to squeeze through sideways, before it stuck.

Nylan edged inside and checked the door. The hinge pins were solid, and the strap plates hadn't moved. He bent down, then nodded. With the moisture, the wood had swelled, and perhaps the latch end had drooped some with the extra weight and usage. Whatever the exact reason, the end of the door was wedged on the stone.

He grunted, and half lifted, half shoved the door back closed.

After closing the door, he took off his jacket and wrung it dry, letting the water spill on the stones by the door. Then he stripped off his boots and the shipsuit and repeated the process with the shipsuit, ignoring the fact that he was standing near-nude by the door. He turned his boots upside down and poured out the remaining water.

As he set them down, the north door eased open, then stuck once more.

Siret squeezed inside, barely able to maneuver her thickening midsection through the narrow opening. Her deep green eyes fixed on him. "Ser?"

"Trying to wring out the worst of the water," he explained.

Siret said nothing, her eyes still on him as he redonned the shipsuit, and he could feel himself blushing. Once he had the damp suit back on, he shoved the door shut, barefoot, his feet sliding on the cold damp stones.

"I'm sorry, ser," Siret finally said. "I should have helped, but I . . . I just . . . I don't know what happened." Her eyes did not meet Nylan's.

"That's all right." He slowly pulled on the damp boots.

"Thank you." Siret turned and headed toward the great room on the other side of the central stairs.

Nylan followed. Even before he was two steps into the great room, he felt the heat, from the hearth, more welcome than the odor of fresh bread coming from the grass baskets. He spread his damp jacket on the shelves beneath the stairs, then walked toward the warmth, glad that his seat was close to the hearth.

The two tables were nearly filled with damp marines. Narliat's dry leathers stood out, as did Kadran's and Kyseen's. The dryness of the cooks' clothing, Nylan could understand, but Narliat sat beside Gerlich, who looked like a drowned rodent, with his damp chestnut beard and longer hair plastered against the back of his neck. Relyn, across the table, was soaked as well, but he offered a smile.

Nylan returned Relyn's smile and nodded when he passed Gerlich, and then eased into the seat at the end of the bench closest to the hearth.

Saryn sat on the end of the table with her back to the windows, across from Nylan. Between her and Ayrlyn sat Hryessa in dampened leathers. Relyn sat to Ayrlyn's left.

"The fire feels good," Nylan observed.

"Since everyone's soaked, it seemed like a good idea." Ryba smiled faintly. "Our resident healer and communicator pointed that out."

"The damp is worse for health than snow would be. So I suggested the fire," Ayrlyn said.

Nylan turned on the bench so that the heat from the hearth would warm his back. While the shipsuits were thin, the synthetics did dry quickly.

The big pot in the center of the table held a soupy stew, to be poured over the bread. Saryn passed him a basket of bread, and he broke off a chunk, then stood and ladled stew over it.

"How did you get soaked?" Ryba asked.

"Cleaning out the drains in the bathhouse so that the foundations wouldn't get washed away. I also checked the other drains and the outfalls."

"It's snowing on the higher peaks," said Ayrlyn. "I wouldn't be surprised if we got snow here within an eight-day or two."

"I hope it holds off. We've still got a bunch to do to get the bathhouse finished."

"Will it take that long?" asked Ryba.

"Long enough," said Nylan, pouring the hot root and bark tea into his mug where, when the hot liquid hit the clay, the mug cracked in two, as if a magical knife had cloven it, and the tea poured across the table.

"Friggin' . . . !" Nylan nearly knocked over the bench as he lurched sideways to avoid the boiling liquid that had started to drip off the table onto his legs. As he stood beside Ryba's chair, he looked around for something to wipe away the tea.

"Ser!" Kyseen stood and tossed a bunched rag toward Nylan, which opened and dropped onto Hryessa's bread and stew.

Hryessa's mouth opened.

"These things happen," said Ayrlyn calmly, as she reclaimed the rag and spread it on the tea puddle.

Hryessa looked at her stew and bread, then at Ayrlyn.

Saryn grinned, shaking her head. "It doesn't look like it's been your morning, Engineer."

Nylan reached forward and gathered the tea- and stew-soaked rag, carefully wringing the liquid into the inside corner of the hearth where the heat would evaporate it. Then he mopped up more of the tea and repeated the process.

In time he sat back down, glad at least that the split mug hadn't poured bark tea over his bread and stew.

"Here's another mug, ser." Rienadre set one in front of him and retreated. "Some of them don't fire right. I'm sorry."

"Would you pour the tea?" Nylan asked. "I haven't had much luck."

Rienadre took the kettle and poured. The mug held.

"Thank you." Nylan took a small sip, marveling that the tea wasn't bad. That alone told him how bedraggled he felt. He took a mouthful of bread and stew, then another, trying to ignore the bitterness of the tubers and onions. From the corner of his eye as he set down his mug, Nylan could see Gerlich bending toward Narliat.

"Finishing the bathhouse with hand tools is going to take time—and dryer weather," the engineer added.

"Cannot a mage do anything?" asked Narliat. "You have builded a tower that reaches to the skies, and you cannot make a few channels in stone?"

Put that way . . . Nylan frowned. "Perhaps I can, after all." The real question was the timing of Narliat's question. Was Gerlich thinking up the nasty questions for the armsman, or was Narliat that disruptive on his own?

"You are a great mage, and great mages do great things," Narliat added.

Nylan wanted to strangle him for the setup. Instead, he turned to the armsman. "I have never claimed to be a great mage. But I have done my best to accomplish what needed to be done, and I will continue to do so." His eyes locked on Narliat until the other looked away.

Then he took another chunk of bread and ate more of the stew, trying to ignore the gamy taste Kyseen had not been able to mask with salt and strong onions.

XLII

As HE WAITED for Ryba, Nylan stood in the darkness at the unshuttered, unglazed window and looked at Freyja, the knife edges of the needle-peak softened but slightly by the starlight and by the snow.

His stomach growled, reminding him that the spiced bear

stew—that was what Kyseen had called it—had not fully agreed with his system. Would it be that way all winter, although he could scarcely call it winter, since only a few dustings of snow had fallen around the tower? Not all of the scrub bushes and deciduous trees had shed their gray leaves, although it was clear most kept about half, shriveled against the winter.

Meals were enough, so far, to keep body together, but not much more, and it wasn't that cold yet.

Nylan leaned forward and looked to the north side of the tower and the half-roofed bathhouse. Almost instinctively, he curled his hands, and his fingertips rested on the callused spots at the base of his fingers. He had far too much to finish, far too much, and, as time passed, fewer and fewer cared, except for the few like Ryba, Ayrlyn, and Huldran, and the guards with children.

He turned toward the stairs as he heard Ryba's steps—heavier now—approaching.

"Dyliess hasn't been kind to my bladder," said the marshal.

"I'm sorry about the tower design," apologized Nylan. "I just wasn't thinking about waste disposal."

In a rough-sewn nightshirt of grayish beaten linen, Ryba sat down heavily on her side of the twin couches. "Narliat and Relyn think this tower is luxury, the sort of place for lords and dukes or whatever. Neither wants to leave. They'll have to, by spring at the latest."

"If they have to leave, why are you letting them stay?"

"I don't want the locals to find out much about us until we've got things in better order. So far, the only people who have left have been those who have fled our weapons, mostly in terror, and traders who have never seen things closely. I'd like to keep it that way for a while longer. And we can learn a few things more from Narliat and Relyn." Ryba shrugged. "Relyn might end up fathering a child or two, and he seems bright enough."

The engineer pulled at his chin. "You're pregnant, and so

are Siret and Ellysia. Isn't that a lot for the numbers we've got?"

"Three or four out of sixteen—not counting Hryessa— that's only about a third, and most will be able to fight by late spring. Most children will be born in winter or early spring in Westwind, anyway."

The calm certainty in Ryba's voice chilled Nylan more than the wind at his back, but he asked, "Four?"

"I think Istril is, also," said Ryba.

"Istril? She doesn't strike me as the type to play around."

"I could be wrong," Ryba said. "I'm not always certain about these things, but she will be sooner or later."

"But who?"

"I can't pry—or see—into everything, Nylan. Right now, I'm just fortunate enough to be gifted, or cursed, with glimpses of what *might* be. That's bad enough. More than enough."

"I'm sorry."

"Do you know what it's like to see pieces of the future? Not to know, for certain, if they're what will be or what might be? Or whether you'll bring them into being by reacting against them?"

Nylan cleared his throat. "I said I was sorry. I hadn't thought about things quite that way."

Ryba looked at the stones of the wall beside Nylan. "You deal with stone and brick and metal—the certain things. I'm wrestling with what will sustain life here for generations to come. What do I do about men who are killers? Or those who will leave? Or may leave?"

"I don't like the implication that I'll leave." Nylan sat down beside the dark-haired woman and touched her shoulder. "I don't have any pat answers. I do what I can, everything that I can think of, as well as I can."

"I know, Nylan. You work like two people. You've done things I don't think are possible, and Westwind wouldn't be without you. But a place isn't a community without traditions, values, that sort of thing, holding it together. That's why we need your tower, Ayrlyn's songs—"

"And your ability to teach and create military strength?"

Ryba nodded. "It's going to be tough."

"It's already hard."

"It's going to get harder," she predicted, looking out at the cold shape of Freyja. "A lot harder."

In the end, they lay skin to skin, and, after a time, Ryba was passionate, demanding, and warm. Predictably, before they had even relaxed, she had to get up.

"You just went," he protested sleepily.

"There are some things, especially now, where I don't control the timing." She pulled her gown down and padded down the stone steps.

Fighting exhaustion and sleep, Nylan tried to analyze the subtle wrongness behind her words . . . but nothing made sense.

Before either solutions or sleep reached him, Ryba padded back up the steps and slipped into the couch. Her cool hand stroked his forehead for a moment. "You're a good man, Nylan. No matter what happens, remember that." She squeezed his shoulder.

He squeezed her hand in return and murmured, "Know you try your best, for everyone."

She shuddered, and let him hold her, but she would not turn to him as she sobbed silently.

XLIII

IN THE NORTH yard outside the bathhouse, Nylan picked up the hammer and chisel. Behind him, on the roof, Denalle and Huldran spiked roof tiles onto the cross-stringers mortised into the main timbers to provide a flat surface.

Overhead, the clouds were white and puffy, like summer clouds, but the chill in the late autumn wind belied that. To the west, the clouds seemed evenly spaced, and Nylan hoped that they would stay that way. His eyes dropped to the pair on the roof—Cessya had ridden off with Ayrlyn.

". . . damned gourds, whatever they were, never ripened . . . bitter in the stew, worse than that rancid bear meat . . ."

"Just keep complaining, Denalle, and I'll spike your hand right under the next tile," snapped Huldran.

"Potatoes are good . . . hope they last . . ."

"More spikes, Denalle."

Nylan let his eyes drop from the unfinished roof to the dark stone before him that would be a water-conduit section.

"And you cannot make a few channels in stone?" Narliat had asked, at Gerlich's prompting. And Ryba had just left Nylan hanging.

His choices were simple. Abandon the idea of showers. Finish the trough pipes in wood, which would need continuous maintenance, or try low-tech stone-cutting methods. In a low-tech culture, cleanliness was important for health and survival, and if he didn't make it easy or halfway convenient, cleanliness would go the way of the *Winterlance*. Besides, abandoning anything would cause problems with Gerlich. He was coming to like the big man less and less. Was that because he was coming to trust his feelings more? And Ryba—how much was she deceiving him, just to ensure that Westwind would survive?

He moistened his lips. In some ways, it didn't matter. He was stuck finishing the bathhouse the hard way. He took a deep breath and studied the chunk of dark stone, letting his senses drop into the heavy mass, following the lines of stress and fault. If he nudged that line . . . and boosted that . . . then, just maybe, the stone would break . . .

He brought the hammer down on the chisel. *Clung!* The impact shivered up his left arm. There was a technique to chiseling stone, and he had no idea of what it was. He raised the hammer again.

Clung! A flake of stone the size of his thumb flew from the chisel, but the reverberation still numbed his arm.

A dozen strokes later, he had learned a better angle and

not to grip the chisel so tightly. He also had only chipped out a narrow groove in the stone.

The clouds had almost disappeared, leaving the sky a bright green-blue, but the wind seemed stronger, and colder.

Even before he heard the hooves, Nylan could sense the approaching horses, knowing that they were marines—and Ayrlyn. There was no sense of the white disorderliness that seemed to accompany the arrival of locals.

The five horses, and the cart acquired from Skiodra and since rebuilt, headed over the ridge and down the track to the tower. The clay remained damp enough from the previous rain that there was no dust. Riding pillion behind Istril was a woman in tattered leathers, with long brown hair. Another refugee? wondered the engineer. And Istril? She wasn't riding any differently. Was that another of Ryba's foresights? Something that *might* be?

Nylan shrugged, wondering how many more women would arrive at Tower Black before the winter closed in. Given the attrition the angels had suffered, more bodies would be helpful—if there were enough food. They had the sheep and the chickens, but how would they feed livestock through the winter? Didn't that mean more grain? Or grass or hay? Or something?

As the horses passed and he saw that Ayrlyn was safe, he picked up the hammer once more, ignoring the numbness in his fingers from the wind and the impact of iron upon steel.

By the time the triangle by the main south entrance to the tower clanged for the midday meal, Nylan had completed rough channels in two stones, each the length of his forearm. His fingers were cramping, and his arms were scratched from the rock fragments that had split and ricocheted. No wonder not much got built quickly—or with any complexity—in a low-tech culture.

Nylan set aside the hammer and chisel and stood stretching as Denalle and Huldran climbed off the roof. The eastern side was more than half finished.

"Looks good," he offered.

"Except we have to mortar it or it'll be dripping melted

snow inside all winter," pointed out Huldran.

"Doing the roof's friggin' hard on the knees," added Denalle.

"You want to wash clothes in the snow?" asked the older guard.

"The way things are going," said Denalle, looking down at her threadbare and tattered working shipsuit, "we won't have anything to wash."

"The healer just brought in a cart of some kind of cloth, and more barrels of flour, it looked like. You'll be spending part of the winter sewing up your kit for next year." Huldran smiled at Nylan.

"I didn't sign up for sewing."

"Neither did the rest of us. Do you want to fight with your bare breasts hanging out?" asked Huldran.

Denalle glared at the ground.

"Let's go eat," suggested the engineer.

As Nylan neared the lower table, Relyn, sitting beside Jaseen, raised his right arm, and the artificial hand, and nodded. The engineer smiled back.

"You made that, ser?" asked Huldran. "Why?"

"So he wouldn't have any excuses to mope around," Nylan said dryly. "You'll note that I made it blunt. Very blunt."

Huldran laughed.

The newcomer was seated between Saryn and Ayrlyn, near the head of the table on the window side. For some reason Narliat was on Ayrlyn's right, with Gerlich on the other side of the former armsman. Nylan surveyed the two tables and found that Hryessa was seated near the foot of the second table, beside Istril and across from Relyn and Jaseen. Istril looked down at her trencher, and her lips curled. Had Ryba been right? Was she pregnant? The engineer glanced toward the hearth and kept walking until he reached the end of the table.

"How is it going?" Ryba asked as Nylan waited for Huldran and then slipped into his end seat beside the marine.

"Huldran and the others are doing well on the roof. Maybe two days before it's tight."

"Could be three," Huldran said, "if we run into trouble."

"And you?" Ryba asked Nylan.

"I'm getting the hang of the stone-cutting, but it's slow."

"The weather will hold for at least several days," Ayrlyn said.

"Good." Nylan poured some of the hot bark-and-root tea and waited. The mug did not crack. He picked it up and took a sip, waiting for Huldran to help herself to the bread in the grass basket. "Another refugee?" The engineer turned to Ayrlyn as he took a chunk of bread and handed the basket to Ryba.

"Thank you," said the marshal.

"This is Murkassa," said Ayrlyn in Old Anglorat. "She's from Gnotos. That's a little town in Gallos, just east of the Westhorns."

The round-faced girl, and she seemed more a girl than a woman, nodded, her long hair so thin that it fell in a cloud over her shoulders.

"This is Nylan. He is an engineer and a mage," Ayrlyn explained, still in Anglorat.

Murkassa's brow furrowed at the word "engineer." She turned to Ayrlyn. "What kind of mage?"

"Black, I'm told," Nylan answered before Narliat could open his mouth and create trouble. "I make things."

Narliat had his mouth open, but Ayrlyn's elbow caught the former armsman in the gut, and he closed it.

"Nylan is—" Gerlich started to speak, then stopped as he realized Murkassa did not understand him.

"How was your luck with the traders, Ayrlyn?" asked Ryba.

"They had some of what we needed, but it cost me three blades and a gold." She glanced at Nylan. "I'm not quite as good as the engineer."

"Any spikes?" Nylan asked, knowing that Huldran wanted to know.

"A small keg—those were half a gold, and they wouldn't budge on that, but you and Huldran put them high on the list."

"We can't finish the bathhouse roof without them," said the marine. "Not without taking all winter."

"What else?"

"Heavy wool cloth. Rough as a new recruit. Some tanned hides for winter gloves, another eight barrels of flour and two of dried fruit. A bag of salt for drying whatever we slaughter or bring in from hunting. Another big kettle for Kyseen. A half-dozen needles—another half gold, but how can anyone sew without needles?—and a roll or spool of heavy thread that's almost twine. And a bunch of little things, some spices, and a big bag of onions and two sacks of potatoes, and a barrel of dried corn for the livestock." The redhead shrugged. "That doesn't leave too much in the Westwind treasury. They said they'd be back in an eight-day, if it doesn't snow."

"After that, we'll probably be on our own, I guess," said Ryba. "The snow line is creeping down the peaks around us." She turned to Murkassa and switched to Anglorat. "How . . . did you . . . come to Westwind?"

"I was sold to be the consort of Jilkar. He is a hauler in Gnotos, and a strong man. He beat his first consort to death because she angered him. She gave him only daughters, and then she ran away with a trooper from Fenard. Jilkar found them and let the man go." Murkassa shrugged. "He would have beaten me. He beats everyone. I heard of the tower of women, and I ran. If I did not find you, I would die in the Westhorns. But I did find you." A fleeting smile crossed her face.

"You are welcome to stay as long as you wish."

"Can I stay forever?"

"If you follow our way," Ryba answered.

"No one said anything to Jilkar?" Ayrlyn's tone suggested she knew the answer.

"No. He is the hauler. He takes the wool to Fenard. He is stronger than any two men, and he has a house on the hill with guards."

As the others drew out the sordid social structure of Gnotos, all too familiar a pattern, from what Nylan could tell, he sipped the tea and ate.

After the midday meal, Nylan returned to the north tower yard, and the cold wind out of the northwest. Huldran, Cessya, and Denalle worked on the roof, with Cessya lugging up the stones, Denalle placing them, and Huldran spiking them in place.

Nylan studied the stone that he was supposed to turn into a conduit. There had to be a faster way to cut the stone, didn't there? For a long time, he let his senses range over the oblong of black rock before him. He'd already discovered that he felt uneasy, so much that his head ached and his stomach twisted, if he even came close to mimicking the white lines of fire that the local mages effected.

After concentrating on the stone for a time, he finally placed the chisel and lifted the hammer. The reverberations seemed to be less when he didn't worry so much about precise chisel placement, but the order of the stone.

His progress was better with the new technique, not anything to boast about compared to the laser, but by the time the triangle clanged again, he had five more lengths of conduit bottom.

After he stacked the conduit in the corner of the bathhouse, on the eastern side under the completed roof, he flexed his sore and increasingly callused fingers—only small blisters.

"You really got that in place," he told Huldran, looking up at the expanse of completed roof tiling.

"Thank darkness that the healer came up with another keg of spikes." The marine reached out and knocked on the side of the crude ladder-pole she had just climbed down. "I never thought so, but you might get your bathhouse and laundry, ser."

"I thought you wanted the showers," Nylan joked.

"Choosing between stinking and bathing in ice water isn't a choice I'd want to make." Huldran lowered the ladder-pole, and she and Denalle laid it down under the completed roof, then gathered the spikes they had dropped.

Every single spike was valuable, Nylan realized, especially in a low-tech culture where each had to be fashioned by hand. He walked around the tower to the stream, hoping it wouldn't be too long before he could use the bathhouse.

After washing his hands and face, he walked back around the tower and, as he neared the almost-completed archway from the bathhouse to the tower, he whistled a few notes. What were the words?

". . . an engineer's work is never done, / not even after the long day's run . . ."

He smiled to himself as he opened the door, which no longer scraped the stones—although it had taken Saryn and Selitra most of a morning to plane and carve it back into shape.

"You seem cheerful, Engineer," said Gerlich. Narliat just bowed.

"The stone-shaping's coming better, and Huldran's got the roof in place."

"Good." Gerlich offered a quick smile, and he and Narliat turned, leaving Nylan as he closed the north door.

The engineer wondered why neither had looked pleased. Did they want to stink or bathe in freezing water? Or was it because each of Nylan's accomplishments boosted Ryba's authority and the satisfaction of the guards with her rule? And it was rule, Nylan knew full well, and there wasn't that much doubt in Nylan's mind that Gerlich would rather be the one doing the ruling—or that having Gerlich in charge would be a disaster. Ryba did what had to be done, but Nylan knew it wasn't always easy for her. Gerlich would end up like every other male tyrant on the planet.

He pulled at his chin, wondering why so many men had to dominate. Then maybe women would be just the same, given the chance. With a shrug, he walked toward the hearth of the great room and the aroma of fresh-baked bread and cooked onions.

XLXIV

HISSL PACES ACROSS the small room, then peers out the window toward the river and the stubbled fields that lie beyond. Although the sun glints off the puddles in the fields, the sky is turning the bluer green-blue that presages winter. The wizard looks away from the distant points of glare and paces back toward the table.

"Nothing! We sit here and wait. And Terek meets with Lord Sillek while I rot here."

He paces back across the small room, passing the table and the screeing glass again, then back to the window. The distant puddles still throw glare at him.

Finally, he seats himself at the table that holds the flat mirrorlike glass. He concentrates. The white mists swirl. He concentrates until the sweat beads on his forehead, although the room is pleasantly cool, filled with the scents from the bakery up the street, and the hum of conversations.

At last, the image appears—that of a black tower, with a second, and lower, building rising beside it, already roofed with the same black slate tiles that cover the taller tower. A short, stone-walled causeway leads to the tower and to a heavy door banded together with strips of metal—not iron, but some metal Hissl does not recognize, though it feels like iron through the glass.

Farther uphill, the angels, some in black and others in leathers, are digging a long ditch in a line that leads toward the tower. On the uphill portion of the ditch, the black mage and an angel are placing lengths of stone in the trench. There is a trough filled with what might be mortar beside the stones.

Hissl squints and tries to focus the image, but the best he can do is catch a glimpse of a section of rock that appears to have a deep trench gouged in it. He slumps back into the chair.

"Black angels and a black mage." He shivers for a moment. No lord he knows could have built a tower like that, and not in a mere two seasons. Yet the black mage who lives with the angels has done so, and the mage has done other things, as well, things that Hissl does not understand.

"Still, they have not felt the winter, and the number of cairns grows. By spring . . ." He raises his eyebrows and smiles.

In the spring and early summer, Ildyrom and his people will be busy planting. Hissl nods to himself.

XLV

A LOW FIRE burned in the bathhouse stove, but the building— still open inside except for the three jakes stalls at the north end—remained chill.

Nylan washed and shaved his several days' worth of beard in one of the laundry tubs. He looked wistfully to his right, at the unfinished showers, and at the piles of slate stone and powdered mortar heaped in the middle of the room. While there was water to the ceramic nozzles, he and Huldran still had to finish the stone floors, or all they would have would be frozen clay. He took a deep breath and splashed away skin, whiskers, and blood.

After washing, he rinsed his waste water down the floor drain, with a breath of relief as the water gurgled out of sight. He hoped the combination of deeply buried drain lines and the outfall covering—and oversizing—would be enough to get them through the winter.

Wearing just a tattered pair of trousers—spoils, again— he walked the length of the bathhouse, along the already packed clay of the east side, and through the archway into the tower and up the stairs, all four flights to the top level.

Ryba had already dressed, and was pulling on her boots as Nylan stripped off the leather trousers and donned his working shipsuit. She stood and straightened the blanket as he struggled into the leather boots.

"It looks like a storm is coming in hard," she said. "Can you finish the bathhouse?"

"The inside will take a day or two more. We've got the jakes and the laundry area finished." Nylan walked over to the sole armaglass window and looked up at the dark clouds boiling out of the northwest, cloaking Freyja in blackness, with snow thickening and dropping to shroud the lower parts of the western peaks and the heights behind the tower.

A thin layer of ice covered the window ledge outside the casement, and the engineer watched as one flake, then another, dropped onto the ice, melding with it and turning transparent, the black-gray stone showing through.

The flakes thickened, and even the lower sections of Freyja disappeared in the snow that seemed so white near the tower and so dark in the distance. The ground remained brown, with a few white patches.

Nylan closed the armaglass window, and the shutters. When he looked down, he realized that he had stood before the open window long enough for a small pile of flakes to accumulate, but as he watched, the whiteness faded into a damp splotch on the roughly smoothed plank floor.

"Why did you close the shutters?" asked Ryba, fully dressed in her shipsuit, and even wearing a black ship jacket. "It looks like midnight in here that way. I can't see in pitch-blackness, the way you can."

"We're going down to the main level, and no one's going to be here." He walked around the couches toward where the marshal of Westwind stood.

"That makes sense, but it still bothers me when it's so dark."

"It's going to be a long and dark winter."

"You are so cheerful this morning."

"I try," he answered.

They walked down the long stone steps, the sounds of their boots echoing away from the stairwell and into the open levels they passed. Several marines were still dressing on the third level, but none looked toward Nylan and Ryba.

The tables were largely full, and even Murkassa sat at the end, on Istril's right, while Hryessa sat on the slim trooper's left. Istril looked at the bread on her trencher, but had not lifted it.

Did she look pale? Nylan smiled, getting a quick and faint smile in return as he followed Ryba toward the head of the table and the hearth.

After he slid onto the bench, Nylan poured the bark-and-root tea into the dark brown mug. The tea's taste was still bitter, but warming. He reached for the dark bread.

"A storm like this won't last," predicted Relyn, sitting at the last seat on the window side of the first table. "The snowflakes are too large."

"The snow will bring a long rest," pronounced Narliat. His cloak was wrapped tightly around him, and he glanced toward the cold hearth.

"I'm glad for the rest," announced Huldran.

"You don't get one. Not yet," said Nylan. "We've still got the shower floors and partitions to install."

"Cessya can help."

Cessya looked at Huldran, her eyes dark.

"It's easier than clearing and packing snow," intervened Nylan.

"What are you talking about?" asked Gerlich.

"We still have to keep the area around the doors, the outfalls, and the trails to the stables and down to the forest open." Nylan pulled at his chin, then looked toward Ayrlyn, then Ryba. Both nodded.

"We'll need to have ways the horses can travel. They'll need some exercise," pointed out Ayrlyn. "We'll need them to bring up more wood." She cleared her throat. "Hryessa, Siret, and Murkassa need to gather more cones."

"Cones?" asked Nylan.

"They have seeds, and they'll help feed the chickens," Ayrlyn said.

"Your chickens, they will taste like the pine trees."

"I'd rather have live pine-tasting chickens than dead tasty ones halfway through the winter. We don't have near enough food for the livestock, and that will help," answered Ayrlyn. "If the traders come back, they're supposed to have some more dried corn. If they come back . . ."

"We can't have people sitting around all winter," added Saryn. "They'd be at each others' throats."

"They can't sit around anyway," said Ryba. "We'll need some additional food, something from hunting, and probably more firewood."

"A lot more firewood," predicted Nylan. "We probably ought to require dragging as much up here as we burn."

"How?"

"If we keep doing it, we should be able to keep a path clear to the forest at the base of the ridge. Ayrlyn—you said we could drag trunks with the horses, and cut them outside the causeway."

"The guards can only stay out so long, and we don't have enough cold-weather clothing for everyone," pointed out Saryn.

"We have wool and thread and needles," said Ayrlyn.

Nylan cleared his throat. "We could dry some of the wood near the furnace, and we need a lot of furnishings—tables, even dressers."

"We don't have that many nails," said Ryba.

"They used to put things together with pegs. We can do that," Ayrlyn pointed out. "It takes more time, but we're going to have a lot of time."

"You can make glue," added Relyn. "The crafters dry and grind hooves, I think, and some parts of the hides and boil them."

"Arms practice. For everyone. I don't want a tower full of crafters come spring," added Ryba. "They'll have to be better than any of the locals when the battles resume."

"I think archery is out," said Nylan.

"Because of the weather? No. There will be enough clear days . . ."

"The clear days are cold enough to a freeze a man's lungs," said Relyn.

"Woolen scarves would help," Ayrlyn said, "but you'd have to hold down heavy exertion and mouth breathing."

"We'll take it as it comes." Ryba broke off a chunk of bread. "There's a lot we can do to get ready for next spring and summer."

"How are we going to get around in this stuff?" asked Huldran, with a gesture toward the window. "We don't have skis or sleds or sled dogs."

"Slowly," says Hryessa. "In the lower Westhorns, the snow gets deeper than a horse's head."

"Snowshoes," Ryba said, "and old-fashioned wooden skis with leather thongs, just like Gerlich and Saryn have been making."

Nylan frowned. Would he have to learn to ski? He didn't look forward to that at all, not at all.

"Have you ever skied?" Ayrlyn asked him.

"No. I never saw the joy of slogging through powdered ice for fun."

"I can learn it, and I'm not even Sybran," insisted Ayrlyn. "I'm mostly Svennish. You're at least half Sybran, aren't you?"

"About half and half. It gets complicated. But my grandfather Weryl was a Svenn. He came to Heaven as a boy. Does that make me more Sybran than if he'd come as an adult?" Nylan laughed. "He didn't ski, either."

"Was he a blond, too, ser?" asked Istril. "Like you used to be?"

"I think so. He died when I was little."

"Just because he didn't ski doesn't mean you can't," pointed out Ayrlyn.

"Especially since you'll have to if you want to go anywhere in the wintertime," added Ryba.

"You make it sound so attractive. I'll have to." Nylan frowned. "Either freeze or be stranded in the tower."

"It's not that bad," said Saryn.

As Nylan thought about a response, he saw Istril hurry from the table, toward the north door, and disappear. Her bread was untouched.

"You'll like it," added Ryba.

Ayrlyn gave a quick grin.

Nylan took a sip of tea, warm tea, and wondered just how badly he would freeze learning to get around on wooden slats.

XLVI

IN HER GREEN tunic and trousers, her hair bound back in a green and black enameled hairband, Zeldyan steps into the tower room. After closing the door, she bows deeply to the lady Ellindyja. "Honor and greetings to you, lady."

"You are now the Lady of Lornth, and I am honored," answers Ellindyja. She does not rise from the cushioned bench in the alcove, but lowers the embroidery hoop to her lap. "Your grace in coming to visit so soon shows great respect for your lord, and I am pleased to see that."

"I respect Sillek, more than most would ever know. You are my consort's mother, and, out of my deep respect for him, always to be honored and respected," says Zeldyan, inclining her head to Ellindyja again.

"I am so pleased to be included in your respects, dear, especially since your mother has always been one of my dearest friends." Ellindyja knots the yellow-green thread with deft motions, and takes up the needle.

"She would count you among her dearest and most trusted friends," answers Zeldyan, stepping toward the alcove where Sillek's mother begins an embroidered leaf on the white linen. "And a wise woman."

"Wise? I would think not," says Ellindyja as the needle

completes another loop of green comprising the leaf. "For my son has less of his heritage than his father."

"I am confident that situation will change, my lady, and that the greatness of Lornth will increase."

"With enemies on three sides, Lady Zeldyan?"

"While I would certainly defer to those who understand arms and other weapons far better than I do, I have great faith in my lord Sillek." Zeldyan pauses. "And great faith that you will offer counsel to him."

"I have always attempted to be of service to the Lords of Lornth, to his father, and to Sillek." Ellindyja completes the small leaf, knots the thread, and rethreads the needle with crimson.

The faint whine of the late fall wind rattles the closed tower window, but neither woman looks to it.

"And you have," responds Zeldyan. "You surely have."

"Thank you, my dear." Ellindyja knots the crimson thread and makes the first stitch in the small segment of the linen that will be a drop of blood. "I understand that your father has remained here in Lornth for a time."

"He plans to leave for Carpa tomorrow, now that he has seen me safely joined to Sillek."

"And your mother?"

"She will arrive to see you presently. I prevailed upon her to allow me a few moments with you to convey my respects."

"You know, my dear, Sillek may have been even wiser than I had thought. Together we might be of great assistance to him." The crimson stitches bring the hint of arterial blood to the linen.

"My lord Sillek respects you greatly, Lady Ellindyja, and I would prefer not to intrude upon that bond or that trust. I would be most happy for any and all advice that you might have."

"As I said, Lady Zeldyan, Sillek chose wisely." Ellindyja's voice is dry, but she holds the needle still for a moment. "I would trust that you might pay some heed to the possibility of ensuring the succession of Lornth."

Zeldyan bows slightly. "I would like nothing better, my lady."

A muffled *thrap* sounds on the door.

"That would be your mother, I presume?"

"Yes, my lady."

"If you would be so kind as to bid her enter?" Ellindyja's needle flashes again as Zeldyan steps toward the door.

"But, of course. She has looked forward to seeing you for some seasons." Zeldyan smiles and opens the door.

"Cakes and sweets should be arriving shortly," announces Ellindyja, "for the three of us. I had hoped we might converse." She stands and sets aside the embroidery hoop. "Erenthla!"

The heavier white-haired woman bends forward and brushes Zeldyan's cheek with her lips before stepping fully into the room and responding. "Ellindyja, I am so pleased to see you."

Zeldyan closes the door and, with a faint smile, stands, waiting.

II.

THE WINTER

II

THE WINTER

XLVII

As he walked back from the bathhouse, and the jakes he was getting gladder and gladder about having completed, Nylan pulled down the ship jacket that had a tendency to ride up over the lined leather trousers. The lining consisted of the synthetic material left from his tattered work shipsuit, inexpertly stitched in place. The combination was warmer than the shipsuit, and certainly less drafty.

In the archway between the bathhouse and the tower, just before the closed north door, ice was already forming on the walls, from the collected and frozen condensation of the breath of those who passed through, and from the moisture coming from the completed showers.

"Too far from the furnace or the water-heating stove." The engineer opened the north door and then closed it behind him, his fingers tingling from the chill metal latch—not quite cold enough to freeze skin to it.

He could sense the residual warmth from the furnace ducts as he walked into the great room, although he could tell from the lack of air motion that no logs had been added to the firebox recently.

He stopped at the staircase when he saw Ayrlyn bent over her lutar. For a time, he listened to the soft words which she half-sang, half-hummed.

On the Roof of the World, all covered with white,
I took up my blade there, and I brought back the night.
With a blade in each hand, there, and the stars at my
* boots,*
With the Legend in song, then, I set down my roots.

The demons have claimed you, forever in light,
But the darkness of order will put them to flight,
Will break them in twain, soon, and return you your
  pride,
For the Legend is kept by the blade at your side.

The blade at your side, now, must always be bright,
and the Legend we hold to is that of the right.
For never will guards lose the heights of the sky,
And never can Westwind this Legend deny . . .
And never can Westwind this Legend deny.

The words echoed softly in the great room, and the wind that hurled the snow against the shutters and windows supplied a backdrop of off-rhythm percussion.

The four armaglass windows in the great hall provided the only exterior light, and that illumination was diminished by the storm and the snow that had gathered in the outside window ledges and half covered each with snow. Snow sifted through the windows that had but shutters and built into miniature drifts on the stone ledges, drifts occasionally swirled by the gusts that forced their way around the edges of the shutters and sent thin tendrils of freezing air across the room.

Nylan waited until Ayrlyn stopped and looked up before he spoke. "That's a haunting melody."

"It should carry the words well enough." Ayrlyn's voice was cool, measured. "That's what she wants."

"Ryba?" Nylan eased himself onto the bench on the other side of the table from the redhead.

"Who else wants songs? Most people work on firewood, food"—she laughed softly—"or bathhouses and towers. I still have to do other things. Skis are what Saryn and I have been doing, but the song comes first, or, at least, not last." Ayrlyn paused. "You haven't made your skis or even tried skiing. That's going to make it hard on you. Even Siret's been out, and in her condition, balancing isn't easy."

"Do I have to?"

"Of course not. You can stay inside all winter or walk the two trails we can keep packed. Anyway . . . I wish I could have spent more time learning the skiing, but Ryba wanted the songs."

The engineer frowned. "She's trying to build a culture, in a hurry."

"I don't object to that. Songs have always been part of any culture, and we need some sort of verbal reminder . . ." Ayrlyn paused. "I just don't know that I like what I'm doing. The words are as much hers as mine, and . . . I just don't know."

"The guards seem to like them."

"Do you?"

The directness of the question stopped Nylan, and he pulled at his chin, then licked his lips. Finally, he answered. "They're too harsh." Then he shrugged. "But people only respond to strength, or force, whether that force is in song or a blade."

"Whether they're angels or demons."

Nylan nodded.

"So the great marshal will use every tool of force necessary."

"I don't see that we've had much choice. Mran, Gerlich, Relyn, bandits . . . all of them wanted to force things their way."

"That's a sad comment on so-called intelligent beings." Ayrlyn glanced toward the stairwell. "So . . . I'll sing this one tonight, after the evening meal. It should please the marshal."

"You're angry."

"It doesn't matter, does it? She's right. This world needs changing. Even I see that. What if I'm just a tool in the process?"

"We're all tools."

"You like that?" asked the redhead.

"No. But you have to survive before you can get beyond being a tool. I just haven't figured out how to get that far."

Ayrlyn shook her head. "I'll see you later, fellow tool. Now that this task is done, it's back to the mundane business of crafting and carving skis." Ayrlyn stood. "You too should join us."

"In what?"

"Making skis and learning to use them."

"Me? I've never skied."

"If you don't want to be walled behind these stones all winter, you'd better learn, and you can't learn if you don't have skis." Ayrlyn picked up the lutar. "It might make it less necessary for you to be a tool."

"That's a great choice. Be imprisoned for half the year or learn to do the unnatural in the middle of powdered ice so cold that walking over it will freeze your breath into ice crystals."

"It's a choice." Ayrlyn lifted her eyebrows, before heading toward the stairwell.

It was a choice. Not the best of choices, but a choice, like all the other choices that seemed to face Nylan.

As Ayrlyn carried her lutar down the stairs to the lower level, another set of steps sounded, coming from the bathhouse. Nylan waited, watched, until Relyn stepped into the great room.

"I hoped I would find you, mage."

Nylan gestured to the table. "Sit down." He sat without waiting for Relyn to do so.

Relyn eased onto the bench, actually using the blunt, half-hooked end of the metal hand to balance, although Nylan caught the wince as the other put too much pressure on the still-tender stump.

"That replacement will take getting used to, I'm afraid," Nylan said. "And it will probably be cold outside unless you cover it. The metal will pick up the chill. I didn't think about that when I crafted it."

Relyn waited for a moment, saying nothing. As the wind rattled the shutters, and more snow sifted onto the inner casement ledges of the windows, he finally spoke. "The hunter . . . he says that you are not really a mage. Is that true?" Relyn struggled with the Sybran/Heaven Temple tongue.

"Gerlich?" Nylan shrugged. "That depends on what you mean by a mage. Can I throw firebolts the way your wizards can? No. Can I tear apart things? No. If that's what you mean by a mage, I'm not, and I never said I was."

Relyn pursed his lips. "You made those devil blades that cut through armor, did you not?" Half his words were Old Anglorat. "And you used the flame of the angels?"

"I did, but that's a form of machine, not magic."

"The singer, she says that you used magery to twist the flame in a way that no one else could."

"I suppose that's true," Nylan admitted. "And I can use that ability to chisel stone a little more easily."

"I saw you carve that hard black stone like it might be wood. No stoneworker I have seen could do that."

"Does a name matter?"

"Names are important," insisted Relyn.

"Are they?" asked Nylan. "Substance lies in what is, not what people say."

Relyn frowned. "Words cause people to act. If someone calls you evil angels, then that gives others a reason to destroy you."

"That's true," Nylan admitted, "but only when you talk about inspiring people to act. Their actions cause destruction, not the words directly. All the words in the world will not make me into a white wizard. All the words in the world will not bring back your hand."

"I do not know about that . . ." Relyn muses. "Do not the white wizards whisper incantations to bring about their actions? Did I not hear you talk to yourself when you guided the green flames of order?"

"Did you not talk to yourself when you practiced with the blade?" countered Nylan. "The actions matter, not the words which surround them . . . although words can certainly inspire actions." He cleared his throat, then paused as a violent gust of wind rattled the windows and shutters and shivered the great south door on its heavy iron hinges. "That's often the problem with rulers. They move people with their words, and because they do, they believe that they can use words to change the physical world. They can change people's minds and feelings, but unless those people use shovels and some form of power, the words will not move the mountains." As he finished, the engineer looked down at the table. "I'm sorry. I shouldn't talk so much."

"You are a mage, a different mage, but a mage, and how will I learn about what you do if I do not listen? I can see your actions"—Relyn lifted the artificial metal hand—"but not your thoughts."

"I'm not sure that my thoughts are terribly important." Nylan laughed. "The marshal's perhaps, but not mine."

"She thinks great and terrible thoughts, I fear."

Nylan thought the same of Ryba's thoughts, but he only answered, "She does think great thoughts, and she will change this world."

"So will you, Mage."

"Me? Only so far as . . ." Nylan stopped. "I do not think so."

Relyn laughed. "More so than you think." He stood. "But I must think more. Thinking is harder than the blade."

Nylan frowned. "There's no reason why you couldn't relearn the blade with your other hand. Saryn could certainly teach you."

Relyn paused. "A left-handed blade?"

"No worse than a black mage," countered Nylan.

Relyn laughed harshly, then turned.

As the former noble walked toward the stairwell and up the steps, Nylan glanced back at the now-empty tables and the cold hearth. After a moment, he crossed the great room and headed down to the tower's lowest level.

In the kitchen, the heat radiated from the stove where the long loaves of bread baked. Nylan took a deep breath, enjoying the aroma. Kyseen and Kadran worked at the blocky worktable, its surface already marked with the imprints of knives, slicing potatoes into circles and dropping them into the largest caldron. Both wore rough shirts with the sleeves rolled up. Kyseen set down her knife and, taking a pad made of rags, opened the stove grate, easing in two chunks of wood, one after the other.

"We'll need to saw some more small stove wood," Kyseen told Kadran, checking the coals in the stove, with the door open.

More heat welled out into the lower level, enough that Nylan, even by the foot of the stairs, could feel himself getting warm and dampness on his forehead. He unfastened the light ship jacket.

"It's your turn," Kadran said back to Kyseen.

"All right."

Cloaks wrapped around them, Narliat, Hryessa, and Murkassa stood in the alcove between the side of the stove and the central stairwell.

"Narliat, and you two—you could do some woodcutting," suggested Nylan. "It might even warm you up."

"Friggin' right," whispered Kyseen to Kadran, who nodded.

"Kyseen will show you what to do," Nylan suggested, before heading toward the other side of the lower level and the rudimentary carpentry which awaited him. Carpentry? He really didn't have that much of a feel for wood, but he had no real tools for working metal. By the next winter, he really should think about building another structure, a small smithy where he could learn, one way or another, more traditional metalworking. Even with his ordering ability, he suspected it would be a long summer and hard work, but there were too many tools and items that Westwind needed—and too few coins to purchase them. On the other hand, with the lander shells, there was metal, even if it did take his strange ability to work it.

Ayrlyn gave him a crooked smile as he stepped toward the planks.

"Where do I start?" he asked, repressing a shudder at the thought of trying to cross deep powdery snow on a pair of carved boards.

XLVIII

WITH A NOD to the guard in the corridor, the Lord of Lornth closes the tower door and crosses the room to the alcove where the lady Ellindyja sits.

"Good day, my lady mother."

"Good day, Sillek. You are kind to continue to visit me."

"Since I have a consort? You will always remain my mother, and a woman from whom I have learned much." As the wind whistles, he turns and eases back toward the window. "The wind is stronger than usual, this time of year."

"It may be a cold winter. It's not been this cold in several years." Ellindyja's eyes drop to the embroidery hoop. "I hope it will not be too chill for your consort."

"Zeldyan? Carpa is almost as close to the Westhorns as Lornth, and farther north. I'm sure she's used to winter. Her father did teach her to hunt and basic blade skills."

"She is rather accomplished." Ellindyja pauses, but Sillek's eyes drift back to the window. She clears her throat. "Sillek, your Zeldyan has been such a dear . . . so solicitous and so faithful in paying her respects to me."

Sillek turns from the fitful flakes of snow that dance outside the tower window and crosses the room, dropping into the chair across from his mother. "She knows that you are very wise. She's told me so."

"She loves you, Sillek. That is very dangerous." Ellindyja lifts the embroidery needle like a scepter and points it toward her son.

"Dangerous?"

"She cares so deeply that she may counsel you against what is best for Lornth out of her fears for you." Ellindyja deftly secures the end of the thread, then begins the first stitch of the sword blade that will be golden.

"I am sure that there are many who will seek to counsel me otherwise," Sillek responds. "It might be refreshing to have someone actually interested in my health. Not necessarily good for Lornth, but refreshing."

"What would be good for Lornth will be good for you, Sillek."

"I would hope so." The Lord of Lornth stands. "I would hope so." His eyes turn back to the window. "Perhaps a long, cold winter will rid us of the evil angels on the Roof of the World."

"Do you believe that?" The embroidery needle flickers through the linen, trailing gold.

"Evil isn't usually dislodged by weather. Still . . . one can hope, and, since spring comes late to the heights, that will give us time to increase our resources before dealing with that problem."

"I am pleased to see you have not put that loss from your mind."

"Neither from my mind, nor from my plans, Mother dear. But I have no desire to leave my back unshielded while venturing into the Westhorns." Sillek studies the dancing flakes beyond the window. "Yes . . . a long, cold winter might be helpful for many reasons." He walks toward the door.

"I am pleased that you are doing well, that you have chosen not to be cloistered, and that Zeldyan pleases you." He smiles as he holds the door ajar. "And I am also pleased that I took your advice and journeyed to Carpa." With a last smile, he half salutes Lady Ellindyja and closes the door.

The north wind rattles the tower window, and the snowflakes dance.

XLIX

CARRYING THE SKIS and the fir poles with the leather straps at one end out through the south door to the tower, Nylan followed Ayrlyn and Saryn up the beaten path toward the stables for several hundred cubits. Where the ground dropped away from the path on the south side, there was a ramp packed through the waist-deep snow, rising gently from the path for perhaps fifty cubits before the ramp merged with the snow. Beyond that point, the snow, swirled in drifts, generally dropped away toward the east.

The cairns down in the south corner of the snow-covered meadow were white hummocks with drifts extending almost to the drop-off that overlooked the forest far below. A light wind blew across the snowfield, lifting and swirling the top powdered snow under a bright sun that gave no warmth and a clear green-blue heaven that seemed to suck the heat out of the engineer, despite the two jackets and heavy woolen scarf he wore.

Nylan set the skis on the flat part of the packed snow ramp, following Ayrlyn's example, and looked along the ramp that sloped gently upward through the walls of snow. A half-dozen dual ski tracks fanned out from the end of the ramp onto the snowfield.

"Who's been out already?" Despite the scarf around his nose and mouth, Nylan's breath formed white clouds in the air, and he could feel the ice forming on the wool of the scarf. As he watched, the ice crystals that had been Saryn's breath fluttered to the powdery surface of the packed snow.

"Gerlich, the hunters," answered Saryn, "and Fierral, Ryba, and the scouts."

If Gerlich could master old-style skis, then Nylan could, he decided, as he bent down and fastened the leather thongs around his boots, boots lined with wool scraps and bulging somewhat at the tops. He had to take off the outer layer of his gloves because they were really leather mittens covering woolen gloves, and he couldn't handle the leather thongs with the fingerless mittens. Neither mittens nor the gloves beneath fit terribly well, since he'd done the cutting and stitching himself.

"Ready?" asked Saryn.

Nylan straightened and pulled the leather mittens back over his gloves, then took a pole in each hand.

"If I can do this, you can," said Saryn, slowly gliding up the ramp.

"Let's hope so," Nylan muttered, but he followed her example and, one pole in each hand, slowly slid the left wooden ski forward. Each ski felt like a building timber, but Ayrlyn had insisted that the skis needed to be wide and long because the snow on the Roof of the World was light and powdery.

As he tried to slide the right ski after the left one, he could feel himself lurching forward, and he leaned back to compensate. Then his left ski started sliding backward, and he jabbed a pole into the packed snow of the ramp, wobbling there before catching his balance.

"Start with slow movements," suggested Saryn, "and keep your weight forward—not too forward—on the skis."

"I've always tried not to be too forward," Nylan retorted, ignoring the cold air that bit into his nose, throat, and lungs.

"Slow movements, one ski at a time," ordered Ayrlyn.

Nylan inched the left ski forward, then the right, then the left until he had crept up the ramp to where the packed area ended. Squinting against the brightness of the sun, he looked out over the nearly flat and powdered snow that covered the meadows more than waist-deep.

"Just follow in my tracks," Ayrlyn instructed.

Nylan edged after the redhead, though her hair and most of her face were well swathed in a gray woolen scarf.

Despite his best efforts, his skis skidded out of the tracks Ayrlyn had made, then sank to knee depth. As the snow piled up in front of his shins, he slowed to a stop. When he shifted his weight, the skis sank even farther until the snow reached his knees.

"Making the first trail is the hardest," called Saryn from beside him, "especially if you're moving slowly. Speed helps—until you fall, and then it's a mess."

Looking at the snow that covered his skis completely and most of his lower legs, Nylan decided it was already a mess.

"Just put one ski in front of the other. Make it a sliding sort of walk."

That Nylan could understand, and the process seemed to work, enough so that he actually had covered several hundred cubits, mostly staying in the trail Ayrlyn had cut through the snow.

"That's it," the singer called. "Just keep up that motion."

At that moment, Nylan reached too far forward with his right pole, lost his balance, flailed, and went down in a heap, his entire upper body plunging through the powdery white crystals until a gloved hand slammed against something hard.

He lay in the snow, his feet pinned together by the skis, breathing both chill air and snow crystals that had oozed around his scarf.

"Straighten your skis."

"How?" he mumbled through the snow.

Finally, he levered his upper body sideways, since his skis would not move, until his legs could separate slightly. Then he bent his knees and curled up into a ball as close to the skis as he could. That allowed him to rock himself over into a half-crouching, half-kneeling position. From there he struggled upright, his snow-covered face finally emerging into the glare, the snow almost chest-deep.

His skis felt mired, but he lifted each in turn, letting snow filter under each, climb-packing his way up until he stood on the skis—merely knee-deep in the powder that leached the heat out of his legs and feet.

"See . . . you can get out of it," said Saryn.

"This time," snorted Nylan, trying to brush the snow off

himself, snow that clung to everything but the leather trousers and packed itself into every bodily crevice.

He started after Ayrlyn even more cautiously than before, then stopped as he saw a pair of figures sweeping from the ridge line above the tower.

Istril and Ryba skied slowly downward, a rope tied to a bundle they towed. As they neared, each leaving a graceful dual line of ski traces in the snow, Nylan could see the bundle consisted of a pale-coated winter deer.

He also marveled at their grace, doubting that he would ever match it. Part of him never wanted to try as the snow melted in cold rivulets down his neck, back, and legs. He forced a wave to the two skiers.

"There's the engineer!" Istril returned his wave.

As he started to follow Ayrlyn's tracks again, in a turn that would carry him back toward the packed trail the horses used, Nylan found himself again wobbling on the skis, conscious that the leather thongs provided no real support. He jabbed his poles back down to balance himself and let himself slide to a halt.

"Watch your balance," said Saryn, nearly beside the engineer, making her own track, the powdery snow nearly to her knees.

"That's easy to say. Doing it is a lot harder."

Istril and Ryba had towed the deer carcass to the tower, unfastened their skis, and lugged their kill and skis inside long before Nylan struggled the few hundred cubits back to the tower.

"That's enough for today," he declared. Maybe forever, he thought, as he gathered skis and poles and trudged back across the causeway. He left a trail of snow and water down to the storeroom beside the furnace, and on the steps on his return trip back up to the great room for the midday meal.

Nylan slumped onto the bench before the hearth, aware that he was sitting in damp trousers. His upper cheeks were nearly flaming red, and his ears ached as they warmed. They hadn't been out in the cold that long—except it appeared that the Roof of the World was even colder than a Sybran winter—and that was cold, indeed.

Although there was no fire in the hearth, the great room was warm by comparison to the frozen wasteland outside, and the bark-and-root tea helped. He poured a second mugful.

"You drank that quickly," said Ryba.

"You would too, if you'd dived into a snowbank and gotten stuck there."

"You wouldn't have had that problem," pointed out Ryba, "if you'd started trying to learn earlier."

Nylan took another sip of the tea. Ayrlyn had already told him as much, far earlier, and he supposed he deserved the reminder, but skiing was a pain, however necessary it might prove.

Ryba raised her eyebrows.

"How were the bows in the cold?" he asked, hoping to change the subject.

"The bows are really good in the cold," Istril said from the foot of the first table.

Nylan nodded. While he hadn't thought about that, both the composite and the endurasteel had been designed to handle the chill of space and the heat of high-temperature reentry, which would make them ideal for the chill of the winter on the Roof of the World.

"Gerlich's already snapped one of his great wooden bows in the cold," Istril added in a lower voice, after looking around and not seeing the hunter. "I'll bet the new bows would be really good in cold-weather warfare."

"Is anyone else crazy enough to be out in this weather?" asked Nylan.

"Well . . . they're good for hunting, too. Even Fierral thinks so, and she's pretty hard on everything."

"Is there that much out in the woods?"

"More than you'd suspect, from the tracks, and that's good for us. You saw the deer. That's a couple of meals, at least, even for twenty of us. There's also a snow cat, almost all white, with big spread paws and claws. I don't know how good the meat is, but I'd bet the fur is warm."

Nylan nodded. After his brief excursion, a warm coat sounded better than wool or a ship jacket, a lot better.

L

NYLAN FASTENED THE ship jacket and pulled on the crudely lined boots that he wore everywhere, even inside the tower. His fingers crossed his stubbly chin, but the chill was so great, even with the heat from the bathhouse stove, that he had not shaved, but only washed his face and hands, before hurrying back up to the tower's top level to dress for the cold day ahead.

The heat from the furnace removed the biting chill of the wind that howled outside the tower's walls, but Nylan's breath turned into a frosty cloud when he stepped away from the heated center of the tower and up to the sole top-level armaglass window to check the sealing. He half rubbed, half scraped away the frost to look outside, but cold air rolled off the glass, and frost re-formed almost as fast as he removed it. Through the little area he could keep clear, he could only see white—white and more white.

For more than two days, the white barrage had continued, and Nylan wasn't certain how much of the snow was new and how much just snow picked up by the roaring wind and flung—and reflung—against the walls.

Most of the exterior tower walls had a spotty coating of ice on the inside stone, except in the kitchen and the furnace room. Kyseen and Kadran had plenty of guards—especially the newer ones—ready to saw and split wood in return for a place around the stove. The number of people willing to work on partitions and stools, or other wooden necessities, in the workroom off the furnace had never been higher.

Could it be the warmth? Nylan grinned at the thought, even as he readied himself to head down to join them.

Ryba was below somewhere; she hadn't said where she was going, but, with the storm still going, she was somewhere in the tower.

A figure huddled by the furnace duct on the fifth level. Nylan paused on the steps. "Relyn?"

"Ser?" The red-haired man stood with his cloak wrapped around him. "A man can never get warm here. It's too cold to do anything except be miserable, and just warm enough so that you never quite freeze." He jerked his head toward the single shuttered window. "I can't even leave. Twenty steps in that, and they'd find me frozen in a block of ice come spring."

Nylan sat on a step, and Relyn sat on the other edge.

"Why are you up here?" asked the engineer.

"It's the only place where I can be alone. Sometimes . . ." Relyn shook his head.

"I'm surprised that you haven't gotten close to one of the guards."

"It is . . . hard . . . to think about, as you put it, getting close to someone who could kill you with one blow."

"Why?" asked Nylan. "Anyone you sleep with anywhere could kill you."

"You always bring up disturbing points, Mage. At home, when I had a home, should anyone have killed me, they would have been tortured and then killed."

"If anyone killed you here, she'd be punished. What's the difference?"

"It is different," pointed out Relyn.

"I suppose so. Here you have to trust someone else, under a . . . ruler . . . you don't know. I think that means you've never really trusted anyone." Nylan stood up.

"Mage . . . were you in Carpa, I would challenge you."

"For what? Is the truth so terrible? Most people with power always say they trust people, and what they mean is that they only trust them so long as they control them. True trust occurs only when you have no control."

"I'd rather have control."

"We all would . . . but even that's an illusion a lot of the time." Nylan recalled Ryba's struggle with her visions. "Even for rulers. If a ruler taxes his people too heavily, some will revolt, and he must kill them."

"As he should," declared Relyn.

"But dead men pay no taxes, and now the ruler must tax the others more heavily to pay the soldiers because there are fewer men to tax. And he will need more soldiers because people will be even more unhappy. More soldiers require even more taxes, and that makes people even less happy. Do you see where that leads?"

"But . . ." Relyn looked up at Nylan.

"Control is not what it seems, young Relyn. If you kill a man, you make an enemy out of his family. How many enemies can a ruler afford? Do you see the marshal eating better food than her guards?"

"No."

"Does she wear jewels or great trappings of wealth?"

"No."

"Will her guards follow her anywhere?"

"I think they would."

Nylan smiled. "Think it over." He walked down the steps, wondering why he had bothered. What he had said would certainly have upset anyone in Relyn's position, and the young noble was probably very upset. But what good had it done? His head throbbed slightly. Why? Because what he'd said wasn't quite true? Ryba did have one thing the others didn't—power. It might be power out of necessity, but it was power. Nylan shook his head. He couldn't even present provoking thoughts that might be misleading without getting a headache, or so it seemed.

Nylan rubbed his forehead as he walked down the steps past the great room, empty except for Ayrlyn, gently strumming the lutar—probably refining or working on another song. He paused for a moment, watching the redhead struggle with a chord or a phrase, but she did not look his way.

He turned toward the south door, where chill winds

seeped through the cracks, and a fine layer of snow covered the stones behind the door, shifting with each gust that buffeted the tower.

Nylan resumed his descent, thinking about the cradle he was crafting. But Dyliess would need somewhere to sleep, and a cradle made sense.

LI

FROM THE INNER corner of the room wells the warmth of a well-banked fire, though Terek still wears a heavy white woolen vest over his robes. The white wizard's face is red with strain, but Sillek ignores the wizard's effort and studies the image in the glass on the table.

In the center of the swirling white mists is a dark tower, rising out of the snows. A beaten path runs uphill from the tower toward a canyon in the base of the higher western slopes. Thin spirals of smoke rise from the twin chimneys in the pyramidal roof of the black tower.

A pair of figures in black coats walk briskly uphill, their breath leaving a thick trail of white. The snow on each side of the path rises above the heads of either.

The flat of the snow before the tower is crossed with sets of flat tracks, ski tracks that spread in all directions, with some circling back to the short causeway before the tower. A second packed-snow trail leads to the ridge separating the tower from the forest below, and a pair of horses drag a tree trunk up the ridge. Beside them walks a figure bearing a pack.

"It looks normal," observed Sillek.

"Have you seen enough, ser?" asks Terek.

"I think so."

The wizard relaxes, and the mists collapse, leaving a blank glass. "It's too normal, ser. That snow is over their heads, and there must be three cubits more packed underfoot. The air is so cold that their very breath falls like snow itself, and they walk to check their mounts—those are stables up in that canyon. Could your armsmen do that?"

"Not for long." Sillek turns to the wizard. "What is your meaning, Ser Wizard?"

"They are evil angels, ser. They must be destroyed, or they will destroy us. No one else could walk the Roof of the World without freezing into ice."

Sillek nods without agreeing. "Thank you, Ser Wizard. If you discover anything new, please let me know."

"Will you destroy them, ser?"

"Ser Terek, as you pointed out, we can do nothing until the snows melt, and it becomes warm enough for normal men on the Roof of the World."

"Yes, Lord Sillek."

"Then we will see what we can do." Sillek nods once more as he leaves the warm quarters of the wizard. His face is impassive as he walks the long corridor and climbs another flight of stairs.

The guard opens the door to his quarters, and he closes it, stepping quietly past the sitting room to the bedchamber where Zeldyan sits in a chair, knitting a small blanket.

She smiles and stands, setting aside her work. "You look glum, Sillek."

The Lord of Lornth hugs his consort, feeling the beginning of a gentle rounding of her figure against him. "How are you doing?"

"Fine. I can feel him kick." Zeldyan smiles as they separate.

"How can you? You're not that far along."

"I can. It's gentle, but he does kick."

"You always call the child 'him.' "

"That's because he is, and we'll call him—"

"Hush. That's bad luck, to name a child before he's born."

"As you say." Zeldyan grins. "Why were you so displeased?"

"I had asked Terek to scree the Roof of the World. My

mother has again pressed the issue. Now Terek is pressing me to attack the Roof of the World. No one else but evil angels could survive that cold." Sillek shrugs. "No one else built a huge stone tower with hearths up there, either, but he says that those women must be destroyed, that they're too evil to live."

"Are they?"

"What do you think?" he counters, glancing back toward the closed doors.

"They're probably no more evil than anyone else. They come from somewhere else, and they have nowhere else to go." Zeldyan smiles momentarily before continuing. "Like those who have nowhere else to go, they will fight to the last to keep what they have. That will make them very dangerous."

"It already has," he points out, looking toward the window and across the light blanket of snow that has already begun to melt, even though the clouds have blocked the winter sun.

"You have already committed to undertake the expedition to Rulyarth." Zeldyan points out. "Though we must say nothing publicly."

"And so I will. If I am successful, though, the wizards, the believers, and everyone else will be pushing me . . ."

"And your mother," Zeldyan adds gently.

"I know." He sighs. "Rulers are always ruled by everyone else's expectations."

Zeldyan steps close to him and takes his face in her gentle hands. "Even I have expectations, love." Her lips brush his.

"Yours I can handle," he whispers and returns the kiss.

LII

DESPITE THE HEAVY woolen blanket that covered the thin thermal blanket and the crude but heavy woolen nightshirt he wore, Nylan was cold. A thin layer of crystals from his own breath scattered off the blanket as he sat up. The room was dark, with only the hint of gray seeping through the thoroughly frosted single armaglass window, although Nylan knew, alerted by the sounds drifting up the steps from the great room, that it was late enough. Another storm had descended upon the Roof of the World, with yet more snow.

As if to punctuate his conclusion, the wind provided a low howl, and the window casements rattled. A few fine flakes sifted around the iced-over shutters as Nylan sat on the edge of the couch and stared at the peg holding clothes he knew would feel like ice against his skin.

"Don't take the covers," said Ryba. "It is cold up here."

"Another furnace day."

"It's been a furnace day every day for the last eight-day, and we're running through wood all too fast. Fierral's coughing out her lungs because she spent too much time in the cold. Istril's not that much better, and I worry because she's pregnant."

"Ayrlyn helped them both."

"There's a limit to what she can do, though."

"Just like there are limits on the way you seem to be able to see pieces of the future," Nylan pointed out.

Ryba sat up on the couch and swirled the covers around her. "I hate feeling this awkward."

"You don't look awkward," Nylan pointed out as he struggled into his clothes. He'd wash later. That bothered him, too, that even for him cleanliness was falling behind the need to keep warm.

"Dyliess is already affecting my balance. My bladder already went." The marshal of Westwind slipped to her feet. "I hate wearing this thing like a tent. At least I can still get into my leathers. Darkness knows how long that will last."

"I'm headed down," Nylan said.

"It might do your image good to arrive before me."

"Thank you, gracious Marshal."

"Oh, Nylan . . . it's just that you're always too busy to be punctual. Go get your tea." Ryba pulled off the woolen gown. Her midsection was only slightly rounded, and the engineer wanted to shake his head. Ryba would feel huge while she was slimmer than most women who weren't even carrying a child.

Nylan pulled on his boots and went. He had not even set foot on the stones of the main level when Kyseen greeted him.

"Ser, the cistern's not filling. It's half-full."

"It'll wait." Nylan walked to the table, looming out of the gloom like a rock out of the fog of a harbor.

"Amazing," whispered Gerlich, just loud enough for most to hear. "The engineer arrived before the marshal."

"Amazing? I suppose so." Nylan wished he could think quickly enough for a clever comment.

"What magic will you create, Mage, to return the waters to the tower?" asked Narliat.

"It's not magic, Narliat. It's a stone conduit that's probably frozen solid because I didn't get it buried far enough below the frost line." Nylan snapped off a piece of bread and dipped it in a brown sauce that was left over from dinner the night before. "I haven't lived here before, and I had to guess. No one around here could even build a tower."

"But you are a mage."

"You said that. I didn't." Nylan took a bite. Both bread and sauce were cool. Even the tea was lukewarm.

Across the table from Nylan, Ayrlyn offered a faint smile of condolence, but said nothing as she sipped her own tea.

The insides of the shuttered windows were masses of ice, created from drifted snow and the condensation from the guards' breath. The four true windows were so heavily frosted that they were solid white. With a shiver, Nylan took a second sip of the warm tea that didn't help all that much, then another mouthful of bread and sauce, followed by the last dried apple slices in the wooden bowl. The single fat candle on the table shed as much greasy smoke as light.

"I'll be getting a few more apples for the marshal, ser," said Kyseen, "and you can have a few, too."

"Thank you," said the engineer, although he wondered why he should be thanking her because the early birds had eaten everything.

The fruit had not made its way up to the table by the time Ryba sat down heavily in the chair with her back to the cold hearth.

"You seem tired, Marshal," offered Gerlich.

Narliat smiled. From the middle of the second table, both Hryessa and Murkassa looked at Ryba and then at Gerlich. Ayrlyn frowned.

"I am tired," Ryba admitted. "I'm especially tired of your superficial cheerfulness, and I'm almost tempted to send you out hunting at this very moment. So don't push it."

Nylan held in a grin.

"I beg your pardon," Gerlich responded.

"No, you don't. You just say you do," said Ryba politely. "Snakes have more integrity than you do, Gerlich. So do the demons."

Beside Istril, at the far end of the second table, Relyn paled.

"You could even say, behind my back, that I'm in a bitchy mood. That's a mildly polite way of putting it." Ryba smiled. "So the next time you attempt to patronize me, you might have to eat steel or ice. You can take your pick."

Kyseen hovered behind Nylan, holding the small bowl of dried fruit, waiting until Ryba turned to the cook and nodded. Kyseen set the bowl between Ryba and Nylan.

"Thank you, Kyseen," said the marshal.

"Thank you," echoed Nylan.

Nylan glanced at Gerlich and caught the under-the-breath

"Thank you, thank you—it makes me puke . . ." With a forced smile, Nylan looked at the hunter and said, "Why, Gerlich, I thought you had better digestion than that. By the way, the reason I'm usually late is that I have better things to do than to sneak around and complain about how things are run around here, or make snide remarks under my breath. Or go out and hide and sulk in the snow while pretending to hunt."

Narliat turned pale; Gerlich opened his mouth, and then shut it.

"You know, Gerlich," added Ryba. "You always did underestimate the engineer. In the end, it's likely to prove fatal."

"Might I be excused?" Gerlich asked quietly.

"Of course." Ryba smiled.

Gerlich stood and bowed, but not too deeply.

"Your timing was excellent, Nylan. That should stop his plotting for a time," said Ryba. "A day or two, perhaps."

"Are you going to kill him?" asked Ayrlyn.

"No," said Ryba. "There's been enough death, and that sort of thing wouldn't play well with the guards. Not yet." Her face held a bitter smile. Then she took a sip of tea. "This is almost as bad as liquid manure. Almost, but not quite."

Nylan took several of the apple slices, but left most of them for Ryba. She needed them, and so far, he didn't. He did refill his mug from the steaming pot that Kadran set on the table. The bark-and-root tea tasted better hot, or perhaps he couldn't taste it so well when it was hot.

He munched another piece of bread.

Ayrlyn rose and nodded to the marshal, then to Nylan. "We'll be doing a lot of woodwork for the next few days, ser, and I need to see to the space, and the glue."

Ryba nodded, as did Nylan, since he didn't have much choice with a mouth full of dry bread.

"We have problems with the water, I understand," Ryba said after Ayrlyn had departed.

"I'd guess the frost line is lower than I'd calculated, but

I'll have to check now that I've eaten and have some strength."

"You made such a to-do about the water . . ."

"I know. I know. It's all my fault." With a groan, Nylan rose and headed down to the lower level and the cistern, Kyseen following closely.

All the guards in the kitchen area watched as he neared the cistern. He opened the cover and peered inside. His eyes saw almost nothing, but his senses could feel that the inlet pipe was mostly filled with ice. The water level had dropped to the half-full point, a good two cubits below the stone inlet conduit. A few drops glistened on the ice-coated inlet spout.

Nylan extended his senses, attempting to hold the feeling similar to the neuronet. So far as his senses could follow the water back up the conduit, he could sense only ice. Finally, he stepped away from the tower's cold south wall, leaving the cover open and turning to Kyseen. "It's frozen. Keeping this open might help, but make sure everyone stays away from it."

"Ser?" asked Kyseen.

"The air here is warmer. It might help thaw the ice inside. The piping wasn't deep enough. I'm pretty sure it's frozen outside as well."

"What do we do? You can't fix it now, can you?" Kyseen made a vague gesture up the steps toward the heavy lower outer door, which continued to vibrate, despite the southern exposure and the heavy windbreaks beyond.

Beyond the stone walls, the wind howled.

"We may not be able to fix it until spring, and that's a long time," answered Nylan. "For now, take the extra caldrons and fill them with snow. Put them by the furnace. When they melt, pour the water into the cistern and start over. If we can get the water level up, and warmer, it might help."

"Should we put some on the stove?"

"Not until after meals are cooked, and don't add any wood to the fire. We really don't have enough wood as it is. The tower's warm enough down here to melt the snow."

Up in the room he and Ryba shared—that was another story. The center space was warm enough, thanks to the furnace ducts, but only when the furnace was burning. The shuttered window had become a mass of immobile ice.

"What about boiling water?" asked Kadran.

"That won't do any good until the water level's up near the inlet spout, and that means melting a lot of water."

"Now what are you going to do?" demanded Kyseen.

"I still have to check the bathhouse," he answered as he crossed the kitchen and headed back up the steps to the north door. "That might tell me where the freezing's happening."

The north archway was cold, as usual, but the bathhouse was tolerable, perhaps because Huldran had a fire going in the stove. Nylan climbed up the brick steps beside the wall—designed for just such a purpose—and checked the water warmer—which was three-quarters full. A thin stream of water trickled into the warmer's reservoir, but only a thin stream, even with the knife gate wide open.

"How long have you had the fire going?" he asked Huldran.

"Not long, ser. Colder than a winter deer's rump in here earlier."

Nylan sighed. "Maybe heating the stove will increase the flow more. If not, we can use the stove to melt snow, and perhaps the heat from that will also keep some water flowing." He paused. "Once the storm lets up, I'll check the outfalls."

"Hope the stove helps, ser," offered Huldran.

"So do I."

He shook his head as he passed through the ice-covered cave that the archway between the tower and bathhouse had become. Chronologically, they weren't quite at midwinter, from what he could figure, and everything was freezing. Maybe more heat would help . . . and maybe not.

Another blast of cold air shivered through the archway following a long low moan from the gale outside, and a short icicle hanging from the bricks overhead broke loose and shattered across the stone floor, several pieces skidding against the tower door.

The unheated archway was better than an open space between tower and bathhouse, but not much, reflected Nylan, as he opened the tower door, stepped inside, and closed it behind him. He stopped shivering when he started down the steps to the almost comfortable lower level of the tower.

On the side of the lower level away from the kitchen—opposite the furnace—Ayrlyn directed a half-dozen marines in their efforts to turn rough wooden slabs and planks into furnishings for the tower—wall partitions, stools, an occasional chair, and several cradles.

Nylan stepped toward the group.

"How is the water going, ser?" asked Siret.

"There's enough in the bathhouse for some washing, a few quick showers, and maybe more as the stove warms things up," Nylan said, inhaling the aroma of baking bread that never quite seemed to leave the kitchen area. Did Kadran and Kyseen do all the baking as much to keep warm as to feed the marines?

"What about the cistern?" asked Istril.

"I can't do much about that now. We'll see if Kadran can get the water level up. That might help." He shrugged. "If I can't fix the water, at least I can do something useful." Nylan picked up the dovetailed section of the cradle that was beginning to resemble a headboard. Carving and fitting the pieces was slow, even with the glue Relyn had developed from ground deer hooves and boiled hide and who knew what else.

After studying the design he had scratched on the wood, he set the headboard down and took out his knife, borrowing the common whetstone to sharpen it.

"Can I follow the same pattern?" asked Istril, as she stepped up beside him, no longer nearly so slim in the midsection as she had been in the summer and early fall. "For the cradle, not the design." Then she covered her mouth and smothered a cough.

"Of course," answered the engineer. "Is there anything I can explain . . . or help with?"

Istril flushed.

So did Nylan, although he didn't know why, and he stammered, "With the woodworking. I'm not an expert. That's Ayrlyn."

"That cradle looks very good, especially for the tools we have," commented Ayrlyn.

"I've had a lot of time," said Nylan. "And probably even more to come."

"He's safer down here," whispered Berlis.

Both Siret and Istril turned toward the mouthy guard, and Berlis stammered, "The marshal . . . she is a little touchy . . . right now . . ."

"You'd be touchy, too," said Saryn, looking up from where she smoothed a curved backpiece for what looked to be a chair. "She has to think of everything and put up with idiots like the great hunter." Saryn glanced toward the corner where Ellysia quietly worked over another plain cradle. "I'm sorry, Ellysia. I didn't—"

"No offense taken, ser. He's a lying cur. I just hope he's got good genes." Ellysia showed broad, even teeth, then looked down over her swollen midsection at the sideboards she was painstakingly rounding.

Nylan studied the design again, the sole tree twisting out of the rocky hillside, then let his senses take in the wood before he lifted the knife.

". . . everything he does is beautiful . . ."

The engineer tried not to flush.

"Not quite everything," quipped Ayrlyn quietly. "You haven't seen him ski, obviously."

Nylan grinned in spite of himself, thinking about the considerable additional practice he would clearly need in that area. Then he slowly drew the knife over the line that represented the right side of the rocky slope, deepening the groove gently . . . gently.

LIII

As he watched Saryn shift her weight on the ungainly skis, Nylan wanted to shake his head, but he had little enough time for that. Just following the former pilot's tracks was proving hard enough even after his determined efforts over the past eight-days. To navigate and shoot a bow on skis remained an effort, but he wasn't plunging headfirst into the snow or leaning backward until his skis slid out from under him and left his shoulders and rump buried in the white powder.

With a passing cloud, a shadow fell across the trail, and Nylan's eyes squinted to adjust to the change in the midday light, but the relative relief of the cloud passed, and the glare returned.

The snow around and across the Roof of the World was more than seven cubits deep, and twice that in drifts. That was deep enough that Nylan could fall into one of those pits and never make his way out, not without turning into a knot and cutting the thongs. There was no way to untie them hanging upside down in a mass of powdered ice or the equivalent. His fingers twitched around his poles as he thought about the knife at his waist.

He blinked as a clot of snow thrown up from Saryn's skis and carried by a gust of wind splattered above his left eye.

Saryn held up a hand, and Nylan coasted to a stop right behind her, proud that he neither hit her nor fell into the deep snow beside the semitrail that the guards had created through the lower forest.

As he caught his breath on the level stretch before a steep descent through the trees, trying not to breathe too deeply, Nylan put off thinking about the climb back up the ridge that would follow the trip.

"I think there are some deer, and maybe a snow leopard, downhill and to the right. The wind's coming uphill here, and I might be able to get close enough," whispered Saryn.

"If I'm not stamping along?"

She nodded.

"Go on. We're always on the verge of running out of meat."

"Can you just wait here?" asked Saryn, her voice still low. "With your bow ready?"

"I'll wait with a bow handy. How much good it will do I'm not sure." Nylan tried to keep his own voice down.

As the wind whispered through the evergreens, clumps of snow splattered around them, leaving pockmarks scattered on the once-smooth white surface, depressions that the wind seemed to begin to fill immediately with feathery white powder that scudded along the snow.

The engineer glanced back uphill. Already, sections of the packed trail they had followed had begun to disappear beneath the drifting snow. Another shadow darkened the Roof of the World, and he looked up at the white cloud that scudded across the sun.

"You'll do fine. Just don't let our supper get away." Saryn raised her left hand and then slipped down the steeper section of the partly packed snow trail ahead. In moments, she was out of sight in the trees, gone as silently as if she had never been there.

Nylan shrugged and unlimbered the composite bow, wishing that he had practiced more with the weapon. The shadow of the cloud passed, and for a long time, nothing moved in the expanse of white beneath the overhanging firs, nothing except snow scudded between trunks by the light wind that rose and fell, rose and fell.

A gray-winged form plunged from nowhere into a swirl of powdered snow, and a quick geyser of white erupted, then died away as the gray-hawk flapped away, a small white-coated rodent in its claws.

As the hawk vanished, Nylan inched forward on the skis, mainly to shift his weight and keep his hips and knees from cramping in the cold. He looked back in the general direction of the tower, but could see nothing but snow, tree trunks, and the white-covered green of the fir branches.

A rhythmic swishing, almost a series of whispering thuds, rose, just barely, over the hissing of the wind.

Nylan squinted, looking downhill, when the snow cat bounded across the hillside toward the trail where he stood, moving so quickly that what had seemed a small figure swelled into a vision of knife claws and glinting teeth even as Nylan released his first arrow and reached for the second, triggering reflex step-up. The second arrow flew as the leopard reached the snow beside the flat section at the crest of the trail.

Both Nylan and the snow cat seemed to be moving in slow motion, but the engineer forced his body to respond. The third arrow left the bowstring as the cat stretched toward Nylan.

Bow still in hand, he managed to dive into the snow at the side of the trail as the snow cat lunged at him. A line of fire slashed down his shoulder as he half twisted away from the mass of fur and claws. His skis linked together, and he toppled like a tree blasted by a microburst into the deep snow, a heavy weight on his back.

That weight did not move, and, in time, Nylan levered it away from him and, through a combination of rolling, twisting, and gasping, finally struggled into the light.

His knees ached. One leg burned, and the other threatened to cramp. Half sitting, half lying in the snow, he managed to reach one of the poles he had abandoned to use the bow, and with it, to retrieve the bow itself. He laid it on the edge of the harder snowpack of the trail. Then he looked at his boots and the mass of snow and ice around the thongs.

With a groan and more rolling he finally managed to totter erect.

The claws had sliced through the heavy leather shoulder of the hunting jacket he had borrowed from Ayrlyn, but blunted the impact enough that the wound was little more than a thin line skin-deep.

He looked at the snow-covered leopard, then downhill, but the forest was silent. After prodding the cat with one of his poles, he took a deep breath, regretting it instantly as the chill bit into his lungs, and then edged his skis toward the dead leopard.

Nylan knelt and removed the first arrow shaft, wiping it clean on the snow, then replacing it in the quiver. Then he searched for the second.

The sun was well past midday when Saryn trudged uphill, pulling the carcass of a winter deer behind her. By then, Nylan had dragged the snow leopard out onto the trail and worked out the three arrows.

"I'm sorry, Nylan, but . . . we do need the meat, and it took me longer—What happened to you?" Saryn stopped and stared at the bedraggled engineer, her eyes going from his shoulder to the body of the snow leopard.

"It decided I'd make a good dinner. I tried not to oblige."

"You were lucky."

Nylan nodded. His jaw still chattered, and his knees were wobbly, especially as he looked at the stretched-out length of the cat.

"But they're all your shafts. So you get the fur. We all share the meat. That's a dubious benefit." Saryn laughed, and Nylan joined her.

Snow-cat meat was tough, gamy, and no pleasure for teeth or tongue, even in a well-cooked stew.

Nylan adjusted the bow in its cover and checked the quiver.

"What will you do with the fur?" Saryn asked. "That's yours, you know."

"Mine?"

"Meat you can split, but not the hide. We all agreed that the choice is up to the one who brings the animal down, especially if you get wounded."

Nylan's eyes flicked to the slash in his jacket. "It's only a cut."

Saryn laughed. "Your skis didn't move much." Her eyes looked to the depression beside the trail.

"That would have been futile," Nylan admitted.

"So you stood there and fired three arrows at a charging leopard?"

"It does sound stupid, when you put it that way."

"Necessary," Saryn said. "What would have happened if you'd tried to ski away?"

"I'd be under ten cubits of snow or a midday meal for the leopard."

"So the pelt is yours. You earned it."

"I suppose it will make a good coverlet for Dyliess. It's light and warmer than anything else."

"Dyliess? Ryba's . . . ?"

Nylan nodded. "Mine, too."

"That's a beautiful cradle you're making."

"Thank you. It's almost done, and that's hard to believe." Nylan took a deep breath. "Don't we have to drag this beast somewhere?"

"You get to drag it home. I've got the deer," Saryn said. "I even have some rope."

"You are so obliging."

"Think nothing of it."

How Nylan got the cat carcass back to the tower he didn't know, only that his legs ached even more, his shoulder burned, as did his eyes, despite the eye black under and around them—which he'd have to wash off sooner or later. He felt light-headed.

He had taken off his skis and leaned against the causeway wall and watched as Kadran and Saryn set up the tripod and skinned and gutted the deer and then the leopard. With the pelt off, the cat's carcass was thin, and Nylan felt almost sorry for the dead animal, even though it had certainly tried to kill him. "Thin," he murmured. "So fearsome, and so thin."

"It's a hard life, even for the animals who live here," answered Saryn.

A taller figure skied to a halt beyond the causeway, then bent and unlaced the thongs of his skis. Gerlich looked at Saryn and Kadran. "So you finally got something besides a deer. A real snow leopard. Congratulations, Saryn."

Saryn smiled politely, pulling her scarf away from her mouth. "Thank you, but it isn't mine. I got the deer. Nylan put three arrows through the cat. All of them in the chest, not much more than a span apart."

"In the chest?"

Saryn rotated the carcass on the fir-limb tripod and pointed. "Here, here, and here."

Gerlich inclined his head to Nylan. "My congratulations to you, then, Engineer. Your bows must carry farther in the winter."

"I wish I'd been able to use them at that range," Nylan offered, pointing to the slash in the jacket. "Then this wouldn't have happened. He got a little closer than I would have ideally preferred. It's hard to fire arrows with claws in your face."

After a moment, Gerlich answered, "I can see that." With a look back at Nylan, he crossed the causeway and entered the tower.

"Ser," said Saryn, "we really don't need you. You might think about cleaning and dressing that slash. Relyn and I— we'll start tanning the pelt . . . don't you worry."

Nylan heaved himself erect and picked up the skis and poles. "Thank you. You're probably right."

After carting the skis down to the lower level and racking them and the poles, he started back up toward the fifth level, where the medical supplies were kept. He stopped at the main level and staggered into the great room, where he slumped at the empty table, too tired to climb the steps.

While he really needed to wash out the cut on his shoulder, that meant climbing four more flights of steps, and digging out the antiseptic, what little there was left, and then going to the bathhouse. He took a deep breath.

The main door opened, and Kadran struggled inside with a deer haunch, followed by Kyseen. Neither looked toward the dimness of the great room.

". . . should have heard the engineer . . . 'got a little closer than I would have ideally preferred.' I thought I'd die. Gerlich was going to shit building stones . . ."

"Engineer's a tough little bastard."

". . . quiet, a lot of the time . . . have to be tough to deal with the marshal . . . leopard's probably easy by comparison . . ."

Ryba, tougher than a snow leopard? Nylan chuckled to himself. No question about that, but he'd prefer to fight neither.

As the two cooks vanished, he stood and walked toward the steps, and the antiseptic, the cleaning he wasn't looking forward to, and soreness in muscles he'd forgotten he had— and the headache, the headache that seemed not quite constant.

LIV

OUTSIDE THE FROSTED window, the day is dull gray. Even the snow on the fields in the distance is gray. That on the roads below Hissl's room has been tramped into a frozen mixture of brown and gray.

The warmth from the small brazier in the corner is more than welcome. Hissl shifts his weight on the stool to warm his right side, without taking his eyes from the glass on the table.

Centered in the swirling white mists are the images of the black mage and the woman warrior. Each drags a carcass, but the mage drags that of a snow cat up the slope toward the line of smoke that rises from the tower chimneys.

Two other figures, also on the long wide skis, sweep down the slope toward the pair.

The mage appears awkward on the skis, but he is the one who drags the snow cat. Their breath puffs through the scarves that cover their faces, then falls in the bright light in powdery crystals toward the snow through which they climb.

Hissl's eyes focus on the bows both carry, then narrow. He smiles. "No thunder-throwers now."

Neither of the two skiers who stop on the white expanse above the toiling pair wear thunder-throwers, either, and Hissl's tight smile broadens. He tries not to think about a mage who will stand fast before a snow leopard, and his eyes flick to the window.

The grasslands beyond Clynya are still covered with white, but the days are again lengthening, and even on the Roof of the World the snows will vanish in time.

LV

CARRYING A CLEAN outfit, Nylan padded down the stairs in his boots and old trousers, trying to ignore the chill that seeped around him. He slowed as he neared the fourth level.

Gerlich unloaded his gear, racking the quiver in the shelf space that was his, and hung the long bow beside it, his fingers running over the wood, almost lovingly. Then he removed the shoulder harness and the great blade.

The big man slid the blade from the scabbard, studied it, and took a small flagon from the bag that hung from one of the pegs. After extracting a pair of rags from the leather bag, he used one rag first to dry the blade and afterward the scabbard, before draping the damp rag over a shoulder-high peg on the long board fastened to the wall. Then he unstoppered the flagon and poured a small amount of oil onto the other rag before closing the flagon. Gently, the hunter oiled the blade from hilt to tip.

As he watched the hunter, Nylan puzzled over several items. Although Gerlich brought back no game, he had brought back fewer arrows, and shafts and arrowheads were not easy to come by. Had Gerlich lost the shafts?

Nylan smiled. Perhaps the great hunter was not so great

after all. He shook his head as he studied Gerlich. Why did the hunter carry the huge blade on a hunting trip? Any sort of sword was difficult to use on skis. In fact, anything was hard to use trying to balance on wooden slats spanning deep powder snow.

Based on his encounter with the leopard, Nylan could certainly testify to that. He lifted his right shoulder, felt the soreness. Despite the antiseptic, one section of the slash had become inflamed, enough so that Ayrlyn had been forced to use her healing talents—a way of forcing out the disorder of infection.

After having watched her do it, Nylan had practiced on the shoulder wound himself, keeping it chaos-free. That talent might come in useful at some point, especially when the few remnants of the medical supplies were exhausted. The talent didn't seem to speed healing much, but it stopped infection and would reduce scarring, Nylan suspected.

"Any luck?" Nylan asked from the steps.

Boredom replaced surprise on Gerlich's face. "Not this time. We've killed most of the dumb animals, and I've got to travel farther every time."

"Sorry to hear that." Nylan nodded and continued down the steps.

There were people near the hearth in the great room, but the engineer continued onward toward the north door. He shivered as he hurried through the ice-lined archway and into the bathhouse. The stove was yet warm, and some water lay on the stone tiles of the first shower stall, but no one remained in the building. Huldran probably had used the shower—or Ryba—or both.

Nylan stripped off the boots and trousers and checked the knife valve. Then he stood under the frigid water only long enough to get thoroughly wet, before lathering himself with the liquid concoction that Ayrlyn had claimed was the local equivalent of soap.

The amber liquid looked like oil laced with sand and flower petals. That was also what it smelled like—rancid flower petals. It felt like liquid sandpaper as Nylan stood, damp and freezing, on the cold stones of a shower stall without a door, trying to scrub grease off his hands, frozen and thawed sweat out of his stiff hair, and grime off most of his body.

He had to wet his body twice more just to get lathered half properly, and then it took three short rinses—just because he couldn't stand under the cold water that long. Cold? The water had been warmed some by the bathhouse stove's water warmer.

The only excuse for a towel was a napless synthetic oblong that might have qualified as a hand towel on Heaven except for the fact that it was designed to shed water—not absorb it. So Nylan had to use it more to wipe the water off his body, letting a combination of evaporation and what felt like sublimation do the rest.

While he looked and smelled more human at the end of the process, the bluish tinge to his skin spoiled the feeling. The goose bumps and shivers remained long after he donned the relatively clean clothes that had taken two days to dry after he had washed them. Finally, his feet were dry enough for him to pull on the wool-lined boots.

The bathhouse remained empty, except for him.

When he had stopped shivering violently, he marched resolutely toward the brick archway that had become a solid arc of ice. The ends of his damp hair still froze before he got into the tower and closed the north door behind him. After carting his old trousers up to the top level, he returned to the great hall, and the coals in the hearth.

In the dimness, Relyn sat on one side, Murkassa on the other, each one's back to the coals. Neither looked at the other. Both shivered.

"A cheerful group," Nylan observed.

"Feeding fowls—that is all I can do that is useful," snapped Relyn, raising his artificial hand. "Or sheep. It is so cold that I can barely hold the bag." His eyes turned on Nylan. "Your hair is wet."

"I couldn't stand being dirty and unshaven any longer. I took a shower."

"You have ice in your veins." Relyn shuddered. "You are more terrible than the women. They are merely angels, trying to live as people."

"That's nonsense," Nylan retorted. "I'm trying just as hard." He stepped toward the residual warmth of the hearth.

"They did not think of the tower and build it. They did not find the water that flows when all is frozen. They did not forge the blades of black lightning. They did not build the small bows that send arrows through plate mail." Relyn stood, but his eyes were on the stones of the floor. "They only fought and grew crops and hunted. You forged Westwind, and all that it will be. I have finally seen the truth. You are the first true black mage."

Nylan snorted. "Me? I'm the man who can barely cross the snows on skis. The one who couldn't get a thunder-thrower to kill anyone . . ."

Relyn laughed . . . gently. "The thunder-throwers do not belong in Candar. Nor did the magical tools you first used. Yet all the weapons you created and all the buildings you built will remain. Everything you forged belongs here on the Roof of the World, and everything will last for generations. If you died today, what you have wrought would remain."

"That was the general idea. You seem to be the first one to fully understand that." Nylan paused, and in the silence could hear the sounds of voices and tools and cooking coming up from the lowest level of the tower. "What's so strange about it? I helped to build a tower, but there are towers all over Candar. I forged some blades, but armsmen all over Candar carry blades. I created bows, but archers have existed for years."

Relyn just shook his head.

"Murkassa?" Nylan turned to the thin and round-faced girl.

"Yes, Ser Mage." Murkassa pursed her lips and waited.

"Tell the honorable Relyn that he's full of sheep manure."

"No, ser. You are the black one, and the marshal is the Angel, and you have brought the Legend to the world." She looked sideways at Relyn. "The men of these lands, mayhap of all lands, are like Jilkar. They respect only the strong. You have made these women strong—"

"They were already strong." Nylan laughed bitterly.

"Then you have kept them strong, and they will force the men of Candar to respect them—and to respect all women."

"That is why Sillek will come to attack Westwind," said Relyn. "After him may come Lord Karthanos of Gallos."

"Is that why Lornth dislikes Jerans?" asked Nylan. "Strong women?"

Relyn nodded.

With the low moaning of the wind, the engineer turned toward the windows. "Some mage I am. I can't even keep this place warm enough."

"It is warm enough for the angels to grow and prosper. It is warm enough that all Candar will tremble at the name of Westwind. I should think that would be warm enough." Relyn's tone is ironic.

"You give me far too much praise, Relyn."

"No . . . ser . . . you do not choose to see that you have changed the world. You have changed me, and you will change others, and in time few indeed will understand the world before the Legend."

"You are different," Murkassa added. "You see women as strong, and as you see them, so are they."

"Women are strong. Stronger than men in many ways," Nylan said.

"As you say, Mage."

Nylan shook his head. Why did they take his words as a statement of faith, as if what he said became true? Outside, the howling of the storm rose, and Nylan wondered, absently, how the sheep, chickens, and horses were faring. The enemy was the winter, not the preconceptions of men in Candar.

Both Relyn and Murkassa exchanged amused smiles, as if Nylan could not see the obvious. Maybe he couldn't.

"I'm going down to work."

"Yes, Mage."

They smiled again.

Change the world? Nylan tried not to frown as he left the slowly chilling great room to descend to the woodworking area and his efforts with the cradle and the rocking chair he was beginning. Changing the world by building a tower with rudimentary water and sanitation? By using a dying laser to forge a handful of blades and a few composite bows? By nearly getting killed by a snow cat or always falling into snow over his head?

He snorted again. He had a cradle to finish—and a rocking chair—and he couldn't afford to be distracted by delusions of grandeur.

LVI

". . . Don't understand why Lord Sillek is receiving this trader with such honor . . ."

As she catches the murmur from halfway down the long table on the low dais, Zeldyan smiles and, under the table, squeezes Sillek's hand.

He turns and smiles at his consort.

"The honorable Lygon of Bleyans!" announces the young armsman-in-training at the doorway to the dining hall, his voice on the edge of cracking.

Retaining the smile on his face, Sillek stands to greet Lygon. Zeldyan rises almost simultaneously. At the end of the table to Sillek's right, the lady Ellindyja smooths her face into a mold of polite interest. At the end to the left, Ser Gethen cultivates a look of indifference.

Lygon, a round-faced man wearing a maroon velvet tunic and a silver chain, marches up between the two rows of tables in the dining hall as the murmurs die away and the leading tradespeople and landowners of Lornth watch.

A quick trumpet fanfare sounds as Lygon steps onto the dais.

Sillek gestures to the empty seat to his right. "Welcome, Lygon. Welcome to Lornth, and to our hospitality." He steps back. "This is Zeldyan, my lady and consort. Zeldyan, this is Lygon, the most honorable trader of Suthya."

"Whenever you rulers call me honorable, Sillek, I want to reach for my purse." Lygon overtops Sillek by half a head, but bows low, first to the Lord of Lornth, and then to Zeldyan. "It is a pleasure to meet you, lady, and to know that Lord Sillek has you to enchant him and grace his towers."

"It is my pleasure to meet you, ser," Zeldyan responds, smiling brightly. "And I will do my best to offer such grace, especially since you do us such honor."

Behind her, Gethen nods minutely.

"We don't want your purse, Lygon, just your presence." Sillek laughs easily and stands until the trader sits.

Around the hall, the murmurs rise again.

Lygon stares frankly at Zeldyan for a moment before his eyes return to Sillek. "Your consort, she is a true beauty." His eyes go back to Zeldyan. "And you are, my lady. Few indeed have your grace and beauty."

"I do my poor best for my lord," Zeldyan answers, "for he is dear to me."

Lygon nods, neither agreeing nor disagreeing as Sillek himself pours the red wine from the pitcher between them into two goblets almost equidistant from each man. The trader takes the goblet fractionally closer to Sillek.

Sillek lifts the one remaining, raises it, and says, "To your continued health and to good trading."

"To health and good trading," affirms Lygon.

Those at the head table drink with Sillek and Lygon, though Zeldyan's lips barely pass the wine.

Lygon sets his goblet before him and studies the great hall below the dais. "Quite a gathering."

"Only the due of a first trader of Suthya." Sillek takes another sip from his goblet. "Even my consort's father made a special trip from Carpa to honor you."

"First trader, twentieth trader—what difference does it

make?" Lygon shakes his head. "We're all traders, and we try to be fair to all."

Lygon's voice carries, but his eyes are on Sillek, and he does not see how Ser Gethen's lips tighten at his words.

"Fairness—that's important to Lornth. It always will be," answers Sillek.

"I had hoped that Lornth would continue the warm relationship enjoyed in the past with the traders of Suthya, and I am pleased to see such hospitality again offered." Lygon downs the remaining wine in his goblet with a single swallow, then slices the pearapple on his plate into slivers and pops a pearapple section and a chunk of Rohrn cheese into his mouth. "Always have good cheeses here."

"I am glad you find them so, and trust you will always do so." Sillek takes a swallow of his wine, a swallow far smaller than it appears.

"The wine's better than what your sire served. Where'd you find it?"

Sillek inclines his head toward Zeldyan. "The uplands of Zeldyan's father's lands produce a good grape, and better wine."

"Ha! Consorted well, for beauty and good wine. You demon, you." Lygon laughs.

Sillek smiles, as does Zeldyan, but, at their respective ends of the table, neither Gethen's nor Ellindyja's face mirrors such apparent pleasure.

"Heard some rumors—you know how things go—some rumors that a bunch of crazy women took over a mountaintop on your eastern marches." Lygon swallows and chews more of the pearapples and cheese. "Some even say," adds the trader through a full mouth, "they're evil angels."

"That has been said," acknowledges Sillek, "and, if they survive the winter, I may well be occupied. Then again," he laughs wryly, "I may be occupied with the Jeranyi. I'm certain you've also heard that rumor. Well . . . it's true. I've got my chief armsman in Clynya. He's not exactly pleased."

"It has also been said that you handed Ildyrom a stinging defeat." Lygon chews through the rest of the pearapple slices, barely avoiding spitting fragments across the linens.

At her end of the table, Lady Ellindyja contains a wince.

"The problem with such victories," Sillek responds, "is that they require maintenance. And supplies," he adds, looking at the trader.

"No business tonight, Lord Sillek," protests Lygon. "It's a cold winter out there, and tonight's the time for warmth and good food."

"I stand corrected." Sillek raises his hands, half in laughter, half in mock defeat.

Zeldyan smiles. So does her father.

LVII

A LOW FIRE, for once, burned in the hearth of the great room.

Ryba sat in the chair at the end of the table, with Saryn on her right and Nylan on the left. Ayrlyn sat beside Saryn, while Fierral sat next to Nylan with Kyseen beside her. Relyn was seated beside Ayrlyn. Gathered around the foot of the first table on the side below Saryn were Gerlich, Narliat, and Selitra. On the side below Nylan were Huldran, Istril, Murkassa, and Hryessa.

"I'd guess you'd call this a status or planning meeting." Ryba's breath created a flicker in the candle at her end of the table. "I wanted to hear from each of you about how your efforts are going, and any suggestions you might have." The marshal looked at Gerlich. "Hunting?"

"It's getting harder," Gerlich said. "The deer we do get are thinner. We haven't seen a snow leopard since the engineer killed his. The big cats have gone to lower grounds—or hibernated. The same for the bears."

"The old ones say the leopards talk to each other," added Murkassa.

Her breath nearly guttered out the other candle, and Huldran reached out and moved it more toward the center of the table.

"What about smaller animals?" asked Ayrlyn.

"It takes a lot of effort to catch them, and what good is a hare when we have to forage for more than a score of people?" Gerlich shrugged, looking toward Kyseen.

"You get me three hares, and I can make a meal," affirmed the cook.

"How are your supplies coming?"

"Not as well as I'd like," admitted Kyseen. "We've been grinding and powdering some of those roots into the flour, and that stretches it. Some of the guards say it's bitter. What can I do? The potatoes are good, but we'll finish those off in another eight-day, maybe two, if we only have them every third day."

"The potatoes are all that stick," said Huldran. "There's not enough meat, and the loaves are getting smaller."

The low moan of the wind outside the great room punctuated her words, and, for a moment, no one spoke.

"Birds?" asked the marshal.

"We've got owls and gray-hawks up here. That's all we've seen, anyway," answered Gerlich. "Neither has much meat, and they're so quick I don't see how you could shoot them."

Ryba nodded and turned to Saryn. "What about the livestock?"

"There isn't enough grass and hay for the horses and the sheep," Saryn said. "We've cut back on the corn for the chickens, and they've cut back on laying. There's not enough grain for the rest of the winter for them, either."

"The chickens, they lay little in the winter," said Hryessa. "I would start killing the older ones and let the young ones live for the year ahead."

"Can you work that out?" asked Ryba.

Saryn glanced at Hryessa, then at Ryba, and nodded. "That still doesn't solve the fodder problem."

"The lander we used for storage is more than a third full," said Selitra.

"I helped fill that full, I did," interjected Narliat.

"We're only about halfway through the winter," pointed out Saryn. "There's no forage out there, and there won't be even after the snow melts."

"There are the fir branches . . ." suggested Murkassa. "Goats sometimes eat them."

"It doesn't do the goats much good," pointed out Relyn, "and sheep can't eat as many things as goats."

"We're getting short of food," Ryba pointed out, "and we don't have enough food for both sheep and mounts." Her eyes narrowed. "We can get more sheep, one way or another, if we have to. Without mounts we're dead."

"We need twenty mounts," said Fierral. "And they can't be skin and bones."

The marshal turned back to Saryn. "Figure out a slaughter schedule for the sheep—and horses, if need be—that will leave us with twenty mounts, if you can, by the time there's something for the sheep and horses to forage on. It would be good to have some sheep left, but . . . we'll need the mounts more to get through the summer."

"That's going to take a day or so."

"A day or so won't make any difference. Also, work it out with Kyseen. That's so she can plan the food schedule to keep everyone as healthy as she can, given this mess."

Saryn nodded.

"What about timber? Firewood?" asked Ryba.

"We're almost out of the green timber for making things," said Saryn flatly. "We've got skis for everyone, and you've seen the chairs and room panels—and the cradles. That's about all we can do this winter. We're running through the stove wood and firewood. We can't even drag enough wood up from the forest to replace what we're burning. If we drag up more than we are now, the horses will need to eat more, and some will get lung burn."

"Should we turn the furniture into heat?" asked Gerlich idly.

"No," answered Ayrlyn. "That wouldn't add two days' heat, and it would be a waste of all that effort. Besides, the impact on people's morale . . ."

"Just asking."

"Try thinking," muttered Huldran under her breath.

Nylan barely kept from nodding at that.

"Anything else?" The marshal looked around the table.

Gerlich nudged the woman beside him.

"The roof in the showers leaks," ventured Selitra.

"We can't do much about that until spring," Nylan admitted.

"Sometimes the water freezes on the stones. That's dangerous," said the lithe guard.

"Getting up on that roof now would be more dangerous," pointed out Nylan. "And it's too cold for the mortar to set. We don't have roofing tar . . . maybe by summer."

"I hope no one falls."

"Is there anything else we can do something about?" asked Ryba. "If not, that's all. Saryn . . . you stay. I'd like your estimates on what livestock should be slaughtered and how that might stretch out the feed and fodder."

As Nylan stood by the window while Saryn provided rough fodder estimates to Ryba, he listened to Hryessa and Murkassa, talking in low voices by the shelves under the stone staircase.

". . . a third of a place filled with hay and grass, and they would start slaughtering now?"

"Would you wait until there was no food, and then kill them all, or have them starve?" asked Murkassa. "These women, they are smart, and the Angel thinks ahead, far ahead."

Perhaps too far, thought Nylan, turning back to the pair at the table. He hadn't liked Gerlich's using Selitra to bring up problems with the bathhouse, either. The engineer forced himself to take several deep slow breaths, then turned his thoughts back to the table, though he remained beside the frosted and snow-covered window.

"I'd say a sheep now, and another one in an eight-day . . . two chickens . . . lay in three days . . . that leaves eight hens and four half-grown chicks."

"Mounts?" asked Ryba.

"There's one nag, gelded, barely gets around."

"See if Kyseen can make something there. Start with the nag, not the sheep. A sheep can give wool and food. A male that can't work and can't stand stud—that's useless."

Nylan half wondered if someday he'd be just like the poor nag. He pursed his lips and waited until Saryn strode out. Then he stepped up as Ryba rose from the chair. "In short," he said, "things are bad and getting worse, and it's going to be a long time before the snow melts."

"That's not a problem," said the marshal. "It's going to warm up within probably three eight-days. But it's likely to be almost eight eight-days before there's any spring growth, even in the woods, that the animals can forage through, or before Ayrlyn can get out and trade for food."

"Eight eight-days? That's going to be hard. Really hard."

"Harder than that. Much harder." Ryba walked toward the steps down to the kitchen area.

LVIII

THE TALL MAN smooths his velvet tunic before stepping into the tower room.

"You do honor to receive me, Lady Ellindyja," offers the tall trader.

Lady Ellindyja steps back from the door and offers a slight head bow. "I do so appreciate your kindness in coming to see one whose time is past." She slips toward her padded bench, leaving Lygon to follow.

As she turns and sits, she picks up the embroidery hoop, and smiles as she finds the needle with the bright red thread.

"Ah . . . my lady, you did—"

"Lygon, you are a trader, and you have dealt fairly with Lornth for nearly a score of years."

"That is true." Lygon runs his hand through the thinning brown hair before settling into the chair opposite Ellindyja.

"I would like to believe I have always been fair. Firm, but fair." He laughs. "Firm they sometimes take for being harsh, but without a profit, there's no trading."

"Just as for lords, without honor, there is no ruling?" asks Ellindyja, her needle still poised above the white fabric of the hoop.

Lygon shifts his weight on the chair. "I would say that both lords and traders need honor."

"What weight does honor add to a trader's purse?" asks Ellindyja, her tone almost idle.

"People must believe you will deliver what you promised, that your goods are what you state they are."

"Do you tell people what to buy?"

Lygon frowns before he answers. "Hardly. You cannot sell what people do not want."

"I fear that is true in ruling, too," offers Ellindyja, her eyes dropping to her embroidery as the needle completes a stitch. "The lords of a land have expectations. Surely, you are familiar with this?"

"I am a trader, lady, not a lord." Lygon shifts his weight.

"I know, and you would like to continue trading in Lornth, would you not?" Ellindyja smiles.

"Lady . . ." Lygon begins to stand.

"Please be seated, trader Lygon. I am not threatening, for I certainly have no power to threaten. I am not plotting or scheming, for I have my son's best interests at heart. But, as any mother does, I have concerns, and my concerns deal with honor." With another bright smile, Ellindyja fixes her eyes on Lygon. "You are an honorable man, and you understand both trade and honor, and I hope to enlist your assistance in allaying my concerns." She raises the hand with the needle slightly to halt his protestation. "What I seek from you will neither cost you coin nor ill will. I seek your words of wisdom with my son, at such time as may be appropriate. That is all."

"I am no sage, no magician." Lygon rubs his forehead.

"I have little use for either," answers Ellindyja dryly. "As you remarked at the dinner the other night, my son faces a difficult situation. Lord Ildyrom has created some difficulties to the south, while the demon women have seized part of his patrimony in the Westhorns. These women are said to be alluring, not just to men, but to malcontented women here in Lornth." She pauses. "And all across the western lands, even in Suthya. Would you want women leaving Suthya to create a land ruled by women? How would you trade with them? Would they not favor traders from, say, Spidlar?"

"I could not say. I have not heard of such." Lygon licks his thick lips.

"Let us trust that such does not come to pass, then." The needle flickers through the white fabric. "Yet how can Lord Sillek my son support such a cause merely because it would benefit the traders of Suthya?"

Lygon's brows furrow. "If you would go on . . ."

"It is simple, honored trader. My son is concerned that the honor of *merely* regaining his patrimony is not enough to justify the deaths and the coins spent. His lords are concerned that their daughters and the daughters on their holdings do not find the wild women alluring, but they cannot speak this because they would be seen as weak or unable to control their own women."

Lygon shakes his head. "What has this to do with trading?"

Ellindyja's lips tighten ever so slightly before she speaks. "We have few weaponsmiths, and armies require supplies. If the honor of upholding your—and our—way of life is not sufficient for you to speak to my son about the need to uphold his honor, and that of his lords, then perhaps the supplies needed in such an effort will offer some inducement. Except you need not speak of supplies to Lord Sillek. That would be too direct, even for him."

"My lady . . . you amaze me. Lord Sillek is fortunate to have a mother such as you."

"I seek only his best interests, trader. Happily, they coincide with yours."

"Indeed." Lygon's eyes wander toward the door.

Lady Ellindyja rises. "You must have matters to attend to more pressing than listening to an old lady. Still, if you could see it in your heart to offer your observations about honor and about how you see that lords would not admit their concerns publicly . . . why, I would be most grateful."

Lygon stands and bows. "I could scarcely do less for a mother so devoted to her son."

"I am deeply devoted to his best interests," Ellindyja reiterates as she escorts the tall trader to the door.

The tower door opens, and Lygon steps into the hallway and strides toward the steps to the lower level, his face impassive, his eyes not catching the blond woman who is descending from the open upper parapets.

As she follows the trader down the steps, Zeldyan's eyes flick to the door to Lady Ellindyja's room, and her mouth tightens.

LIX

IN THE CORNER of the woodworking area of the tower, Nylan slowly traced the circular cuts he needed to make in the scrap of poorly tanned leather. That way, he got longer thongs and could use the leftover scraps. Even so, his makeshift net was turning into a patchwork of cord, leather thongs, and synthcord.

He glanced at the pieces of the unfinished cradle, then at the rocking-chair sections. Both needed more smoothing and crafting before he glued and joined them, but his hands cramped after much time with the smoothing blade—and Siret and Ellysia had a more urgent need to finish their cradles.

From the other side of the tower came the smell of meat— horse meat, cooking slowly in the big oven. There was also the smell of bread, with the hint of bitterness that Huldran and others had noted.

Nylan found himself licking his lips—over horse meat?

It had been a long winter. For a few days, they'd eat well. And then they wouldn't, not for another eight-day or so. He tried not to dwell on the fate of the poor swaybacked and tired gelding and instead looked at the fragile-appearing net.

"How do you catch the snow hares?" Nylan had asked Murkassa.

"Weaving I know, and cows, and sheep, but not hunting. Men hunt, Ser Mage." The round-faced girl had shrugged, as if Nylan should have known such. Then she had added, "It is too cold to hunt here, except for you angels, and I must stay behind the walls."

Hryessa had been more helpful. "My uncle, he once showed me his snares and his nets . . ."

After listening to descriptions of snares and setting them, Nylan had decided nets were more practical in the deep snow of the Roof of the World.

Then, he hadn't considered the sheer tediousness of making the damned net. With a slow deep breath, he started cutting, trying to keep his hands steady, knowing that, as in everything, he really couldn't afford to make any mistakes, to waste any of the leather.

He rubbed his nose, trying to hold back a sneeze. With the dust left over from building and the sawdust from woodworking and the soot from the furnace, he wondered why they weren't all sneezing.

Kkhhhchew! Kkhchew! The engineer rubbed his sore nose again.

"It's hard to keep from sneezing," said Siret from where she smoothed the sideboards of her cradle. "I hate it when I sneeze, especially now."

Behind and around Nylan, guards worked on their own projects. Ayrlyn was attempting a crude lutar, using fiber-cabling from one of the landers as strings. Surprisingly, Hryessa also worked on a lutar.

As he knelt on the slate floor, Nylan caught a glimpse of boots nearing.

"It's getting presentable in size," said Ryba.

Nylan stood. "The net? Yes. Whether it will work is another question, but I thought I'd try for another niche in the ecological framework."

The marshal laughed. "When you talk about hunting, you sometimes still sound like an engineer."

"I probably always will."

"What else are you working on?" Her eyes went to the wood behind Nylan.

He gestured, glad that the cradle's headboard was turned so the carving was to the wall. While he couldn't conceal the cradle itself, he wanted some aspect of it to be a surprise.

"The cradle for Dyliess. A chair." He laughed. "Once the cradle's done, I'll have to start on a bed. Children grow so fast. But that will have to wait a bit, until the snows melt, and until we're in better shape."

"At times, I feel like life here is always a struggle between waiting and acting, and that I'll choose the wrong thing to wait on because we don't have enough of anything." Ryba forced a laugh. "I suppose that's just life anywhere."

"What are you doing?" he asked.

"Checking on what everyone else is doing. Then I'll start pulling out guards for blade practice."

"You're still doing that on the fifth level? It's dark up there."

"It works fine. They really have to concentrate. Besides, using a blade has to be as much or more by feel as by sight." Ryba cleared her throat. "Nylan . . . you need practice with a blade. A lot more practice."

"Another vision?" he answered glumly.

"Another vision." There was nothing light in her voice.

"All right. After I get a little more done on the net."

"I'll be a while. I need to talk to Kyseen." Ryba's eyes passed over the back side of the cradle's headboard without pausing as she turned and crossed the space toward the kitchen.

Nylan's ears followed her progress.

". . . not a warm bone in her body . . ."

". . . like the queen of the world . . ."

". . . even cold with the engineer . . . show him some warmth . . ."

". . . she's not kept in a corner, caged up, like me," added Murkassa. "She can walk the snows."

Istril, almost like a guardian, touched the Gallosian woman's arm. "It is getting warmer. It won't be that long."

". . . too long, already. The stones of the walls will fall in upon me . . ."

All the guards were getting worn and frazzled. Nylan hoped that Istril were right, that it wouldn't be that long, but he wasn't counting on it. That was why he worked on the net.

". . . never loses sight of the weapons, does the marshal?" asked Siret, not looking up from her continued smoothing of the sideboards of the cradle she knelt beside.

"No, and she's right, even if I dread getting bruised and banged up."

"You do better than most, ser."

"You're kind, Siret, but she makes me feel like an awkward child, even when she's carrying extra weight and is off balance."

"What about me, ser?" asked the visibly pregnant guard.

"You're still sparring?"

"She says that the men around here could give a damn if I'm with child. Or have a babe in arms."

"She's probably right about that, too," Nylan answered slowly.

"Sad, isn't it?"

They both took deep breaths, almost simultaneously. Then Siret grinned, and Nylan found himself doing the same.

LX

SILLEK WALKS INTO the armory, followed by Terek. The Lord of Lornth spots the assistant chief armsman, sharpening a blade with a whetstone. "Rimmur?"

The thin man looks up from the stool, then stands quickly. "Yes, ser?"

Behind Sillek, Terek closes the door.

"How can I help you, ser?"

"Since Koric remains to hold Clynya, I need you to make sure that our armsmen are ready to travel as soon as the roads firm. I don't mean an eight-day later. I mean the day I lift my blade. Do you understand?"

"Yes, ser. Where do we make ready to go?"

"I'm not telling you. Nor will I until we start to march." Sillek's smile is grim.

"Ser . . . that'll make it hard . . ." Rimmur's words die under Sillek's glare. "I mean . . . the men . . ."

"Let me explain it," answers Sillek. "I have Ildyrom and the Jeranyi to the west, and these evil angels to the east. If I announce I'm going after the angels, Ildyrom will be in and through Clynya within days after the snows melt, or the rains stop, and the roads firm. If I go after Ildyrom, the traders will raise their prices and lower what they pay, and the angels will be free to take over more of the Westhorns, including the trade routes and the lower pastures. If I do nothing, everyone will think they can make trouble."

"Yes, ser," answered Rimmur. "Which are you going to do?"

Sillek slaps his forehead theatrically and glares at the assistant armsman. "If I tell you and the armsmen of Lornth that I'm going after Ildyrom, then everyone will tell everyone else, and in three days all of Candar will know, and the traders and the angels will make trouble. If I say I'm going after the angels, then Ildyrom and his war-women will make trouble. So I can't say. You just have to get them ready. I'll announce where later."

"Yes, ser. They won't like it, ser."

"Rimmur . . . do they want to know and be dead, or not know and be alive?"

"Ser?"

"If no one knows where we're going, whether it's after Ildyrom or the black angels, then our enemies can't plan. If they can't plan, then fewer of our men get killed. So just get them ready. Tell them what I told you."

"Yes, ser." Rimmur stands and waits.

As Terek and Sillek head up the narrow steps to the upper levels of the tower, the white wizard clears his throat, finally saying, "You never did indicate . . . ser . . ."

"That's right, Terek. I did not. I do not know what sort of screeing or magic the angels have. So my decision remains unspoken until we leave. That way, Ildyrom and the angels have to guess not only which one I intend to attack, but also when."

"As Rimmur said, ser, that makes preparation uncertain."

"Terek . . . before this is all over, we'll end up fighting them both. So prepare for both eventualities." Sillek steps out onto the upper landing and turns. "Your preparations won't be wasted."

"Yes, ser." Terek inclines his head.

"Good." Sillek turns and walks down the corridor to the quarters where Zeldyan waits.

LXI

THE NIGHT WIND whistled outside the tower windows, rattling the shutters on the partitioned-off side so much that small fragments of ice broke off and dropped to the floor inside the sixth level. From the third level below came the faint crying of an infant, Dephnay, but the crying died away, replaced by the faintest of nursing sounds, and gentle words.

On the slightly warmer side of the top level of the tower, protected by the thin door, the recently completed partitions and hangings, Ryba and Nylan lay in the darkness.

Nylan's legs ached from the skiing, the endless attempts to find and track the smaller rodents he knew were in the forests. His arms and shoulders ached from the drubbings he had taken in his last blade-sparring sessions with Saryn and Ryba in the half darkness of the fifth level of the tower. His lungs were heavy from the cold. His guts grumbled from the continual alternation of too much meat and too few carbohydrates with the periods of too little food at all. His upper cheeks burned from near-continual frostbite, and his fingers ached from holding a smoothing blade or a knife too long.

For all his exhaustion, he could not sleep, and his eyes fixed on the patchwork hangings that moved, ever so slightly, to the convection currents between the cold stone walls and the residual warmth of the chimney masonry that ran up the center of the tower.

Ryba lay on her back, nearly motionless, eyes closed, the woolen blanket concealing her swelling abdomen.

In the darkness through which he could see, Nylan studied her profile, chiseled against the darkness like that of a silver coin against black velvet, a profile almost of the Sybran girl-next-door, lacking the regalness that appeared whenever she was awake.

What had made her able to struggle against such odds, going from a steppe nomad child to being one of UFA's top combat commanders and to founding a nation or tradition that seemed almost fated to endure?

Would it endure? How long?

He stifled a sigh. Did it matter? Ryba was going to do what Ryba was going to do, or what her visions told her to do, and for the moment he had no real choices. Nor did any of them, he supposed, not if they wanted to survive. He tried to close his eyes, but they hurt more closed than open, with a gritty burning.

The shutter on the far side of the tower rattled again as the wind forced its way against the tower, and more icicles broke off and shattered across the plank floor. Even the armaglass window creaked and flexed against the storm, although Ayrlyn insisted that, while the storms would be more violent in the eight-days ahead, they represented the warming that was already under way.

Nylan hadn't seen any real warming outside, and the snow was still getting deeper, and the game scarcer, and the livestock thinner, and tempers more frayed.

He tried to close his eyes again, and this time, this time they stayed closed.

LXII

NYLAN LAY IN his snow-covered burrow, the long thong attached to the weighted net suspended over the concealed rabbit run.

Catching even rodents was a pain. First he'd had to put out the nets almost an eight-day before so that the damned frost rabbits would get used to the scent—or that the cold and wind would carry it away. But even when they triggered the net, somehow they never had stayed caught long enough for Nylan to get there.

So he'd been reduced to tending his net traps in person.

It had taken him all morning to get the one dead hare strapped to his pack, and it was well past mid-afternoon. Now, lying covered in the snow, watching the second rabbit run he had discovered, Nylan could sense the snow hare just below the entrance to the burrow. It had poked its head out several times, but not far enough or long enough for Nylan to drop the net.

So the engineer shivered and waited . . . and shivered and waited.

The sun had almost touched the western peaks before the hare finally hopped clear of the burrow.

Nylan jerked the thong and the weighted net fell.

The rabbit twisted, but the crude net held, and in the end, Nylan carried a small heap of thin flesh and matted fur up through the snow. Now he had two thin, dead snow hares—that was all.

He was cold, his trousers half-soaked. The sun was setting, and he had a climb just to get out of the forest, even before the ridge up to Westwind.

All that effort, for two small hares. In the future, could they breed them? Except that meant more forage and grain stored, and there was a limit to what they could buy or grow.

He waded through the snow that was chest-deep downwind to where his skis were. Once he went into a pothole, with the snow sifting around his neck and face. He slowly dug himself out.

His fingers fumbled as he strapped his boots to the skis in the growing purple deeps of twilight. Then he pushed one heavy ski after the other along the slope. When he reached the packed trail the horses used to drag the trees up the ridge, he unfastened the thongs and carried poles and skis up the ridge. By the time he reached the causeway, all the stars were out, and the night air cut at his lungs.

From the darkness outside the tower, he stumbled inside into the gloom of the front entry area inside the south door, carrying skis, poles, and hares.

The warmth of the great room welled out and surrounded him, and the twin candles on the tables seemed like beacons.

Ayrlyn reached him first as he leaned against the steps. "Ryba was worried. It gets cold out there when the sun goes down."

"I know. It took a little longer than I thought." He looked toward the guards at the table, his eyes focusing on the cook near the end of the second table. "Kyseen. My humble offerings." Nylan raised the pair of dead hares.

The dark-haired cook slipped from the table and hurried across the cold slate floor. "All offerings are welcome these days, ser."

Kadran followed her. "If you can bring in a couple more, we can tan the pelts and stitch them together as a coverlet for Ellysia's Dephnay," added the second cook. "This tower's not so warm as it could be for a child . . . begging your pardon, ser, knowing you did the best you could, but it's not."

"By next winter, it will be warmer." Nylan hoped they would be around for next winter.

"You go eat, ser," insisted Kyseen. "I'll dress these quick so they don't spoil, and I'll be back up in an instant."

"Have you eaten?" he asked. "I wouldn't want to spoil your meal . . ."

"I've eaten, and you haven't." Kyseen took the two hares and started down the steps.

Nylan left the skis and poles by the stairs. He'd put them away after he ate.

"Two rabbits? That's all?" asked Gerlich as Nylan walked slowly toward his place at the table.

"I'm still learning." As Nylan sat, heavily, ignoring the cold and dampness in his trousers, he asked, "By the way, when did you last bring in any game?"

Gerlich flushed. "I brought in a winter deer, not a rabbit."

"That was more than two eight-days ago," Ayrlyn said as she reseated herself across from the engineer.

"So?" retorted Gerlich. "Everything's scarce these days, and we've probably already killed the stupid ones."

"We can't live on stupid game," pointed out the singer.

"The hares are another meal." Ryba's voice cut through the argument. "And each meal helps." She smiled for a moment at Nylan, though there was sadness in the expression as well as pleasure and relief.

"It's always cold and dark! Always!"

Nylan turned his head at the loud words from the lower table, where Istril had laid her hand on Murkassa's shoulder.

"The days are getting longer now," pointed out the silverhaired guard. "Before long, it will be getting warmer as well."

"It's still too cold and dark." Murkassa's words seemed lower, though Istril patted her shoulder again. "Even the wall stones are cold and dark."

Turning back to the trencher before him, Nylan took a slow swallow of the warm tea, not even minding the bitterness. He reached for the chunk of bread left for him.

A portion of a mutton stew or soup also remained, only half-warm, but Nylan began to eat, hardly conscious of the coolness of the meat and gravy, or the lumpiness that marked the last of the blue potatoes . . . or of the continuing conversation between Istril and Murkassa.

LXIII

"I CAN'T! I can't!"

From the corner of the furnace and woodworking room where he smoothed the sideboards of the cradle, Nylan looked toward the stone steps.

"NO! I won't. I can't."

Beside him, Siret dropped the polishing cloth, then awkwardly bent over, trying to reach the scrap of fabric. Nylan retrieved it and handed the cloth back to her. "Here."

"Thank you, ser. I feel like I can't do much of anything easily—"

"No! It's too white! It's . . . AEEEiiiii . . ."

Across the room, Ayrlyn set down the lutar bridge she had been working on, nodded to Hryessa, and hurried up the stairs. After a momentary hesitation, Nylan lurched to his feet and followed Ayrlyn, not knowing quite why he did, but feeling that he should.

By the south door to the tower, Jaseen and Istril held a struggling brown-haired figure—Murkassa—dressed in a heavy jacket.

"Too white! It's too white!" Murkassa's flailing arm caught Istril across the cheek, but the silver-haired guard pinned the arm to her anyway, ignoring the red blotch that would be a bruise.

Ayrlyn stepped up to Murkassa, whose body was stiff, and whose screams had become incoherent, and touched her forehead. Murkassa jerked away, but Ayrlyn followed the movements, again touching her forehead.

After a moment, the dark-haired woman slumped, and the two holding her lowered her to the floor.

"Whew!" muttered Jaseen.

Istril put a hand to her cheek.

Ayrlyn bent down and stroked the woman's forehead. "You'll be all right . . ."

Nylan swallowed. Had he felt that unreasoning fear and rage? He studied the figure on the stones. Murkassa's face, though relaxing under the healer's touch, remained drawn. Or was it just thin?

Nylan thought for a moment. Wasn't everyone's face thinner? His trousers were looser.

"Hut fever," Ayrlyn said wryly, straightening up.

"Hut fever?" asked Istril.

"She's not built for the cold—not enough body fat when she came here," explained Ayrlyn. "We really don't have warm enough garments—or sufficient food for a good cold-weather diet. She can't stand the cold. She's afraid of it—with reason—but she can't stand being kept confined." Ayrlyn shrugged. "The conflict just got to her."

"What do we do?" asked the medtech. "There's nothing in the kits, little enough left anyway, and we're saving that for childbirths."

"She'll be all right." Ayrlyn sighed, then sank onto the stairs.

Nylan could feel her exhaustion, almost the way he had felt when he had worked hard manipulating the fields for the laser—or the powernet on the *Winterlance*. The *Winterlance* seemed a lifetime ago, and, in a way, it was.

"Just take her up to her bunk. She'll be all right when she wakes." Ayrlyn's voice was low and hoarse.

"You sure?" asked Jaseen.

The singer and healer nodded.

Jaseen turned and called to Weindre, who stood gaping by the stairs from the lower level. "Give me a hand."

"Istril's there."

"Get your rump over here. Last thing we need is Istril lug-

ging weights up stairs. Then we'll have someone else needing medical care we haven't got the supplies for."

As Weindre neared, Istril said quietly, "I'm sorry."

"You've got nothing to be sorry for," said Jaseen. "Someday it'll be her turn, and she'll need help."

As the two guards carried Murkassa up to the next level,
followed by Istril, Nylan said to Ayrlyn, "Stay here. I'll be
right back."

He hurried down to the kitchen and cornered Kadran. "I
need some bread, something for the healer."

"Healer?"

"Ayrlyn used that healing touch on Murkassa—she went
crazy, Murkassa, I mean—and Ayrlyn looks like she's been
run over by a couple of horses."

Kadran frowned. "Just a little. You never lie anyway, ser,
but some, they'd tell me anything to get more to eat, and we
got to keep it fair."

"I know. I appreciate it."

"Here you go, ser." Kadran cut a thin slice from the end
of a loaf cooling on the table. "Just try not to talk about it,
or everyone will have a tale of some sort."

Nylan nodded wryly. "I'd gathered as much. Thank you."

Nylan carried the thin slice of the bitter and dark bread
up the stairs, where he handed it to Ayrlyn.

The healer took it without speaking and began to eat,
slowly. More slowly, the color returned to her face. "How
did you know?" she asked after she licked the few crumbs
from around her lips.

"I could . . . sense it. You sort of manipulated the whiteness away from her, but that takes energy."

For a moment, neither spoke as Jaseen and Weindre
trudged back down the steps. Nylan moved to let them pass.

"We got her in her bunk. Istril's staying with her," Jaseen
announced.

"Thank you, Jaseen, Weindre," said Ayrlyn.

"No problem. Want you around to do that healing if I need
it." Jaseen offered a smile and a half salute. "We're going
down where it's warm."

After the guards had disappeared into the lower level, Nylan sank back onto the stone step.

"Thank you," Ayrlyn said.

"You're welcome." He added, "I saw Murkassa after you put her to sleep, and I was thinking how thin she was." He shifted his weight on the stone.

"Everyone's thin. Haven't you noticed that?" Ayrlyn glanced down at the entry space by the closed south door, then back at Nylan. "The fact that Istril, Siret, Ryba, and Ellysia are pregnant takes our minds away from it—that and the bulky clothes. We're not on what seems to be a starvation diet, but you need three to four times the food intake if you're active in cold weather, and we have to be active—for a number of reasons—like getting enough wood to keep from freezing. So we really don't have enough food."

"Is it ever going to get warmer?"

"It already is. The ice is thinner on the windows, and before long they'll stay clear all the time." Ayrlyn paused. "I worry about the food, though. Darkness knows what it will be like by early summer."

Nylan nodded. They needed more hares, more game . . . more everything. He knew what he was doing from now on.

"You can't do it all, Nylan," Ayrlyn said softly. "You can't solve every problem."

"But I have to do what I can." His eyes met hers. "How could I live with myself if I didn't?"

After a moment, she looked down at the stones. Then she raised her brown eyes to his. "I appreciate that, but it will always bring you sadness, because people take advantage of it, just like they only respond to force." Her fingers touched his hand for an instant, and he could feel the warmth that was more than physical—and the sweet sadness—before she dropped them.

He nodded. "I know. So do you."

Their eyes met for a moment before he looked away. Why was she the only one who really understood? Or was she?

After another long moment, he asked, "Do you need anything else?"

"No," Ayrlyn answered with a faint and enigmatic smile. "The bread was fine. I don't need anything else to eat."

Nylan nodded again, and helped Ayrlyn to her feet. "I have to get back to woodworking."

"I know."

Again, he could feel her eyes on his back as he went down the stone steps to the lower level.

LXIV

ZELDYAN RESETTLES HERSELF in the large padded chair beside the bed, wearing a green silksheen dressing gown that, while it sets off her golden hair, barely covers her midsection. "He's active," she says, looking down and smiling. "I wish he weren't quite so . . . strong."

"You always say 'he.' " Sillek stands up from the chair that matches the one where Zeldyan sits.

"You always question that. The child is a boy. Even if he were a girl, would it matter? We're young."

"It matters not to me." Sillek steps up beside her chair, bends, and kisses her cheek.

"But it matters to all the holders, and to your enemies." A touch of bitterness creeps into Zeldyan's voice. She shifts her weight in the chair. "I can't ever get comfortable these days."

"A lord is always captive to his people's perceptions." Sillek glances toward the window, beyond which he can glimpse the distant fields, half white, half brown.

"You mean the perceptions of the holders and those with wealth?" Zeldyan again shifts her weight in the chair and glances toward the corner that holds the chamber pot.

"I cannot support a large standing army. So I must have the support of the large holders. They want the succession of Lornth to be ensured."

"If either a son or a daughter could hold Lornth, there would be more stability."

"Not as they see it." Sillek reaches down and squeezes Zeldyan's shoulder. "Only men can be holders."

"Or warriors. Or lords." Zeldyan glances up. "Even your mother feels that way, and she understands more than most men. Yet she pushes and pushes for you to attack those women on the Roof of the World. Even enlisting foreign traders."

"Lygon . . . he can't do that much, and we can make that work to our advantage."

"For now," she agrees. "But how can you put off all these questions of honor that your mother raises or the idea that you are weak if you do not attack the Roof of the World?" Her lips tighten, and she forces them to relax.

"I can put that off for a time," he muses. "But not forever."

"I know. If you fail to strengthen Lornth"—she looks to the closed door—"Ildyrom will likely succeed in taking it. If you are successful, then all the holders will demand you reclaim the Roof of the World."

Sillek nods slowly.

"What real good is that land? Only angels or demons could live there. Was it worth your father's death? If a few damned women want to live there . . ." Zeldyan shakes her head.

"Some women have already deserted their households. One was caught; the others were not."

"Oh . . . so the idea of a refuge where women are not beaten, where they can bear arms—that frightens the strong men of Lornth?" Zeldyan shifts her weight in the chair again. "I'm sorry, Sillek. It's not you. You've been fair and open. And, in his own way, so is my sire."

"I'm still Lord of Lornth, and the men have the power, and they look to me to put things right—as they see it."

"As they see it . . . what they see will be the death of us all."

"I am trying to work around that."

"I know. I know."

"I'll be back." Sillek bends and kisses her cheek again. "At midday?"

"At midday." Her eyes drift toward the chamber pot.

LXV

"IT HURTS . . . NO one said it would hurt like this . . . damn you, Ryba! Damn you!"

Siret's words, muffled by the steps and the ceiling and floor separating the great room from the marine quarters above, were still clear.

Nylan looked at Ryba.

"Childbirth hurts," the marshal said, "as I'm going to find out firsthand before too long." She winced slightly as Siret yelled again.

The space across from Nylan was vacant. Both Ayrlyn and Jaseen were up with Siret. At the base of the table, Gerlich glanced quizzically at Nylan, then whispered something to Narliat. The former armsman raised his eyebrows and looked at Nylan.

Nylan could almost sense the pain rolling down from the upper level. Finally, he stood. "Maybe I can help Ayrlyn."

"You're not a healer or a medtech," pointed out Ryba.

"No . . . but healing takes a sort of . . . field strength . . . and I can help there. Besides," he pointed out, tossing the words back over his shoulder, "I'm not good at standing around and doing nothing."

The silence behind him lasted but a moment, and the buzzing of conversations rose, louder than before, even before he started up the stairs.

Siret's face was red as Nylan approached the couch in the dimness of the candlelit third level. Ayrlyn was pale, and

Jaseen glanced at the engineer as if to ask what he was doing there.

"Good," murmured Ayrlyn.

Without asking, Nylan touched the back of Ayrlyn's neck, trying to extend that sense of ordered power. Through Ayrlyn he could sense the wrongness.

"Need to move her," he said quietly, "the child."

"How?" murmured Ayrlyn.

Nylan didn't know. He knew only that it felt wrong. He let go of Ayrlyn and touched Siret's left arm.

For the first time, she saw him. "You came. You came."

"Hush," he said, embarrassed. "We'll see what we can do."

Jaseen frowned and mouthed behind Ayrlyn's back, "The baby's stuck."

Nylan nodded, but his perceptions reached out again, almost, it seemed, independently, trying to catalogue the problems, from the cord that was around the child's neck to the tightness of the birth canal to . . .

First . . . as though he were guiding a laser, he strengthened the flow of blood, oxygen, life force—in the confusion of mixing systems, he did what felt right, hoping that his feelings were correct, since he was no doctor, only an engineer. But there were no doctors.

"She's breathing easier . . ." murmured Jaseen.

Ayrlyn nodded.

". . . hurts, hurts so much," whimpered Siret.

Nylan's legs were shaking, and he went down on his knees beside the former lander couch, his fingers brushing the silver-haired guard's forehead, then her abdomen as he tried to loosen what needed to be loosened, ever so gently, half wondering if he were dreaming or dead, as the room took on an almost surreal air, as he kept shifting the strange black-tinged forces in a pattern he did not quite understand, but could only feel.

Beside him, he could feel another black-tinged presence, sometimes helping, sometimes leading.

"There!" exclaimed Ayrlyn. "There! Push again!"

"I'm pushing," groaned Siret.

Nylan closed his eyes for a moment, trying to get the room to stop swirling around him.

"You have to push again," announced Jaseen. "You've still got the afterbirth."

"Hurts . . ." Siret's voice was low, but stronger.

"You can do it."

"Good."

After a time, the engineer stood and looked at Ayrlyn. "You did it."

"No, you did it. I didn't have the nerve to try until you started."

"We did it, then."

They looked at Siret, and at the girl she held to her breast, the infant with the silver fuzz on her scalp that would be silver hair like her mother's.

Siret smiled, finally, wanly, and then said, "Thank you. I could feel you changing things . . . somehow. She wouldn't have lived, would she?"

"No," said Jaseen. "But she's a strong little girl. So don't you worry. Now, we've got to get you two cleaned up, and I can do that. Those two"—and she jerked her head toward Nylan and Ayrlyn—"they spent every bit of that magic they had on you. You're a lucky woman."

Siret's green eyes closed for a moment, then opened. "I'm so tired."

Nylan extended his perceptions, afraid she might be hemorrhaging or something worse, but, beyond the damages his mind and senses insisted were normal—he could only find exhaustion.

He shook his head.

"Anything wrong?" asked Jaseen.

"No. Except that everyone insists this is normal."

Ayrlyn and Jaseen laughed.

"I need some tea," Nylan said, "and I can't do anything more here." He felt guilty as he stepped away, but Siret and her baby daughter seemed all right. He tried to ignore the blood that seemed to be everywhere as Jaseen started with the antiseptic.

Slowly, he made his way down the stairs, but a faint smile came to his face as he realized that, strange as it had been, everything had turned out the way it should. He crossed the great room, half aware that the tables were mostly empty and that Ryba had left.

"You look like a proud father," said Gerlich cheerfully.

Narliat smiled nervously.

"You know, Gerlich," Nylan said coldly. "The woman was in pain. For the record, not that it should matter, I never slept with her. And you should know that. So shut up before I stuff you into a piece of stone." He turned and sat down at the end of the table.

Gerlich sat silently, as if stunned, but Nylan didn't care. He was tired of Gerlich's games and insinuations.

Ryba had already left, but Kyseen or Kadran, or someone, had left the bread and some tea. The tea was lukewarm, but tasted good. Nylan ate the bread slowly, sipping the tea.

After a time, Ayrlyn sat down across from him. "Thank you. We might have lost them both."

"You were doing fine. I just made it easier." He cupped his hands around the mug, glancing at the window behind her, aware that the snow had melted and/or sublimated off the armaglass.

"Siret was glad you were there."

"I'm just an engineer, stumbling along and doing what I can." He refilled his mug, then hers. "I make a lot of mistakes."

Her hand touched his wrist, just for a moment, and he felt a sense of warmth. "You're a good man, Nylan. It's . . ." She broke off the words, and repeated, "You're a good man. Don't forget it."

Nylan looked toward the window, hoping spring was coming, and dreading it at the same time. He took another sip of tea, vaguely aware that Ayrlyn had slipped away, as his thoughts skittered across Siret and a silver-haired child, across a tower without enough food, across Gerlich's uncharacteristic silence, across Ayrlyn's warmth.

He sipped more tea, tea that had become cold without his noticing it.

LXVI

As HE HEADED back up to the tower's top level, Nylan paused on the steps, looking into the tower's third level with eyes and senses. There, in the darkness, a silver-haired guard held a silver-haired infant daughter to her breast and gently rocked back and forth on the rocking chair that all the guards, and even Nylan, had helped to make.

"Hush, little Kyalynn, hush little angel . . ." Siret's voice was low, but sweet, and apparently disturbed none of the guards sleeping on the couches in the alcoves spaced along the tower walls and separated by the dividers many had not only crafted, but personally decorated and carved.

Some remained awake.

Nylan could see where one of the other silver-haired marines—Istril—now heavy in her midsection—stared through the darkness in his direction.

Did she have the night vision? Had it been conferred by that underjump on all who had gotten the silver hair? How many of the former marines had strange talents, like his or Ryba's, talents they had never mentioned?

That Nylan did not know, for he had never mentioned that ability, though Ryba had guessed—or learned through her strange fragmentary visions. His eyes slipped back to Siret, his ears picking up the gentle words.

"Hush, little angel and don't you sigh / Mother's going to stay here by and by . . ."

Nylan swallowed. He'd always heard the lullaby with "father" in the words, but he had the feeling that fathers weren't playing that big a part in Ryba's concept of what Westwind should be.

How long he listened he wasn't certain, only that little Kyalynn was asleep, as was Dephnay, and so were their mothers. His feet were cold by the time he slipped into the joined couches up on the sixth level.

"Where were you?" whispered Ryba.

"I went down to the jakes."

"That long?"

"I . . . went . . . to the bathhouse . . . it's more . . . private." He felt embarrassed, but the heavy mutton of the night before clearly hadn't agreed with his system. "The mutton . . ."

"I see . . . I think."

"Then I stopped to listen to Siret singing to her daughter for a moment. You don't—I didn't—really think of her as a mother. You see them with those blades, so effective, so . . ." Nylan paused, searching for the words.

"So good at killing?"

"No. I don't know. It just touched me, that's all. I don't even know why. It's not as though I really even know her. I just helped a little."

A shudder passed through Ryba.

"Are you cold?" He reached out to hold her, but found her shoulders, her body warm, despite the chill in the tower. The rounding that was Dyliess made it difficult for him to comfort her, or to stop her silent shaking.

In the end she turned away, without speaking. Even later, after they had fallen asleep, his arm upon her shoulder, Ryba had said nothing, though her silent shakes—had they been silent sobs?—had subsided.

LXVII

SUNLIGHT POURED THROUGH the narrow open window of the tower. So did a flow of cold air, ruffling the hangings and rattling the thin door that closed off the marshal's quarters.

"We're doing all right with the food," Ryba said. "The snow's beginning to melt off the rocks, and it won't be all that long before we can send out Ayrlyn to trade for some things."

"It is warming up," admitted Nylan. "I hope we can count on it continuing." He peered out the narrow opening, squinting against the bright light, and studying the blanket of white—and the few dark rocks on the heights to the west of the tower.

"A storm or two won't make that much difference," pointed out the marshal of Westwind. "We've still got more than anyone expected."

"You managed it very well," Nylan agreed, looking out the open window—the fresh air, cold as it was, was welcome. "Very realistically."

" 'Realistic,' that's a good term." Ryba shifted her bulk on the lander couch. "Most people aren't realistic. Especially men."

Rather than debate *that,* Nylan asked, "What do you mean by 'realistic'?"

Ryba gestured toward the window. "The locals can't really live up here. It's hard enough for us. Realistically, they should just leave us alone. Over time, we'll be able to make the roads free of bandits, facilitate trade, and stabilize things. Not to mention providing an outlet for abused women, some of them, anyway, which will make men—some of them—less abusive. If they attack us, a lot of people get killed, more of them than of us." She sighed. "That's a realistic, or rational, assessment. But what will happen is different. The local powers—all men—will decide that a bunch of women represent a threat to their way of life, which isn't that great a life anyway, except for a handful of the well-off, and they'll force attacks on us. If they win, they wouldn't have any more than if they hadn't attacked, not really, and when they lose, and they will, they're going to lose a whole lot more over time."

"How would women handle it?" Nylan asked almost idly. "Do you want me to close the window? It's getting colder in here."

"You probably should. A lot of the cold air drops onto the lower floors, even with the door closed." Ryba shifted her weight again. "They say you can never get comfortable in the last part of pregnancy. I believe it. Now . . . how would women handle it? I can't speak for all women, but the smart ones would ask what the cost of an action would be and what they'd get. Why fight if you don't have to?"

"Maybe the smart men do, too, but they don't have any choice," suggested Nylan, stepping over to the window and closing it.

"That could be," admitted Ryba. "But you're conceding that the smart men are surrounded by other men with power and no brains."

Nylan shrugged.

"Too many men want to dominate other people, no matter what the cost. Women, I think, look at the cost."

"Women also manipulate more, I suspect," Nylan answered. "Men—most of them—aren't so good with subtleties. So they dislike the manipulative side of women."

"When it suits them. Manipulation isn't all bad. If you can get something done quietly and without violence, why not?"

"Because men have this thing about being deceived and being out of control." Nylan laughed wryly. "They can go out of control when they find out they've been tricked or manipulated."

"Let me get this straight. Men fight and have wars because they can't manipulate, and then they fight and have wars whenever they feel they are manipulated?"

Nylan frowned. "I don't like the way you put that."

"If you have a better way of putting it, go ahead. Personally, I believe women, given the chance, can do a better job, and, here, I'm going to make sure they get a better chance." Ryba eased herself onto the floor. "I'll be glad when I can get back to serious arms practice. For now, it's just exercise."

"I doubt it's ever just exercise," quipped Nylan, following her down to the dimness of the next level and the practice area.

He paused on the steps, noting that among those already practicing with Saryn and a heavy-bellied Istril were Relyn and Fierral. The one-handed man gripped the fir wand in his left hand with enough confidence that Nylan could see he had been practicing for some time.

Ryba picked up a wand. "Istril? Shall we?"

Istril bowed.

Nylan took a deep breath and headed down to the woodworking area and the unfinished cradle. What Ryba had said about men seemed true enough, but that apparent truth bothered him. It bothered him a lot. Were most men really that irrational? Or that blind?

LXVIII

HALFWAY UP TO the top of the ridge, Nylan looked back, adjusting his snow goggles. Gerlich and Narliat remained out on the sunlit flats, Gerlich shouting instructions as Narliat struggled with a shorter pair of skis. The shorter skis would probably work, Nylan reflected, now that the midday warmth had partly melted the snow and left it heavier and crustier.

As he continued up the ridge, leaving Gerlich and his hapless pupil on the flats before the tower, Nylan wondered why

Gerlich had suddenly taken an interest in instructing Narliat on skis.

Was he becoming a counterfeit Ryba, trusting no men? He didn't distrust Relyn, although he didn't understand the man. Relyn seemed different, as though he had changed and were not sure of himself. Gerlich, on the other hand, seemed ever more foreign, contemptuous, stopping just short of provoking Ryba.

As Nylan reached the top of the ridge, he looked back. Narliat was skiing slowly, following a track already set in the snow, and Gerlich continued to encourage the local.

Nylan used the thongs to fasten his boots in place, then skied down the ridge in the gentle sweeping turns he had never thought he could do. He still lurched and flailed, but did not fall.

He stopped at the bottom of the ridge, searching the trees, then finally pushed his skis west, toward the narrower strip of forest, following his senses. Were the gray leaves on the handful of deciduous trees beginning to unshrivel? They'd have to sooner or later, but Nylan hoped it would be sooner.

As he entered the trees, now bare of snow, the engineer swept the scarf away from his mouth. The wool was too warm, and he couldn't breathe as he slid the heavy skis through the space between the trunks, his perceptions out in front of him, trying to sense any possible game.

He saw older hare tracks, expanded by the faint heat of the midday sun, tree-rat tracks, but nothing larger or newer.

Moving slowly, he paused frequently, letting his senses search for signs of life he could not see. His fingers strayed to the bow at his back.

Something stirred—slightly—beneath a snow-covered hump, but Nylan shook his head. That something was a bear not likely to emerge for a time, and there was no way the engineer was going to try to dig out something far more than twice his size.

He slowed as his eyes caught the tracks in the snow— something like deer tracks, but larger. He turned his skis slightly downhill to follow the tracks, his senses ranging ahead.

From his perceptions the animal seemed to be a large deer—or an elk. Nylan had never paid much attention to those sorts of distinctions, but it definitely offered the promise of a lot of meat.

The big deer had migrated up from the lower elevations, or, thought Nylan, fled local hunters seeking game as the snow in the lower hills melted.

Nylan must have skied nearly another kay before he saw the animal, standing in a slight opening under a large fir. The engineer stopped in the cover of a pine. If he moved farther toward the deer, the animal would see him, yet he was still more than fifty cubits away.

Nylan remained in the shadows of the pine, as silent as he could be, downwind of the deer, finally deciding he was as close as he dared. Slowly, quietly, he withdrew an arrow from the quiver, nocked it, and released it. The next shaft was quicker, as was the third.

The buck snorted, and then ran. Nylan slogged after him, not pressing, but moving steadily. If he had missed, he'd never catch up. If he'd wounded the beast, then he ought to be able to wear it down—if it didn't wear him down first.

Within a few cubits of where the buck had stood were scattered bloodstains. He also found a shaft, wedged in a pine trunk—probably the third shaft. After recovering that— carefully—he replaced it in the quiver and put one ski in front of the other, trudging through the ever-heavier snow along a trail of scattered blood droppings.

Sweat began to ooze from his forehead, and he loosened his jacket and untied the scarf and put it inside the jacket. He didn't want to stop to get into the pack.

A welcome shadow fell across the forest as a single, white puffy cloud covered the sun.

Nylan's legs began to ache, and the buck turned uphill at a slant. Nylan's legs ached more. He glanced ahead, and did not see the hump in the snow—a covered root or low branch.

His left ski caught, and he twisted forward. A line of pain

scored his leg, and he grunted, trying not to yell. For a moment he lay there, letting his perceptions check the leg. The bones seemed sound, but another wave of pain shot down the leg as he rolled into a ball to get up.

Slowly, he stood, casting his senses ahead.

The buck was not that far away, perhaps two hundred cubits, just out of sight, and Nylan slowly slid the left ski forward, then the right.

When he reached the next low crest in the hill, he could see the big deer, almost flailing his way through the snow.

Nylan pushed on, trying to ignore the pain in his leg.

With the sound of the skis on the crusting snow, the deer lunged forward, then sagged into a heap.

Nylan finally stood over the buck, but the animal was not dead. Blood ran from the side of its mouth, and one of the shafts through the shoulder had been snapped off. More blood welled out around the other shaft, the one through the chest. The deer tried to lift his head; then the neck dropped, but he still panted, and the blood still oozed out around the shaft in his chest.

Nylan looked at the deer. Now what? He didn't have anything for a humane quick kill. Finally, he fumbled out the belt knife.

Even using his perceptions, trying to make the kill quick, it took him three tries to cut what he thought was the carotid artery. Three tries, and blood all over his trousers, the snow, and his gloves. Even so, the deer took forever to die, or so it seemed to Nylan, as he stood there in the midday glare and the red-stained snow. The sense of the animal's pain was great enough that, had he eaten recently, he wouldn't have been able to keep that food in his guts. Even though they needed the meat, his eyes burned.

Nylan worked out the one good arrow shaft, cleaned it on the snow, and put it in his quiver. Then he dug out the rope and the sheet of heavy plastic. Awkward as it was working on skis, he left them on, afraid that he'd never get them back on if he took them off.

The poor damned deer was heavy, and the plastic sheeting was smaller than the carcass, which had a tendency to skid sideways as Nylan pulled it. The snow had gotten even damper under the bright sun, and most of the way back was uphill. Nylan's left leg stabbed with each movement of the skis.

The rope cut into his shoulders, despite the heavy jacket, and sweat ran into his eyes. It felt like he had to stop and rest every hundred cubits, sometimes more often.

Mid-afternoon came, and went, before he cleared the forest and reached the bottom of the ridge. There, Nylan dragged everything onto the packed snow surface of the trail, took off his skis, and tied them to the sheeting.

With another series of slow efforts, he started uphill.

Halfway up, two figures skied down and joined him.

"Ser?"

Nylan looked up blankly, then shook his head as he recognized Cessya and Huldran.

"Frigging big animal, ser," observed Huldran with a grin.

"Heavy animal." Nylan nodded tiredly. "I could use some help." That was an understatement.

"We can manage that." Huldran studied the red deer. "Lot of meat here."

"I hope so. I hope so."

As the two marines unfastened their skis, Nylan just sat in the snow beside the trail.

"You all right, ser?"

"I'm a lot better since you arrived." Nylan staggered up as they started to pull his kill uphill once more. The muscles in his left leg still knotted with every step, but the pain was less without the strain of pulling the makeshift sled and deer.

Saryn was waiting, tripod ready, by the time the three reached the causeway.

Nylan set his skis against the tower wall and sat on the causeway wall, too tired to move for a time. The sun had just dropped behind the western peaks, and a chill freeze rose.

"Ser," ventured Huldran, "would you mind if I took your skis and poles down?"

"I definitely wouldn't mind. I'd appreciate that very much."

"Don't stay out too long, ser," added Cessya, picking up his poles.

"I won't." The coldness of the wind felt good against Nylan's face, and he just sat there, staring into space.

Saryn looked up from the deer carcass, then at Nylan. "Good animal, but you sure made a mess."

"I'm a poor killer and a worse butcher," Nylan said, his voice rasping. "I wasn't planning on getting anything this big. I hope I didn't spoil anything by taking so long."

"It's cold enough that it isn't a problem." Saryn grinned. "Gerlich came back earlier. He said there wasn't anything within kays."

"There isn't. I went down that section you call the forest wedge."

"And you carted this back that far? That's a long climb."

"Huldran and Cessya helped me back up the ridge."

Kyseen hurried out the tower door, looked at the deer, then at Nylan.

"Mother of darkness! What am I going to do with that?"

"Cook it," snapped Saryn. "The engineer didn't cart it back to waste."

"Tonight . . . the meal's done."

"I'm sure you can find something to do with this tomorrow, Kyseen," Nylan said. "And they'll eat anything you cook."

"They're already complaining about the chicken soup, and it's not even on the tables. Why didn't I wait for the big deer the engineer brought—that's what Cessya asked."

"Tell her it's worth waiting until tomorrow." Nylan grinned, and slid off the wall, trying not to wince as his leg hit the stones of the causeway. "You mind if I leave you, Saryn?"

"No. You did the hard work. This is simple drudgery." Saryn's skinning knife flashed again.

Nylan limped into the tower, and looked down at his damp and bloody clothes. Should he go straight to the laundry, or up to find something, like his sole remaining shipsuit, that was dry?

"You look even worse than manure." Ayrlyn walked toward him from the stairs leading up from the lower level. "You're limping. Is any of that blood yours?"

"I fell chasing the deer. I don't think any of it's mine."

"Let me see." Her fingers lifted the trouser bottoms and touched his upper calves. "It feels like you ripped the muscles. You shouldn't be skiing or hunting for a while."

Nylan could feel a faint touch of warmth radiating from her fingers, and a lessening of the cramping. The pain subsided, slightly, from an acute stabbing into a duller, but heavy aching.

Ayrlyn straightened. "I hope it was a big deer."

"It's a huge deer," interjected Huldran as she passed, adding, "I'll get the stove in the bathhouse warmed up. You look like you need it, and there's a little wood we can spare."

"I'm all right," Nylan protested, feeling as though he were being humored.

"Enjoy it," Ayrlyn laughed. "People are glad to see another solid meal. And you do look like you need some cleaning up. I'm going to help Saryn. From what everyone's said, she needs it, or she'll be out there all night."

Nylan flushed. "It's not that big."

The healer grinned before she turned.

Nylan looked at the stairs up to the top level. The bathhouse wouldn't have warmed that much yet. He suppressed a groan before he started up the stone steps.

LXIX

IN THE WARM lower level of the tower, Nylan worked only in a light tattered shirt and trousers, occasionally even wiping sweat from his forehead, as he smoothed and evened the cradle's sideboards. At times, he had to stop and massage, gently, the aching left calf that still had a tendency to cramp if he stood on it too long without moving.

A few cubits away, Istril used a single smoothing blade to plane the sideboards of the cradle that could, except for the carvings and designs, have been a mate to the cradle before Nylan.

The engineer glanced at Istril's headboard—which bore a crossed hammer and blade surrounded by a wreath of pine boughs. He nodded at the detail of the pine branches.

"You like it, ser?" She leaned back against the cool wall stones and wiped her forehead.

"You did a much better job on the carving than I did," he admitted. "The pine wreath is good."

"Thank you. I worked hard on it." She grinned, although the grin was wiped away as she stopped and massaged her abdomen. "They say the last part is the hardest."

"Of woodworking?"

"Of bearing a child. I suppose that goes for anything."

Nylan nodded, lowering himself onto his knees to take the weight off his leg, but the stone was hard, and he'd have to switch position before long.

"Jaseen said you and the healer saved Siret and Kyalynn."

"We did what we could. It happened to be enough."

"If . . . I need you . . . would you?"

Nylan nodded. "If you need us, we'll be there."

"Thank you."

He paused. "Istril, could you feel what we did?"

The silver-haired marine blushed slightly. "A little, ser."

"Good. You might try to explore that talent. It could come in useful."

Istril paled. "Ah . . . excuse me, ser." She turned.

"Are you all right?"

"I'm fine. Fine as I can be with someone punching my bladder." The formerly slim guard half walked, half waddled up the tower stairs, even though, except for the distended abdomen, she carried no extra weight.

Nylan couldn't imagine carrying and bearing a child.

Having to experience the pain and discomfort secondhand was bad enough. Maybe Ryba was right. Maybe things would be better if women ran them. Then, again, maybe they'd just get used to abusing power, too. The soreness in his knees from kneeling on the hard rock got to him, and the engineer switched to a sitting position beside the cradle.

He picked up the fine-grained file and studied it, glancing at the assembled cradle in front of him. After looking at the wood, he set the file aside and picked his knife back up.

With long strokes that were as gentle as he could make them, he worked on rounding the left sideboard just a touch more, trying to make the sides match as closely as he could. The relief around the rocky hillside on the headboard needed to be deeper, too, although he sometimes felt as though attempts at art were almost a waste in a community struggling to survive.

He looked up at the sound of boots.

Relyn stood there, studying the cradle. After a moment, the red-haired man asked, "Were you ever a crafter, Ser Mage?"

"No, I can't say that I was." Nylan blotted his forehead with the back of his hand, then shifted his weight on the hard stone floor.

"Then the forces of order have gifted you." Relyn squatted next to the cradle, his fingers not quite touching the carving of the single tree rising out of the rocky hillside.

"It's not as good as Istril's," Nylan said, nodding toward the momentarily abandoned work.

"She is also one of the gifted silver-heads." Relyn eased into a sitting position with his back against the wall.

"Are there many in Lornth with silver hair?"

"None, except the very old, and their hair is a white silver, not the silvered silver of the angels." Relyn tapped the blunt hook that had replaced his right hand against the cut stone of the wall in a series of nervous movements, almost a replacement gesture for tapping fingers or snapping them.

"You look upset," the engineer observed, lowering his voice, although only Rienadre and Denalle remained on the woodworking side of the lower level, and they were laboring together on a chair of some sort across the room, in the area closest to the kitchen space.

Relyn glanced at the other two guards. "It grows warmer. What am I to do? I am not welcome in Lornth. I would have to fight to prove I was no coward."

"I saw you practicing the other day. The blade looks comfortable in your hand."

"I hope to learn enough to defend myself with the bad hand."

Nylan frowned. "Maybe . . . maybe, we could figure out a clamp or something so that you could fix a knife to the hook. Don't some fight with a blade and a knife?"

"That . . . I have not heard of."

"It's been done," Nylan affirmed.

"Since you say it, Mage, that must be so."

"Wouldn't that help? Enemies wouldn't think you were defenseless on your right."

"Again, you prove you are dangerous." Relyn frowned. "Could you make such a device?"

"I'll see what I can do. Let me see your knife, though."

Relyn eased the knife out and passed it hilt-first to the engineer.

Nylan looked at it for a time before speaking. "I think I can, maybe bend some rod locks so they'll hold the hilt." He handed back the knife. "I take it you'd rather not stay in Westwind."

"I am no mage. Nor am I a mighty and powerful warrior like the hunter. Nor did I handle a blade, even with two hands, as well as the best of these guards. Even those bearing a child work and improve their skills—and with those devil blades you forged?" Relyn shook his head. "Also, I do not trust the marshal. She smiles, but she smiled when she took off my hand."

"Why are you telling me?"

"I must talk to someone, and I distrust you the least, because you would build rather than destroy."

"Thanks," answered Nylan dryly. "I suppose I deserve that."

Relyn shrugged apologetically.

"Do you think the marshal will have you killed in your sleep or something?" Nylan asked, wishing he had not even as he spoke.

"It is possible. It is possible that lightning might strike me as well. I do not fear either . . . now."

"Ah . . . but you think your welcome might wear thin?"

"There is not that much food, is there?"

"I did bring in that deer, and that means more game might be moving higher into the mountains."

"That will be true for a time, but only for a time."

"Where could you go?"

"South, north, east—anywhere but west." Relyn grinned briefly. "I do not have to decide that until the snows melt, perhaps later." He paused. "If I should need to depart sooner?"

"I'll let you know if I know." Nylan laughed softly. "Sometimes, I'm among the last to discover things."

"It is often that way when one deals with women."

"Even in Lornth?"

"Even in Lornth, even as a holder's son," Relyn affirmed, as he stood, using the hook to catch the edge of a stone wall block and to help balance him. "Thank you, Ser Mage." He offered Nylan a head bow before turning and heading for the steps.

Nylan looked down at the cradle. A daughter coming? That was hard to believe as well.

LXX

NYLAN TOOK ONE end of the saw and looked across the half-cubit-thick fir trunk to Huldran. "Ready?" Another trunk lay beside the path, ready for their efforts when they finished cutting and splitting the first.

"Ready as you are, ser." The broad-shouldered marine grinned.

"I hope," Nylan grunted as he pulled the blade handle toward him, "you're a lot more ready than that."

"Do we really need this wood now?" asked Huldran.

"We could get more storms. Even if we don't, do you think it will go to waste? After this winter? Besides, we can't plant now. We're just about out of wood planking for new fixtures, and there's only so much equipment for people to hunt. Also, we'll need wood for the kitchen stove and," Nylan laughed, "to defrost the bathhouse."

"You used it more than I did," pointed out Huldran.

"We probably used it more than about half the guards did together."

"If we get more guards, they'll have to use it. You know what standing next to Denalle is like?"

"Do I want to find out?"

Huldran shook her head over the motion of the saw.

"I was afraid you'd say that."

As they sawed, Gerlich opened the tower door, and he and Narliat walked out across the causeway and leaned their skis against the low wall near the end of the causeway. Gerlich carried his great bow, the second one, since the first had broken, and both bore packs.

"Off hunting?" asked Nylan, without stopping his efforts with the saw.

"We'll see what we can find," Gerlich answered. "Now that it's warmer, and Narliat's learned to ski better, he can help me pack back whatever we get." The hunter grinned. "There might even be another one of those big red deer." The grin faded. "Sometimes, Engineer, sometimes . . ."

"I'm just an engineer," Nylan admitted.

"He is also a mage," added Narliat.

"I know that," said Gerlich. "He's the one who doesn't." The tall man hoisted his skis. "We need to be off."

The two carried their skis up the trail toward the top of the ridge.

"That's a case of white demon leading the white demon," puffed out Huldran.

"He brings back food."

"Sometimes . . . and he's not shy about letting the whole tower know."

When Nylan and Huldran finished the first cut, a piece of trunk a little over a cubit in length lay on the stones of the causeway.

"Do we split or keep sawing?" asked Huldran.

"Saw another," suggested Nylan.

"This is a lot of sawing for a trunk that's not all that thick."

"It's as thick as a single horse can drag. Anything bigger, we'd have to saw where it was felled, and I don't want to struggle with a saw in chest-deep snow." Nylan paused, and Huldran staggered.

"Tell me when you're going to stop," she said.

"Sorry." Nylan tried to catch his breath, grateful that the air was no longer cold enough to bite into his lungs.

"Ready?" asked Huldran after several moments. "Let's forget about splitting until we get this thing cut."

They resumed sawing, even as Fierral marched out with nearly a squad of guards. All of them went up to the stable, and brought back three mounts, on which were strapped the other crosscut saw, and two of the four axes.

"More wood?" asked Nylan, pausing with the saw, then adding, too late, to Huldran, "I'm stopping."

Huldran stumbled back several steps, and barely kept from toppling into the deeper snow only by grabbing onto Rienadre.

"I'm sorry, Huldran."

"Ser . . . please?"

Fierral shook her head. "There's not much else we can do right now. So we'll cut and trim as much as we can. We'll leave the smaller limbs in cut lengths for later in the year when we can bring them back with the cart, and we'll drag back the trunks. Saryn thinks we should set aside more and more to start seasoning so that we'll have a supply for making planks."

"She's probably right."

After Fierral and the squad trudged up the trail to the ridge, both Nylan and Huldran took a break, for some water and other necessities, before they resumed. As they sawed, Ayrlyn and Saryn came and trudged up to the stables to feed livestock, along with Istril, who was worried about the mounts.

When the three returned, Nylan and Huldran had only finished five more sections.

"You two are slow," jibed Saryn.

Nylan took his hands off the saw—and Huldran staggered again, almost toppling into the snow—and gestured. "You want to take this end?"

"Ah . . . no, thank you, Nylan. I'm working on finishing those dividers for the fourth level."

"I thought we were out of wood for that sort of thing," said Huldran, leaning on the now-immobile saw.

"They were rough-cut eight-days ago. The finish work is what takes the time," answered Saryn.

"What about you, Ayrlyn?" asked Nylan. "Room dividers?"

"Healing. I'm worried about this rash little Dephnay's got. It keeps coming back. And Ellysia's having trouble nursing, and there aren't any milk substitutes here."

"We need a few goats or cows, you think?" asked the engineer.

"We need everything." Ayrlyn shook her head as she left with the others.

"Ser, if you stop to talk to everyone, this trunk's still going to be here by the time we plant crops." Huldran cleared her throat. "And I did ask if you'd let me know when you stop sawing. Twice."

"Sorry." Nylan looked down at the slush underfoot and used his boot to sweep it away from where he stood. "All right?"

Before the next interruption, they managed almost a dozen more cuts, leaving them with most of the first trunk cut into lengths to be split. Despite the gloves, Nylan could feel blisters forming on his hands, and the soreness growing in his arms and shoulders.

They were halfway through yet another cut, one that would leave only a few more cuts to finish the second trunk, when the horses reappeared on the ridge, dragging more fir trunks—two each—down the not-quite-slushy packed snow of the trail toward the tower.

Fierral and her squad were laughing by the time they reached the causeway and stacked the six trunks up.

"You two are so slow."

"Do you want to do this?" asked Huldran, without slowing her sawing.

With grins, Denalle and Rienadre shook their heads.

"We'll just bring in the trunks, thank you," added Fierral. "Has Kadran rung the triangle yet?"

"No." But as Nylan spoke, Kadran came out and rang the triangle for the midday meal.

"Good timing," added Selitra.

Huldran let go of the saw, and Nylan stumbled forward and rammed the saw handle into his gut, so hard that he exhaled with a grunt.

"So sorry, ser." She grinned.

"All right," Nylan mumbled. "Next time I'll remember."

"What was all that about?" asked Kadran.

"Nothing," answered Nylan. "What are you serving?"

"Venison, your leftover venison, spiced with pine tips, a few not quite moldy potatoes, and a handful of softened pine nuts. The bread is more bitter than ever, but the healer says it's edible."

"It's better than starving."

"Not much," commented Berlis, as she followed Denalle and Rienadre into the tower.

Fierral, Selitra, and Weindre did not go inside, but led the horses back up to the stables.

"More wood will help," said the cook. "When will you have some split?"

"Mid-afternoon," Nylan guessed.

"I'll send Hryessa and Murkassa out for it. They can take

that kind of cold." Kadran paused. "It's not really that cold anymore, but they think it is. Flatlanders!" She snorted.

"You can tell she's from the Purgatory Mountains," said Huldran as Kadran left. "Let's finish the last cut before we eat. Fierral and the others will take that long to get the horses settled anyway. Then we can try splitting what we've sawed when we get back."

Nylan took up his end of the saw once more.

After the midday meal, Nylan picked up one of the axes and looked at the sections of trunk. "I don't know."

He lifted the axe and brought it down. The axe head buried itself in the wood, which creaked, but did not split. He lifted the axe, and the wood came with it. So he brought wood and axe down on the frozen ground together. It took him two more attempts before the circular chunk of wood split into two unequal sections.

"I think sawing is easier." Nylan panted as he half leaned on the axe handle.

"Let me try."

"Be my guest." Nylan handed the axe to Huldran.

Her first attempt also stuck in the larger log section, but the second effort split that section in two. "Only took me two." The blond guard smiled at Nylan. "Splitting's easier."

"You were working on a smaller section. Try one of the big ones."

Huldran shrugged and lifted the axe again. It took her two attempts to split the log chunk. "It's tough. Maybe we don't have the technique."

"Green wood is harder, I think."

They alternated efforts, slowly improving, until they had reduced the sawed sections into chunks of stove and furnace wood. The guards who passed the wood-splitting avoided commenting after a quick look at Nylan's face.

About mid-afternoon, as promised by Kadran, Hryessa and Murkassa peered out from the tower door, some time after Nylan and Huldran had returned to sawing another green fir trunk.

"We've got plenty there for you," said the engineer.

Hryessa stepped out quickly, then stopped by the pile of split wood, looking at the open jackets and the two sweating figures. Her breath formed a faint white cloud as she spoke. "It's still cold here. It is not as bad as before, but . . ." She shrugged. "Yet you are hot."

"It's so cold up here that you'd think the lowlanders would leave us alone, wouldn't you?" asked Huldran, not stopping her sawing.

Nylan just kept moving his end of the saw.

Murkassa, stooping to fill her arms with split wood, shook her head sadly. "They are men."

"It is sad, in a way," added Hryessa, as she struggled back into the tower, leaving Huldran and Nylan to their sawing.

"I'm not sure it's sad being a man," Nylan puffed as he kept the blade moving.

"It is if you're as hidebound as the locals are."

"The women have it much worse."

"For now," pointed out Huldran.

"Point taken," Nylan said. "Let's take a break." As he slowed the saw, he glanced to the west where the sun hung just above the Westhorns.

The tower door opened, and Murkassa and Hryessa trooped out again, this time accompanied by Jaseen and Kadran.

"They said you had a lot of wood here," explained Jaseen, glancing over the pile. "You two make a good team."

"True," said Huldran. "I don't like taking breaks, and he won't quit until the job's done."

"I need something to drink," Nylan told Huldran. She nodded, and he walked into the tower and then out through the north door and through the archway, where most of the ice had slowly melted, leaving the split stone floor perpetually damp. He made his way to the laundry area where both tubs, full of clothes and chill water, stood with no one nearby. Nylan held out a hand toward the stove. It was warm.

He shrugged. With little soap, soaking helped. He wondered if some of the recently cut and split wood had found its way into the bathhouse warming stove. Why not, now?

The water was beginning to flow more regularly, and Nylan drank from the laundry tap, trying not to spill too much on the floor, then used the jakes. As he walked back, he passed Siret, carrying Kyalynn, as he started through the north tower door.

"You have the laundry detail?" he asked.

"Yes, ser. It's better that way now that I'm so far along. I still do my blade practice and exercises, though."

Nylan shook his head. "Don't worry about it. Letting the water warm to room temperature probably helps get things cleaner, too."

"I hadn't planned it that way . . ."

"Don't tell anyone." With a grin, Nylan held the door, then closed it after them.

"You took long enough," said Huldran.

"Some things take a little time." He took up his end of the saw, looking at the third or so of the trunk that remained to be cut.

Before they finished cutting two more lengths, the kitchen crew had carted off all the split wood, and Nylan had asked Jaseen to carry one armful out to the bathhouse stove.

"You might get cleaner clothes that way . . . also warmer wash water," he told the medtech. *Except she's more like a healer now. No medtechs on the Roof of the World,* he thought.

"Sounds like a good idea." Jaseen winked at him.

Nylan ignored the wink, wondering why she had offered the gesture, and kept sawing. After they finished sawing their fifth trunk, with the sun starting to drop behind the western peaks, they began splitting.

Whheeeee . . . eeeee . . .

At the sound of horses, Nylan glanced uphill. Fierral led the three horses over the ridge, each dragging two mid-sized trunks.

Huldran and Nylan looked at each other, then at the three trunks piled by the trail road.

"We're never going to get caught up."

"Just think of it this way. We're working on next winter.

So we can burn wood all winter long and be warm," said Nylan. "And have warm showers and water that's only cold, not liquid ice."

"It does sound better when you put it that way." Huldran picked up the axe again and split a half-trunk section into quarters, then the larger quarter in half, before handing the axe back to Nylan.

"You're going to be stiff, Engineer," laughed Fierral as the logging crew stacked six more long trunks beside the trail path.

"Since you're done for the day," grunted Nylan, splitting another section, "let Huldran have the other axe so we can finish this. Then, your people can take down the split wood when they go in."

Fierral unstrapped the axe, and Huldran took it.

Denalle, winding up one of the hauling ropes, groaned.

"You want to do what the engineer's doing?" asked Fierral.

"Been doing it all day . . ." mumbled Rienadre.

"You got breaks. There were six of us." Fierral raised her voice. "Denalle, Rienadre, and Berlis—you don't have to climb to the stable, but you get to cart in wood. Selitra, Weindre, and I will stable and rub down the horses."

Several groans echoed around the causeway.

"You want to be warm—you cart wood."

Fierral, Selitra, and Weindre started up the shadowed snow trail to the stables with the horses. The other three guards carried sets of skis into the tower, then straggled back across the causeway to stack wood in their arms.

Huldran held her axe for a moment and looked at Nylan. They both grinned. Then, Nylan set down his axe and massaged his right shoulder with his gloved left hand.

"I'm already sore, and there's two days' work stacked behind us."

"We want to be warm next winter. Someone told me that," returned the stocky blond guard.

Nylan looked at the four cut, but unsplit, trunk sections. "There aren't too many left here."

"Here comes Gerlich," said Huldran, "but I don't see Narliat."

"Maybe he's following the great hunter."

"Maybe . . . except he always likes to get to the food first." Huldran brought the axe down again.

Nylan followed her example, and by the time Gerlich dragged his bundle up to the causeway, they were cleaning the axes. Rienadre was stacking another armful of wood, but the other guards had not returned for their third load.

"Where's Narliat?" asked Huldran.

"Gone," answered Gerlich. "I was trying to pack this boar-thing up the slope, and when I stopped, he was gone." The hunter gestured to the dead boar. "This is heavy. Maybe not quite as heavy as a red deer, but there's a lot of meat there."

Again, Nylan could sense the wrongness about Gerlich's words, and he instinctively looked for Ayrlyn, but the healer was nowhere around, not that she had any reason to be out in the twilight and cold.

"It does look like a lot," Nylan temporized.

"Sneaky little bastard, anyway," said Rienadre as she staggered away under a load of wood.

"He was born here, not on Heaven," said Gerlich, setting his skis against the wall by the door. "I'm going to get Saryn, to see if she can help me butcher this."

As he went inside, Kadran came out to ring the triangle. She looked toward the carcass. "The hunter's back. What's that?"

"Gerlich brought back a boar," answered Huldran. "Of course, he lost Narliat along the way."

"Why does this happen to us?" asked the cook. "We've got a thin soup and barely enough bread, and he brings in a juicy boar, and everyone's going to complain and ask why we've got soup." She rang the triangle.

"We're coming!" called Fierral.

Saryn and Ayrlyn followed Gerlich across the causeway, Saryn bearing the tripod and the hooks. Gerlich hoisted the carcass into place after Saryn set the tripod into the packed snow of the trail beyond the end of the causeway stones.

"We'll gut this and rough-cut it now," said Saryn, "and stack the sections in the archway by the north door. That's plenty cold. Then Kyseen and Kadran can figure out what to cook and when later tonight or in the morning."

"Fine," said Gerlich. "Fine."

"Another good meal," offered Weindre as she, Selitra, and Fierral passed the tripod.

"Not tonight," said Ayrlyn. "Tomorrow."

Selitra nodded to Gerlich, but the hunter did not return the gesture.

"Let's take some wood." Fierral looked at the remaining split sections.

"Trust Denalle to leave some," muttered Weindre, bending to scoop lengths into her arms.

"There's not that much left," said Fierral.

"I'll take a load, too," said Nylan. "That should do it."

"I'll rack the axes," offered Huldran.

"Thanks." Nylan followed the guards down to the lower level and into the far kitchen corner, and the makeshift wood bins there.

"See!" snapped Kyseen, stirring a kettle. "Even the engineer carts wood."

Nylan nodded after dumping his armload and trudged to the bathhouse to wash up. The wash tubs were empty, and tilted to dry. He supposed the clothes were hanging on lines around the tower, on one side of the fifth level, usually.

Fierral stood in one shower stall, using the tap to rinse her face and hands. In another was Selitra, stripped to the waist. Nylan passed and quickly looked away.

He used the tap valve in the laundry area to wash his hands and face, blotting the chill water from his face with his hands, and shaking the water off his hands in turn.

"Still better than trying to find the stream." Fierral laughed as she joined him in walking back to the great room.

"That's true. I hope we can get enough wood to keep the place warmer next winter."

"That would be nice."

Nylan slipped into his spot on the bench before Ryba or

Gerlich had arrived. For a moment, he just sat, his head in his hands, realizing just how tired he was, and how sore he was going to be—and there were days more of wood sawing and splitting to come! Maybe it would improve his muscular condition, but would he survive it?

Ayrlyn sat down across from him. Neither spoke for a time, until Nylan finally lifted his head.

"Hard day?" Ayrlyn asked.

"Yes. I wasn't built to be a lumberjack."

"Thin soup, again," said Ayrlyn. "They won't like it."

Kadran's and Ayrlyn's prediction seemed fulfilled. As the seats filled, Nylan listened.

". . . thin soup, and there's a big pig carcass in the back archway . . ."

". . . always hold out a good meal for tomorrow when we get crap today . . ."

"Why do the hunters always bring the good stuff in late?"

Holding Dephnay in a half pack, Ellysia sat at the second table, beside Siret and Kyalynn. Siret cradled Kyalynn in her arms. Dephnay kept squirming until Ellysia put the child up to her shoulder and patted her back.

Istril sat down heavily across from Siret and beside Hryessa, and then Ryba walked past the two mothers and eased herself into her chair. "I see Gerlich isn't here."

"Not yet."

"He's washing," added Ayrlyn.

Ryba waited until Gerlich sat down. "I understand that Narliat left," she said evenly.

Gerlich turned to face the marshal. "I was pulling the carcass up the hill. When I looked back he was gone."

"Just like that?"

"That boar was heavy, and I didn't have enough rope for both of us."

"Did Narliat say anything before he left?" Ryba nodded to Ayrlyn.

"No. He talked about how he'd never be an armsman again, but he's said that a number of times." Gerlich took a short swallow of tea from his mug.

Again, Nylan could sense the whiteness, the partial wrongness surrounding the hunter's answers.

Kyseen set one of the heavy caldrons on the table, then used the ladle to fill Ryba's bowl/trencher. Kadran followed with the baskets of bread.

"Did he say anything else?" Ryba asked.

"Nothing special."

"Where do you think he went?"

"I don't know. He was headed west, I think, but he could have doubled back or turned north or south."

"He won't go south, not far," said Ayrlyn. "Straight south is just more mountains. Southwest leads to the local equivalent of the hottest demons' hell. It's a place called the Grass Hills, except there's not much grass, they say."

"West or north, then," observed Ryba with a nod. "And that means the locals will know more about us. Well . . . they would sooner or later." She paused, then added, "I'm glad you were able to bring back that boar."

"My pleasure, Ryba. My pleasure."

Nylan and Ayrlyn exchanged glances, and Ryba shook her head.

Gerlich frowned.

"We'll have solid meals tomorrow," Ryba added. "Might I have some bread?"

Nylan passed her the basket. The soup was more tasty than many previous efforts, and hot, for which he was grateful. The bread was bitter, but the bitterness didn't bother him. His shoulders were tight and ached, and while the tea helped, it didn't help enough.

Later, after a meal of small talk and speculation about how soon the snow would really melt, Nylan dragged himself up to the top level, following Ryba.

He sat on the end of the couch. "Gerlich isn't telling everything."

"He's lying," Ryba said tiredly, shifting her weight on the couch. "I didn't need you and Ayrlyn to tell me that. He's lied from the beginning."

"Are you going to let him keep doing this? You killed Mran."

"Gerlich hasn't openly defied me, or you, or anyone. We know he's lying, but knowing and proving it aren't the same thing." Ryba eased her legs into another position. "I hate this. Now my legs get swollen all the time. I'm already regarded as a tyrant by some, and I can't throw him out or kill him until he gives some obvious reason. He won't, though, because he can't stand the hot weather below, and that makes it even worse. He wants to be marshal, and he's plotting to replace me."

"How? No one likes him, except maybe Selitra."

"Who said anything about liking him? He's using Narliat, I'm sure, although I can't see it clearly, to try to find some local backing."

"Local backing?"

Ryba laughed harshly. "Gerlich is a man. He can make the argument that the locals can't take Westwind, but they can ensure that one of their kind—a good old boy—runs it. He'll try to join the local gentry, or whatever passes for it . . . and, if we're not careful, he could."

"What about your . . . visions?"

"They show Westwind surviving. But it could survive under Gerlich's descendants as well." Ryba took a deep breath and shifted position again. "I hate this."

Nylan frowned. Like Gerlich, Ryba wasn't telling the whole story. Then again, were any of them telling the whole story? He licked his lips.

"We need some rest." Ryba leaned over and blew out the small candle, then stripped off her leathers and eased into her tentlike nightgown.

Nylan undressed in the dark.

LXXI

NYLAN SET THE cradle—pale wood glistening in the indirect light that filtered through the single armaglass window of the tower's top level—where Ryba would see it.

Then he drew into the dimness behind the stones of the chimney and central pedestal and waited, sensing her climbing the steps. In time, the sound of her steps, slower slightly with each passing day and heavy with the weight of the child she carried, announced her arrival.

Nylan watched as she bent down, as her fingers touched the wood, stroked the curved edges of the side panels, as her eyes focused on the single tree rising out of the rocky landscape in the center of the headboard.

"Do you like it?" He stepped out from the corner. While the cradle was no surprise to her, he had tried to keep the details from her as he had finished the carving and smoothing—all the laborious finish work.

Ryba straightened, her face solemn. "Yes. I like it. So will she, when she is older, and so will her children."

"Another vision?" he asked, trying to keep his voice light.

"You make everything well, Nylan, from towers to cradles." Ryba sank onto the end of the bed.

"I didn't do so well with the bathhouse."

"Even that will be fine. We just didn't have enough wood this winter to keep it as warm as we needed."

"The water lines needed to be covered more deeply." His eyes went to the cradle again.

So did Ryba's. "It is beautiful. What do you want me to say?"

"I don't know." Nylan didn't know, only that, again, something was missing. "I don't know."

III.

THE SPRING
OF WESTWIND

LXXII

IN THE COLD starlight, the short man struggles through the knee-deep snow, snow that is heavy and damp, that clings to everything but his leathers. The snow glistens with a whiteness that provides enough light for him to continue. His boots crunch through the icy crust covering the road that will not be used by others for at least another handful of eight-days.

The soft sound of wings mixes with the light breeze that sifts through the limbs of the pines and firs, and a dark shadow crosses the sky, then dives into a distant clearing.

The traveler shivers, but his feet keep moving, mechanically, as if he is afraid to stop.

Occasionally, he glances back over his shoulder, as though he flees from someone, but his tracks remain the only ones on the slow-melting snow. On his back he carries a pack, nearly empty.

As he lifts one foot and then the other, his mittened fingers touch the outline of the cylindrical object in the pouch that swings around his neck under jacket, tunic, and shirt. He tries not to shiver as he thinks of the object, instead continuing to concentrate on reaching the warmer lands beyond the Westhorns, the lower lands where the heights do not freeze a man into solid ice.

He puts one foot in front of the other.

LXXIII

NYLAN GLANCED FROM the bed to the half-open tower window. Outside, the sun shone across the snowfields, and rivulets formed pathways on the snow, draining off the grainy white surface and into the now-slushy roads and pathways. In a few scattered places, the brown of earth, the dark gray of rock, or the bleached tan of dead grass peered through the disappearing snow cover. Despite the carpet of fir branches, much of the road from the tower up to the stables was more quagmire than path.

The east side of the tower was half ringed with meltwater that froze at night and cleared by day, so much that from the eastern approach to the causeway, the tower resembled the moated castle that Nylan had rejected building.

His eyes flicked from the window back to Ryba, whose own eyes were glazed with concentration and the effort of measured breathing. On the other side of the lander couch stood Ayrlyn, her fingers resting lightly on Ryba's enlarged abdomen. Beside her was Jaseen.

"I'm hot," panted the marshal.

The joined couches had been moved toward the window because the ice and snow melting off the slate stone roof had revealed more than a few leaks that dripped down into the top level of the tower.

Nylan used the clean but tattered cloth to blot the dampness off Ryba's face, then put his hand on her forehead.

"That feels good."

"Good," affirmed Nylan.

"Just a gentle push . . . gentle . . ."

"Hurts . . . tight . . ." the marshal responded. "Dyliess?"

"She's doing fine, Ryba," said Ayrlyn.

"I'm . . . not . . ." Ryba shivered. "Cold now."

After he drew the blankets around her shoulders, Nylan blotted Ryba's damp forehead again. "Easy," he said. "You're doing fine, too."

"Easy . . . for you . . . to say."

"I know." Nylan kept his tone light, although, with his perceptions, he could sense that Ryba's labor was going well, if any labor, and the effort and pain involved, could be said to be going well.

"Push . . . a little harder."

"Am pushing . . ."

"Stop . . ."

". . . tell me to push, then not push . . . make up your mind . . ."

Nylan held back an inadvertent grin at Ryba's asperity.

"We're trying to do this with as little stress on you and Dyliess as possible."

". . . little stress?"

Jaseen nodded, but said nothing.

Nylan patted away the sweat on Ryba's forehead, then squeezed her arm gently.

"Push!" demanded Ayrlyn.

The marshal pushed, turning red.

"You have to breathe, too," reminded Ayrlyn after the push.

"Hot . . ." gasped Ryba.

Nylan eased the blankets away from her shoulders.

"All right . . . get ready . . ." said Ayrlyn.

Through it all, Nylan stood by, occasionally touching Ryba, infusing a sense of order, though that order was not essential. In the end, a small head crowned, and Jaseen eased the small bloody figure into the light, and onto the Roof of the World.

"In a bit, you'll need to push again," said Ayrlyn.

"I . . . know . . . let me see her," panted Ryba.

When the cord was tied and cut, Ayrlyn eased the small figure onto Ryba's chest. Dyliess seemed to look around, then turned toward her mother's breast, her mouth opening and fastening in place.

"You little piglet," murmured Ryba.

"Like her mother," affirmed Nylan. "She's concentrating on what's important."

His senses extended over his daughter, taking in the hair that would be silver and the narrower face that was also from his Svennish heritage. In some ways, almost, she felt like Kyalynn, Siret's silver-haired daughter.

Nylan swallowed, then looked away toward the window, back out to the spring, and the melting snow, back out to the few green shoots that hurried through the patches of white.

Not now, he thought, *not now,* and he forced a smile, which turned into a real one as he watched Dyliess, even though his chest was tight, and a sense of chaos swirled through his thoughts.

"They're both fine," Ayrlyn affirmed.

Jaseen nodded.

Ryba's eyes closed, a half-smile on her face.

LXXIV

"DON'T WE KNOW where we're heading? Or when?" Hissl walks to the barracks door. By looking out and down the street, he can see the haze of light green—the grasslands that stretch all the way from Clynya to the South Branch of the River Jeryna.

Koric shrugs. "Lord Sillek is not telling anyone. We know we will be moving against either Lord Ildyrom or against those angels on the Roof of the World. One way or the other . . . we have to be ready."

"He hasn't said?" asks the white wizard.

"No. Rimmur said he almost took off his head for asking." Koric laughs. "I can't say as I blame Lord Sillek. If people knew where or when, they'd be ready, and our armsmen would be killed. As it is, everyone's waiting for him to make a mistake, any mistake. Everyone talks. You know how hard it is to keep things quiet. Ildyrom probably has spies in every tavern in Clynya, and a few other places as well, if you know as to what I mean."

"Yes, I know." Hissl smiles faintly.

"You seen any sign of the Jeranyi, yet, in your glass?" Koric asks.

"Not anywhere close to the grasslands, but the grass is short, and the way's still muddy."

"Could they come up the river? Don't you wizards have trouble with running water?" Koric fingers the hilt of the big blade on the bench before him.

"I can see what's on the water, not what's in it or under it. But they wouldn't swim all the way upstream from Berlitos." Hissl forces a chuckle.

"No, Wizard, I guess they wouldn't. But you be looking for them. I wouldn't want any surprises. Neither would Lord Sillek."

"I'll be looking," Hissl replies. "I'll certainly be looking."

LXXV

FROM THE CAUSEWAY, Ayrlyn and Nylan looked at the fields and the stretches of mud that had been crude roads the previous fall and snow-covered trails through the winter. The fields and meadows were white and brown, still primarily white, although long green shoots poked through the white in places.

"Snow lilies." Ayrlyn pointed to a green stem rising from the snow.

"Some things will grow in the strangest conditions," mused Nylan. "They grow through the snow, and we can't even walk up the hill without sinking knee-deep in mud.

We're not moving much anywhere for a while."

"The stables are even more of a mess because all that packed snow turned into ice and then melted all at once. Fierral's in a terrible mood. Then, I'm surprised she's not that way more often."

"Why?" asked the engineer.

"How would you like to be the chief armsmaster under Ryba? Fierral knows that nothing she does will ever match Ryba. That means she'll always be the chief flunky."

"Hadn't thought about that, but it makes sense."

"Of course it does." Ayrlyn snorted.

"We won't be seeing any bandits or invaders for a while, I'd bet."

"No traders, either," pointed out Ayrlyn.

"You could ride out, and it would be dry when you returned."

"If it didn't rain, but I couldn't bring much back without the cart, and how would I get it out of here?"

"Hadn't thought about mud." Nylan turned his eyes downhill and to the east. Below the lower outfalls, the cold rushing water, both from the runoff diverted from around the bathhouse and tower and from the drainage system, had cut an even deeper gouge through the low point of the muddy swathe that had been a road, a depression that was fast becoming a small gorge.

"I knew I should have built a culvert there," muttered Nylan.

"Exactly when did you have time?" asked Ayrlyn.

"The road to the ridge needs to be paved." Nylan ignored her question, since the only free time he'd had, had been after the snow had fallen. "It's almost impossible to leave the tower anyway." He glanced toward the fir trunks stacked beyond the causeway, noting that the trunks on the bottom of the pile were more than half sunk into the mud. "I suppose we can cut and split the rest of that wood."

"You always have to have something to do, don't you?"

"There's always more to do than time to do it," he pointed out.

She nodded slowly. "Do you think that when you die someone will build a huge stone memorial that says, 'he accomplished the impossible'? Or 'he did more than any three other people'?"

"No one will build me any memorials, Ryba's prophecies notwithstanding." Nylan paused, and then his voice turned sardonic. "Don't you know that's why I built the tower? It's the only memorial I'll ever have, and I'm the only one who knows it—except you."

"You're impossible, Engineer." Ayrlyn turned to him, and her eyes were dark behind the brown. "She sees the future, but you take the weight of that future."

"I suppose so." Nylan shrugged. "But who else will? The guards, even Ryba, laugh at my building, my obsession— I'm sure that's what it's called. The predictably obsessed engineer." His words turned bitter. "If this were a novel or a trideo thriller, the editors would cut out all the parts about building. That's boring. You know, heroes are supposed to slay the enemy, but no one has to worry about shelter or heat or coins or stables or whether the roads need to be paved or whether you need bridges or culverts to keep them from being impassible. Bathhouses are supposed to build themselves, didn't you know? Ryba orders sanitation, and it just happens. No matter that the snow is deep enough to sink a horse without a sign. No matter that most guards would rather stink than use cold water. No matter that poor sanitation kills more people in low-tech cultures than battles. But building is boring. So is making better weapons, I suppose. Using them is respected and glorious and fires the imagination. Frig . . . every mythological smith has been the butt of jokes, and I'm beginning to understand why."

"You're angry, aren't you?"

"Me? The calm, contained engineer? Angry?" Nylan swallowed. "Never mind. I didn't mean to upset you."

"You didn't upset me, Nylan. And I do understand. Do you think that going out trading is any different? We need all these goods to survive, but trading isn't glamorous like winning battles. Do you know what it's like to have every man stare at your hair and run his eyes over you as if you wore nothing? To know you can't lift a blade because women are less than commodities, and almost anything goes? And if you do use your blade, you won't be able to trade for what you need?" Her voice softened and took on an ironic tone. "Besides, no one wants to trade with someone who kills some idiot and then has to empty her guts on her own boots." The redhead laughed. "They don't do trideo dramas about people who trade for flour and chickens, either."

"No. They focus on the great heroes," Nylan said. "Like Ryba."

"Part of that's not easy, either," Ayrlyn pointed out. "She does see things, you know."

"I know."

"It must be terrible."

"I suppose so." Nylan didn't want to say more, feeling as though he'd poured out more than he'd ever intended, and Ayrlyn wasn't even the one with whom he slept.

"I mean it. If she has a vision, or whatever it is, can she trust it? Does she dare to oppose it? What should she do to make it occur, if it's an outcome she wants? What are the options and trade-offs?"

"You still talk like a comm officer, sometimes."

"I probably always will." A brief laugh followed. "Don't you see, though? What she has is a terrible curse. It's much easier to be a healer, or a black mage. We do the best we can, and, if we make mistakes, we aren't faced with the idea that we *knew* in advance and still failed."

"She doesn't see everything."

"That's worse. How can she tell what might be a wish, or what leads to what she sees?" Ayrlyn shivered.

Nylan moistened his lips, and his eyes flicked toward the top of the tower. The wind rose, and a fluffy white cloud covered the sun, and Nylan shivered also, but not because of the darkness or the chill that swept across Tower Black and the causeway where they stood.

LXXVI

"YOUR SON, LORD Sillek." The midwife turns to Sillek, her face blank with the concealed expression of one who felt Sillek had no rights to be in the room.

Sillek glances from the small figure in the midwife's arms to Zeldyan's washed-out and sweat-plastered face, then back to the child and the fuzz upon his scalp that already bears a blond tinge. He smiles broadly at both his son and his consort.

"Have you a name?" asks the midwife.

Sillek ignores the question and bends over the wide bed. His lips brush Zeldyan's cheek. "I love you." His fingers squeeze hers for a moment. "Thank you. He's healthy and wonderful. You are, too."

"May I?" asks the Lady of Lornth, her arms reaching for the infant as Sillek steps back.

"You?" asks the midwife.

"He's my son."

Sillek's eyes fasten on the midwife until she lowers the boy into Zeldyan's arms.

Zeldyan eases the seeking mouth into place and smiles faintly. "His name is Nesslek, after his father and grandsire."

"Nesslek . . ." muses Sillek. "You had that thought out all along, didn't you?"

"Of course." Zeldyan's quick grin fades. "I still feel like a herd of something ran over me."

"Would you like a wet nurse now?" asks the midwife. "Lady Ellindyja . . ."

"No. Thank you. Not now." Zeldyan's arms tighten ever so slightly around her son.

Sillek watches both, a smile on his lips and in his eyes.

LXXVII

TWO HUNDRED CUBITS uphill from Tower Black, still well below the rocks that rose into the sides of the stable canyon, Nylan looked at his forge site. Four corners marked with rocks, that was all, not that there was much he could do until the planting was complete—food was the first priority.

With a forge, he might be able to make a simple plow, if he could bend metal around a wooden frame. He certainly wouldn't have the heat to forge metal lander alloys—soften them, perhaps, and even that would be hard. He'd also need charcoal, lots of it, and that meant work down in the forest, after it dried out more.

He turned toward the greenery below, the sprigs of grass sprouting even in the field area, and the sprays of thin white lacy flowers that seemed to have sprung up everywhere.

Despite the chill that had him in his worn ship jacket, the engineer took a deep breath of the clean air, glad to be out of the tower. Then he started up to the stables. His first job was to fix the road, and he needed the crude cart to lug down rocks, piles of rocks. As he passed the lander, now used for fodder storage, he could hear Ayrlyn and the guards as the healer organized the planting detail.

"Those are potatoes? Where did you get these?" demanded Denalle.

"We grew them. The ones we saved are known as seed potatoes," said Ayrlyn, almost tiredly. "The number of potatoes we saved for seed wouldn't have fed anyone for more than an eight-day—and then what would we have to plant for the next year?"

"We're hungry now."

"Shut up, Denalle," added Rienadre. "Someone's got to

think ahead. You think there's a food market over the next hill? Or a seed store?"

"Stuff it! I'm tired of your superiority. I'm tired of you, and I'm tired of this whole planet. I just want out. Out! Do you hear me?"

"I think the whole Roof of the World hears you," added Nylan before the healer could speak. "The marshal will let you leave anytime. The only question is whether you want to be beaten, raped, killed, or just be a paid slut once you reach a town." He shrugged. "Who knows? You might find some peasant nice enough to feed you, shelter you, and give you a dozen kids."

Denalle glared at the engineer. Nylan met her eyes evenly. Then she looked down. "I hate this place."

"I don't think any of us would have chosen it," Nylan said quietly. "We just have to make the best of it. You have any ideas to make it better, let someone know. We are listening." He started toward the cart, then stopped and asked Ayrlyn, "You don't mind if I use the cart around here? I'm going to cart stones."

"Stones?" asked Ayrlyn.

"I'm going to build a stone culvert and crude bridge where the outfalls cut through the road. Unless I fix that, it will just get worse. Then, as I can, I'll be using stones to pave the road from the causeway to the bridge, and then up the ridge. Someday, we won't have to worry about the mud, then."

"I thought you were going to work on a forge."

"I'll probably do both. I can't use the forge until I make charcoal. I'd need help with the logs, and that'll have to wait until after planting."

"That's a lot of stones," said Ayrlyn. "You can have the cart. It's not as though we couldn't come and get it almost immediately."

Nylan grinned and walked toward the stables.

"Use the gray," Ayrlyn called. "She's used to the cart."

By the time the engineer had the gray harnessed and the cart ready, the planting detail had left.

He had tucked his blade and scabbard in the narrow space beside the seat, so he could get it quickly—Ryba had insisted he have it near—and flicked the worn leather leads. "Come on, old lady."

His eyes went to the blade. With the practice that Ryba had also insisted upon, he was improving, but he still wasn't comfortable with the blade, even as he found that he could now usually keep from getting spitted—or the equivalent with the wooden practice blades—and could actually strike most of the other guards at will, except for Ryba and Saryn. He could also run through the exercises with his own blades—finally—without danger of taking off an ear or other limbs.

He flicked the leads once more, and the gray tossed her head vigorously but followed him through the mud toward the outcroppings farther up the gorge from the stable.

Rough stones there were, more than enough, and Nylan slowly filled the cart until it seemed to sag over the wheels. By then his back felt as if it were sagging as well.

"Hard labor—they never told me about this in engineer's school," he mumbled to the gray.

The mare didn't answer, but chewed the few green shoots she could reach from where Nylan had tethered her. She kept chewing as he untethered her and slowly led her and the creaking wagon down past the stables, past the smithy site, past the tower and causeway to the gaping hole in the muddy patch that passed for a road.

Then he began to unload the stones, one after the other, stacking each where he thought it would be closest to where it would be needed. After the wagon was empty, he flicked the reins, half dragging the mare from cropping the white flowers and the tender leaves beneath, and headed back up-hill.

"Nice day, ser," called Hryessa from the causeway, where she had taken off her boots and was knocking the mud from them against the stones of the causeway wall.

Behind her, in the low-walled practice area, Llyselle and Siret sparred with wands, their mounts standing by, since

Ryba had decreed that at least two outriders were to be ready at all times.

"It is, at last." He waved to Hryessa and kept leading the mare uphill.

For the second load, Nylan concentrated on finding larger chunks of stone, the kind he could use to frame a large culvert. Two long green trunks might help. Ideally, stone alone would last, but he couldn't always afford to do the ideal.

After he finished loading the cart, he stretched and tried to massage his back. The planting detail was still struggling with mud and seeds when he returned to the road and began stacking the stones from his second load.

He glanced to the tower as the triangle sounded once. Almost before its echoes died away, Siret and Llyselle galloped up the hill. The guards in the planting group laid aside shovels, hoes, and warrens, and reclaimed bows and blades.

Nylan continued to unload stones until he heard hoofbeats on the trail down from the ridge. Then he dropped the last stone and strapped his scabbard in place. Only the two Westwind mounts returned, but Llyselle and Siret each carried another rider.

As the two slowed and picked their way around the gap in the road, and the gray and the cart, Nylan studied the newcomers—both women, one brown-haired, one black. Then he walked toward the causeway.

The silver-haired guards set the two women on the stones at the end of the causeway. Both staggered as their feet hit the hard rock.

Nylan arrived after the armed and curious guards of the planting detail. The black-haired woman, thin-faced, glanced at Nylan, then at Siret, then at Llyselle, and back at Nylan.

The engineer glanced around. Ryba was still in the tower. Saryn was out hunting, although Nylan suspected she was as much keeping an eye on Gerlich as hunting. Ayrlyn had been supervising the crop planting and stood at the back of the now-armed planting group.

"I think they're asking for shelter, ser," said Llyselle, "but I still have problems with the local tongue."

"I don't trust the dark one," added Siret.

Nylan turned his perceptions on the black-haired woman, wincing as he did. An aura of white chaos, laced with red, surrounded her.

"See what I mean, ser?"

Nylan grinned at Siret. "Your night vision is a lot better than it used to be, isn't it?"

She looked down.

"Don't worry." He glanced at Llyselle. "Yours is too, isn't it?"

Llyselle looked bewildered. "I thought most everyone's was. So I didn't say anything. Besides, I hate night duty."

Ayrlyn made her way around the half-dozen guards who had been planting and stepped up beside Nylan. He realized that, in their muddy and tattered work garb, none of them looked terribly prepossessing.

Ryba stepped out of the tower doorway, dressed in clean leathers, both blades at her waist. Just inside the door, Nylan could make out Ellysia, Dyliess in one arm, Dephnay in the other. The marshal surveyed the group, her eyes halting on the two women.

Both would-be refugees prostrated themselves. "Refuge, Angel of Darkness."

"You can get up," she said wryly in Old Anglorat. "I'm the marshal of Westwind, not an angel of darkness." She turned to Nylan and asked, "Have you talked with them?"

"No. The brunette seems all right. The black-haired one is trouble, filled with chaos."

"Chaos?"

"The white stuff that means no good. It's like an aura." Nylan glanced around. "She's like a white wizard."

Ryba winced, then turned to Ayrlyn. "You're the healer. What do you think?"

"I'd go with the engineer's assessment."

Ryba looked at the black-haired woman. "You still carry the evils of men, and of chaos. We will not harm you. We will not receive you. We will give you food and let you make your own way."

The black-haired woman swayed, and put a hand out to hold the causeway wall.

"She's acting," snapped Ayrlyn.

"Faker," added Siret in a low voice.

Nylan nodded in agreement.

"You're sure?" Ryba asked Ayrlyn.

"Yes."

"You are bid to leave," ordered Ryba. "Now. Walk up to the—"

The dark-haired woman turned. Something glinted in her hand, and she jumped toward the healer.

Siret's blade flashed down, almost in reflex, cutting across the dark-haired woman's shoulder and into her chest. Blood splashed, striking the stones of the causeway almost as fast as the corpse from which it came.

Nylan staggered at the wave of whiteness coming from the death. His skull felt as if it might split for an instant, before the sensation subsided to a dull aching.

Ayrlyn eased back and quietly retched into the depression behind the causeway.

The brown-haired woman flattened herself on the stones. "Spare me!"

Denalle stepped forward and kicked back the dead woman's hand. Under it was a dagger with a jagged blade.

"Nice," said Ryba dryly. "What about the other?" Her eyes went to the groveling brunette.

"No chaos. We can't tell intent," Nylan said, his eyes darting toward Ayrlyn, who had finally straightened up. Their eyes crossed, sharing the knowledge and the chaotic feeling of death.

"Ayrlyn? Would you and one of the guards—and the mage"—her eyes focused on Nylan—"talk with the other one? If she seems all right, have Hryessa and Istril get her set up. If not, feed her, and send her on her way with some food, not a lot."

Nylan glanced at the marshal, as if to ask if she had any visions.

"Not this time. They're not always reliable."

Although Rienadre looked puzzled at the exchange, she said nothing. Ayrlyn nodded almost imperceptibly.

"We've all got work to do. Let's get on with it." Ryba turned and went back into the tower.

"You may rise, woman," Nylan said in Old Anglorat.

The brunette looked up, her eyes going to Siret, who remained mounted, cleaning the black blade on a scrap of cloth, then to the closed tower door.

Ayrlyn glanced at Denalle. "Would you and Rienadre bury . . . don't make a big deal of it, out by the bandits, deep enough . . ."

"We'll take care of it, healer," answered Rienadre.

Denalle glanced at Nylan and nodded.

"The rest of you can get back to planting. I'll be there before too long," said Ayrlyn. "Siret and Llyselle, and the mage, are enough guard for one woman."

Denalle slipped the jagged blade into her belt before she and Rienadre lugged off the body.

The brunette had gathered herself into a sitting position on the stones as the majority of the guards left. The entire left side of her face was yellow and green from a recent series of bruises.

"Who are you?" began Ayrlyn.

"Blynnal . . . I'm from Rohrn . . . I . . . we heard . . . there was a place . . ." Tears began to stream down her cheeks. "But . . . women . . . don't . . . kill . . ."

"Why not?" asked Ayrlyn. "Men do. Women have strong arms, too."

"But . . ."

"Child . . ." said Ayrlyn softly. "If we are attacked, we defend ourselves. Is that wrong?"

"Jrenya, she was strong. She said no man would ever force her, and you killed her."

"Why did you and Jrenya come here?" asked Nylan.

Blynnal's eyes dropped to the stones, to the patch of blood that marked where Jrenya had fallen.

Ayrlyn and Nylan waited. So did Siret and Llyselle. Llyselle's mount *whuffed,* and the guard patted its neck.

"Dyemeni, he was my consort, he beat me after Kyel died . . . he kept beating me . . ." More tears rolled down Blynnal's face. "Jrenya said it was wrong. She said we needed to do something. When . . . the snows melted . . . Dyemeni, he took out his big leather belt . . . he did . . . things . . ."

"What about Jrenya?" asked Nylan, ignoring the faint glare from Ayrlyn. "Why did she come with you?"

"She . . . she said, Nortya was mean . . ."

"Did Nortya beat her?" asked Nylan. "Did Jrenya have bruises like yours?"

"No . . . but . . . he was mean."

"How was he mean?" pressed Nylan. "Did you see him hurt her?"

"No . . . but she hated him . . . she said . . . her father made her join him . . . because he was the factor's only son."

"So . . . you left Rohrn because your consort beat you?"

Blynnal nodded.

"Did Jrenya kill Dyemeni?" asked Nylan.

Ayrlyn's eyes widened, as did Siret's.

Blynnal looked down at the stones.

"Did she?"

"I . . . don't know . . . She stabbed him, and we ran. We meant to leave anyway, but he came home early, and he saw the packs, and he hit me. He didn't see her."

"What about her consort?"

Again the brunette looked down at the stones.

"She killed him, too, I suppose?"

The faintest of nods answered Nylan.

He looked at Ayrlyn. "I don't know. She's weak—probably because everyone beat her up. She doesn't seem evil or chaotic . . . but two murders?"

"The dead one did both," pointed out Siret.

"I . . . was glad . . ." admitted Blynnal. "Dyemeni . . . hurt me . . . so much . . ."

"Honesty helps," Nylan offered.

The brunette sat on the dust and mud of the causeway stones in her tattered trousers and tunic.

Ayrlyn glanced from the green and purple side of Blynnal's face to the two mounted guards. "What do you two think? She'll be sharing your quarters."

"Her problem seems to be men, and we sure don't have too many around here, especially since the weasel left," said Llyselle.

"The weasel?" Nylan said inadvertently.

"Narliat."

Ayrlyn looked at Siret.

"I'd say to give her a chance. First mistake, and she's gone."

The healer looked to Nylan.

"That's my reaction . . . but I'm a man."

As the conversation proceeded, Blynnal had turned from one face to the next, eyes puzzled, almost like a trapped hare.

"I think we agree," said Ayrlyn, "and none of us are exactly happy about it." She turned to Blynnal and switched to Old Anglorat. "We are not happy with how you came . . ."

Tears oozed from the local woman's eyes.

". . . but . . . you will have a chance to prove yourself."

Blynnal threw her arms around Ayrlyn's legs. "Thank you, great lady. Thank you! I will be good. I will cook. I will scrub, but do not send me away."

"You may cook or scrub—we all do. Even the mage digs and lifts rocks. But once you prove yourself, we will also teach you the blade."

Blynnal's eyes widened. "I had not thought . . ."

"You will learn when to use it—and when not to. Both are important." Ayrlyn glanced at Nylan. "I just hope . . ."

"So do I."

"She'll be all right," said Siret softly. "She's just a scared little rabbit who got with the wrong people. That other one, though . . ."

"Very bad person." Llyselle shook her head. "Very bad."

"Anything else?" asked the healer, looking toward the tower.

"Before you go . . . I had a question," said Nylan. "Could I get two green trunks, around a half cubit thick, for the bridge?"

Ayrlyn looked over his shoulder at the stones stacked around the gorge through the road. "I'll talk to you about that after I get Blynnal organized with Istril. But I think we can manage that—if it doesn't rain." She gave Nylan a brief smile and touched Blynnal on the shoulder. "You need to wash, and to have your hair cut and to get clean garments . . ."

As Ayrlyn and her charge left, Llyselle looked to the sky. "It won't rain. I can tell."

Nylan wondered what else the silver-haired guard could tell. He looked back at the cart and the stones. Then he took a deep breath and started back toward the unbuilt bridge, trying to ignore the thoughts of the unbuilt smithy.

LXXVIII

THRAP!

Hissl glances up from the table to the half-open door to the outside landing, half-open to allow in the spring breeze.

"Yes?"

"I seek the great wizard Hissl," comes the voice from beyond the door.

Hissl rises and picks up the white bronze dagger from the table as he steps toward the door. "And why might you seek him?"

The door swings open, but the hooded figure standing there does not enter the room.

"I'm not exactly interested in cutthroats sneaking around with their faces hidden." Hissl's tone is faintly ironic.

"I am not a cutthroat, and I offer you the key to your wishes, honored Wizard," begins the hooded figure.

"My wishes? How would you presume to know my wishes?" asks Hissl.

"An unnamed brethren of yours presumes, not I." The

hooded figure extends an object . . . very slowly.

Hissl reaches, then draws back his hand. "Iron! That is no token of friendship!" His fingers tighten around the dagger.

"Look again, I was told to tell you."

Hissl's eyes narrow, but he studies the object on the other's palm. "Chaos, bound in iron, and yet, the chaos binds the iron. How can that be?"

The hooded man steps forward and sets the object on the white oak table. "I will leave that for you, and for you to consider." He turns and walks down the narrow steps from the upper room.

Behind him, Hissl studies the iron and the chaos which surrounds it. "But how? How?"

He finally glances out into the afternoon, but the hooded figure has vanished into the streets of Clynya, and the spring wind bears no hint of the stranger or his origin.

LXXIX

THIS TIME, AT the low cries, and the sense of pain, Nylan had not waited, but followed Ayrlyn up to the third level, and to Istril.

"It'll be all right," insisted the silver-haired guard. "It will be. I know." Her breathing increased, and lines of pain creased her face. "But I feel better with both of you here."

"You know a lot," said Ayrlyn. "More than I do."

"What about me?" said Jaseen.

"You . . . too . . ." puffed Istril.

"Don't push yet," cautioned the healer. "You're not ready."

"Feels that way . . ." grunted the silver-haired guard. "Want to push . . . whole body says I should."

"Don't . . . not yet . . . pant . . . puff, but don't push."

Nylan stood beside the bed that had been a lander couch, waiting, hoping he would not be needed, feeling, again, almost like an intruder, for all that he had promised Istril that he and Ayrlyn would be there.

In the end, besides providing order support, and a touch of healing, he was not needed, and Istril cuddled her son in her arms, and dampness streaked her cheeks.

"What are you going to call him?" asked Ayrlyn.

"Weryl."

Nylan paused. "Weryl? That was my grandfather's name, too."

"I know. I liked the name." Istril's hand stroked the boy's cheek. "So small." Her eyes closed momentarily. "Tired . . . worse than riding all day . . . hurts a lot more, too."

"You'll heal fine," Ayrlyn assured her.

"Just let me finish getting you cleaned up," muttered Jaseen, adding to Ayrlyn, "That's about the last of that antiseptic."

"We're going to have to develop some local substitutes—something."

Nylan stepped back away from the couch, then stopped and looked at the boy, another child with the silver fuzz on his scalp, foreshadowing silver hair like his mother's. Istril's eyes closed again, and her breathing smoothed, but she opened them and looked at Nylan.

"Glad . . . you keep promises . . ."

Although he felt awkward, Nylan stepped forward and touched her wrist. "You just rest and take care of your son."

"He . . . I will," answered Istril, seemingly fighting both pain and exhaustion.

"Just rest," added Ayrlyn.

Nylan took a last look at the two and then walked to the steps and down toward the now-empty great room. Ayrlyn followed.

The engineer looked at the empty tables, then walked to the one window that was open. He stood there, in the cool wind that carried the smell of turned earth, spring flowers, and damp pine needles into the tower.

"Sometimes . . ." For a time, he did not finish the sentence.

"Sometimes, I feel like there's so much I should see, like the children."

"Both Istril and Siret had silver-headed children," said Ayrlyn. "That's more than a little strange, since Gerlich is dark-haired."

"Does Relyn have anyone in his family with silver hair?" asked Nylan.

"I don't know, but I got the impression that no one has seen anyone with silver hair like the four of you anywhere on this planet."

"Maybe it's dominant?" Nylan shook his head.

"That's asking a lot," said Ayrlyn. "Our hair colors get changed from this switch from universe to universe. That I can buy, in a weird sort of way. But changing a recessive into a dominant gene? I don't know about that." She pauses. "Are you sure you don't know more about this?"

"I've only slept with one person."

"You're telling the truth, and that bothers me. Because . . ."

"I know," Nylan sighed. "Kyalynn, Dyliess, and Weryl all feel the same, with our senses . . . don't they?"

Ayrlyn nodded.

"I need to talk to Ryba."

"I'll be here," Ayrlyn said. "Remember that. I'll be here."

Nylan looked at the redhead, but she just repeated her words. "I'll be here, if you need to talk."

"Thank you." He took a deep breath and headed for the steps.

Ryba was easing Dyliess into the cradle. So Nylan waited for a time until his daughter half snorted and slipped into sleep to the gentle rocking of the cradle. Already, she seemed larger.

"How is Istril?" asked Ryba, her tone that of professional concern, even before Nylan could speak.

"She's fine. So's her son." Nylan watched Ryba.

A faint shadow crossed the marshal's face. "She had a son?"

"She named him Weryl."

"How touching."

Nylan swallowed. "Dyliess isn't the only one, is she? How did you do it?"

"How does it feel? I promised you a son. I didn't realize it would be this soon."

"I don't like it—but how did you manage it? You're the only one . . . I mean, I'm not like Gerlich, bedding every willing marine."

Ryba turned toward the window, walking past the cradle, where Dyliess gave a little snort. Ryba paused and smiled briefly at the infant before speaking. "You don't have to bed anyone but me. We do have some remnants of medical technology. And I know how to use the local net, or whatever you want to call it, also, at least enough to ensure that our child would be a daughter." Ryba looked back at the silver-haired girl in the cradle. "I thought that Istril's child would be a girl."

Nylan decided against mentioning Istril's slow-emerging abilities. He walked to the other tower window, and looked out past the folded-back shutters. "Why?"

"Isn't it obvious?" Ryba brushed the short dark hair out of her face. "We're stuck here. We need to prepare for the next generation. Interbreeding with the locals runs risks we don't even know about. With Mertin's death, you and Gerlich are the only ones with verifiably compatible genes. You're hung up on being with one person . . . which is . . . reassuring . . . for me, but not terribly effective. This way we can assure staggered pregnancies. Besides, we don't have many men. Look what happened to Mertin. At least now we've saved your genes."

"And so many girls?"

"I'm not about to let male brute force undo what we've built. There will be a few more sons, though."

"Stud value," said Nylan bitterly.

"Eventually, we'll have to bring in locals, but not until we've widened the gene pool enough, and until the girls are socialized the right way."

"The feminine utopia."

"You've seen this planet. Boys are more fragile than girls;

so more boys are born in times of stress. Put those together, and natural selection would have all our daughters barefoot and pregnant in fifteen years. Twenty at the outside. No, thank you."

Nylan could see dark gray clouds massing on the northern horizon, just above the western peaks. "You could have told me, rather than let me guess."

"I couldn't risk it." Ryba looked down at the floor, then to the cradle. "It's not you. You're basically a gentle man . . . but . . . I know what works, and there's too much at stake. Do I tell you, when I know that I'll have a bright and talented daughter if I don't? Or that . . . I don't dare tell you that, either." She shook her head helplessly. "I know just enough."

"You're a captive of your visions. Life isn't just following what you know will work. Can't you dare to make it better?"

"I have," answered Ryba bleakly. "That's why three guards are dead. I saw myself being more brutal than in dealing with Mran, and I wouldn't do it. I wasn't quite that bad after Frelita died, but I should have been, because more guards died being careless, because people only respect force. You don't think I've tried? Or that it doesn't bother me?"

"It doesn't bother you enough."

"It bothers me a lot! I suggest, and, unless I've got a hand on a blade and madness in my eyes, half of them won't listen. You think I enjoy that?"

"But you do it . . ."

"You don't see how much it upsets me, and you never will, and that's just another reason why I don't ever want many men around. And you're one of the best. Most of them are like Gerlich or that weasel Narliat."

Nylan shook his head. "I'm not them."

"No, you're not. What would you have me do? Don't give me generalities, either. What action do you want?"

"Don't turn me into a stud through artificial insemination."

"Fine. Will you promise me to bed three more guards—of my choice—late this summer?"

"I'm not like Gerlich."

"No. But we need children if Westwind is to survive. And if Westwind doesn't survive, most women on this planet won't have a life worth living."

"You need a purpose, don't you?" asked Nylan. "You have to have something that makes it all worthwhile."

"It took you this long to figure that out?" Ryba gave a harsh bark, not quite a laugh, and Dyliess murmured and turned on the coarse sheet. The marshal bent down and rocked the cradle. "I'm not satisfied with mere survival, and you aren't either, Nylan. You just won't admit it. You'll nearly kill yourself to build a tower that will last for centuries, but you won't admit it. You'll risk ridicule for being obsessed with building, but you won't admit you need a larger purpose, too." The marshal paused, then added, "You still didn't answer my question. You asked me to do something, and I said I would—if you'd give me an alternative."

"I don't know." Nylan looked down at Dyliess.

"I always thought men liked the idea of harems." Ryba shrugged. "Or we can keep on the way we are. It's a little messy, but . . ."

"I'm not Gerlich, and I need to think about it." With a last look at Dyliess, Nylan turned and walked down the steps—out through the big south door and out into the shadows that were falling from the cold north across the Roof of the World. His feet carried him to the smithy site, and the rocks and the mortar. At least what he built was solid. At least he could see what happened with mortar and stone and timber.

He needed to talk with Ayrlyn. He needed that, but not yet. Not yet.

LXXX

"THAT'S IT." NYLAN tapped the last wedge into place, ensuring that the fourth fir trunk would remain in place over the stone culvert. Ryba had declared that food and planting came first. So he'd done the bridge and culvert backward, putting the heavy rock riprap in place on both uphill and downhill sides of the culvert first, doing everything he could do alone until Saryn and the others could fell and bring him the trunks he needed.

"Last year, this was just bushes and grass," said Huldran, setting down a heavy stone just beyond the footings that held the bridge timbers. She looked down at the stone-lined channel. "Do you think we need this big a bridge?"

"I hope it's big enough," the engineer answered. He gestured toward the tower and the bathhouse behind it. "We're changing the land, and the guard will keep expanding—according to the marshal. The more hard roads and buildings, the more runoff. This is to keep it channeled from the fields."

"What if there's no rain?" grunted Cessya, mixing water into the dry ingredients of the mortar.

"That's next year's project," laughed Nylan, slightly nervously. "See that swale down there? If we dam it at the north end, then we can put a spillway, a little one, in the middle, and run a ditch from the south end down to the fields."

"The Rats'd have your head, Engineer, for all this land-changing," Huldran commented.

"They'd do the same if they were trying to survive here."

"They like hotter places."

"They can have 'em," snapped Cessya. "Mortar's ready."

The three lugged the battered and leaking mortar tub up to the flat spot beyond the end of the timbers. Huldran and

Nylan began to fill the spaces between the heavy rocks, the wedges, and the timbers.

Once the mortar dried and held the trunks, then Nylan could complete the bridge's roadbed, not so wide as he would have liked, but wide enough for a good-sized wagon and a wall on each side.

As he paused before taking another trowel of mortar, he took in the short stretch of paving stones that extended from the west end of the unfinished structure toward the causeway before the tower. Westwind was looking more and more permanent.

Nylan eased the mortar into place, while Huldran took the cart back up beyond the tower and to the base of the rocky hills to bring back more stones for both the bridge roadbed and for fill.

In the low-walled flat beyond the causeway, blade practice had begun again. Ryba had handed the carry-pack with Dyliess in it to Selitra. Facing her was Blynnal, and the local woman cowered once she held the wooden wand.

Saryn stood beside Blynnal, correcting her.

Behind Saryn, Hryessa and Murkassa practiced, already, from what Nylan could tell, making good progress toward achieving Ryba's standards for all the guards, whether originally angel marines or local refugees.

The engineer pursed his lips as he bent for more mortar. Results—Ryba got them. He just wasn't fond of the tactics.

"Working hard again, I see."

Nylan glanced up to see Ayrlyn standing there. "What else do obsessed engineers do?"

"I'm leaving tomorrow morning . . ." The redhead let her words trail off.

"All right." This time, Nylan understood. "Can I finish up this batch of mortar?"

She nodded.

The engineer turned to Cessya. "I'll finish here. Would you go find Huldran and tell her just to unload the stones and then take the cart back. I need to talk to Ayrlyn about what we need from her next trading trip."

"Yes, ser." Cessya grinned. "Walking's easier than moving stones."

"We'll make up for it after the noon meal," Nylan promised, returning her grin, then looking back down at the stone in front of him.

"I'm still looking for an anvil?" Ayrlyn asked as Cessya started uphill, toward the tower and the rock-strewn canyon beyond the stable canyon.

"We need spikes, and nails, almost any kind of hardware. A set of hammers, I'd guess, big ones for the forge." Nylan troweled the mortar smooth in the joints between two stones. "And some circular saw blades for the sawmill."

"We don't have one," the redhead pointed out with a smile. "We don't have a forge, either."

"We'll have both, before the end of the year." The smith extended the trowel for more mortar.

"Nylan . . . why do you drive yourself so hard?"

"Because . . . what else can I do? Ryba wants to change this world to one where women rule, and she'll leave the ground soaked with blood, including mine, if I try to stop her. Besides, she's right about the way women are treated, and you can't change that without even greater force." He paused and wiped his forehead with the back of his forearm.

"Building things won't change that," Ayrlyn reflected. "You're just allowing her to do more."

"What am I supposed to do? I've got three children, and I only knew about one of them until they were born. Am I just going to condemn them to a short and nasty life? If they have strong walls and warmth and clean water, that leaves them less at the mercy of this friggin' world. I don't like it, but Ryba's the only ship in port."

"What do *you* want?"

The smith finished the joint, and extended the trowel to the battered tub for more mortar. "I don't know. I know what I don't want. I don't want killing after killing. I don't want to be cold and dirty and hungry. I don't want that for Dyliess or Weryl or Kyalynn." He shrugged, then applied the trowel again.

"You want to be appreciated, but you don't want to force people to appreciate you. You want to be loved, but not used."

"You might say that," he admitted. "But that's true of most people. Don't you feel that way?"

"Yes"—Ayrlyn smiled warmly—"but I thought we were talking about you. You feel responsible for all your children, and yet you feel used. And you won't say anything about it. You don't like to talk about your feelings, not directly, and you try to avoid it. Was it that way growing up?"

"My mother always said there was no use in complaining. No one cared, and we might as well save our breath. So Karista and I didn't. The older I got, the truer it seemed." He set down the trowel as he finished the last of the mixed mortar. "What about you?"

"There you go again. Two sentences about you, and switch the subject to me." Ayrlyn laughed. "My father was the warm one, and he joked a lot. He was quiet about it, but he also made it known, like your mother, that outside the family, no matter what people said, most didn't care."

"It sounds like he cared."

"Your mother didn't? I'm sure she did."

"Oh, she did," Nylan admitted, "but she felt it should be obvious, and why belabor the obvious? Actions speak louder than words—that was her maxim."

"So you keep trying to make your actions do the speaking?" The redhead shook her head. "Most people don't read actions very well. They need words as well, lots of them, preferably words that say how wonderful they are."

"You're more cynical than I am."

"You're not cynical at all, Nylan." Ayrlyn reached down and touched his arm gently, her fingers warm and cool at the same time. "You're a caring man who's never allowed himself to express what he feels. You feel guilty and self-indulgent when you even think about what you feel. So you keep doing things and hope people understand."

"Probably."

Ayrlyn snorted and squeezed his arm.

"What about you? After last fall, aren't there going to be armsmen out there looking for a trader with flame-red hair?"

"It's getting cut shorter, and I'll be wearing a hat. If they notice, well, it takes time to send messages in this culture, and we'll try to stay ahead of Lord Sillek's authorities."

"I'm not sure I like that."

"What else can I do? We need the goods, and now is better than later."

The engineer nodded reluctantly, then stood as the bell rang for the midday meal.

"Time to eat? You headed my way?" asked Ayrlyn.

"Is there any other way?" Nylan swallowed. "Don't answer that."

"I won't, but I'll remember that you asked it." She smiled gently, and Nylan smiled back.

LXXXI

ZELDYAN SITS, PROPPED on the edge of the bed, Nesslek at her breast, wearing a green silksheen dressing gown that sets off her golden hair.

"He's mostly good," she says, looking down and smiling.

"Except when he cries in the middle of the night." Sillek rubs his eyes and yawns, then walks to the window of the room. The fields beyond Lornth, those he can see, have turned green, the light green of crops recently sprouted, with a hint of brown underlying the green. "Some night— just a night—couldn't he stay with a nurse?"

"When he's older, but he's not even a season yet," points out Zeldyan. "Would you want to trust the heir of Lornth out of our sight so young?" She offers an open smile.

"I may not survive another season." Sillek laughs. "Undertaking this campaign may get me more sleep than staying in my own bed."

"I'm glad it's only sleep you're wishing."

He turns from the window and steps to the bed, bending and brushing her cheek with his lips. "It's not all I'm wishing, but I want you well."

Zeldyan flushes, ever so slightly. Then she frowns. "I still worry about your being so far from Lornth."

"Whatever I do, it will be far from Lornth. I have two enemies trying to bleed us dry, and another one that my own holders won't let me forget. Or my mother."

"Has she done anything beyond talking to Lygon?" asks Zeldyan.

Sillek frowns faintly, then turns to the window.

"I'm sorry. I didn't mean . . ."

"That's all right." Sillek strokes his black beard without turning. "Lord Megarth approached me. So did Lord Fysor. They were old friends of my sire." He shrugs and turns, his eyes bleak. "What can I do?"

"I'm sorry," Zeldyan repeats.

"So am I."

"It all seems so stupid." Zeldyan lifts her free left hand to stop his objection. "I know. I know. You've explained, and so has your mother, and so did my father when he disowned Relyn, but it's still stupid."

"Has anyone heard from Relyn?"

"No. Father thinks the angel women have kept him captive. Have your wizards seen him?"

"No. That doesn't mean much, though. They can't scree inside that black stone tower, and during the winter how could anyone tell one person from another in those heavy coats and scarves?" Sillek sits in the chair beside the bed and yawns. His hand strokes her cheek for a moment.

Nesslek gurgles, makes a soft sneezing sound, and returns to nursing.

"You just get to eat and sleep and be close to your mother," says Sillek to his son. "And keep me awake." He stands.

Zeldyan reaches out and touches his hand. He wraps his fingers around hers for a moment, and then their fingers part.

LXXXII

RIENADRE GESTURED TOWARD the brick forms stacked in rows on the crude trestles. "It'll be another few days before these are ready."

"We do what we can." Nylan needed more of the bricks so that he could finish the smithy and the forge.

"That we do." Rienadre picked up the axe.

Nylan flicked the leads, and the gray mare *whuffled*. The cart creaked as it rocked forward under the load of building bricks. A heavy gust of wind whipped through Nylan's hair, then dropped away. Overhead, high cumulus clouds dotted the sky, some showing dark centers, for all that it was only slightly before midday. The gray *whuffled* again, and the cart creaked, and Nylan walked beside, along the rutted trail that was not quite a road.

Whufff . . .

"I know. It's no fun carting bricks uphill. Well . . . it's no fun walking alongside you, either."

The cart—the one Saryn and Ayrlyn had built, not the one that they'd obtained from Skiodra and repaired—creaked again. The other was with Ayrlyn, and Nylan wondered if she would be able to obtain saw blades on her trading run. Then he, in his copious spare time and with his great ignorance of low technology, would attempt to build a sawmill.

He snorted. The healer had perhaps four golds, and several blades. What were they going to do to get through the early summer? He swallowed, thinking about her flame-red hair and the anger Westwind was generating.

A flash of yellow-banded black wings crossed the trail, and the yellow and black bird alighted on the end of a dead pine branch and cocked its head in an almost inquiring attitude at Nylan.

"Hello there," said the would-be smith.

Twirrrppp . . . twirrrppp . . .

The cart *creaked* once more, and the bird responded to that as well.

"I think you like noise."

At that comment, the wings spread, and the bird departed.

Ahead, Nylan heard voices, and saws, and the regular *thump-chop* of an axe. Fierral and the timber crew were at it, and before long, he'd have to come down and turn the piles of limbs, the crooked ones, the stumps, and the other sections unsuited to timber, into charcoal. The idea was simple enough, a controlled burn under low-oxygen conditions. That meant burying most of the wood, probably in a long pile and lighting one end. How many times would he have to try it before he got it right?

He flicked the reins again.

Before long, the cart crossed another low rise in the trail. To the right, downhill, was a clearing filled with stumps. At the east end was a pile of limbs, odd pieces of trees, flanked by a tall brush pile. Along the traillike road were two low piles, one of squarish timbers and one of planks.

From a pole fastened between two smaller pines and fashioned from a roughly smoothed and stripped fir limb hung four gutted hares.

Nylan's eyebrows rose, and he slowed to examine the game.

"Hryessa," explained Fierral, walking up. "She made some snares. Can you take those up to Blynnal and Kadran?"

"Where's Kyseen?"

"Working with us. There was a general consensus that she's better with a blade and an axe or saw than in the kitchen, and I really doubt that Blynnal will ever be much with a blade. Hryessa and Murkassa—they'll be good, but not poor Blynnal. On the other hand—"

Both turned at the sound of hoofs.

"Weapons! Blades and bows!" Fierral's blue eyes turned cold, cold as the ice on Freyja.

A black-haired woman clung to what seemed to be the plow-harness or horse collar of a big brown beast that lumbered down the slope toward the guards. Before her on the horse was a small, dark-haired child. With each step, they bounced, and Nylan winced.

Hryessa arrived almost instantly, and Berlis wasn't that far behind. Weindre stood by one end of the pole with the hares on it, her bow in hand.

The woman pulled at the leads, and the plow horse slowed.

Fierral glanced uphill, then stepped forward and caught the leads up short, just beyond the harness. Foam streaked the gelding's muzzle.

The dark-haired woman straightened on the horse's back, holding her head higher, her arm around the girl who sat before her. Their brown tunics had recently been cleaned, but both riders were mottled with dust, and muddy patches appeared on the mother's cheeks.

"Are you . . . the . . . mountain women?" asked the woman in a hoarse voice.

"We live here," answered Fierral in accented Old Anglorat.

"I would like to claim refuge. For my daughter and me."

Fierral looked at Nylan. "What can you tell?"

Nylan took a breath and tried to let his feelings, through what he still conceived of as the local magic net, sense the woman. After a moment, he turned to Fierral. "None of that white stuff, that chaos that's almost like evil. She's tired, almost ready to collapse, probably ridden that beast a long way. All that doesn't mean she's good, though. The child's hungry," he added as an afterthought.

"It's a start," pointed out Fierral, who looked back at the exhausted riders. "We will not send you away, but the marshal must—"

"Decide," finished Nylan.

"Please . . . help. Surba . . . he follows, and Pretar is with him." With a convulsive gesture, the woman half climbed, half fell, off the horse. Her bare feet hit the ground hard, and she turned and lifted her daughter down.

Nylan shuddered. His feet would have hurt from hitting the rocky ground that hard, but the woman seemed unfazed by that. Instead she looked back uphill. The child looked boldly at Nylan, and he smiled back. She remained solemnly wide-eyed, her head reaching not quite to his chest.

"Hryessa—take your mount and get the marshal—and some reinforcements. Let the marshal decide, but tell her we have a refugee and a couple of incoming troublemakers."

"Incoming?" asked the locally raised guard as she mounted.

"Bad men who are on their way here," Fierral rephrased.

Berlis offered a brief grin at the rewording. Hryessa urged her mount uphill.

"Who might you be?" Nylan asked.

"Nistayna. I rode all the way from Linspros." Her eyes darted back uphill, her hands remaining on the girl's shoulders.

"Stand by for company!" ordered Fierral. "Berlis—you get over there on the other side where you've got a clear shot."

The guard eased her way across the trail.

"And Linspros is where?" asked Nylan.

Her eyes widened. "Is it true that you fell from the skies?"

"Yes, in a way," answered Nylan tiredly. "Now . . . where is Linspros?" He added to Fierral, "I'd like to know where else we're going to be making enemies."

The chief guard, or armsmaster or armsmistress—she had to be something like that in this culture now, Nylan reflected—responded with a grim smile, then motioned to Weindre. "They need something to drink."

"Linspros . . ." Nistayna mumbled.

Nylan walked to the nearest stump, leading the cart horse, and tied the leads to a protruding root. Then he turned and extended a hand to the apparently tottering woman.

Nistayna shied away, her arms shielding the girl.

"Fine." He motioned to Weindre, who approached with a plastic water bottle, one of the few remaining. "You get them to sit down before they both fall over."

Fierral tied the plow horse to another tree, and glanced back uphill. Hryessa was already nearly to the top of the ridge and almost out of sight.

After the black-haired local slumped onto the stump, she took the bottle and offered it to the girl. After the child drank, and after the mother took several swallows of water, Nylan tried again. "We are strangers. Where is Linspros? Is it near Gnotos?"

"Oh, no. Linspros is between Analeria and Gallos in the great west valley."

"It's east of the mountains. How long did it take you to find us?"

"Days . . . many days, and yesterday . . . I saw Surba. I was on the heights, but he has Pretar. He is a hunter and a tracker. They will be here soon. We could not ride as fast as they can." Again, she looked to the east.

"This refugee bit always disrupts work," said Fierral dryly.

"We've gotten a good cook, a good rabbit hunter, and some blades."

"We'll need a lot more, the way things are going."

"Why did you leave Linspros?" asked Nylan.

"Surba . . . only a woman would know. Only a mother." Her eyes fell.

"Sexual abuse?" Nylan asked the redheaded head of the guards.

"Probably, but who knows? Any kind of abuse seems to be fair on this friggin' planet. Maybe the girl."

Nylan bridled inside, but only said, "That's not representative. We only see the ones who are abused. The happy ones, or those from places where the women have some power, won't be the ones seeking out the angels."

Fierral opened her mouth, then paused. "You could be right."

"Maybe what this shows is that the society doesn't offer a place for those that don't fit in, but it doesn't mean every woman is degraded or oppressed."

"No," said Fierral. "Just those who want to be treated equally."

"Maybe," said Nylan. "Maybe not. Do we know enough?"

They looked back at Nistayna. She, in turn, kept her eyes on the ground, but clutched the plastic water bottle, then offered it to her daughter again. The child drank, but kept her eyes on Nylan.

For a time, they all waited. How long, Nylan wasn't certain. Then he frowned. Did he hear hooves? Ryba?

"Ready!" snapped Fierral.

Across the trail road, Berlis checked her bow.

Weindre checked her bow and held an arrow, almost ready to nock it.

Behind Fierral, Llyselle appeared, also carrying her composite bow, flanked by Kyseen, the former cook, who grinned shyly at Nylan.

Ryba rode down the trail, and the guards lowered their bows.

"Don't relax too much," said the marshal as she and Hryessa rode up together. "Your incomings are headed this way."

"Will they go up to the tower?" asked Nylan.

"They might, but they won't get far. Everyone else, except Ellysia and Blynnal, is waiting on the top of the ridge. And Gerlich, of course—he's out hunting."

Ryba surveyed the area. "If we have to go to weapons, use the bows first. I don't want any of us hurt if we can avoid it." Then she eased the big roan up next to the stump where the dark-haired Nistayna now stood.

"You are the Angel?"

"I'm Ryba, the marshal of Westwind."

Nistayna bowed her head. "Please . . . save us . . . take us in. Do not make me return. If you must, I will leave, but please take Niera. She must not . . ."

Nylan's lips tightened. He didn't like Surba, and the man hadn't even appeared.

Ryba glanced to Nylan.

"No chaos. Seems honest."

"So long as you live by our rules, you may stay." Ryba paused, and then added, "Westwind is not always an easy place, and we already have powerful enemies—" She broke off at the sound of hooves.

Two riders eased their way down the slope. On the lead

horse, a black stallion, rode a burly man dressed in a green shirt and tunic and brown leather trousers. Behind him rode a thin-faced blond man with a large bow across his back.

The thin man started to reach for the bow.

"I would not touch that bow, not if you wish to live," said Ryba, her voice carrying across the suddenly silent trail and woods.

The burly man reined in the black stallion, a trace of foam at the edge of his mouth, and skittering at his rider's rough handling.

"Nistayna's my woman, and no mountain women are going to take her away. You keep her, and I'll have every man in Linspros here to tear down your fancy tower. Yes, we've heard about your tower, and no tower's going to stop us."

"That would mean a lot of graves," pointed out Ryba.

Nistayna shivered, but stood straight.

"I want my woman back. Now."

"You don't own her." Without taking her eyes off Surba, Ryba asked, "Do you wish to return with him?"

"No. I would die first." The words were soft, but firm. "We both would."

Ryba's lips curled. "They do not like you much."

"They are mine, and they will return with me."

"I think not."

Surba looked at the four bows trained on him. Then he looked at Nylan, who had drawn his blade, but not lifted it. His eyes darted to the blond man, who shook his head. Finally, he answered Ryba, "There are a lot more of you than us, but we'll be back, and we'll tear that tower down stone by stone."

"I see," said Ryba. "So you and your friend just rode after this woman, and I'll bet you didn't even bother to tell anyone where you were going. You just thought you'd ride her down and beat her and take her back. Is that it?"

"Real men don't have to tell anyone where they're going." He shrugged. "All of Linspros knows me. No one walks on Surba."

"I wouldn't think of it," murmured Ryba. She nodded at Berlis, then slowly took out her throwing blade. She rode forward slowly, stopping a dozen paces away from the stallion. "Do you know what this is?"

"It's a toy blade."

Ryba smiled, and the blade flashed from her hand.

The burly man slumped over the saddle, tried to straighten up, and finally did. "Bitch . . . dirty . . . bitch." The stallion whickered and skittered sideways. ". . . unfair . . ."

Nistayna's hand went to her mouth, then her arms went around her daughter, and she turned so the child looked to the forest.

"It's so fair to beat someone who can't flee or fight back," murmured the marshal. "So honorable . . ."

The slender hard-faced man took one look at the dying man, ducked to one side of his mount, and spurred the beast toward the woods.

"Get him!" Ryba ordered, urging the roan after Pretar.

Fierral nocked and released an arrow. So did the other four guards.

The blond man and the horse went down, the horse screaming.

Nylan's legs felt weak, and he forced himself to remain erect, despite the white flashes of death that washed over him. He was glad he hadn't been forced to use his blade, but how often could he avoid it on this frigging brutal planet?

"Damn!" muttered Fierral. "That was a good horse."

Ryba studied the two corpses before riding back to Nistayna. "One always pays for freedom." Her voice was cold. "I hope you will use that freedom well."

Nistayna looked from the marshal to Nylan.

"Angels are not sweet, lady," he added. "They are often just and terrible, and few indeed are strong enough for justice." Even as he spoke, he wondered how just murdering two men had been.

With a sigh, he walked toward Fierral. "Put the bodies on the cart. I'll take them up to the tower. Then, after I unload, I'll send someone down with the cart for the horse. Maybe Blynnal can make a few meals out of it."

Nylan glanced from Fierral to Ryba, still seated on the

roan. Ryba shifted her weight in the saddle, and he realized that the ride had been painful for her.

"This was a setup." She answered his unspoken question. "Either they brought her back, and that proved we could be intimidated or taken, or they came back empty-handed, and set it up for an army. This way, no one knows for sure." She shrugged. "People don't like to send out armies or armed forces when they don't know what happened."

She turned the roan back toward the tower. "Hryessa?"

The young guard drew her mount beside the marshal as the two horses slowly walked uphill.

"Stupid . . . they were stupid . . ." muttered Berlis.

Nylan looked from Ryba to the two refugees, and then to the bodies on the cart. While he understood Ryba's logic, he couldn't say he was pleased with the speed with which it was made and the dispatch with which it was executed. Literally executed, he reflected sardonically.

He turned toward the gray mare, wondering again. Ryba anticipated trouble, and in any "civilized" world, that would be called murder. Yet . . . was preventing abuse and death through death exactly wrong? He shook his head. The problem was that you couldn't always be sure that a killing before the fact was justified, visions or no visions.

He untied the leather leads to the cart horse and flicked them. The wheels *creaakked* as he resumed the long climb up to the ridge, the tower, and the smithy site.

LXXXIII

AT THE *THRAP* on the door, Hissl turns from the window. The knocking continues when he does not move.

"Just a moment." The wizard composes himself and steps forward, his fingers on the hilt of the white-bronze dagger at his belt.

A hooded figure stands at the outside door to Hissl's room and bows. "Have you thought about the keys to your wishes?"

"The keys to my wishes? How would you presume?"

"You are tired of being thought of as the second wizard, as a tool to be used and left aside. You would like position and power in your own right." The hooded figure remains on the landing.

"Stay there." Hissl takes two steps back, still watching his visitor, then circles behind the table with the glass. He looks from the hooded figure to the glass, then concentrates.

Slowly, a shape appears in the swirling mists, the figure of an armsman in brown leathers with a purple sash across the thin breastplate. Behind the figure is a black stone tower.

Hissl does not wipe his sweating brow as he releases his hold upon the glass.

"You are an armsman, but you come from the black tower of the devil angels. I could kill you." He pauses. "I should kill you."

The armsman takes one step into the room and stops. He extends his right hand, missing the index finger and thumb, but does not throw back the hood, for all that his features had just appeared in the screeing glass. "The angels took those from me. I cannot return to Lornth or my family. I offer you the chance for power and position."

"How can you offer me power and position? You have nothing." Hissl laughs. "And you have returned to the lands of Lornth, if not Lornth itself."

"My . . . patron would like to see Westwind fall."

"Westwind?"

"That is what the evil angels call their tower and the lands they stole from the Lord of Lornth."

"If your patron is so powerful, why does he not take this . . . Westwind himself?"

The armsman shrugs. "Lord Nessil could not, not with threescore armsmen. You and the great hunter could, knowing what he knows and what you know, and what I know."

"And what is that?"

"He will have to tell you that."

"I am supposed to take that on faith? Ha!" Hissl laughs again.

"Here is another token." Slowly, the armsman extends an object, bending forward and setting it on the table beside the glass.

Hissl looks at the thunder-thrower, smaller than he had realized. "Why would I need that?"

"So you will not take the hunter on faith."

Hissl licks his lips as he regards the metal object that radiates both chaos and order. Finally, he says, "What does the hunter want?"

"To meet with you. To plan the conquest of Westwind."

"Ha! Young Relyn of Gethen had nearly twoscore armsmen, and he failed. So did Lord Nessil. You, your hunter, and I are supposed to succeed when they did not?"

"I was bid to tell you that more than a third of the angels who faced Lord Nessil are dead. Four are with child or have a babe, and only one thunder-thrower still works. Many of the angels are unhappy with the highest angel, and the black mage has lost much of his magic."

Hissl shrugs. "If your . . . patron is so eager to see me . . . why, have him come to Clynya."

The hooded figure nods. "He said you would bid me so. Before long, he will come."

"I would like to see him." Hissl forces a smile. "That I would."

LXXXIV

"I'LL TAKE HER." In the darkness, Nylan slipped out of his side of the bed, his former lander couch, and picked up Dyliess. "She can't be hungry. You just fed the little pig."

He checked her makeshift diaper—too much remained makeshift within Tower Black—but she was dry. Nylan eased into the rocking chair. "Now . . . now . . . little one . . ."

Despite his gentle singing, Dyliess's moans changed into a full-fledged crying.

Ryba sat up. "I'm tired, but not enough to sleep through that."

The engineer kept rocking, kept singing. Ryba flopped back on one side and rubbed her forehead. Outside the tower, the night wind whispered, its gentle hissing lost behind the cries and songs in the tower.

Dyliess continued to cry for a time. Then her cries dropped off to moans, and the moans to sniffles. Finally, she gave a last snuffle. Nylan continued to rock, and the wind whispered through the cracks in the shutters.

"I can't sleep, now," said Ryba, just above a whisper. "And I have a headache."

Nylan refrained from saying that he had several, and instead patted Dyliess on the back and stood, walking back and forth between the partly open armaglass window and the cradle. Finally sensing she was asleep, he eased Dyliess into the cradle, then immediately knelt and patted her back with one hand while rocking the cradle with the other.

Dyliess took three noisy breaths and settled back to sleep, but Nylan eased off the rocking slowly. After a time, he stopped and returned to his side of the bed, where he sat on the edge, eyes closed, and rubbed his temples with the fingers of his right hand.

"We haven't talked about children," Ryba said quietly into the darkness.

"What about them?"

"You never answered my question. You're being difficult."

"Probably."

"Do you want everything we represent lost?"

Nylan took a deep breath. "I don't know. It seems as though, so long as I build towers, and bridges, and bathhouses, and smithies, everything is fine, but when I say . . .

oh . . . never mind . . . I can't explain how I feel."

"You haven't tried," said Ryba in a reasonable tone.

"You have everything figured out. If we don't kill these two men, dozens will arrive, and we'll have to kill them, too, or be killed. If we don't use the two men as studs, we might have our gene pool contaminated too soon . . ."

"Aren't you being harsh?"

"You've said or done all those." Nylan's shoulders slumped in the darkness, and his eyes dropped to the cradle. Would Dyliess be as coldly reasonable as her mother?

"We landed with twenty-seven women. No sooner had we landed than a local lord showed up wanting to turn us all into serfs or concubines, or worse, and probably to slaughter all three of you men. Since then, we have made not one aggressive gesture toward the locals. We have not raided; we have not stolen. All we have done is build a place to live where they can't and try to survive. The locals are still trying to kill us or cheat us . . . or both. The local women, some of them at least, are risking death to find refuge here. Maybe all this local male behavior is mere lousy socialization. Maybe it's not. Do you want me to gamble after everything that's happened? Do you really want Gerlich's genes to dominate Westwind?"

Nylan rubbed his temples again. Finally, he said, "The killing hurts. Even when I don't do it, it hurts."

"You think I like it?"

"I know you don't," Nylan said. "I'm telling you something different. It's part of this net, or whatever it is, but when someone's killed, a wave of whiteness, like mental acid or something, washes through me."

"Ayrlyn told me the same thing happens to her." Ryba paused. "You both have that ability to help healing. They're probably tied together."

"I wouldn't be surprised."

"We still haven't dealt with the children problem. Do you want me to risk—"

Nylan raised a hand to wave off the question, but realized that Ryba couldn't see the gesture. "You've been right about most things, but . . . and this sounds like a woman . . . I still feel violated."

"I've noticed that. You stay on your side of the couches. Are you . . . do you need time?"

Nylan took a slow deep breath, wondering if time would ever heal anything: "I don't know that time would heal things." He paused. "Do you want me to move my stuff elsewhere?"

"No." Ryba's voice was cool.

"What do you want?"

"I want you to think about things. We can move the couches apart, if that will help."

Nylan puzzled at Ryba's tone, wondering about the wrongness again. "More visions?"

"You could say that."

Nylan could sense the sadness and reserve in the tired voice, and the anger. "I'm sorry."

"So am I, but being sorry doesn't solve things."

He eased his body next to hers, putting his arms around her shoulders.

She pushed him away. "I don't need your comfort."

"Ryba . . ." He put his arms back around her. Who else could hold her, and who else besides Ryba was strong enough to bring them through? His eyes burned, even as his own anger seethed, but he whispered, "Even marshals need to be held."

"I don't need you . . . I don't need anyone."

In the end, he looked into the darkness, while Ryba, the marshal, the farsighted, sobbed silently, again, with her face away from him.

Dyliess slept, and the wind hissed through the window.

LXXXV

THE WATCH TRIANGLE rang once, well before mid-morning, and Nylan ignored the summons to the tower, continuing to lay brick, although he hoped that it signaled Ayrlyn's return, and that she'd been able to find saw blades.

The back wall was complete, and the side walls were thigh-high. Where the front wall would be, the space for the double doors was framed in brick—but only knee-high—and he needed to leave spaces for two windows.

By the time he finished using the last of the mortar, Ayrlyn and the cart were headed down from the ridge. Nylan squinted. There were two people on the cart seat, and two in the cart, and five on horseback. A stranger accompanied the four guards who had gone with the healer on her trading run.

The engineer wiped his forehead with the back of his hand, then looked down at the empty mortar tub. Beside it were the baskets of crushed lava, clay, and what passed for lime. He set the trowel down and started downhill.

Four strange women stood by the causeway with the healer, three shifting their weight nervously from one foot to the other, while the shorter dark-haired woman on one end gentled her mount.

Ayrlyn was supervising the unloading. "The barrels of flour and meal go down to the big shelves in the corner off the kitchen."

With that, Weindre carted off a large barrel.

"The saw blade is for Nylan, but put it up on the fifth level. We haven't built a sawmill yet."

Murkassa laughed at the comment as Ayrlyn handed the blade to Berlis.

"He says he will—then he will." Ayrlyn turned. "Speak of the demon."

"I see you got the saw blade."

"Just one, and it was nearly a gold itself, and I had to promise that it was going up on the Westhorns. That was an easy promise."

"I see you brought some recruits. We picked up one—with a daughter."

"Word is getting around." Ayrlyn gestured toward the tower. "Selitra went to find Ryba."

"I suppose you took them all." Gerlich stepped up beside Ayrlyn.

"Hardly. I must have been approached by a dozen women. I settled on these four."

"Only four. Imagine that."

"Don't push it, Gerlich," Nylan said quietly. "I haven't seen too much game lately, and you don't offer much besides that."

"Game is scarce." Gerlich eased away to the other side of the cart, frankly appraising the three women. Relyn stood beside Cessya, an ironic smile on his face, his semihook resting on his belt.

Nylan still had to make and deliver the clamp for the one-armed man—another area where he'd fallen short, but he didn't have the smithy working.

With the sound of hoofs on the short stretch of pavement heading up toward the stables, the engineer turned. Ryba sat easily on the roan, though Nylan knew riding was slightly painful, but not so painful as their uneasy peace, a peace held together by separated couches, necessity . . . and Dyliess.

All four women turned to Ryba as well, the tallest shivering enough that her discomfiture was obvious to all the guards gathered round.

Ryba reined up, but did not dismount. "So you wish to join the guard of Westwind?"

"If it pleases you, Angel," answered the dark-haired woman, the shortest of the group.

"That's Ydrall," whispered Ayrlyn. "She even had her family's permission, and brought a few things we could use—needles, a few silvers . . . and some dried fruit from their trees—pearapples, they're called. She rides well and can use a blade."

"I'm no angel. I'm the marshal of Westwind. If you choose to remain here, you will have to fight for it. It appears half the men in Candar would wish to beat you down and to tear down our tower stone by stone. Are you willing to fight them, even if they are cousins?" Ryba's voice was hard. "If one is your sister's consort?" Ryba straightened in the saddle. "If you are that determined, you may share what we have, and we will teach you the way of the blade and bow."

The four nodded, and several quietly said, "Yes."

Ryba's eyes turned to Gerlich for a moment, then passed to Fierral. "Will you make the arrangements, guard leader?"

"Yes, Marshal." Fierral turned to the four. "Bring your gear, your things, with me, and we'll find you space on the third level . . ."

As Ryba turned her mount back up toward the stables, and as the four left following Fierral, Nylan remarked, "Too many more, and we'll have to start making bunks and mattresses or pallets."

"We'd better start now," answered the healer. "I've avoided any large towns, places where there would be armsmen, but everywhere I've been, there are women ready to leave. There aren't too many in any one place, but . . ."

"I'm glad you avoided the armsmen. It has to be getting more dangerous." Nylan added quickly, "What do we make mattresses from?"

"I tried not to be too obvious . . . and thank you for saying that you care." Ayrlyn smiled as Nylan swallowed, then said, "Grasses might do for mattress filling, if they're dried well and thoroughly debugged, but we don't have that much cloth to cover them, or sew them."

"I wouldn't sew them all the way," suggested Nylan. "Leave an end open so it could be folded shut. That way—"

"That makes sense. We could tuck dried flowers in there. They might help." Ayrlyn glanced at Cessya. "We need to finish unloading the cart."

Nylan shifted his weight from one sore foot to the other. "I've got more brickwork to do, and I need to raid a lander lock. Maybe I'll do that first."

"A lander lock?" asked Ayrlyn.

"Something I promised for Relyn."

"That's something I like about you, Nylan, another thing," Ayrlyn said before turning to Cessya. "You keep your promises."

A small face peered out the window from the great room, and Nylan waved to Niera. Was she helping with the infants? Or just keeping their mothers company or running errands?

Niera gave the smallest of waves, then ducked back from the window. Nylan crossed the causeway and headed inside.

After reclaiming a tool kit from the fifth level of the tower, Nylan trudged uphill to the lander used for grass storage. "I promised him eight-days ago, longer." He shook his head.

The lander door was ajar, as always, since the lock mechanism had been disconnected and the lock plates removed, and most of the guards didn't bother using the sliding bolt that had replaced the automated system.

After removing three access plates, and sneezing intermittently the whole time from the hay and grass dust that rose every time he moved his boots, he found something that might work—more like an inside lock-plate shim with large screw holes at each end. If he could bend a control arm. That meant removing another access plate and disconnecting the other end of the rod.

Nylan was sweating, his tattered work shirt soaked through, by the time he had all the miscellaneous parts he needed—or thought he needed. But he smiled as he carried them, and the tools, back to the smithy where Cessya greeted him.

"Now that we stowed the trading goods, the healer said I'm supposed to make myself useful, ser," she announced, "and I've got no interest in pulling weeds or sawing timbers. What do you need?"

"More mortar." Nylan grinned. "Are you sure you want to make yourself useful here?"

"Grinding that lava rock for mortar is better than grubbing through the mud or having that fir sap fall all over you. The rock dust washes off. Besides, what you do lasts, and I can say that I helped do it."

"Well . . . I appreciate that honesty. We'll all learn, you and Huldran and I, how to build and operate a smithy."

"Sounds good. I'll be back in a bit. I need to get those mallets and a bucket of water." Cessya inclined her head and was gone.

Nylan set the tools and parts in the corner. Because he needed some of the cruder and heavier tools in the lower level of the tower, he'd start work on Relyn's knife-holder-grip after the midday meal, hoping he wouldn't need to actually forge it, but just bend metal.

He looked around the unfinished smithy. With Cessya's help, it might not be that long before they had the building and the forge done. The charcoal was another story, and trying to forge metal was going to be a disaster.

"A smith, yet? Probably not . . ." He shook his head, then began to carry in bricks.

LXXXVI

NYLAN STUDIED THE completed rear wall of the would-be smithy, and took a deep breath. He was getting tired of the building that seemed endless. His eyes flicked to the high puffy clouds. Would it never end?

His mother had been right, though. No one else cared about his troubles, except Ayrlyn. He smiled, tentatively, then blanked his face at the sound of boots on the road.

"How soon will you have this forge operating?" asked Fierral as she stepped within the uncompleted walls.

Nylan glanced around the area, trying to estimate. "A

while," he finally said. "Only have half the walls done. The forge itself . . ." He shook his head.

The guard leader frowned.

"Why?"

"We don't have that long. We're reaching the limits of the blades you forged. We've never had enough of those bows. And we're getting more and more women showing up. They don't have the training the best locals do. Most of us don't, but we're getting there." Fierral ran her hand through her short-cropped fire-red hair. "What gives us a chance is your weapons."

"But you need more?" asked the engineer.

"We need more of everything. Arrowheads first. Frigging Gerlich—he took off hunting this morning with a good fifty shafts. Showed how few we have left."

Nylan pursed his lips. Gerlich, again. Now what was the man up to?

"Ser . . ." Fierral asked quietly. "Do you really need a smithy built like the tower? We just can't wait for that. The locals won't."

Nylan looked around again. "I can put together a forge of some sort in the next few days—I have to have that—and develop a bellows of some sort. And you'll have to help me make charcoal. You can't smith without coal or charcoal."

"Whatever it takes, ser." Fierral's eyes drifted to the practice yard below the front of the tower. "I'm just a guard leader. I'll never be that much more, not like you or the marshal. But the guards, all of the women, they need the weapons."

Nylan understood that the words were as close to a plea as Fierral would ever offer; that, like him, she kept the doubts and fears and concerns held tightly.

"I'll get working on it," he promised.

"Thank you."

Nylan did not sigh until she was halfway back to the practice yard.

LXXXVII

THE SCOUTS RIDE vanguard nearly a kay before the column that follows, riders under the purpled banners of Lornth and trailed by a far longer column of foot soldiers, levies leavened with professionals from Carpa, Lornth itself, and even from Spidlar and far Lydiar.

As it takes the road skirting the rapids, the army approaches the ford that prefaces the split in the trading road. Less than a kay below the rapids lies the junction of the greater and lesser rivers. Another kay below that is the ford, and beyond that the river flows smooth and deep on its northward course to Rulyarth. On the east side of the ford, the road splits, the left-hand highway following the river, the right slowly rising into the hills until it reaches the west branch of the River Arma where it follows Arma all the way to the city of Armat, capital of Suthya.

By straining, Sillek can see the edge of the fields in the flat below and to the northwest of the hills through which the road passes and the river rapids pass. Those fields are a lighter green than those in Lornth, and half the ground shows brown where the crops have not spread so early in the year.

With the wind out of the east, occasional drops of moisture fly from the rapids to the road, and more than once Sillek looks to the clear sky in surprise, before turning his head toward the dull roaring of the river.

On Sillek's right rides Ser Gethen. Behind them, flanked on each side by hard-faced armsmen, ride Terek and Jissek.

"Fornal was reluctant to remain at the Groves," says Gethen.

"Someone we can trust has to," answered Sillek easily.

"Don't speak of trust loudly, Lord Sillek. Soldiers might presume that such planning implies an expectation of failure." Gethen laughs. "Call that the insight of an old man."

"You're scarcely old, with those few gray hairs," points out the younger man, looking to the low hill beyond, the last hill before the ford. His face tightens as one of the scouts in the van pauses his mount at the hill crest, then turns and gallops back toward the main force.

"I'd say that means a Suthyan force holds the ford," Gethen says.

"Probably."

They continue to ride toward the messenger.

"Suthyans, Lord Sillek," announces the rider in the purple tunic.

"How many?"

"Not more than score twenty, I'd say. Two- to threescore mounted, and none are archers."

Sillek nods. "Stay back on the hill. Don't let them see you. We'll be there presently."

"Yes, ser." The messenger heads back toward the five other scouts.

"What do you plan, Lord?" asks Gethen.

"To destroy them," answers Sillek.

"You have more than enough forces to make them retreat." Gethen turns in the saddle to survey the more than two thousand troops following.

"If I let them escape, then I'll have to fight them later."

"They are outnumbered, and will fight desperately, and that will cost you disproportionately," advises Gethen.

"In a head-to-head battle, yes."

The older man waits. "I await your orders, Lord."

"With the option to disengage if I plan something too stupid, Ser Gethen?" asks Sillek with a smile.

"You are both your father's and your mother's son, I think."

They proceed to the grassy back side of the hill overlooking the ford—and the Suthyans—where Sillek gathers in the chief armsmen and the two wizards.

"Hold the body of the troops just below the hill crest on this side," Sillek orders the chief armsmen. "Keep them still.

About half the mounted troopers will come with me. We'll hold the hill crest in full view of the Suthyans."

Gethen frowns, but says nothing.

Sillek turns to Terek and continues with his instructions. "You and Jissek will be with us, and when I give the order, you're to start casting those firebolts into their ranks. We'll start downhill, slowly, but stay short of really effective bow range. They don't have any Bleyani bowmen, thank the light."

Sillek pauses and scans the faces, then bites back the words he might have said, instead adding, "We'll be showing less force than they have, and by coming downhill, we're also showing that I'm young and inexperienced. The firebolts will get them angry, because that's not fighting fair, and they'll come charging after us—"

"If they don't?" asks Gethen.

Sillek shrugs. "Then we stop a third of the way down the hill and let Terek and Jissek fry as many of them as we can. I'm not in this for honor. The idea is to take the river and Rulyarth as effectively as possible. If you would, Ser Gethen, I'd like you to arrange the forces here so as to trap the Suthyans once they cross the hill crest. Could we set the pikes so their horse couldn't stop in time?"

Gethen purses his lips. Then his lips twist. "You have a nasty turn of thought, Lord Sillek. Nasty . . . but it should work."

The chief armsmen nod in agreement.

Sillek looks to the armsmen. "Don't let anyone charge down that hill. If anyone tries it, I'll have Terek turn him into charred bacon. Let them all know that, if you have to."

The grizzle-bearded armsman on the right coughs and spits from his saddle and onto the damp grass. "Isn't that being a mite hard, ser? Especially when it's an easy fight, us havin' so many more than them?"

"No. We'll need every man we have alive and well when we reach Rulyarth. I'm not interested in glory hounds. You can tell them that, too. I want to win with the fewest lives lost."

The slightest nod from the oldest armsman greets his statement.

Shortly, Sillek leads more than twoscore mounted troops over the hill crest and slowly downhill under a pair of purpled banners. To the right of the hill is the river, and from farther east comes the muted rumbling of rapids above the point where the two rivers meet.

A trumpet sounds from the Suthyan forces, and the Suthyan horse, numbering nearly twice those Sillek leads, form up on the flat before the long gentle slope that leads up toward the banners of Lornth.

The Suthyans wait as Sillek's troop descends. In time, Sillek gestures, and his troopers rein up.

The Suthyans continue to wait.

Sillek shrugs and says, "Make ready, Wizards."

"We are ready, Lord," answers Terek.

"Now!" orders Sillek.

Terek concentrates, almost wavering in his saddle, but a white-red bolt of fire arcs downhill and into the mounted Suthyans.

A single horse rears, flame rising from where the rider had been, and screams as only a horse in pain and agony can.

Jissek follows with a second firebolt, then Terek with a third.

By the time a half-dozen Suthyans have been brought down with wizard fire, some of the horse troopers trot uphill. Then, the trumpet sounds, and all the Suthyans begin the charge toward the apparently outnumbered Lornians.

"A few more firebolts," orders Sillek, before turning to the armsman mounted on the horse beside him. "Let them get within a hundred cubits."

"That's too close, ser. They'll chase if they get to two hundred."

"Two hundred, then. Would you suggest a flat gallop, or a quick trot?"

The other grins. "A *good* commander would order a gallop, get you clear, then a walk. A dumb one always orders a quick trot, then a gallop, and your mount's got nothing left."

Sillek grins back. "A quick trot to the top of the hill, then."

As they have talked, three more Suthyan troopers have been incinerated, and the Suthyan mounted are riding quickly toward them.

"Back!" orders Sillek, after a quick glance at the armsman, who nods. "Quick trot!"

The Suthyans are less than a hundred cubits behind when Sillek's horse crosses the hill crest and he orders his mounted troop to swing to the west.

"Get the pikes set!" snaps Gethen. "Horse on the flanks! Archers—stand fast! Between horse and flank!"

The Suthyan horse is a ragged line by the time the riders surge over the crest chasing the "fleeing" Lornian forces.

Fully twenty horse and riders are spitted on the waiting pikes. The others slow into a milling mass.

"Archers!" shouts Gethen, and the arrows turn half the remaining Suthyans into pincushions.

Perhaps a dozen horse troopers swing out to the flanks, only to be encircled and brought down by Sillek's troopers on the left, and Gethen's reserves on the right.

"Move up! Move up!" snaps Gethen, and the pikemen and the foot move forward.

"Measured pace! Measured pace! Archers forward and to the flanks," orders Gethen.

Sillek brings the wizards back to the hill crest. By now the Suthyan foot are more than halfway up the hill.

"Firebolts!" he orders.

Jissek strains, and a small ball arches into the left side. Greasy smoke rises, along with the shriek of a man who rolls in the damp grass—in vain as he writhes before subsiding into a blackened lump.

"Terek."

The chief wizard casts another bolt, and two Suthyan troopers turn to flaming brands.

A trumpet bugles, and the Suthyan forces begin to trot uphill.

"Idiots," mutters Sillek, looking over his shoulder to see

that the pikes are set in the forward position. Then he signals, and his horse troopers reform in a double line, waiting.

As the Suthyan forces halt at the hill crest, wavering in sight of the pikes, Gethen drops his arm, and arrows sheet through the Suthyans.

The line wavers, and then breaks, ignoring the shouted commands from the Suthyan commanders.

Gethen swings his arm, and the Lornian horse charges.

Less than twoscore Suthyans scramble into the river, and less than half those make it across the ford.

On the west side of the river, Sillek reins up and watches. His eyes stray, not to the hundreds of Suthyan bodies, nor to the fallen horse, but to the relative handful of fallen Lornians. He turns to Gethen.

Gethen cleans his blade and turns to Sillek. "They'll call you a butcher, Lord."

"I don't care what they call me, just so long as they respect me." Sillek takes a deep breath and looks to see that they are beyond easy earshot of the wizards and the chief armsmen, who are directing the looting and burial details. "Fighting is not glorious, and anyone who thinks so . . ." He does not finish the thought, but shakes his head.

"Many in your land would dispute that, Lord."

"Even as I save their sons, yet." Sillek laughs harshly. "Would you dispute me, Gethen?"

"No." Gethen laughs harshly. "You have learned young what many never learn. But do not speak it except to those as gray-haired as I, or those who have buried sons lost in useless battles, not unless you wish to kill them."

"I won't." Sillek tightens his lips. "Is this useless battle?"

"It is less useless than most, My Lord. Else I would not be here."

"On to Rulyarth."

"On to Rulyarth," echoes Gethen.

"After our gloriously victorious troops claim their just rewards," Sillek adds darkly and under his breath.

LXXXVIII

NYLAN TAPPED THE brick level on the mortar and troweled away the excess mortar. That finished the base of the forge. Sometime, Huldran and Cessya and the others could set the roof timbers. He had to finish the forge and start making more weapons . . . for more killing.

"Need more mortar, ser?" asked Huldran.

"No." He glanced toward the west, but the sun was just above the peaks, and they wouldn't have much time before the evening triangle rang. He rubbed his shoulders. After a year, things should be easier, but it didn't seem that way. He paused as he saw Ayrlyn hurrying toward the unfinished smithy. "I sense trouble."

"We've got more than enough, ser," said Huldran. "That new one, Desain, she thinks that showers are unhealthy, and the other one, Ryllya, she had a fit when the healer cut her hair. Said her strength was in her hair. Things like that remind me how strange this place is."

"It is strange." Nylan wondered what was driving Ayrlyn.

"Here comes the healer," announced Huldran.

"Gerlich is gone," Ayrlyn announced even before she stepped inside the brick-framed doorway of the smithy. Her face was flushed.

"How do you know?"

"Day before yesterday, he said he'd be gone for two days—that he'd been having trouble finding game. He took a mount and the old gray for a pack animal. Llyselle found that out when she was cleaning the stables. She told me, and I told Ryba. Today, I happened to look at his space, and both bows were gone. There were rags folded where his clothes were. I started checking, and he took all the coins in the strongbox I had hidden on the fifth level." Ayrlyn wiped her forehead. "Ryba has the golds somewhere, but that's a lot of silvers, and a bunch of coppers. He also made off with a handful of blades—the poor ones in the back of the chest."

Nylan nodded. "He's also been sneaking arrows out of the tower."

"You didn't say anything?"

Huldran's eyes widened as they moved from Ayrlyn to Nylan and back again.

"I didn't know. All I knew was that every time he went hunting he came back with a few arrows missing, sometimes more than a few shafts. Then the morning he left, Fierral told me he'd taken fifty shafts hunting. I just thought he was a poor shot, but didn't want to admit it. Now . . ."

"It makes sense," pointed out Ayrlyn.

"Narliat's departure was no accident, either, then," Nylan continued. "That bastard Gerlich has something arranged." He turned to Huldran. "Can you clean up? The healer and I need to find the marshal."

"Yes, ser."

The engineer and the healer headed toward the tower.

"Where is she?" asked Ayrlyn.

"Up in the tower, I think. I carted Dyliess around this morning. Bricklaying is slow with an infant strapped to you, but she liked the motion. I only had trouble if I stood still."

Nylan and Ayrlyn found the marshal on the fifth level, working with one of the newcomers. Saryn sparred with another and Fierral with a third. At a break in the sparring, Nylan motioned to Ryba.

The marshal stopped. "With two of you, it must be serious." Ryba turned to Saryn. "Desain needs to stop letting her wrist droop."

"I can manage that." Saryn laughed.

"And Fierral," added Ryba. "Nistayna doesn't have any follow-through. She's afraid she'll hurt someone. If she doesn't, they'll kill her."

Ryba racked her wand, and the three walked up the stone steps.

On the top level of the tower, Ellysia sat in the rocking

chair, holding Dephnay on her knee with one hand and rocking the cradle containing Dyliess with the other, the cradle
that now rested at the foot of the two separated lander
couches.

"Thank you, Ellysia," said Ryba. "You can go now." She
crossed the room and opened both windows wide.

Behind her Ellysia shivered as the wind gusted into the
room, then stood and picked up Dephnay. Dyliess started to
murmur the moment the unattended cradle began to slow.

As Ellysia, shivering, her face flushed, started down the
steps, Ryba eased Dyliess from the cradle. "You're about to
wake up anyway, little one."

Ryba sat in the rocking chair and unfastened her shirt.
Dyliess began to nurse, as greedily as always, reflected
Nylan.

"What is this problem?" asked the marshal.

"Gerlich is gone," said Ayrlyn. "He also took all the silvers from the lower strongbox."

"I checked the golds this morning. They're all here," Ryba
said flatly. "He doesn't have enough coin to do that much."

"He still stole close to four golds in silver and copper,"
pointed out Ayrlyn.

"He took everything he could sneak out, including more
than fifty arrows, a packhorse, and some of the more battered blades," Nylan added.

"Those blades he took are worth close to five golds. He
could buy close to a score of armsmen," explained Ayrlyn.
"Hired blades are cheap here."

"Life is cheap here," said Ryba. "Look at those cairns."
Her head inclined toward the open tower window.

"You think he'll do that?" Nylan's guts already gave him
one answer.

"He will, and he will be back, with an army behind him,"
agreed Ryba tiredly, shifting Dyliess from one breast to the
other.

"You see this?" asked Nylan.

"Not all of it, just a fragment, just enough."

Ayrlyn frowned, but said nothing.

"What Gerlich took won't be enough, and he knows it," Ryba pointed out.

"Narliat left earlier than Gerlich," said Ayrlyn.

The triangle rang for the evening meal.

"He's acting as Gerlich's advance agent. Gerlich tries to let someone else face the dangers first." Ryba looked down at Dyliess. "Easy there . . . easy . . ." A rueful smile crossed her face.

"Should we beef up the standing guard?" asked Ayrlyn.

"For how long? We still need food. We need to get more things working, like the smithy, and possibly a few cows or goats. Not every guard can nurse, and we won't always have guards with infants at the same time. Guards have to work and guard, or Westwind will fall. I don't know when Gerlich will try his attack. The only thing we can do is make sure that all the guards have their weapons at hand, whatever they're doing. Fierral can build a permanent watchpost on top of the ridge, with another warning triangle. Outside of that . . ." Ryba shrugged.

Nylan and Ayrlyn exchanged glances.

"What can we do, besides what we're already doing?" asked Ryba. "Let's go eat." She slipped Dyliess from her lap into the carrypack, stood, and headed down the stairs. "You've eaten, little pig. It's your mother's turn."

Ayrlyn glanced at Nylan and shrugged.

He shrugged back.

As they entered the great room, guards were still straggling in. Nylan almost stopped short at the third table below the first two. It only had one bench, but three of the new guards sat there, flanking Istril and Weryl.

Nylan paused. "Hello there, young fellow."

Weryl gurgled. Nylan patted his shoulder.

Istril smiled. "He's good."

"I'm sure he is." Nylan returned the smile, hiding a certain dismay. How had he ended up with three children born within a season of each other? His eyes flicked to Ryba's back, but he kept smiling as he nodded to the three newcomers before turning. One was called Nistayna—that he remembered.

A spicy scent Nylan had not smelled before filled the area, and he looked toward the big pot that Kadran set in the middle of the table.

"Something new," announced the cook. "You take one of those flat biscuit things and pour a ladle of this over the biscuit."

"It better be good," muttered Weindre, loud enough for those at all three tables to hear.

"It's too good for you," snapped Kadran.

Even the newcomers at the third table smiled briefly.

Ryba slid into her chair, and Nylan and Ayrlyn sat on the benches across from each other.

When the woven grass basket came to Nylan, he broke off a piece of bread, sniffed it, and drew in the spicy aroma. "This even smells good."

"That's Blynnal's new bread," mumbled Relyn from beside Ayrlyn. "It's much better."

"It tastes like real bread," added Huldran.

Nylan took a thick biscuit and then two ladles full of the main course, a thin stew or thick sauce filled with chunks of meat and assorted chunks of other things, presumably roots or other vegetable matter, and poured it over the flat biscuit.

He looked at the brown mass dubiously, then sniffed. Nothing smelled burned or rancid. In fact, the aroma was pleasant, somewhere between minty and something else. Finally, he took a mouthful of meat, sauce, and biscuit.

Ayrlyn and Ryba watched.

"You're braver than I am," murmured the healer.

Nylan nodded, chewed, and swallowed. "It's good. I can't tell what's in it, but it's good." As he spoke, he could feel his forehead warming, then his face, and then his mouth and throat. "Whewww!" He reached for his mug and downed the cold water. It didn't help, but the bread did.

"Do you still think it's good?" asked Ryba with a smile, patting Dyliess's back as she squirmed in the chest carrypack.

Nylan nodded, and took a second mouthful, a much smaller one.

"Another Blynnal special?" Ayrlyn asked Relyn.

He looked puzzled.

"Did Blynnal cook this?"

"Yes. She is a good cook. You are fortunate to have her." Relyn ate without water, and without apparent discomfort.

"They clearly like food hotter than we're used to," observed Ryba.

After taking a very small bite of her dinner, Ayrlyn nodded.

Nylan broke off another chunk of bread, but kept eating, ignoring Ayrlyn's amused smile.

LXXXIX

NYLAN WIPED HIS forehead and looked down at the coals, at his quick-built forge. Without a chimney and in a structure without completed walls, with no doors, open gaps for windows, and no roof, Nylan was trying to implement a combination of basic metallurgy and low-level technology, and use his particular abilities with the local magic field to create a piece of metal shaped and strong enough to pierce plate armor and to maim or kill those who wore such armor—or do worse to those who didn't.

He'd already tried to melt the iron, and that hadn't worked. It took both charcoal and green wood, and the bellows, and half the time the iron burned rather than melted.

As he thought of the arrows and blades Fierral had pleaded for, he sighed twice—once for the thought that damned little was settled in human affairs without some kind of force and once for his unfulfilled promise. He still hadn't finished the clamp device he'd promised Relyn—another tool of war, except, for the one-handed man, it seemed more defensive than offensive.

Nylan raised his eyes to Huldran, standing by the bellows. The bellows hadn't been that hard, just three pieces of wood joined with leftover synthetic sheeting and using flap valves and a nozzle. Creating a tube under the center of the thrown-together brick forge had been tricky, finally accomplished by having Rienadre fire more than a dozen bricks with a hole in the center and lining them up and mortaring them in place. The air nozzle was a modified lander fuel sieve—greatly modified.

The first charcoal burn hadn't worked. More than half the wood turned into ashes. Another quarter hadn't burned at all. About a quarter had been transformed into charcoal. The second burn had gone better. Maybe half the wood had become charcoal. So after more than an eight-day, Nylan had two heaping piles of charcoal behind the smithy and a half-dozen disgruntled and sooty guards. They hadn't cared that he was sooty.

It was early summer, and the purple starflowers had bloomed and were fading, and the crops seemed to be taking, at least the potatoes, which were critical. One of the remaining ewes had lambed, and three of the mares had foaled, and yet another woman, older than the others, had claimed refuge. Nylan was losing track of all the names of the newcomers. Names or not, Fierral slammed them into blade and bow training, and into logging or field work—except for the timid Blynnal, who had transformed mealtime from an ordeal into something less arduous.

Nylan looked down at the open forge. To save the charcoal, he had built the fire with wood and let it burn down to coals before easing the charcoal into place.

Now, he had two hammers, and a makeshift anvil created by cold-hammering sheet alloy around a stone block wedged between the sides of a green spruce log buried in the ground. The anvil, such as it was, stood waist-high. Nylan hoped that was correct. He had one chisel, and a makeshift pair of tongs.

Huldran still stood by the bellows, waiting. "Tell me when, ser."

"I wish I really knew," Nylan muttered to himself, as he took the square of alloy, one of the ones he knew was iron-based and lower-temperature-rated, in the tongs and thrust it into the coals. "Now . . . slowly."

The engineer watched until the metal finally turned cherry-red, when he put it on the anvil and picked up the chisel. "Hit the chisel," he told Huldran, and the guard struck the chisel squarely.

Nylan tried not to wince. "You hold the tongs, and let me have the hammer."

Huldran took the tongs without comment, and Nylan brought the hammer down, trying to use his senses to find some grain, some pattern in the metal. In a dozen strikes, he finally had a shape that looked remotely like the war arrow that lay in the unframed and unshuttered front window.

Nylan reclaimed the tongs, and sent Huldran back to the bellows.

After the next heat, he bent the sides back and forged or welded them back on each other. With the third heat, he drew out the edges. With the fourth came more ordering through his senses, and finally a slightly overlarge arrowhead lay on the alloy anvil.

"Going to have to do this quicker—or find some other way."

"Could you cast them?" asked Huldran.

"Right now, I don't see how. This is as hot as I can get this with just charcoal, and the metal's nowhere close to melting. Casting would be a lot easier, but I can't seem to melt it without burning it."

"What about copper or bronze?"

Nylan shrugged. "Even if we melted down the copper buried in the landers, copper arrowheads wouldn't do much good against even iron plate."

"Oh . . ."

"Exactly." Nylan lifted the tongs. "So I'd best get a lot faster."

When Nylan looked up from the sixth arrowhead, he could sense that the charcoal was almost gone. Each of the killer arrowheads had been easier, but each still took time.

Since the wood made a good base and stretched the charcoal, he set down the hammer. "We'll build up the fire with those heartwood logs. Then we'll take a break while it burns down to coals. All right?"

"That's fine by me, ser." Huldran blotted her sweat-dampened forehead. "Do you think smithing's always this hard?"

"We're making a lot of mistakes. I just don't know what they are, but it's always been hard work." He walked out through the open space that was meant for doors to the pile of split and cut logs. Huldran followed.

Once the open forge was blazing, and Nylan hoped the heat wouldn't crack too many bricks, he headed down the road toward the tower. Under the clear sky, the sun beat down, so much that he still did not cool off much once he was away from the forge.

He walked across the short causeway, but stopped short of the door. He could sense people in the great room—guards and infants. Between meals, the great room had become almost a de facto nursery, which made a sort of sense to Nylan, because it had the most ventilation and the best light.

After entering the tower, he slipped along the side away from the great room and to the bathhouse, where he managed to remove some sweat, soot, and grime. Then he squared his shoulders and headed for the great room.

Siret was the closest to the door, and she had Kyalynn in one arm, and Dephnay in the other.

Nylan looked down at his silver-haired daughter, her eyes the darker green of Siret's. Kyalynn looked back. He smiled. She did not, although her mother did. Slowly, he extended his index finger, gently letting it slide into Kyalynn's open palm. Almost as slowly, her chubby fingers wrapped around his finger. He wiggled his finger, and her hands tightened. He wiggled again, and Kyalynn gurgled.

"She's strong," he said.

"Yes." Siret smiled again.

"I'm sorry. I didn't know," he confessed.

"I know that. The marshal told me a long time ago. Do you mind?"

"Mind?" asked Nylan, wiggling his finger to keep Kyalynn interested.

"That I agreed to have your child? After the battle with the demons, I thought . . . I never would have a child." The silver-haired guard shook her head gravely. "I hadn't thought that would ever upset me, but it did. It really did. Then after the first battle here, I decided that . . ." Siret paused. "You're not mad at me?"

"I was a little upset—but not at you," he admitted.

"You came when I—when we—needed you."

"I didn't know then, either, but I knew you needed help."

Siret looked down for a moment, then met his eyes. "I am not yours, and I will never belong to any man. But . . . I'm glad you are Kyalynn's father."

Nylan finally looked away. "It's hard for me."

"You are a healer, as well as an engineer. The other healer . . . you know that she cries when she thinks no one is listening?"

Ayrlyn, the self-contained and competent healer and trader? "No. I didn't know. Or . . . maybe I didn't want to see it." He paused. "And you, Siret, what about you? The night vision, the feeling that you can sense things you cannot see?"

"They help. This is a strange world, but in many ways better than what I left."

"I trust you will always find it that way." Nylan cleared his throat. "And that you keep working on those new skills."

"I hope that Kyalynn has such skills. I wouldn't want her to be just a guard." Siret's green eyes darted toward the stairs, as if to ask if Ryba were descending.

Kyalynn yawned.

"Well . . . work on your own skills." Nylan wiggled his finger out of the sleepy Kyalynn's hand and stood.

Siret offered a smile and rose. "I need to put them to sleep while I can. Ellysia can watch them while I practice and do a few things for me."

Istril and Weryl were at the next table, and Nylan crossed the stone tiles. Weryl's eyes were already green, and they locked in on Nylan as the engineer approached his son.

"He knows his father," Istril said quietly.

"I should have realized earlier. There were clues there, but I just never thought . . ." Nylan shook his head.

"I'm not upset. It was my choice. You've saved my life twice, you know." Istril gave a wry smile. "And I don't even know what to call you. Part of me thinks of you as an officer and 'ser,' and part as Nylan."

"Whatever you feel comfortable with."

" 'Nylan' in private and 'ser' in public."

Nylan smiled. "All right."

"You know," Istril said quietly, "I'm stuck here. When I've been hunting, I've gone down lower, especially last summer. The air was so hot and thick that I felt like I couldn't breathe. Ayrlyn can do it. She's from Svenn. I couldn't. The guards that go with her—they all lose weight, and it takes them days to feel good after they return. That's why Ayrlyn takes different ones each time. You're only half Sybran. You could handle the heat and thick air. So could Weryl. He's young . . . but I couldn't." She shrugged. "It's not bad here, though, and it's getting better. I'm glad Blynnal came."

Weryl made a stretching motion, as if to reach out to Nylan. Nylan took the small hand and let Weryl's fingers curl around his.

"Oooohhh . . ."

"He likes you." Istril shifted the boy onto her other knee, closer to Nylan.

"I'd hope so."

"What are you going to do?"

"Right now, I'm trying to figure out a faster way to forge arrowheads. We need a lot of them. If I can solve that problem, I might go to work on planning and building a sawmill . . ."

In time, Nylan finally stood.

"I understand, Nylan, if you don't want to spend too much time with me. But keep stopping to see Weryl." Istril's face was calm, somewhere between content and resigned.

"I will." *What else can I do?* he thought. *They are my children. Why . . . why did you do this to me? Why did I refuse to see what was happening? Because it was easier?* He forced a smile, which softened as Weryl "gooed" again.

Either Istril or Siret would have been warmer to him than Ryba, and Siret really wasn't that interested—or so she said—in any man. Yet he never even considered them—because he was still bound in the officer-marine separation? And Ayrlyn, crying in the night?

Again, nothing was quite what it seemed on the surface, even with people. He supposed people still thought he and Ryba slept together. That was another problem they hadn't resolved—or he hadn't. Surprisingly, Ryba hadn't pushed. What else did she know?

He snorted once, ironically, as he started up the steps to the fifth level. Wasn't that always the way it was? Ryba knowing, and not saying, and Nylan the great mage, bewildered and struggling. He snorted again.

In the dimness of the fifth level, Ellysia was practicing, puffing, with Saryn, Hryessa, and Ydrall. Nylan eased around the sparring and toward the section of storage shelves above the unused weapons laser. He scooped the parts he had taken from the lander and roughly bent into shape into a worn leather bag that had been some poor raider's purse.

Then he headed back down to the lower level. As he passed the third level, he saw Siret rocking Kyalynn to sleep. Dephnay, on her knee, looked wide awake. Nylan found Relyn in the space off the kitchen, laboriously smoothing what looked to be a wooden tray.

"That looks good," observed the smith-engineer.

"I said I'd help her. She's too quiet." Relyn looked up. "Blynnal. She won't ask for anything."

"Some people won't. She's improved the food a lot."

Relyn grinned. "Sometimes, I get a little extra."

"I haven't forgotten my promise," Nylan said, taking out the pieces of metal. "Like everything around here, it's taking longer. If you'll come here, I'd like to measure these. I'll probably have to hot-hammer—or whatever they call it—these together, but I wanted to check the fit first."

Relyn extended his hook.

Nylan slipped the pieces in place, then nodded toward the knife. "I need to see how tight it should be."

"As tight as you can make it, Mage."

The knife slid into the makeshift clamp easily, too easily. Nylan studied the construction, then took his own knife and scratched where the changes should be.

"We'll try again."

"You do not admit failure, do you?"

Nylan laughed, harshly. "Life is trial and error. Those who succeed are those who survive their failures and keep trying. So far, I've been lucky."

Relyn looked back at the tray. "It is not luck—that I know. You understand how the world works." He smiled wryly. "I hope to learn that, too."

"You probably know more about that than I do," admitted Nylan.

"Never, Mage. You refuse to accept how much you do know."

"That's all," Nylan said, uneasy with Relyn's words. "Now, I have to make it work, and then forge scores and scores of arrowheads."

"You will," promised Relyn.

"I hope so." Nylan wished he were as sure as the young man from Carpa, but when he returned to the smithy, he carried the pieces for Relyn's clamp.

Huldran was waiting, and they loaded more of the charcoal into the forge.

XC

ZELDYAN EASES HERSELF into the armchair facing the alcove where the lady Ellindyja embroiders.

"You do me honor, Lady," offers Ellindyja.

"You are the Lady of Lornth," responds Zeldyan easily.

"No longer. That is your position, now, but you are most kind to recall my past . . . honor." The needle carries crimson thread into the white fabric. "How might I be of help?"

"I thought you might like to hear. There was a dispatch from Lord Sillek, Lady," answers Zeldyan.

"And you were thoughtful enough to come to tell me, and in your condition, too. I appreciate that. I do." Ellindyja knots the crimson strand and threads green through the eye of the needle.

"I am well indeed, only sore, and that is passing. Nesslek is strong, and healthy indeed, and for that I am glad." Zeldyan laughs. "But I stray. Lord Sillek has taken the ford below the great fork and nears Rulyarth. According to the dispatch, they have destroyed nearly a thousand Suthyans, and less than that number stands ready to defend Rulyarth. The city was never walled, you know," she adds conversationally.

"I had heard that somewhere," Ellindyja assents. "You understand these things, I can tell. It must help, being raised in an honorable warrior's holding."

"I was fortunate," Zeldyan says, shifting her slender figure in the chair. "My mother was learned, and taught my father and her children. My father was skilled in arms and taught her and us both honor and arms."

"He taught arms to the lady Erenthla?" Ellindyja raises her eyebrows.

"But, of course. He wanted no helpless women in his

holding." Zeldyan smiles as she rises. "I must go, but I did want you to know that Lord Sillek is well."

"I appreciate your thoughtfulness, Lady."

Zeldyan inclines her head.

As the door closes behind her, Ellindyja snaps the green thread, and knots it in a quick, hard motion.

XCI

THE ALLOY IN the tongs began to change color, getting redder under the influence of the coals. Above the open doorway to the unfinished smithy, a fly droned, circling toward the sweating smith-engineer.

Arrowheads! Nylan was already sick of dealing with them, despite the acclaim the product had received from Istril and Fierral. Roughly two hundred had been finished. Nylan smiled. That meant two hundred that Fierral and the marines had to smooth and sharpen and fletch—and that also meant netting birds. Relyn had proved helpful there, explaining how to net them and which ones worked better.

With the tongs, Nylan flipped the red-hot metal onto the now-dented makeshift anvil, then began hot-cutting the shape of the arrowhead with the chisel and hammer while Huldran took over the tongs.

The hammer rose, and fell, and Nylan moved the chisel. Sparks of metal flew with each impact. One rough shape lay on the anvil, and Nylan began the cutting on the next. He concentrated on following the hidden grain of the metal, letting his senses guide him, even more than his sight.

That guidance resulted in stronger arrowheads, but each was subtly different from the next—not enough, Nylan hoped, to affect their flight.

Through the roof beams, the sun beat into the smithy, and sweat dripped down Nylan's face. He brushed back a fly, twice, before it buzzed across the meadow toward the smelly sheep from whence it had probably come. Nylan blinked back sweat. While he and Huldran forged, around them Cessya and, surprisingly to Nylan, Nistayna had worked on getting the roof timbers in place, but the roof had to wait for the completion of the forge itself.

Each day, after completing forging, Nylan mixed up some mortar and added to the hood and chimney of the forge. The door and windows could wait.

Before the metal cooled enough to need reheating, he had five shapes cut. With each day, his strokes, while probably crude compared to the local smiths, had gotten surer, and the finished product needed less and less smoothing.

Nylan nodded, and Huldran swung the uncut section of metal back into the coals. The smith-engineer brushed the sweat off his forehead with the back of his forearm, then took the tongs. "Need more air, Huldran."

The stocky blonde began to pump the bellows. While some air wheezed out through the sides of the bellows, most came up through the air nozzle, and the coals glowed hotter.

Nylan walked out to the dwindling pile of charcoal—another problem—and used a shovel to bring in another scoop, which he distributed evenly. Then he flipped the metal to get a better heat distribution.

He lifted the metal onto the anvil and turned to Huldran. "You try one."

Huldran just nodded and slowly picked up the hammer and chisel.

Clung!

Nylan winced as he felt the shiver up the guard's arm. "Angle the chisel a shade—to the outside. It cuts cleaner, and it doesn't hurt as much."

The second blow did not ring quite so off-key. Huldran finished two rough arrow-shaped forms before Nylan lifted the metal back into the forge.

"Harder than it looks, ser," Huldran admitted as she pumped the bellows.

"Yes. You didn't do badly. My first were pretty crude. I'll do the next batch, and then you can do some."

"You're a lot faster, and Fierral needs a lot of arrows."

"I know, but you need some practice, too. Westwind needs more than one person who can handle things like this. Otherwise, an accident—or an arrow from one of the locals— could wipe out everything I've learned."

When the metal came out of the forge again, cherry-red, Nylan resumed cutting. The two kept working until past mid-morning, when they came to the end of the sheet of alloy. All that remained were a few scraps that Nylan swept into an already battered wooden bucket.

"Someday, I'll work on reforging the scraps into stock. I think that's what they call it." He wiped his forehead. "We need a break, and I need to find another panel in one of the landers that won't take forever to unfasten."

"I'll bank the fire," Huldran volunteered.

"Thanks." Nylan blotted the sweat out of his eyes again, then began to walk downhill along the trail he hoped would someday be a real road.

To the south, by the cairns, grazed the handful of sheep. Desain and Ryllya were weeding and working the fields, along with Selitra, who was supervising while weeding and cleaning out the small irrigation ditches.

A cart, carrying a stack of rough-cut planks for the smithy roof—slate was out, now that the laser was gone—creaked down from the ridge. Weindre walked beside the cart horse, one hand briefly touching her blade.

On the flat exercise area beyond the causeway, two figures sparred.

One was Cessya, the other Relyn. Relyn was using the knife and clamp over his hook, but had fashioned a wooden cover for the blade.

Nylan stopped and watched for a time as the wooden wands flashed.

The two paused, and Relyn turned to Nylan. "It works. I have much to learn about using a blade left-handed, but the knife helps."

"He's . . . better . . . than that . . ." puffed Cessya. "Glad he wasn't this good back when he attacked."

"I must be better," Relyn said. "My left arm is not as strong as my right."

"Manure," responded Cessya.

Nylan offered a wave that was a half-salute and started across the causeway. His arms still ached. Would he ever get used to the heavy labor involved with smithing—or everything in a low-tech culture?

He crossed the causeway, but stopped short of the tower door, thinking about the children and their mothers in the great room. He didn't want to face company, not when three of the four children were his, and he'd be obligated to comment on each, play with each, and possibly even sing a lullaby to each. He did most of the time, anyway, since he'd finally made his uneasy peace with himself, if not with Ryba. Her high-handedness still made him seethe, but that wasn't his children's fault. Still, he wasn't up to infants this particular morning.

Their mothers don't have any choice. He pursed his lips, then, after a moment, headed for the sheltered corner formed between the bathhouse and tower walls. He just wanted to be alone.

That wasn't going to be. As Nylan neared the corner of the tower wall, he heard the sound of the lutar. He stopped and listened, recognizing Ayrlyn's clear voice.

Oh, Nylan was a smith, and a mighty mage was he.
With lightning hammer and an anvil of night forged he.
From the Westhorns tall came the blades and bows of the
*   night,*
Their lightning edges gave the angels forever the height.

Oh, Nylan was a mage, and a mighty smith was he.
With rock from the heights and a lightning blade built he.
On the Westhorns tall stands a tower of blackest stone,
And it holds back the winter's snows and storms all
*   alone . . .*

When the notes died, Nylan stepped around the corner and looked at Ayrlyn, sitting on a stone above the ditching.

"That's awful," muttered Nylan. "Just awful."

"Who was it that told me the songs that people remember and love to sing are generally awful?"

"Those weren't about me."

"That makes it different?" asked the healer.

Nylan eased himself onto the ground. His feet and legs were tired, too, and it wasn't even midday.

"You're still doing arrowheads?"

He nodded. "I wish I could get the coals hot enough to melt the metal and cast them, but when I try that it takes green heartwood, and the metal burns, and I can't damp it. With plain charcoal, it's hard enough just to get the metal hot enough for cutting them. Some of those arrowheads are going to rip up the people they hit."

"Isn't that the idea?"

"Unfortunately, but I still have trouble with the idea that people only respond to force."

"It's especially clear on this planet."

"It's clear everywhere, but in a high-technology setting, it's easier to ignore. On the powernet, you see a de-energizer beam, and a mirror tower, and, poof, the tower's gone. You don't see the demons die. If someone commits a murder, the government carts them off, and, poof, they're lase-flashed into dust. Here it's obvious and slow. I seem to feel it more and more." His eyes turned to Ayrlyn. "I suspect you do, too."

"I get so nauseated I can't hold anything down." Her eyes dropped. "It seems so . . . weak. I tell myself it must be in my mind, but the reaction's so immediate, so physical . . ."

"It's more like a splitting headache for me. The last few times, it's been so intense I couldn't see or move for a moment or two."

"Great survival reactions for a violent culture." Ayrlyn's tone was dry.

"It's more violent here because Ryba's changing things, and change usually is violent."

"We're part of that change," Ayrlyn said. "And there's not much way to get around that."

After a long silence, Nylan finally asked, "You're really not going to sing that song, are you?"

"No. I've got another trading run to make." Ayrlyn laughed. "So I won't be singing it. Not now. I'll teach it to Istril. It's simple enough, and she's actually getting passable with the simple lutar we built. It doesn't have the depth of tone this one does, but it works."

"Why are you going to teach her that song?"

"Why not?" answered Ayrlyn. "As many untrustworthy people have said, 'Trust me.'"

"I guess I have to." He stood. "But the song's awful . . . 'a mighty mage'? You have to be joking." He paused, then asked, "Is it safe for you to keep trading?"

"It's as safe as sitting here waiting to be attacked, if I'm careful. We avoid the larger towns, and I've got some ideas where this Lord Sillek has his garrisons."

"I don't know. I don't like it." He shook his head.

"I'll be all right."

"Be careful."

"I will."

"And try not to sing that song anywhere."

"As these things go, it's a good song."

"Try not to have it sung for a while." *Not until I'm dead, preferably, and I hope that's a long while,* he added to himself.

"After I teach it to Istril . . . we'll think about it."

"Please don't." Nylan frowned. "I've sat around too long. After I get something to drink, I've got to find another lander panel to turn into low-tech weapons of destruction."

"Good luck." Ayrlyn rose. "I'm going back down to the loggers. It's amazing how experience changes people's views. After the cold of the winter, now all they can think about is making sure there's enough wood for next winter. That bothered them more than the short rations."

"Food wasn't that short. How are we doing now?"

"Those horses have helped a lot, and so have our local re-

cruits. There's more out there in the forest than we knew."
Ayrlyn shrugged. "For now, we're all right, but we'll need a
lot more coin for supplies—a lot more."

Nylan started back uphill, conscious that Ayrlyn's eyes
stayed on his back for a long time.

XCII

HISSL GLANCES AT the candle, then at the darkness outside.
A lamp in the barracks courtyard casts a faint glow across
the wooden steps that lead up to his quarters.

He looks at the beaker of wine on the table, already beginning to turn, for all that he has had the bottle less than a
day, then back out through the window. Beyond the courtyard, on the far side, the windows of Koric's room are dark.

"Out with his woman," snorts Hissl. "He has his power
and his woman, and Terek rides beside Sillek, and I . . . I wait
for an attack that will never come, not while I am here. Not
while Ildyrom knows I am here."

He fills the beaker from the bottle and drinks fully half
what he has poured, wincing as he swallows.

A sense of unease fills him, and he looks at the flat glass
on the table. Leaving the beaker half-full, he walks to the
doorway.

A tall figure slips up the stairs, gracefully, yet not
furtively, followed by a second smaller figure.

Hissl touches his dagger, but does not draw it as the others approach. Instead, he opens the door and waits.

The man who stops in the doorway fills it, and towers over
both Hissl and the sturdy armsman in the cloak behind the
stranger.

"I understand you bid me visit you, Wizard?" asks the visitor in accented speech. The tall man wears only a sleeve-
less tunic in the cool evening, yet his brow is damp, and his

face appears flushed in the indirect light.

Hissl nods. "I did. What would a warrior, a true warrior from the Roof of the World, wish from a poor wizard?"

"To make our fortune. To keep the world from being changed. To provide you with fame and position." The tall stranger glances toward the table and the flat glass and the beaker. "Might we come in?"

"Of course." Hissl steps back and offers a deep and ironic bow. "My humble quarters await you."

The tall man takes the high stool and leans forward, waiting until Hissl seats himself. The cloaked armsman stands by the door.

"Why have you taken so long?" Hissl begins.

"I beg your pardon, Ser Wizard, but it has taken somewhat longer to accomplish the necessary."

"The necessary?"

The stranger smiles coldly. "To travel here. To raise coins. Such coins, I understand, are necessary. Gold, after all, is the mother's milk of ambition, is it not?"

"I had not heard it expressed quite that way," admits Hissl.

"You wish position and power. I offer that. With your help, we can take Westwind—"

"Westwind?"

"The Roof of the World. Once we take Westwind, the Lord of Lornth, I understand, will be most suitably grateful." The tall man wipes his forehead again.

"That is what has been said," offers Hissl cautiously.

"To take Westwind will require four things: good tactics based on knowledge, an adequate number of armsmen, a good leader, and a very good wizard." The stranger looks straight at Hissl. "You are said to be a very good wizard. You also must have some coins and contacts which would supplement our coins in hiring armsmen."

"Many would claim what you propose is impossible. Many have already died." Hissl's eyes stray to the blank glass on the table and then to the half beaker of wine.

"Hardly impossible. Difficult, perhaps, but nothing is impossible."

Hissl raises his eyebrows.

"When we take Westwind, you may have the lands and title that Lord Sillek offers. I will take Westwind, and offer immediate and faithful homage to His Lordship. I think he will accept it," the stranger says.

"How can I trust you?" asks Hissl bluntly. "You ask me to risk much. Why would you offer me the leopard's share?"

The stranger spreads his hands, then wipes his forehead. "Look. You wear warm clothes. Na— The armsman wears a cloak. I wear as little as I can, and I am hot. Given any choice, I would never leave the high peaks. I would die during a long hot summer in the lowlands." The man shudders. "I could not take lowlands if they were forced upon me."

"How would I know this?"

The stranger glances at the glass and then at Hissl. "You know."

"Why do you come to me, and not to Lord Sillek?"

"Because that would place him, and me, in a most difficult position. He cannot deal directly with a man associated with the angels, but he could accept the return of his lands, especially if that return is accomplished with the help of one of his loyal wizards.

"To some degree, I am gambling that he will accept a man who is a stranger paying homage to him. But he has said that he will reward the man who overthrows the evil angels and returns the lands to Lornth. Because you are a loyal subject and of Lornth, he will certainly reward you." The stranger smiles again.

"How, exactly, would you accomplish this?"

"By wizardry, and by unexpected attacks." The stranger clears his throat. "Are you interested?"

After a time, Hissl nods. "Yes."

XCIII

NYLAN BRUSHED AWAY a persistent fly, the kind that hurt when it bit, as he had learned the painful way, before pulling the alloy from the forge. He blinked as he turned. Although the brick forge now almost reached the roof line, it did not block the direct afternoon sun that beamed down on his dented, and oft-reflattened and -smoothed makeshift anvil.

Huldran took the tongs. Nylan lifted the hammer once more, ready to hot-cut, wondering if Fierral's endless appetite for arrowheads would ever be sated. Then, again, did any military commander ever have enough ammunition?

He laughed as he finished the blank.

"Ser?" asked Huldran.

"Military commanders never have enough ammunition."

"If you say so, ser." Huldran looked puzzled.

Nylan lifted the hammer again, then paused as he glimpsed a motion from the corner of his eye. He turned his head. Ydrall, her dark hair now cut short, ran up the road. Nylan lowered the hammer, then raised it again and kept cutting until the new guard actually entered the smithy.

"Ser?" gasped Ydrall.

Nylan set the hammer aside, and brushed back another of the scattered but persistent flies. "Yes?"

"Istril and Jaseen, they said you should come," she said in Old Anglorat. "Ellysia is sick, very sick, and the other healer, she is off trading."

"What's that about Ellysia?" asked Huldran.

"She's sick. Very sick." Nylan set down the hammer. "It's your turn to do what you can all alone. I'll send someone up to hold the tongs for you."

Nylan hurried, not quite running, first to the bathhouse to rid himself of dirt and grime, and then back into the tower.

Still damp, the engineer returned to the tower through the connecting south door.

Ryba, carrying Dyliess in the chest pack, met him at the foot of the stairs. "They called you? Good. She's really sick."

"I'll do what I can. Ayrlyn would be better." He paused. "Could you arrange to send a guard up to help Huldran while I'm gone? Cessya, Weindre, someone like that? She's trying to keep forging arrowheads."

"I'll take care of it."

"Thank you." Nylan hurried up the stairs.

Jaseen sat beside the bed. On her bed, a dozen cubits away, Istril held Dephnay and rocked the cradle holding Weryl. Ellysia's face was blotched and pale, and Nylan could feel the heat welling off her face. Her entire body was drenched, both in sweat and in an unseen ugly whiteness.

"What is this?" muttered Nylan to Jaseen.

"Massive systemic infection, I'd guess. We don't have any diagnostics, or those fancy nanotech probes."

"Please . . . help me, ser." Ellysia's voice was less than a whisper.

Nylan took a deep breath, sending his perceptions out, trying to find a nexus, a center for the infection, but there seemed to be none. The ugly whiteness oozed from everywhere within the stricken woman.

He wished he knew more about medicine and bodily systems. After a brief respite, he eased his senses out again, this time concentrating on her circulatory system, trying to strengthen the minuscule order he found there.

Had a touch of color returned to Ellysia's face? Was there a trace less of the whiteness around her?

"Still . . . so hot . . . do something . . . just look at me . . ."

"He is doing something, Ellysia. Healers do it with their thoughts," insisted Istril from behind Nylan.

Even as he watched, Nylan could sense the faint order he had instilled crumble. Again, he forced himself out, to try to strengthen the ailing woman's internal order, to build dikes against the infection.

His own eyes blurred, and his head ached, and he looked

blindly at the floor, seeing nothing. His knees started to shake, and he sank down on the planks beside the lander couch, trying to keep the room from swimming around him, even as he knew that what he'd done hadn't been enough.

He reached out, but it was too late. He slumped into darkness.

Someone was applying a damp cloth to his forehead when he woke. His eyes fixed on the silver hair.

"Ellysia?" he asked.

Istril shook her head. "She was better, but it didn't last."

Nylan started to shake his head, then stopped. Even that slight motion hurt too much.

Istril blotted his forehead again. "You tried to do too much. Even I could feel it."

". . . wasn't enough . . ."

"You need to drink something." She held a mug.

Nylan struggled up into a half-sitting position. His head felt like his own hammers were pounding on it. The triangle rang for the evening meal, but he concentrated on sipping the water. By the time he had finished the mug, the hammering inside his skull had diminished to a dull thumping.

"Try this." Istril handed him a slice of bread.

Nylan could hear the whimpering from the cradle. "Take care of Weryl. I'm feeling better." He paused. "Dephnay?"

"Siret has her now. Over there."

As he chewed the thin slice of bread, Nylan's eyes jumped to the next alcove, where Siret held two infants.

Istril eased Weryl out of the cradle and to her breast. The whimpering was replaced with sucking, interspersed with a noise sounding to Nylan suspiciously like a slurp.

"He likes to eat," said the smith.

"I've started giving him a few mushy things. The solids seem to help him sleep a little longer, but he still nurses a lot." Istril looked down at her son. "Little pig."

Some of Nylan's dizziness passed, and he eased himself into a sitting position. He noticed that Ellysia's bed was vacant.

"Jaseen moved her. Said she wanted her in the ground as quick as possible."

Nylan nodded.

"I don't understand," Istril said. "No one got sick all winter, and it was cold, and we didn't really have enough to eat. Why now?"

"Because it was cold," Nylan tried to explain, as much for himself as for Istril. "It was too cold for mosquitoes, flies, and insects that carry diseases. We didn't see any traders. Now, after the winter, there are a lot more ways to catch things, and Ellysia was just worn out."

He didn't add that not having two healers around probably hadn't helped either, but with the raging infection that had surged through Ellysia, he wondered whether even both he and Ayrlyn would have been able to do anything.

His head turned toward the dark-haired baby girl Siret held. "She'll have to be fed. I don't suppose she's had much solid food."

"I can nurse Dephnay some," volunteered Istril.

"I can, too," added Siret.

"I suppose I can make it down to eat." Nylan eased himself erect.

"Are you sure?" asked Istril.

"I'll manage." Since Nylan finally could move without his head spinning, he tottered down the single flight of stairs and into the great room, followed by Siret and Istril, and the three infants.

". . . silver-haired bunch . . ."

". . . they look after him."

"Engineer . . . looks like shit . . ."

". . . nearly killed himself . . . they said . . ."

". . . more dead than alive . . ." murmured Selitra.

"I'm not that bad," he rasped back. "I can still hear whispers."

Selitra blushed.

Nylan continued past the lower tables and slid into his place. He immediately broke off a chunk of bread and began to chew.

"You're still pale." Ryba patted Dyliess in the carrypack on her chest.

Huldran, beside Nylan, nodded.

"Healing's harder than smithing or stone masonry," Nylan grunted after chewing the first mouthful of bread.

"Ooo . . ." interjected Dyliess.

"I'm glad you agree," said Nylan. "A daughter's opinion is important."

"Oooo . . ."

Huldran grinned.

Nylan finally took a chunk of the sauce-covered unknown meat. He barely had to use his knife. The brown sauce wasn't the burning dish that Blynnal called burkha, but a cinnamon mint, hot but not too hot. It also concealed whatever the meat was, and that, Nylan decided, was fine with him. He broke off another chunk of bread and dipped the end into the sauce, then took a sip of the cool tealike drink that was also new, and less bitter than the hot bark-and-root tea of winter had been.

When Nylan stopped and took a last sip of the cool tea, Ryba slipped Dyliess out of the carrypack.

"Would you hold her for a bit?"

Nylan extended his arms.

"Oooooo . . ."

"I'm glad you agree, daughter."

Ryba stood, looking imperious. Nylan cradled Dyliess in his right arm.

"Ellysia died," Ryba began. "You all know that. You may be the best blades on the face of the world, but that doesn't make you immune to disease. The engineer built a bath-house. I expect you all to use it—regularly. Cleanliness is about the only defense against disease we have left." The marshal turned to Blynnal and Kadran. "Everything you prepare is to be washed, cooked at least to a dull pink if it's meat, and all the way through if it's one of those wild pigs or a chicken. The same with eggs."

". . . tastes . . . terrible . . ." came a murmur.

"Do you want to have good-tasting food and die?" snapped Ryba. "There was a reason for all those primitive dietary laws we've abandoned. Just as there's a reason why the engineer nearly killed himself to build that bathhouse." Her eyes raked the group, and the silence was absolute, except for a faint infant whimper from the second table.

Nylan patted Dyliess on the back and chewed another chunk of bread as Ryba took her seat.

XCIV

"IT'S REALLY A pity, you know," Sillek says conversationally, as he bends forward in the saddle for a moment to stretch. "The harbor at Rulyarth is far better than the one at Armat. But the Suthyans are blessed with three decent harbors, and so they make the middle one their main trading point."

"Devalonia is icebound a third of the year," points out Gethen.

"So is Armat. That's my point. We could do wonders—"

"Let's not talk about wonders, Lord Sillek, not until we have Rulyarth and its harbor and can hold it." Gethen coughs and clears his throat, glancing up through the mist that is not quite rain toward the clouds that seemingly shift endlessly and yet do not move at all. "I hate this rain."

Sillek nods behind them. "Not so much as my poor wizards."

A messenger gallops toward them from the vanguard, and the two men wait.

"Where the road narrows and goes through a gap in the hills ahead, there is a force drawn up behind a barricade of stone."

Gethen raises his eyebrows. "Plans for the harbor?"

Sillek shakes his head. "I defer to the experience of wisdom and age."

The messenger glances from one lord to the other.

"Have the van halt. We'll be there presently," orders Sillek.

As the messenger rides north, Gethen asks, "Have you any miraculous plans?"

"Not yet. I have an idea."

"I hope it's as effective as the last one."

"So do I." Sillek gestures toward the chief armsman. "Rimmur! Have the force hold here in readiness. There's a Suthyan force behind those stones by the hill ahead."

"Yes, ser."

The two lords ride until they reach the van, and the rolling downhill stretch below the mounted foreguard. There Sillek reins up and studies the terrain. So does Gethen.

In time, he motions to Gethen, and the two ride aside from the others.

"They don't have more than fourscore there—mostly foot levies," points out Sillek. "The hill on the north side of the road is rocky, and they've only a handful of troops there. If we take the wizards, we should be able to use their firebolts and take the crest. From there, we can roll down rocks on them—rocks and firebolts."

"What if they reinforce the hilltop?" asks Gethen.

"The hillside is exposed. You have our archers fire at them. We can get rid of their hill guards before they can send others up the hillside. Then it will be too late." Sillek smiles.

"They'll start sending reinforcements as soon as they see what you're doing."

"But they won't see that. You're going to draw up our forces just about a double bow-shot length from them and go through elaborate preparations for an attack."

Gethen nods, then asks, "What if they attack?"

"Can you deploy the forces to kill them without losing many?"

"With more than ten times their forces and archers, I can manage that." Gethen smiles grimly. "I would still point out that you have a nasty turn of thought, Lord Sillek."

"That's because I dislike fighting."

"So did I. I still do."

Both men shake their heads before Gethen turns his mount toward the main body of troops.

XCV

THIN HAZY CLOUDS covered the blue-green sky, not totally blocking the sky, but reducing the sun's glare and direct heat. The usual breeze was absent, and the meadow grasses hung limp and still. The lack of wind left the early afternoon almost hotter than if there had been a breeze and no clouds.

Nylan was crossing the causeway, on the way back to the smithy, when the outer triangle, located in the small brick tower recently completed on the top of the ridge, rang three times. He had scarcely taken two steps when the triplet clanged again.

Across the fields, guards dropped warrens and hoes and scrambled toward the tower, fastening blades in place. As Nylan watched, two duty guards—Cessya and Nistayna, one of the older new guards—rode up toward the ridge. Before he could reach the smithy, Istril had ridden down past Nylan, leading three saddled mounts, taken immediately by Weindre, Kyseen, and Kadran, who all rode toward the watch tower.

Istril frowned, but did not ride out with the three, instead spurring her mount back toward the stables, as Ydrall rode down leading three more mounts.

Nylan nodded. Fierral, or someone, had figured out how to get the kitchen and the field details into the saddle quickly. They were still fortunate that the timber detail was involved in expanding the stables, rather than working down in the woods.

Ydrall's mounts included Ryba's roan, Fierral's mount, and a horse taken by Berlis.

The engineer had just reached the front of the smithy when Istril rode back down with another set of three mounts. Behind her and the riderless three mounts rode Llyselle,

Jaseen, and Murkassa. Murkassa's face was pale.

At the tower, three more guards were waiting—Saryn, Selitra, and Hryessa.

"Move it!" Saryn's voice carried as she vaulted into the saddle, leading the six riders up toward the watch tower.

Nylan paused as Istril turned and headed her mount back uphill. He waited outside the smithy for the silent silver-haired guard.

She reined up and looked down. "With Ellysia dead, until the little ones are old enough to eat solid food, I'm ordered away from battle, unless attackers reach the tower itself." Istril glanced toward the tower. "Siret has them now."

"You don't have to explain to me, Istril. You've put your life on the line plenty." Nylan gave the silver-haired guard a ragged smile. "You don't see me charging out there, either."

"That's different. If anything happens to you . . ." She turned her mount uphill. "I've got to get more mounts ready."

Nylan watched her for a moment before entering the smithy. Huldran was forging arrowheads, letting Desain, one of the newer guards, hold the tongs.

"Over now. Easy."

When the triangle rang a third time, Nylan looked at Huldran. "We'd better get moving, too."

"The forge?"

"Let it burn." Nylan turned to Desain. "Find your blade, and then go down to the tower. Listen to Istril or the guards there."

At her puzzled look, Nylan repeated himself in Old Anglorat to her before turning to Huldran. "We'll head up to the stables."

They didn't have to go that far. Istril met them with two more mounts at the opening to the small canyon where Nylan climbed onto a brown mare he'd never ridden before. She seemed responsive enough and not ready to throw him every which way.

"Take care, ser," Istril said. "Don't lead the charge."

"I won't."

"That one cares for you, ser," Huldran said quietly.

"I know. She's good, and she works hard." He glanced toward the tower, where Fierral and Ryba, already mounted, waited for them just beyond the end of the causeway. "I worry about her."

"You worry about a lot of people."

"One of my undoings," quipped Nylan.

"Come on!" Ryba waved a blade, and Nylan urged the mare into a trot, wincing at the jolting, and then feeling guilty as he thought about how much harder that kind of jolting had to be on Ryba or Istril.

As the four rode two by two across the narrow bridge over the tower outfall drainageway, Ryba said, "The bridge is solid, and the paved part feels that way, too."

"I wish we had time to pave more."

"Once we get the new ones more settled, maybe we can have a stone-paving crew. It's good exercise."

"That's true," agreed Fierral, "but let's worry about what's over the hill right now. There's another group of mounted brigands coming up the ridge. They're wearing purple, but it's not that light purple of Lornth. It's darker."

"Darker purple? Who could that be?" asked Nylan.

"Does it matter?" retorted Ryba. "How many?"

"A little less than twoscore."

"Any archers or bows?"

"No. But this group carries round shields that look pretty thick."

"Arrows are faster than shields," Ryba pointed out.

"We don't even have a score of guards up there."

"Use the arrows first," said Ryba.

"I'd planned to." Fierral glanced at Nylan. "Now that we have some, I told Saryn to make them count, but not to worry if a few shafts fall by the way so long as most of them hit something."

When Nylan looked back toward the tower, he saw one more rider, Ayrlyn, following, with several large saddlebags. Medical supplies, such as they had remaining, he guessed.

More than a dozen guards, all mounted and bearing bows and blades, forged by Nylan, waited at the ridge top, facing downhill and to the west.

"They seem to be waiting for us," Saryn announced. "But they can wait a long time. I'd rather hold the heights."

"Idiots," murmured Ryba as she saw the darker purple banners drawn up on the flat below the ridge. "They should have just attacked." Beyond the banners, almost out of sight, were tethered what appeared to be packhorses.

"Don't put down male chivalry too much," cautioned Nylan. "If they hadn't waited to set up a formal battle, it would have been a mess."

Both Fierral and Ryba looked sideways at the engineer.

"You keep up the direct and brutal business," added Nylan, "and they'll do the same. At least, after word gets around, they will."

Huldran nodded minutely, although the gesture was lost on the other two women.

The ridge top darkened as a larger and more substantial cloud buried in the high haze drifted across the sun.

"They're out of bow shot."

"We need to make them come to us," Ryba said.

"Do they want to fight at all?" asked Nylan.

"They won't admit that. First, they'll make some statement about how they come in peace to reclaim whatever they think is theirs. Then will come threats, and then they'll ride downhill and charge back up."

Nylan said nothing, instead trying to send his perceptions out to see if the apparent attackers were more deceptive than they appeared. As he swayed in the saddle, straining at the limits of his abilities, he could sense that matters were not quite as they seemed.

"Hold it," he gasped, raising a hand.

"What?" said Ryba almost impatiently.

"This one's a setup, I think," Nylan explained. "See the trees to the right, where they bulge out on the lower side?"

"Someone there?" asked Fierral.

"Archers, it feels like. I'll bet their mounts are in with the packhorses down there. The woods are too steep there for horses."

"That means ten to fifteen archers." Ryba nodded. "So they'll come a quarter of the way up the hill under a white banner, make an impossible demand, and as they turn, we'll get sleeted with a cross fire?"

The engineer shrugged. "I don't know tactics, but I'd guess something like that."

Ryba studied the ground, then looked downhill and out at the flat where a rider was lifting up a white banner. "They don't want to give us much time, either."

"Can't imagine why . . ." muttered Nylan under his breath, wondering if the guards' reputation for instant and unforgiving action had already crossed most of Candar by rumor.

"How far will their arrows go—uphill?" asked Ryba.

"We could only descend another four hundred cubits or so before we'd be at the outer range, probably," hazarded Fierral.

"Fine. We'll go down to the edge of that range and wait."

"And?" asked Fierral.

"We'll insult their manhood. That might get them mad enough to charge after us," said Ryba.

"They can't be that stupid," pointed out Fierral.

"Probably not. But there's nothing that says we have to fight. We ride away. If they want to fight, they'll either have to bring up their archers out of the woods—or leave them behind." The marshal smiled coldly.

"They won't leave them, not after bringing them all the way up here."

"No, they won't. But our bows have a longer effective range than theirs, because they're your specials, and because the height should give us a little more impact, and they won't expect that power from mounted archers." Ryba laughed. "If they're better, we retreat to the rocks by the watchtower. That covers the road, and they'll have trouble."

"What if they retreat?" asked Nylan.

"They won't."

As the rider bearing the limp white banner rode uphill, followed by three riders, Ryba, Fierral, and Berlis rode down the ridge more slowly, drawing up well short of the midpoint between the two forces.

The leaders of the purple forces stopped exactly where predicted and waited.

Ryba, Fierral, and Cessya waited.

Nearly half a kay separated the two groups.

Finally, the man bearing the banner—alone—rode up the hill.

Drawing on his senses, Nylan strained to hear, but could only catch the general sense of the conversation, and the scathing scorn in Ryba's voice.

The central rider of the attackers' leaders raised a gloved fist. Ryba's laugh echoed down the hill. Then the three Westwind riders turned their backs on the others, and rode back up the hill.

Several arrows arched out of the lower forest, but fell short. Neither Ryba nor Fierral even looked back.

After a time, the armsman with the banner rode back down to the three others.

"They've got a problem." Ryba's voice contained a hint of laughter as she reined up before the Westwind guards. "They were sent to rout us out. If they go back, they won't be in good standing. If they've got any brains, the last thing they're going to want to do is ride up the ridge . . . but in this kind of culture, if you don't take the fight to the enemy you're a coward, and that's either a death sentence or an endless round of duels and hassles."

"Are you sure?"

"What did they say?" asked Cessya.

"Just about what you'd expect. They claimed that we had insulted the sovereignty of Gallos by enticing various inhabitants to join us. He couldn't even bring himself to say 'women.' "

"What now?" asked Fierral.

"We wait."

Finally, a trumpet sounded.

"They'll take the horses up to the archers, and have them

ride to about where we waited for them," said Ryba. "That would give them enough bow range to drop arrows on the ridge top here, and that's supposedly beyond the range of horse-carried bows. Don't do anything—just watch—until all the archers are well within range. Then hit them with everything we can fire.

"The horse will charge at that point, and we'll start potting horsemen then. Some will get through, but try to make it as few as possible."

Nylan looked over at Ayrlyn, who had just reined up beside him, and they exchanged glances. The healer nodded sadly.

As Ryba had predicted, several armsmen led the dozen mounts to the once-hidden archers. The archers mounted and began to ride farther uphill. At the same time, the main mounted force began to walk up the center of the ridge, slowly.

As the archers dismounted, Ryba said quietly, "Fire. Try to make each shaft count."

Since he had no bow, Nylan watched. So did Ayrlyn.

Within moments, half the Gallosian archers were down or wounded.

The horn sounded, and the nearly twoscore mounted armsmen urged their mounts uphill.

"You three at the end, keep working on the archers. The rest of you take the mounted!" snapped Ryba.

Nylan touched his blade, then drew it, waiting as the Gallosians rumbled up the gentle, but barren, slope.

Despite the shields, the purple-clad armsmen began to fall more than two hundred cubits from the Westwind forces.

Nylan couldn't see how many made it to the ridge top, because two of them were headed toward the left end of the Westwind line, where he and Ayrlyn had reined up.

The engineer swallowed, then urged the mare forward, hoping he could stay in the saddle, but knowing that he would be dead meat if he sat rock-still.

The oncoming rider carried a long blade, not so long as the monster Gerlich used, but long enough that Nylan felt his black blade was less than a toothpick in comparison.

All the engineer could do was to slide the other's blade past him, then tighten his knees and try to turn the mare.

His senses, rather than his eyes, warned him of the next Gallosian, and Nylan just slashed, nearly wildly, but successfully enough, his arm propelled by something akin to pure terror, to drive the other's blade down almost into the Gallosian's mount.

Struggling to recover control of both mount and blade, Nylan plunged after the two as they bore down on Ayrlyn. She had the first, on her left, held off, but the second raised his blade on her unprotected side.

Nylan, with few options, hurled the black blade, again reaching for the air, the sense of smooth flow.

The Gallosian crumpled across his mount, Nylan's blade through his body.

Nylan winced, his head splitting as though his blade had cloven his own skull, and he clutched the mare's mane with his now-free sword hand, eyes filled with blinding white and unable to see.

He blinked, slowly able to catch glimpses of the ground ahead and the horse bearing the dead Gallosian. As the engineer trotted after the dead Gallosian, and his blade, his vision slowly returned, but his head continued to feel as though someone had driven an arrow or a blade through his skull. Each time he opened his eyes, knives stabbed through them. A quick look back reassured him that the guards had matters in hand, and he could see that Saryn had come to Ayrlyn's aid, and dispatched the other attacker.

Nylan rode nearly a kay before managing to catch and calm the skittish horse that still bore the dead man. By the time he recovered his blade and rode back, there were no Gallosians left standing. Two of the archers had reclaimed mounts and rode furiously down the lower part of the ridge, followed by a single armsman.

Nearly a dozen horses lay across the battle site.

Fierral looked sourly at Nylan as he rode up. "We'll need more arrows." Her eyes took in the dead body. "Yours?"

The engineer nodded.

"You must be surprising with that blade."

"He threw it through him," Ayrlyn said tiredly, rubbing her forehead, as she stood by her mount and began to unload medical supplies.

"Through him?"

Fierral rode closer and lifted the corpse half off the saddle, then levered the inert form out of the saddle. The corpse hit the ground with a dull thud. "You're as bad as the marshal."

Except she doesn't get splitting headaches that almost knock her off her horse, thought Nylan.

Murkassa rode up, holding her arm, and slowly dismounted.

Ayrlyn looked at the slash on the newer guard's arm. "It's only a little more than skin-deep. Get that grime washed out good, and then see me or the engineer." She looked toward Nylan.

He nodded. "That I can do."

Ryba rode over, shaking her head.

"What?" asked Ayrlyn.

"I just told her to stay back. She shouldn't have been in the front row. Ryllya, she's dead," added the marshal. "The newest ones aren't ready for this."

Ayrlyn walked across the rocky ground to where Hryessa looked down at a handsome brown-bearded man. Blood welled out from his left shoulder and above the breastplate.

"He's dying, and I killed him."

"He would have killed you," Ayrlyn said gently. "That's what happens when people fight. They could have left us alone. They didn't."

"Lyntar . . . said . . . beautiful women . . . golds . . . there for the taking . . ." The brown-bearded man forced a smile, then tried to hold back a cough. His face paled, and the strangled cough brought up only blood—bright blood. ". . . wrong . . . he was . . . about the taking . . ." He looked at Hryessa. "So slender . . . like . . . dagger . . ." His lips moved, but no sound issued forth, and his eyes glazed over.

Beyond the dead Gallosian was another . . . of more than a score strewn across the slope.

"Nistayna!" ordered Ryba. "You and Cessya bring back the carts. We've got a lot of hauling to do."

"I don't understand it," Ayrlyn said. "They just kept coming. Half of them were dead before they even reached us. It was as though they couldn't believe they were being killed."

"They couldn't," snapped Fierral. "In their mind-set, women can't even try to kill, except maybe to protect their children. These idiots'd rather give up their lives than their beliefs."

"That just might change after a few battles," Nylan said heavily from his saddle. "You'll be devils, and they'll try to kill you without mercy."

"There are rumors everywhere," said Ryba, reining the roan up beside Nylan. "We're angels; we're devil women. We're beautiful; we're hags. The rumors don't matter. What matters is that we've got to get better. Every guard has to handle a bow and blade as well as Fierral or Istril. It would help if they could also throw a blade like you can because things are just going to get worse." Ryba surveyed the battlefield, where women in leathers stripped and stacked bodies and loot, where other women collected horses.

The creaking from below the ridge indicated that the carts were on the way to recover the assorted leavings and loot.

"With each success and each new rumor," said Ryba, "we'll get more women trying to escape, and more armsmen and brigands looking for easy loot because they can't believe we're real. Then, as Nylan says, one day, they'll believe it, and someone will head up here with a real army, and we'd better be ready. We'll need more arrowheads."

"More arrowheads," groaned Nylan.

"It's better than having to meet them blade to blade, and, speaking of blades, can you make any more?"

Nylan looked at Ryba. "We're having enough trouble with arrowheads. I made those blades out of structural braces, and I barely could handle those with a laser. All that charcoal I've got up wouldn't warm one lousy brace."

"We need something."

"I'll see about reworking some of the locals' blades—the terrible ones," said the engineer-smith, "if you don't mind the potential revenue loss."

"Good." Ryba paused, then added, "At least all this loot will help us get supplies for winter."

Nylan and Ayrlyn rubbed their foreheads and exchanged glances.

XCVI

AFTER THE LONG afternoon of cleaning up carnage and wounds, and building a cairn for Ryllya, the guard he'd never known, and an evening meal filled with quiet and exhaustion, Nylan sat in the rocking chair, holding Dyliess. Ryba lay in the darkness, silent on her separate couch.

For whatever reason, rocking his daughter in the gloom of the tower helped his throbbing head, more than the darkness or the hot and welcome meal prepared by Blynnal.

. . . and who will rock you to sleep?

Your daddy will rock and sing you a song,
There's only a cradle and nothing is wrong.
When the sun has set and the stars are so high,
I'll rock you and hold you 'til morning is nigh . . .

By the time Dyliess dropped off and he had slipped into his separate couch bed, the throbbing inside his skull had subsided to a dull echo of the former hammering.

After a quick flash of light through the window, the evening breeze brought the rumble of distant thunder over the western peaks and then the dampness of air that had held rain. Perhaps the rain would wash the sense and stench of killing off the Roof of the World. Perhaps sleep would help.

Again, not for the first time, nor for the last, Nylan wondered why so many people respected only force. He tried not to sigh.

"The killing is hard on you," Ryba observed.

"You've noticed." He tried to keep the bitterness from his voice, knowing he failed.

"You're good for about one killing a battle, aren't you?" asked Ryba quietly. "That makes it hard when people are riding around with blades."

"Very hard, especially when you're on a horse and can't see." Nylan stretched. His legs and arms were sore, from some combination of riding and smithing, neither of which he did terribly efficiently, he feared.

"Why?"

"With every killing, there's a whiteness that fills the field, or the local net, or whatever you want to call it. It goes through me like an invisible but very sharp dagger."

"This place . . ." said Ryba heavily. "The more we succeed, the more everyone wants to destroy us."

"That's true everywhere." Nylan yawned. "It's just more obvious here."

"We're going to get more women, and that means we'll need more weapons."

"More arrowheads," groaned Nylan, trying to put aside the thought of more deaths.

"Can't you make any more blades? We need both. I'd really like each guard to have two blades. That way they could throw one if they had to. The more standoff capability we have . . ."

Nylan wanted to laugh at the thought of a throwing blade being a standoff capability. How far they'd fallen from lasers and de-energizer beams, although the weapons laser still remained mostly intact. "We're having enough trouble with arrowheads."

"We need something."

"I told you. I'll try to rework some of the captured

blades—the terrible ones," said the engineer-smith, "that's if you don't mind losing some coins."

"After today, we have enough coins and blades that you can have a few of them to work with. I'm sure you can figure out something."

Nylan yawned again, wishing he were that certain.

XCVII

ZELDYAN RISES FROM the scrolls that are stacked on the desk by the window and turns to greet her visitor. "Lady Ellindyja, I must apologize for a certain disarray." Despite her apology, every blond hair is in place under the silver hairband inlaid with malachite, and her green tunic and trousers are spotless.

" 'Disarray' is not a term I would ever think of applying to you, dear," responds Ellindyja. "You are always prepared."

"I thank you for your kindness, and I am most happy to see you. Is there anything in particular to which I owe this happy visit?"

"I understand that a force of Gallosians attacked the Roof of the World an eight-day ago," begins the lady Ellindyja. "You, of course, as Lady of Lornth, would know more of this than I. Perhaps you could enlighten me?"

"I would be more than pleased to share what little knowledge I have, although you doubtless have many more sources than do I." Zeldyan picks up the small bell off the table and rings it. "Please, do be seated, and I will have cool, sweetened green juice sent up." She gestures to the largest armchair in the sitting room.

"I so appreciate your kindness." Ellindyja smiles and eases her bulk into the large chair. Her eyes cross the room to the cradle. "You are sure that ringing will not wake young Nesslek?"

"If it should wake him, I will hold him." Zeldyan smiles. "Children, I have seen, grow so quickly, and I am not yet tired of enjoying him while my comfort means much to him."

"They do grow quickly, and you are to be commended for your care and concern."

A stocky serving maid appears and bows to Zeldyan. "Yes, my lady?"

"A carafe of the cold fresh green juice, with honey, and some of the fresh pastries, if you please."

The dark-haired maid nods and slips out through the door.

Zeldyan steps toward the cradle and studies her sleeping son, then takes the straight-backed chair across the low table from her consort's mother. "I received a report from one of the wizards—he sent a report directly to Lord Sillek as well—that a Gallosian force attempted to attack the angel outpost on the Roof of the World. The Gallosians lost many armsmen. The wizard was uncertain if any of the angels were killed, but some were wounded."

"That must have been Hissl. He is never certain about anything. Except his own importance," Ellindyja adds.

"Still . . . wizards, uncertain or not, have a usefulness."

"This . . . incursion . . . has a disturbing flavor. I was also under the impression that a dispatch arrived from Gallos, something about the inability of Lornth to control the depredations of its inhabitants?" Ellindyja smiles sweetly.

"Yes," replies Zeldyan. "As you doubtless know from the dispatch, though it was addressed to Lord Sillek, Lord Karthanos expressed his regrets. He wrote that he felt compelled to take action because the situation on the Roof of the World had become most distressing to his holders. Lord Karthanos expressed the hope that Lord Sillek, once he returned to Lornth, would redress the situation on the Roof of the World."

"I had gathered it was something like that."

The door opens, and the serving maid returns with a silver tray, on which there are a crystal carafe filled with a green liquid, two empty goblets, and a pale green china plate on which are heaped a number of miniature pastries. The maid sets the tray on the table, bows, and retreats, closing the door behind her.

Zeldyan pours two goblets and waits for Ellindyja to take one.

The older woman also takes a small pastry and eats it delicately. "These are good. I recall something of the like from when I visited your mother—a family recipe, perhaps?"

"I learned a great deal from Mother, for which I am most thankful." Zeldyan takes a sip of her green juice, holding the goblet and waiting.

"You can see, I am sure," the lady Ellindyja finally continues, "the difficulty this situation has raised."

"Yes. It is rather clear. The male holders on each side of the Westhorns are outraged that a group of women has created what appears to be an independent land. If Sillek refuses to conquer them, then he faces dissatisfaction here in Lornth, and possible greater loss of face and lands if Lord Karthanos takes matters even more into his hands." Zeldyan sets the goblet down and smiles. "Of course, Karthanos was unsuccessful, and that may be why he is requesting, so politely and indirectly, that Lord Sillek put his lands in order."

Ellindyja sips the green juice, blots her lips with a silk-sheen cloth, and replaces the goblet on the table. "You are suggesting something, my dear, but I am afraid that suggestion is not as clear as it might be."

Zeldyan shrugs. "Lord Karthanos is known for his cunning. Perhaps he has judged that this would-be country of women cannot be taken."

"That would seem unlikely. A mere handful of women?"

"Unlikely it might be, but were it so, and were my lord to squander his funds and forces upon the Roof of the World, then what would there be to keep Karthanos from acknowledging these women and then expanding his domains into such areas as Middlevale or eastern Cerlyn?"

Lady Ellindyja purses her lips, but for a sole moment. "You are dubious about the skills and valor of your lord?"

"I love, honor, and respect my lord, and that love, honor,

and respect demand that I offer him my best judgment. No one stood against the eagles of the demons when they landed ages ago in Analeria, and I would rather my lord be cautious than suffer the fate of Lord Pertelo."

"Such caution would be wise, save that such caution would have all holders on both sides of the Westhorns clamoring for your lord's early departure from his stewardship."

"You may well be right, my lady, for most men are ever fools, and those who are not, such as my lord, are often captives of the multitudes," Zeldyan acknowledges.

"Lord Sillek must make his own destiny, and reclaim his patrimony. Would you have him do otherwise?" Ellindyja holds the glass, but does not sip from it.

"My lord must follow his destiny, as you have pointed out so clearly," answers Zeldyan. "Do have another pastry."

"One more," agrees the lady Ellindyja.

"Some more juice?"

"I think not, but you are so kind."

Zeldyan pours herself another half goblet, and her eyes flick, ever so briefly, to the cradle.

XCVIII

A FAINT LINE of sunlight crossed Nylan's face as he loaded more charcoal onto the forge coals started from wood. The basic planks for the smithy roof were in place, set almost clinker fashion, but in one or two places, thin beams of sunlight shone through.

There were no shutters, nor doors, nor a real floor. The only reason he had a roof was that Ryba and Fierral needed weapons, and that meant the ability to forge in poor weather. Would Westwind always rest on weapons?

The engineer-smith picked up the heavy iron/steel blade and extended his senses, studying the metal, following the grain. His lips curled as he felt the weakness that ran up what he would have called the spine of the blade. Not only did he not know smithing—he didn't even know the right terms.

He had no real tools, no real idea of how iron should be forged—just a basic understanding that a sort of waffled forging and reforging of steel and iron, combined with a quench that he developed more by feel than by physics, might improve the local product.

He laughed. Might improve? It also might turn a dull and serviceable crowbar of a weapon into scrap metal. But the marshal of Westwind needed better weapons for the new recruits, blades sharper, tougher, and lighter than the huge metal bars favored by the locals.

There was another difference. The locals seemed to want to beat each other to death. It almost seemed that the equivalent of cavalry sabres were looked down on, as though it were a badge of honor to carry the biggest and heaviest weapon possible. Ryba just wanted to find the quickest and most efficient way to win.

"Are you ready for this?" he asked Huldran as he set the blade aside on the brick forge shelf to the right side of the forge proper. He picked up a thin strip of alloy with the tongs, setting it on the coals.

Huldran pumped the bellows slowly and without comment. The alloy began to heat, more slowly than the local blade would. After a bit, Nylan eased the blade into the coals, almost next to the alloy, and waited for it to heat.

Once the crude steel blade had heated, he laid it on his makeshift forge. Then he eased the hot alloy strip on top of the cherry-red blade, and lifted the hammer, his senses extended as he tried to feel how he would meld the two.

Three blows later, he knew he was in trouble. The alloy went right into the local steel like a chisel through wood.

"Frigging alloy," he mumbled under his breath. "Of course it wouldn't work the simple way."

"It never does, ser," pointed out Huldran.

"Unfortunately."

It took Nylan longer to separate the barely hammered pieces than it had to half join them.

"If that doesn't work . . ." He walked to the unfinished smithy door. High cumulus clouds—with dark centers that promised lightning, thunder, and high winds—filled the sky. Too bad he couldn't harness lightning bolts into an electric furnace. "Right!" he snorted as he walked back to the forge.

What if he flattened the alloy into a paper-thin sheet and then smoothed the local steel over it? Then if he heated the sheets and folded them back and flattened them together— always with a layer of the alloy on the bottom—would that work?

He set aside the mangled blade and used the tongs to put the alloy into the forge.

"You think you can make this work?" asked Huldran, pumping the bellows, sweat running out of her short blond hair.

"For a while. We're just about out of the thin alloy sheets from partitions and the like. I don't have the tools to take apart the lander hulls. If I had the tools and talents of a good local smith, I might be able to, but I don't."

After a time, he eased the alloy from the forge and began to hammer it into a flatter sheet. The alloy lost heat quickly, and he had to reheat it before he was even a third of the way down the narrow strip.

It took until mid-morning just for Nylan to flatten the alloy and the blade, and to hammer-fold the two together once. His arms ached. His shoulders were sore; his hands were tired; and he understood why the old pictures showed smiths as men with arms like tree trunks.

He eased the once-folded metal onto the side of the forge.

"Now what?" asked Huldran.

"We take a break. Then we go back to work."

"You mean this works?"

"Oh, it's working. It's slow, like everything in a low-tech culture." Nylan stood and stretched, trying not to wince too much. "Why do you think that even a terrible blade is worth

almost a gold?" He took a deep breath and lifted and lowered his shoulders, trying to loosen them. "I read somewhere that a good smith might have to fold and refold iron
and steel together dozens of times to get the right kind of
blade."

"Dozens of times. It took half the morning for once."

"That's what I meant," pointed out Nylan dryly. "Lasers
and lots of energy make that sort of thing a lot easier. Now
all we've got is charcoal and hammers and muscles. It takes
longer." He walked toward the tower.

After a moment, Huldran followed.

XCIX

SILLEK STANDS ON the pier. Gethen stands several paces in-
shore of him. The armsmen at the foot of the old pier hold
torches, but the light barely carries to where the Lord of
Lornth stands a dozen cubits out on the rickety structure that
sways with the incoming tide. The sound of surf rises beyond the bay. The harbor is empty. So are the warehouses
that held goods, though a handful still hold grain.

"Only because they couldn't get enough ships in," Sillek
says to himself.

"What did you say?" asks Gethen.

"Nothing. Nothing."

"You thought this might happen, didn't you, Sillek?"
Gethen looks down at the dark water. "That the traders
would pull out without a fight?"

Below them bobs a waterlogged chunk of wood, and beyond that some unidentifiable bit of moss-covered and slimy
debris. The cold air coming off the Northern Ocean smells
of salt with a hint of rotten fish and ocean-damp wood.

"I hoped they would. Wars cost money, and they've always
kept Rulyarth as a place to bleed, not to fight over. This was

the easy part. Now it gets harder." Sillek looks into the darkness. "We'll have to bribe the independent traders, with something, and rebuild at least one of the piers. And probably reinstate the barges on the lower section below the rapids."

"You'll get some cargoes. My wines alone—"

"Your wines will likely save us, Gethen. For that I am grateful."

"I've been tired of seeing the Suthyans eat up the profits with their port charges." Gethen kicks the rotten wood of the pier, and a chunk flies out into the dark water of the harbor.

"We'll need some charges, or we won't have a port," cautions Sillek. "We've got some hungry people here who are going to be very unhappy. And then there's Ildyrom."

"He hasn't moved on Clynya."

"No, but that ties up more armsmen and a wizard. I really can't afford another campaign this year. That's why that business with Karthanos bothers me. I could care less about the middle of the Westhorns. The land doesn't feed my people, and there aren't any precious metals there. But because a bunch of women took it over, it's going to create a real problem with a lot of the traditional holders." Sillek takes another few steps seaward, testing the planks underfoot. One creaks and bends under his weight. He shakes his head. "When you solve one problem, you get two more."

"You're right about the Roof of the World." Gethen laughs. "That's why I'm glad you're the lord, and I'm not."

"Well . . . if anything happens to me, you'll inherit the mess. So don't laugh too hard."

"Me?" Gethen's amazement is unfeigned.

"Who else? The holders wouldn't accept my mother as regent, for which I am grateful, or Zeldyan, for which I am not. So I've named you as head of the regency council, with Zeldyan and Fornal as the other two counselors. You're respected, and your blood runs in Nesslek. Besides, you don't want the job—not that I hope you ever get it, you understand." Sillek's voice turns dry with his last words.

Both men laugh.

Behind them the torches flicker in the wind, and before them the faint phosphorescence of the waves outlines the distant breakwaters.

C

THE STOCKY CLOAKED figure climbs the outside stairs to Hissl's quarters and waits outside the door, silhouetted against the late twilight horizon of summer.

Hissl opens the door.

"I have come to see how things are going," says the cloaked armsman.

"Matters are not so simple as the great hunter would think," snaps Hissl, motioning the other into his rooms, but leaving the door ajar. "If I leave here while Lord Ildyrom remains a threat, no amount of success on the Roof of the World will leave my head attached to my body, unless I stay on the Roof of the World." The wizard glares at the arms-man. "How did you like winter on the Roof of the World?"

"I am not a wizard, ser," answers the armsman.

"I am not a devil angel, either, raised in the cold of Heaven and suckled on teats of ice."

"How soon can you gather what you promised?"

"Lord Sillek is still in Rulyarth, and may well be there until close to the end of summer."

"The end of summer?"

"The great hunter wishes a reward. The reward must come from Lord Sillek. If we offend him . . ." Hissl shrugs. "So we must wait, until I can be relieved, for when he returns, I can certainly request relief for a time after a year in this hole. Wizards are not that easy to come by."

"If your good lord does not wish to relieve you?"

"Then I can leave my position—but I would leave in good

enough humor to claim His Lordship's reward. Not so if I deserted, especially not when he is waging war, such as it is, against the Suthyans." Hissl smiles sardonically.

"Can you get armsmen that late in the year?"

"I have the coin. With coin, I can obtain twoscore of armsmen, maybe more if the harvest is poor." Hissl looks toward the window and the darkening courtyard below. "Come back when you hear that Lord Sillek is returning."

"I will be back." The armsman bows and slips out the door.

Hissl's eyes turn to the blank glass. He smiles.

CI

As THE SUN neared the western peaks, Nylan eased the blade he had labored over for more than a day into the quench, watching the color intently, noting the flickering effect created by the wavelike patterns of the hard-forged intertwinings of alloy and steel. When the purplish shade crossed the edge he eased the weapon out of the liquid and onto the bricks to cool in the gentle and dying heat from the forge.

The slightly curved blade, similar to but subtly different from the laser-forged blades, carried order and strength without as much of a black sheen to the metal.

"Another good one," offered Huldran.

"Tomorrow, you can start one."

"Me? It won't be near as good as yours."

"Mine weren't as good as mine when I started, either, but I'll be demon-damned if I'm going to be the only one slaving over weapons. Let's bank this down. I've had it."

Huldran nodded. "Cessya's working on doors and shutters for us, sometimes."

"Good. We might get them before the frosts."

"That's a season away, ser."

"I know." After piling the coals into the corner of the forge, Nylan took a strawgrass broom and began to sweep the now-packed clay floor clean. "The paving crew's going to put in a stone floor next eight-day."

"Do we need it?"

"No more than doors and windows."

The blond guard gave the engineer-smith a crooked smile as she racked the tongs and the hammers.

A cough caught Nylan, and he looked up.

Relyn stood in the unfinished door. He pointed to the cooling blade. "That is better than those you forged with the fires of Heaven."

"I don't know about that," Nylan said slowly, setting down the broom. "I do know that it's slower—a lot slower."

The one-handed man gave a single headshake. "With a simple forge, you create almost a master blade a day. No smith I know could touch that. It is as though you could see inside the metal."

"Not that fast." Nylan frowned. He did see into the metal with his senses, but didn't most smiths on this crazy planet? He looked down at his hands. "I need to wash up."

"I'll finish here, ser. You did the hard work."

"Pumping that bellows is no fun."

"You can do that tomorrow," Huldran suggested as Nylan walked out into the cooler air outside the smithy.

Relyn followed.

"What have you been doing?" Nylan turned downhill.

"What a one-handed man can do. Gather grasses for drying, find leaves from the teaberry bush for Blynnal, lead cart horses with loads of paving stones. I keep busy. This is not a place where a man should be lazy."

"You could slip away."

"Where would I go?" asked Relyn. "I am nothing in Lornth, and anywhere he is not known, a one-handed man is first considered a thief."

"They don't cut off hands for that here?"

"Not everywhere, but it is said they do in Certis and Lydiar. So . . ." Relyn shrugged. "I make myself useful here.

Some of the women, like poor Blynnal, do talk to me. None of the angels do, except you, the healer, and some of the other silver-heads. You are the true angels, the ones who can hold the black of order."

"I don't think you have to have silver hair to appreciate order," Nylan answered, his boots scuffing on the stone of the road.

The paved sections of the road ran from the causeway past the smithy and up to the mouth of the stable canyon and to the bridge over the outfall. Piles of stones lined the upper section of the road leading to the ridge, indicating where the next paving and road-building would occur.

A cart full of cut wood creaked toward the castle, the cart horse being led by Kyseen, who flicked the long leather leads not quite impatiently. Already, long piles of cut wood more than guard-high stretched in three rows along the west side of the road leading to the causeway, forming another wall between the low crude one that marked the exercise yard and the road and causeway to the south door of the tower.

Nylan sniffed the air. The wind out of the south carried the smell of damp ground from the irrigated fields, and the fresher smell of cut grass. On the air, also, was the sound of wooden wands against each other on the open expanse of the south exercise yard.

In the late afternoon, Saryn and Ryba, helped by Istril and Kadran, drilled the newer guards with wands that resembled the blades of Westwind.

Nylan permitted himself a half-bitter smile. His legacies would probably be Tower Black and the shape and killing ability of the guard blades. Sooner or later, if not for years, the composite bows would fail, but his efforts in the smithy proved that, to some degree, he could replicate blades without the laser. While the alloys helped, he suspected that a good local smith could do the same entirely with local steels.

As he paused to watch the practice, he noted that Ryba alone wore a slug-thrower, in addition to her twin blades, for the first time in seasons.

"Nylan! You can spare a moment to spar with us," called Ryba.

He shrugged and walked forward.

"You know Nistayna. This is Liethya, and this is Quilyn." Ryba surveyed the three. "Nistayna, you're the farthest along." Then she handed Nylan the wand she had used.

"So long as this isn't for blood. I'm stiff," protested Nylan.

"Wands up," ordered the marshal.

Nylan lifted his wand, trying to get into the spirit of the sparring.

Nistayna seemed almost diffident, and Nylan easily slid around her wand and tapped a shoulder.

"Nistayna! You'll get killed that way!" snapped Ryba. "Let me have your wand."

Nylan began to understand what was happening, and he waited as Ryba squared her shoulders and lifted the wand.

Then he attacked, as well as he could. Ryba parried, and cut back. Nylan backpedaled. The wooden wands hurt, especially with the force Ryba used.

The engineer-smith tried to gather to himself some of the feeling of order and pattern he felt within the smithy and with a metal blade, and, as he did, the wand seemed lighter, and almost wove a moving net with Ryba's wand.

For a time, neither he nor Ryba seemed able to touch the other. But Nylan's legs, rather than his arms, gave out, and he stumbled. Ryba's wand cracked his ribs.

"All right," he groaned, with a forced laugh.

Ryba handed the wand to Nistayna, whose eyes were wide. "That is how good you must be."

"The mage—he is better than any armsman I have seen."

"He's better than any I've seen," added a male voice from the causeway, "and I've seen a few." Relyn gave a crooked grin. "And she's better than he is. Not by much, but enough for it to count in a battle."

Ryba erased a momentarily puzzled look from her face, as she said to Nylan, "You've gotten better, much better. You aren't practicing that much."

"Smithing the hard way is good for arm strength," he said

wryly, handing the wand back to Ryba. "It's my footwork that suffers."

Liethya and Quilyn still looked from Ryba to Nylan and back again.

"I'm going to wash up before the evening meal." The smith pushed hair that needed cutting back off his damp forehead.

"You're quitting before the sun sets and before it's pitch-dark?" Ryba asked in mock amazement.

"I got to a stopping place. I've got another blade finished that needs to be wrapped and sharpened."

"I'll have Fierral get it in the morning, if that's all right."

"Fine."

"Back to your drills!" snapped Ryba. "You'll drill until you can hold off anyone who's not as good as the mage—or until your arms drop off."

Nylan could sense the unvoiced groans. He would have groaned, too.

Siret, Istril, and Niera had the youngsters in one corner of the third level as Nylan trudged up. He waved, briefly, and got a smile from Niera. Istril had her back to the stairs, nursing Weryl, and Siret was juggling Kyalynn and Dephnay.

Shortly, Nylan trudged back down toward the bathhouse and a shower, carrying his cleaner leathers, the ones he wore when he wasn't dealing with coals, metals, and sweat.

The bathhouse was warm, hot, with a fire in the stove. While the showers were empty and the fire burning down, the floor stones in two of the stalls were still wet. Nylan stripped and soaked himself. The water was not freezing, but not quite lukewarm, either, but he was hot enough that it didn't matter as he took what passed for soap and lathered up. Then he shaved, by feel, no longer needing a mirror.

After he dried off, a process more like wiping the water off his body and letting the rest evaporate than toweling dry, he eased into the cleaner shirt and leather trousers and boots.

As he passed through the archway, he nearly ran into Huldran.

"How's the water, ser?" Huldran was smeared with soot,

and her hair was sweaty and plastered to her skull.

"Someone fired up the stove. It's not bad." He looked at the guard.

"I had Denize do it."

"Thank you."

"It was as much for me as you, ser," said Huldran with a grin.

"I still appreciate it. Enjoy your shower."

Huldran gave a half-nod as she padded barefoot toward the showers. Nylan opened the north door, noting that the archway didn't seem to trap moisture in the summer the way it had in the winter.

"Excuse me, ser." Kadran scurried past him and out the big south door to ring the triangle for the evening meal.

Almost before the echoes died away, guards appeared from everywhere—outside following Kadran in, and from the third level, trooping down to the main floor of the tower.

Nylan stood back in the generally unused space on the east side. If they could bring in more glass, then perhaps the space could be used for the children, eventually space for schooling. And that was something else—books. They needed to preserve the knowledge base.

He took a deep breath, trying to regain his mental balance before crossing the foyer area into the great room. The great room now held five tables, although the fifth was sometimes not used, and not full when in use.

As Nylan passed the empty fifth table, and then the fourth, most of the newer guards looked down, almost as much as when Ryba passed. Unlike the others, Nistayna offered a faint smile, and Niera just looked up with wide eyes.

"Better eat all your dinner," he told the girl, feeling awkward, but feeling he should say something.

Istril stood, awkwardly holding a squirming Weryl. Nylan extended his hands, and Weryl thrust out his pudgy hands.

"All right, Weryl." As the boy smiled, Nylan grinned and scooped him up. "He's growing. You must be feeding him right."

Both Istril and Nylan blushed when he realized the inappropriateness of the remark.

"I tried one of the new blades," began Istril after the awkward silence. "I like it even better than the others, even if I won't be using it in battle for some time yet."

"The new ones are a lot more work." Nylan paused and shifted Weryl as his son's fingers probed at his jaw. "Why do you like it better?"

"It feels more solid."

"It's heavier. That might be one reason. There's more iron in it."

"Not that much. The balance could be better."

Blynnal passed, carrying one of the caldrons filled with sauce and meat.

"The last of the salted horse meat, dressed and sauced to disguise the taste."

"Not the last," prophesied Istril.

Nylan glanced across the table, but Siret was not around.

"She's up nursing Dephnay. Kyalynn was still sleeping," Istril explained. "I'll feed Dephnay later."

"How is that going?" Nylan shifted Weryl again to keep from being poked in the eye.

"Not that well. It's a good thing both Siret and I can nurse. Dephnay has trouble with even the softest solid foods."

Kadran passed them, hauling a second caldron, this one filled with what looked to be noodles.

"Fire noodles," laughed Istril.

"They're not bad."

"How would anyone know? They're so hot you can't taste anything."

Ryba entered the great room, holding Dyliess to her shoulder, and walked down the other side of the tables.

"Come on, Weryl," said Istril, taking her son back. "Your father needs to eat, too. You already did."

"Oooo . . ."

Nylan gently disengaged Weryl's fingers and made his way to his place at the first table.

"Do you want to eat first or second?" he asked Ryba.

"First, if you don't mind."

"No problem." He reached out and eased Dyliess into his lap.

"I can't tell which of you she looks like," offered Ayrlyn, sitting across from Nylan. "When I look at you, Ryba, and then at Dyliess, you look the same, except for the hair. But the same thing is true when I look at Nylan."

Huldran slid into the seat next to Nylan. "Too early to tell, but she seems to favor both. Doesn't matter. She'll be a handsome woman whichever way."

"What do you think of the new blades, Huldran?" Ryba asked after chewing and swallowing a mouthful of meat, sauce, and noodles.

Nylan eased Dyliess to his left knee and sipped the cool tea, then reached for the bread and awkwardly broke off a dark steaming chunk.

"Some ways, I like them better. There's more weight there, and they seem to be just as tough. Maybe we should give the older ones, the first ones, to the smaller guards, or the newer ones."

Her mouth full, Ryba nodded.

"The engineer, he's teaching me how." Huldran shook her head. "Never thought making a single small piece of steel would take so much work. But the new blades, they've got enough heft to make it easier to stand up to those crowbars—the kind Gerlich liked."

When Ryba did not respond immediately, Ayrlyn asked, "Do we have any idea what he's up to? Gerlich, I mean?"

"He doesn't like the heat. So I can't imagine he's too far down in the lowlands," mused Nylan.

"He's trying to gather an army to attack Westwind. I suppose," Ryba added after a pause.

Nylan's stomach sank at the timing of the pause. Ryba wasn't guessing.

"Do you think he'll be successful?" asked Huldran.

"He took a lot of coin and some old weapons," said Ayrlyn.

"I'd guess we'd see him in late summer, before harvest,"

speculated Ryba. "Hired armsmen would be cheaper then."

"He'll try something sneaky. He's that type," said Huldran.

"True," agreed Ryba.

Nylan grabbed Dyliess's wandering hand just in time to keep his mug from being knocked over. "Hold it, little one. You don't drink tea. I do."

Ryba continued to eat, almost silently, her eyes half glazed over. When she was done, she held out her arms, and Nylan ate.

Dyliess began to fuss, and Ryba rose, nodding. "Excuse me, but my young friend here has some plans for me." With a quick smile, the marshal was gone.

"She's preoccupied," Ayrlyn observed.

"Wouldn't you be?" offered Huldran. "She's got a lot to worry about."

So do we all, thought Nylan, without speaking his thoughts. *So do we all.*

After the evening meal, Nylan walked uphill in the twilight, past the doorless and windowless smithy, and then northward until he came to a small hillock of rocks that overlooked the lander shell still used to store grasses and hay. The drying racks, half filled with grass, stretched across the space between the meadow and the rising rocky hills to the west. One empty rack lay broken and sprawled on the rocky ground.

The brighter stars were appearing in the south, one on each side of the ice-tipped Freyja. As the evening deepened, more points of light appeared, and no star looked that different to Nylan from those he had seen from Heaven. Only the patterns in the sky were different.

The wind had switched, and blew cooler and out of the north. Nylan sat on a smooth boulder and looked at the bulk of Tower Black, and at the dark fields beyond, and the lighter stones of the cairns to the southeast. So many cairns for such a short time, and he had no illusions. The number of cairns would continue to grow.

"Nylan?"

He looked down in the direction of the drying racks.

Ayrlyn stood at the base of the rocks. "Would you mind if I climbed up to talk to you? You look like you need someone to talk to. I do."

Nylan waved her up and waited until she settled on a boulder beside him. Unlike Nylan, who sat in the dark in a shirt, the healer wore shirt, tunic, and a light ship jacket.

"Neither you and Ryba talk much anymore."

"What is there to talk about? The situation seems impossible, that's all. I feel so awkward. Weryl's my son, and Kyalynn's my daughter, and I've never touched Istril or Siret." He laughed, a soft harsh sound. "Except with a wand in sparring. Yet I feel that Ryba wants me to ignore them. Even though it wasn't my idea, they are my children."

"You try so hard. Siret and Istril know that."

"Does trying count? Or is Ryba right, that, in the end, only survival and results count?" He cleared his throat. "Oh, there are all the religions and philosophies about life being worth nothing if it isn't lived well—but all that's written for people who have the time and the resources to read, not for a bunch of high-tech refugees trying to scrape together a future on a cold mountaintop."

"Go on," said Ayrlyn.

"All I do is cobble together infrastructures that most places have years, if not decades, to build—and figure out better low-tech weapons for Ryba to train people to use. Every time someone dies, it hurts."

Ayrlyn nodded.

"But I'm supposed to ignore that, too." He paused. "I'm feeling too sorry for myself. The deaths hurt you, too."

"Death's everywhere, Nylan. We could have died on the *Winterlance*. Maybe we did. Maybe this is all an elaborate illusion."

"It's no illusion." He glanced up at the cold stars. "There, I didn't feel each death personally."

"This might be better," reflected Ayrlyn. "Death was a sanitary and distant occurrence there. It just happened— light-minutes away at the end of a de-energizer. No more demons. Or no more angels. And we could ignore it. Here we can't."

"Most people can—here or there. We just can't."

Ayrlyn's hand touched his forearm.

"Your fingers are cold." He took her hand in his, then looked up again. The stars above were bright. Bright and unfamiliar. Bright and cold. He squeezed her fingers, gently.

CII

SILLEK TOSSES THE scroll, wrinkled and smudged, with fragments of wax still clinging to one edge, on the sitting room table. Then he bends over Zeldyan and scoops Nesslek out of his consort's arms.

"You're the best thing I've seen today, except for your mother."

"I'm a thing now?" Zeldyan's voice carries but a faint edge.

"Of course not. That wasn't what I meant." He looks down at his son in his arms and puts his forehead gently against the boy's. "Was it? We didn't mean any insults to your mother."

"Oooooo . . ." offers Nesslek.

"That's what he thinks," responds Zeldyan, "for all your fancy words." She smiles fondly at her consort.

"Would you read that abomination I dropped on the table and tell me what you think?"

"A lordly matter? Your mother would not approve, my lord." Zeldyan smiles again, more ironically, as she lifts the scroll. "Why do you want me to read it?"

"You know why," Sillek counters with a laugh, "but I'll tell you anyway. Because you're your father's daughter, and you can think. He's stuck in Rulyarth trying to rebuild that mess the traders left, and I need someone with brains that I can also trust."

"Your mother would definitely not approve of that."

"Of course not. You have brains, and you love me. She didn't approve of our joining after she found out I'd fallen in love with you. 'Love is dangerous for rulers, Sillek.' It gets in the way of honor and patrimony." He walks to the window and stands there, still carrying Nesslek, waiting as Zeldyan reads through the scroll.

After a time, he finally asks, "Have you got it?"

"It's a letter from Ildyrom, renouncing all interest in the grasslands. There are many flowery phrases, but that's what it says . . . I think."

"Exactly." Sillek bites off the word. "Exactly. It came with a small chest of golds."

"That seems odd," muses Zeldyan. "Last year he built that fort to try to take them from you. I wouldn't trust him."

"I don't, but I think the gesture is real, and it's a danger."

"Not having to fight over the grasslands is a danger?"

"All my holders will know that Ildyrom has sued for peace. Your father holds Rulyarth, and the locals there seem to be pleased with his efforts. We offered a percentage of our trade revenues from Rulyarth to the Suthyan trade council—"

"You did?"

"It was your father's idea—much cheaper for both of us. They couldn't really maintain three ports anyway."

"And we can even if the traders couldn't?"

"If we expand trade, we can. They just wanted quick golds." Sillek shrugs and lifts Nesslek to his shoulder. The infant burps—loudly. "The bay is much better than Armat . . ."

Zeldyan laughs. "I've heard this before. What about Ildyrom?"

"It's demonish. We have peace with both Suthya and Ildyrom. All our borders are secure—except for those devil women on the Westhorns."

"Oh." The smile fades from Zeldyan's face.

"You see? The chest of golds—that's already known. You can't keep that a secret. It even means I can hire mercenaries. More women have left the holdings. Genglois had three petitions waiting for me—demanding I do something." Sillek lowers Nesslek and wipes his mouth gently.

"What will you do?"

"Stall." Sillek lowers his voice. "Make obvious preparations. Send dispatches to your father. Stall and hope. Hope for an early winter, or the need to do something urgent in Rulyarth or the grasslands."

"And neither Ildyrom nor the traders will offer the slightest pretext while your stodgy traditional holders bombard you with demands to reclaim the Roof of the World."

"That's the way I see it." Sillek sighs. "But I have a little time. Not much, but a little. I can hope."

A frown crosses Zeldyan's forehead, but she forces a smile.

CIII

"WE DON'T TALK much anymore," Ryba said quietly. "I miss that."

"I'm sorry. I guess I don't much feel like talking a lot of the time," Nylan said quietly, as he rocked the cradle and watched his daughter's face through the darkness.

"Could I ask why?" The marshal's voice was calm, soft. "Is it just me? You go off and talk to Ayrlyn."

"I worry, and I worry about things that seem set in stone. I feel like, when I talk to you, we talk in circles." When Ryba did not answer, he continued, his eyes still on Dyliess. "We go back and forth saying the same things. If you try to avoid using force, people die. If I don't build towers and weapons and what amounts to a low-tech military infrastructure, people will die. If you don't play tyrant and I won't play stud, our children won't have any future." His voice dropped into silence.

Again, Ryba was silent, and he continued to rock the cradle and to watch the sleeping Dyliess. In time, he spoke. "Even as each killing hurts more, I become better at making weapons and using them. I can't walk away from you, or Istril, or Siret, or little Dephnay who won't know her mother or her father—not now—but I keep asking myself how long I can continue doing this." He gave a rueful grin he doubted Ryba could see through the darkness. "How long before I'm so blind in a battle that I get spitted? And if I don't kill my allotted one or two, who else will get killed?"

"You think I like it?" asked Ryba, her voice still calm. "I can't ask anything without the threat of some sort of force. I can't get anyone to see what I see. If I try to use reason, even you fight me. If I use coercion and trickery, then what does that make me? But I have to, if I want a daughter, and if I want her to have a future. There aren't any choices for me, Nylan. And there aren't many for you."

Nylan looked back at Dyliess's peaceful and innocent face, asking himself, *Were we like that once? Does life force us into the use of force and violence, just to survive?*

"You have visions of what must be, and when you don't follow those, people suffer and die," Nylan finally said. "You've told me that, and I see that. I see it, but that doesn't mean I have to like it."

"All I want is for us to be free, for the guards, me, Dyliess, not to be trapped in a culture in which some horses are treated better than women. That's not asking a lot."

"It doesn't seem so," agreed Nylan. "But for us to be free seems to require more recruits and more and more weapons. More recruits makes the locals madder, and that means we have to defend ourselves, which leads to more deaths, and more plunder. That allows us to get stronger, but only if we keep our deaths few, which means better training and more weapons. Better training means less food-growing and hunting, and that means a military culture, probably eventually hiring out to the powers that be." Nylan cleared his throat.

"Is that what you see? Is that what you want?"

"I wish I could see a more peaceful way, but I don't. West-wind will have to hire out some guards, but from what little I do see, we will be able to prosper by building better trade roads, by levying tariffs on them, and by protecting them." Ryba paused. "I don't see this as the clear and unified picture you paint, either. I catch an image here, or there, and I have to try to visualize how it fits. I always worry that I won't put the pieces of this puzzle together right, and that I'll fail and someone else will die who shouldn't."

Nylan slowly eased the cradle to a stop. Dyliess gave the smallest of snores, then sighed. He slipped under the light and thin blanket that was all he needed in the summer evening.

"Would you hold me?" asked Ryba. "I know you've been forced, tricked, and coerced, and I'm not proud of it. But it's lonely. I'm not asking for love. Just hold me."

In the darkness Nylan slipped from his couch to hers, where, uncertain as he was, Nylan put his arms around her, his eyes open to the rough planking overhead, wondering how long he could hold her, yet knowing she had no one else.

CIV

"Hissl has requested relief from his post in Clynya for three eight-days," Sillek says, looking up from the table and stifling a yawn. His breath causes the candles in the nearer candelabra to flicker.

"He's been there for a while, hasn't he?" asks Zeldyan, gently bouncing Nesslek on one knee, while occasionally picking up a morsel from the small sitting room table and eating it.

"Yes."

"Why does it bother you?"

"Terek says he's up to something, something not exactly wizardly. Strange people have been visiting him—armsmen no one recognizes. He's been laying up enough provisions for a small army. Koric told me that. He laughed. Said that Hissl has no idea how to do something secretly."

"He's not . . . surely he wouldn't try to . . . he's not stupid enough for treason."

"No. And he's not subtle enough to try it that way. If he were out to overthrow me, his best chance would have been to murder Koric and open the grasslands to Ildyrom in return for support from Jerans. He is smart enough to consider that. Since he didn't, it's something else." Sillek yawns and looks at his son. "When will he go to sleep?"

"Soon," says Zeldyan with a laugh. "Keep talking. Your voice soothes him. So what is Hissl doing?"

"I'm just guessing, but I'd say he's going to mount his own expedition to the Roof of the World."

"Why? He wouldn't know a sword from a dagger."

"He is a wizard, and he told Terek last year that he thought the thunder-throwers of those angel women would not last a year."

Zeldyan frowns. "Why would he risk such a thing?"

"He dislikes being second to Terek. He would like lands in his own right and a title. I could not back down on my promise on that, especially if Hissl defeats them, and he knows that. My word would be forfeit to every holder *and* every wizard in Candar." Sillek frowns, then stifles another yawn.

"You're more tired than your son. Perhaps you should be the one going to sleep."

"I'm not that tired."

Zeldyan laughs and cradles Nesslek in her arms. "His eyes are drooping, and I'll be able to put him in the cradle soon. Your mother thinks ill of my closeness with him."

"I know. She says nothing, though."

"You don't mind, do you? He'll grow so fast. I saw that happen with Fornal and Relyn."

"Have you heard anything about Relyn?"

Zeldyan shakes her head. "Why are you worried if Hissl is going to attack the Roof of the World? If he wins, you don't have to go. If he loses, he still may weaken them."

"I'm no longer sure about that. I wonder if I see Ildyrom's fine hand behind all this."

"Keep talking," says Zeldyan as she slips to her feet and steps toward the cradle.

"Terek says that every time that someone has attacked those devil women, the women have gotten a lot of plunder. They're selling a lot of plate armor and blades to traveling traders for supplies. They've got mounts and some livestock, and a tower and they're building more buildings . . ."

Zeldyan nods to Sillek to keep speaking as she eases Nesslek into the cradle and starts to rock it gently.

". . . now Ildyrom is as devious as a giant water lizard and about twice as dangerous. What if he's backing Hissl, not directly, but through some adventurers? Ildyrom can't lose. If Hissl wins, I lose the wizard that's kept him at bay. I also lose face, and that's a problem with the holders that will tie me up. If Hissl loses, that's worse. Those angels will have enough plunder that it will take all the free armsmen in Candar to pry them out. And even more women will start fleeing unhappy situations here and in Gallos, and whatever it is, those people on the Roof of the World know how to fight and to teach other to fight. So all my holders will be up in arms if I don't act. So will Karthanos. And Ildyrom, with his pledge not to take the grasslands, loses nothing, only a small chest of coins. Even if I win, it will be a bloody mess, and it will be years before we could consider more than holding on to what we already have."

"That's more than enough now," Zeldyan points out.

"I know that. But from Ildyrom's position, a few coins behind Hissl is a cheap way to weaken Lornth no matter what happens. And I can't afford to stop Hissl, either. That's what's so demonish about it."

Zeldyan lets the cradle slow and steps back. Nesslek snuffles momentarily, but continues to sleep. She turns to Sillek.

"You can tell me more later. We can talk when he's awake. Unless you're too sleepy?"

"Never."

"Good." She leans over and blows out the candles.

CV

THE AIR WAS still, hot, and humid—for the Roof of the World—in the brickworks canyon. The three who toiled beside the stream were soaked in sweat, except where their boots and trousers were damp from the running water.

One knee-high line of rocks and bricks mortared together ran from the north side of the stream to the canyon wall. On the south side of the stream a trench extended toward the hill that straddled the middle of the canyon. There, Rienadre, Denalle, and Nylan struggled to remove the silty and clay-filled soil, at least enough to provide footings for the crude retaining wall that would, Nylan hoped, form the millpond.

Nylan paused and leaned on the shovel, wishing he had explosives, even crude black powder, but while he could make charcoal, he hadn't seen or heard of anything resembling sulfur or potassium nitrate. As for more sophisticated explosives—gun cotton or blasting gelatin—he was no chemist. None of them were.

Clank . . .

"Friggin' rocks," muttered Denalle, attempting to lever a stone more than a cubit long and half as thick and wide out of the trench. Nylan lifted his shovel, and the two of them levered it out of the way.

The engineer-smith blotted his forehead and began digging again.

Rienadre walked up from where she had been toiling nearer the stream, halted by Nylan, and gestured. "Is where I've outlined that second channel far enough from the first?"

Nylan stopped digging momentarily. His eyes followed her gesture. "Should be. We'll put a small gate in each spot. That way we can drain the pond if it's necessary for repairs."

"Why two?" puffed Denalle.

"The stream has to have somewhere to go while we're working on the first one," answered Rienadre for Nylan. "Same's true when we go back to work on the second one."

"Just when I think we're done making bricks," commented Denalle as Rienadre passed, "the engineer comes up with something else. We'll never be done."

"We weren't ever done when we were marines, either." Rienadre started to walk down toward the stream. "Rather take my chances against the locals than the demons of light."

"Maybe," grunted Denalle as she thrust the shovel into the ground. "But dying here is dirty, and it hurts more."

As Nylan kept digging, his thoughts spun through the shafts, the gearing and mill structure. He was probably stuck with an overshot wheel, just because he knew how to make that work, but somewhere he had the notion that an undershot wheel was more efficient—or was it the other way around? How would he have known that kind of knowledge would come in useful?

Nylan lifted out another shovelful of dirt and clay. He had to have thought of a sawmill, hadn't he? And half the guards had to bitch about it, because none of them could see that the mill mechanism could be used for dozens of applications. Why was it that no one ever liked the practical side of things, in songs, trideo dramas, or in real life? No, the people who were practical always lost to the warriors and the glory hounds. He shook his head and kept digging.

CVI

CLOUDS SCUDDED QUICKLY across the greenish-blue morning sky, leaving the Roof of the World intermittently darkened by fast-moving shadows. Gusts of wind, cooled by the ice-capped peaks to the west, whipped back and forth those few scrawny firs that clung to crevices in the walls of the narrow canyon above the Westwind stables.

Nylan checked the shovels and other gear strapped to the back of the mare's saddle. Another long day of earth-moving and rock-mortaring! In an eight-day or so, they might even be able to start work on the mill's foundation. He patted the mare's shoulder and led her out into the light. "Come on, lady."

At the end of the stables, Ryba stood, talking to Istril, Hryessa, and Ydrall. All three guards stood before saddled mounts, and all three were fully armed with twin blades and bows.

Nylan paused, then strained to listen, his hand absently patting the mare to quiet her.

". . . they won't try a frontal attack. Even Gerlich isn't that stupid. So your job is to scout around the area and discover any possible place they could bring up horses and armed men . . . start with the second canyon there. Look for traces on the trees and bushes, up high. Remember, the snow was deep . . ."

The engineer-smith swung up into the saddle, teetering there awkwardly for a moment. He still wasn't totally comfortable riding, but one way or another he'd eventually learned. He didn't have any real alternatives to horses and skis, it appeared. He flicked the brown mare's reins and slowly rode toward the three guards who listened intently to Ryba.

"Just a moment. I need a word with the engineer before he heads off down to the lower works," Ryba said, stepping back from the guards and turning toward Nylan.

The engineer-smith reined up.

"Do what you can down at the mill over the next few days." Ryba lowered her voice. "After that, I'd like you and Rienadre and Denalle to stay close to the tower."

"Gerlich?"

Ryba nodded. "I can't tell when, but it feels like it won't be long."

"Do you want me to get the weapons laser ready?"

"No. We'll need that later, when we face a real army."

"If we don't stop Gerlich, there won't be a later."

"I know."

The flatness of her voice stopped Nylan. After a moment, he said, "All right."

After another silence, she added, "You can work on more blades, if you would. We'll need those, too, as many as you and Huldran can make."

"A good anvil would help," Nylan said.

"Tell Ayrlyn. It's a good investment." She flashed him a quick smile, bright and shallow.

"We'll hold off on the millrace and the mill. We might get the pond finished in the next few days. Then, we can certainly go back to forging a few blades."

"Good." Ryba turned back to the guards, continuing almost as though she hadn't talked to Nylan. "Gerlich should have left traces, bent branches, scars. He might even have marked a trail. Look for them . . ."

Nylan flicked the reins gently, then leaned forward and patted the mare on the shoulder again as she *whuffed* and stepped sideways before walking downhill toward the smithy and the tower.

CVII

SILLEK STEPS INTO the hot tower room, dim despite the blazing summer sun outside, and hot and close, even with the breeze seeping through the two open windows.

Despite his light shirt and thin trousers, Sillek begins to sweat almost immediately.

"Lord Sillek," says Terek, standing, "I found what you were seeking." The white wizard rubs his forehead, then gestures to the blank glass. "If you're ready, I'll try to call it up again."

"Please do."

Terek seats himself on the high-backed stool, shifting his weight from side to side for a moment. White mists swirl across the silver of the glass. Then, in the midst of the white mists in the glass, an image forms. A line of horsemen winds its way along a narrow mountain road in the glare of the midday sun.

"Yes?" Sillek's eyes narrow, and he strains to discern details which would identify the horsemen. "Who are they? Where are they going?"

Sweat drips from Terek's face, and the lines in his forehead deepen as he concentrates. "I'll try to get a closer picture."

After a moment, the image shifts slightly, to the head of the column where a white-coated figure rides between two armed men. The taller figure wears a huge blade across his shoulders.

"That's Hissl, all right," murmurs Sillek. "And the smaller one, he looks familiar, but I don't know why." He studies the image for a time longer. "That looks like the road past the Ironwoods into the Westhorns, just into the real mountains."

Terek, sweat now pouring down his cheeks, clears his

throat. "Ah . . . ser . . . do you need to see . . . any more?"

"Oh, no." Sillek pauses, then asks, "Do you know who the other fellow was? The big one?"

Terek clears his throat, once, twice. "No, ser. He feels a little like a beginning white wizard, but I know I've never seen him." Terek takes out a large white square of cloth and slowly blots his forehead. After a time, he slides off the stool and shakes the white robes away from his body.

"Hissl must have gathered twoscore armsmen there." Sillek purses his lips.

"He wants to be Lord of the Ironwoods." Terek's voice is flat.

"If he can defeat those angel women, I'd be most happy to grant him the title and those lands." Sillek forces a laugh. "It would take a wizard to make that maze of thorn trees productive."

"I wish him well," adds Terek.

"I know you do. He's difficult to work with, isn't he?" Sillek's eyes fix on the white wizard.

Terek takes a long look at the Lord of Lornth, then speaks in measured tones. "Hissl has a great willingness to work hard, great talent, and a great opinion of that talent."

"As I said . . . difficult to work with." Sillek chuckles. "Don't mind me, Master Wizard. And I thank you for your images. They make things clearer."

He turns and walks from the small room, adding under his breath, "But not that much clearer."

CVIII

NYLAN DISMOUNTED AND led the brown mare into the stable. His working clothes were almost tatters, and damp through, either from sweat or water, and his feet squished in his boots with each step he took. Mud streaked his arms and his clothes. As always, his arms ached, and so did his legs, and most of his muscles.

Still, the footings and the base of the millpond wall were completed, and he had another day before he had to return to smithing. Behind him, Rienadre led her mount into the stables. If anything, she was damper and muddier than Nylan.

The engineer-smith struggled with the cinch and girth, and finally unsaddled the mare. Mechanically, he brushed her, occasionally patting her flanks or neck. After stalling her and ensuring that her manger was full, he walked silently down the road and past the now-deserted smithy. The sun was almost touching the western peaks. Behind the faint chirping of insects and the intermittent songs of the green and yellow birds came the low baaing of the sheep grazing around the cairns.

He shivered slightly, knowing there would be more cairns, and hoping that he would not be laid under those rocks.

He crossed the causeway, entered the tower, and paused. Ryba, Fierral, and three guards were clustered around the last table in the great room. Nylan extended his perceptions, feeling faintly guilty for his magical eavesdropping but being curious nonetheless.

"The second canyon over—the one that looked like a dead end? It's not," declared Istril. "It's narrow. Then it climbs before it widens, and it's almost a flat run down to the trading road. I can't say that Gerlich was there, but there are some marks on the trees, a good four to six cubits up in places, small crosses, and they were made recently."

"How recently?" asked Fierral.

"Last spring or late winter. The bark's puckered a bit. In one place, there's a broken limb that has growth buds that died."

Hryessa nodded.

"Anything else?" asked Ryba, her eyes circling the table. After a long silence, she continued. "We'll need a place for an outpost—one that can be watched, but isn't in the canyon itself—and a clear route to get back to the tower. I want two guards there all the time from now on."

"Two?"

"One to watch, and one to get back the warning to us."

"Why don't we just block the canyon?"

"Because then I don't know where Gerlich will attack from," pointed out Ryba. "Oh . . . there's a back path from the canyon to the stable—or a way Gerlich's men will take to try to fire the stables. Find it, and work out the best place for an ambush. That will be a quick way to take out four of his armsmen, and they won't be expecting it at dawn."

Fierral and Saryn exchanged glances.

Nylan slipped past the stairs and headed for the north door and the bathhouse. He hoped that Ryba's visions were correct, but he wasn't about to question her, not when her perceptions had been so accurate so far. And this time, if Gerlich did as she foresaw, there wouldn't be any question of guilt.

CIX

GERLICH HOLDS UP his hand, and the column slows to a halt. The early-morning mist rises out of the trees to the east of the road that continues to climb as it turns northward.

"All right, Ser Wizard," the big man announces. "Get out your glass or whatever you need, and scout out that trail." He points to a gap between the trees on the side of the road. "I want you to make sure no one is on it."

"That's not even a real trail, and it goes right into the mountain," protests Hissl. "What good will that do?"

"It is a trail," answers Gerlich. "I've scouted it, and it curves through this slope and rocky ridge and comes out right behind the tower—inside their watch posts and defenses. And it's close enough so that there's a back way to their stables. You have the map on that, Nirso." The hunter nods to the squat armsman riding behind Narliat.

Narliat's eyes flick from the wizard, who dismounts and eases a padded and leather-covered glass from one saddle-bag, to Gerlich and then to the road ahead. His lips tighten.

"Worried, friend Narliat? You have seen what I can do with the blade and bow, and they certainly will not be expecting an attack—especially from here." Gerlich laughs.

Hissl squats on the ground, concentrating on the glass before him, and the mists that appear. After a time, he rises, wipes his forehead, and repacks the glass.

"Well?"

"There is no one on the trail. It is narrow, but I could see no tracks and no horses."

"Good." Gerlich turns his mount uphill, and the others follow.

CX

"FRIED RODENT, AGAIN," muttered Huldran from beside Nylan. "Demon-damned stuff to put in your guts before smithing."

"The rodents serve two saving purposes," answered Ayrlyn with a smile. "Serving them saves other food for the winter, and killing them keeps them from eating the crops. They like the beans and, for some reason, they want to dig up the potatoes. So they also serve who are served."

Nylan hastily washed down a mouthful of fried rodent meat. "That's a terrible pun." He followed his comment with a mouthful of cold bread.

"Oooo," commented Dyliess from the carrypack Ryba wore.

"That's fine, dear," said Ryba, "but you're not the one who has to eat it." Her eyes flicked toward the doorway, again.

Ryba seemed on edge all the time, Nylan reflected, but especially in the morning, as the days had dragged out since Istril had discovered what seemed to be Gerlich's back route to the Roof of the World.

"How soon, do you think?" he asked.

Ayrlyn rubbed her forehead, and Nylan smiled faintly. Thinking about a battle and all those who would need healing would certainly give any healer a headache—at least, he thought it would.

The sound of hoofbeats on the paved section of the road from the smithy to the tower rat-a-tatted in through the open windows to the great room. Ryba stood, unstrapping the carrypack, even before Liethya burst into the room. The young guard glanced toward the marshal and then to Fierral, as if uncertain as to whom she should report.

"I presume the traitor has returned," Ryba said, her voice hard as she eased Dyliess, still in the carrypack, to Nylan.

"There are armsmen on the trail, ser." Liethya's voice trembled slightly.

Fierral stood. So did Saryn.

Saryn motioned. "Stable detail. Let's go." She left the room almost at a run, followed by Hryessa, Jaseen, and Selitra.

Fierral added, "The rest of you to the stables—with full weapons."

All the guards at the tables, except for Istril, boiled off the benches and toward the end of the great room, some hurrying up the stone steps, presumably for weapons and gear, others straight out the main door.

Ryba touched Nylan on the shoulder. He turned, the carrypack unfastened, Dyliess in it and looking wide-eyed at him.

"Blynnal and Niera will take care of the children. Relyn, Siret, and Istril will hold the tower, if necessary. Join us as soon as you can," Ryba whispered to Nylan as he took their daughter. Then she was hurrying for the door as well, picking up her bow and a full quiver from the shelves by the stairs.

"Off to the slaughter," announced Ayrlyn. "Sometimes, I wonder if it will ever stop."

"Not until they destroy us or it's clear we're strong enough to destroy them." Nylan shifted Dyliess into a more comfortable position to carry her.

"Demon-hell of a world," said Ayrlyn with a laugh. She gulped down the last of her cool tea and added, "Just like every other world."

"You're so cheerful."

"Cynically realistic, Nylan. I'd like to change things, but I haven't figured out how."

"That makes two of us. I'd better stop talking, though, and start moving." Carrying Dyliess in his arms, not bothering to strap the carrypack in place, Nylan half walked, half ran up to the fifth level, breathing heavily by the time he stopped in front of the space where he kept his weapons.

Dyliess whimpered, jolted by his running, and he patted her back and laid her on the floor momentarily as he pulled out the second blade—one of the newer iron ones—and strapped it in place. That way, as Ryba had suggested, he could throw one, if he needed to, and still defend himself. Privately, he wondered if he'd be in any shape to defend himself if the first blade were accurate. Then, he could miss, and without the second blade, he'd be dead meat.

He picked up Dyliess and patted her again and again, before starting down to the third level, where Blynnal and Niera were rearranging cradles. Dephnay and Kyalynn were in two of them, and Niera held Weryl. The girl handed Weryl to Blynnal, who eased the squirming boy into an empty cradle.

"Blynnal?"

"Ser?"

"Here's Dyliess. I need to go." Nylan brushed his daughter's forehead with his lips.

"We'll keep her safe." The dark-haired guard and cook took Dyliess, carrypack and all. "Now, you take care, Ser Mage."

"I'll try." Nylan took a last look at the children, trying not to shake his head at the thought that three of the four were his.

He headed down the stairs, then stopped as he saw Siret laying out quivers by the first window to the right of the south door.

"Do you have plenty of arrows?" he asked.

"Two quivers."

"If any of them even look like they're getting close, pick them off." Nylan paused and pointed to the timbers behind the heavy plank door. "As soon as the last guard leaves, drop those in place. Don't wait. And barricade the north door, too."

"I will, Father Brood Hen." Siret gave him a crooked grin. "I'll even close all the tower shutters and windows except the ones that Istril and I are using to shoot from. She's up on the fourth level. That way we have two different angles."

"See that you keep them closed," Nylan said with mock gruffness. He turned to go.

"Ser?"

Nylan turned back to meet the deep green eyes.

"I'm glad you took a moment. I'll tell Istril."

A dull thump echoed through the lower level, followed by a second thump, and then a third. They both looked toward the north side of the tower.

Relyn strolled forward from the north door. "The north door's barricaded. So is the outside door to the bathhouse, but they could break through that pretty quickly." He slipped on the clamp and the knife over his hook, then the wooden sheath. "I hope I don't have to use these."

So did Nylan.

"I'd better go." The engineer-smith nodded to both, and slipped out the south door, hurrying uphill.

In the east, the sun hung just above the great forest beyond the drop-off, and tendrils of mist cloaked the taller distant firs. Nylan turned uphill. To the west, the morning mist was still rising off the hills.

As he half walked, half ran up the road, Nylan realized one other thing. The warning triangle had never rung. Then, he nodded. Gerlich knew what the triangle meant.

By the time he reached the stable, almost all the guards were mounted, and the three who had left the tower's great room with Saryn were riding farther up the canyon behind the former second pilot.

Llyselle held the reins of the brown mare for Nylan. "We thought you'd need this, ser."

Nylan, still breathing heavily, shook his head. His slowness in saddling his mounts was unfortunately all too well known.

"Follow your squad leaders!" ordered Ryba.

Nylan swung himself up into the saddle, the scabbard on his right side banging against the side of his leg as he thrust it across the saddle.

"Squad one!" Fierral raised her blade.

Across the grim-faced riders, Nylan caught Ayrlyn's eyes and pantomimed the question, "Which squad?"

Ayrlyn shrugged.

"Let's go," called Fierral, and almost a dozen riders followed her. The remainder followed Ryba.

After a moment of hesitation, Nylan rode after Ryba's group, where he and Ayrlyn brought up the rear.

"Do you know the plan?" he asked quietly.

"Not exactly. Gerlich is coming down the second canyon, and they'll try to use the ledges to pick them off, some anyway, before they can get out of the canyon. Saryn's supposed to get the ones headed for the stable, and then rejoin the main group."

"Not terribly well organized," mused Nylan.

"How can it be? Ryba can't station people everywhere eight-days on end. What if Gerlich never showed up? She's probably got plans for a dozen different cases."

"Still, it seems risky going out after him."

"It is, and Gerlich probably would have trouble cracking the tower. But we couldn't survive another winter without livestock and mounts, and he knows it."

Nylan nodded. So, to protect the outbuildings and what they contained, the guards had to take the fight to Gerlich, before he knew it. He also realized why ancient castles held *everything*—a realization that, as seemed all too frequent, came too late.

"Pickets here!" called Fierral. The newest guards— Denize, Liethya, Miergin, and Quilyn—served as pickets, holding mounts ready, as the more experienced guards, or at least those more trained, swarmed up the ropes already fastened in place on the slope.

Nylan nodded as he dismounted and handed the mare's reins to Quilyn. Maybe things weren't so disorganized. He and Ayrlyn were the last on top of the ridgelike overlook.

"Down," whispered Ryba.

Nylan went to his knees. So did Ayrlyn.

Ryba had lined up the guards in two rows, sitting or kneeling, behind the low scrub on a flat ledge that overlooked the widening opening of the second canyon. Fierral was crouched at the uphill end, Ryba at the lower end.

Nylan studied the placement—hardly ideal, since the canyon walls were too steep for anything but a mountain goat farther uphill and since Gerlich's troops only would be in a field of arrow fire for a short time. Still, if attrition were the idea, it might work, because it would take time for Gerlich's armsmen to circle the hills, assuming they knew from where the arrows came.

"Listen!" hissed Ryba. "You fire four arrows—just four— as accurately as you can. You know which row to aim for. Then you bat-ass down to your mounts and form up, just like we practiced. Now . . . quiet. We wait."

Nylan had no bow. That was no great loss, since his accuracy with the weapon was less than most of the guards, especially at a distance, and the number of bows—the good composite ones—was limited. Besides, with everything else, he had scarcely practiced with the bow since winter.

He looked at Ayrlyn, also without a bow, and motioned to the ropes behind them. "We leave after they start to fire," he mouthed.

She raised her eyebrows.

Nylan repeated his words, and she nodded.

The sun, early as it was, warmed Nylan's back, but the end of the canyon remained in shadow.

Nylan nodded again as he realized Ryba had planned better than he had thought. Gerlich's troops would come around the final turn in the canyon with their eyes facing right into the rising sun: Nylan bet the big hunter hadn't even considered that fact, but he hadn't the slightest doubts that Ryba had. When it came to using force, she tried to consider everything.

The sun climbed a bit higher, and the air remained still. Not even a bird chirped, and Nylan worried about that. Would Gerlich sense the unnatural quiet?

The faintest of clinks echoed across the rocks.

Ryba raised her hand, and nearly a score of guards nocked arrows, but Ryba kept her hand just above shoulder level.

A single rider turned the corner into the low-angled sunlight, his hand up to shield his eyes. Two more followed, their mounts walking easily. Ryba's hand remained up until more than a score of armsmen squinted their way into the sunlight.

Then her hand snapped down.

The second snap was that of bowstrings.

Nylan saw several riders pitch forward and one reach for a shaft through his upper arm.

"Arrows!" came Gerlich's bellow. The big man dropped down low on his mount almost as the shafts flew. "Follow me!"

Nylan scrambled back and down the rope, noting just as he ducked that the armsman he thought was Narliat had gone down with at least two shafts through him. The white wizard and his mount vanished, just as the one had in the very first battle on the Roof of the World.

Nylan came down the hillside in a haze of dust and struggled up into his saddle, trying to get the mare moving toward the canyon mouth, realizing that, for all Ryba's training, the guards might be too slow if someone weren't near the canyon mouth to slow the attacking armsmen.

He leaned back and whacked the mare's flank, and she jumped forward so quickly that Nylan almost lurched backward out of the saddle. He grabbed the front rim of the saddle with his free hand and levered himself forward, wondering what he was doing trying to hold off a charge of horsemen by himself.

Another horse drew up beside him on his right.

"Demon-damned way to run a battle," yelled Ayrlyn.

"Not exactly the best people to blunt an attack," he answered without looking at her, just doing his best to guide the mare around the rocky hill and toward the mouth of the canyon.

He glanced ahead to his right. The canyon opening was ahead, and none of the attackers had emerged. Maybe Ryba had planned it right. He hazarded a quick glance over his shoulder. At least a handful of guards were mounted and following them.

He looked back ahead, and the first armsman came charging out of the canyon, almost without seeing Ayrlyn, lost in the glare of the early sun. Although the invader turned toward her and raised a long blade, she slipped under it, and her own blade flashed, driving into the angle between chest and neck. Blood welled up everywhere, as did a white haze that shivered the healer where she rode, even as she beat back a feeble thrust from the dying armsman by instinct.

"Back off!" called Nylan, knowing that she could not see. That white impact of death had seemingly shivered against him, against his blade, but he shook it off. He hadn't done the killing, and that helped.

Another handful of riders rode out of the canyon, circling south, so as to avoid riding straight into the sun, and reforming into a line.

Behind him, Nylan could hear hoofbeats. He hoped there were enough.

An arrow arched over him and toward the invaders, but passed through them. Nylan half wondered who was good enough even to shoot while riding. That took two free hands, and half the time, he needed one hand to grab the mare's mane or the saddle to keep from getting jounced off.

A firebolt *hhissssed* past Nylan, its heat skin-searing. The wizard had reappeared beside Gerlich, who waved the big sword in Nylan's general direction.

Another firebolt flared across the distance between the mounted groups.

Aeeeiii!

The sickening scream was cut short, as if by a knife.

"Aim for the wizard!" ordered Nylan, and almost immediately several shafts arrowed toward the white-clad man.

Nylan could sense the white wizard throwing up some short of shields, and parts of the arrows flared into flame. The arrowheads tumbled forward untouched.

"More!" snapped Ryba. "He can't use his powers while cold iron's flying at him."

How did Ryba know that? wondered Nylan. It made sense, but how had she known?

HHHssstttt!

Another of the wizard's firebolts flared toward Ryba, and she raised her blade and half ducked, half parried it.

"To the tower!" ordered Gerlich, spearheading a wedge of horsemen aimed slightly to the left of the center of the guards.

The invading horsemen charged forward, and the wizard vanished. Nylan extended his senses, probing for the wizard . . . and finding him behind a wall of unseen white. Maybe . . . maybe, he could do something like that, or figure out a way to break down—

"Nylan!"

At the scream, Nylan blinked, then lifted his blade as a bearded armsman bore down. The engineer wanted to turn and flee, but he'd just get himself cut down from behind.

Nylan barely managed to get the blade up to deflect the smashing blow, and his entire arm ached. He urged the mare sideways, raising his own weapon again, and hacking the bearded man, who caught Nylan's blade with the big crowbar. Again, Nylan's arm shivered, but he actually gouged a chunk of iron from the huge sword.

He wished he had had the time to try his shield idea, but the armsman brought the huge blade around in a sweeping, screaming arc, and the engineer was forced back in the saddle. He could no longer see what else was happening, though he could feel the lines of white-red force flying toward and around Ryba.

Almost automatically, as the attacking armsman overbalanced, Nylan felt the moves that Saryn and Ryba had drilled into him taking over, and his blade flashed—once . . . twice.

The bearded man's surprised look stayed on his dead face, even as the white shock of his death shivered through Nylan.

"Move, ser! Move!"

At the sound of Huldran's voice, Nylan forced his eyes back open, despite the needles of pain that shivered through them, and weakly lifted his blade. Three guards had swept in before him and seemed to hold back twice their number.

His guts churned, and his eyes burned. His arm just hurt.

Another armsman rode up, circling toward Huldran's blind side, and Nylan, again mostly reacting, threw the heavy balanced blade, and immediately grabbed for his second blade.

As the thrown blade sliced through the armsman's chest, Nylan's fingers groped for, and almost lost, his other blade. For a moment he sat on the mare, paralyzed, knives of liquid lightning stabbing through his eyes, and lines of ionized fire streaming down his arms.

He forced his blade up, but, for the moment, it wasn't needed. The last armsman attacking Cessya wheeled his mount, turned, and started to flee. Cessya threw one of her blades through his back, then rode after the trotting mount to reclaim it.

HHHssttt!

Nylan's stomach churned as the ashes that had been Cessya flared into the morning air, but he forced himself to turn the mare toward the white-clad figure and raised his remaining blade. "Let's go."

Extending his perceptions again, ignoring the fire that ran through his body, he let the mare trot forward, afraid a run would jolt him right out of the saddle.

Huldran rode on his right, Weindre on his left, and two

others he didn't look back to identify slightly behind.

Another firebolt flared, but Nylan raised his blade, using his senses somehow to deflect it.

A third firebolt slammed at Nylan, cascading around his blade, and almost singeing his hair.

The engineer felt as though he were riding in slow motion, but he kept moving, holding the blade like a talisman, ignoring the soreness in his muscles as he and the guards narrowed the distance between them and the wizard.

Two firebolts, in quick succession, flashed toward them, but Nylan, with his senses, eased them aside.

As the white wizard saw the guards beating their way through the armsmen, he glanced left, then right, and squinted.

Nylan could feel the sense of distortion, the wrenching feeling twisting at his sight, and he fought it, muttering under his breath, "I will. I will see what is. I will . . . will . . ."

His head seemed to split as unseen lines of fire stretched from the wizard to him, but he held firm, his eyes blurring, only knowing that the wizard's defenders were melting under the flashing, often crudely hacking, blades of the Westwind guards.

Suddenly, the wizard turned his mount and started to gallop away. Two blades flashed through the air. One struck, almost a glancing blow, Nylan thought, but the wizard almost seemed to disintegrate.

"Get those blades!" ordered Huldran.

Nylan, ignoring the blinding knives that accompanied each glance at the bodies strewn across the area around the fields, and the gash in his arm that he had not even noticed before, urged the mare toward the knot of armsmen besieging Ryba and the guards around her.

As the two guards reclaimed their blades, Huldran, Weindre, and Nylan rode over the corner of the bean field toward the dust-shrouded figures struggling in the mid-morning light.

Gerlich loomed over the group, and his blade cleared a guard from her mount, almost bisecting her.

Nylan winced at the additional pain of more death, but leaned forward in the saddle, still gripping his blade.

"Now, we'll see, Angel and Marshal!" yelled Gerlich, spurring his mount toward Ryba, pushing aside one of his own armsmen as he came up on her left side, the huge blade spinning like night toward the marshal, even as she turned.

The dark-haired leader dived sideways as the blade clove through the neck of the roan. The big red horse crumbled, but Ryba tucked and rolled out, staggering erect into a space in the midst of the dust and horses.

One of Ryba's arms hung loosely as Gerlich wheeled his mount toward her.

Her shoulders slumped, and Nylan watched helplessly. Gerlich's blade rose again.

At the last moment, the forgotten slug-thrower came up . . . and four even shots stitched four welts of red across Gerlich's chest. The big blade slipped from his fingers as his mouth dropped open.

As the ten or so armsmen turned, as if to attack the dismounted marshal, Saryn lifted both her blades. Each glittered like black fire in the midday sun, each impossibly reflecting the sun. Saryn and the half-dozen guards beside her charged the remaining armsmen, splitting off half the group and backing them away from Ryba. The guards' black blades glittered in the late morning light, glimmered like black fire.

A second group of five guards, led by Fierral, formed a tight circle around Ryba against nearly twice their number.

Nylan turned toward Ryba's attackers, and the mare pulled up short, almost slamming into an armsman's mount from behind. As the man turned, seemingly in slow motion, Nylan's iron blade slashed.

With the cold white of another death, Nylan shuddered, and his senses screamed.

No matter how hard he tried to hold on, the engineer

could feel himself slumping in the saddle, almost in slow motion, as the power of that exploding whiteness slammed into him, and his fingers grasped at the mare's mane, trying to hold on. Trying . . .

CXI

ZELDYAN SITS NEARLY upright in the rocking chair, Nesslek on her shoulder, patting him as he cries. "Now . . . now . . ." She nods to Sillek. "What did Terek tell you? You went running out of here like the Westhorns had burst into flame."

Sillek looks down at the uneaten remnants of his midday meal. "I'm worried."

"That is obvious." She continues to pat Nesslek.

Her son arches his back slightly and gives an *uuurpppp*.

"There . . . does little Nesslek's tummy feel better? There . . ." Zeldyan raises an eyebrow. "Does this have to do with your adventuresome wizard's exploits?"

"He's dead. Somehow they turned his wizardry back on him and cut him down with cold iron." Sillek stands and walks to the window, his eyes looking toward the fields filled with grain turning gold, a gold he does not see though his eyes rest upon the fields. "They have demon blades—or angel blades—or something. Hissl threw his fire at the head angel, and she turned it with her blade. I didn't see it in the glass, but Terek swears it happened."

"Do you believe him?"

Nesslek whimpers again, and Zeldyan brings him up to her shoulder, patting him once more.

"I've never seen him look that shaken."

"How many of Hissl's armsmen survived?"

"A handful, if that. They were led by a big man who was one of the best I've seen. He had a big blade, as big as my father's, and he used it like a toothpick. It wasn't enough."

"What about the angels?"

Sillek turns from the sunlight and the window. "They lost some. How many I couldn't say, but there seem to be as many as before. Their leader was wounded, but she was still giving orders. I don't know about their mage. They were carrying him off the field, but the glass didn't show any blood. Terek thinks he was only stunned, says that he tied Hissl's magic in knots at the end."

"You're very worried."

"You know why," Sillek answers. "They'll get more women after this. They know how to train them. They have blades that turn wizards' fire and cut through plate armor. They have bows that send arrows through anything. I have Ildyrom stirring up rumors that I'm a coward, and that I intend to turn Lornth over to the women. I have my own holders who will demand that I destroy this abomination, and what will I get out of it?" Sillek snorts. "If I'm unlucky, I'm dead. If I'm lucky, I'll win a victory that will destroy me. To win, I'll need to raise an army—not a force, but an army as big as the one that took Rulyarth—and I can't pull your father out of Rulyarth, or the forces that support him. So I need more mercenaries and levies, and both are expensive. That means a tax on the holders. Who else has got coins? That will make them mad, and they won't remember that it's their bitching that created the mess."

"It is that bad, isn't it?"

Nesslek burps again before his father can respond.

"It's worse. I hate those women. Just by existing, they're going to destroy me, one way or another."

"No they won't. Life is never easy, but you can defeat them. I know you don't want to, and I don't, either, but we don't want a holder revolt, either." Zeldyan smiles. "When you come back, then you certainly won't have any trouble with Ildyrom."

"No. That's true. One way or another I won't have to worry about Ildyrom." He walks over to the chair. "Let me take Nesslek. You haven't had a bite to eat, and all I've done is talk."

"Careful," says Zeldyan with a laugh. "You shouldn't let anyone see you acting like a nursemaid."

"Bother that," mutters Sillek, lifting Nesslek up to his shoulder. "I'm a nursemaid to all those holders who are afraid that, if those women survive up on that mountain, they won't be able to keep beating their own up."

"I never would have thought you'd say that."

"I've learned a lot from you." Sillek pats his son on the back and smiles at Zeldyan.

CXII

WHEN NYLAN WOKE, he was lying on his lander cot bed. The light from the windows, while dim, burned through his eyes. He turned his head slightly, eyes slit, and a sledge smashed across his temples. Whiteness and blackness washed over him for a time, and he lay motionless, eyes closed, until the hammering and the knives that slashed at his eyes subsided.

Slowly, without moving his head, he eased his eyes open.

The gentle creaking of the cradle seemed more like the rumbling of a mill beside his head, and Dyliess's breathing like a high wind that whipped through the tower.

Ryba sat in the rocking chair, one arm bound tightly in a sling, the other rocking the cradle. The left side of her face was scraped and blackish blue, with thin red lines running across her cheek.

"You . . ." rasped Nylan. His eyes still burned.

"I know," she said. "You look almost as bad. They had to pry your fingers out of your poor mount's mane."

Nylan tried to move his fingers. They were stiff, sore. His head throbbed even with the attempted movement.

"You don't look that wonderful," he said after a time.

"It's not too bad. It was only dislocated, but badly. Istril has some of the healing talent. It must go with the silver hair.

It's a good thing, too, because whatever you did to that wizard backfired all over both you and Ayrlyn. Last time I looked she was flattened like you."

"No . . ." Nylan tried to moisten his lips. "I got . . . through the wizard. It was the killing. Killing's hard on me, hard on healers."

"The killing was the easy part," said Ryba, as though she had not even heard Nylan's last words. "Getting guards trained is the hard thing, and making sure they do what they're supposed to. These women, half are scared to lift a blade against a man. Got to change that." She coughed, wincing.

"Sore ribs, too?"

"I don't notice you doing much moving."

"If I did, my head would fall off," Nylan admitted.

"Denize, she froze, just sat there on her mount," Ryba continued, again almost as though she had not heard Nylan. "They hacked her apart, and I couldn't reach her in time. Desain, Miergin, and poor Nistayna, they did their best and it wasn't enough. The wizard got Jaseen and Berlis, too." Ryba shivered, then stopped rocking the cradle. "Killing's easy. Too easy for men."

Nylan closed his eyes. He didn't feel like arguing. Maybe killing was easy, but feeling the deaths of those you killed wasn't. Yet what else could they have done? He could feel himself drifting back into darkness, and he let it happen.

CXIII

THE WARM WIND coming through the open windows raised dust off the floor of the great room, dust that appeared no matter how often the stones were swept or washed.

Nylan rested his elbows on the table and closed his eyes. Finally, he opened them and took a sip of the cold water. His

body still felt as if it had been pummeled in a landslide of
building stones and sharp-edged bricks.

He couldn't rest, even though Ryba and Dyliess were, and
Ayrlyn was. So were most of the children. He took another
sip of the water and glanced through the nearest narrow
window slot at the green-blue sky and the scattered clouds
of late summer. Then he held his aching head in his hands.

Relyn eased into the room. The former noble wore a hand-
dyed black cloak over equally black trousers and shirt.

"Relyn?"

"I came to thank you."

"Thank me?" Nylan wanted to laugh. "For what?"

"For making things clear, ser." Relyn eased onto the bench
across the table from Nylan.

Nylan studied the man in black. "My head still hurts, and
I guess I'm not thinking too well. Just how did I make things
clear?"

Relyn scratched his head, then rubbed his nose. "First, I
thought you had magic that you brought from Heaven. When
the magic from Heaven died, I thought you had tools from
Heaven. Then I watched as you kept building things, and I
thought that the greatest magic is in a man's mind."

"It helps to have knowledge," Nylan said wryly. "Sometimes, the biggest hurdle is just knowing that something can
be done. Or that it can't."

Relyn smiled apologetically, but did not speak.

Nylan took another sip of water. "Now what are you going
to do?" he asked after he set down the mug.

"For a time, I will try to learn more of the way of the Legend, and the way of order, so long as you and the singer will
teach me. In time, I will leave and teach others."

"Teach them what?"

"What I have learned. That what a man does must be in
harmony with what he thinks. That order is the greatest
force of all." Relyn shrugged. "You know."

Nylan wasn't sure what he knew. "That may not make you
all that popular, Relyn."

"I have already decided that. I will have to go east, or circle Lornth and go far to the west. I would not be well received in Lornth, especially after Lornth is vanquished."

"From what the healer has discovered from the traders, Lord Sillek has hired mercenaries, and has more resources than ever before. Yet you think he will be vanquished." Nylan's arm swept across the great room. "We have perhaps a score and a half, twoscore at the most, and how many will he bring? Fivescore? Six? Twentyscore? Fortyscore?"

"They will not be enough." Relyn smiled. "Three more women arrived at Tower Black today. There was one yesterday, and two the day before. They brought blades, and some brought coins. One rode up bringing her own pack-horse loaded with goods. She was willing to give them to the angel even if she could not stay."

Nylan took a deep breath. "The women of this world are fed up."

"If I understand you, that is true." Relyn's smile vanished. "The longer Lord Sillek waits, the more guards and goods Westwind will have. Two of those who rode up today already had their own blades and could use them."

"I'm afraid that is why your Lord Sillek will not wait."

"He is not my Lord Sillek. A disowned man has no lord. That is one of the few benefits." Relyn laughed. "And few would attack a one-armed man, for there is no honor in that. So, when the time comes, I will depart."

"Why don't you leave now?"

"I would see the destruction of Lornth. Then I can tell the world of the power of the Legend."

"You have a great deal of faith." *Far more than I do,* thought Nylan. *Far more.*

"No. This is something I know." Relyn slipped off the bench. "You are tired, and I would not weary you more."

For a time, Nylan sat, eyes closed, but his head ached, and he did not feel sleepy. Relyn was talking as though Ayrlyn and Nylan were the prophets of some new faith, and that bothered the smith, as if his head didn't hurt enough already.

Finally, he stood and walked to the open south door and crossed the causeway. The large cairn was now twice its for-

mer length, and Nylan could no longer distinguish the separate smaller cairns that dotted the southeast section of the
meadow, almost opposite the mouth of the second canyon
from which Gerlich's men had poured.

A crew of new guards, led by Saryn, had already blocked
the narrow passage at the upper end of the canyon and
erected a small and hidden watchtower that overlooked the
trail leading there.

How much did you let happen, Ryba, wondered Nylan, *because you dared not risk going against your visions? Maybe
. . . maybe there are worse things than feeling deaths. Is feeling the deaths of those I killed so difficult compared to your
causing deaths that may have been unnecessary—and knowing that those deaths may have been unnecessary . . . and
living with those deaths forever?*

A small figure sat on the end of the causeway wall, looking toward the cairns. Suddenly, she turned and asked, "Why
didn't you save Mother?"

Nylan tried not to recoil from the directness of the question.

After a moment, he said slowly, "I tried to save as many
as I could." *By killing as many of the invaders as I could,* he
added to himself.

"They weren't Mother." Niera's dark eyes bored into
Nylan. "They weren't Mother. The angel let the other mothers stay in the tower."

"Did your mother wish to stay in the tower?"

"No. You and the angel should have made her stay!"

Nylan had no ready answer for that, not a totally honest
one, but he continued to meet the girl's eyes. Then he said,
"Perhaps we should have, but I cannot change what should
have been."

At that, Niera turned and looked at the cairns, and her thin
frame shook. Nylan stepped up beside her, and lightly
touched her shoulder. Without looking, she pushed his hand
away. So he just stood there while she silently sobbed.

CXIV

A STIFF AND cool breeze, foreshadowing fall, swept from the sunlit meadows and fields through the open and newly hung doors of the smithy. With the air came the scent of cut grass, of dust raised by the passing horses, and of recently sawn fir timbers. Inside, the air smelled of hot metal, forge coals, and sweat—of burned impurities, scalded quench steam, and oil.

Nylan brought the hammer down on the faintly red alloy, scattering sparklets of oxides. The anvil—a real anvil, heavy as ice two on a gas giant, if battered around the edges—and the hammer rang. Nylan couldn't help smiling.

"Is it good?" asked Ayrlyn. "I've been looking for one all summer. I got this from a widow not far from Gnotos."

"It's good. Very good. It feels good."

"You look happy when you work here, when you build or make things, and I can almost feel the order you put in them."

"You two," said Huldran, easing more charcoal into the forge. "You talk about feeling. It's as though you feel what you do more than you see it."

"He does," said Ayrlyn. "He can sense the grain of the metal."

Nylan grinned at the healer. "She can sense sickness in the body."

Huldran shook her head, and the short blond hair flared away from her face. "I've always thought that. I don't think I really wanted to know. With the laser, I figured that was because it was like the engineer's powernet . . . Is all the magic in this place like that, something that has to be felt, that can't really be seen?"

"In a way you can see it," responded Ayrlyn, brushing the

flame-red hair back over her ear. "It's a flow. If it's good, it's smooth, like a dark current in a river."

"I don't know that it's really magic," mused Nylan, looking at the cooling metal and then taking the tongs to slip it back into the forge. As the lander alloy reheated, his eyes flicked to the iron that had come from a broken blade. It waited by the forge for the next step of his blade-making when he would have to flatten the two and then start hammer-folding them together and drawing them out—only to refold and draw, refold and draw. If only the smithing weren't for blades . . . He licked his lips and then he continued. "You can feel—"

"You can. I can't," pointed out Huldran.

"You may be better off that you can't in some ways," replied Ayrlyn.

"You can feel," Nylan repeated, "flows of two kinds of energies. Apparently, the ones I can use are the black ones, or at least they say I'm a black wizard, and you can build and heal, or they help build and heal. The stuff the wizard that came with Gerlich had, and Relyn thinks he was the same one that was in the first attack, is white, and it feels ugly, and tinged with red. It's almost like the chaotic element in a powernet, the fluxes that aren't that can still tear a net apart. Well, that's what the firebolts he was throwing felt like."

"Like a powernet chaos flux?" asked Ayrlyn with a slight wince.

"Worse, in some ways." Nylan looked at the alloy on the coals, barely red, but that was as hot as it was going to get. Initially, working with it was a cross between hot and cold forging, and slow as a glacier on Heaven. "I've got to get back to this. With all these recruits showing up, the marshal wants more blades, and Saryn wants more arrowheads."

"You know, ser," pointed out Huldran. "I could use the old anvil to make arrowheads or whatever, and we could bring in some help with the tongs and bellows."

Nylan nodded, ruefully. "I should have thought of that."

"Does this mean we really need another anvil?" asked Ayrlyn.

"Well . . ." began Nylan. "Since you asked . . ."

"I search and search and finally get you an anvil, and now you want two." Ayrlyn gave an overdramatic sigh. "Nothing's ever enough, is it?"

"No. But no one pays any attention when I say it. We make hundreds of arrowheads, arrowheads that really ought to be cast, and Saryn and Fierral just want more. Ryba wants more blades." Nylan gave back an equally overdramatic sigh and pulled the metal from the coals and eased it onto the anvil. "And it's time to work on this blade." He looked at Huldran. "I can handle this alone. You go find an assistant. One, to begin with."

"I thought . . ." began the blond guard.

"Rule three hundred of obscure leadership. If it's your idea, you get to implement it."

Ayrlyn laughed. After a moment, so did Huldran.

Nylan lifted the hammer.

The cooling wind swept into the smithy, bringing with it the sound of the sheep on the hillside, the shouted instructions, and the clatter of wooden wands from the space outside the tower. The hammer fell on the alloy that would be the heart of yet another blade for the guards of Westwind.

Ayrlyn looked at the hammer, the anvil, and the face of the engineer-smith and shivered. Neither Nylan nor Huldran saw the shiver or the darkness behind her eyes.

CXV

SILLEK STEPS INTO the small upper tower room after a preemptory knock.

The mists in the glass vanish, and Terek stands. Despite the heat in the room and the lack of wind from the two open and narrow windows, the white wizard appears cool.

Sillek blots the dampness from his forehead, but remains standing.

"I have but a few moments, Ser Wizard, but since we last talked," asks Sillek, "what have you discovered about the angel women on the Roof of the World?"

"Discovering matters through a glass is slow and difficult. One sees but dimly."

"Dimly or not, you must have discovered something."

"Hissl was correct in one particular," Terek admits slowly. "The angel women have no thunder-throwers remaining."

"What else have you discovered?" asks Sillek.

"He underestimated the talents of the black mage."

"We knew that. Anything else?"

"The black mage is a smith, and even without his fires from Heaven he can forge those devil blades that seem able to slice through plate and chain mail. He and his assistant are also forging arrowheads."

"Forging? That is odd."

Terek shrugs. "It is slow, but the arrowheads are like the blades, much stronger, and they can cut some mail."

"Can you tell how many of these angels there are?"

"There are more than twoscore, perhaps threescore, women on the Roof of the World. A dozen or so remain of the original angels, and only the one man."

Sillek nods. "Then we should have less trouble than my sire."

"I would not be that certain," offers Terek. "Those who remain seem very good, and they are spending much time training the newcomers. I am not an armsman, but it seems to me that they are very good at teaching our women, or those who were our women before they fled Lornth. Some of the women who fled to the angels killed quite a few of Hissl's armsmen."

Sillek purses his lips. "That would mean that the longer we wait, the better the forces they will have?"

"You would know that better than I, ser." Terek shrugs. "I can tell that the mage is also getting stronger. He is also building something else, it appears to be a mill of some sort. Their smithy is largely complete, and they seem to have more livestock."

"Demons!" Sillek looks at the blank glass and then at Terek. His voice softens slightly. "I am not angry at you, Terek."

"I understand, ser. This situation is not . . . what it might be."

"No. It's not." Sillek offers a head bow. "Thank you."

After he leaves the tower room, Sillek adjusts the heavy green ceremonial tunic and heads for the Great Hall.

By the side entrance, Genglois waits for him. "You have a moment, ser?"

"I suppose so. Do we know what this envoy of Karthanos wants?"

Genglois shrugs, and his jowls wobble as his shoulders fall. "It is said he has brought a heavy chest with him."

"That's not good. It's either a veiled threat or a bribe. Or both, which would be even worse." The Lord of Lornth stands for a moment, motionless, then opens the door and steps into the hall, where he walks to the dais and sits on the green cushion—the only soft part of the dark wooden high-backed chair that dates nearly to the founding of Lornth. He gestures.

A trumpet sounds, and the end doors open.

"Ser Viendros of Gallos, envoy from Lord Karthanos, Liege Lord of Gallos and Protector of the Plains." The voice of the young armsman-in-training almost cracks.

As Viendros marches in followed by two husky and weaponless armsmen carrying a small but heavy chest, Sillek stands and waits for the swarthy envoy to reach the dais.

Viendros offers a deep bow, not shallow enough to be insulting nor deep enough to be mocking, then straightens. "Your Lordship."

"Welcome, Ser Viendros. Welcome." Sillek gestures to the chair beside his. As he does, the armsman behind him turns his heavy chair. "Please be seated. You have had a long journey."

Viendros offers a head bow. "My thanks, Lord Sillek." He sits without further ceremony, as does Sillek.

"What brings you to Lornth?"

"My lord Karthanos would wish to ensure that you do not misunderstand the events of earlier this summer. I was sent to convey both his deepest apologies, and his regrets, and his tokens of apology."

Sillek forces his face to remain polite, his voice even. "Misunderstandings do occur, and we are more than willing to help resolve them."

Viendros glances around the Great Hall, then lowers his voice slightly. "I am not an envoy by choice, My Lord. I do not know the fancy words. I was sent because I am an armsman from a long family of those who have served Gallos."

"Gallos has been well served by those who bear its blades," Sillek agrees.

"Lord Karthanos was—how can I say it?—surprised by the unfortunate occurrence which befell your sire on the Roof of the World. He was further . . . upset, if I might be frank, that you chose to do nothing about that occurrence, especially when it became clear that the evil angels were luring women from Lornth to the Roof of the World. With the best of intentions, that of assisting you in regaining control of that portion of your realm, he dispatched a small force, well armed." Viendros takes a deep breath. "My brother was the chief armsman of that force. He did not return."

"I understand few returned," Sillek says quietly.

"Lord Karthanos also understands that a force led by one of your wizards recently traveled to the Roof of the World and failed to return."

"That is true," Sillek admits. "Although I must point out that while that effort had my blessing, it was not backed by my coin or men."

Viendros swallows. "This is difficult, you understand. I know that your sire and Lord Karthanos had other . . . misunderstandings in the past, but such . . . misunderstandings should be put aside, if possible."

"What does your lord have in mind?" asks Sillek.

Viendros holds up his right hand. "A few words more, first, if you please." He clears his throat. "Lord Karthanos was fortunate to have a wizard, not so powerful as yours, but one skilled with the glass, and thus Lord Karthanos saw a portion of the battle. I would call it a slaughter myself," added Viendros. "Now, after seeing that fight, he understands the cruel position in which fate has placed you. He also understands the reasons for your ignoring the Roof of the World while reclaiming the ancient right to the river to the Northern Ocean."

Sillek nods and waits.

"Lornth is respected, most respected, and Lord Karthanos has been most impressed with the manner in which you have conducted your armsmen. Yet you have refrained from attacking the Roof of the World until your borders were more secure to the west and the north. Again, this appears most wise, especially considering the might of arms of the angels. Yet my lord Karthanos is greatly concerned—"

"As am I," interjects Sillek. "You may understand, however, that it will take a considerable force to subdue the angels, and one removed a great distance from Lornth itself."

"Yes. This also occurred to Lord Karthanos." Viendros turned to the armsmen who stand by the chest. "The chest contains a thousand golds for your use in reclaiming the Roof of the World." Viendros withdraws a scroll and extends it. "I am also bid to tell you that Lord Karthanos will place score forty armsmen under your orders for this campaign. All will be paid from his treasury. They will be under my command, and subject to your orders."

"That is most brotherly . . . and *most* generous," says Sillek. "I am overwhelmed."

Viendros snorts. "I am not a diplomat, Lord Sillek. It is not generous. It is a necessity. Those women have already created much trouble, both for Gallos and for Lornth, and those troubles will only get worse. You cannot, without the support of Lord Ildyrom and Lord Karthanos, afford to hazard your forces so far from Lornth. Nor would Lord Karthanos expect that, given the surprising abilities of these strange angels." The envoy/armsman shrugs. "There you have it."

"Yes, we do." Sillek smiles, a warm smile, yet somehow distant. "Will you remain with me to assist in planning this campaign, or will we meet later to discuss the particulars?"

"I am at your immediate disposal."

"Then let us find something to eat." Sillek rises. "We have much to do before the rains of autumn arrive."

Viendros smiles, the smile of an armsman awaiting a mighty battle.

CXVI

NYLAN STUDIED THE timber that would be the shaft linking the unbuilt wheel with the unforged collar. The shaft, a smoothed and peeled log, lay on the clay next to the wall that would hold it.

With the charcoal stick Nylan made a template on the wooden disc he had brought for the purpose, noting the dimensions with one of the pocket rules from the landers. Then he wrapped the disk in a rag and carried it to the brown mare, where he eased it into a saddlebag.

Then he walked back up on the mill foundation and surveyed the layout again. He frowned. Bearings—he really needed bearings—but a grease collar would have to do.

"You don't like it, after all this work?" asked Ayrlyn.

"It's fine. I was thinking about bearings. And about the wheel itself. And the gears we need to get the blade moving fast enough to cut." His eyes darted to the millpond walls, and the water sluicing out of the open gate, and then to the nearly completed millrace where Weindre and Quilyn were laying the last stones.

Next would come the actual walls, built up from the mill's foundation, and eventually the mill itself, assuming that

Nylan could forge or otherwise make the reducing and transforming gears, assuming that Ayrlyn and Saryn could build the mill wheel. Assuming, assuming . . .

He wanted to shake his head and scream. Nothing was ever enough. From brickworks to smithy to sawmill to who knew what next. From blades to arrows to throwing blades to strange magic. And with each new building, each new idea, he could sense ever-growing resistance. Why couldn't they see?

"Are you all right?" asked the healer.

Nylan forced himself to take a long slow breath, then another. "As right as anyone else here, in this crazy world where nothing is ever enough."

Ayrlyn looked at him. "That was true on Heaven, and I imagine it's true everywhere, in every universe that has some form of human being. The general condition of being human is that nothing satisfies most people for long. Those with no power want power. Those with power want more power. Those with food want more food or luxuries. Those with a roof over their heads want a castle. But everyone wants someone else to do the work." She shrugged. "So what else is new?"

"Thanks for cheering me up." He walked down off the mill foundation and toward the brown mare.

"Nylan, please don't get short with me. I'm not a demon or a local. I don't take glory in killing, and I don't like weapons, and I've more than tried to be helpful."

The smith paused. He took another deep breath. "I'm sorry. What you said upset me. I *know* human beings are human beings, but I guess that I felt that the 'nothing is ever enough' feelings were the result of our modern technology, and you're telling me—rightly, it appears—that, even when people can barely survive, they'd still rather kill and plunder because someone else has more. Or build arsenals of crudely effective weapons because other people feel that way." He untied the mare, then climbed into the saddle.

Ayrlyn mounted the gelding. "Generally, there's more charity and less violent self-interest in more technological societies than in low-tech ones. You can't get to high-tech levels without a greater degree of cooperation—not usually, anyway."

"Great. You're telling me that technology enables ethics." He flicked the reins, and the mare began to walk toward the trail that circled the cliffs and would eventually lead them to the ridge road.

"Not exactly. Stop playing bitter and dumb. You know it's not that way. Technology allows, in most cases, comparative abundance. Comparative abundance means that the powerful and greedy can amass power and goods without starving substantial chunks of society to death—in some societies, anyway. Sometimes, it just leads to the technological society being more merciful to its own underclass while exploiting the light out of another society. Technology doesn't make people better. Sometimes, though, it mitigates their cruelties."

"You're even more cynical than I am."

"You're not cynical, Nylan," Ayrlyn said gently as she rode up beside him. "You're angry. You want to know why, because you thought it would be different here, and it's not. Power still rules, and if you want to control your own life, you have to be powerful. Especially in a low-tech world. Ryba understood that from the first."

"She certainly did." Nylan looked at the road ahead, uphill all the way to Westwind. "She certainly did."

"What do you want to do about it?" asked the healer.

"I don't know. Everyone else has answers." He flicked the reins. "Relyn's turning what I believe into a frigging religion; Ryba's turned power into a belief system; Fierral accepts Ryba as marshal and goddess. Me—I just want to build a safe place, and I keep finding out that it takes more and more building, more and more weapons, and more and more killing. We're in the most remote place on the continent, and it's still that way."

"You're angry." Ayrlyn's voice was soft. "You're angry because what you see seems so obvious, and no one else seems to understand. People want what you build, but they ever so reluctantly and quietly want to help less and less."

"So I look more and more unreasonable, more and more obsessed, more and more like a joke, because people don't understand what it really takes to build an infrastructure." Nylan snorted. "Ryba says that's the way it is, and that I have to accept it. I'm angry because . . . frig! I don't know. There ought to be some way to change it, and I can't find it."

"You're a builder, Nylan, a maker, and you want to make the world better. Everyone else wants control, not real change." Ayrlyn paused. "Except Relyn, and he's not just founding a new religion; he's making you its prophet."

"Me?"

"Who else? Prophets have to be men." She shrugged. "This place could use a new religion, but new religions don't always follow their prophet's words."

Nylan shook his head. Relyn couldn't be that crazy, could he? The engineer's free hand brushed the front rim of the saddle. Then he swallowed.

CXVII

SILLEK MUNCHES THROUGH a honey cake, trying not to scatter too many crumbs on the small table. From the cradle in the corner of the sitting room comes an occasional snuffle or snore.

"I can't believe it. I'm here, and he's actually sleeping. He's really sleeping."

"He does sleep," points out Zeldyan.

"Not often. Not when I'm around." He forces a leer at his blond consort.

"Later," she says, gently taking his hand. "You're still upset."

"Upset? Me? The oh-so-cool and disinterested Lord of Lornth. How could I be upset? Lornth is more prosperous and secure now than in any time in centuries. Is anyone happy? Of course not. All the holders are ready to throw me out unless I march an army to the Roof of the World and destroy a tower and twoscore women, and, yes, one black mage, whose crime seems to be that he builds good towers, and forges excellent weapons of self-defense. Actually, they wouldn't throw me out. They'd execute me for treason. And you and Nesslek as well, at least Nesslek. Why? Because they're afraid that they'll have to treat women more like people.

"If it weren't for their demon-damned pigheadedness, we'd be doing well. We've gotten back the grasslands. Your father is getting Rulyarth organized, and trade duties are beginning to flow in, and soon your brother can take over there." Sillek takes a deep pull of wine from the goblet.

"Why would you have Fornal there?" asks Zeldyan.

"Your father has asked that he not be my permanent representative there. I could use his counsel closer, and both Fornal and I could benefit from Fornal's service in Rulyarth. So, I imagine, could your father," adds Sillek dryly.

"Yes, Fornal does chafe at Father's counsel." Zeldyan smiles. "But you really think you must attack the Roof of the World?"

"No more than fish must swim, birds fly, and men die, and they will. Between Karthanos, Ildyrom, and my own beloved holders, I'm going to have to attack the Roof of the World. Karthanos got rid of any choice I might have had, without saying a word."

"How?" asks Zeldyan. Her voice conveys that she knows the answer, but she wants Sillek to speak.

"He sent me a thousand golds and offered score forty armsmen, as well as an experienced commander. What does that tell you about his resources?"

"Are you suggesting that the most honorable Karthanos has intimated that, unless you remove the women from the Roof of the World, he will indeed remove you as Lord of Lornth?"

"Unless I overlooked something, I think that was the message." Sillek downs the rest of the wine in a single gulp.

"Perhaps you should talk to your mother," suggests Zeldyan. "She has much experience in such intricacies."

"She'll only suggest that I take all the coins and all the armsmen and reclaim my patrimony. She's played that tune from the beginning—with all her little talks with 'old' friends and her letters—all the signs she thinks I'm too stupid to see. And I can do nothing because all those old friends would agree with her, and I'd have even more trouble. After all, I only told her not to talk to me of honor." He toys with the goblet, then sets it down hard. "Besides, even I can see I have no choices."

"Then let her convince you," suggests Zeldyan. "It will make her happy."

"No, only justified, but it's a good idea. I don't know how I managed without you, dear one." Sillek laughs, rises, steps around the table, and lifts her into his arms. "It's later, now."

"You are impossible." But she lifts her lips to his.

CXVIII

DRY DUST SWIRLED into the smithy, both from the road and from fields that had not seen rain in more than an eight-day.

Clung! Clung!

Nylan struggled with the metal on the anvil, a chunk of iron that neither looked circular nor like a gear. Even the hole in the center was lopsided. Finally, he took the tongs and set the misshapen mass on the forge bricks, then wiped his forehead with the back of his forearm.

"Does the whole thing have to be of metal, ser?" asked Huldran from behind the older, makeshift anvil, where she continued to hammer out the arrowheads that ought to have been cast.

"It would be stronger."

"Couldn't the wood people make something like a wheel, with holes in it where you put through sort of square metal pegs? You could put flanges on the bottom so they wouldn't slip out, and a smaller wheel inside the other."

Nylan squinted, trying to visualize what the blond guard had suggested. Then he shook his head and laughed. "It would probably work better than what I've been trying to do. In making wooden wheels you can wet-bend the wood. Yes, it would work."

"You think so?"

Nylan pointed to the misshappen metal. "Look at that. That's workable?"

A thin woman, painfully thin, wearing leathers from the plunder piles, with dark smears that had been blood, stepped into the smithy. "Ser?"

Nylan turned. "Yes."

"I was bid . . . If you please, ser . . . the marshal . . . she . . . ser—"

"I take it that the marshal requests my presence?" Nylan asked to cut off the painfully slow speech for the new guard.

"Yes, ser."

"Fine." He set aside the hammer. "I assume I'll be back before too long, Huldran. Use the good anvil." Nylan looked back at the messenger. "I don't know everyone anymore. Who are you?"

"Meyin, ser."

"Where are you from?" The smith stepped from behind the anvil.

"Dinoz, ser."

Nylan had never heard of Dinoz, but he'd never heard of most of the small towns from which the new guards had fled. "East or west of the mountains?"

"It's in Gallos, ser."

"Let's go."

Nylan followed Meyin down the road toward the tower. Nearly a dozen new guard recruits were practicing on the sparring ground. On the stretch of meadow between the road and the fields another handful ran through exercises with wands on horseback.

"Looks more like a boot camp . . ." Nylan muttered to himself. "Then it is." How long could Ryba build her forces before someone else decided to take a crack at Westwind? An eight-day? A year? Who knew?

Ryba sat behind a small flat table in the corner of the top level of Tower Black, military and cool-looking in the gray leathers. She nodded, pushing aside the quill pen and the scroll. Nylan stepped into the room, and Meyin slipped down the steps, closing the door behind her.

As he eased onto the stool, Nylan's eyes flicked to the empty cradle.

"She's down in the nursery area with Niera and Antyl."

The smith-engineer looked blankly at the marshal.

"Antyl's the one who's so pregnant that I couldn't figure out how she got here."

"Oh, the one with the burns?"

Ryba nodded. "What were you working on?"

"Gears for the sawmill. I managed to get the collar for the mill wheel done, but I was having trouble. Huldran came up with a better idea." Nylan shrugged. "I should have thought of it—or asked—sooner."

"The sawmill will have to wait—maybe until next year."

"Trouble?"

"We've had trouble from the day the landers planetfell." Ryba glanced to the window, her eyes traveling to the ice needle that was Freyja and then to the western peaks. "It's beautiful here. If they'd just leave us alone—but they won't. We're going to have to win a big battle. Soon."

"How big? How soon?"

"Before mid-fall, perhaps sooner. I can't tell yet, but some of the latest recruits have been bringing tales of armsmen gathering in Lornth, and of lots of mercenaries being hired. I sent Ayrlyn out to get more supplies, and more information."

"Maybe Lornth expects trouble elsewhere." Nylan worried about another scouting run for Ayrlyn, but forced his concerns to the back of his mind.

"No."

"Visions? Images?"

"Those and all the scattered reports."

"So we need a superweapon? A magic sword that slices armsmen in quarters without anyone holding it? Or perhaps a magic bow?"

"Nylan." Ryba's voice was as cold as the ice on Freyja.

"I'm sorry. What am I supposed to do? Make more blades? Even with better blades, we still lost a lot of good guards." He cleared his throat, his eyes flicking to the window and Freyja, the ice-needle that sometimes seemed warmer and more approachable than Ryba.

"We can't afford those kinds of losses again," Ryba said. "Even with all the new recruits . . . we can't train them well that fast, and half are scared to death of men with weapons. It takes time to overcome that."

Nylan rubbed his forehead. At times, especially when he thought of weapons, his head still ached. "Huldran is working on arrowheads. She can't give them that final ordering, but she makes good arrowheads. I can make more, too. I don't like it, but I can. Or blades. What do you want?"

"The weapons laser. I told you we'd need it for the big battle. How usable is it?"

"We've got one bank of firin cells left. They're at about eighty percent and deteriorating—probably won't be much good past the coming winter. The generator's gone; so we're stuck with what we have in the cells." He looked at the marshal. "How big a battle?"

"I don't know the exact numbers, but they'll have enough troops to cover the ridge fields. They'll have some siege engines for the tower. That's why I told you to save the laser for the battle with this Lord Sillek. He's supposedly using all his loot from taking over that seaport for just two things. Fortifying his hold on the conquered city . . . and building up and buying armsmen."

"The laser won't be enough, then." Nylan massaged his

forehead again. "We need some defensive emplacements. I have an idea—if I can have some guards."

"How many? I don't have that many of the original marines left."

"New ones will be fine, with maybe one experienced one."

"Can you tell me what you have in mind?"

"It's an idea. Call it a booby trap. One way or another, it will work." He sighed. "It will work. Everything I build works."

"All right, but stop feeling sorry for yourself about it. It takes strength to survive here, and there's nothing either one of us can do about that." The marshal paused, her eyes straying to the window again, before she continued. "There's another thing. From what Relyn learned from the two survivors, before we sent them off, Gerlich was stupid, and this Lord Sillek isn't."

"Stupid in what way?" asked Nylan.

"Gerlich got caught up in the fighting and forgot his original plan. The wizard was supposed to throw firebolts at the guards and incinerate them one by one. Instead, Gerlich charged, and when everyone got mixed together, the wizard couldn't."

"That was probably because you parried that wizard's fire," Nylan said.

"Parried? I didn't do that."

"I saw it. You threw up the blade, and the firebolt turned."

"It must be your blades, then," Ryba laughed. "The great smith Nylan whose blades turned back the wizards' fire."

Nylan not only doubted her analysis, but failed to see the humor. "That's probably why Gerlich ordered the charge. He thought the wizard's fire wouldn't work, and that the guards would pick off his men one by one."

"Our arrows can't pick off a thousand invaders."

"That many?"

"That few, if we're lucky."

Nylan stood. "I think I'd better figure out more than a few tricks."

"Nylan . . . we still need arrows and the laser."

"I know—and magic blades, and a complete set of armaments from the *Winterlance*." He tempered his words with a forced grin. "And a lot of luck."

"We can't count on luck."

"Of course not. We're angels." He inclined his head. "Maybe Relyn can pray to his new religion."

For the first time in seasons, Ryba looked surprised. "His what?"

"Once we destroy Lornth, he's going out to preach the faith of the angels, the way of black order—something like that. He's convinced you and I and Ayrlyn will change the world."

"I can't say I like that. Not at all." Ryba's fingers seemed to inch toward the blade at her hip.

"Let him go," Nylan said wearily. "If we win, we can use all the propaganda we can get, and religion's good propaganda. If not . . . it doesn't matter."

"It won't be the same. It won't be Westwind—what we believe. The last thing this forsaken planet needs is a new messianic religion."

"No, Ryba, he won't follow your vision. You're the only one with your vision, but I'd trust his version more than any alternatives that might crop up." He took a deep breath. "Let's worry about this later."

Ryba shook her head.

"Relyn's one man. We have to fight a frigging army first. A lot of your guards respect Relyn. It wouldn't exactly help morale . . ."

"All right . . . but after this is over . . . we'll have to settle that."

Nylan nodded and rose. "I'll see you later." He knew how she would settle the issue, and that bothered him, too. Would she always be like that?

"Nylan . . . just do what you can. You work hard, and it will be enough. Trust me."

"I have, and I am." As he stepped back, before turning toward the door and the steps, he gave another not quite false smile, thinking, *And look where it's gotten me!*

CXIX

SILLEK PAUSES BEFORE the open tower window, letting the faint breeze, warm as it is, lift the sweat off his face.

Despite the late-summer heat, the lady Ellindyja sits in the alcove, away from the breeze, wearing a long-sleeved shirt and an overtunic. The embroidery hoop in her lap shows the figure of a lord, wearing a gold circlet, with an enormous glittering blade ready to fall upon a woman warrior in black. The face of the lord is blank, unfinished.

"How nice to see you, my lord," she says politely.

"You are looking well, Lady Mother." He offers a slight bow as he turns from the window and steps toward the straight chair.

"Well enough for an old woman who has outlived her usefulness." She threads the needle with crimson thread, her fingers steady and sure.

"Old? Scarcely." Sillek laughs as he seats himself opposite her.

"Like any grandmother, I suppose, I see more of my grandson than his father. He looks much like you. And your lady is most solicitous of my health and opinions."

"You imply that I am not." Sillek shrugs. "I am here."

Ellindyja knots the crimson thread and takes the first stitch, beginning a drop of blood that falls from the left arm of the lord in the embroidery hoop.

"You know of Ildyrom's envoy, and his proposal . . ." Sillek lets the words trail off.

"I was under the impression that it was somewhat more than a proposal. He sent a sealed agreement, a chest of golds, and removed all his troops back to Berlitos." Ellindyja completes another loop in the first droplet of blood. "That should free you to reclaim your patrimony."

"With what?" Sillek laughs. "I have nearly a thousand armsmen still in Rulyarth, and that doesn't count those supplied by Gethen."

"I understand—or was I mistaken?—that Lord Karthanos offered to place score forty troops under your command for the purpose of taking the Roof of the World."

"You understand correctly." Sillek leans back in the chair. "It is truly amazing that my former foes have suddenly become so solicitous of my need to reclaim my patrimony. Truly amazing."

"Those who do not use resources while they can often wish they had." The needle flashes, as though it contained a silver flame.

"A good thought, provided one knows the price of such resources." Sillek leans forward slightly.

"You lost a wizard—a foolish one, but a strong one—because you attempted to regain your heritage indirectly. Indirection does not become your father's son." The first droplet of blood is complete, and Ellindyja's needle begins the second, darting through the pale linen like a rapier.

"I suppose you're right, especially since I have no choice."

Ellindyja sets the embroidery hoop down, and her eyes fix on her son's. "Lord, you never had a choice. A lord whose holders believe he cannot hold his own lands will not trust him to guard theirs. A lord who allows their women to flee will find his holders demanding his women, and his head. A lord who will not protect his holders against attacks on what they hold dear cannot long count on holding even his own tower, let alone his lands." She lifts the embroidery, and the needle flashes.

Sillek nods ever so slightly, but says nothing.

"It has been so nice that you came to visit me, dear," Ellindyja says sweetly. "And do tell your lady that I appreciate her kindness. I would not keep you now, for there must be much you must do." The needle knots at the back of the second droplet of blood.

Sillek rises. "I do appreciate your wisdom, Mother, and your indirectly forthright expressions, as well as all those conversations with your old friends, which have helped to leave me little choice. Still, I trust you will recall that I sought your counsel before I began my preparations to reclaim my patrimony. And I will certainly convey your thanks to Zeldyan. She is most respectful of you."

"And I of her, dear." Ellindyja smiles as Sillek bows before departing. "And I of her."

CXX

"EASY, EASY . . ." THE three new guards, led by Ydrall, eased the heavy section of log into the hole.

Nylan nodded. "Wedge it in place with the heavy stones."

Two of the guards began to roll a round stone toward the hole while the other two braced the log in place.

Nylan surveyed the two lines of holes. Each hole was about eight cubits from the next, and the first line lay just short of the top of the ridge on the tower side, below the narrowest point between the rock outcroppings that constricted the open space on each end. Still, the distance was over two hundred cubits, and that was a lot of engineering in what might be a very short time.

If he couldn't complete the pike line he had in mind, perhaps a cable that could be raised at the last moment would provide some carnage. Nylan massaged his temples. Ryba's thoughts about power notwithstanding, designing destructive systems still gave him headaches.

A single horse broke away from the mounted drills and started up toward Nylan and his crew. After leaving the paved lower section of the road by the tower, Saryn turned her mount from the packed clay trail and rode up across the grassy slope toward Nylan.

"The marshal said you were going to try something else," Saryn said as she reined up. "Are you putting up a fence?

Those posts are more than a half cubit across, and you've sunk them nearly two cubits deep. Isn't that a lot of work? A fence isn't going to stop a horde of armsmen, not for long, anyway."

"It's not a fence." Nylan offered a wry smile. "And it is a lot of work. If I get time, there will be two lines of these posts, and what goes with them." Nylan wiped his damp forehead.

"Do you want to explain?" Saryn surveyed the lines of holes, turning in the saddle.

"Not really, except that I'm trying to put something together to cause trouble for any attackers. If I can get it in place and it works, then I'll let you know. If I don't, then I won't feel so stupid for promising something."

Saryn shook her head as she rode back toward the road.

Ydrall watched the exchange with a puzzled look.

Nylan hoped everyone stayed puzzled.

The idea was simple enough—semiautomatic pikes—a whole line of pikes attached to stringers or crossbeams, weighted to slip up at the right angle and set to ground if a horse and rider impacted them.

Nylan had set them on the flat just over the crest of the hill. All an attacker would see would be a line of squat pillars, with nothing between them until the last moment—he hoped.

As the crew finished wedging the second post in place, he nodded to the third hole. "Let's try for another." He picked up one section of the harness, and they began to drag the log toward the next hole, while behind them, two of the guards tamped soil in between the wedging rocks.

Below them, another crew supervised by Weindre was building a fortified platform for the weapons laser—to the east of the road leading down from the ridge. The platform would allow the laser a sweep of the entire downslope.

Lasers and semiautomatic pikes—what a strange combination of weaponry. Would it be enough against thousands of attackers?

Nylan doubted it, but what choices did they have? The locals seemed enraged enough to tear apart anyone from Westwind if they tried to flee, and most of those on the Roof of the World, for one reason or another, could not survive elsewhere.

"All right," Nylan said. "Let's get this one in place."

The sound of stonework drifted up from below, along with those of practice wands, and horse drills, carried by the wind that bore the faintest hint of fall.

CXXI

SILLEK WEARS A purple tunic over a lighter shirt, and maroon leather trousers. The scabbard holding the sabre at his side and his riding boots are both scarred and workmanlike. He carries a heavy leather jacket in his left arm as he stands by the door. "I need to go."

"I know." Zeldyan offers a gentle smile. "Be careful."

"I always am."

"Don't be a hero," says Zeldyan quietly, holding a squirming Nesslek, whose fingers grasp for the blond strands held back from his hands by her green and silver hairband.

"I have no intentions that way—as you know. My idea is to win, not to follow some outdated idea of honor."

"Please remember that."

"I will. If . . . though . . . If it comes to that, you have what you need . . . Summon your father . . ." His voice turns husky for a moment.

"I know. It won't be necessary." Her tone is bright, despite the darkness in her eyes.

Sillek enfolds them both in his arms, and his lips and Zeldyan's touch, gently, desperately gently.

Nesslek's fingers seize his father's tunic and twist.

Sillek reaches up and disengages the chubby fingers. "You, young imp. Always grabbing."

"Like his father," Zeldyan says gently.

Sillek holds his son's fingers, and his and Zeldyan's lips brush again, more delicately, more longingly than the last time.

CXXII

". . . WHAT NEWS DO you have, Ayrlyn?" asked Ryba.

Five people and an infant had gathered around the head table in the great room—Ryba, Saryn, Fierral, Ayrlyn, Nylan, and Dyliess. Dyliess dozed in the carrypack on Nylan's chest although, he reflected, she was already growing too big for it, and her upper body half sprawled out of the pouch and across Nylan's chest. He patted his daughter's back gently.

The two fat candles on the table created a circle of dim light that barely included the table and those around it.

In the gloom, Nylan glanced across the table at Ayrlyn, her hair still damp from the shower she had taken immediately upon her return from her latest trading/scouting venture. She returned his glance with a faint smile, then turned toward Ryba, and began to speak.

With his free left hand, Nylan idly brushed the bread crumbs off the table as he listened, ignoring the creaks of the crickets that had begun to invade the tower.

"There's nothing absolute yet, except that Lord Sillek has either just begun to move his army, or that he will shortly. Everyone seems certain that he is getting reinforcements from the Lord of Gallos, and that the Lord of Jerans has sent gold and a pledge of peace." Ayrlyn took a sip of cold tea from her mug, then set it back on the table.

"In effect, we have three local kingdoms determined to wipe us out, just because we've armed some women and given others a place to flee to." Ryba laughed harshly. "It's wonderful to be so well liked."

"Giving women an option is radical, even revolutionary, in this culture. It has been in most noncold-climate cultures," pointed out Ayrlyn. "People with power don't like change. Just by existing, we're creating change."

"We'll keep doing it," said Ryba, asking, after a moment, "How did you do with your trading?"

"Trading—not that well. The word is out everywhere. We couldn't trade for much. All the traders felt we should be paying double or triple." Ayrlyn gave a half smile as if she were anticipating the next question.

"But the carts were full," said Fierral, as if on cue.

"Peasant women, herders' women, even a trader's consort—they *gave* me things. There are linens, bandages, salves, and food—all in small packages. There are even coppers and silvers."

"You can't tell me that every woman in Candar is praying for us," said Saryn.

"Hardly," answered Ayrlyn. "Some in the small towns, places without names, spat at us. Some towns closed their shutters. But we must have traveled through ten towns." She shrugged. "Figure two women a town and every tenth herder's woman, and those who gave were generous. We had to keep ahead of reports that would have sent a large force of armsmen after us. The locals wouldn't dare."

"Any other word on Lord Sillek?" asked Ryba.

Dyliess murmured, and Nylan patted her back.

"There are plenty of rumors. He's hired score ten mercenaries from someplace called Lydiar. He's raised score fifty armsmen in levies. Lord Karthanos is sending score forty armsmen and siege engines. The Jeranyi women will ride against the evil angels—"

"Forget that one," Ryba suggested. "There won't be a woman in those forces. Not a one."

"—a dozen wizards will join Lord Sillek. Not a single wizard will oppose the angels. For almost every rumor, there's one on the other side."

"Wizards? They can be nasty," pointed out Saryn, "especially if there are a lot with this Lord Sillek."

"According to Relyn," Nylan pointed out, "good wizards are rare. One thing that's kept all of Sillek's enemies from overwhelming him has been the fact that he had three. One we killed. That leaves two. I'd guess we'll face both, and I doubt anyone else will risk lending their wizards."

"Two wizards, and up to two thousand troops. We've got sixty bodies—not guards, just warm bodies, one sort of wizard"—Fierral nods toward Nylan—"a few gadgets, and one laser good for a very short time. I can't say any objective assessment of our situation would give us much of a chance."

Ryba's glance turned to Nylan. "How is your work coming?"

"The pikes have been the hard part, even without iron tips. Tomorrow we should finish the first line up on the ridge. Two more days should see the second line done. The laser emplacement walls are complete, and we can have the laser in place almost in moments."

"What exactly are your defensive surprises?" asked Fierral. "You only test them when it's raining or in the darkness."

"That's because of something Relyn said. Narliat mentioned it earlier. I'd forgotten, though. Ryba knows." Nylan looked at the marshal.

She shrugged.

"These wizards seem to know a lot. Relyn says that some have a special mirrorlike glass and that they can see events through it. They can't do it well in the dark or through running water. Rain is running water." He cleared his throat and patted Dyliess again. "What's up there are what I'd call automatic pikes. When I pull a cord, they'll snap up into place."

"That means someone will have to be up there," pointed out Fierral.

"That's one reason why there are two lines," answered Nylan. "There's about thirty cubits from the rise to the first row. I checked the line of sight, and you can't see the posts until you pass the crest. Now, if they charge quickly, then a bunch of them are going to get spitted. If they go slowly, they'll have to stop, and that should make them good targets for arrows." He shrugged. "I know it means four to eight guards will be exposed, but they can lie flat behind the posts until they trigger them. After that, I really don't think, if they hurry back to the second line and trigger those, that anyone will be paying attention to them."

"How well do these work?"

"So far, every time." Nylan gave a sardonic smile. "That means something will go wrong when it counts. Even if one or two don't work, it's going to slow them down a lot and allow you to pump a lot more shafts into them."

Fierral nodded. "I can see that. I hope that we can get maximum impact from everything."

"When will they get here?" asked Saryn.

"Sometime in the next three to five days, I'd guess," answered Ryba. "Unlike the bandits, or Gerlich, this won't be a sneak attack. They'll attempt to move in mass and not get picked off piece by piece."

"Why?" questioned Saryn.

"Because they don't have high-tech communications. Everything's line of sight or sound."

"What are we going to do?" asked Nylan.

"That's simple," snapped Fierral. "Shoot a lot of arrows from cover as they advance. That's so they stay bunched up and use those little shields. Then we'll form up out of their bow range and try to delay them so the entire attacking force is concentrated on the tower side of the ridge. After that, we hope you and the laser, and anything else you can come up with, can incinerate most of them. Otherwise, we're dead, and so is Westwind."

"I think Fierral has stated our basic strategy clearly," said Ryba. "Is there anything else?"

After a long silence, she stood.

Ayrlyn looked at Nylan, giving him the faintest of headshakes. He offered a small nod in return.

As the silence continued, punctuated by the crickets, the others rose, Nylan the last of all as he eased off the bench slowly, trying not to wake Dyliess.

Nylan and Ryba walked up to the top level of the tower without speaking. Ryba closed the door, and Nylan eased Dyliess out of the carrypack and into the cradle.

Later, in the darkness, as he rocked the cradle gently, Nylan asked, "Even if we win—"

"We will win," Ryba snapped, "if we just do what we can."

"Fine. Then what? The laser's gone. Probably half the guards or more will be gone. What happens with the next attack?"

"There won't be one."

"Why do you say that? We've been attacked for almost two solid years. What would change that?" He tried to keep the cradle rocking evenly. "You're the one who tells me that force wins, and that people keep trying."

Ryba shrugged. "After the destruction of the combined army of three local nations, who could afford to even suggest another attack immediately? And if he did, how could he be sure that his enemies wouldn't find his undefended lands easier pickings?"

"Sooner or later, someone will try."

"Three years from now, Westwind will have a considerable army of its own, with alliances and a treasury."

Nylan shook his head, glad Ryba did not have his night vision.

"Don't doubt me on this, Nylan. I'm not saying it won't be costly, or that it will be easy. I am saying that we can win. And that it will be worth it, because no one in our lifetime will try again—if we do it right."

Dyliess snuffled, then settled into a deeper sleep, and Nylan slowly eased the cradle to a stop. Before long, it seemed, she'd be too big for the cradle. He wondered if he'd see that day. Ryba had said Westwind would prevail. That didn't mean he would, and he wasn't about to ask—not now. He wondered if he really wanted to know—or feared the answer.

He eased into his separate couch, looking past Ryba's open eyes to the cold stars above the western peaks.

CXXIII

NYLAN RAISED THE hammer and let it fall, cutting yet another arrowhead, knowing that it might not matter, but not knowing what else he could do while they waited for the ponderous advance of the Lornian forces. Not that one more arrowhead probably ever made a difference in a big battle, except to the man it killed.

He lifted the hammer, and let it fall, lifted, and let fall, and as he did, from the smithy, he could see the constant flow of messengers and scouts, tracking the oncoming force and reporting to Ryba and Fierral or Saryn.

As he set the iron into the forge to reheat, the triangle rang, twice, then twice again.

"That's it, ser," announced Huldran. "Time to make ready."

"Ready for what?" Nylan hadn't paid that much attention to the signal codes. Two and two, he thought, meant the arrival of Sillek's force in the general area.

"The scouts and the pick-off efforts." Huldran set down the hammer and the hot set she had been working with and racked both. Nylan followed her example with his tools. It wouldn't hurt to check on his pike arrays and make sure all the laser components were ready to set up.

After banking the fire, as he left the smithy, he glanced at the afternoon sky, with the scattered thunderclouds of late summer rising over the peaks. Surely, the Lornians wouldn't attack late in the afternoon?

He headed down to the tower. When he started across the causeway, he looked up to see Ayrlyn waiting by the door.

"The end of the golden age," she said ironically.

"What?" Her words halted him in his steps. "What do you mean by that?"

Her brown eyes seemed to flash that dark blue shade, and then her lips quirked. "If the angels win, then women will throw off their shackles, and men will see the past as the golden age. If we lose, why then, we will have been that bright shining age forever aborted by the cruelty and stupidity of men." Her tone turned from faintly ironic to bitterly sardonic. "I think that's the party line."

Nylan thought for a moment. "I suppose that is the official line. The problem is that it's got a lot of truth within it, especially on this planet."

Ayrlyn gestured to the causeway wall. "Why don't you sit down? They really don't have any use for a healer who loses her guts when they kill someone, or for an engineer who'd rather build than kill. Not today. Tomorrow they'll need us both."

Nylan hoisted himself up on the low wall. "I haven't seen you this bitter, I don't think ever."

"I haven't been." She paused while she climbed onto the wall. "I'm tired, Nylan. I'm tired of having to heal people because no one can ever solve anything except with force. I'm tired of being thought of as some sort of weakling because killing men upsets me. Frig it! Killing anything upsets me. It's just that a lot more men have been killed around here lately."

"That's true."

"I'm tired of traveling and trading, and seeing women with terror in their eyes, seeing women barely more than girls pregnant and not much more than brood mares. Ryba may be right, that force applied in large enough quantities is the only solution, but I'm tired of it."

"So am I," Nylan said, almost without thinking. "And I'm tired because nothing is enough. More arrowheads, more blades, more violence. And what happens? We've got one of the biggest armies in this culture's history marching after us. And if we do manage to destroy it? What then?"

"Why . . . everything will be roses and good crops and strong healthy baby girls, won't it?" Ayrlyn sighed. "And warm fires, and good meals, and smithies and sawmills and . . . and . . . and . . ."

"Of course. Isn't that the way the story's supposed to end?"

Ayrlyn laughed, harshly. "Frig . . . frig, frig . . . the story never ends. People fight, and fight, and fight. If you win, you have to keep fighting so others won't take it away. If you lose and survive, you have to fight to live and to regain what you lost. Why?"

"Because nothing is ever enough," Nylan said harshly. "We talked about this before."

"And nothing ever changes?"

"Not yet. Not that I've been able to figure out."

"Nylan . . . ?"

"Yes."

"If we get through this, can we try to change things . . . so it's not just fight, fight, fight?"

He nodded.

"You promise?"

"Promise."

For a time, they sat there silently, hands clasped, watching the departures and the hurrying guards, until Kadran came out and rang the triangle to announce supper for those few left in Tower Black.

CXXIV

NYLAN LAY AWAKE on his couch, his ears and senses listening to the gentle sound of Dyliess's breathing, his thoughts on scattered feelings and images—including an evening meal with only a handful of guards even there, most gone out into the twilight with full quivers; including the idea that the whole world was decided by violence and where no achievement or possession was ever enough.

His breath hissed out between clenched teeth.

"Are you awake?" Ryba asked quietly from across the gap between them.

"Yes. It's a little hard to get to sleep, no matter how much you need the rest, thinking of two thousand men who want to kill you and destroy all you've built." Nylan really didn't want to discuss the problems of violence and greed with Ryba.

"They won't do it. Not if we all do our parts."

"You've said that before. I know in my head that you're probably right, but my emotions don't always follow reason. You seem to have more faith than I do that we can destroy a force close to fifty times our size."

"Fierral thinks our archers have already taken out between a hundred and two hundred of their armsmen. She still has a few out there, the ones with night vision," Ryba said. "Tomorrow, if we can take out another two hundred and get them in a murderous mood coming up the ridge, your little traps could add a hundred or two more. We might get them down to an even thousand before you have to use the laser."

"And . . . poof . . . just like that, our troubles are over?"

"What's gotten into you, Nylan? I know you don't like all the killing, but, outside of dying or running like outlaws until we're hunted down, what choices do we have?" She paused. "Oh, I forgot. We could spend the rest of our very short lives barefoot and pregnant and beaten, unless we were fortunate enough to subject ourselves to someone who's as kind as you are, and I've met exactly one of you in a life a decade longer than yours."

Nylan had no answer, not one that made sense. Logically, what Ryba said made sense, but he wanted to scream, to ask why logic dictated violence and killing, when the only answer was that only violence answered violence, and that some people refused to give up violence.

"Your problem is that you're basically good and kind, and you really have trouble accepting that most people aren't, that most people require force or discipline to live in any sort of order."

"I see that part," Nylan conceded. "What I don't see is *why* people are like that. War leaves a few people better off, but most worse off. Sometimes, it's even necessary to survive, but that means that the other side doesn't."

"Look at those Gallosian men who attacked earlier this summer." Ryba's voice was low and cool. "They couldn't conceive of women like us. They wouldn't face it. They would rather have died than faced the idea that women could be as tough and as smart—and they did. You have to face the facts, Nylan. Most people's beliefs aren't rational. They wouldn't do what they do if they were. But they do, and that's the proof."

"I suppose so." Nylan took another deep breath, trying to keep it low and quiet. He didn't want to talk about it anymore. He just wanted to know why people were so blind. Sure—violence was always successful for the strongest, but only one person could ever be the strongest. So why did so many people delude themselves into thinking they were that person? "I suppose so . . . and I can see what you say. I don't have to like it."

"Neither do I." Ryba yawned. "But I can't change people."

Nylan wondered if she really wanted to, but said nothing in the darkness. He turned to watch the cradle, hoping that Dyliess might understand, yet fearing that, if she did, she would not survive. He studied her profile in the silence until his eyes got heavy, until he dropped into an uneasy sleep, far too late, and far too close to an early dawn.

CXXV

THE TRIANGLE RANG in the darkness, and Nylan bolted upright.

Ryba moaned in her sleep, and Dyliess snuffled and

shifted on the lumpy cradle mattress. Slowly, the smith-engineer swung his feet onto the floor. He sat on the edge of the bed for a time, until Dyliess began to whimper. Then he eased his daughter from the cradle, and half sat, half fell into the rocking chair, with her on his chest, where he began to rock and pat her back.

The triangle sounded again, once, and Ryba mumbled, "Not yet."

Nylan agreed with the sentiment, but waited until Ryba shifted her weight again with another groan.

"The great day has arrived," said Nylan. "I hope it's great. Better yet, I hope they just take their army and turn around."

"That won't happen," mumbled Ryba groggily as she turned in his direction. In the dark, she fumbled with the striker for a time before she could get the candle lit. "I still don't understand how you can see in pitch-darkness. Demons, it's early."

Nylan patted Dyliess, but her whimpers rapidly progressed toward wails.

"She's hungry," he pointed out.

"I can hear that. Just let me get half-dressed." Ryba pulled leather trousers off the pegs and stuffed her legs into them, then pulled on her boots, leaving the thin sleeping gown in place over trousers and boots as she walked toward Nylan and their daughter. "Would you take Dyliess's cradle down to the main level while I feed her?" asked Ryba. "After you get dressed, I mean."

"You can feed her now?"

"Who else?"

Nylan stood, then handed Dyliess to her mother. Even before Dyliess started to nurse, the wails stopped.

"Greedy little piglet."

"She's not so little anymore," Nylan observed as he began to don his leathers.

"She's still greedy."

Like the whole world, thought Nylan, *but maybe I can change her a little.* After he dressed and strapped the pair of blades in place, he lifted the cradle, stepping carefully so that he didn't trip on either cradle or blades. He snorted, thinking how pointless it would all be if he tumbled down four flights of stone steps before the battle.

"I'll bring her down in a moment," Ryba said. "Go ahead and eat."

"Fine," he grunted, struggling through the door with his burden.

After he slowly trudged down the steps and set the cradle next to the others carried down by either Siret or Istril or those who had helped them, Nylan paused. He saw a hand wiggling and walked over to look down at Weryl. Flat on his back, his son studied his own chubby hands, his short fingers intertwining, then separating, as if they were not really connected to his own body. Antyl—the new and very pregnant guard—stood watching.

Nylan bent down and touched Weryl's arm lightly, trying to offer some cheer. After a bit, he straightened. In the next cradle lay Kyalynn, being rocked by Niera. His other daughter's eyes were wide in the dimness, but she only looked, first at Niera, and then at Nylan.

Nylan walked around the cradle so that he could bend down without getting in Niera's way, and he touched Kyalynn's wrist. Her eyes turned to him, deep green and serious as he looked at her.

Finally, his eyes burning, he stood. He swallowed, took a deep breath, and started toward the great room. Though his guts were tight, he knew he had to eat, as much as he could stomach.

"I saw that, Nylan."

He looked up as Istril stood there. Then he shrugged. "What can I say? I didn't have a lot to do with their birth, but nothing can change that they're my children."

"You had a lot to do with their birth, just not their conception." Istril swallowed. "I hope Weryl grows up like you."

"I hope he grows up," Nylan said bleakly.

"He will. I can see that."

"You, too?" Nylan forced a chuckle.

"Me, too." Istril paused. "You're not riding with the guard?"

"No. I'm supposed to stay with the laser, and try to hold off their wizards in some way that I haven't really figured out. So I don't have to worry, in the beginning, anyway, about arrows and blades."

"That doesn't reassure me, Nylan."

"What you're wearing doesn't reassure me much, either." Nylan looked at the silver-haired guard, in full battle dress with twin blades, and the bow and quiver in her hands. "What about . . . ?"

"Weryl? There are more than score eighty armsmen out there, and two of those small siege engines. Every person counts. Siret and I drew straws. I won, or lost, depending on how it goes. Yesterday, she went out with the sniping detail. You know they got almost two hundred of the Lornians, especially in the darkness?"

"What about their wizards?"

"They can't see that well in the dark, and Saryn had the tactics laid out well. Only one shot from each position, then move. When you've got twenty kays of trail to leapfrog along and they don't dare leave formation, it's not that hard."

"Of course," Nylan said, "by this morning those fifteen hundred or so who are left are ready to kill us all, preferably by attaching sections of our anatomy to horses traveling at high rates of speed in different directions."

"Probably. We just have to kill all of them. Then they won't be a problem."

Nylan looked at her. He thought he saw a faint hint of a smile. Then again, maybe he hadn't. "That's not a solution that works well over time."

"No. It'd be a lot easier if most men were more like you, but they seem to be more like Gerlich."

Nylan's stomach growled, and his head felt faint.

"You need to eat, and so do I."

Nylan nodded, and they walked toward the great room, where the tables were mostly filled. The candles helped dispel some of the predawn gloom, but not much, and they flickered with the breeze through the open windows.

Istril sat down at the second table.

Ayrlyn—dark circles under her eyes—nodded as Nylan sat down at the head table.

"You're tired," Nylan said, reaching for the pot that held the bitter tea he needed—badly.

"It was a late night."

"You went with the archers?"

Ayrlyn finished the mug of tea. "I can see in the dark. It helps."

Sensing her exhaustion, Nylan stretched across the table and refilled her mug.

"Thank you." The healer put a chunk of bread in her mouth almost mechanically, as if each bite were an effort.

"Do you want some meat?"

"No . . . thank you," the redhead added. "It's not your fault, Nylan, but it *was* a long and hard night." She slowly chewed another piece of bread.

"It's too early," grumbled Huldran. "Bad business to fight before dawn."

"We're not fighting before dawn," said Fierral. "We're eating."

"How did it go last night?" asked Nylan.

"Well enough that any other idiot would have turned around. There are bodies everywhere along the road. Their commander was smart enough to keep them moving, and not try burial. They've got a half-fortified encampment a valley or so down out on a rise that's surrounded by grass." Fierral chewed through a thick chunk of bread, and then a lukewarm strip of unidentified meat that Nylan had tried and choked down despite a taste like gamy venison. "We didn't get many after they camped. Too open."

"We got a lot, and lost a few ourselves," Ayrlyn said tiredly.

Nylan understood her exhaustion went beyond mere tiredness, and he wondered how many she had healed, or had been unable to heal.

Ryba, fully dressed, had carried Dyliess into the great

room, although she had left her bow and blades on the shelves by the stairs. As she seated herself, and Dyliess, she answered Ayrlyn's comment. "That leaves a lot, and us with fewer guards."

Nylan repressed a wince, wondering how Ryba could sometimes be so insensitive—or so strong—as to ignore such pain. Which was it? he wondered. Then his eyes crossed Ayrlyn's, and he offered a quick and apologetic smile.

He got a brief one in return.

"We'll have the first of the picket posts set in a bit, ser," said Fierral. "I had some of the newer guards out real early, scrounging shafts and weapons from the ones that fell last night. They should be back not too long after dawn, well before the army starts moving."

"Men are slow in the morning," mumbled Huldran. "Excepting you, ser," she added to Nylan.

The smith-engineer wondered why he was the exception to everything—or was that just because Ryba needed him? Or because he disliked the use of force to solve everything, even when he was guilty, or more guilty than just about anyone, of employing it? He took a sip of tea, then lowered the mug to his chin, letting the steam seep around his face.

After a few more sips, he slowly chewed a strip of hot-sauced venison, and then another, and then some more bread. All of it tasted flat, but he kept eating.

". . . engineer's off somewhere . . . got that look . . ."

". . . wouldn't want to be in his boots . . ."

"I would."

"That's not what I meant . . ."

In time, he looked up. Ayrlyn and Fierral were gone. The tables were half-empty, and Ryba was wiping her face one-handed, juggling Dyliess on her leg.

"Can you take her?" asked the marshal. "Antyl and Blynnal are keeping the children, while Siret holds the tower . . ."

"I know. Istril told me." He stood, then took his daughter, still looking at her mother.

"You know what you're going to do?" Ryba asked.

"It's pretty simple, in theory anyway. You and the guards

get them bunched on the hillside, and I fry them. That doesn't take into account that they may not want to bunch or that their wizards may have other ideas, or that the wizards may be able to block the effect of the laser. Or that the wizards may be able to fry me. But," he concluded, "I understand the plan." He paused. "Was there any problem getting some of the newer guards to trip the pikes?"

"No. There were a handful who'd have done it on a suicide basis."

Nylan winced. "There's a lot of hatred here."

"There's been a lot of hidden hatred between men and women in a lot of cultures, Nylan. It's just more obvious here." Ryba half turned. "I've got to go. I'll either check with you or send a messenger once we're set."

Nylan shifted Dyliess to his shoulder and patted her back as he walked slowly to the other side of the tower, trying and succeeding in not tripping over the pair of blades he wore.

He eased Dyliess into the cradle, then patted her arm and touched her smooth cheek. She smiled, then threatened to cry as he stood.

"Istril told me you were here earlier." Siret had just handed Kyalynn to Antyl, and she stepped toward Nylan. The silver-haired guard had deep circles under her green eyes, and a narrow slash across her cheek.

Nylan reached out and touched the skin beside the wound, letting a little order seep into it.

"You didn't have to do that."

"You didn't have to go out last night and try to reduce the odds against us."

They just looked at each other for a long moment.

Then Nylan cleared his throat. "Take care of them. Just . . . take care of them."

He turned and headed up the steps to the fifth level and the components of the weapons laser. Huldran joined him on the way up.

The sun had just begun to ease above the great forest to the east of the cliffs when Nylan carried the weapons laser head and cables across the lower meadow to the crude brick revetment. From the raised position on its platform on the highest point of ground east of the tower, amid the fields, the weapons laser had a clean field of fire in nearly any direction.

Behind him followed Huldran and three of the newer recruits, none of whose names Nylan knew, carrying the heavy firin cell block and the rest of the equipment.

Nylan positioned the tripod, then clicked the firing head onto the swivel. After that came the power cable.

"Let's move the cells to the center here," he suggested, and one of the new guards, a mahogany redhead, helped.

After that he straightened and looked at the three new guards. "That's all we need for now. Go do whatever you're supposed to do."

"We're supposed to guard you," the redhead said.

"Oh . . . all right. Then get as many shafts as you can and whatever else you need and report back here. When the time comes, try to use arrows and keep them at a distance. The farther away the better."

"Yes, ser."

The three guards started walking toward the tower.

Nylan shook his head and turned to Huldran. "I'll check this out while you get our mounts. When you get back, I want to inspect the pike lines. Is that all right?"

"I get to walk up to get the horses and bring them back, and you get to ride?" asked Huldran, raising her eyebrows.

"I thought it was a good idea," said Nylan.

"Sometimes, ser, you still have certain male characteristics."

They both laughed. Then Huldran trotted uphill along the paved road to the stables and the corrals where not only the horses were, but where the sheep had been gathered.

As the early golden light fell across the meadows, and the fields, Nylan slowly went through each and every connection, letting his senses check the lines where the flows would follow. He did not power up the system. He could sense that it would work, and he knew that he would need every erg of power, and probably a lot more.

When he had finished, Huldran had not returned, and he looked out to the west, to Tower Black standing in the light against the shadowed rocky hills that rose eventually into the higher peaks of the Westhorns. In the flat morning light, the Roof of the World was quiet except for the steps of the last guards heading up to the stables. The grass hung limp in the stillness, dew glittering like tiny diamonds in the light. The scene appeared almost pastoral.

As Huldran rode across the grass, leading the brown mare, Nylan took another deep breath, conscious that he had recently been taking a lot of deep breaths, a whole lot—and that nothing had changed. He still had to destroy hundreds of men, just so Westwind would be left alone. He walked behind the emplacement and started to check the mare's saddle before he mounted.

The triangle rang three times—twice. A squad or group of guards rode down past the smithy and the tower, and over Nylan's short bridge and up the hill past the end of the paving. As they vanished over the crest of the ridge, the triangle rang again in triplets, and Nylan swung into the mare's saddle and started toward the pike emplacements.

Another set of riders passed the tower, and one turned her horse toward the laser emplacement, then changed her direction toward Nylan.

Behind her, the three newer guards hurried across the meadows, followed by a man in black—Relyn.

Nylan reined up and waited for Ryba.

The marshal drew up beside him, and began to speak. "The Lornians are forming up and beginning to march toward the flat down on the other side of the ridge. The scouts say that they're two kays down past the flat." The marshal glanced toward the sun. "I'd guess it would be after midmorning before they'll be in your range. Longer if we're successful."

"Then I hope you are most successful," Nylan said.

"We'll see. That's something I don't know. I'll try to send you messengers, if we have any to spare." Her eyes were bleak.

"Don't worry," he answered. "I'll do what I can." *As if I had any real choice at all, between you and them.*

As Ryba spurred her horse back toward her guards, Nylan glanced to the great forest beyond the steep eastern cliff that dropped away in its nearly sheer fall. The forest was almost a black outline against the morning sun, and Nylan's eyes rose to Freyja, glittering mercilessly in the cool and the clear morning light.

After a moment, he urged the mare up the hill.

Rather than dismount and risk revealing too much, just in case the Lornians' wizard could see what he did, he rode past each post of the lower line slowly, letting his senses range over what he had constructed. The weights and links seemed sound, and all the cords were in place. Then he repeated the effort with the upper line before easing the mare up to the crest of the ridge.

All he saw on the northeastern side was what he always saw. There were no massed bodies, no horse soldiers, just grasses and road and trees.

He squinted and studied the area to the west. Perhaps there was a low cloud of dust rising above the trees that bordered the wide meadows leading toward Westwind, but the trees shielded his vision.

After a time, he turned the mare and rode back down the road and across the meadow to the laser.

"See anything, ser?" asked Huldran as he rode past the front of the quickly bricked emplacement.

"Some dust, I think, but it wasn't moving that fast."

"It never is," said Relyn, "unless it's on the field and moving right toward you. Then the horses and dust rush at you. At the same time, you feel like they move so slowly."

Nylan reined up and tied the mare in back, beside Huldran's mount where she would be largely sheltered from stray arrows or crossbow bolts or whatever missiles the Lornians might employ. Then he checked the laser again.

For a while, as the sun climbed, and he began to sweat under the leathers, he walked back and forth. Then he wandered out into the grass. Except for the six of them, the entire Roof of the World appeared empty. The tower was barred and silent, and even the insects seemed quieter than normal. Or was that his imagination?

"Why are battles always fought on clear days?" asked Nylan to no one in particular as he sat down in the narrow slit entry, his boots resting on packed clay that had once been grass.

"They are not," answered Relyn from the left side of the emplacement. "I have fought in rain and mud. Not snow."

The smith-engineer nodded. Then he looked at the man in black. After a time, he got up and walked back and forth behind the silent and still unpowered laser. He looked at Relyn a moment, then beckoned, and walked away from the emplacement, letting the one-armed man follow. He stopped a hundred cubits out into the meadow and turned.

Relyn frowned. "What is it?"

"After this is over, it's time for you to leave—as soon as you can." Nylan glanced uphill, but nothing had changed.

"The Angel?"

Nylan nodded. "One way or another, I won't be in very good shape after this. Too much killing is hard on me." He met Relyn's eyes. "I promised. But don't lay a hand on anyone, or I'll chase you to the demon's depths."

Relyn shivered. "I would not, not after all this. Not after what I owe you." He shrugged, then smiled bitterly. "First, we must triumph."

"Don't prophets always win?" Nylan gave a wry grin and walked back toward the laser emplacement.

Relyn followed more slowly, fingering his chin with his left hand.

Huldran glanced from Nylan to Relyn, then just shook her head.

Shortly, a small group of riders appeared just over the crest of the hill, but turned their mounts to face the other way, presumably down on the advancing Lornians. Nylan thought he saw Ryba's latest roan, but he couldn't be quite sure.

Nylan was blotting his forehead, and even Relyn had opened his jacket by the time a single rider cantered down the road from the ridge. Nylan didn't know her name, though he had seen her in training, and she rode well.

"Ser! The enemy is about a third of the way up the ridge. The marshal said that she won't be able to send any more reports."

"Fine. Tell her to make sure the field is clear when the enemy comes down. Do you understand that?"

The guard's face crinkled. "The field must be clear when the enemy comes down?"

"The field must be clear of guards when the enemy comes down." Nylan corrected himself. "Do you have it?"

She repeated the words, and Nylan nodded. Then she turned her mount and started back up toward the ridge.

Relyn looked at Nylan's face. "You plan some terrible magic."

"It's not magic. Not mostly," Nylan added as his head throbbed as if to remind him not to lie, "but, if it works, it will be terrible." He muttered under his breath afterward, "And if it doesn't work, it's going to be terrible in a different way."

"What do you want us to do?" asked one of the new guards.

"When the engineer works his magic," answered Huldran, "his body will be here, but his thoughts will not. Our job is to protect him from anyone who would attack."

Nylan hoped no one got that near, but somehow nothing worked quite the way it was planned in any battle. *Or in anything,* he added mentally.

As the faint and distant sounds of the tumult mounted and purple-clad riders finally crested the ridge, Nylan powered up the firin cell assembly—seventy-seven point five percent. Could he smooth the flows for the fiery weapons head, the way he had for the industrial laser heads?

Another wave of purple riders reached the ridge top, and the Westwind guards began falling back, drawing back across the ridge top, sliding westward toward the road to the tower.

The Lornian forces slowed where the pikes should have

triggered, but Nylan could not see what exactly had occurred, except for the unseen whiteness that signified death and more death.

Nylan sent out his perceptions, his eyes still on the hillside above. He could almost sense the Lornian commander, the arrows falling around him as the man gestured with the big blade. Idly, Nylan thought that he could have shot the man. Then he nodded, and his stomach chilled into ice. Ryba had ordered her guards not to kill him. She was not aiming for the defeat of the Lornians. She wanted to keep the Lornian army whole and moving into the laser's range, and she was gambling on the laser and Nylan to destroy them totally.

"Damn you! Damn you . . ." he muttered.

Suddenly, as the Lornian forces began to move again, to flow around the east end of the pike defenses, the remaining visible guards seemed to peel off the hillside behind the pike lines and ride westward toward the tower. The flow of arrows dropped to a few intermittent shafts.

Ryba reined up on the lower hillside, just above Nylan's bridge, and the remainder of the guards did also—not much more than half a score. Even if some guards remained in the rocks and in the ridge trees, casualties had been high—as usual.

Nylan hadn't seen Ayrlyn, not since breakfast. Why did he keep thinking about her—because she was one of the few that seemed to care about more than force? Because he had come to care for her? He shook his head. The only thing he could do now was use the laser. His thoughts traced the power lines, and slowly smoothed out the fluxes and the swirls within the cells.

Slowly, slowly, the black and purple mass on the hillside continued to move, mostly westward, holding to the high part of the ridge slope, although a lobe of forces seemed to swing downhill.

Nylan let his senses settle into the laser, let himself feel the equipment again, as his eyes and senses also measured the hillside, and he took a deep breath. More than a third of the attackers remained shielded by the curve of the hill.

"Why is he waiting?" whispered a voice.

"Leave him alone. He's got to get them all at once. Too many are hidden by the slope of the hill," hissed Huldran.

As the sweat dripped from his forehead, and he absently brushed it away from his eyes, Nylan continued to watch, to sense. As the dark forces swelled and surged across the hillside toward the thin line of guards, he waited.

Finally, as he tasted salt and blood, he triggered the laser, and the beam flared, and spread into a cast of light that did nothing, just sprayed reddish light across the advancing Lornians.

"What's with the laser?" snapped Huldran. "We've got power."

"The wizards. They've got shields." Nylan extended his senses toward the focal point of the shields, stepping toward Huldran as he did. "Ease it right, more, more. Hold it there!"

White-faced, Huldran helped him ease the laser eastward.

The focal change failed to help, and another flare of light lit the hillside, even as the Lornian forces reached a point less than two hundred cubits from Ryba and the guards.

"Shit!" He could sense the interlocked shields of the two wizards on the hillside, and his mind and fingers tried to tighten the focus of the beam, to swing it right against those red-white shields.

The energy in the firin cells seemed to build, and Nylan could sense the surging power, surges with far more energy than those cells could have possibly contained, as well as the invisible hands of the white wizard, probing, jabbing.

The engineer concentrated, ignoring the nearing hoofbeats, ignoring the raging chaos in the power cells behind him, trying to focus his energy and order into the thinnest, sharpest needle of order and power.

The white shields pulsed, and the needle halted.

Nylan concentrated harder, and the black needle probed at the reddish-white shields, narrowing, narrowing. Nylan squeezed all the firin cell energy into that needle, driving it, hammering like a smith might hammer a needle-thin chisel against the joints in armor, relentlessly probing.

His eyes burned; his head felt like an anvil he was using, as though each thrust of the laser and the chaos somehow added by the white wizards rebounded back through him. His fingers were locked on the laser, as though held there by an electric current that flayed his nerves.

Still, Nylan hammered the needle against the white-red shields, forcing more and more power into that thrust, more and more chaos, more and more disruption, fighting the chaos backlash, and the lines of fire that felt as if they streamed from the white wizards and fell like lashes across his mind and body.

The shields of the white wizards wavered, and Nylan eased every erg of energy, chaotic and nonchaotic, smoothing it into an overwhelming tide of massed energy that cascaded against the pulsing white shields of the struggling Lornian wizards.

Something has to give . . . has to . . . has to, thought Nylan as he strained against the barriers that protected the Lornians.

CRRUMMMMMPTTT!

Energy flared across the Roof of the World, and the sky shivered and the ground shook, and all three wizards were clothed in flame and chaos. At that moment, Tower Black, rearing mounts, guards, armsmen, and wizards were suspended in a timeless instant—bathed in fire, bathed in chaos, bathed in order.

CXXVI

"LEAVE THE SIEGE engines at the bottom there," Sillek orders Viendros.

Viendros nods, as does Koric from beyond the Gallosian commander. If they can clear the field, then there will be time for the engines. If not, they will never get close enough to use them. The Gallosian rides back toward the lagging equipment.

Arrows continue to fly from the trees on the left, and from the rocky jumble on the right. Sillek occasionally glimpses a slim figure retreating uphill as the Lornian force, under the two differently shaded purple banners, continues forward. The lancers advance almost in circles, keeping the horses moving at angles and turning abruptly to cut down on the ability of the angel archers to predict where the horsemen will be.

The foot keep their small shields raised, and many arrows either stick in the shields or bounce off. A fair number penetrate defenses and bodies, and several dozen bodies sprawl across the hillside behind the advance, as has been the case for kays.

"Keep moving!" Sillek orders. A flicker of something catches his eye, and he turns to see a squad of fast-moving angels riding toward the lead lancers. Almost before he can see what has happened, the angels have ridden farther uphill and into the dark cover of the high firs.

What Sillek can see are four or five riderless mounts and a slight slowing of the advance.

"Send a troop after them!" he orders Koric.

Koric looks puzzled.

"They'll do it again. After the next quick attack send twice that many riders after them."

"Ser . . ."

"I know. Most of them will get killed. But if we let them slow us down much more . . . we'll take even more losses from those damned arrows."

"We could turn back."

Sillek laughs. "I wouldn't last two days if I brought back an army and no victory."

"We could wait."

"Every day we'd lose another hundred troops. How long would they stand it? How long before I had no army?" He raises the sabre for emphasis.

Koric nods reluctantly, then summons a messenger, who

rides around the main body and to the vanguard.

Halfway up the long slope another squad of angels darts from the woods, slashing at the left flank of the lancers. Two squads of purple tunics race after them, catching one trailing rider, and slashing her from her mount.

The lancers slow, but do not stop as they near the trees, then vanish.

No one else attacks while the main force slogs another three hundred cubits uphill, while Viendros rejoins Sillek and Koric. Then a single mount staggers out of the trees, a purple figure sagging in the saddle. No other lancers return.

"Demons!" mutters Koric. "They're worse than the Jeranyi."

"Far worse," agrees Viendros.

"Keep moving! Do the same thing if they attack from the flank again. One more attack, and we'll have the crest." Sillek turns to Terek. "Is the crest still clear, Ser Wizard? No pits in the ground?"

Terek bounces in the saddle, then answers. "No pits. I can sense that. The ground is solid, and clear except for some posts. They look like they started to build some fences. I saw them working on the fences days ago, but they're gone now. All that's left are the posts. Can your horsemen avoid them?"

"How big are they?"

"Like a tree trunk, shoulder-high. I would say ten cubits apart."

"That shouldn't be a problem." Sillek nods to Koric.

"We need to charge them, to cut them off," says Viendros.

Another squad of angel riders flashes down to less than a hundred cubits from the advancing lancers, reins up, where the riders draw short bows. The two dozen arrows almost wipe out the front row of horsemen, and the advance slows. A second angel squad appears on the right quarter, and also lets loose their arrows.

"Shit . . ." mutters someone. "No one shoots that hard from horseback."

Sillek wants to agree, but looks at Koric, then turns to

Terek. "Are there any foot, any pikes, anything like that on the hill crest or beyond?

"Just the posts, ser."

"Koric," Sillek orders, "send all our lancers right after those riders. Clear the hill crest!"

"Yes, ser!" Koric nods, and beside him the trumpet sounds, and sounds again.

"Mine too, I think!" snaps Viendros, and he spurs his horse uphill.

Almost in insolence as nearly two hundred lancers begin to trot forward, sabres at the ready, the angels wait, and loose another horseback volley. Only a dozen riders stagger in their saddles or fall, and the angels fall back. In fact, they gallop away as though demons were pursuing them, and the lancers charge over the hill crest, pressing their mounts.

The hill seems to shiver, ever so slightly. Then, a wave of screams, mostly horse screams, echoes down the hillside.

"What?" Sillek turns to Terek.

"A terrible hidden thing . . ." stammers the wizard.

"You said that there were no pits, and that they had ridden over the entire hillside!" Sillek rides around his own forces, ignoring the wizard and heading over the hill crest, ignoring Koric and his own guards.

As he crosses the crest, he reins in, staring at the mangled remains of more than fifty horse impaled on the line of pikes that had appeared from nowhere, suspended on heavy cross poles from the so-called fence posts.

Arrows start to fall once more, centered on the foot trying to hack through or climb or slip through the pike wall. Behind the pikes, those foot levies not struggling to chop the wooden pikes clear of the stout frames are dragging bodies away from the pike line. Yet the arrows, the demon-damned arrows, sleet down from everywhere.

Sillek waves to the first rank of the foot. "Clear those pikes. Now! Clear them!"

Viendros, from the western side of the field, echoes the orders.

Koric, riding hard, has caught up with his lord, and he repeats the command.

By standing in the saddle, Sillek can make out a second line of posts, almost concealed in the high meadow grasses beyond the lower grass of the ridge crest.

"Stand down," hisses Koric. "You're making yourself a target."

Sillek lowers himself into the saddle.

"Charge again!" demands Koric.

"No! Not yet." Sillek twists in the saddle. "Terek! That second line of posts down the hill. Burn down the post on the end. The last one. Turn it into cinders."

The white wizard frowns.

"Do it. There are more of those demonish pikes attached there. You burn it, and we can sweep around those defenses on the left side away from the tower and the road."

"There are archers on that side," points out Koric.

"There are archers everywhere, it seems."

As Sillek and Koric talk, the two wizards concentrate. Then one firebolt and another flash toward the big squat post. The post remains standing.

"Well?" asks Sillek.

"It's green wood, ser, and it's infused with order."

Another volley of the deadly arrows sheets into the front ranks, and horses and men fall.

"You sure they are only score two?" rasps Koric.

"They're angels, remember?" counters Sillek. "Do you want to fight them when they've built up to score twenty?"

Koric shakes his head. "We'll get them."

Another set of firebolts flare at the post, and another.

As the wizards work to destroy the lynch post, as the foot levies and engineers hack away the barrier of pikes and bodies, the arrows keep falling, and horses and men scream.

Then one line of the crude angel pikes falls, and another, and the remaining lancers start forward.

"To the left!" yells Koric, riding forward, and sending his remaining messengers out.

The left end lynch post of the second pike line crumbles

into ashes, but the next line of pikes springs up to the west of the last section, and a handful of angels sprint downhill from behind the posts. A half-dozen overeager lancers spit themselves on the second line of pikes, but one of the few crossbowmen slams a bolt between the shoulder blades of a fleeing angel, and the woman pitches headfirst into the grass.

"One less evil angel," mutters Terek.

Sillek studies the field, watching as the remnants of the angels, a handful on foot, less than a score on mounts, draw up on the new paved road above a new stone bridge, a thin line between the advancing forces and the tower. "It's almost a pity," he murmurs. "A waste."

"Don't feel sorry now, My Lord," rumbles Koric.

Sillek shakes off the feeling and sheaths the sabre. Then he pulls forth the great blade from the shoulder scabbard, a blade as near a duplicate to his father's as he has been able to have forged.

"Ser!" yells Terek. "The wizard's down there, in that little stone fort, and he's doing something."

"Well, undo it!" snaps Sillek. "That's your job." He glances over his shoulder to see that the last of his forces are clear of the demonish pikes and ready for the assault on the remaining angels.

The trumpet sounds, and the Lornian forces move forward, a trot for the lancers, a quickstep for the foot, ready at last to avenge all the hurts, the wounds, the deaths suffered on this campaign into the cold and unfriendly Westhorns.

Sillek raises his blade and rides forward. So does Viendros.

As they do, the hillside is bathed in red light—a red light that burns faintly, as though the sun had grown hotter, or Sillek had stood too close to the fire. The Lord of Lornth turns in the saddle, not slowing, to see Terek and Jissek, almost frozen in their saddles. Even Sillek can sense the immense forces that surge between the two wizards and the small fort on the flat below.

"Faster!" he yells to Koric.

Koric looks to the wizards, and then jabs the bugler, and the quick advance call rings out over the hillside.

Sillek gallops toward the angels, aiming himself toward the tall black-haired woman.

Another wave of red light flashes across the downslope, and Sillek urges his mount forward, knowing he *must* reach the angels quickly.

The ground trembles.

Sillek spurs his horse forward. Yet another two hundred cubits separate him from the angel forces, and the ground trembles again.

Then, a single shriek and a dull rumbling sound that lasts forever and yet is instantaneous cross the hillside, and Sillek feels as though a mighty blade of fire and destruction slams toward the hillside, toward him, as the heavens turn brilliant, burning white, as the air sears hotter than noon in the Stone Hills.

"Govern well, Gethen," whispers Sillek, and, as the incredible flare of whiteness flashes out from that focal point around Terek and Jissek, Sillek feels himself flaming, and he holds, for a moment, the images of Zeldyan and Nesslek, even as his great sword melts in his hand, and he with it.

The hillside shudders, and a dull huge clap echoes off the rocks and the surrounding higher peaks, echoes, and re-echoes, like a chain of images trapped in mirrors facing each other, getting fainter and fainter, and stretching farther and farther away. The earth tremors echo each other, and flashes of light, like whole-sky lightning, blaze across the Roof of the World.

Then . . . ashes fall like snow across the hillside, burning like fire as they touch the dry grass west of the devastation.

CXXVII

CRUUMPPTTT!!!

The building of intertwined chaos and order stretched and stretched through an endless and timeless moment, then . . .

A miniature sun—a green and gold fireball—flared in the middle of the hillside below the ridge and east of Tower Black, transforming the soldiers and horses around it into statues of gray ash, then flattening those fragile shapes with its shock wave. The incineration and flattening effect flared through those Lornians farther away as the circle of destruction widened almost instantaneously.

For a fraction of an instant two white-clad figures seemed to stand out against the tide of destruction, as if standing on a crumbling cliff before a tsunami of chaos washed over them, before they too flashed into fire and ashes.

Nylan staggered, but continued to concentrate on focusing the laser even as he felt that wave of whiteness and mass death screaming toward him. With eyes already blind, knives stabbing through his skull, he forced the last ergs of power across the hillside, incinerating all that moved toward the road, raising instant funeral pyres—and the shock waves echoed and reechoed across the Roof of the World.

Perhaps a handful of riders pounded downhill toward the laser, toward the smith who wielded its dying hammer against the remnants of the Lornian forces on the hillside.

As Nylan shuddered under the first of the chaos waves that battered him, clinging to the laser, the five lancers charged the small fort.

For a moment, nothing happened, as the new guards stood stunned, eyes wide at the conflagration and shock waves that had roared across the hillside, at the swirls of ashes and flame, at the charred shapes heaped and tossed like burned limbs from a wildfire, then swirled into less than ashes. At the outskirts of the destruction, charred bodies tumbled into heaps.

"Fight! Frig it!" yelled Huldran, and her throwing blade cleared the wall and slammed into a lancer's shoulder.

Then the others, the white-faced guards, reacted, and three arrows flew, one striking another lancer.

Relyn jumped before Nylan, and the short blade he had once scorned flashed. The lancer fell.

The smith-engineer sagged against the burned-out laser, and his body still shook as the waves of unseen whiteness hammered at him, as he twitched in the grip of chaos and terror unseen to those beside him and around him.

On the western fringe of the hillside perhaps half the Westwind guards stirred, but nothing else moved, except the fine ashes that rained across the Roof of the World, except the last dying flames.

The rapidly mushrooming storm cloud that had begun to cover the entire sky, growing blacker by the moment, swallowed the sun, and the dimness of an early twilight covered the Roof of the World.

Then Nylan's legs collapsed as he slid to the packed clay beside the tripod base of the laser.

The single remaining Lornian lancer spurred his horse northward and up the east side of the ridge. No one pursued, and ashes and rain fell across the Roof of the World.

Soon, so did thunder and rain and hail, the hailstones falling and clumping in piles, white as bleached bones, cold as death.

CXXVIII

"RYBA, THE LEAST of the rulers of angels, thus became the last of the rulers, and the angels, having fallen from the stars after the time of the great burning, came unto the Roof of the World, where they had descended on the winds from Heaven.

"There, in the tower called black, builded by the great smith Nylan at the behest of Ryba, there they took shelter and gathered their strength together, and abided until the winter should lift.

"Yet since then, upon the Roof of the World, as a memory of the fall of the angels, winter yet remains.

"When the first great winter had passed, then Nylan the smith builded yet another forge, a forge of men, not of Heaven, and with hammer and anvil, forged yet more of the black blades of death, the twin swords of Westwind, and after that, forged he the bows of winter, small enough to be carried on horse and powerful enough to split plate armor, and Ryba the angel was pleased.

"Then, as prophesied by the demons, then came those men who were the descendants of the ancient demons, and with their fires of chaos, fell they upon the angels, for the descendants of the demons were fair determined to drive the angels from the world, and to ensure that no woman should prevail, nor rule herself nor others.

"The lightnings were cast against the tower called black, yet that tower held fast against the lightnings of chaos, and against legions of armsmen more vast than the flow of the great rivers, more numerous than the locusts.

"When she determined that the men who assaulted Westwind were of the demons, with a great sigh, Ryba reclaimed the fires of winter and with those fires and with the black blades of Nylan that were sharper than the edge of night, she and her angels smote the demons. They destroyed all but one, and drove him into the east, leaving none upon the Roof of the World.

"So after that time, whenever angels departed the Roof of the World, whether unto the southlands or the western ways, they carried forth the message of Ryba: Remember whence you came, and suffer not any man to lead you, for that is how the angels fell . . ."

Book of Ryba
Canto 1, Section II
[Original text]

CXXIX

NYLAN WOKE, BUT could not move. His face burned, and his eyes stabbed so much he could neither open them, nor see. He listened, and even the words fell on him like hammers, most rebounding, their meaning lost in the force of their impact.

". . . not a mark on him . . ."

". . . more than that *in* him . . . who else . . . strong enough to hold a thousand deaths . . ."

". . . it's all in his mind . . . guards died . . ."

Ryba's words—"guards died"—stabbed through his ears, and he would have lifted his hands to close them, but could move neither hands nor head, and again he sank, not into darkness, but into a sea of white chaos that burned his body and soul, into a river of fire that flared from the sky he could not see and singed his body like an ox upon a slowly turning spit.

An ox, he thought, *a dumb ox . . .* and then, for a time, he thought no more.

Cool cloths bathed his face when he awoke again, if indeed it were the second time, for that was what he remembered.

Blinding light flared through his eyes, tightly squeezed shut as they were.

"Are you awake, Nylan?" asked a husky voice—Ayrlyn's voice.

He started to nod, but white needles stabbed through his brain, and instead he rasped, "Yes," afraid to move his head. Even thinking hurt, each thought like a thin knife.

"You need to drink, or you'll die. I'm going to put a cup to your mouth. Don't worry if you get wet."

Nylan eased his mouth open, and swallowed, then opened and swallowed, ignoring the unseen white knives that slashed his face but left no marks, just pain. Some little of the blinding agony eased as he drank, as the water ran across his cheeks and chin, as Ayrlyn softly blotted away the dampness, a dampness welcome for its cooling.

"In a bit, you'll need more."

"All . . . right . . . now."

He drank more, and the dryness in his throat subsided, and he slept, still flayed with red-tinged white whips that left no marks, but scarred his sleep and soul.

Over the next uncounted days, he drank and slept and drank and slept, and finally ate, until one morning, he could finally leave the single lander couch with Istril's and Ayrlyn's help and sit in the rocking chair that had been moved beside the couch for him.

But the pain and glare were so bright when he tried to open his eyes that he nearly doubled over.

"Ooooo . . . I even felt that," said Ayrlyn quietly.

"So did I," added Istril. "I think it will be a while before you want to try to see again."

"What's wrong?"

"We don't know," admitted Ayrlyn. "You ought to be able to see, but whatever you did with that laser had a backlash, and it's not exactly psychological—it had an effect on your entire nervous system. It should wear off, but it's going to be eight-days or longer, maybe years before the pain leaves totally."

Nylan didn't want to deal with that, not then, not ever, but it didn't seem like he had much choice. "Where am I?"

"You're on the other side of the sixth level. Ryba was afraid that Dyliess would disturb you, and here was the best place. Also, with her shattered arm—"

"Shattered arm?"

"Flying debris," Ayrlyn said dryly. "Everything was either blown off that part of the hill or turned to ashes."

"What's left?" he asked.

"Away from the hill above the tower . . . most everything," Istril answered. "We had another rush of women. We're short of trained guards, but there are more than enough bodies to keep things going. Saryn's working on training, and Siret and Weindre are helping. Huldran's trying to forge the pieces for the sawmill, and in time we might be able to sell timber or planking. Blynnal's found another cook, and the food is better yet."

"I have noticed that." Nylan paused. "What about Fierral?"

The silence gave the answer.

"Who else?"

After a moment, Istril answered. "Denalle, Selitra, Quilyn—those are the ones you knew."

"So . . ." Nylan tried to count them all in his head. "We landed with thirty. We have nine left. Great survival ratio."

"It's better than everyone dying in orbit," said Ayrlyn.

"Or being a slave," added Istril.

"What a wonderful world. What a wonderful life . . ." He stopped. "Don't mind me. It's just hard. Darkness, it's hard." His mouth and throat were dry, and though he swallowed, they remained dry.

Ayrlyn's hand touched his, and he was surprised at the warmth, and the huskiness in her voice. "We know."

"We know," echoed Istril.

Later, as he rocked slowly in the chair, steps echoed through the white darkness that enshrouded Nylan, hard firm steps that Nylan recognized as Ryba's.

In the darkness, he might be able to open his eyes for a few moments before the pain became too great, and, in time, he supposed, his normal vision might return. But he preferred to keep his eyes closed when he had no immediate need to see, and he had no need or any desire to look upon Ryba.

"How's your arm?" he asked.

"Ayrlyn says it will heal straight. So does Istril. She's giving up the blade, except as necessary in emergencies, to be a healer. She had to. Ayrlyn was down for quite a while."

"I thought that might happen." Eyes still closed, he massaged his temples, and then his neck, hoping that would help relieve the pain. "What else is new in the sovereign domain of Westwind?"

"I'm sending Lord Sillek's blade back, and his ring—a bit melted around the edges—that was all we could find in that mess. With them go some fancy language. It's an effort to make peace—in return for keeping the Westhorns, this part, anyway, clear of bandits." Ryba cleared her throat, and Nylan could sense that she leaned against the lander couch.

"Will it work?"

"Yes," Ryba said calmly. "Lord Karthanos has already sent an envoy disavowing the use of his troops and a small chest of golds as a payment for our efforts to maintain the Westhorns, as he put it, 'clear of any impediments to travel and trade.' "

"Convenient to blame poor dead Lord Sillek. He probably wasn't even a bad sort," Nylan said. "Like a lot of us, he probably just got pushed into a situation from which there wasn't any escape."

"He was bad enough to kill a lot of guards, and bad enough to lose an entire army. That will do for me, thank you. And anyone who lets himself be pushed into that kind of situation probably shouldn't be running a country."

"We didn't do much better. Nine out of thirty, isn't it? And how many of those who came to us are dead?"

"It's better than the alternative. Over time, probably only you, Saryn, and Ayrlyn could have survived in the lowlands. The rest of us were all Sybran."

"That's true. We didn't have too many good alternatives,

and the locals left us even less choice." Nylan didn't feel like arguing, not when he knew there was no purpose to be served. Not when he knew that Ryba was right. Right she might be, but again, he realized he wanted to be neither captain nor marshal. Apparently, neither he nor poor dead Lord Sillek had any business running a country—or a ship—not when men and women only respected force and always wanted more.

"And your friend Relyn disappeared right after the battle. He was considerate, though. He took a Lornian horse and not a thing from us. You warned him, didn't you?"

"Yes."

"I trust we don't live to see his new faith threaten us all," Ryba said tiredly.

"It won't." Nylan could feel that it wouldn't; despite his threats to Relyn, he'd felt that way for seasons. Relyn needed the faith of order, and others would, too.

"I hope you're as good a prophet as an engineer."

So did Nylan, but instead of admitting that openly, he asked the question to which he already knew the answer. "Would you mind if I just turned this side of the tower into my quarters for now?"

"No. I wondered when you'd ask."

Nylan heard the sadness, and the acceptance, and the inevitability in her voice, and he nodded, saying, "I know you did what had to be done, and I did what I did in full knowledge." *But it hurts, and it always will, and every time I open my eyes for the rest of my life, I'll know what I did, and you don't even understand why I did it.*

"You'll go down as one of the great ones, Nylan, and you're a good man, but you still don't accept that the world is governed by force. Cold iron is master of them all."

"Now," he agreed, without opening his eyes. "Now." *But we can try to change that, and that's worthwhile.*

"Always," answered Ryba. "Always."

CXXX

ZELDYAN ENTERS THE tower room, flanked by Gethen and Fornal. All wear white armbands, and the faces of all three are stern. They glance toward the alcove.

Lady Ellindyja rises, setting the embroidery on the far end of the bench. "Your Grace." Her eyes fix on the blond woman, as if Zeldyan's father and brother were not present.

"My lady Ellindyja, and grandmother of my son, I came to wish you well in your time of grief and loss." Zeldyan offers a head bow, one which is but the minimal formality.

"Your courtesy does you well, inasmuch as your grief must be even greater than mine own to have lost a mate and a lover and your son's father all at once."

"Great is my grief, as is yours. Yet I thought of you, and of how painful it must be for you to remain here, where you have lost so much." Zeldyan takes one step beyond those of her father and brother, so that she stands that much closer to Ellindyja.

"This little is all I require." Ellindyja's eyes harden. "And I trust, regents of Lornth, that you will not take this from me."

"As regents, we must look to the welfare of Lornth, and ensure that the gains made by Lord Sillek are preserved for his heir and his people." Zeldyan's voice is smooth, almost soft. "He sacrificed much to the cause of Lornth, and I would not see that squandered."

"You are all so devoted to Lornth. So devoted that you ensured that the one who showed the greatest concern would not be considered as one of my son's son's regents." Ellindyja turns her eyes on the gray-haired Gethen.

He does not flinch, and his gaze is steady as he answers. "That decision was his, My Lady. You know that. Know also that we, and the holders, agree in that decision. Those same holders also felt that the gains attained from the acquisition of Rulyarth should not be jeopardized by any effort to reclaim the wilderness on the Roof of the World."

"Wilderness now? I can recall when the area was prime summer pasturage. And when they were screaming to reclaim it."

"Wilderness," affirms Gethen. "My losses there have matched yours, and the holders scream no longer."

"Your losses are nothing as to what will happen to Lornth if those angels are not driven back to whence they came."

"There are times, lady," returns Zeldyan, "when the wisest course is to recognize what is. For a modest sum from us—"

"One might term it tribute."

"—they have agreed to maintain the new borders and to ensure the peace in the Westhorns."

"Whatever one calls it, the service is worth the price," adds Fornal. "They have destroyed every raiding band in their territory, and they have made the mid-Westhorn road the preferred trading route from Gallos. Already the traders are talking of doubling their runs and using Rulyarth instead of Armat."

"Those women will destroy Lornth."

"Attempting to defeat them has nearly destroyed us already," answers Gethen. "Karthanos has disavowed his agreements, and without the buffer of Westwind, we would be hard-pressed to hold Rulyarth."

"Westwind? You have recognized this . . . bastard . . . tabletop . . . a place that has less than score two in their keep?"

"The number is more like fivescore now," says Fornal dryly. "With a mere twoscore, they destroyed more than two thousand armsmen. Would you care to lead the next force, Lady?"

"Do not be unkind, Fornal," says Zeldyan. "Lady Ellindyja has suffered deeply, as have we all. As have many of her old friends." Zeldyan bows deeply, cutting off the discussion, her high-collared tunic severe against her chest and beneath her silver-corded hair and coronet. "The world should see more of you, Lady Ellindyja."

"I have no desire to see more of the world."

"Alas . . ." Zeldyan inclines her head slightly. "For the sake of Lornth, and for the sake of your son's son, the time has come for you to be seen in the world."

"You would take what little that remains to me?"

"The world would take it, Lady. You may leave of your choice or face a hearing of holders, who may not be so generous." Ser Gethen bows.

"A hearing of mongrel landowners?"

Fornal takes a half step. "I lost my brother to your devices. My sister has lost her lord, who wished not to face the witches of heaven, and you sit here and deny your schemes, the ideas you placed?"

Gethen extends a hand. "We wish you the best, Lady. My lady Erenthla bids you join her in Carpa."

"Oh, a gilded prison, now?"

Gethen shrugs. Zeldyan's eyes harden, as do Fornal's. All three stand like crags of the Westhorns—looming over a field to be stripped and turned.

Ellindyja bends and picks up the embroidery. "Never let it be said that I would stand in the way of Lornth. And it has been a long time since I have talked to Erenthla."

She nods to the three. "I will make ready."

EPILOGUE

NYLAN EASED OPEN the south door to Tower Black one-handed, carrying Dyliess in his right arm. He stepped out into the dampness. To the south, all but the base of Freyja was shrouded in the heavy clouds, but even the lower cliffs that Nylan could see were already sheathed in snow.

For a moment, the smith and mage rested his cheek against his daughter's forehead, ignoring the questing fingers that pulled at his ears. He let his eyes fall on the small brick fort—now empty—that had held the laser, and the rows of cairns in the southeast corner of the Roof of the World, cairns from which bloodflowers had sprouted and half wilted.

Despite the fine mist that dropped from the dark clouds, mixed with the smallest of ice flakes, Nylan walked out across the causeway. There he turned and forced himself to look up to the ridge.

The paved section of the road nearly reached the ridge crest, and the darker hues of the newer stones showed the progress made since the battle. A pile of unused stones stood at the end of the paved section, waiting to be used to transform more mud and clay into an all-year road.

Nylan's eyes slowly moved eastward across the hillside. In the damp late autumn air, after the rains, the black and white had faded into gray, and a few sprigs of fireweed had sprouted, along with some grass.

For a moment, he closed his eyes, then opened them. The expanse that had been seared by the laser remained gray, faded gray.

He supposed everything faded in time. And in time, new life filled in for the old. He disengaged Dyliess's fingers from his earlobe and held them, his green eyes meeting his daughter's green eyes.

Behind him, he heard the tower door open and close, but he continued to stand on the damp stones of the road, ignoring the small, sharp knives in his eyes, holding Dyliess and taking in the sodden gray ashes that had been flame and fire, man and mount, green and grass.

Then he turned to see who had followed him.

Ayrlyn, red hair as intense as the gray ashes were dull, crossed the causeway, carrying Weryl. She smiled. "He wanted to see where you had gone. So I brought him."

Nylan smiled at the healer who had begun to heal him, and they turned back and looked once more at the gray hillside, framed by rock and tree, where life again had begun to sprout.